NAKED EMPIRE

Voyager

NAKED EMPIRE

TERRY GOODKIND

HarperCollins*Publishers*

Voyager
An Imprint of HarperCollins*Publishers*
77–85 Fulham Palace Road,
Hammersmith, London w6 8jb

www.voyager-books.com

Published by *Voyager* 2003
1 3 5 7 9 8 6 4 2

Copyright © Terry Goodkind 2003

The Author asserts the moral right to
be identified as the author of this work

A catalogue record of this book
is available from the British Library

ISBN 0 00 714557 8

Typeset in Janson Text by
Palimpsest Book Production Limited,
Polmont, Stirlingshire

Printed and bound in Great Britain by
Clays Limited, St Ives plc

To Tom Doherty,
always a champion in the struggle of good against evil.

NAKED EMPIRE

CHAPTER 1

"You knew they were there, didn't you?" Kahlan asked in a hushed tone as she leaned closer.

Against the darkening sky, she could just make out the shapes of three black-tipped races taking to wing, beginning their nightly hunt. That was why he'd stopped. That was what he'd been watching as the rest of them waited in uneasy silence.

"Yes," Richard said. He gestured over his shoulder without turning to look. "There are two more, back there."

Kahlan briefly scanned the dark jumble of rock, but she didn't see any others.

Lightly grasping the silver pommel with two fingers, Richard lifted his sword a few inches, checking that it was clear in its scabbard. A last fleeting glimmer of amber light played across his golden cape as he let the sword drop back in place. In the gathering gloom of dusk, his familiar tall, powerful contour seemed as if it were no more than an apparition made of shadows.

Just then, two more of the huge birds shot by right overhead. One, wings stretched wide, let out a piercing scream as it banked into a tight gliding turn, circling once in assessment of the five people below before stroking its powerful wings to catch its departing comrades in their swift journey west.

This night they would find ample food.

Kahlan expected that as Richard watched them he was thinking of the half brother that until just recently he hadn't known existed. That brother now lay a hard day's travel to the west in a place so naked to the burning sun that few people ever ventured there. Fewer still ever returned. The searing heat, though, had not been the worst of it.

Beyond those desolate lowlands, the dying light silhouetted a remote rim of mountains, making them look as if they had been charred black by the furnace of the underworld itself. As dark as those mountains, as implacable, as perilous, the flight of five pursued the departing light.

Jennsen, standing to the far side of Richard, watched in astonishment. "What in the world . . . ?"

"Black-tipped races," Richard said.

Jennsen mulled over the unfamiliar name. "I've often watched hawks and falcons and such," she said at last, "but I've never seen any birds of prey that hunt at night, other than owls—and these aren't owls."

As Richard watched the races, he idly gathered small pebbles from the crumbling jut of rock beside him, rattling them in a loose fist. "I'd never seen them before, either, until I came down here. People we've spoken with say they began appearing only in the last year or two, depending on who's telling the story. Everyone agrees, though, that they never saw the races before then."

"Last couple of years . . ." Jennsen wondered aloud.

Almost against her will, Kahlan found herself recalling the stories they'd heard, the rumors, the whispered assertions.

Richard cast the pebbles back down the hardpan trail. "I believe they're related to falcons."

Jennsen finally crouched to comfort her brown goat, Betty, pressing up against her skirts. "They can't be falcons." Betty's little white twins, usually either capering, suckling, or sleeping, now huddled mute beneath their mother's round belly. "They're too big to be falcons—they're bigger than hawks, bigger than golden eagles. No falcon is that big."

Richard finally withdrew his glare from the birds and bent to help console the trembling twins. One, eager for reassurance, anxiously peered up at him, licking out its little pink tongue before deciding to rest a tiny black hoof in his palm. With a thumb, Richard stroked the kid's spindly white-haired leg.

A smile softened his features as well as his voice. "Are you saying you choose not to see what you've just seen, then?"

Jennsen smoothed Betty's drooping ears. "I guess the hair standing on end at the back of my neck must believe what I saw."

Richard rested his forearm across his knee as he glanced toward the grim horizon. "The races have sleek bodies with round heads and long pointed wings similar to all the falcons I've seen. Their tails often fan out when they soar but otherwise are narrow in flight."

Jennsen nodded, seeming to recognize his description of relevant attributes. To Kahlan, a bird was a bird. These, though, with red streaks on their chests and crimson at the base of their flight feathers, she had come to recognize.

"They're fast, powerful, and aggressive," Richard added. "I saw one easily chase down a prairie falcon and snatch it out of midair in its talons."

Jennsen looked to be struck speechless by such an account.

Richard had grown up in the vast forests of Westland and had gone on to be a woods guide. He knew a great deal about the outdoors and about animals. Such an upbringing seemed exotic to Kahlan, who had grown up in a palace in the Midlands. She loved learning about nature from Richard, loved sharing his excitement over the wonders of the world, of life. Of course, he had long since come to be more than a woods guide. It seemed a lifetime ago when she'd first met him in those woods of his, but in fact it had only been little more than two and a half years.

Now they were a long way from Richard's simple boyhood home or Kahlan's grand childhood haunts. Had they a choice, they would choose to be in either place, or just about anywhere else, other than where they were. But at least they were together.

After all she and Richard had been through—the dangers, the anguish, the heartache of losing friends and loved ones—Kahlan jealously savored every moment with him, even if it was in the heart of enemy territory.

In addition to only just finding out that he had a half brother, they had also learned that Richard had a half sister: Jennsen. From what they had gathered since they'd met her the day before, she, too, had grown up in the woods. It was heartwarming to see her simple and sincere joy at having discovered a close relation with whom she had much in common. Only her fascination with her new big brother exceeded Jennsen's wide-eyed curiosity about Kahlan and her mysterious upbringing in the Confessors' Palace in the far-off city of Aydindril.

Jennsen had had a different mother to Richard, but the same brutal tyrant, Darken Rahl, had fathered them both. Jennsen was younger, just past twenty, with sky blue eyes and ringlets of red hair down onto her shoulders. She had inherited some of Darken Rahl's cruelly perfect features, but her maternal heritage and guileless nature altered them into bewitching femininity. While Richard's raptor gaze attested to his Rahl paternity, his countenance, and his bearing, so manifest in his gray eyes, was uniquely his own.

"I've seen falcons rip apart small animals," Jennsen said. "I don't believe I much like thinking about a falcon that big, much less five of them together."

Her goat, Betty, looked to share the sentiment.

"We take turns standing watch at night," Kahlan said, answering Jennsen's unspoken fear. While that was hardly the only reason, it was enough.

In the eerie silence, withering waves of heat rose from the lifeless rock all around. It had been an arduous day's journey out from the center of the valley wasteland and across the surrounding flat plain, but none of them complained about the brutal pace. The torturous heat, though, had left Kahlan with a pounding headache. While she was dead tired, she knew that in recent days Richard had gotten far less sleep than any of the rest of them. She could read that exhaustion in his eyes, if not in his stride.

Kahlan realized, then, what it was that had her nerves so on edge: it was the silence. There were no yips of coyotes, no howls of distant wolves, no flutter of bats, no rustle of a raccoon, no soft scramble of a vole—not even the buzz and chirp of insects. In the past, when all those things went silent it had meant potential danger. Here, it was dead silent because nothing lived in this place, no coyotes or wolves or bats or mice or even bugs. Few living things ever trespassed this barren land. Here, the night was as soundless as the stars.

Despite the heat, the oppressive silence ran a chill shiver up through Kahlan's shoulders.

She peered off once more at the races barely still visible against the violet blush of the western sky. They, too, would not stay long in this wasteland where they did not belong.

"Kind of unnerving to encounter such a menacing creature when you never even knew such a thing existed," Jennsen said. She used her sleeve to wipe sweat from her brow as she changed the subject. "I've heard it said that a bird of prey wheeling over you at the beginning of a journey is a warning."

Cara, until then content to remain silent, leaned in past Kahlan. "Just let me get close enough and I'll pluck their wretched feathers." Long blond hair, pulled back into the traditional single braid of her profession, framed Cara's heated expression. "We'll see how much of an omen they are, then."

Cara's glare turned as dark as the races whenever she saw the huge birds. Being swathed from head to foot in a protective layer of gauzy black cloth, as were all of them except Richard, only added to her intimidating presence. When Richard had unexpectedly inherited rule, he had been further surprised to discover that Cara and her sister Mord-Sith were part of the legacy.

Richard returned the little white kid to its watchful mother and stood, hooking his thumbs behind his multilayered leather belt. At each wrist, wide, leather-padded silver bands bearing linked rings and strange symbols seemed to gather and reflect what little light remained. "I once had a hawk circle over me at the beginning of a journey."

"And what happened?" Jennsen asked, earnestly, as if his pronouncement might settle once and for all the old superstition.

Richard's smile widened into a grin. "I ended up marrying Kahlan."

Cara folded her arms. "That only proves it was a warning for the Mother Confessor, not you, Lord Rahl."

Richard's arm gently encircled Kahlan's waist. She smiled with him as she leaned against his embrace in answer to the wordless gesture. That that journey had eventually brought them to be husband and wife seemed more astonishing than anything she would ever have dared dream. Women like her—Confessors—dared not dream of love. Because of Richard, she had dared and had gained it.

Kahlan shuddered to think of the terrible times she had feared he was dead, or worse. There had been so many times she had ached to be with him, to simply feel his warm touch, or to even be granted the mercy of knowing he was safe.

Jennsen glanced at Richard and Kahlan to see that neither took Cara's admonition as anything but fond heckling. Kahlan supposed that to a stranger, especially one from the land of D'Hara, as was Jennsen, Cara's gibes at Richard would defy reason; guards did not bait their masters, especially when their master was the Lord Rahl, the master of D'Hara.

Protecting the Lord Rahl with their lives had always been the blind duty of the Mord-Sith. In a perverse way, Cara's irreverence toward Richard was a celebration of her freedom, paid in homage to the one who had granted it.

By free choice, the Mord-Sith had decided to be Richard's closest protectors. They had given Richard no say in the matter. They often paid little heed to his orders unless they deemed them important enough; they were, after all, now free to pursue what was important to them, and what the Mord-Sith considered important above all else was keeping Richard safe.

Over time, Cara, their ever-present bodyguard, had gradually become like family. Now that family had unexpectedly grown.

Jennsen, for her part, was awestruck to find herself welcomed. From what they had so far learned, Jennsen had grown up in hiding, always fearful that the former Lord Rahl, her father, would finally find her and murder her as he murdered any other ungifted offspring he found.

Richard signaled to Tom and Friedrich, back with the wagon and horses, that they would stop for the night. Tom lifted an arm in acknowledgment and then set to unhitching his team.

No longer able to see the races in the dark void of the western sky, Jennsen turned back to Richard. "I take it their feathers are tipped in black."

Before Richard had a chance to answer, Cara spoke in a silken voice that was pure menace. "They look like death itself drips from the tips of their feathers—like the Keeper of the underworld has been using their wicked quills to write death warrants."

Cara loathed seeing those birds anywhere near Richard or Kahlan. Kahlan shared the sentiment.

Jennsen's gaze fled Cara's heated expression. She redirected her suspicion to Richard.

"Are they causing you . . . some kind of trouble?"

Kahlan pressed a fist to her abdomen, against the ache of dread stirred by the question.

Richard appraised Jennsen's troubled eyes. "The races are tracking us."

CHAPTER 2

Jennsen frowned. "What?"

Richard gestured between Kahlan and himself. "The races, they're tracking us."

"You mean they followed you out into this wasteland and they're watching you, waiting to see if you'll die of thirst or something so they can pick your bones clean."

Richard slowly shook his head. "No, I mean they're following us, keeping track of where we are."

"I don't understand how you can possibly know—"

"We know," Cara snapped. Her shapely form was as spare, as sleek, as aggressive-looking as the races themselves and, swathed in the black garb of the nomadic people who sometimes traveled the outer fringes of the vast desert, just as sinister-looking.

With the back of his hand against her shoulder, Richard gently eased Cara back as he went on. "We were looking into it when Friedrich found us and told us about you."

Jennsen glanced over at the two men back with the wagon. The sharp sliver of moon floating above the black drape of distant mountains provided just enough light for Kahlan to see that Tom was working at removing the trace chains from his big draft horses while Friedrich unsaddled the others.

Jennsen's gaze returned to search Richard's eyes. "What have you been able to find out, so far?"

"We never had a chance to really find out much of anything. Oba, our surprise half brother lying dead back there, kind of diverted our attention when he tried to kill us." Richard unhooked a waterskin from his belt. "But the races are still watching us."

He handed Kahlan his waterskin, since she had left hers hanging on her saddle. It had been hours since they had last stopped. She was tired from riding and weary from walking when they had needed to rest the horses.

Kahlan lifted the waterskin to her lips only to be reacquainted with how bad hot water tasted. At least they had water. Without water, death came quickly in the unrelenting heat of the seemingly endless, barren expanse around the forsaken place called the Pillars of Creation.

Jennsen slipped the strap of her waterskin off her shoulder before hesitantly starting again. "I know it's easy to misconstrue things. Look at how I was tricked into thinking you wanted to kill me just like Darken Rahl had. I really believed it, and there were so many things that seemed to me to prove it, but I had it all wrong. I guess I was just so afraid it was true, I believed it."

Richard and Kahlan both knew it hadn't been Jennsen's doing— she had merely been a means for others to get at Richard—but it had squandered precious time.

Jennsen took a long drink. Still grimacing at the taste of the water, she lifted the waterskin toward the empty desert behind them. "I mean, there isn't much alive out here—it might actually be that the races are hungry and are simply waiting to see if you die out here and, because they do keep watching and waiting, you've begun to think it's more." She gave Richard a demure glance, bolstered by a smile, as if hoping to cloak the admonishment as a suggestion. "Maybe that's all it really is."

"They aren't waiting to see if we die out here," Kahlan said, wanting to end the discussion so they could eat and Richard could get some sleep. "They were watching us before we had to come here. They've been watching us since we were back in the forests to the northeast. Now, let's have some supper and—"

"But why? That's not the way birds behave. Why would they do that?"

"I think they're keeping track of us for someone," Richard said. "More precisely, I think someone is using them to hunt us."

Kahlan had known various people in the Midlands, from simple people living in the wilds to nobles living in great cities, who hunted with falcons. This, though, was different. Even if she didn't fully understand Richard's meaning, much less the reasons for his conviction, she knew he hadn't meant it in the traditional sense.

With abrupt realization, Jennsen paused in the middle of another drink. "That's why you've started scattering pebbles along the wind-blown places in the trail."

Richard smiled in confirmation. He took his waterskin when Kahlan handed it back. Cara frowned up at him as he took a long drink.

"You've been throwing pebbles along the trail? Why?"

Jennsen eagerly answered in his place. "The open rock gets blown clean by the wind. He's been making sure that if anyone tries to sneak up on us in the dark, the pebbles strewn across those open patches will crunch underfoot and alert us."

Cara wrinkled a questioning brow at Richard. "Really?"

He shrugged as he passed her his waterskin so that she wouldn't have to dig hers out from beneath her desert garb. "Just a little extra precaution in case anyone is close, and careless. Sometimes people don't expect the simple things and that catches them up."

"But not you," Jennsen said, hooking the strap of her waterskin back over her shoulder. "You think of even the simple things."

Richard chuckled softly. "If you think I don't make mistakes, Jennsen, you're wrong. While it's dangerous to assume that those who wish you harm are stupid, it can't hurt to spread out a little gravel just in case someone thinks they can sneak across windswept rock in the dark without being heard."

Any trace of amusement faded as Richard stared off toward the western horizon where stars had yet to appear. "But I fear that pebbles strewn along the ground won't do any good for eyes watching from a dark sky." He turned back to Jennsen, brightening, as if remembering he had been speaking to her. "Still, everyone makes mistakes."

Cara wiped droplets of water from her sly smile as she handed Richard back his waterskin. "Lord Rahl is always making mistakes, especially simple ones. That's why he needs me around."

"Is that right, little miss perfect?" Richard chided as he snatched the waterskin from her hand. "Maybe if you weren't 'helping' keep me out of trouble, we wouldn't have black-tipped races shadowing us."

"What else could I do?" Cara blurted out. "I was trying to help—to protect you both." Her smile had withered. "I'm sorry, Lord Rahl."

Richard sighed. "I know," he admitted as he reassuringly squeezed her shoulder. "We'll figure it out."

Richard turned back to Jennsen. "Everyone makes mistakes. How a person deals with their mistakes is a mark of their character."

Jennsen nodded as she thought it over. "My mother was always afraid of making a mistake that would get us killed. She used to do things like you did, in case my father's men were trying to sneak up on us. We always lived in forests, though, so it was dry twigs, rather than pebbles, that she often scattered around us."

Jennsen pulled on a ringlet of her hair as she stared off into dark memories. "It was raining the night they came. If those men stepped on twigs, she wouldn't have been able to hear it." She ran trembling fingers over the silver hilt of the knife at her belt. "They were big, and they surprised her, but still, she got one of them before they . . ."

Darken Rahl had wanted Jennsen dead because she had been born ungifted. Any ruler of that bloodline killed offspring such as she. Richard and Kahlan believed that a person's life was their own to live, and that birth did not qualify that right.

Jennsen's haunted eyes turned up to Richard. "She got one of them before they killed her."

With one arm, Richard pulled Jennsen into a tender embrace. They all understood such terrible loss. The man who had lovingly raised Richard had been killed by Darken Rahl himself. Darken Rahl had ordered the murders of all of Kahlan's sister Confessors. The men who had killed Jennsen's mother, though, were men from the Imperial Order sent to trick her, to murder in order to make her believe it was Richard who was after her.

Kahlan felt a forlorn wave of helplessness at all they faced. She knew what it was to be alone, afraid, and overwhelmed by powerful men filled with blind faith and the lust for blood, men devoutly believing that mankind's salvation required slaughter.

"I'd give anything for her to know that it wasn't you who sent those men." Jennsen's soft voice held the dejected sum of what it was to have suffered such a loss, to have no solution to the crushing solitude it left in its wake. "I wish my mother could have known the truth, known what you two are really like."

"She's with the good spirits and finally at peace," Kahlan whispered in sympathy, even if she now had reason to question the enduring validity of such things.

Jennsen nodded as she swiped her fingers across her cheek. "What mistake did you make, Cara?" she finally asked.

Rather than be angered by the question, and perhaps because it had been asked in innocent empathy, Cara answered with quiet candor. "It has to do with that little problem we mentioned before."

"You mean it's about the thing you want me to touch?"

By the light of the moon's narrow crescent, Kahlan could see Cara's scowl return. "And the sooner the better."

Richard rubbed his fingertips across his brow. "I'm not sure about that."

Kahlan, too, thought that Cara's notion was too simplistic.

Cara threw her arms up. "But Lord Rahl, we can't just leave it—"

"Let's get camp set up before it's pitch dark," Richard said in quiet command. "What we need right now is food and sleep."

For once, Cara saw the sense in his orders and didn't object. When he had earlier been out scouting alone, she had confided in Kahlan that she was worried at how weary Richard looked and had suggested that, since there were enough other people, they shouldn't wake him for a turn at watch that night.

"I'll check the area," Cara said, "and make sure there aren't any more of those birds sitting on a rock watching us with those black eyes of theirs."

Jennsen peered around as if fearing that a black-tipped race might swoop in out of the darkness.

Richard countermanded Cara's plans with a dismissive shake of his head. "They're gone for now."

"You said they were tracking you." Jennsen stroked Betty's neck when the goat nudged her, seeking comfort. The twins were still hiding under their mother's round belly. "I never saw them before now. They weren't around yesterday, or today. They didn't show up until just this evening. If they really were tracking you, then they wouldn't be gone for such a stretch. They'd have to stick close to you all the time."

"They can leave us for a time in order to hunt—or to make us doubt our suspicion of their true intent—and, even if we keep going, they can easily find us when they return. That's the advantage the black-tipped races have: they don't need to watch us every moment."

Jennsen planted her fists on her hips. "Then how in the world could you possibly be sure they're tracking you?" She flicked a hand out toward the darkness beyond. "You often see the same kind of birds. You see ravens, sparrows, geese, finches, hummingbirds, doves—how do you know that any one of them aren't following you and that the black-tipped races are?"

"I know," Richard said as he turned and started back toward the wagon. "Now, let's get our things out and set up camp."

Kahlan caught Jennsen's arm as she headed after him, about to renew her objections. "Let him be for tonight, Jennsen?" Kahlan lifted an eyebrow. "Please? About this, anyway."

Kahlan was pretty sure that the black-tipped races really were following them, but it wasn't so much an issue of her being sure of it herself. Rather, she had confidence in Richard's word in matters such as this. Kahlan was versed in affairs of state, protocol, ceremony and royalty; she was familiar with various cultures, the origins of ancient disputes between lands, and the history of treaties; and she was conversant in any number of languages, including the duplicitous dialect of diplomacy. In such areas, Richard trusted her word when she expressed her conviction.

In matters about something so odd as strange birds following them, she knew better than to question Richard's word.

Kahlan knew, too, that he didn't yet have all the answers. She had seen him like this before, distant and withdrawn, as he struggled to understand the important connections and patterns in relevant details only he perceived. She knew that he needed to be left alone about it. Pestering him for answers before he had them only served to distract him from what he needed to do.

Watching Richard's back as he walked away, Jennsen finally forced a smile of agreement. Then, as if struck with another thought, her eyes widened. She leaned close to Kahlan and whispered, "Is this about magic?"

"We don't know what it's about."

Jennsen nodded. "I'll help. Whatever I can do, I want to help."

For the time being, Kahlan kept her worries to herself as she circled an arm around the young woman's shoulders in an appreciative embrace and walked her back toward the wagon.

CHAPTER 3

In the immense, silent void of night, Kahlan could clearly hear Friedrich, off to the side, speaking gently to the horses. He patted their shoulders or ran a hand along their flanks each time on his way by as he went about grooming and picketing them for the night. With darkness shrouding the empty expanse beyond, the familiar task of caring for the animals made the unfamiliar surroundings seem a little less forbidding.

Friedrich was an older, unassuming man of average height. Despite his age, he had undertaken a long and difficult journey to the Old World to find Richard. Friedrich had undertaken that journey, carrying with him important information, soon after his wife had died. The terrible sadness of that loss still haunted his gentle features. Kahlan supposed that it always would.

In the dim light, she saw Jennsen smile as Tom looked her way. A boyish grin momentarily overcame the big, blond-headed D'Haran when he spotted her, but he quickly bent back to work, pulling bedrolls from a corner beneath the seat. He stepped over supplies in his wagon and handed a load down to Richard.

"There's no wood for a fire, Lord Rahl." Tom rested a foot on the chafing rail, laying a forearm over his bent knee. "But, if you like, I have a little charcoal to use for cooking."

"What I'd really like is for you to stop calling me 'Lord Rahl.' If we're anywhere near the wrong people and you slip up and call me that, we'll all be in a great deal of trouble."

Tom grinned and patted the ornate letter "R" on the silver handle of the knife at his belt. "Not to worry, Lord Rahl. Steel against steel."

Richard sighed at the oft-repeated maxim involving the bond of the D'Haran people to their Lord Rahl, and he to them. Tom and Friedrich had promised they wouldn't use Richard's and Kahlan's titles around other people. A lifetime's habits were difficult to change, though, and Kahlan knew that they felt uncomfortable not using titles when they were so obviously alone.

"So," Tom said as he handed down the last bedroll, "would you like a small fire for cooking?"

"Hot as it is, it seems to me we could do without any more heat." Richard set the bedrolls atop a sack of oats already unloaded. "Besides, I'd prefer not to take the time. I'd like be on our way at first light and we need to get a good rest."

"Can't argue with you there," Tom said, straightening his big frame. "I don't like us being so out in the open where we could easily be spotted."

Richard swept his hand in a suggestive arc across the dark vault above.

Tom cast a wary eye skyward. He nodded reluctantly before turning back to the task of digging out tools to mend the breeching and wooden buckets to water the horses. Richard put a boot on a spoke of the cargo wagon's stout rear wheel and climbed up to help.

Tom, a shy but cheerful man who had appeared only the day before, right after they'd encountered Jennsen, looked to be a merchant who hauled trade goods. Hauling goods in his wagon, Kahlan and Richard had learned, gave him an excuse to travel where and when he needed as a member of a covert group whose true profession was to protect the Lord Rahl from unseen plots and threats.

Speaking in a low voice, Jennsen leaned closer to Kahlan. "Vultures can tell you, from a great distance, where a kill lies—by the way they circle and gather, I mean. I guess I can see how the races could be like that—birds that someone could spot from afar in order to know there was something below."

Kahlan didn't say anything. Her head ached, she was hungry, and she just wanted to go to sleep, not to discuss things she couldn't answer. She wondered how many times Richard had viewed her own insistent questions in the same way she now viewed Jennsen's. Kahlan silently vowed to try to be at least half as patient as Richard always was.

"The thing is," Jennsen went on, matter-of-factly, "how would someone get birds to . . . well, you know, circle around you like vultures over a carcass in order to know where you were?" Jennsen leaned in again and whispered so as to be sure that Richard wouldn't hear. "Maybe they're sent with magic to follow specific people."

Cara fixed Jennsen with a murderous glare. Kahlan idly wondered if the Mord-Sith would clobber Richard's sister, or extend her leniency because she was family. Discussions about magic, especially in the context of its danger to Richard or Kahlan, made Cara testy. Mord-Sith were fearless in the face of death, but they did not like magic and weren't shy about making their distaste clear.

In a way, such hostility toward magic characterized the nature and purpose of Mord-Sith; they were singularly able to appropriate the gifted's power and use it to destroy them. Mord-Sith had been mercilessly trained to be ruthless at their task. It was from the madness of this duty that Richard had freed them.

It seemed obvious enough to Kahlan, though, that if the races really were tracking them it would have to involve conjuring of some sort. It was the questions raised by that assumption that so worried her.

When Kahlan didn't debate the theory, Jennsen asked, "Why do you think someone would be using the races to track you?"

Kahlan lifted an eyebrow at the young woman. "Jennsen, we're in the middle of the Old World. Being hunted in enemy territory is hardly surprising."

"I guess you're right," Jennsen admitted. "It just seems that there would have to be more to it." Despite the heat, she rubbed her arms as if a chill had just run through her. "You have no idea how much Emperor Jagang wants to catch you."

Kahlan smiled to herself. "Oh, I think I do."

Jennsen watched Richard a moment as he filled the buckets with water from barrels carried in the wagon. Richard leaned down and handed one to Friedrich. Ears turned attentively ahead, the horses all watched, eager for a drink. Betty, also watching as her twins suckled, bleated her longing for a drink. After filling the buckets, Richard submerged his waterskin to fill it, too.

Jennsen shook her head and looked again into Kahlan's eyes. "Emperor Jagang tricked me into thinking Richard wanted me dead." She glanced briefly over at the men engaged in their work before she went on. "I was there with Jagang when he attacked Aydindril."

Kahlan felt as if her heart came up in her throat at hearing first-hand confirmation of that brute invading the place where she'd grown up. She didn't think she could bear to hear the answer, but she had to ask. "Did he destroy the city?"

After Richard had been captured and taken from her, Kahlan, with Cara at her side, had led the D'Haran army against Jagang's vast invading horde from the Old World. Month after month, Kahlan and the army fought against impossible odds, retreating all the way up through the Midlands.

By the time they lost the battle for the Midlands, it had been over a year since Kahlan had seen Richard; he had seemingly been cast into oblivion. When at last she learned where he was being held, Kahlan and Cara had raced south, to the Old World, only to arrive just as Richard ignited a firestorm of revolution in the heart of Jagang's homeland.

Before she'd left, Kahlan had evacuated Aydindril and left the Confessors' Palace empty of all those who called it home. Life, not a place, was what mattered.

"He never got a chance to destroy the city," Jennsen said. "When we arrived at the Confessors' Palace, Emperor Jagang thought he had you and Richard cornered. But out in front waited a spear holding the head of the emperor's revered spiritual leader: Brother Narev." Her voice lowered meaningfully. "Jagang found the message left with the head."

Kahlan remembered well the day Richard had sent the head of that evil man, along with a message for Jagang, on the long journey north. "'Compliments of Richard Rahl.'"

"That's right," Jennsen said. "You can't imagine Jagang's rage." She paused to be certain Kahlan heeded her warning. "He'll do anything to get his hands on you and Richard."

Kahlan hardly needed Jennsen to tell her how much Jagang wanted them.

"All the more reason to get away—hide somewhere," Cara said.

"And the races?" Kahlan reminded her.

Cara cast a suggestive look at Jennsen before speaking in a quiet voice to Kahlan. "If we do something about the rest of it, maybe that problem would go away, too." Cara's goal was to protect Richard. She would be perfectly happy to put him in a hole somewhere and board him over if she thought doing so would keep harm from reaching him.

Jennsen waited, watching the two of them. Kahlan wasn't at all sure there was anything Jennsen could do. Richard had thought it over and had come to have serious doubts. Kahlan had been amply skeptical without Richard's doubts. Still . . .

"Maybe" was all she said.

"If there's anything I can do, I want to try it." Jennsen fussed with a button on the front of her dress. "Richard doesn't think I can help. If it involves magic, wouldn't he know? Richard is a wizard, he would know about magic."

Kahlan sighed. There was so much more to it. "Richard was raised in Westland—far from the Midlands, even farther from D'Hara. He grew up in isolation from the rest of the New World, never knowing anything at all about the gift. Despite all he's so far learned and some of the remarkable things he's accomplished, he still knows very little of his birthright."

They had already told Jennsen this, but she seemed skeptical, as if she suspected there was a certain amount of exaggeration in what they were telling her about Richard's unfamiliarity with his own gift. Her big brother had, after all, in one day rescued her from a lifetime of terror. Such a profound awakening probably seemed tangled in magic to one so devoid of it. Perhaps it was.

"Well, if Richard is as ignorant of magic as you say," Jennsen pressed in a meaningful voice, finally having arrived at the heart of her purpose, "then maybe we shouldn't worry so much about what he thinks. Maybe we should just not tell him and go ahead and do whatever it is Cara wants me to do to fix your problem and get the races off your backs."

Nearby, Betty contentedly licked clean her little white twins. The sweltering darkness and vast weight of the surrounding silence seemed as eternal as death itself.

Kahlan gently took hold of Jennsen's collar. "I grew up walking the corridors of the Wizard's Keep and the Confessors' Palace. I know a lot about magic."

She pulled the young woman closer. "I can tell you that such naive notions, when applied to ominous matters like this, can easily get people killed. There is always the possibility that it's as simple as you fancy, but most likely it's complex beyond your imagination and any rash attempt at a remedy could ignite a conflagration that would consume us all. Added to all that is the grave peril of not knowing how someone, such as yourself, someone so pristinely ungifted as to be forewarned of in that ancient book Richard has, might affect the equation.

"There are times when there is no choice but to act immediately; even then it must be with your best judgment, using all your experience and everything you do know. As long as there's a choice, though, you don't act in matters of magic until you can be sure of the consequence. You don't ever just take a stab in the dark."

Kahlan knew all too well the terrible truth of such an admonition. Jennsen seemed unconvinced. "But if he doesn't really know much about magic, his fears might only be—"

"I've walked through dead cities, walked among the mutilated bodies of men, women, and children the Imperial Order has left in their wake. I've seen young women not as old as you make thoughtless, innocent mistakes and end up chained to a stake to be used by gangs of soldiers for days before being tortured to death just for the amusement of men who get sick pleasure out of raping a woman as she's in the throes of death."

Kahlan gritted her teeth as memories flashed mercilessly before her mind's eye. She tightened her grip on Jennsen's collar.

"All of my sister Confessors died in such a fashion, and they knew about their power and how to use it. The men who caught them knew, too, and used that knowledge against them. My closest girlhood friend died in my arms after such men were finished with her.

"Life means nothing to people like that; they worship death.

"Those are the kind of people who butchered your mother. Those are the kind of people who will have us, too, if we make a mistake. Those are the kind of people laying traps for us—including traps constructed of magic.

"As for Richard not knowing about magic, there are times when he is so ignorant of the simplest things that I can scarcely believe it and must remind myself that he grew up not being taught anything at all about his gift. In those things, I try to be patient and to guide him as best I can. He takes very seriously what I tell him.

"There are other times when I suspect that he actually grasps complexities of magic that neither I nor anyone alive has ever before fathomed or even so much as imagined. In those things he must be his own guide.

"The lives of a great many good people depend on us not making careless mistakes, especially careless mistakes with magic. As the Mother Confessor I'll not allow reckless whim to jeopardize all those lives. Now, do you understand me?"

Kahlan had nightmares about the things she had seen, about those who had been caught, about those who had made a simple mistake and paid the price with their life. She was not many years beyond Jennsen's age, but right then that gulf was vastly more than a mere handful of years.

Kahlan gave Jennsen's collar a sharp yank. "Do you understand me?"

Wide-eyed, Jennsen swallowed. "Yes, Mother Confessor." Finally, her gaze broke toward the ground.

Only then did Kahlan release her.

CHAPTER 4

"Anyone hungry?" Tom called to the three women.

Richard pulled a lantern from the wagon and, after finally getting it lit with a steel and flint, set it on a shelf of rock. He passed a suspicious look among the three women as they approached, but apparently thought better of saying anything.

As Kahlan sat close at Richard's side, Tom offered him the first chunk he sliced from a long length of sausage. When Richard declined, Kahlan accepted it. Tom sliced off another piece and passed it to Cara and then another to Friedrich.

Jennsen had gone to the wagon to search through her pack. Kahlan thought that maybe she just wanted to be alone a moment to collect herself. Kahlan knew how harsh her words had sounded, but she couldn't allow herself to do Jennsen the disservice of coddling her with pleasing lies.

With Jennsen reassuringly close by, Betty lay down beside Rusty, Jennsen's red roan mare. The horse and the goat were fast friends. The other horses seemed pleased by the visitor and took keen interest in her two kids, giving them a good sniff when they came close enough.

When Jennsen walked over displaying a small piece of carrot, Betty rose up in a rush. Her tail went into a blur of expectant wagging. The horses whinnied and tossed their heads, hoping not to be left out. Each in turn received a small treat and a scratch behind the ears.

Had they a fire, they could have cooked a stew, rice, or beans; griddled some bannock; or maybe have made a nice soup. Despite how hungry she was, Kahlan didn't think she would have had the energy to cook, so she was content to settle for what was at hand. Jennsen retrieved strips of dried meat from her pack, offering them around. Richard declined this, too, instead eating hard travel biscuits, nuts, and dried fruit.

"But don't you want any meat?" Jennsen asked as she sat down on her bedroll opposite him. "You need more than that to eat. You need something substantial."

"I can't eat meat. Not since the gift came to life in me."

Jennsen wrinkled her nose with a puzzled look. "Why would your gift not allow you to eat meat?"

Richard leaned to the side, resting his weight on an elbow as he momentarily surveyed the sweep of stars, searching for the words to explain. "Balance, in nature," he said at last, "is a condition resulting from the interaction of all things in existence. On a simple level, look at how predators and prey are in balance. If there were too many predators, and the prey were all eaten, then the thriving predators, too, would end up starving and dying out.

"The lack of balance would be deadly to both prey and predator; the world, for them both, would end. They exist in balance because acting in accordance with their nature results in balance. Balance is not their conscious intent.

"People are different. Without our conscious intent, we don't necessarily achieve the balance that our survival often requires.

"We must learn to use our minds, to think, if we're to survive. We plant crops, we hunt for fur to keep us warm, or raise sheep and gather their wool and learn how to weave it into cloth. We have to learn how to build shelter. We balance the value of one thing against another and trade goods to exchange what we've made for what we need that others have made or grown or built or woven or hunted.

"We balance what we need with what we know of the realities of the world. We balance what we want against our rational self-interest, not against fulfilling a momentary impulse, because we know that our long-term survival requires it. We use wood to build a fire in the hearth in order to keep from freezing on a winter night, but, despite how cold we might be when we're building the fire, we don't build the fire too big, knowing that to do so would risk burning our shelter down after we're warm and asleep."

"But people also act out of shortsighted selfishness, greed, and lust for power. They destroy lives." Jennsen lifted her arm out toward the darkness. "Look at what the Imperial Order is doing—and succeeding at. They don't care about weaving wool or building houses or trading goods. They slaughter people just for conquest. They take what they want."

"And we resist them. We've learned to understand the value of life, so we fight to re-establish reason. We are the balance."

Jennsen hooked some of her hair back behind an ear. "What does all this have to do with not eating meat?"

"I was told that wizards, too, must balance themselves, their gift—their power—in the things they do. I fight against those, like the Imperial Order, who would destroy life because it has no value to them, but that requires that I do the same terrible thing by destroying what is my highest value—life. Since my gift has to do with being a warrior, abstinence from eating meat is believed to be the balance for the killing I'm forced to do."

"What happens if you eat meat?"

Kahlan knew that Richard had cause, from only the day before, to need the balance of not eating meat.

"Even the idea of eating meat nauseates me. I've done it when I've had to, but it's something I avoid if at all possible. Magic deprived of balance has grave consequences, just like building too big a fire in the hearth."

The thought occurred to Kahlan that Richard carried the Sword of Truth, and perhaps that weapon also imposed its own need for balance. Richard had been rightly named the Seeker of Truth by the First Wizard himself, Zeddicus Zu'l Zorander—Zedd—Richard's grandfather, the man who had helped raise him, and from whom Richard had additionally inherited the gift. Richard's gift had been passed down not only from the Rahl bloodline, but the Zorander as well. Balance indeed.

Rightly-named Seekers had been carrying that very same sword for nearly three thousand years. Perhaps Richard's understanding of the need for balance had helped him to survive the things he'd faced.

With her teeth, Jennsen tugged off a strip of dried meat as she thought it over. "So, because you have to fight and sometimes kill people, you can't eat meat as the balance for that terrible act?"

Richard nodded as he chewed dried apricots.

"It must be dreadful to have the gift," Jennsen said in a quiet voice. "To have something so destructive that it requires you balance it in some way."

She looked away from Richard's gray eyes. Kahlan knew what a difficult experience it sometimes was to meet his direct and incisive gaze.

"I used to feel that way," he said, "when I first was named the Seeker and given the sword, and even more so later, when I learned that I had the gift. I didn't want to have the gift, didn't want the things the gift could do, just as I hadn't wanted the sword because of the things in me that I thought shouldn't ever be brought out."

"But now you don't mind as much, having the sword, or the gift?"

"You have a knife and have used it." Richard leaned toward her, holding out his hands. "You have hands. Do you hate your knife, or hands?"

"Of course not. But what does that have to do with having the gift?"

"Having the gift is simply how I was born, like being born male, or female, or with blue, or brown, or green eyes—or with two hands. I don't hate my hands because I could potentially strangle someone with them. It's my mind that directs my hands. My hands don't act of their own accord; to think so is to ignore the truth of what each thing is, its true nature. You have to recognize the truth of things if you're to achieve balance—or come to truly understand anything, for that matter."

Kahlan wondered why she didn't require balance the way Richard did. Why was it so vital for him, but not for her? Despite how much she wanted to go to sleep, she couldn't keep silent. "I often use my Confessor's power for that same end—to kill—and I don't have to keep in balance by not eating meat."

"The Sisters of the Light claim that the veil that separates the world of the living from the world of the dead is maintained through magic. More precisely, they claim that the veil is here," Richard said, tapping the side of his temple, "in those of us who have the gift—wizards and to a lesser extent sorceresses. They claim that balance for those of us with the gift is essential because in us, within our gift, resides the veil, making us, in essence, the guardians of the veil, the balance between worlds.

"Maybe they're right. I have both sides of the gift: Additive and Subtractive. Maybe that makes it different for me. Maybe having both sides makes it more important than usual for me to keep my gift in balance."

Kahlan wondered just how much of that might be true. She feared to think how extensively the balance of magic itself had been altered by her doing.

The world was unraveling, in more ways than one. But there had been no choice.

Cara dismissively waggled a piece of dried meat before them. "All this balance business is just a message from the good spirits—in that other world—telling Lord Rahl to leave such fighting to us. If he did, then he wouldn't have to worry about balance, or what he can and can't eat. If he would stop putting himself in mortal danger then his balance would be just fine and he could eat a whole goat."

Jennsen's eyebrows went up.

"You know what I mean," Cara grumbled.

Tom leaned in. "Maybe Mistress Cara is right, Lord Rahl. You have people to protect you. You should let them do it and you could better put your abilities to the task of being the Lord Rahl."

Richard closed his eyes and rubbed his temples with his fingertips. "If I had to wait for Cara to save me all the time, I'm afraid I'd have to do without a head."

Cara rolled her eyes at his wisp of a smile and went back to her sausage.

Studying his face in the dim light as he sucked on a small bite of dried biscuit, Kahlan thought that Richard didn't look well, and that it was more than simply being exhausted. The soft glow of light from the lantern lit one side of his face, leaving the rest in darkness, as if he were only half there, half in this world and half in the world of darkness, as if he were the veil between.

She leaned close and brushed back the hair that had fallen across his forehead, using the excuse to feel his brow. He felt hot, but they were all hot and sweating, so she couldn't really tell if he had a fever, but she didn't think so.

Her hand slipped down to cup his face, kindling his smile. She thought she could lose herself in the pleasure of just looking into his eyes. It made her heart ache with joy to see his smile. She smiled back, a smile she gave no one but him.

Kahlan had an urge to kiss him, too, but there always seemed to be people around and the kind of kiss she really wanted to give him wasn't the kind of kiss you gave in front of others.

"It seems so hard to imagine," Friedrich said to Richard. "I mean, the Lord Rahl himself, not knowing about the gift as he grew up." Friedrich shook his head. "It seems so hard to believe."

"My grandfather, Zedd, has the gift," Richard said as he leaned back. "He wanted to help raise me away from magic, much like Jennsen—hidden away where Darken Rahl couldn't get at me. That's why he wanted me raised in Westland, on the other side of the boundary from magic."

"And even your grandfather—a wizard—never let on that he was gifted?" Tom asked.

"No, not until Kahlan came to Westland. Looking back on it, I realize that there were a lot of little things that told me he was more than he seemed, but growing up I never knew. He just always seemed wizardly to me in the sense that he seemed to know about everything in the world around us. He opened up that world for me, making me want to all the time know more, but the gift wasn't ever the magic he showed me—life was what he showed me."

"It's really true, then," Friedrich said, "that Westland was set aside to be a place without magic."

Richard smiled at the mention of his home of Westland. "It is. I grew up in the Hartland woods, right near the boundary and I never saw magic. Except maybe for Chase."

"Chase?" Tom asked.

"A friend of mine—a boundary warden. Fellow about your size, Tom. Whereas you serve to protect the Lord Rahl, Chase's charge was the boundary, or rather, keeping people away from it. He told me that his job was keeping away the prey—people—so that the things that come out of the boundary wouldn't get any stronger. He worked to maintain balance." Richard smiled to himself. "He didn't have the gift, but I often thought that the things that man could pull off had to be magic."

Friedrich, too, was smiling at Richard's story. "I lived in D'Hara all my life. When I was young those men who guarded the boundary were my heroes and I wanted to join them."

"Why didn't you?" Richard asked.

"When the boundary went up I was too young." Friedrich stared off into memories, then sought to change the subject. "How much longer until we get out of this wasteland, Lord Rahl?"

Richard looked east, as if he could see off into the black of night beyond the dim circle of lantern light. "If we keep up our pace, a few more days and we'll be out of the worst of it, I'd say. It gets rockier now as the ground continues to rise up toward the distant mountains. The traveling will be more difficult but at least as we get higher it shouldn't be quite so hot."

"How far to this thing that . . . that Cara thinks I should touch?" Jennsen asked.

Richard studied her face a moment. "I'm not so sure that's a good idea."

"But we are going there?"

"Yes."

Jennsen picked at the strip of dried meat. "What is this thing that Cara touched, anyway? Cara and Kahlan don't seem to want to tell me."

"I asked them not to tell you," Richard said.

"But why? If we're going to see it, then why wouldn't you want to tell me what it is?"

"Because you don't have the gift," Richard said. "I don't want to influence what you see."

Jennsen blinked. "What difference could that make?"

"I haven't had time to translate much of it yet, but from what I gather from the book Friedrich brought me, even those who don't have the gift, in the common sense, have at least some tiny spark of it. In that way they are able to interact with the magic in the world—much like you must be born with eyes to see color. Being born with eyes, you can see and understand a grand painting, even though you many not have the ability to create such a painting yourself.

"The gifted Lord Rahl gives birth to only one gifted heir. He may have other children, but rarely are any of them ever also gifted. Still, they do have this infinitesimal spark, as does everyone else. Even they, so to speak, can see color.

"The book says, though, that there are rare offspring of a gifted Lord Rahl, like you, who are born devoid of any trace whatsoever of the gift. The book calls them pillars of Creation. Much like those born without eyes can't perceive color, those born like you can't perceive magic.

"But even that is imprecise, because with you it's more than simply not perceiving magic. For someone born blind, color exists, they just aren't able to see it. For you, though, it isn't that you simply can't perceive magic; for you magic does not exist—it isn't a reality."

"How is such a thing possible?" Jennsen asked.

"I don't know," Richard said. "When our ancestors created the bond of the Lord Rahl to the D'Haran people, it carried the unique ability to consistently bear a gifted heir. Magic needs balance. Maybe they had to make it work like this, have this counter of those born like you, in order for the magic they created to work; maybe they didn't realize what would happen and inadvertently created the balance."

Jennsen cleared her throat. "What would happen if . . . you know, if I were to have children?"

Richard surveyed Jennsen's eyes for what seemed a painfully long time. "You would bear offspring like you."

Jennsen sat forward, her hands reflecting her emotional entreaty. "Even if I marry someone with that spark of the gift? Someone able to perceive color, as you called it? Even then my child would be like me?"

"Even then and every time," Richard said with quiet certitude. "You are a broken link in the chain of the gift. According to the book, once the line of all those born with the spark of the gift, including those with the gift as it is in me, going back thousands of years, going back forever, is broken, it is broken for all time. It cannot be restored. Once forfeited in such a marriage, no descendant of that line can ever restore the link to the gift. When these children marry, they too would be as you, breaking the chain in the line of those they marry. Their children would be the same, and so on.

"That's why the Lord Rahl always hunted down ungifted offspring and eliminated them. You would be the genesis of something the world has never had before: those untouched by the gift. Every offspring of every descendant would end the line of the spark of the gift in everyone they married. The world, mankind, would be changed forever.

"This is the reason the book calls those like you 'Pillars of Creation.'"

The silence seemed brittle.

"And that's what this place is called, too," Tom said as he pointed a thumb back over his shoulder, seeming to feel the need to say something into the quiet, "the Pillars of Creation." He looked at the faces surrounding the weak light coming from the sputtering lantern. "Seems a strange coincidence that both those like Jennsen and this place would be called the same thing."

Richard stared off into the darkness toward that terrible place where Kahlan would have died had he made a mistake with the magic involved. "I don't think it's a coincidence. They are connected, somehow."

The book—*The Pillars of Creation*—describing those born like Jennsen was written in the ancient language of High D'Haran. Few people still living understood High D'Haran. Richard had begun to learn it in order to unravel important information in other books they'd found that were from the time of the great war.

That war, extinguished three thousand years before, had somehow ignited once again, and was burning uncontrolled through the world.

Kahlan feared to think of the central—if inadvertent—part she and Richard had played in making it possible.

Jennsen leaned in, as if looking for some thread of hope. "How do you think the two might be connected?"

Richard let out a tired sigh. "I don't know, yet."

With a finger, Jennsen rolled a pebble around in a small circle, leaving a tiny rut in the dust. "All of those things about me being a pillar of Creation, being the break in the link of the gift, makes me feel somehow . . . dirty."

"Dirty?" Tom asked, looking hurt to hear her even suggest such a thing. "Jennsen, why would you feel that way?"

"Those like me are also called 'holes in the world.' I guess I can see why, now."

Richard leaned forward, resting his elbows on his knees. "I know what it's like to feel regret for how you were born, for what you have, or don't have. I hated being born the way I was—with the gift. But I came to realize how senseless such feelings are, how completely wrong it was to think that way."

"But it's different with me," she said as she pushed at the sand with a finger, erasing the little rut she'd made with the pebble. "There are others like you—wizards or sorceresses with the gift. Everyone else can at least see colors, as you put it. I'm the only one like this."

Richard gazed at his half sister, a beautiful, bright, ungifted half sister that any previous Lord Rahl would have murdered on the spot, and was overcome with a radiant smile. "Jennsen, I think of you as born pure. You're like a new snowflake, different to any other, and startlingly beautiful."

Looking up at him, Jennsen was overcome with a smile of her own. "I never thought of it that way." Her smile withered as she thought about his words. "But still, I'd be destroying—"

"You would be creating, not destroying," Richard said. "Magic exists. It cannot possess the 'right' to exist. To think so would be to ignore the true nature—the reality—of things. People, if they don't take the lives of others, have the right to live their life. You can't say that because you were born with red hair you supplanted the 'right' of brown hair to be born on your head."

Jennsen giggled at such a concept. It was good to see the smile taking firmer hold. By the look on Tom's face, he agreed.

"So," Jennsen finally asked, "what about this thing we're going to see?"

"If the thing Cara touched has been altered by someone with the gift, then since you can't see the magic, you might see something we can't see: what lies beneath that magic."

Jennsen rubbed the edge of her boot heel. "And you think that will tell you something important?"

"I don't know. It may be useful, or it may not, but I want to know what you see—with your special vision—without any suggestion from us."

"If you're so worried about it, why did you leave it? Aren't you afraid someone might come across it and take it?"

"I worry about a lot of things," Richard said.

"Even if it really is something altered by magic and she sees it for what it truly is," Cara said, "that doesn't mean that it still isn't what it seems to us, or that it isn't just as dangerous."

Richard nodded. "At least we'll know that much more about it. Anything we learn might help us in some way."

Cara scowled. "I just want her to turn it back over."

Richard gave her a look designed to keep her from saying anything else about it. Cara huffed, leaned in, and took one of Richard's dried apricots. She scowled at him as she popped the apricot in her mouth.

As soon as supper was finished, Jennsen suggested that they pack all the food safely back in the wagon so that Betty wouldn't help herself to it in the night. Betty was always hungry. At least, with her two kids, she now had a taste of what it was like to be badgered for food.

Kahlan thought that Friedrich should be given consideration, because of his age, so she asked him if he'd like to take first watch. First watch was easier than being awakened in the middle of the night to stand watch between stretches of sleep. He smiled his appreciation as he nodded his agreement.

After opening his and Kahlan's bedroll, Richard doused the

lantern. The night was sweltering but crystal clear so that, after Kahlan's eyes adjusted, the sweep of stars was enough to see by, if not very well. One of the white twins thought the newly unfurled bedrolls would be a perfect place to romp. Kahlan scooped up the leggy bundle and returned it to its tail-wagging mother.

As she lay down beside Richard, Kahlan saw the dark shape of Jennsen curl up by Betty and collect the twins in the tender bed of her arms, where they quickly settled down.

Richard leaned over and gently kissed Kahlan's lips. "I love you, you know."

"If we're ever alone, Lord Rahl," Kahlan whispered back, "I'd like to have more than a quick kiss."

He laughed softly and kissed her forehead before lying on his side, away from her. She had been expecting an intimate promise, or at least a lighthearted remark.

Kahlan curled up behind him and rested a hand on his shoulder. "Richard," she whispered, "are you all right?"

It took him longer to answer than she would have liked. "I have a splitting headache."

She wanted to ask what kind of headache, but she didn't want the tiny spark of fear she harbored to gain the glow of credence by voicing it aloud.

"It's different from the headaches I had before," Richard said, as if in answer to her thoughts. "I suppose it's this wicked heat on top of not having had any sleep for so long."

"I suppose." Kahlan bunched up the blanket she was using for a pillow to make a lump that would press against the sore spot at the base of her skull. "The heat is making my head pound, too." She gently rubbed the back of his shoulder. "Have a good sleep, then."

She was exhausted and aching all over, and it felt delicious to lie down. Her head felt better, too, with the soft lump of blanket pressed against the back of her neck. With her hand resting against Richard's shoulder, feeling his slow breathing, Kahlan fell into a dead sleep.

CHAPTER 5

As tired as she was, it was a marvelous sensation being beside Richard and letting herself go, letting her concerns and worries go for the time being, and so effortlessly sinking into sleep.

But the sleep seemed only just started when she woke to find Cara gently shaking her shoulder.

Kahlan blinked up at the familiar silhouette standing over her. She ached to go back to sleep, to be left alone to be so wonderfully asleep again.

"My watch?" Kahlan asked.

Cara nodded. "I'll stand it if you'd like."

Kahlan glanced over her shoulder as she sat up, seeing that Richard was still fast asleep. "No," she whispered. "You get some sleep. You need rest, too."

Kahlan yawned and stretched her back. She took Cara's elbow and pulled her a short distance away, out of earshot, and leaned close. "I think you're right. There's more than enough of us to stand watch and all still get enough rest. Let's let Richard sleep till morning."

Cara smiled her agreement before heading for her bedroll. Conspiracy designed to protect Richard suited the Mord-Sith.

Kahlan yawned and stretched again, at the same time forcing herself to shake the lingering haze of sleep from her mind, to be alert. Pulling her hair back from her face and flipping it over her shoulder, she scanned the wasteland all around, looking for anything out of the ordinary. Everything beyond their camp was as still as death. Mountains blacked out the glittering sweep of stars in a jagged line all the way around the horizon.

Kahlan took careful assessment of everyone, making sure they were all accounted for. Cara already looked comfortable. Tom slept not far from the horses. Friedrich was asleep on the other side of the horses. Jennsen was curled up beside Betty, but by her movements, the way she turned from her side to her back, didn't look asleep. The babies had moved and now lay sprawled with their heads butted up tight against their mother.

Kahlan was always especially vigilant right at change of watch. Change of watch was a prime time for attack; she knew, for she had often initiated raids around change of watch. Those just going off watch were often tired and already thinking of other things, considering watch the duty of the next guard. Those just coming on watch were often not mentally prepared for a sudden attack. People tended to think that the enemy would not come until they were properly settled in and on the lookout. Victory favored those who were ready. Defeat stalked those who were unwary.

Kahlan made her way to a formation of rock not far from Richard. She scooted back, sitting atop a high spot in order to get a better view of the lifeless surroundings. Even in the middle of the night, the rough rock still radiated the fierce heat of the previous day.

Kahlan pulled a skein of damp hair away from her neck, wishing there were a breeze. There had been times, in winter, when she had nearly frozen to death. Try as she might, she couldn't seem to recall what it felt like to be truly cold.

It wasn't long after Kahlan had gotten herself situated before she saw Jennsen get up and step quietly through their camp, trying not to wake the others.

"All right if I sit with you?" she asked when she finally reached Kahlan.

"Of course."

Jennsen pushed her bottom back up onto the rock beside Kahlan, pulled her knees up, and wrapped her arms around them, hugging them close to her body. For a time she just gazed out at the night.

"Kahlan, I'm sorry—about before." Despite the dark, Kahlan thought she could see that the young woman looked miserable. "I didn't mean to sound like a fool who would do something without thinking. I'd never do anything to hurt any of you."

"I know you wouldn't deliberately do any such thing. It's the things you might do unwittingly that concern me."

Jennsen nodded. "I think I understand a little better, now, about how complicated everything is and how much I really don't know. I'll not do anything unless you or Richard tells me to, I promise."

Kahlan smiled and ran a hand down the back of Jennsen's head, letting it come to rest on her shoulder. "I only told you those things because I care about you, Jennsen." She gave the shoulder a compassionate squeeze. "I guess I'm worried for you the same way Betty worries for her innocent twins, knowing the dangers all around when they rarely do.

"You need to understand that if you go out on thin ice, it doesn't matter if the lake was frozen over by a cold spell, or a magic spell. If you don't know where you're stepping, so to speak, you could fall into the cold dark arms of death. It matters not what made the ice—dead is dead. My point is that you don't go out on that thin ice unless you have a very powerful need, because it very well could cost you your life."

"But I'm not touched by magic. Like Richard said, I'm like someone born without eyes who can't see color. I'm a broken link in the chain of magic. Wouldn't that mean that I can't accidentally get into trouble with it?"

"And if someone pushes a boulder off a cliff and it crushes you, does it matter if that boulder was sent crashing over the edge by a man with a lever, or by a sorceress wielding the gift?"

Jennsen's voice took on a troubled tone. "I see what you mean. I guess that I never looked at it that way."

"I'm only trying to help you because I know how easy it is to make a mistake."

She watched Kahlan in the dark for a moment. "You know about magic. What kind of mistake could you make?"

"All kinds."

"Like what?

Kahlan stared off into the memories. "I once delayed for half a second in killing someone."

"But I thought you said that it was wrong to be too rash."

"Sometimes the most foolhardy thing you can do is to delay. She was a sorceress. By the time I acted it was already too late. Because of my mistake she captured Richard and took him away. For a year, I didn't know what had happened to him. I thought I would never see him again, that I would die of heartache."

Jennsen stared in astonishment. "When did you find him again?"

"Not long ago. That's why we're down here in the Old World—she brought him here. At least I found him. I've made other mistakes, and they, too, have resulted in no end of trouble. So has Richard. Like he said, we all make mistakes. If I can, I want to spare you from making a needless mistake, at least."

Jennsen looked away. "Like believing in that man I was with yesterday—Sebastian. Because of him, my mother was murdered and I almost got you killed. I feel like such a fool."

"You didn't make that mistake out of carelessness, Jennsen. They deceived you, used you. More importantly, in the end you used your head and were willing to face the truth."

Jennsen nodded.

"What should we name the twins?" she finally asked.

Kahlan didn't think that naming the twins was a good idea, not yet anyway, but she was reluctant to say it.

"I don't know. What names were you thinking?"

Jennsen let out a heavy breath. "It was a shock to suddenly have Betty back with me, and even more of a surprise to see that she had babies of her own. I never considered that before. I haven't even had time to think about names."

"You will."

Jennsen smiled at the thought. Her smile grew, as if at the thought of something more.

"You know," she said, "I think I understand what Richard meant about thinking of his grandfather as wizardly, even though he never saw him do magic."

"What do you mean?"

"Well, I can't see magic, so to speak, and Richard didn't do any tonight—at least none I know of." She laughed softly, as pleasing a laugh as Kahlan had ever heard, full of life and joy. It had a quality to it much like Richard's, the feminine balance to Richard's masculine laugh, two facets of the same delight.

"And yet," Jennsen went on, "the things he said made me think of him in that way—wizardly—like he said about Zedd. When he was saying that, I knew just what he meant, just how he'd felt, because Richard has opened up the world for me, but the gift wasn't the magic he showed me. It was him showing me life, that my life is mine, and worth living."

Kahlan smiled to herself, at how very much that described her own feeling of what Richard had done for her, how he had brought her to cherish life and believe in it not just for others, but, most importantly, for herself.

For a time they sat together, silently watching the empty wasteland. Kahlan kept an eye on Richard as he tossed in his sleep.

With growing concern, Jennsen, too, watched Richard. "It looks like there's something wrong with him," she whispered as she leaned close.

"He's having a nightmare."

Kahlan watched, as she had so many times before, as Richard made fists in his sleep, as he struggled silently against some private terror.

"It's scary to see him like that," Jennsen said. "He seems so different. When he's awake he always seems so . . . reasoned."

"You can't reason with a nightmare," Kahlan said in quiet sorrow.

CHAPTER 6

Richard woke with a start.

They were back.

He had been having a bad dream. Like all of his dreams, he didn't remember it. He only knew it was a bad dream because it left behind the shapeless feeling of breathless, heart-pounding, undefined, frantic terror. He threw off the lingering pall of the nightmare as he would throw off a tangled blanket. Even though it felt as if the dark things in lingering remnants of the dream were still clawing at him, trying to drag him back into their world, he knew that dreams were immaterial, and so he dismissed it. Now that he was awake, the feeling of dread rapidly began to dissolve, like fog burning off under hot sunlight.

Still, he had to make an effort to slow his breathing.

What was important was that they were back. He didn't always know when they returned, but this time, for some reason, he was sure of it.

Sometime in the night, too, the wind had come up. It buffeted him, pulling at his clothes, tearing at his hair. Out on the sweltering waste, the scorching gusts offered no relief from the heat. Rather than being refreshing, the wind was so hot that it felt as though the door to a blast furnace had opened and that the heat were broiling his flesh.

Groping for his waterskin, he didn't find it immediately at hand. He tried to recall exactly where he'd laid it, but, with other thoughts screaming for his attention, he couldn't remember. He would have to worry about a drink later.

Kahlan lay close, turned toward him. She had gathered her long hair in a loose fist beneath her chin. The wind whipped stray strands across her cheek. Richard loved just to sit and look at her face; this time, though, he delayed but a moment, looking at her only long enough in the faint starlight to note her even breathing. She was sound asleep.

As he scanned their camp, he could just make out a weak blush in the eastern sky. Dawn was still some time off.

He realized that he'd slept through his watch. Cara and Kahlan had no doubt decided that he needed the sleep more than he was needed for standing a watch and had conspired to not wake him. They were probably right. He had been so exhausted that he'd slept right through the night. Now, though, he was wide awake.

His headache, too, was gone.

Silently, carefully, Richard slipped away from Kahlan so as not to wake her. He instinctively reached for his sword lying at his other side. The metal was warm beneath his touch as his fingers curled around the familiar silver-and-gold-wrought scabbard. It was always reassuring to find the sword at the ready, but even more so at that moment. As he silently rolled to his feet, he slipped the baldric over his head, placing the familiar supple leather across his right shoulder. As he rose up, his sword was already at his hip, ready to do his bidding.

Despite how reassuring it was to have the weapon at his side, after the carnage back at the place called the Pillars of Creation the thought of drawing it sickened him. He recoiled from the mental image of the things he had done. Had he not, though, Kahlan wouldn't be sleeping peacefully; she would be dead, or worse.

Other good had come of it, too. Jennsen had been pulled back from the brink. He saw her curled up beside her beloved goat, her arm corralling Betty's two sleeping kids. He smiled at seeing her, at what a marvel it was to have a sister, smiled at how smart she was and all the wonders of life she had ahead of her. It made him happy that she was eager to be around him, but being around him made him worry for her safety, too. There really wasn't any place safe, though, unless the forces of the Order that had been unleashed could be defeated, or at least bottled back up.

A heavy gust tore through their camp, raising even thicker clouds of dirt. Richard blinked, trying to keep the blowing sand out of his eyes. The sound of the wind in his ears was aggravating because it masked other sounds. Though he listened carefully, he could hear only the wind.

Squinting against the blowing grit, he saw that Tom was sitting atop his wagon, looking this way and that, keeping watch. Friedrich was asleep on the other side of the horses, Cara not far away on the desert side of Kahlan, putting herself between them and anything that might be out beyond. In the dim starlight Tom hadn't spotted Richard. When Tom scanned the night in the opposite direction, Richard moved away from camp, leaving Tom to watch over the others.

Richard was comfortable in the cloak of darkness. Years of practice had taught him to slip unseen through shadows, to move silently in the darkness. He did that now, moving away from camp as he focused on what had awakened him, on what others standing watch would not sense.

Unlike Tom, the races did not miss Richard's movements. They wheeled high overhead as they watched him, following him as he made his way out along the broken ground. They were almost invisible against the dark sky, but Richard could make them out as they blacked out stars, like telltale shadows against the sparkling black curtain of night—shadows that he thought he could feel as well as he could see.

That the crushing headache was gone was a great relief, but that it had vanished in the manner that it had was also a cause for concern. The torment often vanished when he was distracted by something important. Something dangerous. At the same time, even though the pain was gone, it felt as if it were simply hiding in the shadows of his mind, waiting for him to relax so that it could pounce.

When the headaches surged through him, the nauseating pain was so intense that it made him feel sick in every fiber of his being. Even though the crushing pain at times made it difficult for him to stand, to put one foot in front of the other, he had known that to remain behind, where they were, would have meant certain death. While the headaches were bad in and of themselves, Richard wasn't so much concerned about the pain as he was about the nature of the headaches—their cause.

They weren't the same as the headaches he'd had before that he so feared—the headaches brought on by the gift—but they weren't like those he considered to be normal headaches, either. Throughout his life he'd occasionally had terrible headaches, the same as his mother used to have on a more regular basis. She'd called them "my grim headaches." Richard thoroughly understood her meaning.

These, however grim, were not like those. He worried that they might be caused by the gift.

He'd had the headaches brought on by the gift before. He had been told that as he grew older, as his ability grew, as he came to understand more, he would, at times later in his life, be confronted with headaches brought on by the gift. The remedy was supposedly simple. He had only to seek the help of another wizard and have him assist with the necessary next level of awareness and comprehension of the nature of the gift within himself. That mental awareness and understanding would enable him to control and thereby eliminate the pain—to douse the flare-up. At least, that's what he had been told.

Of course, in the absence of another wizard to help, the Sisters of the Light would gladly put a collar around his neck to help control the runaway power of the gift.

He had been told that such headaches, if not properly tended to, were lethal. This much of it, at least, he knew was true. He couldn't afford to have that problem now, on top of all his others. Right now there was nothing he could do about it; there was no one anywhere near who could help him with that kind of headache—no wizard, and even though he would never allow it, no Sister of the Light to put him in a collar again.

Richard once more reminded himself that it wasn't the same kind of pain as the last time, when it had been brought on by the gift. He reminded himself not to invent trouble he didn't have.

He had enough real trouble.

He heard the whoosh as one of the huge birds shot past low overhead. The race twisted in flight, lifting on a gust of wind, to peer back at him.

Another followed in its wake, and then a third, a fourth, and a fifth. They slipped silently away, out across the open ground, following one another roughly in a line. Their wings rocked as they worked to stabilize themselves in the gusty air. Some distance away, they soared into a gliding, climbing turn back toward him.

Before they returned, the races tightened their flight into a circle. When they stroked their huge wings, Richard could usually hear their feathers whisper through the air, although now, with the sound of the wind, he couldn't. Their black eyes watched him watching them. He wanted them to know he was aware of them, that he hadn't slept through their nocturnal return.

Were he not so concerned about the meaning of the races, he might think they were beautiful, their sleek black shapes silhouetted majestically against the crimson flush coming to the sky.

As he watched, though, Richard couldn't imagine what they were doing. He'd seen this behavior from them before and hadn't understood it then, either. He realized, suddenly, that those other times when they'd returned to circle in this curious fashion, he had also been aware of them. He wasn't always aware of them or aware of when they returned. If he had a headache, though, it vanished when they returned.

The hot wind ruffled Richard's hair as he gazed out across wasteland obscured by the dusty predawn gloom. He didn't like this dead place. Dawn here would offer no promise of a world coming to life. He wished Kahlan and he were back in his woods. He couldn't help smiling as he recalled the place in the mountains where the year before they had spent the summer. The place was so wondrous that it had even managed to mellow Cara.

In the faint but gathering light, the black-tipped races circled, as they always did when they performed this curious maneuver, not over him, but a short distance away, this time out over the open desert where the buffeting wind unfurled diaphanous curtains of sandy grit. The other times it had been over forested hills, or open grassland. This time, as he watched the races, he had to squint to keep the blowing sand from getting in his eyes.

Abruptly tipping their broad wings, the races tightened their circle as they descended closer to the desert floor. He knew that they would do this for a short while before breaking up their formation to resume their normal flight. They sometimes flew in pairs and performed spectacular aerial stunts, each gracefully matching the other's every move, as ravens sometimes did, but otherwise they never flew in anything like the compact group of their sporadic circling.

And then, as the inky shapes wheeled around in a tight vortex, Richard realized that the trailers of blowing sand below them weren't simply snaking and curling aimlessly in the wind, but were flowing over something that wasn't there.

The hair along his arms stood stiffly up.

Richard blinked, squinting into the wind, trying to see better in the howling storm of blowing sand. Yet more dust and dirt lifted in the blast of a heavy gust. As the twisting eddies raced across the flat ground and passed beneath the races, they swirled around and over something below, making the shape more distinct.

It appeared to be the form of a person.

The dirt swirled around the empty void, silhouetting it, defining it, revealing what was there, but not. Whenever the wind lifted and carried with it a heavy load, the outline of the shape, bounded by the swirling sand, looked like the outline of a man shrouded in hooded robes.

Richard's right hand found the hilt of his sword.

There was nothing to the shape save the sand that flowed over the contours of what wasn't there, the way muddy water streaming around a clear glass bottle revealed its covert contour. The form seemed to be standing still, watching him.

There were, of course, no eyes in the empty sockets of blowing sand, but Richard could feel them on him.

"What is it?" Jennsen asked in a worried whisper as she rushed up beside him. "What's the matter? Do you see something?"

With his left hand, Richard pushed her back, out of his way. So urgent was his headlong rush of need that it took concentrated effort to be gentle about it. He was gripping the hilt of his sword so tightly that he could feel the raised letters of the word TRUTH woven in gold wire through the silver.

Richard was invoking from within the sword its purpose for being, the very core of its creation. In answer, the might of the sword's power ignited.

Beyond the veil of rage, though, in the shadows of his mind, even as the anger of the sword thundered through him, Richard dimly perceived an unexpected opposition on the part of the flux of magic to rise to the summons.

It was like heading out a door and leaning his weight into the howl of a gale, and stumbling forward a step at unexpectedly finding less resistance than anticipated.

Before Richard could question the sensation, the wave of wrath flooded through him, saturating him in the cold fury of the storm that was the sword's power.

As the races wheeled, their circle began coming closer. This, too, they had done before, but this time the shape that moved with them was betrayed by the swirl of sand and grit. It appeared that the intangible hooded man was being pulled closer by the black-tipped races.

The distinctive ring of steel announced the arrival of the Sword of Truth in the hot dawn air.

Jennsen squeaked at this sudden movement and jumped back.

The races answered with piercing, mocking cries that carried on the howling wind.

The unmistakable sound of Richard's sword being drawn brought Kahlan and Cara at a dead run. Cara would have leapt protectively ahead, but she knew better than to get in front of him when he had the sword out. Cara had her Agiel, the weapon of a Mord-Sith that looked like nothing more than a small red leather rod, clenched in her fist. She skidded to a halt off to the side, crouched and at the ready, a powerful cat ready to spring.

"What is it?" Kahlan asked as she ran up behind him, gaping out at the pattern in the wind.

"It's the races," came Jennsen's worried voice. "They've come back."

Kahlan stared incredulously at her. "The races don't look like the worst of it."

Sword in hand, Richard watched the thing below the wheeling races. Feeling the sword in his grip, its power sizzling through the very marrow of his bones, he felt a flash of hesitation, of doubt. With no time to waste, he turned back to Tom, just starting away from securing the lead lines to his big draft horses. Richard mimed shooting an arrow. Grasping Richard's meaning, Tom skidded to a halt and spun back to the wagon. Friedrich urgently seized the tethers to the other horses, working to keep them calm, keeping them from spooking. Leaning in the wagon, Tom threw gear aside as he searched for Richard's bow and quiver.

Jennsen peered from one grim face to another. "What do you mean the races aren't the worst of it?"

Cara pointed with her Agiel. "That . . . that figure. That man."

Frowning in confusion, Jennsen looked back and forth between Cara and the blowing sand.

"What do you see?" Richard asked.

Jennsen threw her hands up in a gesture of frustration. "Black-tipped races. Five of them. That, and the blinding blowing sand is all. Is there someone out there? Do you see people coming?"

She didn't see it.

Tom pulled the bow and quiver from the wagon and ran for the rest of them. Two of the races, as if noting Tom running in with the bow, lifted a wing and circled wider. They swept around him once before disappearing into the darkness. The other three, though, continued to circle, as if bearing the floating form in the blowing sand beneath them.

Closer still the races came, and the form with them. Richard couldn't imagine what it was, but the sense of dread it engendered rivaled any nightmare. The power from the sword surging through him had no such fear or doubt. Then why did he? Storms of magic within, beyond anything storming across the wasteland, spiraled up through him, fighting for release. With grim effort, Richard contained the need, focused it on the task of doing his bidding should he choose to release it. He was the master of the sword and had at all times to consciously exert that mastery. By the sword's reaction to what the currents of sand revealed, there could be no doubt as to Richard's conviction of the nature of what stood before him. Then what was it he sensed from the sword?

From back by the wagon, a horse screamed. A quick glance over his shoulder revealed Friedrich trying to calm them. All three horses reared against the rope he held fast. They came down stamping their hooves and snorting. From the corner of his eye, Richard saw twin streaks of black shoot in out of the darkness, skimming in just above the ground. Betty let out a terrible wail.

And then, as quickly as they'd appeared, they were gone, vanished back into the thick gloom.

"No!" Jennsen cried out as she ran for the animals.

Before them, the unmoving shape watched. Tom reached out, trying to stop Jennsen on the way past. She tore away from him. For a moment, Richard worried that Tom might go after her, but then he was again running for Richard.

Out of the dark swirling murk, the two races suddenly appeared, so close Richard could see the quills running down through their flight feathers spread wide in the wind. Swooping in out of the swirling storm of dust to rejoin the circle, each carried a small, limp, white form in its powerful talons.

Tom ran up holding the bow out in one hand and the quiver in the other. Making his choice, Richard slammed his sword into its scabbard and snatched up the bow.

With one smooth motion he bent the bow and attached the string. He yanked an arrow from the leather quiver Tom held out in his big fist.

As Richard turned to the target, he already had the arrow nocked and was drawing back the string. Distantly, it felt good to feel his muscles straining against the weight, straining against the spring of the bow, loading its force for release. It felt good to rely on his strength, his skill, his endless hours of practice, and not have to depend on magic.

The still form of the man who wasn't there seemed to watch. Eddies of sand sluiced over the shape, marking the outline. Richard glared at the head of the form beyond the razor-sharp steel tip of the arrow. Like all blades, it fell comfortingly familiar to Richard. With a blade in his hands, he was in his element and it mattered not if it was stone dust his blade drew, or blood. The steel-tipped arrow was squarely centered on the empty spot in the curve of blowing sand that formed the head.

The piercing cry of races carried above the howl of the wind.

String to his cheek, Richard savored the tension in his muscles, the weight of the bow, the feathers touching his flesh, the distance between blade and objective filled with swirling sand, the pull of the wind against his arm, the bow, and the arrow. Each of those factors and a hundred more went into an inner calculation that after a lifetime of practice required no conscious computation yet decided where the point of the arrow belonged once he called the target.

The form before him stood watching.

Richard abruptly raised the bow and called the target.

The world became not only still but silent for him as the distance seemed to contract. His body was drawn as taut as the bow, the arrow becoming a projection of his fluid focused intent, the mark before the arrow his purpose for being. His conscious intent invoked the instant sum of the calculation needed to connect arrow and target.

The swirling sand seemed to slow as the races, wings spread wide, dragged through the thick air. There was no doubt in Richard's mind what the arrow would find at the end of a journey only just begun. He felt the string hit his wrist. He saw the feathers clear the bow above his fist. The arrow's shaft flexed slightly as it sprang away and took flight.

Richard was already drawing the second arrow from the quiver in Tom's fist as the first found its target. Black feathers exploded in the crimson dawn. The bird tumbled gracelessly through the air and with a hard thud hit the ground not far from the shape floating just above the ground. The bloody white form was free of the talons, but it was too late.

The four remaining races screamed in fury. As the birds pumped their wings, clawing for height, one railed at Richard with a shrill scream. Richard called the target.

The second arrow was off.

The arrow ripped right into the race's open throat and out the back of the head, cutting off the angry cry. The flightless weight plummeted to the ground.

The form below the remaining three races began to dissolve in the swirling sand.

The three remaining birds, as if abandoning their charge, wheeled around, racing toward Richard with angry intent. He calmly considered them from behind feathers of his own. The third arrow was away. The race in the center lifted its right wing, trying to change direction, but took the arrow through its heart. Rolling wing over wing, it spiraled down through the blowing sand, crashing to the hardpan out ahead of Richard.

The remaining two birds, screeching defiant cries, plunged toward him.

Richard pulled string to cheek, placing the fourth arrow on target. The range was swiftly closing. The arrow was away in an instant. It tore through the body of the black-tipped race still clutching in its talons the bloody corpse of the tiny kid.

Wings raked back, the last angry race dove toward Richard. As soon as Richard snatched an arrow from the quiver an impatient Tom held out, the big D'Haran heaved his knife. Before Richard could nock the arrow, the whirling knife ripped into the raptor. Richard stepped aside as the huge bird shot past in a lifeless drop and slammed into the ground right behind him. As it tumbled, blood sprayed across the windswept rock and black-tipped feathers flew everywhere.

The dawn, only moments ago filled with the bloodcurdling screams of the black-tipped races, was suddenly quiet but for the low moan of the wind. Black feathers lifted in that wind, floating out across the open expanse beneath a yellow-orange sky.

At that moment, the sun broke the horizon, throwing long shadows out over the wasteland.

Jennsen clutched one of the limp white twins to her breast. Betty, bleating plaintively, blood running from a gash on her side, stood on her hind legs trying to arouse her still kid in Jennsen's arms.

Jennsen bent to the other twin sprawled on the ground and laid her lifeless charge beside it. Betty urgently licked at the bloody carcasses. Jennsen hugged Betty's neck a moment before trying to pull the goat away. Betty dug in her hooves, not wanting to leave her stricken kids. Jennsen could do no more than to offer her friend consoling words choked with tears.

When she stood, unable to turn Betty from her dead offspring, Richard sheltered Jennsen under his arm.

"Why would the races suddenly do that?"

"I don't know," Richard said. "You didn't see anything other than the races, then?"

Jennsen leaned against Richard, holding her face in her hands, giving in briefly to the tears. "I just saw the birds," she said as she used the back of her sleeve to wipe her cheeks.

"What about the shape defined by the blowing sand?" Kahlan asked as she placed a comforting hand on Jennsen's shoulder.

"Shape?" She looked from Kahlan to Richard. "What shape?"

"It looked like a man's shape." Kahlan drew the curves of an outline in the air before her with both hands. "Like the outline of a man wearing a hooded cape."

"I didn't see anything but black-tipped races and the clouds of blowing sand."

"And you didn't see the sand blowing around anything?" Richard asked. "You didn't see any shape defined by the sand?"

Jennsen shook her head insistently before returning to Betty's side.

"If the shape involved magic," Kahlan said in a confidential tone to Richard, "she wouldn't see that, but why wouldn't she see the sand?"

"To her, the magic wasn't there."

"But the sand was."

"The color is there on a painting but a blind person can't see it, nor can they see the shapes that the brush strokes, laden with color, help define." He shook his head in wonder as he watched Jennsen. "We don't really know to what degree someone is affected by other things when they can't perceive the magic that interacts with those other things. For all we know, it could be that her mind simply fails to recognize the pattern caused by magic and just reads it as blowing sand. It could even be that because there is a pattern to the magic, only we can see those particles of sand directly involved with defining the pattern, while she sees them all and therefore the subordinate pattern is lost to her eyes.

"It could even be that it's something like the boundaries were; two worlds existing in the same place at the same time. Jennsen and we could be looking at the same thing, and see it through different eyes—through different worlds."

Kahlan nodded as Richard bent to one knee beside Jennsen to inspect the gash through the goat's wiry brown hair.

"We'd better stitch this," he told Jennsen. "It's not life-threatening, but it needs attention."

Jennsen snuffled back her tears as Richard stood. "It was magic, then—the thing you saw?"

Richard stared off toward where the form had appeared in the blowing sand. "Something evil."

Off behind them, Rusty tossed her head and whinnied in sympathy with inconsolable Betty. When Tom laid a sorrowful hand on Jennsen's shoulder, she seized it as if for strength and held it to her cheek.

Jennsen finally stood, shielding her eyes against the blowing dust as she looked to the horizon. "At least we're rid of the filthy races."

"Not for long," Richard said.

His headache came slamming back with such force that it nearly took him from his feet. He had learned a great deal about controlling pain, about how to disregard it. He did that now.

There were bigger worries.

C H A P T E R 7

Around mid-afternoon, as they were walking across the scorching desert, Kahlan noticed Richard carefully watching his shadow stretched out before him.

"What is it?" she asked. "What's the matter?"

He gestured at the shadow before him. "Races. Ten or twelve. They just glided up behind us. They're hiding in the sun."

"Hiding in the sun?"

"They're flying high and in the spot where their shadow falls on us. If we were to look up in the sky we wouldn't be able to see them because we'd have to look right into the sun."

Kahlan turned and, with her hand shielding her eyes, tried to see for herself, but it was too painful to try to look up anywhere near the merciless sun. When she looked back, Richard, who hadn't turned to look with her, again flicked his hand toward the shadows.

"If you look carefully at the ground around your shadow, you can just make out the distortion in the light. It's them."

Kahlan might have thought that Richard was having a little fun with her were it not about a matter as serious as the races. She searched the ground around their shadows until she finally saw what he was talking about. At such a distance, the races' shadows were little more than shifting irregularities in the light.

Kahlan glanced back at the wagon. Tom was driving, with Friedrich sitting up on the seat beside him. Richard and Kahlan were giving the horses a rest from being ridden, so they were tethered to the wagon.

Jennsen sat on blankets in the back of the wagon, comforting

Betty as she bleated in misery. Kahlan didn't think the goat had been silent for more than a minute or two all day. The gash wasn't bad; Betty's suffering was from other pain. At least the poor goat had Jennsen for solace.

From what Kahlan had learned, Jennsen had had Betty for half her life. Moving around as she and her mother had, running from Darken Rahl, hiding, staying away from people so as not to reveal themselves and risk word drifting back to Darken Rahl's ears, Jennsen had never had a chance to have childhood friends. Her mother had gotten her the goat as a companion. In her constant effort to keep Jennsen out of the hands of a monster, it was the best she could offer.

Kahlan wiped the stinging sweat from her eyes. She took in the four black feathers Richard had bundled together and strung on his upper right arm. He had taken the feathers when he'd retrieved the arrows that were still good. Richard had given the last feather to Tom for killing the fifth race with his knife. Tom wore his single feather like Richard, on his arm. Tom thought of it as a trophy, of sorts, awarded by the Lord Rahl.

Kahlan knew that Richard wore his four feathers for a different reason: it was a warning for all to see.

Kahlan pulled her hair back over her shoulder. "Do you think that was a man below the races? A man watching us?"

Richard shrugged. "You know more about magic than me. You tell me."

"I've never seen anything like it." She frowned over at him. "If it was a man . . . or something like that, why do you think he finally decided to reveal himself?"

"I don't think he did decide to reveal himself." Richard's intent gray eyes turned toward her. "I think it was an accident."

"How could it be an accident?"

"If it's someone using the races to track us, and he can somehow see us—"

"See us how?"

"I don't know. See us through the eyes of the races."

"You can't do that with magic."

Richard fixed her with a trenchant look. "Fine. Then what was it?"

Kahlan looked back at the shadows stretching out before them on the buckskin-colored rock, back at the small bleary shapes moving around the shadow of her head, like flies around a corpse. "I don't know. You were saying? . . . About someone using the races to track us, to see us?"

"I think," Richard said, "that someone is watching us, through the races or with their aid—or something like that—and they can't really see everything. They can't see clearly."

"So?"

"So, since he can't see with clarity, I think maybe he didn't realize that there was a sandstorm. He didn't anticipate what the blowing sand would reveal. I don't think he intended to give himself away." Richard looked over at her again. "I think he made a mistake. I think he showed himself accidentally."

Kahlan let out a measured, exasperated breath. She had no argument for such a preposterous notion. It was no wonder he hadn't told her the full extent of his theory. She had been thinking, when he said the races were tracking them, that probably a web had been cast and then some event had triggered it—most likely Cara's innocent touch—and that spell had then attached to them, causing the races to follow that marker of magic. Then, as Jennsen had suggested, someone was simply watching where the races were in order to get a pretty good idea of where Richard and Kahlan were. Kahlan had thought of it in terms of the way Darken Rahl had once hooked a tracer cloud to Richard in order to know where they were. Richard wasn't thinking in terms of what had happened before; he was looking at it through the prism of a Seeker.

There were still a number of things about Richard's notion that didn't make sense to her, but she knew better than to discount what he thought simply because she had never heard of such a thing before.

"Maybe it's not a 'he,'" she finally said. "Maybe it's a she. Maybe a Sister of the Dark."

Sisters of the Dark, once Sisters of the Light who had sworn allegiance to the Keeper of the underworld, worked covertly. In return for that allegiance, they gained a limited use of powers not available to Sisters of the Light.

Richard gave Kahlan another look, but this one was more worry than anything else. "Whoever it is—whatever it is—I don't think it can be anything good."

Kahlan couldn't argue that much of it, but still, she couldn't reconcile such a notion. "Well, let's say it's like you think it is—that we spotted him spying on us, by accident. Why did the races then attack us?"

Dust rose from Richard's boot as he casually kicked a small stone. "I don't know. Maybe he was just angry that he'd given himself away."

"He was angry, so he had the races kill Betty's kids? And attack you?"

Richard shrugged. "I'm just guessing because you asked; I'm not saying I think it's so." The long feathers, blood-red at their base, turning to a dark gray and then to inky black at the tip, ruffled in the gusts of wind.

As he thought it over, his tone turned more speculative. "It could even be that whoever it was using the races to watch us had nothing at all to do with the attack. Maybe the races decided to attack on their own."

"They simply took the reins from whoever it was that was taking them for the ride?"

"Maybe. Maybe he can send them to us so he can have a peek at where we are, where we're going, but can't control them much more than that."

In frustration, Kahlan let out a sigh. "Richard," she said, unable to hold back her doubts, "I know a good deal about all sorts of magic and I've never heard of anything like this being possible."

Richard leaned close, again taking her in with those arresting gray eyes of his. "You know about all sorts of things magic from the Midlands. Maybe down here they have something you never encountered before. After all, had you ever heard of a dream walker before we encountered Jagang? Or even thought such a thing was possible?"

Kahlan pulled her lower lip through her teeth as she studied his grim expression for a long moment. Richard hadn't grown up around magic—it was all new to him. In some ways, though, that was a strength, because he didn't have preconceived notions about what was possible and what wasn't. Sometimes, the things they'd encountered were unprecedented.

To Richard, just about all magic was unprecedented.

"So, what do you think we should do?" she finally asked in a confidential tone.

"What we planned." He glanced over his shoulder to see Cara scouting a goodly distance off to their left side. "It has to be connected to the rest of it."

"Cara only meant to protect us."

"I know. And who knows, maybe it would have been worse if she hadn't touched it. It could even be that by doing what she did, she actually bought us time."

Kahlan swallowed at the feeling of dread churning in her. "Do you think we still have enough time?"

"We'll think of something. We don't even know yet for sure what it could mean."

"When the sand finally runs out of an hourglass, it usually means the goose is cooked."

"We'll find an answer."

"Promise?"

Richard reached over and gently caressed the back of her neck. "Promise."

Kahlan loved his smile, the way it sparkled in his eyes. Somewhere in the back of her mind she knew that he always kept his promises. His eyes held something else, though, and that distracted her from asking if he believed the answer he promised would come in time, or even if it would be an answer that could help them.

"You have a headache, don't you?" she said.

"Yes." His smile had vanished. "It's different from before, but I'm pretty sure it's caused by the same thing."

The gift. That's what he meant.

"What do you mean it's different? And if it's different, then what makes you think the cause is the same?"

He thought about this for a moment. "Remember when I was explaining to Jennsen about how the gift needs to be balanced, how I have to balance the fighting I do by not eating meat?" When she nodded he went on. "It got worse right then."

"Headaches, even those kind, vary."

"No . . ." he said, frowning as he tried to find the words. "No, it was almost as if talking about—thinking about—the need not to eat meat in order to balance the gift somehow brought it more to the fore and made the headaches worse."

Kahlan didn't at all like that concept. "You mean like maybe the gift within you that is the cause of the headaches is trying to impress upon you the importance of balance in what you do with the gift."

Richard raked his fingers back through his hair. "I don't know. There's more to it. I just can't seem to get it all worked out. Sometimes when I try, when I go down that line of reasoning, about how I need to balance the fighting I do, the pain starts to get so bad I can't dwell on it.

"And something else," he added. "There might be a problem with my connection to the magic of the sword."

"What? How can that be?"

"I don't know."

Kahlan tried to keep the alarm out of her voice. "Are you sure?"

He shook his head in frustration. "No, I'm not sure. It just seemed different when I felt the need of it and drew the sword this morning. It was as if the sword's magic was reluctant to rise to the need."

Kahlan thought it over a moment. "Maybe that means that the headaches are something different, this time. Maybe they aren't really caused by the gift."

"Even if some of it is different, I still think its cause is the gift," he said. "One thing they do have in common with the last time is that they're gradually getting worse."

"What do you want to do?"

He lifted his arms out to the sides and let them fall back. "For now, we don't have much of a choice—we have to do what we planned."

"We could go to Zedd. If it is the gift, as you think, then Zedd would know what to do. He could help you."

"Kahlan, do you honestly believe that we have any chance in Creation of making it all the way to Aydindril in time? Even if it weren't for the rest of it, if the headaches are from the gift, I'd be dead weeks before we could travel all the way to Aydindril. And that's not even taking into account how difficult it's bound to be getting past Jagang's army all throughout the Midlands and especially the troops around Aydindril."

"Maybe he's not there now."

Richard kicked at another stone in the path. "You think Jagang is just going to leave the Wizard's Keep and all it contains—leave it all for us to use against him?"

Zedd was First Wizard. For someone of his ability, defending the Wizard's Keep wouldn't be too difficult. He also had Adie there with him to help. The old sorceress, alone, could probably defend a place such as the Keep. Zedd knew what the Keep would mean to Jagang, could he gain it. Zedd would protect the Keep no matter what.

"There's no way for Jagang to get past the barriers in that place," Kahlan said. That much of it was one worry they could set aside. "Jagang knows that and might not waste time holding an army there for nothing."

"You may be right, but that still doesn't do us any good—it's too far."

Too far. Kahlan seized Richard's arm and dragged him to a halt. "The sliph. If we can find one of her wells, we could travel in the sliph. If nothing else, we know there's the well down here in the Old World—in Tanimura. Even that's a lot closer than a journey overland all the way to Aydindril."

Richard looked north. "That might work. We wouldn't have to make it past Jagang's army. We could come right up inside the Keep." He put his arm around her shoulders. "First, though, we have to see to this other business."

Kahlan grinned. "All right. We take care of me first, then we see to taking care of you."

She felt a heady sense of relief that there was a solution at hand. The rest of them couldn't travel in the sliph—they didn't have the required magic—but Richard, Kahlan, and Cara certainly could. They could come up right in the Keep itself.

The Keep was immense, and thousands of years old. Kahlan had spent much of her life there, but she had seen only a fraction of the place. Even Zedd hadn't seen it all, because of some of the shields that had been placed there ages ago by those with both sides of the gift, and Zedd had only the Additive side. Rare and dangerous items of magic had been stored there for eons, along with records and countless books. By now it was possible that Zedd and Adie had found something in the Keep that would help drive the Imperial Order back to the Old World.

Not only would going to the Keep be a way to solve Richard's problem with the gift, but it might provide them with something they needed to swing the tide of the war back to their side.

Suddenly, seeing Zedd, Aydindril, and the Keep seemed only a short time away.

With a renewed sense of optimism, Kahlan squeezed Richard's hand. She knew that he wanted to keep scouting ahead. "I'm going to go back and see how Jennsen is doing."

As Richard moved on and Kahlan slowed, letting the wagon catch up with her, another dozen black-tipped races drifted in on the air currents high above the burning plain. They stayed close to the sun, and well out of range of Richard's arrows, but they stayed within sight.

Tom handed a waterskin down to Kahlan when the bouncing wagon rattled up beside her. She was so dry that she gulped the hot water without caring how bad it tasted. As she let the wagon roll past, she put a boot in the iron rung and boosted herself up and over the side.

Jennsen looked to be happy for the company as Kahlan climbed in. Kahlan returned the smile before sitting beside Richard's sister and the puling Betty.

"How is she?" Kahlan asked, gently stroking Betty's floppy ears.

Jennsen shook her head. "I've never seen her like this. It's breaking my heart. It reminds me of how hard it was for me when I lost my mother. It's breaking my heart."

As she sat back on her heels, Kahlan squeezed Jennsen's hand sympathetically. "I know it's hard, but it's easier for an animal to get over something like this than for people to do the same. Don't compare it to you and your mother. Sad as this is, it's different. Betty can have more kids and she'll forget all about this. You or I never could."

Before the words were out, Kahlan felt a sudden stab of pain for the unborn child she had lost. How could she ever get over losing her and Richard's child? Even if she ever had others, she would never be able to forget what was lost at the hands of brutes.

She idly turned the small dark stone on the necklace she wore, wondering if she ever would have a child, wondering if there would ever be a world safe for a child of theirs.

"Are you all right?"

Kahlan realized that Jennsen was watching her face.

Kahlan forced herself to put on a smile. "I'm just sad for Betty."

Jennsen ran a tender hand over the top of Betty's head. "Me too."

"But I know that she'll be all right."

Kahlan watched the endless expanse of ground slowly slide by to either side of the wagon. Waves of heat made the horizon liquid, with detached pools of ground floating up into the sky. Still, they saw nothing growing. The land was slowly rising, though, as they came ever closer to distant mountains. She knew that it was only a matter of time until they reached life again, but right then it felt like they never would.

"I don't understand about something," Jennsen said. "You told me how I shouldn't do anything rash, when it came to magic, unless I was sure of what would happen. You said it was dangerous. You said not to act in matters of magic until you can be sure of the consequence."

Kahlan knew what Jennsen was driving at. "That's right."

"Well, that back there pretty much seemed like one of those stabs in the dark you warned me about."

"I also told you that sometimes you had no choice but to act immediately. That's what Richard did. I know him. He used his best judgment."

Jennsen looked to be satisfied. "I'm not suggesting that he was wrong. I'm just saying that I don't understand. It seemed pretty reckless to me. How am I supposed to know what you mean when you tell me not to do anything reckless if it involves magic?"

Kahlan smiled. "Welcome to life with Richard. Half the time I don't know what's in his head. I've often thought he was acting recklessly and it turned out to be the right thing, the only thing, he could have done. That's part of the reason he was named Seeker. I'm sure he took into account things he sensed that even I couldn't."

"But how does he know those things? How can he know what to do?"

"Often times he's just as confused as you, or even me. But he's different, too, and he's sure when we wouldn't be."

"Different?"

Kahlan looked over at the young woman, at her red hair shining in the afternoon sunlight. "He was born with both sides of the gift. All those born with the gift in the last three thousand years have been born with Additive Magic only. Some, like Darken Rahl and the Sisters of the Dark, have been able to use Subtractive Magic, but only through the Keeper's help—not on their own. Richard alone has been born with Subtractive Magic."

"That's what you mentioned last night, but I don't know anything about magic, so I don't know what that means."

"We're not exactly sure of everything it means ourselves. Additive Magic uses what is there, and adds to it, or changes it somehow. The magic of the Sword of Truth, for example, uses anger, and adds to it, takes power from it, adds to it until it's something else. With Additive, for example, the gifted can heal.

"Subtractive Magic is the undoing of things. It can take things and make them nothing. According to Zedd, Subtractive Magic is the counter to Additive, as night is to day. Yet it is all part of the same thing.

"Commanding Subtractive, as Darken Rahl did, is one thing, but to be born with it is quite another.

"Long ago, unlike now, being born with the gift—both sides of the gift—was common. The great war then resulted in a barrier sealing the New World off from the Old. That's kept the peace all this time, but things have changed since then. After that time, not only have those born with the gift gradually become exceedingly rare, but those who have been born with the gift haven't been born with the Subtractive side of it.

"Richard was born of two lines of wizards, Darken Rahl and his grandfather Zedd. He's also the first in thousands of years to be born with both sides of the gift.

"All of our abilities contribute to how we're able to react to situations. We don't know how having both sides contributes to Richard's ability to read a situation and do what's necessary. I suspect he may be guided by his gift, perhaps more than he believes."

Jennsen let out a troubled sigh. "After all this time, how did this barrier come to be down, anyway?"

"Richard destroyed it."

Jennsen looked up in astonishment. "Then it's true. Sebastian told me that the Lord Rahl—Richard—had brought the barrier down. Sebastian said it was so that Richard could invade and conquer the Old World."

Kahlan smiled at such a grandiose lie. "You don't believe that part of it, do you?"

"No, not now."

"Now that the barrier is down, the Imperial Order is flooding up into the New World, destroying or enslaving everything before them."

"Where can people live that's safe? Where can we?"

"Until they're stopped or driven back, there is no safe place to live."

Jennsen thought it over a moment. "If the barrier coming down let the Imperial Order flood in to conquer the New World, why would Richard have destroyed it?"

With one hand, Kahlan held on to the side of the wagon as it rocked over a rough patch of ground. She stared ahead, watching Richard walking through the glaring light of the wasteland.

"Because of me," Kahlan said in a quiet voice. "One of those mistakes I told you about." She let out a tired sigh. "One of those stabs in the dark."

CHAPTER 8

Richard squatted down, resting his forearms across his thighs as he studied the curious patch of rock. His head was pounding with pain; he was doing his best to ignore it. The headache had come and gone seemingly without reason. At times he had begun to think that it just might be the heat after all, and not the gift.

As he considered the signs on the ground, he forgot about his headache.

Something about the rock seemed familiar. Not simply familiar, but unsettlingly familiar.

Hooves partially covered by long wisps of wiry brown hair came to an expectant halt beside him. With the top of her head, Betty gently butted his shoulder, hoping for a snack, or at least a scratch.

Richard looked up at the goat's intent, floppy-eared expression. As Betty watched him watching her, her tail went into a blur of wagging. Richard smiled and scratched behind her ears. Betty bleated her pleasure at the scratch, but it sounded to him like she would have preferred a snack.

After not eating for two days as she lay in misery in the wagon, the goat seemed to come back to life and begin to recover from the loss of her two kids. Along with her appetite, Betty's curiosity had returned. She especially enjoyed scouting with Richard, when he would let her come along. It made Jennsen laugh to watch the goat trotting after him like a puppy. Maybe what really made her laugh was that Betty was getting back to her old self.

In recent days the land had changed, too. They had begun to see the return of life. At first, it had simply been the rusty discoloration of lichen growing on the fragmented rock. Soon after, they spotted a small thorny bush growing in a low place. Now the rugged plants grew at widely spaced intervals, dotting the landscape. Betty appreciated the tough bushes, dining on them as if they were the finest salad greens. On occasion the horses sampled the brush, then turned away, never finding it to their liking.

Lichen that had begun to grow on the rock appeared as crusty splotches streaked with color. In some places it was dark, thick, and leathery, while in other spots it was no more than what almost appeared to be a coat of thin green paint. The greenish discoloration filled cracks and crevasses and coated the underside of stones where the sun didn't bleach it out. Rocks sticking partway out of the crumbly ground could be pulled up to reveal thin tendrils of dark brown subterranean fungal growth.

Tiny insects with long feelers skittered from rock to rock or hid in holes in the scattering of rocks lying about on the ground that looked as if they had once been boiling and bubbling, and had suddenly turned to stone, leaving the bubbles forever set in place. An occasional glossy green beetle, bearing wide pincer jaws, waddled through the sand. Small red ants stacked steep ruddy mounds of dirt around their holes. There were cottony webs of spiders in the crotches of the isolated, small, spindly brush growing sporadically across the ever-rising plain. Slender light green lizards sat on rocks basking in the sun, watching the people pass. If they came too close, the little creatures, lightning quick, darted for cover.

The signs of life Richard had so far seen were still a long way from being anything substantial enough to support people, but it was at least a relief to once again feel like he was rejoining the world of the living. He knew, too, that up beyond the first wall of mountains they would at last encounter life in abundance. He also knew that there they would again begin to encounter people.

Birds, as well, were just beginning to become a common sight. Most were small—strawberry-colored finches, ash-colored gnatcatchers, rock wrens and black-throated sparrows. In the distance Richard saw single birds winging through the blue sky, while sparrows congregated in small skittish flocks. Here and there, birds lit on the scraggly brush, flitting about looking for seeds and bugs. The birds disappeared instantly whenever the races glided into sight.

Staring at the expanse of rock and open ground before him, Richard rose up, startled, as the reason it looked unsettlingly familiar came to him. At the same time as the realization came to him, his headache vanished.

Off to his right, Richard saw Kahlan, with Cara at her side, making their way out to where Richard stood staring down at the aston-ishing stretch of rock. The wagon, with Tom, Friedrich, and Jennsen, rumbled on in the distance to the south. The dust raised by the wagon and horses hung in the dead air and could be seen for miles. Richard supposed that with the races periodically paying them a visit, the telltale of the dust didn't much matter. Still, he would be glad when they reached ground where they could at least have a chance to try to remain a little more inconspicuous.

"Find anything interesting?" Kahlan asked as she wiped her sleeve across her forehead.

Richard cast a few small pebbles down at the stretch of rock he'd been studying. "Tell me what you think of that."

"I think you look like you feel better," Kahlan said.

Her eyes on his, she gave him her special smile, the smile she gave no one but him. He couldn't help grinning.

Cara, ignoring the smiles that passed between Richard and Kahlan, leaned in for a gander. "I think Lord Rahl has been looking at too many rocks. This is more rock, just like all the rest."

"Is it?" Richard asked. He gestured at the area he'd been scruti-nizing and then pointed at another place by where Kahlan and Cara stood. "Is it the same as that?"

Cara peered at both areas briefly before she folded her arms. "The rock over there that you've been looking at is just a paler brown, that's all."

Kahlan shrugged. "I think she's right, Richard. It looks like the same kind of rock, maybe just a little more of a tan color." She thought it over a moment as she scanned the ground, then added to her assess-ment. "I guess it looks more like the rock we've been walking across for days until we started encountering a little bit of grass and brush."

Richard put his hands on his hips as he stared back at the remarkable stretch of rock he'd found. "Tell me, then, what characterized the rock in the place where we were before—a few days ago, back closer to the Pillars of Creation?"

Kahlan looked over at an expressionless Cara and then frowned at Richard. "Characterized it? Nothing. It was a dead place. Nothing grew there."

Richard waved his hand around, indicating the land through which they were now traveling. "And this?"

"Now things are growing," Cara said, becoming increasingly disinterested in his study of flora and fauna.

Richard held a hand out. "And there?"

"Nothing is growing there, yet," Cara said in an exasperated sigh. "There are a lot of spots around where nothing is growing yet. It's still a wasteland. Just have patience, Lord Rahl, and we will soon enough be back among the fields and forests."

Kahlan wasn't paying attention to what Cara was saying; she was frowning as she leaned closer.

"The place where things begin to grow seems to start all at once," Kahlan said, almost to herself. "Isn't that curious?"

"I certainly think so," Richard said.

"I think Lord Rahl needs to drink more water," Cara sniped.

Richard smiled. "Here. Stand over here," he told her. "Stand over by me and look again."

Cara, her curiosity aroused, did as he asked. She looked down at the ground, and then frowned at the places where things grew.

"The Mother Confessor is right." Cara's voice had taken on a decidedly businesslike tone. "Do you think it's important? Or somehow a danger?"

"Yes—to the first, anyway," Richard said.

He squatted down beside Kahlan. "Now, look at this."

As Kahlan and Cara knelt down beside him, leaning forward, looking closely at the rock, Richard had to push a curious Betty back out of the way. He then pointed out a patch of yellow-streaked lichen.

"Look here," he said. "See this medallion of lichen? It's lopsided. This side is round, but this side, near where nothing grows, is flatter."

Kahlan looked up at him. "Lichen grows on rocks in all kinds of shapes."

"Yes, but look at how the rock over where there is lichen and brush growing is spotted all over with little bits of growth. Here, beyond the stunted side of the lichen, there is nearly nothing. The rock almost looks scoured clean.

"If you look closely there were a few tiny things, things that have started to grow only in the last couple of years, but they have yet to really begin to take hold."

"Yes," Kahlan said in a cautious drawl, "it is odd, but I'm not sure what you're getting at."

"Look at where things are growing, and where they aren't."

"Well, yes, on that side there's nothing growing, and over here there is."

"Don't just look down." Richard lifted her chin. "Look out at the boundary between the two—look at the whole pattern."

Kahlan frowned off into the distance. All of a sudden, the color drained from her face.

"Dear spirits . . ." she whispered.

Richard smiled that she finally saw what he was talking about.

"What are you two mooning over?" Cara complained.

Richard put his hand behind Cara's neck and pulled her head in to look at what he and Kahlan were seeing.

"That's odd," she said, squinting off into the distance. "The place where things are growing seems to stop in a comparatively clean line—like someone had made an invisible fence running east."

"Right," Richard said as he got up, brushing his hands clean.

"Now, come on." He started walking north. Kahlan and Cara scrambled to their feet and followed behind as he marched across the lifeless rock. Betty bleated and trotted after them.

"Where are we going?" Cara asked as she caught up with him.

"Just come on," Richard told her.

For half an hour they followed his brisk pace as he headed in a straight line to the north, across rocky ground and gravelly patches where nothing at all grew. The day was sweltering, but Richard almost didn't notice the heat, so focused was he on the lifeless expanse they were crossing. He hadn't yet gone to see what lay at the other side, but he was convinced of what they would find once they reached it.

The other two were sweating profusely as they chased behind him. Betty bleated occasionally as she brought up the rear.

When they finally reached the place he was looking for, the place where lichen and scraggly brush once again began to appear, he brought them to a halt. Betty poked her head between Kahlan and Cara for a look.

"Now, look at this," Richard said. "See what I mean?"

Kahlan was breathing hard from the brisk walk in the heat. She pulled her waterskin off her shoulder and gulped water. She passed the waterskin to Richard. He watched Cara study the patch of ground as he drank.

"The growing things start again over here," Cara said. She absently scratched behind Betty's ears when the goat rubbed the top of her head impatiently against Cara's thigh. "They start to appear in the same kind of line as the other side, back there, where we were."

"Right," Richard said, handing Cara the waterskin. "Now, follow me."

Cara threw up her arms. "We just came from that way!"

"Come on," Richard called back over his shoulder.

He headed south again, back toward the center of the lifeless patch of rock, the small group in tow. Betty bleated her displeasure at the pace of the hot dusty excursion. If Kahlan or Cara shared Betty's opinion, they didn't voice the complaint.

When Richard judged they were back somewhere in the middle, he stood with his feet spread, his fists on his hips, and looked east again. From where they stood, they couldn't make out the sides of the lifeless stretch, the places where growth began.

Looking to the east, though, the pattern was evident. A clearly defined strip—miles wide—ran off into the distance.

Nothing grew within the bounds of the straight strip of lifeless desert, whether going over rock or sandy ground. To either side the ground with widely spaced brush and lichen growing on the rock was darker. The place where nothing grew was a lighter tan. In the distance the discrepancy in the color was even more apparent.

The lifeless strip ran straight for mile after mile toward the far mountains, gradually becoming but a faint line following the rise of the ground until, finally, in the hazy distance, it could no longer be seen.

"Are you thinking what I'm thinking?" Kahlan asked in a low, troubled voice.

"What?" Cara asked. "What are you thinking?"

Richard studied the confused concern on the Mord-Sith's face. "What kept Darken Rahl's armies in D'Hara? What prevented him, for so many years, from invading the Midlands and taking it, even though he wanted it?"

"He couldn't cross the boundary," Cara said as if he must be having heat stroke.

"And what made up the boundary?"

At last, Cara's face, framed by the black desert garb, went white, too. "The boundary was the underworld?"

Richard nodded. "It was like a rip in the veil, where the underworld existed in this world. Zedd told us about it. He put the boundary up with a spell he found in the Keep—a spell from those ancient times of the great war. Once up, the boundary was a place in this world where the world of the dead also existed. In that place, where both worlds touched, nothing could grow."

"But are you so sure things wouldn't still grow there?" Cara asked. "It was still our world, after all—the world of life."

"It would be impossible for anything to grow there. The world of life was there, in that spot—the ground was there—but life couldn't exist there on that ground because it shared that same space with the world of the dead. Anything there would be touched by death."

Cara looked out at the straight, lifeless strip running off into the wavering distance. "So you think what? . . . This is a boundary?"

"Was."

Cara looked from his face, to Kahlan, and again out to the distance. "Dividing what?"

Overhead a flight of black-tipped races came into sight, riding the high currents, turning lazy circles as they watched.

"I don't know," Richard admitted.

He looked west again, back down the gradual slope running away from the mountains, back to where they had been.

"But look," Richard said, gesturing out into the burning wasteland from where they had come. "It runs back toward the Pillars of Creation."

As the things growing thinned and eventually ceased to be back that way, so too did the lifeless strip. It became indistinguishable from the surrounding wasteland because there was no life to mark where the line had been.

"There's no telling how far it runs. For all I know," Richard said, "it's possible that it runs all the way back to the valley itself."

"That part makes no sense to me," Kahlan said. "I can see what you mean about it maybe being like the boundaries up in the New World, the boundaries between Westland, the Midlands, and D'Hara. That much I follow. But the spirits take me, I don't get why it would run to the Pillars of Creation. That part just strikes me as more than odd."

Richard turned and gazed back to the east, where they were headed, to the rumpled gray wall of mountains rising steeply up from the broad desert floor, studying the distant notch that sat a little north of where the boundary line ran toward those mountains.

He looked south, to the wagon making its way toward those mountains.

"We better catch up with the others," Richard finally said. "I need to get back to translating the book."

CHAPTER 9

The spectral spires around Richard glowed under the lingering caress of the low sun. In the amber light, as he scouted the forsaken brink of the towering mountains beyond, long pools of shadow were darkening to the blue-black color of bruises. The pinnacles of reddish rock stood like stony guardians along the lower reaches of the desolate foothills, as if listening for the echoing crunch of his footsteps along the meandering gravel beds.

Richard had felt like being alone to think, so he had set out to scout by himself. It was hard to think when people were constantly asking questions.

He was frustrated that the book hadn't yet told him anything that would in any way help explain the presence of the strange boundary line, much less the connection of the book's title, the place called the Pillars of Creation, and those ungifted people like Jennsen. The book, in the beginning that he'd so far translated, anyway, appeared mostly to be a historical record dealing with unanticipated matters involving occurrences of "pillars of Creation," as those like Jennsen were called, and the unsuccessful attempts at "curing" those "unfortunates."

Richard was beginning to get the clear sense that the book was laying a careful foundation of early details in preparation for something calamitous. The nearly quaking care of the recounting of every possible course of action that had been investigated gave him the feeling that whoever wrote the book was being painstaking for reasons of consequence.

Not daring to slow their pace, Richard had been translating while riding in the wagon. The dialect was slightly different from the High D'Haran he was used to reading, so working out the translation was slow going, especially sitting in the back of the bouncing wagon. He had no way of knowing if the book would eventually offer any answers, but he felt a gnawing worry over what the unfolding account was working up to. He would have jumped ahead, but he'd learned in the past that doing so often wasted more time than it saved, since it interfered with accurately grasping the whole picture, which sometimes led to dangerously erroneous conclusions. He would just have to keep at it.

After working all day, focused intently on the book, he'd ended up with a fierce headache. He'd had days without them, but now when they came it seemed they were worse each time. He didn't tell Kahlan how concerned he was that he wouldn't make it to the sliph's well in Tanimura. Besides working at translating, he racked his brain trying to find a solution.

While he had no idea what the key to the headaches brought on by the gift was, he had the nagging feeling that it was within himself. He feared it was a matter of balance he was failing to see. He had even resorted when out alone, once, to sitting and meditating as the Sisters had once taught him in order to try to focus on the gift within. It had been to no avail.

It would be dark soon and they would need to stop for the night. Since the terrain had changed, it was no longer a simple task to see if the area all around them was clear. Now there were places where an army could lie in wait. With the races shadowing them, there was no telling who might know where to find them. Besides simply wanting a break to think about what he'd read and what he might find within himself to answer the problem of his headaches, Richard wanted to check the surrounding area himself.

Richard paused for a moment to watch a family of quail, the juveniles fully grown, hurry across an open patch of ground. They trotted across the exposed gravel in a line while the father, perched atop a rock, stood lookout. As soon as they melted into the brush, they were again invisible.

Small scraggly pine trees dotted the sweep of irregular hills, gullies, and rocky outcroppings at the fringe of the mountains. Up higher, on the nearby slopes, larger conifers grew in greater abundance. In low, sheltered places clumps of brush lay in thick clusters. Thin grasses covered some of the open ground.

Richard wiped sweat from his eyes. He hoped that with the sun going down the air might cool a little. As he made his way along the concealment of the base of a runoff channel in a fold of two hills, he reached for the strap of his waterskin, about to take a long drink, when movement on a far hillside caught his attention.

He slipped behind the screen of a long shelf of rock to stay out of sight. Taking a careful peek, he saw a man making his way down the loose scree on the side of the hill. The sound of the rock crunching underfoot and sliding down the slope sent a distant echo through the rocky canyons.

Richard had expected that as they left the forbidding wasteland they might at any time begin encountering people, so he had had everyone change out of the black outfits of the nomadic desert people and back into their unassuming traveling clothes. While he was in black trousers and simple shirt, his sword was hardly inconspicuous. Kahlan, as well, had put on simple clothes that were more in keeping with the impoverished people of the Old World, but on Kahlan they didn't seem to make much difference; it was hard to hide her figure and her hair, but most of all her presence. Once those green eyes of hers fixed on people, they usually had an urge to drop to a knee and bow their head. Her clothes made little difference.

No doubt Emperor Jagang had spread their description far and wide and had offered a reward large enough that even his enemies would find it hard to resist. For many in the Old World, though, the price of continued life under the brutal rule of the Imperial Order was too high. Despite the reward, there were many who hungered to live free and were willing to act to gain that goal.

There was also the problem of the bond the Lord Rahl had with the D'Haran people; through that ancient bond forged by Richard's ancestors, D'Harans could sense where the Lord Rahl was. The Imperial Order could discover where Richard was by that bond, too. All they had to do was torture the information out of a D'Haran. If one person failed to talk under torture, they would not be shy about trying others until they learned what they wanted.

As Richard watched, the lone man, once he reached the bottom of the hill, made his way along the gravel beds lining the bottom of the rocky gullies. Off to Richard's right the wagon and horses were lifting a long trail of dust. That was where the man seemed to be headed.

At such a distance it was hard to tell for sure, but Richard doubted that the man was a soldier. He wouldn't likely be a scout, not in his own homeland, and they weren't near the hotbeds of the revolt against the rule of the Imperial Order. Richard didn't think there would be any reason for soldiers to be going this way, through such uninhabited areas. That was, after all, why he had picked this route, heading east to the shadow of the mountains before turning to a more northerly route back to where they had been.

There was also the possibility that the bond had inadvertently revealed Richard's whereabouts and an army was out looking for him. If the man was a soldier, there could shortly be many more, like ants, swarming down out of the hills.

Richard climbed the back side of a short rocky prominence and lay on his stomach, watching over the top. As the man got closer, Richard could see that he looked young, under thirty years, a bit scrawny, and was dressed nothing at all like a soldier. By the way he stumbled, he was not used to the terrain, or maybe just not used to traveling. It was tiring walking over ground of loose, sharp, broken rock, especially if it was on a slope, since it never provided any solid place for a steady stride.

The man stopped, stretching his neck to peer at the wagon. Panting from the effort of making it down the slope, he combed his fine blond hair back repeatedly with his fingers, then bent at the waist and rested a hand on a knee while he caught his breath.

When the man straightened and started out once more, crunching through the gravel at the bottom of the wash, Richard slid back down the rock. He used the intervening lay of the land and patches of scraggly pine to screen himself from sight. He paused from time to time, as he moved closer, to listen for the heavy footsteps and labored breathing, checking his dead-reckoning estimation of where the man would be.

From behind a freestanding wall of rock a good sixty feet tall, Richard carefully peered out for a look. He had managed to close most of the distance without the man being aware of his presence. Richard moved silently from tree to rock to the back side of slopes, until he was out ahead of the man and in his line of travel.

Still as stone behind a twisted reddish spire of rock jutting from the broken ground, Richard listened to the crunch of footfalls approaching, listened to the man gulping for breath as he climbed over fingers of rock that lay in his way.

When the man was not six feet away, Richard stepped out right in front of him.

The man gasped, clutching his light travel coat beneath his chin as he cringed back a step.

Richard regarded the man without outward emotion, but inside the sword's power churned with the menace of rage restrained. For an instant, Richard felt the power falter. The magic of the sword keyed off its master's perception of danger, so such hesitation could be because the smaller man didn't appear to be an immediate threat.

The man's clothes, brown trousers, flaxen shirt and a light, frayed fustian coat, had seen better days. He looked to have had a rough time of his journey—but then, Richard, too, had put on unassuming clothes in order not to raise suspicion. The man's backpack looked to hold precious little. Two waterskins, their straps crisscrossed across his chest, bunching the light coat, were flat and empty. He carried no weapons that Richard saw, not even a knife.

The man waited expectantly, as if he feared to be the first to speak.

"You appear to be headed for my friends," Richard said, tipping his head toward the thin golden plume of dust hanging like a beacon in the sunlight above the darkening plain, giving the man a chance to explain himself.

The man, wide-eyed, shoulders hunched, raked back his hair several times. Richard stood before him like a stone pillar, blocking his way. The man's blue eyes turned to each side, apparently checking to see if he had an escape route should he decide to bolt.

"I mean you no harm," Richard said. "I just want to know what you're up to."

"Up to?"

"Why you're headed for the wagon."

The man glanced toward the wagon, not visible beyond the craggy folds of rock, then down at Richard's sword, and finally up into his eyes.

"I'm . . . looking for help," he finally said.

"Help?"

The man nodded. "Yes. I'm searching for the one whose craft is fighting."

Richard cocked his head. "You're looking for a soldier of some kind?"

He swallowed at the frown on Richard's face. "Yes, that's right."

Richard shrugged. "The Imperial Order has lots of soldiers. I'm sure that if you keep looking you will come across some."

The man shook his head. "No. I seek the man from far away—from far to the north. The man who came to bring freedom to many of the oppressed people of the Old World. The man who gives us all hope that the Imperial Order—may the Creator forgive their misguided ways—will be cast out of our lives so that we can be at peace once again."

"Sorry," Richard said, "I don't know anyone like that."

The man didn't look disappointed by Richard's words. He looked more like he simply didn't believe them. His fine features were pleasant-looking, even though he appeared unconvinced.

"Do you think you could" —the man hesitantly lifted an arm out, pointing— "at least . . . let me have a drink?"

Richard relaxed a bit. "Sure."

He pulled the strap off his shoulder and tossed his waterskin to the man. He caught it as if it were precious glass he feared to drop. He pried at the stopper, finally getting it free, and started gulping the water.

He stopped abruptly, lowering the waterskin. "I'm sorry. I didn't mean to start drinking all your water right down."

"It's all right." Richard gestured for him to drink up. "I have more back at the wagon. You look to need it."

As Richard hooked a thumb behind his wide leather belt, the man bowed his head in thanks before tipping the waterskin up for a long drink.

"Where did you hear about this man who fights for freedom?" Richard asked.

The man brought the waterskin down again, his eyes never leaving Richard as he paused to catch his breath. "From many a tongue. The freedom he has spread down here in the Old World has brought hope to us all."

Richard smiled inwardly at how the bright hope of freedom burned even in a dark place like the heart of the Old World. There were people everywhere who hungered for the same things in life, for a chance to live their life free and by their own labor to better themselves.

Overhead a black-tipped race, wings spread wide, popped into sight as it glided across the open swath of sky above the rise of rock to each side. Richard didn't have his bow, but the race stayed out of range, anyway.

The man shrank at seeing the race the way a rabbit would shrink when it saw a hawk.

"Sorry I can't help you," Richard said when the race had disappeared. He checked behind, in the direction of the wagon, out beyond the nearby hill. "I'm traveling with my wife and family, looking for work, for a place to mind our own business."

Richard's business was the revolution, if he was to have a chance for his plan to work, and there were a number of people waiting on him in that regard. He had more urgent problems, first, though.

"But, Lord Rahl, my people need—"

Richard spun back around. "Why would you call me that?"

"I'm, I'm sorry." The man swallowed. "I didn't mean to anger you."

"What makes you think I'm this Lord Rahl?"

The man painted his hand up and down in front of Richard as he sputtered, trying to find words. "You, you, you just . . . are. I can't imagine . . . what else you want me to say. I'm sorry if I have offended you by being so forward, Lord Rahl."

Cara stalked out from behind a rocky spire. "What have we here?"

The man gasped in surprise at seeing her as he flinched back yet another step, clutching the waterskin to his chest as if it were a shield of steel.

Tom, his silver knife to hand, stepped up out of a gully behind the man, blocking the way should the man decide to run back the way he'd come.

The man turned in a circle to see Tom towering behind. As he finally came back around and saw Kahlan standing beside Richard, he let out another gasp. They all were wearing dusty traveling clothes, but somehow Richard didn't suppose that at that moment they looked at all like simple travelers in search of work.

"Please," the man said, "I don't mean any harm."

"Take it easy," Richard said as he stole a sidelong glance at Cara—his words meant not only for the man but for the Mord-Sith as well. "Are you alone?" Richard asked him.

"Yes, Lord Rahl. I'm on a mission for my people, just as I told you. You are of course to be forgiven your aggressive nature—I would expect nothing less. I want you to know I hold no feelings of resentment toward you."

"Why does he think you're the Lord Rahl?" Cara said to Richard in a tone that sounded more accusation than question.

"I've heard the descriptions," the man put in. Still clutching the waterskin to his chest, he pointed with the other hand. "And that sword. I've heard about Lord Rahl's sword." His gaze moved cautiously to Kahlan. "And the Mother Confessor, of course," he added, dipping his head.

"Of course," Richard sighed.

He'd expected that he would have to hide the sword around strangers, but now he knew just how important that was going to be whenever they went into any populated areas. The sword would be relatively easy to hide. Not so with Kahlan. He thought that maybe they could cover her in rags and say she was a leper.

The man leaned cautiously out, arm extended, and handed Richard his waterskin. "Thank you, Lord Rahl."

Richard took a long drink of the terrible-tasting water before offering it to Kahlan. She lifted hers out for him to see as she declined with a single shake of her head. Richard took another long swig before replacing the stopper and slinging the strap back over his shoulder.

"What's your name?" he asked.

"Owen."

"Well, Owen, why don't you come back to camp with us for the night. We can fill up your waterskins for you, at least, before you're on your way in the morning."

Cara was near to bursting as she gritted her teeth at Richard. "Why don't you just let me see to—"

"I think Owen has problems we can all understand. He's concerned for his friends and family. In the morning, he can be on his way, and we can be on ours."

Richard didn't want the man out there somewhere, in the dark, where they couldn't as easily keep an eye on him as they could if he were in camp. In the morning it would be easy enough to make sure that he wasn't following them. Cara finally understood Richard's intent and relaxed. He knew she would want any stranger in her sight while Richard and Kahlan were sleeping.

Kahlan at his side, Richard started back to the wagon. The man followed, his head swiveling side to side, from Tom to Cara, and back again.

Since they were headed back to the wagon, Richard finished what water remained in his waterskin while, behind, Owen thanked him for the invitation and promised not to be any trouble.

Richard intended to see to it that Owen kept his promise.

CHAPTER 10

Up in the wagon, Richard dunked Owen's two waterskins in the barrel that still had water. Owen, sitting with his back pressed against a wheel, glanced up at Richard from time to time, watching expectantly, as Cara glared at him. Cara clearly didn't like the fellow, but as protective as Mord-Sith were, that didn't necessarily mean that it was warranted.

For some reason, though, Richard didn't care for the man, either. It wasn't so much that he disliked him, just that he couldn't warm to the fellow. He was polite and certainly didn't look threatening, but there was something about the man's attitude that made Richard feel . . . edgy.

Tom and Friedrich broke up dried wood they'd collected, feeding it into the small fire. The wonderful aroma of pine pitch covered the smell of the nearby horses.

From time to time Owen cast a fearful eye at Cara, Kahlan, Tom, and Friedrich. By far, though, he seemed most uneasy about Jennsen. He tried to avert his eyes from her, tried not to look her directly in the eye, but his gaze kept being drawn to her red hair shining in the firelight. When Betty approached to investigate the stranger, Owen stopped breathing. Richard told Owen that the goat just wanted attention. Owen gingerly patted the top of Betty's head as if the goat were a gar that might take off his arm if he weren't careful.

Jennsen, with a smile and ignoring the way he stared at her hair, offered Owen some of her dried meat.

Owen just stared wide-eyed up at her leaning down over him.

"I'm not a witch," she said to Owen. "People think my red hair is a sign that I'm a witch. I'm not. I can assure you, I have no magic."

The edge in her voice surprised Richard, reminding him that there was iron under the feminine grace.

Still wide-eyed, Owen said, "Of course not. I, I . . . just never saw such . . . beautiful hair before, that's all."

"Why, thank you," Jennsen said, her smile returning. She again offered him a piece of dried meat.

"I'm sorry," Owen said in polite apology, "but I prefer not to eat meat, if it's all right with you."

He quickly reached in his pocket, bringing out a cloth pouch holding dried biscuit. He forced a smile at Jennsen as he held out the biscuits.

"Would you like one of mine?"

Tom started, glaring at Owen.

"Thanks, no," Jennsen said as she withdrew her extended hand and sat down on a low, flat rock. She snagged Betty by an ear and made her lie down at her feet. "You'd best eat the biscuits yourself if you don't want meat," she said to Owen. "I'm afraid we don't have a lot that isn't."

"Why don't you eat meat?" Richard asked.

Owen looked up over his shoulder at Richard in the wagon above him. "I don't like the thought of harming animals just to satisfy my want of food."

Jennsen smiled politely. "That's a kindhearted sentiment."

Owen twitched a smile before his gaze was drawn once again to her hair. "It's just the way I feel," he said, finally looking away from her.

"Darken Rahl felt the same way," Cara said, turning the glare on Jennsen. "I saw him horsewhip a woman to death because he caught her eating a sausage in the halls of the People's Palace. It struck him as disrespectful of his feelings."

Jennsen stared in astonishment.

"Another time," Cara went on as she chewed a bite of sausage, "I was with him when he came around a corner outside, near the gardens. He spotted a cavalryman atop his horse eating a meat pie.

Darken Rahl lashed out with a flash of conjured lightning, beheading the man's horse in an instant—thump, it dropped into the hedge. The man managed to land on his feet as the rest of his horse crashed to the ground. Darken Rahl reached out, drew the man's sword, and in a fit of anger slashed the belly of the horse open. Then he seized the soldier by the scruff of his neck and shoved his face into the horse's innards, screaming at him to eat. The man tried his best, but ended up suffocated in the horse's warm viscera."

Owen covered his mouth as he closed his eyes.

Cara waved her sausage as if indicating Darken Rahl standing before her. "He turned to me, the fire gone out of him, and asked me how people could be so cruel as to eat meat."

Jennsen, her mouth hanging open, asked, "What did you say?"

Cara shrugged. "What could I say? I told him I didn't know."

"But why would people eat meat, then, if he was like that?" Jennsen asked.

"Most of the time, he wasn't. Vendors sold meat at the palace and he usually paid it no mind. Sometimes he would shake his head in disgust, or call them cruel, but usually he didn't even take notice of it."

Friedrich was nodding. "That was the thing about the man—you never knew what he was going to do. He might smile at a person, or have them tortured to death. You never knew."

Cara stared into the low flames of the fire before her. "There was no way to reason out how he would react to anything." Her voice took on a quiet, haunted quality. "A lot of people simply decided that it was only a matter of time until he killed them, too, and so they lived their lives as the condemned would, waiting for the axe to fall, taking no pleasure in life or the thought of their future."

Tom nodded his grim agreement with Cara's assessment of life in D'Hara as he fed a crook of driftwood into the fire.

"Is that what you did, Cara?" Jennsen asked.

Cara looked up and scowled. "I am Mord-Sith. Mord-Sith are always ready to embrace death. We do not wish to die old and toothless."

Owen, nibbling his dried biscuit as if out of obligation to eat since the rest of them were, was clearly shaken by the story. "I can't imagine life with such savagery as all of you must live it. Was this Darken Rahl related to you, Lord Rahl?" Owen suddenly seemed to think he might have made a mistake, and rushed to amend his question. "He has the same name . . . so I thought, well, I just thought—but I didn't mean to imply that I thought you were like him . . ."

Stepping down from the wagon, Richard handed Owen his full waterskins. "He was my father."

"I didn't mean anything by the question. I would never intentionally cast aspersions on a man's father, especially a man who—"

"I killed him," Richard said.

Richard didn't feel like elaborating. He recoiled from the very thought of going into the whole dreadful tale.

Owen gaped around as if he were a fawn surrounded by wolves.

"He was a monster," Cara said, appearing to feel the need to rise to Richard's defense. "Now the people of D'Hara have a chance to look forward to a future of living their lives as they wish."

Richard sat down beside Kahlan. "At least they will if they can be free of the Imperial Order."

Head down, Owen nibbled on his biscuit as he watched the others.

When no one else spoke, Kahlan did. "Why don't you tell us your reasons for coming here, Owen?"

Richard recognized her tone as that of the Mother Confessor asking a polite question meant to put a frightened petitioner at ease.

He dipped his head respectfully. "Yes, Mother Confessor."

"You know her, too?" Richard asked.

Owen nodded. "Yes, Lord Rahl."

"How?"

The man's gaze shifted from Richard to Kahlan and back again.

"Word of you and the Mother Confessor has spread everywhere. Word of the way you freed the people of Altur'Rang from the oppression of the Imperial Order is known far and wide. Those who want freedom know that you are the one who gives it."

Richard frowned. "What do you mean, I'm the one who gives it?"

"Well, before, the Imperial Order ruled. They are brutal—forgive me, they are misguided and don't know any better. That is why their rule is so brutal. Perhaps it isn't their fault. It is not for me to say." Owen looked away as he tried to come up with words while apparently seeing his own visions of what the Imperial Order had done to convince him of their brutality. "Then you came and gave people freedom—just as you did in Altur'Rang."

Richard wiped a hand across his face. He needed to translate the book, he needed to find out what was behind the thing Cara had touched and the black-tipped races following them, he needed to get back to Victor and those who were engaged in the revolt against the Order, he was past due to meet Nicci, and he needed to deal with his headaches. At least, maybe Nicci could help with that much of it.

"Owen, I don't 'give' people freedom."

"Yes, Lord Rahl."

Owen evidently took Richard's words as something he dared not argue with, but his eyes clearly said that he didn't believe it.

"Owen, what do you mean when you say that you think I give people freedom?"

Owen took a tiny bite of his biscuit as he glanced around at the others. He squirmed his shoulders in a self-conscious shrug. Finally, he cleared his throat.

"Well, you, you do what the Imperial Order does—you kill people." He waved his biscuit awkwardly, as if it were a sword, stabbing the air. "You kill those who enslave people, and then you give the people who were enslaved their freedom so that peace can return."

Richard took a deep breath. He wasn't sure if Owen meant it the way it came out, or if it was just that he was having difficulty explaining himself in front of people who made him nervous.

"That's not exactly the way it is," Richard said.

"But that's why you came down here. Everyone knows it. You came down here to the Old World to give people freedom."

Elbows on his knees, Richard leaned forward rubbing his palms together as he thought about how much he wanted to explain. He felt a wave of calmness when Kahlan draped a gentle, comforting hand over the back of his shoulder. He didn't want to go into the horror of how he had been taken prisoner and taken from Kahlan, thinking he would never see her again.

Richard put the whole weight of emotion over that long ordeal aside and took another approach. "Owen, I'm from up in the New World—"

"Yes, I know," Owen said as he nodded. "And you came here to free people from—"

"No. That's not the truth of it. We lived in the New World. We were once at peace, apparently much like your people were. Emperor Jagang—"

"The dream walker."

"Yes, Emperor Jagang, the dream walker, sent his armies to conquer the New World, to enslave our people—"

"My people, too."

Richard nodded. "I understand. I know what a horror that is. His soldiers are rampaging up through the New World, murdering, enslaving our people."

Owen turned his watery gaze off into the darkness as he nodded. "My people, too."

"We tried to fight back," Kahlan told him. "But there are too many. Their army is far too vast for us to drive them out of our land."

Owen nibbled his biscuit again, not meeting her gaze. "My people are terrified of the men of the Order—may the Creator forgive their misguided ways."

"May they scream in agony for all eternity in the darkest shadow of the Keeper of the underworld," Cara said in merciless correction.

Owen stared slack-jawed at such a curse spoken aloud.

"We couldn't fight them like that—simply drive them back to the Old World," Richard said, bringing Owen's gaze back to him as he went on with the story. "So I'm down here, in Jagang's homeland, helping people who hunger to be free to cast off the shackles of the Order. While he's away conquering our land, he has left his own homeland open to those who hunger for freedom. With Jagang and his armies away, that gives us a chance to strike at Jagang's soft underbelly, to do him meaningful harm.

"I'm doing this because it's the only way we can fight back against the Imperial Order—our only means to succeed. If I weaken his foundation, his source of men and support, then he will have to withdraw his army from our land and return south to defend his own.

"Tyranny cannot endure forever. By its very nature it rots everything it rules, including itself. But that can take lifetimes. I'm trying to accelerate that process so that I and those I love can be free in our lifetimes—free to live our own lives. If enough people rise up against the Imperial Order's rule, it may even loosen Jagang's grip on power and bring him and the Order down.

"That's how I'm fighting him, how I'm trying to defeat him, how I'm trying to get him out of my land."

Owen nodded. "This is what we need, too. We are victims of fate. We need for you to come and get his men out of our land, and then to withdraw your sword, your ways, from our people so we may live in tranquility again. We need you to give us freedom."

The driftwood popped, sending a glowing swirl of sparks skyward. Richard, hanging his head, tapped his fingertips together. He didn't think the man had heard a word he'd said. They needed rest. He needed to translate the book. They needed to get to where they were going. At least he didn't have a headache.

"Owen, I'm sorry," he finally said in a quiet voice. "I can't help you in so direct a manner. But I would like you to understand that my cause is to your advantage, too, and that what I'm doing will also cause Jagang to eventually pull his troops out of your homeland as well, or at least weaken their presence so that you can throw them out yourselves."

"No," Owen said. "His men will not leave my land until you come and . . ." Owen winced. "And destroy them."

The very word, the implication, looked sickening to the man.

"Tomorrow," Richard said, no longer bothering to try to sound polite, "we have to be on our way. You will have to be on your way as well. I wish you success in ridding your people of the Imperial Order."

"We cannot do such a thing," Owen protested. He sat up

straighter. "We are not savages. You and those like you—the unenlightened ones—it is up to you to do it and give us freedom. I am the only one who can bring you. You must come and do as your kind does. You must give our empire freedom."

Richard rubbed his fingertips across the furrows of his brow. Cara started to rise. A look from Richard sat her back down.

"I gave you water," Richard said as he stood. "I can't give you freedom."

"But you must—"

"Double watch tonight," Richard said as he turned to Cara, cutting Owen off.

Cara nodded once as her mouth twisted with a satisfied smile of iron determination.

"In the morning," Richard added, "Owen will be on his way."

"Yes," she said, her blue-eyed glare sliding to Owen, "he certainly will be."

CHAPTER 11

"What is it?" Kahlan asked as she rode up beside the wagon.

Richard looked to be furious about something. She saw then that he had the book in one hand; his other was a fist. He opened his mouth, about to speak, but when Jennsen, up on the seat beside Tom, turned back to see what was going on, Richard said to her instead, "Kahlan and I are going to check the road up ahead. Keep your eye on Betty so she doesn't jump out, will you, Jenn?"

Jennsen smiled at him and nodded.

"If Betty gives you any trouble," Tom said, "just let me know and I'll take her to a lady I know and have some goat sausages made up."

Jennsen grinned at their private joke and gave Tom a good-natured elbow in his ribs. As Richard climbed over the side of the wagon and dropped to the ground, she snapped her fingers at the tail-wagging goat.

"Betty! You just stay there. Richard doesn't need you tagging along every single time."

Betty, front hooves on the chafing rail, bleated as she looked up at Jennsen, as if asking for her to reconsider.

"Down," Jennsen said in admonishment. "Lie down."

Betty bleated and reluctantly hopped back down into the wagon bed, but she would settle for no less than a scratch behind the ears as consolation before she would lie down.

Kahlan leaned over from her seat in the saddle and untied the reins to Richard's horse from the back of the wagon. He stepped into the stirrup and gracefully swung up in one fluid motion. She could see that he was agitated about something, but it made her heart sing just to look at him.

He shifted his weight forward slightly, urging his horse ahead. Kahlan squeezed her legs to the side of her own horse to spur her into a canter to keep up with Richard. He rode out ahead, rounding several turns in the flatter land among the rough hillsides, until he caught up with Cara and Friedrich, patrolling out in the lead.

"We're going to check out front for a while," he told them. "Why don't you fall back and check behind?"

Kahlan knew that Richard was sending them to the back because if he took Kahlan to the back under the pretense of watching anything that might come up on them from behind, Cara would keep falling back to check on them. If they were out front, Cara wouldn't worry about them dropping back and getting lost.

Cara laid her reins over and turned back. Sweat stuck Kahlan's shirt to her back as she leaned over her horse's withers, urging her ahead as Richard's horse sprang away. Despite the clumps of tall grass dotting the foothills and occasional sparse patches of woods, the heat was still with them. It cooled some at night, now, but the days were hot, with the humidity increasing as the clouds built up against the wall of mountains to their right.

Up close, the barrier of rugged mountains to the east was an intimidating sight. Sheer rock walls rose up below projecting plateaus heaped to their very edge with loose rock crumbled from yet higher plateaus and walls, as if the entire range was all gradually crumbling. With drops of thousands of feet at the fringe of overhanging shelves of rock, climbing such unstable scree would be impossible. If there were passes through the arid slopes, they were no doubt few and would prove difficult.

But making it past those gray mountains of scorching rock, they could now see, was hardly the biggest problem.

Those closer mountains spreading north and south in the burning heat at the edge of the desert partially hid what lay to the other side—a far more daunting range of snowcapped peaks rising up to completely block any passage east. Those imposing mountains were beyond the scale of any Kahlan had ever seen. Not even the most rugged of the Rang'Shada Mountains in the Midlands were their match. These mountains were like a race of giants. Precipitous walls of rock soared thousands of feet straight up. Harrowing slopes rose unbroken by any pass or rift and were so arduous that few trees could find a foothold. Lofty snow-packed peaks that ascended majestically above windswept clouds were jammed so close together that it reminded her more of a knife's long jagged edge than separate summits.

The day before, when Kahlan had seen Richard studying those imposing mountains, she had asked him if he thought there was any way across them. He had said no, that the only way he could see to get beyond was possibly the notch he'd spotted before, when he had found the place where the strange boundary had once been, and that notch still lay some distance north.

For now, they skirted the dry side of the closer mountains as that range made its way north along the more easily traversed lowlands.

Along the base of a gentle hill covered in clumps of brown grasses, Richard finally slowed his horse. He turned in his saddle, checking that the others were still coming, if a goodly distance behind.

He pulled his horse close beside her. "I skipped ahead in the book."

Kahlan didn't like the sound of that. "When I asked you before why you didn't skip ahead, you said that it wasn't a wise thing to do."

"I know, but I wasn't really getting anywhere and we need answers." As their horses settled into a comfortable walk, Richard rubbed his shoulders. "After all that heat I can't believe how cold it's getting."

"Cold? What are you—"

"You know those rare people like Jennsen?" The leather of his saddle squeaked as he leaned toward her. "Ones born pristinely ungifted—without even that tiny spark of the gift? The pillars of Creation? Well, back when this book was written, they weren't so rare."

"You mean it was more common for them to be born?"

"No, the ones who had been born began to grow up, get married, and have children—ungifted children."

Kahlan looked over in surprise. "The broken links in the chain of the gift that you were talking about before?"

Richard nodded. "They were children of the Lord Rahl. Back then, it wasn't like it has been in recent times with Darken Rahl, or his father. From what I can tell, all the children of the Lord Rahl and his wife were part of his family, and treated as such, even though they were born with this problem. It seems that the wizards tried to help them—both the direct offspring, and then their children, and their children. They tried to cure them."

"Cure them? Cure them of what?"

Richard lifted his arms in a heated gesture of frustration. "Of being born ungifted—of being born without even that tiny spark of the gift like everyone else has. The wizards back then tried to restore the breaks in the link."

"How did they think they would be able to cure someone of not having even the spark of the gift?"

Richard pressed his lips together as he thought of a way to explain it. "Well, you know the wizards who sent you across the boundary to find Zedd?"

"Yes," Kahlan said in a suspicious drawl.

"They weren't born with the gift—born wizards, that is. What were they—second or third wizards? Something like that? You told me about them, once." He snapped his fingers as it came to him. "Wizards of the Third Order. Right?"

"Yes. Just one, Giller, was the Second Order. None were able to pass the tests to be a wizard of the First Order, like Zedd, because they didn't have the gift. Being wizards was their calling, but they weren't gifted in the conventional sense—but they still had that spark of the gift that everyone has."

"That's what I'm talking about," Richard said. "They weren't born with the gift to be wizards—just the spark of it like everyone else. Yet Zedd somehow trained them to be able to use magic—to be wizards—even though they weren't born that way, born with the gift to be wizards."

"Richard, that was a lifetime of work."

"I know, but the point is that Zedd was able to help them to be wizards—at least wizards enough to pass his tests and conjure magic."

"Yes, I suppose. When I was young they taught me about the workings of magic and the Wizard's Keep, about those people and creatures in the Midlands with magic. They may not have been born with the gift, but they had worked a lifetime to become wizards. They *were* wizards," she insisted.

Richard's mouth turned up with the kind of smile that told her that she had just framed the essence of his argument for him. "But they had not been born with that aspect, that attribute, of the gift." He leaned toward her. "Zedd, besides training them, must have used magic to help them become wizards, right?"

Kahlan frowned at the thought. "I don't know. They never told me about their training to become wizards. That was never germane to their relationship with me or my training."

"But Zedd has Additive magic," Richard pressed. "Additive can change things, add to them, make them more than they are."

"All right," Kahlan cautiously agreed. "What's the point?"

"The point is that Zedd took people who weren't born with the gift to be wizards and he trained them but—more importantly—he must have also used his power to help them along that path by altering how they were born. He had to have added to their gift to make them more than they were born to be." Richard glanced over at her as his horse stepped around a small, scraggly pine. "He altered people with magic."

Kahlan let out a deep breath as she looked away from Richard and ahead at the gentle spread of grassy hills to either side of them, as she tried to fully grasp the concept of what he was saying.

"I never considered that before, but all right," she finally said. "So, what of it?"

"We thought that only the wizards of old could do such a thing, but, apparently, it's not a lost art nor would it be entirely so far-fetched as I had imagined for the wizards back then to believe they could change what was into what they thought it ought to be. What I'm saying is that, like what Zedd did to give people that with which they were not born, so too did the wizards of old try to give people born as pillars of Creation a spark of the gift."

Kahlan felt a chill of realization. The implication was staggering. Not just the wizards of old, but Zedd, too, had used magic to alter the very nature of people, the very nature of what they were, how they were born.

She supposed that he had only helped them to achieve what was their greatest ambition in life—their calling—by enhancing what they already had been born with. He helped them to reach their full potential. But that was for men who had the innate potential. While the wizards of long ago probably had done similar things to help people, they had also sometimes used their power for less benevolent reasons.

"So," he said, "the wizards back then, who were experienced in altering people's abilities, thought that these people called the pillars of Creation could be cured."

"Cured of not having been born gifted," she said in a flat tone of incredulity.

"Not exactly. They weren't trying to make them into wizards, but they thought they could at least be cured of not having that infinitesimal spark of the gift that simply enabled them to interact with magic."

Kahlan took a purging breath. "So then what happened?"

"This book was written after the great war had ended—after the barrier had been created and the Old World had been sealed away. It was written after the New World was at peace or, at least, after the barrier kept the Old World contained.

"But remember what we found out before? That we think that during the war Wizard Ricker and his team had done something to halt Subtractive Magic's ability to be passed on to the offspring of wizards? Well, after the war, those born with the gift started becoming increasingly uncommon, and those who were being born were being born without the Subtractive side."

"So, after the war," she said, "those who were born with the gift of both Additive and Subtractive were rapidly becoming nonexistent. We already knew that."

"Right." Richard leaned toward her and lifted the book. "But then, when there are fewer wizards being born, all of a sudden the wizards additionally realize that they have all these pristinely ungifted—breaks altogether in the link to magic—on their hands. Suddenly, on top of the problem of the birth rate of those with the gift to be wizards dropping, they were faced with what they called pillars of Creation."

Kahlan swayed in the saddle as she thought about it, trying to imagine the situation at the Keep at the time. "I can see that they would have been pretty concerned."

His voice lowered meaningfully. "They were desperate."

Kahlan laid her reins over, moving in behind Richard as his horse stepped around an ancient, fallen tree that had been bleached silver by the sweltering sun.

"So, I suppose," Kahlan asked as she walked her horse back up beside him, "that the wizards started to do the same thing Zedd did? Trained those who had the calling—those who wished to be wizards but had not been born with the gift?"

"Yes, but back then," Richard said, "they trained those with only Additive to be able to use the Subtractive, too, like full wizards of the time. As time went on, though, even that was being lost to them, and they were only able to do what Zedd did—train men to be wizards but they could only wield Additive Magic.

"But that isn't really what the book is about," Richard said as he gestured dismissively. "That was just a side point to record what they had attempted. They started out with confidence. They thought that these pillars of Creation could be cured of being pristinely ungifted, much like wizards with only Additive could be trained to use both sides of the magic, and those without the gift for wizardry could be made wizards able to use at least the Additive side of it."

The way he used his hands when he talked reminded her of the way Zedd did when he became worked up. "They tried to modify the very nature of how these people had been born. They tried to take people without any spark of the gift, and alter them in a desperate attempt to give them the ability to interact with magic. They weren't just adding or enhancing, they were trying to create something out of nothing."

Kahlan didn't like the sound of that. They knew that in those ancient times the wizards had great power, and they altered people with the gift, manipulated their gift, to suit a specific purpose.

They created weapons out of people.

In the great war, Jagang's ancestors were one such weapon: dream walkers. Dream walkers were created to be able to take over the minds of people in the New World and control them. Out of desperation, the bond of the Lord Rahl was created to counter that weapon, to protect a people from the dream walkers.

Any number of human weapons were conjured from the gifted. Such changes were often profound, and they were irrevocable. At times, the creations were monsters of boundless cruelty. From this heritage, Jagang had been born.

During that great war, one of the wizards who had been put on trial for treason refused to reveal what damage he had done. When even torture failed to gain the man's confession, the wizards conducting the trial turned to the talents of a wizard named Merritt and ordered the creation of a Confessor. Magda Searus, the first Confessor, extracted the man's confession. The tribunal was so pleased with the results of Wizard Merritt's conjuring that they commanded that an order of Confessors be created.

Kahlan felt no different to what other people felt, she was no less human, no less a woman, loved life no less, but her Confessor's power was the result of that conjuring. She, too, was a descendant of women altered to be weapons—in this case weapons designed to find the truth.

"What's the matter?" Richard asked.

She glanced over and saw the look of concern on his face. Kahlan forced a smile and shook her head that it was nothing.

"So what is it that you discovered by jumping ahead in the book?"

Richard took a deep breath as he folded his hands over the pommel of the saddle. "Essentially, they were attempting to use color in order to help people born without eyes . . . to see."

From Kahlan's understanding of magic and of history, this was fundamentally different from even the most malevolent experiments to alter people into weapons. Even in the most vile of these instances, they were attempting to take away some attribute of their humanity and at the same time add to or enhance an elemental ability. In none of them were they trying to create that which was not there at all.

"In other words," Kahlan summed up, "they failed."

Richard nodded. "So, here they were, the great war was long over and the Old World—those who had wanted to end magic, much like the Imperial Order—was safely sealed away beyond the barrier that had been created. Now they find out that the birth rate of those carrying the gift of wizardry is plummeting, and that the magic engendered by the House of Rahl, the bond with his people designed to stop the dream walkers from taking them, has an unexpected consequence—it also gives birth to the pristinely ungifted, who are an irreversible break in the lineage of magic."

"They have two problems, then," Kahlan said. "They have fewer wizards being born to deal with problems of magic, and they have people being born with no link at all to the magic."

"That's right. And the second problem was growing faster than the first. In the beginning, they thought they would find a solution, a cure. They didn't. Worse, as I explained before, those born of the pristinely ungifted, like Jennsen, always bear children the same as themselves. In a few generations, the number of the people without the link to the gift was growing faster than anyone ever expected."

Kahlan let out a deep breath. "Desperate indeed."

"It was becoming chaos."

She hooked a loose strand of hair back. "What did they decide?"

Richard regarded her with one of those looks that told her he was pretty disturbed by what he'd found.

"They chose magic over people. They deemed that this attribute— magic, or those who possessed it—was more important than human life." His voice rose. "Here they took the very thing they fought the war over, the right of those who were born the way they were—in that case people born with magic—to their own lives, to exist, and they turned it all around to be that this attribute was more impor- tant than the life which held it!"

He let out a breath and lowered his voice. "There were too many to execute, so they did the next best thing—they banished them."

Kahlan's eyebrows went up. "Banished them? To where?"

Richard leaned toward her with fire in his eyes. "The Old World."

"What!"

Richard shrugged, as if speaking on behalf of the wizards back then, mocking their reasoning. "What else could they do? They could hardly execute them; they were friends and family. Many of those normal people with the spark of the gift—but who were not gifted as wizards or sorceresses and so didn't think of themselves as gifted—had sons, daughters, brothers, sisters, uncles, aunts, cousins, neighbors who had married these pristinely ungifted, these pillars of Creation. They were part of society—a society which was less and less populated by the truly gifted.

"In a society where they were increasingly outnumbered and mistrusted, the ruling gifted couldn't bring themselves to put all these tainted people to death."

"You mean they even considered it?"

Richard's eyes told her that they had and what he thought of the notion. "But in the end, they couldn't. At the same time, after trying everything, they now realized that they couldn't ever restore the link to magic once it was broken by these people, and such people were marrying and having children, and the children were marrying and having children—who in every case passed along this taint. And, those so tainted were increasing in numbers faster than anyone had imagined.

"As far as the gifted were concerned, their very world was threatened, in much the same way it had been threatened by the war. That was, after all, what those in the Old World had been trying to do—destroy magic—and here it was, the very thing they feared, happening.

"They couldn't repair the damage, they couldn't stop it from spreading, and they couldn't put to death all those among them. At the same time, with the taint multiplying, they knew that they were running out of time. So, they settled on what to them was the only way out—banishment."

"And they could cross the barrier?" she asked.

"Those with the gift, for all practical purposes, were prevented from crossing the barrier, but for those who were pillars of Creation, magic didn't exist; they were unaffected by it, so, to them, the barrier was not an obstacle."

"How could those in charge be sure they had all the pillars of Creation? If any escaped, the banishment would fail to solve their problem."

"Those with the gift—wizards and sorceresses—can somehow recognize the pristinely ungifted for what they are: holes in the world, as Jennsen said those like her were called. The gifted can see them, but not sense them with their gift. Apparently, it wasn't a problem to know who the pillars of Creation were."

"Can you tell any difference?" Kahlan asked. "Can you sense Jennsen as being different? Being a hole in the world?"

"No. But I've not been taught to use my ability. How about you?"

Kahlan shook her head. "I'm not a sorceress, so I guess that I don't have the ability to detect those like her." She shifted her weight in her saddle. "So, what happened with those people back then?"

"The people of the New World collected all those ungifted offspring of the House of Rahl and their every single last descendant, and sent the whole lot of them across the great barrier, to the Old World, where the people had professed that they wanted mankind to be free of magic."

Richard smiled with the irony, even of such a grim event as this. "The wizards of the New World, in essence, gave their enemy in the Old World exactly what they professed to want, what they had been fighting for: mankind without magic."

His smile withered. "Can you imagine deciding that we had to banish Jennsen and send her into some fearful unknown, simply because of the fact that she can't see magic?"

Kahlan shook her head as she tried to envision such a time. "What a horror, to be uprooted and sent away, especially to the enemy of your own people."

Richard rode in silence for a time. Finally, he went on with the story. "It was a terrifying event for those banished, but it was also traumatic almost beyond endurance to those who were left. Can you even imagine what it must have been like? All those friends and relatives suddenly ripped out of your life, your family? The disruption to trade and livelihood?" Richard's words came with bitter finality. "All because they decided some attribute was more important than human life."

Just listening to the story, Kahlan felt as if she had been through an ordeal. She watched Richard riding beside her, staring off, lost in his own thoughts.

"Then what?" she finally asked. "Did they ever hear from those who were banished?"

He shook his head. "No, nothing. They were now beyond the great barrier. They were gone."

Kahlan stroked her horse's neck, just to feel the comfort of something alive. "What did they do about those who were born after that?"

Still he stared off. "Killed them."

Kahlan swallowed in revulsion. "I can't imagine how they could do that."

"They could tell, once the child was born, if it was ungifted. It was said to be easier then, before it was named."

Kahlan couldn't find her voice for a moment. "Still," she said in a weak voice, "I can't imagine it."

"It's no different from what Confessors did about the birth of male Confessors."

His words cut through her. She hated the memory of those times. Hated the memory of a male child being born to a Confessor. Hated the memory of one being put to death by command of the mother.

There was said to be no choice. Male Confessors in the past had had no self-control over their power. They became monsters, started wars, caused unimaginable suffering.

It was argued that there was no choice but to put a male child of a Confessor to death, before they were named.

Kahlan couldn't force herself to look up into Richard's eyes. The witch woman, Shota, had foretold that she and Richard would conceive a male child. Neither Kahlan nor Richard would ever for an instant consider harming any child of theirs, a child resulting from their love for one another, from their love of life. She couldn't imagine putting a child of theirs to death for being born a male child of her as a Confessor, or an ungifted male or female child of Richard for being a Rahl. How could anyone say that such a life had no right to exist because of who they were, what they were like, or what they might possibly become?

"Somewhere along the line after this book was written," Richard said in a quiet voice, "things changed. When this book was written, the Lord Rahl of D'Hara always married, and they knew when he produced offspring. When the child was pristinely ungifted, they ended its life as mercifully as they could.

"At some point, ruling wizards of the House of Rahl became like Darken Rahl. They took any woman they wanted, whenever they wanted. The details, such as if an ungifted child born of those couplings was actually a pillar of Creation, became unimportant to them. They simply killed any offspring, except the gifted heir."

"But they were wizards—they could have told which ones were like that and at least not killed the rest."

"If they wanted, I suppose they could have, but, like Darken Rahl, their only interest was in the single gifted heir. They simply killed the rest."

"So, such offspring hid for fear of their life and one managed to escape the grasp of Darken Rahl until you killed him first. And so you have a sister, Jennsen."

Richard's smile returned. "And so I do."

Kahlan followed his gaze and saw distant specks, black-tipped races, watching, as they soared on the updrafts of the high cliffs of the mountains to the east.

She took a purging breath of the hot, humid air. "Richard, those ungifted offspring that were banished to the Old World, do you think they survived?"

"If the wizards in the Old World didn't slaughter them."

"But everyone down here in the Old World is the same as in the New World. I've fought against the soldiers from here—with Zedd and the Sisters of the Light. We used magic of every sort to try to halt the Order's advance. I can tell you firsthand that all those from the Old World are affected by magic, so that means they all are born with that spark of the gift. There are no broken links in the chain of magic in the Old World."

"From everything I've seen down here, I'd have to agree."

Kahlan wiped sweat from her brow. It was running into her eyes. "So what happened to those banished people?"

Richard gazed off toward the mountains beneath the races. "I can't imagine. But it must have been horrifying for them."

"So you think that maybe that was the end of them? That maybe they perished, or were put to death?"

He regarded her with a sidelong glance. "I don't know. But what I'd like to know is why that place back there is named the same as they were called in this book: the Pillars of Creation." His eyes took on a menacing gleam. "And far worse yet, I'd like to know why, as Jennsen told us, a copy of this book is among Jagang's most prized possessions."

That troublesome thought had been running through Kahlan's mind as well.

She looked up at him from beneath a frown. "Maybe you shouldn't have skipped ahead in your reading of the book, Lord Rahl."

Richard's fleeting smile wasn't all she'd hoped for. "I'll be relieved if that's the biggest mistake I've made, lately."

"What do you mean?"

He raked his hair back. "Is anything different about your Confessor's power?"

"Different?" Almost involuntarily, his question caused her to draw back, to focus inwardly, to take stock of the force she always felt within herself. "No. It feels the same as always."

The power coiled in the core of her being did not need to be summoned when there was need of it. As always, it was there at the ready; it only required that she release her restraint of it for it to be unleashed.

"There's something wrong with the sword," he said, catching her by surprise. "Wrong with its power."

Kahlan couldn't imagine what to make of such a notion. "How can you tell? What's different?"

Richard idly stroked his thumbs along the reins turned back over his fingers. "It's hard to define exactly what's different. I'm just used to the feeling of it being at my beck and call. It responds when I need it, but for some reason it seems to be hesitant about doing so."

Kahlan felt that now, more than ever, they needed to get back to Aydindril and see Zedd. Zedd was the keeper of the sword. Even though they couldn't take the sword through the sliph because the presence of its magic would kill anyone in the sliph, Zedd would be able to give them insight about any nuance of its power. He would know what to do. He would be able to help Richard with the headaches, too.

And Kahlan knew that Richard needed help. She could see that he wasn't himself. His gray eyes held a glaze of pain, but there was something more etched in his expression, in the way he moved, the way he carried himself.

The whole explanation of the book and what he had discovered seemed to have sapped his strength.

She was beginning to think that it wasn't she, after all, who was the one running out of time, but that it was Richard. That thought, despite the warm afternoon sun, sent cold terror racing through her.

Richard checked the others over his shoulder. "Let's go back to the wagon. I need to get something warmer to put on. It's freezing today."

CHAPTER 12

Zedd peered up the deserted street. He could have sworn that he saw someone. Using his gift to search for any sign of life told him that there was no one anywhere around. Still, he remained motionless as he stared.

The warm breeze pressed his simple robes against his bony frame and gently ruffled his disheveled white hair. A tattered, sun-faded blue dress that someone had pinned to a second-floor balcony railing to dry flapped like a flag in the wind. The dress, along with a city full of personal possessions, had long ago been left behind.

The buildings, their walls painted various colors from rusty red to yellow with shutters in bright, contrasting hues stuck out to slightly varying degrees on either side of the narrow cobbled street, making a canyon of colorful walls. Most of the second stories overhung the bottom floors by a few feet, and, with their eaves hanging out even more, the buildings closed off the better part of the sky except for a snaking slit of afternoon sunlight that followed the sinuous course of the street up and over the gentle hill. The doors were all tightly shut, most of the windows shuttered. A pale green gate to an alleyway hung open, squeaking as it swung to and fro in the breeze.

Zedd decided that it must have been a trick of the light that he'd seen, maybe a windowpane that had moved in the wind sending a flicker of light across a wall.

When he was at last sure that he had been mistaken about seeing anyone, Zedd started back down the street, yet remained close to one side, walking as quietly as possible. The Imperial Order army had not returned to the city since Zedd had unleashed the light web that had killed an enormous number of their force, but that didn't mean that there couldn't be dangers about.

No doubt Emperor Jagang still wanted the city, and especially the Keep, but he was no fool and he knew that a few more light webs ignited among his army, no matter how vast it was, would in that instant reduce his force by such staggering numbers that it could alter the course of the war. Jagang had fought against the Midland and D'Haran forces for a year and in all those battles he had not lost as many men as he'd lost in that one blinding moment. He would not casually risk another such event.

After such a blow Jagang would want to capture the Keep more than he had ever wanted it before. He would want Zedd more than ever before.

Had Zedd more of the light webs like the one his frantic search through the Keep had turned up, he would have already unleashed them all on the Order. He sighed. If only he had more.

Still, Jagang didn't know that he had no more such constructed spells. As long as Jagang feared that there were more, it served Zedd's purpose in keeping the Imperial Order out of Aydindril and away from the Wizard's Keep.

Some harm had been done to the Confessors' Palace when Jagang had been gulled into attacking, but Zedd judged that trying that trick had been worth the regrettable damage; it had almost netted him and Adie the emperor's hide. Damage could always be repaired. He vowed that it would be repaired.

Zedd clenched a fist at how close he had come to finishing Jagang that day. At least he had dealt a mighty blow to his army.

And Zedd might have had Jagang had it not been for that strange young woman. He shook his head at the memory of actually seeing one who could not be touched by magic. He'd known, in theory, of their existence, but had never before known it for certain to be true. Vague references in old books made for interesting abstract speculation, but seeing it with his own eyes was quite something else.

It had been an unsettling sight. Adie had been shaken by the encounter even more than he; she was blind, yet with the aid of the gift could see better than he could. That day, she had not been able to see the young woman who was there but, in some ways, not there. To Zedd's eyes, if not his gift, she was a beautiful sight, with some of Darken Rahl's looks, but different and altogether captivating. That she was half sister to Richard was clear; she shared some of his features, especially the eyes. If only Zedd could have stopped her, kept her out of the way, convinced her that she was making a terrible mistake by being with the Order, or even if he could have killed her, Jagang would not have escaped justice.

Still, Zedd held no illusions about ending the threat of the Imperial Order simply by killing Jagang. Jagang was merely the brute who led other brutes in enforcing blind faith in the Order, a blind faith that embraced death as salvation from what it preached was the corrupt misery of life, a blind faith in which life itself had no value but as a bloody sacrifice upon the altar of altruism, a blind faith that blamed the failure of its own ideas on mankind for being wicked and for failing to offer sufficient sacrifice in an endless quest for some illusive greater good that grew ever more distant, a blind faith in an Order that clung to power by feeding off the carcasses of the productive lives it ruined.

A faith that by its very beliefs rejected reason and embraced the irrational could not long endure without intimidation and force—without brutes like Jagang to enforce such faith.

While Emperor Jagang was brutally effective, it was a mistake to think that if Jagang were to die that very day it would end the threat of the Order. It was the Order's ideas that were so dangerous; the priests of the Order would find other brutes.

The only real way to end the Order's reign of terror was to expose the naked evil of its teachings to the light of truth, and for those suffering under its doctrines to throw off the Order's yoke. Until then, they would have to fight the Imperial Order back as best they could, hoping at least to eventually contain them.

Zedd poked his head around a corner, watching, listening, sniffing the wind for any trace of anyone who might be lurking about. The city was deserted, but on a number of occasions stray Imperial Order soldiers had wandered in out of the mountains.

After the destruction caused by the light web, panic had swept through the Order's encampment. Many soldiers had scattered to the hills. Once the army had regrouped, a large number of men had decided to desert instead of returning to their units. Tens of thousands of such deserters were rounded up and executed, their bodies left to rot as a warning of what happened to those who abandoned the cause of the greater glory of the Imperial Order, or as the Order liked to put it, the cause of the greater good. Most of the rest of the men who had run to the hills had then had a change of heart and straggled back into camp.

There were still some, though, who had not wanted to go back and had not been caught. For a time, after Jagang's army had moved on, they had wandered into the city, sometimes alone, sometimes in small groups, half starved, to search for food and to loot. Zedd had lost count of how many such men he had killed.

He was reasonably sure that all of those stragglers were dead, now. The Order was made up of men mostly from cities and towns. Such men weren't used to living in the wild. Their job was to overwhelm the enemy, to kill, rape, terrorize, and plunder. A whole corps of logistics personnel provided them with support, delivering and dispensing a constant stream of supplies that rolled in to feed and care for the soldiers. They were violent men, but they were men who needed to be tended, who depended on the group for their survival. They didn't last long on their own in the trackless forested mountains surrounding Aydindril.

But Zedd hadn't seen any of them for quite some time. He was reasonably sure that the stragglers had starved, been killed, or had long ago headed back south, to the Old World.

There was always the possibility, though, that Jagang had sent assassins to Aydindril; some of those assassins could be Sisters of the Light, or worse, Sisters of the Dark. For that reason, Zedd rarely left the safety of the Keep, and when he did, he was cautious.

Also, he hated poking around the city, seeing it so devoid of life. This had been his home for much of his life. He remembered the days when the Keep was a hub of activity—not as it once had been, he knew, but alive with people of all sorts. He found himself smiling at the memory.

His smile faded. Now the city was a joyless sight, forlorn without people filling the streets, people talking from one balcony to a neighbor across the street in another window, people gathering to trade goods in the market. Not so long ago men would have stopped to have conversations in doorways while vendors pulled carts of their wares along the narrow streets and children at play skipped through the throngs. Zedd sighed at the sad sight of such lifeless streets.

At least those lives were safe, if a long way from home. Although he had many fundamental differences with the Sisters of the Light, he knew that their Prelate, Verna, and the rest of the free Sisters would watch over them.

The only problem was that now that Jagang had nothing in Aydindril of any real value to conquer except the Keep, and much to lose, he had wheeled his army east toward the remnants of the Midland forces. To be sure, the D'Haran army waited across those mountains to the east and Zedd knew how formidable they were, but he couldn't fool himself that they stood a chance against a force as immense as the Imperial Order.

Jagang had left the city in order to go after those D'Haran forces. The Imperial Order could not win the war by occupying an empty city; they needed to crush any resistance once and for all so that there would be no people left who could, by living prosperous, happy, peaceful lives, put the lie to the Order's teachings.

Now that Jagang had come all the way up through the Midlands, he had cleaved the New World. Forces had been left all along the route to occupy cities and towns. Now the main force of the Order would turn its bloodlust east, on a lone D'Hara. By dividing the New World in such a way, Jagang would be able to more efficiently crush opposition.

Zedd knew that it wasn't for lack of trying that the New World had given ground. He and Kahlan, among a great many others, had worked themselves sick, month after month, trying to find a way to stop Jagang's forces.

Zedd clutched his robes at his throat, at the painful memory of such ferocious fighting, at how nothing had worked against Jagang's numbers, at the death and dying, at the friends he had lost. It was only a matter of time until all was lost to the hordes from the Old World.

Richard and Kahlan would not survive such a conquest by the Imperial Order. Zedd's thin fingers covered his trembling lips at the ghastly thought of them being lost, too. They were the only family he had left. They were everything to him.

Zedd felt a crushing wave of hopelessness, and had to sit on the stump of a log section set outside a shoe shop that had been boarded closed. Once the Imperial Order finally annihilated all opposition, Jagang would return to take the city and lay siege to the Keep. Sooner or later, he would have it all.

The future, as Zedd imagined it, seemed to be a world shrouded in the gray pall of life under the Imperial Order. If the world fell under that pall, it would probably be a very long time before mankind ever emerged to live free again. Once liberty was surrendered to tyranny, it could be smothered for centuries before its flames again sprang to life and brightened the world.

Zedd hadn't sat for long when he forced himself to his feet. He was First Wizard. He had been in hopeless straits before and had seen the foe turned back. There was still the possibility that he and Adie could find something in the Keep that would aid them, or that they might yet discover information in the libraries that would give them a valuable advantage.

As long as there was life, they could fight on toward their goal. They still had the ability to triumph.

He harrumphed to himself. He would triumph.

Zedd was glad that Adie wasn't with him to see him in such a sorry state that he would have—if even momentarily—considered defeat. Adie would have never let him hear the end of it, and deservedly so.

He harrumphed again. He was hardly inexperienced, hardly without the wherewithal to handle challenges that arose. And if there were assassins about, gifted or not, they would find themselves caught by one of the many little surprises he had left around. Very nasty surprises.

Chin up, Zedd smiled to himself as he turned down a narrow

alley, making his way past a patchwork of yards with empty pens that had once held chickens, geese, ducks, and pigeons. His gaze passed over small back courtyards, their herbs and flowers growing untended, their wash lines empty, their wood and other materials stacked to the sides, waiting for people to return and work them into something useful.

Along the way he stopped in various vegetable gardens, harvesting the volunteer crops that had sprung up. There was lettuce aplenty, spinach, some small squash, green tomatoes and still a few peas. He collected his bounty in a canvas sack and slung it over a shoulder as he walked the garden plots, checking on the progress of irregular patches of onions, beets, beans, and turnips. Still some growing to do, he concluded.

While the vegetables weren't thick from a careful planting, the random growth in yards all over the city meant that he and Adie would have fresh vegetables for some time to come. Maybe she might even take to putting some things up for next winter. They could store root crops in the colder places in the Keep, and preserve more perishable vegetables. They would have more food than they could eat.

On his way up the alley, Zedd spied a bush off toward the corner, sprawled green and lush over a short back fence between two homes. The blackberry bush was loaded with ripe berries. He paused occasionally to check up and down the streets beyond while he made a nice-sized pile of the dark, plump berries in a square of cloth, then tied it up and placed it atop the heavier goods in his sack.

There were still plenty of ripe berries, and he hated to let them go to waste, or to the birds, so he worked at filling his pockets. He didn't worry that it would spoil his dinner; it was a long walk back up the mountain to the Wizard's Keep, so he could use a snack. Adie was making a thick stew from cured ham. There was no danger that he would spoil his appetite on mere berries. She would be pleased by the vegetables he brought and would no doubt want to add them to the stew straight away. Adie was a wonderful cook, although he dared not admit it to her lest she get a big head.

*   *   *

Before the stone bridge, Zedd paused, gazing back down the wide road leading up the mountainside. Only the wind in the trees and their shimmering leaves created any sound or movement. For a long moment, though, he stared down at the empty road.

Finally, he turned back to the bridge that in less than three hundred paces spanned a chasm with near vertical sides dropping away for thousands of feet. Clouds far below hung hard against the sheer rock walls. Despite the countless times he had walked over the stone bridge, it still made him feel just a little queasy. Without wings, though, there was but this single way into the Keep—except for the little trick passage he had used as a boy.

Because of their strategic role, Zedd had placed enough snares and traps along the bridge and the rest of the road up to the Keep that no one was going to live for more than a few paces once they came close. Not even a Sister of the Dark could trespass here. A few Sisters had attempted the impossible, and had paid with their lives.

They would have suspected such webs laid by the First Wizard himself, and felt some of the warning shields, but no doubt Jagang had given them no choice in the matter and had sent them to attempt entry, sacrificing their lives for the greater good of the Order.

Verna had once briefly been taken captive by the dream walker and she had told Zedd all about the experience in the hope that they might find a counter, other than swearing loyalty in one's heart to the Lord Rahl and thereby invoking the protection of the bond. Zedd had tried, but there was no countermagic he could provide. In the great war, wizards far more talented than he, and with both sides of the gift, had tried to devise defenses against dream walkers. Once the dream walker had taken over a person's mind, there was no defense; you had to do his bidding, regardless of the cost, even if the cost was your life.

Zedd suspected that for a few, death was a coveted release from the agony of possession by the dream walker. Suicide was a course blocked by Jagang; he needed the talents of the Sisters and other gifted. He couldn't have them all kill themselves for release from the misery of life as his chattel. But if he sent them to their certain death, such as attempting to enter the Keep, then they could at last be free of the agony that had become their life.

Ahead, the Keep towered on the mountainside. The soaring walls of dark stone, intimidating to most people, offered Zedd the warm sense of home. His eyes roamed the ramparts, and he remembered strolling there with his wife so many years ago—a lifetime ago, it seemed. From the towers he had often looked down at the beautiful sight of Aydindril below. He had once marched across the bridges and passageways to deliver orders defending the Midlands from an invasion from D'Hara, led by Darken Rahl's father.

That, too, seemed a lifetime ago. Now Richard, his grandson, was the Lord Rahl, and had succeeded in uniting most of the Midlands under the rule of the D'Haran Empire. Zedd shook his head at the wonder of it, at the thought of how Richard had changed everything. By Richard's hand, Zedd was now a subject of the D'Haran Empire. What a wonder indeed.

Before he reached the far side of the bridge, Zedd glanced down into the chasm. Movement caught his attention. Putting his bony fingers on the rough stone, he leaned out a little for a look. Below, but above the clouds, he saw two huge birds, black as moonless midnight, gliding along through the split in the mountain. Zedd had never seen the like of them. He couldn't imagine what to make of the sight.

When he turned back to the Keep, he thought he saw three more of the same kind of large black birds flying together, high above the Keep. He decided that they had to be ravens. Ravens were big. He must simply be misjudging the distance—probably from lack of food. Concluding that they had to be ravens, he tried to adjust his estimation of their distance, but they were already gone. He glanced down, but didn't see the other two, either.

As he passed under the iron portcullis, feeling the warm embrace of the Keep's spell, Zedd felt a wave of loneliness. He so missed Erilyn, his long-dead wife, as well as his long-passed daughter, Richard's mother, and, dear spirits, he missed Richard. He smiled then, thinking of Richard being with his own wife, now. It was still sometimes hard for him to think of Richard as grown into a man. He had had a wondrous time helping to raise Richard. What a time that had been in his life, off in Westland, away from the Midlands, away from magic and responsibility, with just that ever-curious boy and a whole world of wonders to explore and show him. What a time indeed.

Inside the Keep, lamps along the wall obediently sprang to flame as First Wizard Zeddicus Zu'l Zorander made his way along passageways and through grand rooms, deeper into the immense mountain fortress. As he passed the webs he'd placed, he checked the texture of their magic to find that they were undisturbed. He sighed in relief. He didn't expect that anyone would be foolish enough to try to enter the Keep, but the world had fools to spare. He didn't really like leaving such dangerous webs cast all about the place, in addition to the often dangerous shields already guarding the Keep, but he dared not relax his guard.

As he passed a long side table in a towering gathering hall, Zedd, as he had done since he was a boy, ran his finger along the smooth groove in the edge of the variegated chocolate-brown marble top. He stopped, frowning down at the table, and realized that it contained something he suddenly felt the want of: a ball of fine black cord left there years ago to tie ribbons and other decorations on the lamp brackets in the gathering hall to mark the harvest festival.

Sure enough, in the center drawer, he found the ball of fine cord. He snatched it up and slipped it into a pocket long emptied of its load of berries. From the wall bracket beside the table, he lifted a wand with six small bells. The wand, one of hundreds if not thousands throughout the Keep, was once used to summon servants. He sighed inwardly. It had been decades since servants and their families last lived in the Wizard's Keep. He remembered their children running and playing in the halls. He remembered the joy of laughter echoing throughout the Keep, bringing life to the place.

Zedd told himself that one day children would again run and laugh in the halls, Richard and Kahlan's children, and a broad smile stretched his cheeks.

There were windows and openings in the stone that let light spill into many halls and rooms, but there were other places less well lit. Zedd found one of those darker places that was dim enough to satisfy him. He stretched a piece of the black cord, strung with one of the bells, across the doorway, winding it around coarse stone molding to each side. Moving deeper through the labyrinth of halls and passageways, he stopped and strung more strings with a bell at places where it would be hard to see. He had to collect several more of the servant wands for a supply of bells.

Although there were shields of magic laced everywhere, there was no telling what powers some of the Sisters of the Dark possessed. They would be looking for magic, not bells. It couldn't hurt to take the extra precaution.

Zedd made mental notes of where he strung the fine black cord—he would have to let Adie know. He doubted, though, that with her gifted sight she would need the warning. He was sure that with her blind eyes she could see better than anyone.

Following the wonderful aroma of ham stew, Zedd made his way to the comfortable room lined with bookshelves they used most of the time. Adie had hung spices to dry from the low beams carved with ancient designs. A leather couch sat before a broad fireplace and comfortable chairs beside a silver-inlaid table placed in front of a diamond-patterned leaded window with a breathtaking view over-looking Aydindril.

The sun was setting, leaving the city below bathed in a warm light. It almost looked like it always did, except there was no tell-tale smoke curling up from cooking fires.

Zedd set his burlap sack loaded with his harvest on piles of books atop a round mahogany table behind the couch. He shuffled closer to the fire, all the while taking deep breaths to inhale the intoxicating aroma of the stew.

"Adie," he called, "this smells delightful! Have you looked outside today? I saw the oddest birds."

He smiled as he inhaled another whiff.

"Adie—I think it must be done by now," he called toward the doorway to the side pantry room. "I think we ought to taste it, at least. Can't hurt to check, you know."

Zedd glanced back over his shoulder. "Adie? Are you listening to me?"

He went to the doorway and peered into the pantry, but it was empty.

"Adie?" he called down the stairs at the back of the pantry. "Are you down there?"

Zedd's mouth twisted with discontentment when she didn't answer.

"Adie?" he called again. "Bags, woman, where are you?"

He turned back, peering at the stew bubbling in the kettle hung on the crane over the fire.

Zedd scooped up a long wooden spoon from a pantry cupboard.

Spoon in hand, he stopped and leaned back toward the stairs. "Take your time, Adie. I'll just be up here . . . reading."

Zedd grinned and hurried for the stew.

CHAPTER 13

Richard rose in a rush when he saw Cara marching up a ravine toward camp, pushing ahead of her a man Richard vaguely recognized. In the failing light, he couldn't make out the man's face. Richard scanned the surrounding flat washes, rocky hills, and steep tree-covered slopes beyond, but didn't see anyone else.

Friedrich was off to the south and Tom to the west, checking the surrounding country, as Cara had been, to be sure there was no one about and that it was a safe place to spend the night; they were exhausted from picking a sinuous route through the increasingly rugged country. Cara had been checking north—the direction they were headed and the direction Richard considered potentially the most dangerous. Jennsen turned from the animals, waiting to see who the Mord-Sith had with her.

Once on his feet, Richard wished he hadn't gotten up quite so quickly—doing so had made him light-headed. He couldn't seem to shake the odd, disconnected sensation he felt, as if he were watching someone else react, talk, move. When he concentrated, forcing himself to focus his attention, the feeling would sometimes drift at least partly away and he would begin to wonder if it was only his imagination.

Kahlan's hand slipped up on his arm, gripping him as if she thought he might fall.

"Are you all right?" she whispered.

He nodded as he watched Cara and the man as he also kept an eye on the surrounding countryside. By the end of their ride earlier that afternoon to discuss the book, Kahlan had become even more worried about him. They were both troubled about what he'd read, but Kahlan was far more concerned, at the moment, anyway, about him.

Richard suspected that he might be coming down with a fever. That would explain why he was feeling so cold when everyone else was hot. From time to time, Kahlan would feel his forehead or place the back of her hand against his cheek. Her touch warmed his heart; she ignored his smiles as she fretted over him. She thought that he might be slightly feverish. Once she had Jennsen feel his forehead to see if she thought he might be warmer than he should be. Jennsen, too, thought that, if he did have a fever, it was minor. Cara, so far, had been satisfied by Kahlan's report that he didn't feel feverish, and hadn't deemed it necessary to see for herself.

A fever was just about the last thing Richard needed. There were important . . . important, something. He couldn't seem to recall at the moment. He concentrated on trying to remember the young man's name, or at least where he'd seen him before.

The last rays of the setting sun cast a pink glow across the mountains to the east. The closer hills were dimming to a soft gray in the gathering dusk. As darkness approached, the low fire was beginning to tint everything close around it a warm yellow-orange. Richard had kept the cook fire small, not wanting it to signal their location any more than necessary.

"Lord Rahl," the man said in a reverent tone as he stepped into camp. He dipped his head forward in a hesitant bow, apparently not sure if it was proper to bow or not. "It's an honor to see you again."

He was perhaps a couple of years younger than Richard, with curly black hair that brushed the broad shoulders of his buckskin tunic. He wore a long knife at his belt but no sword. His ears stuck out to the sides of his head as if he were straining to listen to every little sound. Richard imagined that as a boy he'd probably endured a lot of taunts about his ears, but now that he was a man his ears made him look rather intent and serious. As muscular as the man was, Richard doubted that he still had to contend with taunts.

"I'm . . . I'm sorry, but I can't quite seem to recall . . ."

"Oh, no, you wouldn't remember me, Lord Rahl. I was only—"

"Sabar," Richard said as it came to him. "Sabar. You loaded the furnaces in Priska's foundry, back in Altur'Rang."

Sabar beamed. "That's right. I can't believe you remember me."

Sabar had been one of the men at the foundry able to have work because of the supplies Richard hauled to Priska when no one else could. Sabar had understood how hard Priska worked just to keep his foundry alive under the oppressive, endless, and contradictory mandates of the Order. Sabar had been there the day the statue Richard carved had been unveiled; he had seen it before it was destroyed. He had been there at the beginning of the revolution in Altur'Rang, fighting close alongside Victor, Priska, and all the others who had seized the moment when it was upon them. Sabar had fought to help gain freedom for himself, his friends, and for his city.

That had been a day everything had changed.

Even though this man, like many others, had been a subject of the Imperial Order—one of the enemy—he wanted to live his own life under just laws, rather than under the dictates of despots who extinguished any hope of bettering oneself beneath the crushing burden of the cruel illusion of a greater good.

Richard noticed, then, that everyone was standing in tense anticipation, as if they had expected this to be trouble.

Richard smiled at Cara. "It's all right. I know him."

"So he told me," Cara said. She put a hand on Sabar's shoulder and pushed him down. "Have a seat."

"Yes," Richard said, glad to see that Cara had been fairly amiable about it. "Sit down and tell us why you're here."

"Nicci sent me."

Richard rose again in a rush, Kahlan coming up right beside him. "Nicci? We're on our way to meet her."

Sabar nodded, rising into a half crouch, seeming not to be sure if he was supposed to stand, since Richard and Kahlan had, or stay seated. Cara hadn't sat down; she stood behind Sabar like an executioner. Cara had been there when the revolution in Altur'Rang had started and might remember Sabar, but that would make no difference. Cara trusted no one where the safety of Richard and Kahlan was concerned.

Richard gestured for Sabar to remain seated. "Where is she?" Richard asked as he and Kahlan sat down again, sharing a seat on a bedroll. "Is she coming soon?"

"Nicci said to tell you that she waited as long as she could, but there have been some urgent developments and she could wait no longer."

Richard let out a disappointed sigh. "Some things came up for us, too." Kahlan had been captured and taken to the Pillars of Creation as bait to lure Richard into a trap. Rather than go into all that, he kept the story short and to the point. "We were trying to get to Nicci, but needed to go elsewhere. It was unavoidable."

Sabar nodded. "I was worried when she returned to us and said that you had not shown up at your meeting place, but she told us that she was sure you were busy taking care of something important and that was the reason you had not come.

"Victor Cascella, the blacksmith, was very worried, too, when Nicci told us this. He was thinking you would be returning with Nicci. He said that other places he knows, places he and Priska have dealings with for supplies and such, are on the verge of revolt. These people have heard about Altur'Rang, how the Order has been over-thrown there, and how people are beginning to prosper. He said that he knows free men in these places who struggle to survive under the oppression of the Order as we once did, and they hunger to be free. They want Victor's help.

"Some of the Brothers in the Fellowship of the Order who escaped from Altur'Rang have gone to these other places to insure that such revolt does not spread there. Their cruelty in punishing any they suspect of insurrection is costing the lives of many people, both the innocent and those valuable to the cause of overthrowing the Imperial Order.

"In order to insure their control of the gears of governance and to ready the Order's defense against the spread of the revolt, Brothers of the Order have gone to all the important cities. Surely, some of these priests have also gone to report to Jagang the fall of Altur'Rang, of the loss of so many officials in the fighting there, and of the deaths of Brother Narev and many of his close circle of disciples."

"Jagang already knows of the death of Brother Narev," Jennsen said, offering him a cup of water.

Sabar smiled his satisfaction at her news. He thanked her for the water, then leaned forward toward Richard and Kahlan as he went on with his story.

"Priska thinks the Order will want to sweep away the success of the revolt in Altur'Rang—that they can't afford to let it stand. He said that instead of worrying about spreading the revolt, we must prepare, make defenses, and have every man stand ready because the Order will return with the intent of slaughtering every last person in Altur'Rang."

Sabar hesitated, clearly worried about Priska's warning. "Victor, though, said we should hammer the iron while it is hot and create a just and secure future for ourselves, rather than wait for the Order to gather their strength to deny us that future. He says that if the revolt is spreading everywhere, the Order will not so easily stamp it out."

Richard ran a weary hand across his face. "Victor is right. If those in Altur'Rang try to sit alone as a singular place of freedom in the heart of hostile enemy territory, the Order will sweep in and cut out that heart. The Order can't survive on its perverted ideals and they know it; that's why they must use pressure to sustain their beliefs. Without that bully of force, the Order will crumble.

"Jagang spent twenty years creating a system of roads to knit a diverse and fractured Old World together into the Imperial Order. That was but part of the means of how he succeeded. Many resisted the rantings of his priests. With roads to swiftly respond to any dissent, though, Jagang was able to react quickly, to sweep in and kill those who openly opposed his new Order.

"More importantly, after eliminating those who resisted the Order's teachings, he filled the minds of children, who didn't know any better, with blind faith in those teachings, turning them into zealots eager to die for what they were taught was a noble cause— sacrifice to some all-consuming greater good.

"Those young men, their minds twisted with the teachings of the

Order, are now off to the north conquering the New World, butchering any who will not take up their altruistic tenets.

"But while Jagang and his vast army are to the north, that strength there leaves the Order weak here. That weakness is our opportunity and we must capitalize on it. Now, while Jagang and his men are absent, those same roads he built down here will be our means of rapidly spreading the struggle for freedom far and wide.

"The torch of freedom has been lit by the will of those like you, those in Altur'Rang who seized liberty for themselves. The flames of that torch must be held high, giving others the chance to see its light. If hidden and insulated, such flames will be extinguished by the Order. There may never be another chance in our lifetimes, or our children's lifetimes, to seize control of our own lives. That torch must be carried to other places."

Sabar smiled, filled with quiet pride that he had been a part of it all coming to be. "I know that Victor would like for others, like Priska, to be reminded of such things, of what the Lord Rahl would say about what we must do. Victor wants to talk to you before he goes to these places to 'pump the bellows,' as he put it. Victor said that he awaits your word on how you would move next, on how best to 'put the white-hot iron to them'—again, his words."

"So Nicci sent you to find me."

"Yes. I was happy to go to you when she asked me. Victor will be happy, too, not only that you are well but to hear what the Lord Rahl would say to him."

While Victor was awaiting word, Richard also knew that absent such word, Victor would act. The revolution did not revolve around Richard—it couldn't to be successful—but around the hunger of people to have their lives back. Still, Richard needed to help coordinate the spreading revolt in order to be sure it was as effective as possible, not just at bringing freedom to those who sought it, but at crumbling the foundation of the Order in the Old World. Only if they were successful in toppling the rule of the Order in the Old World would Jagang's attention be pulled away—and many of his men—from conquering the New World.

Jagang intended to conquer the New World by first dividing it.

Richard had to do the same if he was to succeed. Only dividing the Order's forces could defeat it.

Richard knew that with everyone evacuated from Aydindril, the Imperial Order would now turn its swords on D'Hara. Despite the competence of the D'Haran troops, they would be overwhelmed by the numbers that Jagang would throw at them. If the Order was not diverted from its cause, or at least divided into smaller forces, D'Hara would fall under the shadow of the Order. The D'Haran Empire, forged to unite the New World against tyranny, would end before it had really gotten started.

Richard had to get back to Victor and Nicci so that they could all continue what they had begun—devising the most effective strategy to overthrow the Imperial Order.

But they were running out of time to resolve another problem, a problem they didn't yet understand.

"I'm glad you found us, Sabar. You can tell Victor and Nicci that we need to see to something first, but as soon as we do, we'll be able to help them with their plans."

Sabar looked relieved. "Everyone will be happy to hear this."

Sabar hesitated, then tilted his head, gesturing north. "Lord Rahl, when I came to find you, following the directions Nicci gave me, I went past the area where she was to meet with you, and then I continued coming south." Worry stole into his expression. "Not many days ago, I came to a place, miles wide, that was dead."

Richard looked up. He realized that his headache seemed to be suddenly gone. "What do you mean, dead?"

Sabar waved his hand out toward the evening gloom. "The area where I was traveling was much like this place; there were some trees, clumps of grass, thickets of brush." His voice lowered. "But then I came to a place where everything that grew ended. All at the same place. There was nothing but rock beyond. Nicci had not told me that I would come to such a place. I admit, I was afraid."

Richard glanced to his right—to the east—to the mountains that lay beyond. "How long did this dead place last?"

"I walked, leaving life behind, and I thought I might be walking into the underworld itself." Sabar looked away from Richard's eyes.

"Or into the jaws of some new weapon the Order had created to destroy us all.

"I came to be very afraid and I was going to turn back. But then I thought about how the Order made me afraid my whole life, and I didn't like that feeling. Worse, I thought about how I would stand before Nicci and tell her I turned around rather than go to Lord Rahl as she asked of me, and that thought made me ashamed, so I went on. In several miles I came again to growing things." He let out a breath. "I was greatly relieved, and then I felt a little foolish that I had been afraid."

Two. That now made two of the strange boundaries.

"I've been to places like that, Sabar, and I can tell you that I, too, have been afraid."

Sabar broke into a grin. "Then I was not so foolish to be afraid."

"Not foolish at all. Could you tell if this dead area was extensive? Could you tell if it was more than just a patch of open rock in that one place? Could you see if it ran in a line, ran in any direction in particular?"

"It was like you say, like a line." Sabar flicked his hand toward the east. "It came down out of the far mountains, north of that depression." He held his hand flat like a cleaver, and sliced it downward in the other direction. "It ran off to the southwest, into that wasteland."

Toward the Pillars of Creation.

Kahlan leaned close and spoke under her breath. "That would be almost parallel to the boundary we crossed not far back to the south. Why would there be two boundaries so close together? That makes no sense."

"I don't know," Richard whispered to her. "Maybe whatever the boundary was protecting was so dangerous that whoever placed it feared that one might not be enough."

Kahlan rubbed her upper arms but didn't comment. By the look on her face, Richard knew how she felt about such a notion—especially considering that those boundaries were now down.

"Anyway," Sabar said with a self-conscious shrug, "I was happy I did not turn back, or I would have had to face Nicci after she had asked me to help Lord Rahl—my friend Richard."

Richard smiled. "I'm glad, too, Sabar. I don't think that place you went through is a danger any longer, at least not a danger the way it was once."

Jennsen could contain her curiosity no longer. "Who is this Nicci?"

"Nicci is a sorceress," Richard said. "She used to be a Sister of the Dark."

Jennsen's eyebrows went up. "Used to?"

Richard nodded. "She worked to further Jagang's cause, but she finally came to see how wrong she had been and joined our side." It was a story he didn't really feel like going into. "She now fights for us. Her help has been invaluable."

Jennsen leaned in, even more astonished. "But can you trust someone like that, someone who had labored on behalf of Jagang? Worse, a Sister of the Dark? Richard, I've been with some of those women, I know how ruthless they are. They may have to do as Jagang makes them, but they're devoted to the Keeper of the underworld. Do you really think you can trust with your life that she will not betray you?"

Richard looked Jennsen in the eye. "I trust you with a knife while I sleep."

Jennsen sat back up. She smiled, more out of embarrassment than anything else, Richard thought. "I guess I see your point."

"What else did Nicci say?" Kahlan asked, keen to get back to the matter at hand.

"Only that I must go in her place and meet you," Sabar said.

Richard knew that Nicci was being cautious. She didn't want to tell the young man too much in case he was caught.

"How did she know where I was?"

"She said that she was able to tell where you were by magic. Nicci is as powerful with magic as she is beautiful."

Sabar said this in a tone of awe. He didn't know the half of it. Nicci was one of the most powerful sorceresses ever to have lived. Sabar didn't know that when Nicci was laboring toward the ends sought by the Order, she was known as Death's Mistress.

Richard surmised that Nicci had somehow used the bond to the Lord Rahl to find him. That bond was loyalty sworn in the heart, not by rote, and its power protected those so sworn from the dream walker entering their minds. Full-blooded D'Harans, like Cara, could tell through the bond where the Lord Rahl was. Kahlan had confided to him that she found it unnerving the way Cara always knew where Richard was. Nicci wasn't D'Haran, but she was a sorceress and she was bonded to Richard, so she might have been able to manipulate that bond to tell where he was.

"Sabar, Nicci must have sent you to us for a reason," Richard said, "other than to say that she couldn't wait for us at our meeting place."

"Yes, of course," Sabar said as he nodded hastily, as if chagrined to have to be reminded. "When I asked her what I was to say to you, she told me that she had put it all in a letter." Sabar opened the leather flap of the pouch at his belt. "She said that when she realized how far away you really were, she was distraught and couldn't take the time to journey to you. She told me that it was important for me to be sure I found you and gave you her letter. She said the letter would explain why she could not wait."

With one finger and a thumb, Sabar lifted out the letter, looking as if he were handling a deadly viper instead of a small roll sealed with red wax.

"Nicci told me that this is dangerous," he explained, looking up into Richard's eyes. "She said that if anyone but you opened it, I should not be standing too close or I would die with them."

Sabar carefully laid the rolled letter on Richard's palm. It warmed appreciably in his hand. The red wax brightened, as if lit by a ray of sunlight even though it was getting dark. The glow spread from the wax to envelop the whole length of the rolled letter. Fine cracks raced all across the red wax, like autumn ice on a pond breaking up under the weight of a foot placed on it. The wax suddenly shattered and crumbled away.

Sabar swallowed. "I hate to think of what would have happened had anyone but you tried to open it."

Jennsen leaned in again. "Was that magic?"

"Must have been," Richard told her as he started to unroll the letter.

"But I saw it fall apart," she said in a confidential tone.

"Did you see anything else?"

"No, it just all of a sudden crumbled."

With a thumb and finger, Richard lifted some of the disintegrated wax from his palm. "She probably put a web of magic around the letter and keyed that spell to my touch. If anyone else had tried to break that web to open the letter it would have ignited the spell. I guess that my touch unlocked the seal. You saw the result of the magic—the broken seal—not the magic itself."

"Oh, wait!" Sabar smacked his forehead with the flat of his palm. "What am I thinking? I'm supposed to give you this, too."

Shrugging the straps off his shoulders and down his arms, he pulled his pack around onto his lap. He quickly undid the leather thongs and reached inside, then carefully lifted out something wrapped in black quilted material. It was only about a foot tall but not very big around. By the way Sabar handled it, it appeared to be somewhat heavy.

Sabar set the wrapped object on the ground, upright, in front of the fire. "Nicci told me that I should give this to you, that the letter would explain it."

Jennsen leaned in a little, fascinated by the mystery of the tightly-wrapped object. "What is it?"

Sabar shrugged. "Nicci didn't tell me." He made a face that suggested he was somewhat uncomfortable with the way he was in the dark about much of the mission he'd been sent on. "When Nicci looks at you and tells you to do something, it goes out of your head to ask questions."

Richard smiled to himself as he began to unroll the letter. He knew all too well what Sabar meant.

"Did Nicci say anything about who could unwrap that thing?"

"No, Lord Rahl. She just said to give it to you, that the letter would explain it."

"If it had a web around it, like the letter, she would have warned you." Richard looked up. "Cara," he said, gesturing at the bundled package sitting before the fire, "why don't you unwrap it while Kahlan and I read the letter."

As Cara sat cross-legged on the ground and started working on

the knots in the leather thongs around the black quilted wrap,
Richard held the letter sideways a bit so that Kahlan could read it
silently along with him.

Dear Richard and Kahlan,

*I am sorry that I cannot tell you everything right now that I
would have you know, but there are urgent matters I must see to
and I dare not delay. Jagang has initiated something I considered
impossible. Through his ability as a dream walker, he has forced
Sisters of the Dark he controls to attempt to create weapons out of
people, as was done during the great war. This is dangerous
enough in itself, but because Jagang does not have the gift, his
understanding of such things is very crude. He is a blundering bull
trying to use his horns to knit lace. They are using the lives of
wizards as the fodder for his experiments. I don't yet know the
exact extent of their success, but I fear to discover the results. More
of this in a moment.*

*First, the object I sent. When I picked up your trail and began
tracking it to where we were to meet, I discovered this. I believe
you have already come across it because it has been touched by a
principal involved in the matter or involved with you.*

*The object is a warning beacon. It has been activated—not by
this touch, but by events. I cannot overstate the danger it repre-
sents.*

*Such objects could only be made by the wizards of ancient times;
the creation of such an object required both Additive and
Subtractive Magic, and required the gift of both to be innate.
Even then, they are so rare that I have never actually seen one.*

*I have, however, read about them down in the vaults at the
Palace of the Prophets. Such warning beacons are kept viable by a
link to the dead wizard who created them.*

Richard sat back and let out a troubled breath.

"How can such a link be possible?" Kahlan asked.

He hardly had to read between the lines to be able to tell that
Nicci was warning him in the gravest possible terms.

"It has to be linked somehow to the underworld," Richard whispered back.

Little points of firelight danced in her green eyes as she stared at him.

Kahlan glanced again at Cara as she worked at the knots, pulling off one of the leather thongs around an object linked to a dead wizard in the underworld. Kahlan held up the edge of the letter as she urgently read along with him.

From what I know of such warning beacons, they monitor powerful and vital protective shields created to seal away something profoundly dangerous. They are paired. The first beacon is always amber. It is meant to be a warning to the one who caused the breach of the seal. The touch of a principal or one involved with a principal kindles it so it may be recognized for what it is and serve as it was intended—as a warning to those involved. Only after alerting the one it is meant to warn can it be destroyed. I send it to be absolutely certain you have seen it.

The precise nature of the second beacon is unknown to me, but that beacon is meant for the one able to replace the seal.

I don't know the nature of the seal or what it was protecting. Without doubt, though, the seal has been breached.

The source of the breach, while not the specific cause activating this beacon, is self-evident.

"Oh, now wait a minute," Cara said, standing, backing away as if she had released a deadly plague from the black quilting, "it isn't my fault this time." She pointed down at it. "You told me to, this time."

The translucent statue Cara had touched before now stood in the center of its unfolded black quilted wrapping.

It was the same statue: a statue of Kahlan.

The statue's left arm was pressed to its side, the right arm was raised, pointing. The statue, in an hourglass shape, looked as if it were made of transparent amber, allowing them to see inside.

Sand trickled out of the top half of the hourglass, through the narrowed waist, into the bottom of the full dress of the Mother Confessor.

The sand was still trickling down, just as it had been the last time Richard had seen the thing. At that time, the top half had been more full than the bottom half. Now, the top held less sand than the bottom.

Kahlan's face had gone ashen.

When he'd first seen it, Richard wouldn't have needed Nicci to tell him how dangerous such a thing was. He hadn't wanted any of them to touch it. When they had first come across it, in a recess of rock beside the trail, looking almost like part of the rock itself, the thing was opaque, with a dull, dark surface, yet it was clearly recognizable as Kahlan. It was lying on its side.

Cara wasn't pleased to find such a thing and didn't want to leave a representation of Kahlan lying about for anyone to find and to pick up for who-knew-what. Cara snatched it up, then, even though Richard started to yell at her to leave such a thing be.

When she picked it up, it started turning translucent.

In a panic, Cara set it back down.

That was when the right arm had lifted and pointed east.

That was when they could begin to see through the thing, to see the sand inside trickling down.

The implied danger of the sand running out had them all upset. Cara wanted to pick it up again and turn it over, to stop the sand from falling. Richard, not knowing anything about such an object and doubting that so simple a solution would have any beneficial effect, hadn't allowed Cara to touch it again. He had piled rocks and brush around it so no one else would know it was there. Obviously, that hadn't worked.

He knew now that Cara's touch had nothing to do with what was happening, except to initiate the warning, so he thought to confirm his original belief. "Cara, put it down."

"Down?"

"On its side—like you wanted to do the last time—to see if that will stop the sand."

Cara stared at him for a moment and then used the toe of her boot to tip the figure over on its side.

The sand continued to run as if it still stood upright.

"How can the sand do that?" Jennsen asked, sounding quite shaken. "How can the sand still fall—how can it fall sideways?"

"You can see it?" Kahlan asked. "You can see the sand falling?"

Jennsen nodded. "I sure can, and I have to tell you, it's giving my goose bumps goose bumps."

Richard could only stare at her staring at the statue of Kahlan lying on its side. If nothing else, the sand running sideways through the statue had to be magic. Jennsen was a pillar of Creation, a hole in the world, a pristinely ungifted offspring of Darken Rahl. She should not be able to see magic.

And yet, she was seeing it.

"I have to agree with the young lady," Sabar said. "That's even more frightening than those big black birds that I've seen circling for the last week."

Kahlan straightened. "You've been seeing—"

When he heard Tom's urgent warning yell, Richard rose up in a rush, drawing his sword in one swift movement. The unique sound of ringing steel filled the night air.

The magic did not come out with the sword.

CHAPTER 14

Kahlan ducked to the side, out of harm's way, as Richard pulled his sword free. The distinctive ring of steel being drawn in anger fused with Tom's warning yell still echoing through the surrounding hills to send a flash of fright tingling across her flesh. As she stared out into the empty blackness of the surrounding night, her instinct was to reach for her own sword, but she had packed it in the wagon rather than wear it, so as not to raise suspicions about who they might be—women in the Old World did not carry weapons.

By the light of the fire, Kahlan could clearly see Richard's face. She had seen him draw the Sword of Truth countless times and in a variety of situations, from that very first time when Zedd, after giving him the sword, had commanded him to draw it and Richard tentatively pulled it from its scabbard, to times he pulled it free in the heat of battle, to times like this when he drew it suddenly in defense.

When Richard drew the sword, he was also drawing its attendant magic. That was the function of the weapon; the magic had not been created simply to defend the sword's true owner, but, more importantly, to be a projection of his intent. The Sword of Truth was not even really a talisman, but rather a tool, of the Seeker of Truth.

The true weapon was the rightly named Seeker who wielded the sword. The sword's magic answered to him.

Each and every one of the times Richard had drawn the sword, Kahlan had seen that magic dancing dangerously in his gray eyes.

This was the first time he had drawn the sword that she didn't see the magic in his eyes; the raptor's glare was pure Richard.

While seeing him draw the sword without seeing its concomitant magic evident in his eyes shocked her, it seemed to surprise Richard even more. For an instant he hesitated, as if mentally stumbling.

Before they had time to even wonder what had prompted Tom's warning yell, shadowy shapes slipping through the cover of the nearby trees suddenly stormed out of the darkness and into their midst. The sudden sound and fury of bloodcurdling cries filled the night air as men rampaged into the camp, lit at last by firelight.

They didn't appear to be soldiers—they weren't wearing uniforms—and they weren't attacking as soldiers would, with weapons drawn. Kahlan didn't see any of the men brandishing swords or axes or even knives.

Weapons or not, there were a lot of men and they yelled fierce battle cries as if they intended nothing short of bloody murder. She knew, though, that the sudden shock of deafening noise was a tactic designed to render the intended target powerless with fright, making them easier to cut down. She knew because she used such tactics herself.

Blade in hand, Richard was fully in his element; focused, resolute, ruthlessly committed—even without his sword's attendant magic.

As assailants charged in, the sword, driven by Richard's own wrath, flashed through the air, a flash of crimson light from the fire's flames reflected along the blade's length, lending it a fleeting stain of red. In that charged moment of attack met, there was a split second when Kahlan feared that without the sword's magic, it all might go terribly wrong.

In an instant, the camp that had been so quietly tense became pandemonium. Although the attackers weren't dressed like soldiers, they were all big and as they swept in there was no doubt whatsoever as to their hostile intent.

A man rushing onward threw his arms up to seize Richard before his sword could be brought to bear. The sword's tip whistled as it came around, driven by deadly commitment. The blade severed one of the man's raised arms before exploding through his skull. The air above the fire filled with a spray of blood, bone, and brain. Another man lunged. Richard's sword ripped through his chest. In the space of two blinks, two men were dead.

The magic at last seemed to slam into Richard's eyes, as if finally catching up with his intent.

Kahlan couldn't make sense of what the men were doing. They attacked without weapons drawn, but they seemed no less fierce for it. Their speed, numbers and size, and the angry look of them were enough to make most anyone tremble in fright.

From the darkness, more men rushed in on them. Cara stepped into the path of the attack, lashing out with her Agiel. Men cried out in horrifying pain when her weapon made contact, causing hesitation among the attackers. Sabar, knife in hand, tumbled to the ground with one of the men who had seized him from behind. Jennsen ducked away from another man snatching for her hair. As she spun away from him, she slashed his face with her knife. His cries joined a strident chorus of others.

Kahlan realized that it wasn't just men yelling, but the horses were also screaming in fright. Cara's Agiel against a bull-like neck brought a terrifying shriek. Men yelled with effort and shouted orders that were cut off abruptly as Richard's sword tore through them. All the yelling seemed directed at the task of overwhelming the four of them.

Kahlan understood, then, what was going on. This was not an attempt to kill, but to capture. For these men, killing would be a great mercy compared to what they intended.

Two of the burly men dove across the fire, arms spread wide as if to tackle Richard and Kahlan. Cara reached out and seized a fistful of shirt, abruptly spinning one of them around. She drove her Agiel into his gut, dropping him to his knees. The other man unexpectedly encountered Richard's sword thrust straight in with formidable muscle driving it. The scream of mortal pain was brief before the sword slashed his throat. Cara, standing above the man on his knees, pressed her Agiel to his chest and gave it a twist that dropped him instantly.

Already, Richard was leaping over the fire to penetrate into the brunt of the attack. As his boots landed with a thud, his sword cut the man atop Sabar nearly in two, spilling his viscera across the ground.

The man Jennsen had slashed rose up only to be met by her knife driven by desperate fright. She jumped back as he tumbled forward, clutching the base of his throat where she had severed his windpipe. Cara snagged the man Jennsen didn't see going for her back. The Mord-Sith, her face a picture of savage resolve, held her Agiel to his throat, following him to the ground as he choked on his own blood.

Then, among the men Richard ripped into, Kahlan saw the knives coming out. The men abandoned their failed attempt to bring him down by grabbing and overpowering him, and decided, instead, to knife him. If anything, the threat of the knives served only to further unleash Richard's fury. By the look in his eyes, the sword's magic seemed to be fully engaged in the battle.

For an instant, Kahlan stood transfixed by the sight of Richard so ruthlessly committed to self-defense that the act of killing became a graceful manifestation of art—a dance with death. Compared with Richard's fluid movements, the men blundered like bulls. Without wasted motion, Richard slipped among them as if they were statues, his sword delivering unrestrained violence. Each thrust met a vital area of the enemy. Each swing sliced through flesh and bone. Each turn met an attack and crushed it. There was no lost opportunity, no slash that missed, no thrust gone wide, no bobble that only slightly wounded. Each time he spun past the thrust of a blade, met a rush, or turned to a new attack, he cut without mercy.

Kahlan was furious that she didn't have her sword. There was no telling how many more men there were. She knew all too well what it was like to be helpless and overwhelmed by a gang of men. She started edging toward the wagon.

Jennsen and Sabar were both tackled by a burly man diving in out of the darkness. As they hit the ground, the man landed atop them, knocking the wind from them. His big hands pinned their wrists to the ground, keeping their knives at bay.

Richard's blade swept past with lightning speed, slicing across the man's back, severing his spine. Richard went to a knee as he turned, whipping the sword around to impale another attacker rushing in at a dead run, trying to get to Richard before he could recover. The look on the man's face was a picture of horrified surprise as he ran instead onto Richard's sword, running it into his own chest up to the hilt. The heavy man atop Jennsen and Sabar convulsed, unable to draw a breath, as they threw him off. Richard, still on one knee, yanked the sword free as the mortally wounded man fell past him.

As another man rushed into camp, looking around, trying to get his bearings, Cara slammed her Agiel against his neck. As he crumbled, she drove her elbow up to smash the face of a man following the first in, trying to grab her from behind while she was occupied. Crying out, his hands covered crushed bone and gushing blood. She spun and kicked him between the legs. As he fell forward, his hands going to his groin, she broke his jaw with her knee, turned, and dropped a third man by slamming her Agiel to his chest.

Another attacker threw himself at Sabar, knocking him back. Sabar lashed out with his knife, making solid contact. Another man saw the opening and snatched up Nicci's letter lying on the ground. Kahlan dove for the letter in his fist, but missed as he yanked his hand back before dashing away. Jennsen blocked his escape. He straight-armed her as he charged past. Jennsen was knocked reeling, but came around to bury her knife between his shoulder blades.

Jennsen managed to keep hold of her knife, twisting it forcefully, as the man arched his back with a gasp of pain and then a bellow of anger that withered to a wet burble before it was fully out of his lungs. Jennsen's knife had found his heart. He staggered, stumbled, and fell onto the fire. The flames whooshed to life as his clothing ignited. Kahlan tried to snatch the letter from his fist as he writhed in horrifying pain, but, with the intensity of the heat, she couldn't get close enough.

It was already too late, though; the letter she and Richard had only had a chance to partially read flared briefly before transforming to black ash that disintegrated and lifted skyward in the roar of flames.

Kahlan covered her mouth and nose, gagging on the stench of burning hair and flesh as she was driven back by the heat. Though it seemed like hours of fighting, the assault had only just begun and already men lay dead everywhere as yet more of the big men joined the attack.

As she recoiled from the flames and her futile attempt to recover the lost letter, Kahlan turned again toward the wagon, toward her sword. She looked up and saw a man who seemed as big as a mountain charging right at her, blocking her way. He grinned at seeing that he had run down a woman without a weapon.

Beyond the man, Kahlan saw Richard. Their eyes met. He had taken his sword to the bulk of the attack, trying to cut it down before it could get to the rest of them, trying to end it before harm could get to any of them.

He couldn't be everywhere at once.

He wasn't close enough to get to her in time. That didn't stop him from trying. Even as he did, Kahlan discounted the attempt. He was too far away. The effort was futile.

Looking into the eyes of the man she loved more than life itself, she saw his pure rage; she knew that Richard was seeing a face that showed nothing: a Confessor's face, as her mother had taught her. And then the racing enemy came between them, blocking their sight of one another.

Kahlan's vision focused on the man bearing down on her. His arms lifted like a bear lost in a mad charge. His teeth were gritted with determination. A grimace twisted his face in his wild effort to reach her before she could dodge to the side, before she had a chance to escape.

She knew he was too close for her to have that chance and so she didn't waste any effort in a useless attempt.

This one had made it past the killing. He had avoided Jennsen and Sabar. He had figured his attack to skirt Richard's blade while making it past Cara's Agiel as she turned to another man. He hadn't charged in madly like the rest; he had delayed just enough to time his onslaught perfectly.

This one knew he was on the verge of having what he sought.

He was far less than a heartbeat away, plunging toward her at full speed.

Kahlan could hear Richard's scream even as her gaze met the gleam of the man's dark eyes.

The man let out a cry of rage as he lunged. His feet left the ground as he sailed through the air toward her. His wicked grin betrayed his confidence.

Kahlan could see his eyeteeth hooked over his cracked lower lip, saw the dark tooth in the front of the top row between his other yellow teeth, saw the little white hook of a scar, as if he had once been eating with a knife and had accidentally sliced the corner of his mouth. His stubble looked like wire. His left eye didn't open as wide as his right. His right ear had a big V-shaped notch taken out of the upper portion. It reminded her of the way some farmers marked their swine.

She could see her own reflection in his dark eyes as her right arm came up.

Kahlan wondered if he had a wife, a woman who cared for him, missed him, pined for him. She wondered if he might have children, and, if he did, what a man like this would teach his children. She had a momentary flash of the ugliness it would be to have this beast atop her, his wire stubble scraping her cheek raw, his cracked lips on hers, his yellow teeth raking her neck as he lost himself in what he wanted.

Time twisted.

She held out her arm. The man crashed in toward her. She felt the coarse weave of his dark brown shirt as the flat of her hand met the center of his chest.

That heartbeat of time she had before he was atop her had not yet begun. Richard had not yet managed to take a single frantic step.

The weight of the bear of a man against her hand felt as if it were but a baby's breath. To Kahlan, it seemed as if he were frozen in space before her.

Time was hers.

He was hers.

The rush of combat, the cries, the yells, the screams; the stink of sweat and blood; the flash of steel, the clash of bodies; the curses and growls; the fear, the terror, the heart-pounding dread . . . the rage . . . was no longer there for her. She was in a silent world all her own.

Even though she had been born with it and had always felt it there in the core of her being, the awesome power within, in many ways, seemed incomprehensible, inconceivable, unimaginable, remote. She knew it would seem that way until she let her restraint slip, and then she would once again be joined with a force of such breathtaking magnitude that it could only be fully comprehended as it was being experienced. Although she had unleashed it more times than she could remember, no matter how prepared she was the extraordinary violence of it always still astonished her.

She regarded the man before her with cold calculation, ready for that violence.

As he had charged in on her, time had belonged to this man.

Now time belonged to her.

She could feel the thread count of the fabric of his shirt, feel his woolly chest hairs beneath it.

The heart-pounding shock of the sudden attack, the violence of it, was gone now. Now there was only this man and her, forever linked by what was to happen. This man had unconsciously chosen his own fate when he chose to attack them. Her certainty of what was called for carried her beyond the need for the assessment of emotion, and she felt none—no joy, not even relief; no hate, not even aversion; no compassion, not even sorrow.

Kahlan shed those emotions to make way for the rush of power, to give it free run.

Now he had no chance.

He was hers.

The man's face was contorted with the intoxicated, gloating glee of his certitude that he was the glorious victor who would have her, that he was now the one to decide what was to become of her life, that she was but his to plunder.

Kahlan unleashed her power.

By her deliberate intent, the subordinate state of her birthright instantly altered into overpowering force able to alter the very nature of consciousness.

In the man's dark eyes had come the spark of suspicion that something which he could not comprehend had irrevocably begun. And then there came the lightning recognition that his life, as he had known it, was over. Everything he wanted, thought about, worked toward, hoped for, prayed for, possessed, loved, hated . . . was ended.

In her eyes he saw no mercy, and that, more than anything, brought him stark terror.

Thunder without sound jolted the air.

In that instant, the violence of it was as pristine, as beautiful, as exquisite, as it was horrific.

That heartbeat of time Kahlan had before he was on her had still not yet begun.

She could see in the man's eyes that even thought itself was too late for him, now. Perception itself was being outpaced by the race of brutal magic tearing through his mind, destroying forever who this man had been.

The force of the concussion jolted the air.

The stars shuddered.

Sparks from the fire lashed along the ground as the shock spread outward in a ring, driving dust before its passing. Trees shook when hit by the blow, shedding needles and leaves as the raging wave swept past.

He was hers.

His full weight flying forward knocked Kahlan back a step as she twisted out of the way. The man flew past her and crashed to the ground, sprawling on his face.

Without an instant of hesitation, he scrambled up onto his knees. His hands came up in prayerful supplication. Tears flooded his eyes. His mouth, which only an instant before was so warped with perverted expectation, now distorted with the agony of pure anguish.

"Please, Mistress," he wailed, "command me!"

Kahlan regarded him, for the first time in his new life, with an emotion: contempt.

CHAPTER 15

Only the sound of Betty's soft, frightened bleating drifted out over the otherwise silent campsite. Bodies lay sprawled haphazardly across the ground. The attack appeared to be over. Richard, sword in hand, rushed through the carnage to get to Kahlan. Jennsen stood near the edge of the fire's light, while Cara checked the bodies for any sign of life.

Kahlan left the man she had just touched with her power kneeling in the dirt, stalking past him toward Jennsen. Richard met her halfway there, his free arm sweeping around her with relief.

"Are you all right?"

Kahlan nodded, quickly appraising their camp, on the lookout for any more attackers, but saw only the men who were dead.

"What about you?" she asked.

Richard didn't seem to hear her question. His arm slipped from her waist. "Dear spirits," he said, as he rushed to one of the bodies lying on its side.

It was Sabar.

Jennsen stood not far away, trembling with terror, her knife held up defensively in a fist, her eyes wide. Kahlan gathered Jennsen in her arms, whispering assurance that it was over, that it was ended, that she was all right.

Jennsen clutched at Kahlan. "Sabar—he was—protecting me—"

"I know, I know," Kahlan comforted.

She could see that there was no urgency in Richard's movements as he laid Sabar on his back. The young man's arm flopped lifelessly to the side. Kahlan's heart sank.

Tom ran into camp, gasping for air. He was streaked with blood and sweat. Jennsen wailed and flew into his arms. He embraced her protectively, holding her head to his shoulder as he tried to regain his breath.

Betty bleated in dismay from beneath the wagon, hesitantly emerging only after Jennsen called repeated encouragement to her. The puling goat finally rushed to Jennsen and huddled trembling against her skirts. Tom kept a wary watch of the surrounding darkness.

Cara calmly walked among the bodies, surveying them for any sign of life. With most, there could be no question. Here and there she nudged one with the toe of her boot, or with the tip of her Agiel. By her lack of urgency, there was no question that they were all dead.

Kahlan put a tender hand to Richard's back as he crouched beside Sabar's body.

"How many people must die," he asked in a low, bitter voice, "for the crime of wanting to be free, for the sin of wanting to live their own life?"

She saw that he still held the Sword of Truth in a white-knuckled fist. The sword's magic, which had come out so reluctantly, still danced dangerously in his eyes.

"How many?" he repeated.

"I don't know, Richard," Kahlan whispered.

Richard turned a glare toward the man across the camp, still on his knees, his hands pressed together in a beseeching gesture begging to be commanded, fearing to speak.

Once touched by a Confessor, the person was no longer who they had once been. That part of their mind was forever gone. Who they were, what they were, no longer existed.

In its place the magic of a Confessor's power placed unqualified devotion to the wants and wishes of the Confessor who had touched them. Nothing else mattered. Their only purpose in life, now, was to fulfill her commands, to do her bidding, to answer her every question.

For one thus touched, there was no crime they wouldn't confess, if she asked it of them. It was for this alone that Confessors had been created. Their purpose, in a way, was the same as the Seeker's—the truth. In war, as in all other aspects of life, there was no more important commodity for survival than the truth.

This man, kneeling not far away, cried in abject misery because Kahlan had asked nothing of him. There could be no agony more ghastly, no void more terrifying, than to be empty of knowing her wish. Existence without her wish was pointless. In the absence of her command, men touched by a Confessor had been known to die.

Anything she now asked of him, whether it be to tell her his name, confess his true love's name, or to murder his beloved mother, would bring him boundless joy because he would finally have a task to carry out for her.

"Let's find out what this is all about," Richard said in a low growl.

In exhaustion, Kahlan stared at the man on his knees. She was so weary she could hardly stand. Sweat trickled down between her breasts. She needed rest, but this problem was more immediate and needed to be attended to first.

On their way to the man waiting on his knees, his eyes turned expectantly up toward Kahlan, Richard halted. There, in the dirt before his boots, was the remains of the statue Sabar had brought to them. It was broken into a hundred pieces, none of them any longer recognizable except that those pieces were still a translucent amber color.

Nicci's letter had said that they didn't need the statue, now that it had given its warning—a warning that Kahlan had somehow broken a protective shield sealing away something profoundly dangerous.

Kahlan didn't know what the seal protected, but she feared that she knew all too well what she had done to break it.

She feared even more that, because of her, the magic of Richard's sword had begun to falter.

As Kahlan stood staring down at the amber fragments ground into the dirt, despair flooded into her.

Richard's arm circled her waist. "Don't let your imagination get carried away. We don't know what this is about, yet. We can't even be certain that it's true—it could even be some kind of mistake."

Kahlan wished that she could believe that.

Richard finally slid his sword back into its scabbard. "Do you want to rest first, sit for a bit?"

His concern for her took precedence over everything. From the first day she met him, it always had. Right then, it was his well-being that concerned her.

Using her power sapped a Confessor of strength. It had left Kahlan feeling not only weak but, this time, nauseated. She had been named to the post of Mother Confessor, in part, because her power was so strong that she was able to recover it in hours; for others it had taken a day or sometimes two. At the thought of all those other Confessors, some of whom she'd dearly loved, being long dead, Kahlan felt the weight of hopelessness pulling her even lower.

To fully recover her strength, she would need a night's rest. At the moment, though, there were more important considerations, not the least of which was Richard.

"No," she said. "I'm all right. I can rest later. Let's ask him what you will."

Richard's gaze moved over the campsite littered with limbs, entrails, bodies. The ground was soaked with blood. The stench of it all, along with the still-smoldering body beside the fire, was making Kahlan sicker by the second. She turned away from the man on his knees, toward Richard, into the protection of his arms. She was exhausted.

"And then let's get away from this place," she said. "We need to get away from here. There might be more men coming." Kahlan worried that if he had to draw the sword again, he might not have the help of its magic. "We need to find a more secure camp."

Richard nodded his agreement. He looked over her head as he held her to his chest. Despite everything, or perhaps because of everything, it felt wonderful simply to be held. She could hear Friedrich just rushing back into camp, panting as he ran. He stumbled to a halt as he let out a moan of astonishment mixed with revulsion at what he saw.

"Tom, Friedrich," Richard asked, "do you have any idea if there are any more men coming?"

"I don't think so," Tom said. "I think they were together. I caught them coming up a gully. I was going to try to make it back here to warn you, but four of them came over a rise and jumped me while the rest ran for our camp."

"I didn't see anyone, Lord Rahl," Friedrich said, catching his breath. "I came running when I heard the yelling."

Richard acknowledged Friedrich's words with a reassuring hand on the man's shoulder. "Help Tom get the horses hitched. I don't want to spend the night here."

As the two men sprang into action, Richard turned to Jennsen.

"Please lay out some bedrolls in the back of the wagon, will you? I'd like Kahlan to be able to lie down and rest when we move out."

Jennsen patted Betty's shoulder, urging the goat to follow her. "Of course, Richard." She hurried off to the wagon, Betty trotting along close at her side.

As everyone rushed as quickly as possible to get their things together, Richard went by himself to an open patch of ground nearby to dig a shallow grave. There was no time for a funeral pyre. A lonely grave was the best they could do, but Sabar's spirit was gone, and wouldn't fault the necessity of their hurried care for his body.

Kahlan reconsidered her thought. After the letter from Nicci and learning the meaning of the warning beacon, she now had even more reason to doubt that many things, including spirits, were still true. The world of the dead was connected to the world of the living by links of magic. The veil itself was magic and said to be within those like Richard. They had learned that without magic those links themselves could fail and that, since those other worlds couldn't exist independent of the world of life, but only existed in relational sense to the world of life, should the links fail completely, those other worlds might very well cease to exist—much as, without the sun, the concept of daytime would not exist.

It was now clear to Kahlan that the world's hold on magic was slipping, and had been slipping for several years.

She knew the reason.

Spirits, the good and the bad, and the existence of everything else that depended on magic, might soon be lost. That meant that death would become final, in every sense of the word. It could even be that there was no longer the possibility of being with a loved one after death, or of being with the good spirits. The good spirits, even the underworld itself, might be passing into nothingness.

When Richard was finished, Tom helped him gently place Sabar's body in the ground. After Tom spoke quiet words asking the good spirits to watch over one of their own, he and Richard covered the body over.

"Lord Rahl," Tom said in a low voice when they were finished, "while some of the men began the attack on you, here, others slit the horses' throats before joining their fellows to come after you four."

"All the horses?"

"Except mine. My draft horses are pretty big. The men were probably worried about getting trampled. They left some men to take care of me, so these here thought they had me out of the way. They probably figured they could worry about the draft horses later, after they had the rest of you." Tom shrugged his broad shoulders. "Maybe they even planned to capture you, tie you up, and take you in the wagon."

Richard acknowledged Tom's words with a single nod. He wiped his fingers across his forehead. Kahlan thought he looked worse than she felt. She could see that the headache had returned and was crushing him under the weight of its pain.

Tom looked around their camp, his gaze playing over the fallen men. "What should we do with the rest of the bodies?"

"The races can have the rest of them," Richard said without hesitation.

Tom didn't look to have any disagreement with that. "I'd better go help Friedrich finish getting the horses hitched to the wagon. They'll be a handful with the scent of blood in their nostrils and the sight of the others dead."

As Tom went to see to his horses, Richard called to Cara. "Count the bodies," he told her. "We need to know the total."

"Richard," Kahlan asked in a confidential tone after Tom was out of earshot and Cara had started stepping over some of the bodies and between others, going about the task of taking a count, "what happened when you drew the sword?"

He didn't ask what she meant or try to spare her from worry. "There's something wrong with its magic. When I drew the sword, it failed to heed my call. The men were rushing in and I couldn't delay in what I had to do. Once I met the attack, the magic finally reacted.

"It's probably due to the headaches from the gift—they must be interfering with my ability to join with the sword's magic."

"The last time you had the headaches they didn't interfere with the sword's power."

"I told you, don't let your imagination get carried away. This has only happened since I've started getting the headaches again. That has to be the reason."

Kahlan didn't know if she dared believe him, or if he really even believed it himself. He was right, though. The problem with the sword's magic had only recently developed—after he started getting the headaches.

"They're getting worse, aren't they?"

He nodded. "Come on, let's get what answers we can."

Kahlan let out a tired sigh, resigned to that part of it. They had to use this chance to find out what information was now available to them.

Kahlan turned to the man still on his knees.

CHAPTER 16

The man's tearful eyes gazed pleadingly up at Kahlan as she stepped in front of him. He had been waiting, alone and without her wishes, for quite a while and as a result was in a state of dire misery.

"You are to come with us," Kahlan told him in a cold tone. "You are to walk in front of the wagon for now, where we can keep an eye on you. You will obey the orders of any of the others with me as you would obey my orders. You will answer all questions truthfully."

The man fell to his belly on the ground, in tears, kissing her feet, thanking her profusely for at last commanding him. Groveling on the ground, with that V-shaped notch in his ear, he reminded her of nothing so much as a swine.

Fists at her side, Kahlan screamed, "Stop that!" She didn't want this murdering pig touching her.

He sprang back instantly, aghast at the rage in her voice, horror-struck that she was displeased with him. He cringed motionless at her feet, his eyes wide, fearful that he would do something else to displease her.

"You aren't in a uniform," Richard said to the man. "You and the other men aren't soldiers?"

"We're soldiers, just not regular soldiers," the man said with eager excitement to be able to answer the question and thus do Kahlan's bidding. "We're special men serving with the Imperial Order."

"Special? How are you special?"

With a hint of uncertainty in his wet eyes, the man looked nervously up at Kahlan. She gave him no sign. She had already told him that he was to follow all their orders. The man, at last certain of her intention, rushed to go on.

"We're a special unit of men—with the army—our task is to capture enemies of the Order—we have to pass tests to be sure we're able men—loyal men—and that we can accomplish the missions we're sent on—"

"Slow down," Richard said. "You're talking too fast."

The man glanced quickly at Kahlan, his eyes filling with tears that he might have displeased her, too.

"Go on," she said.

"We don't wear uniforms or let our purpose be known," the man said with obvious relief that if he continued it would satisfy her. "Usually we work in cities, searching out insurrectionists. We mingle with people, get them to think of us as one of them. When they plot against the Order, we go along until we find out the names of all those involved and then we capture them and turn them over for questioning."

Richard stared down at the man for a long time, his face showing no reaction. Richard had been in the hands of the Order and "questioned". Kahlan could only imagine what he must have been thinking.

"And do you hand over only those who you know to be plotting against the Order?" Richard asked. "Or do you simply turn in those you suspect and anyone who they know?"

"If we suspect they might be plotting—like if they keep to themselves and their own group, and won't open their lives to other citizens, then we turn them in to be questioned so that it can be determined what they might be hiding." The man licked his lips, keen to tell them the full extent of his methods. "We talk to those they work with, or neighbors, and get the names of anyone they associate with, any of their friends—sometimes even their closest family members. We usually take at least some of them, too, and turn them over for questioning. When they're questioned, they all confess their crimes against the Order so that proves our suspicions about them were right."

Kahlan thought that Richard might draw his sword and behead the man on the spot. Richard knew all too well what they did to those who were brought in, knew how hopeless was their plight.

Confessions obtained under torture often provided names of anyone who might be suspicious for any reason, making the job of torturing a very busy profession. The people of the Old World lived in constant fear that they would be taken to one of the many places where people were questioned.

Those pulled in were rarely guilty of plotting against the Order; most people were too busy just trying to survive, trying to feed their families, to have time to plot to overthrow the rule of the Imperial Order. Many people did, however, talk about a better life, about what they would like to do, to grow, to create, to own, about their hopes that their children would have a better life than theirs. Since mankind's duty was sacrifice to the betterment of their fellow man, not to their own betterment, that, to the Imperial Order, was not just insurrection, but blasphemy. In the Old World, misery was a widespread virtue, a duty to a higher calling.

There were others who didn't dream of a better life, but dreamed of helping the Order by turning in the names of those who spoke ill of the Order, or hid food or even a bit of money, or talked of a better life. Turning in such "disloyal citizens" kept yet other fingers from pointing at the informer. Informing became an indicator of sanctity.

Instead of drawing his sword, Richard changed the subject. "How many of you were there, tonight?"

"Including me, twenty-eight," the man said without delay.

"Were you all together in one group when you attacked?"

The man nodded, keen to admit their whole plan and thus gain Kahlan's approval. "We wanted to make sure you and, and . . ." his eyes turned to Kahlan as he realized the incompatibility of his two goals—confessing, and pleasing the Mother Confessor.

He burst into tears, clasping his hands prayerfully. "Forgive me, Mistress! Please, forgive me!"

If his voice was the quintessence of emotion, hers was the opposite. "Answer the question."

He brought his sobbing to a halt in order to speak as he had been commanded. Tears, though, continued to stream down his filthy cheeks. "We stayed together for a focused attack, so we could be sure that we captured Lord Rahl and, and . . . you, Mother Confessor. When trying to capture a good-size group we split up, with half holding back to look for anyone who might try to slip away, but I told the men that I wanted the both of you, and you were said to be together, so this was our chance. I didn't want to run the risk that you would have any hope of fighting us off, so I ordered all the men to the attack, having some cut the throats of the saddle horses, first, to prevent any possibility of escape."

His face brightened. "I never suspected that we might fail."

"Who sent you?" Kahlan asked.

The man shuffled forward on his knees, his hand tentatively coming up to touch her leg. Kahlan remained motionless, but by her icy glare let him know that touching her would displease her greatly. The hand backed away.

"Nicholas," he said.

Kahlan's brow twitched. She had been expecting him to say Jagang had sent him.

She was wary of the possibility that the dream walker might be watching through this man's eyes. Jagang had in the past sent assassins after he had slipped into their thoughts. With Jagang in a person's mind, he dominated and directed them, and even Cara could not control them. Nor, for that matter, could Kahlan.

"You're lying to me. Jagang sent you."

The man fell to pitiful weeping. "No, Mistress! I've never had any dealings with His Excellency. The army is vast and far-flung. I take my orders from those in my section. I don't think that the ones they take orders from, or their commanders, or even theirs, are worthy of His Excellency's attention. His Excellency is far to the north, bringing the word of the Order's salvation to a lawless and savage people; he would not even be aware of us.

"We are but a lowly squad of men with the muscle to snatch people the Order wants, either for questioning or to silence them. We are all from this part of the empire and so we were called upon because we were here. I am not worthy of the attention of His Excellency."

"But Jagang has visited you—in your dreams. He has visited your mind."

"Mistress?" The man looked terrified to have to question her rather than answer her question. "I don't understand."

Kahlan stared. "Jagang has come into your mind. He has spoken to you."

He looked sincerely puzzled as he shook his head. "No, Mistress. I have never met His Excellency. I have never dreamed about him—I don't know anything about him, except that Altur'Rang has the honor of being the place where he was born.

"Would you like me to kill him for you, Mistress? Please, if it is your wish, allow me to kill him for you?"

The man didn't know how preposterous such a notion was; in his desire to please her, though, if she commanded it he would be only too happy to make the attempt. Kahlan turned her back on the man as Richard watched him.

She leaned toward Richard a bit as she spoke quietly, so the man wouldn't hear. "I don't know if those visited by the dream walker must always be mindful of it, but I think they would be. The ones I've seen before were aware of Jagang's presence in their mind."

"Couldn't the dream walker slip into a person's mind without their being aware of it just so he could watch us?"

"I suppose it's possible," she said. "But think of all the millions of people in the Old World—he can't know whose mind to enter so he can watch. Dream walker or not, he is only one man."

"Are you gifted?" Richard asked the man.

"No."

"Well," Richard whispered, "Nicci told me that Jagang rarely bothers with the ungifted. She said that it was difficult for him to take the mind of the ungifted, so he simply uses the gifted he controls and has them control the ungifted for him. He has all the Sisters he's captured to worry about. He has to maintain his control over them and direct their actions—including what we started to read in Nicci's letter—about how he's guiding the Sisters in altering people into weapons. Besides that he heads the army and plans strategy. He has a lot of things to manage, so he usually confines himself to the minds of the gifted."

"But not always. If he has to, if he needs to, if he wants to, he can enter the minds of the ungifted. If we were smart," Kahlan whispered, "we would kill this man now."

As they spoke, Richard's glare never left the man. She knew he would not hesitate to agree unless he thought the man might still be of use.

"I have but to command it," Kahlan reminded him, "and he will drop dead."

Richard took in her eyes for a moment, then turned back to the man and frowned. "You said someone named Nicholas sent you. Who is this Nicholas?"

"Nicholas is a fearsome wizard in the service of the Order."

"You saw him. He gave you these orders?"

"No. We are too lowly for one such as he to bother with us. He sent orders that were passed down."

"How did you know where we were?" Richard asked.

"The orders included the general area. They said that we should look for you coming north at the eastern edge of the desert wasteland and if we found you we were to capture you."

"How did Nicholas know where we were?"

The man blinked, as if searching his mind to see if he had the answer. "I don't know. We weren't told how he knew. We were told only that we were to search this area and if we found you we were to bring you both in, alive. The commander who passed on the orders told me not to fail or the Slide would be very displeased with us."

"Who would be displeased? . . . The Slide?"

"Nicholas the Slide. That is what he's called. Some people just call him 'the Slide.'"

Frowning, Kahlan turned back to the man. "The what?"

The man began trembling at her frown. "The Slide, Mistress."

"What does that mean? The Slide?"

The man fell to wailing, his hands clasped together again as he begged her forgiveness. "I don't know, Mistress. I don't know. You asked who sent me, that is his name. Nicholas. People call him the Slide."

"Where is he?" Richard asked.

"I don't know," the man blurted out as he wept. "I received my orders from my commander. He said that a Brother of the Order brought the orders to his commander."

Richard took a deep breath as he rubbed the back of his neck. "What else do you know about this Nicholas, other than that he's a wizard and he's called 'the Slide?'"

"I only know to fear him, as do my commanders."

"Why? What happens if you displease him?" Kahlan asked.

"He impales those who displease him."

With the stench of blood and burning flesh, along with the things she was hearing, it was all Kahlan could do to keep from being sick. She didn't know how much longer her stomach could take it if they stayed in this place, if this man told her anything else.

Kahlan gently grasped Richard's forearm. "Please, Richard," she whispered, "this isn't really getting us anything very useful. Please, let's get out of here? If we think of anything, we can question him more later."

"Get out in front of the wagon," Richard said without hesitation. "I don't want her having to look at you."

The man bobbed his head and scrambled away.

"I don't think Jagang is in his mind," Kahlan said, "but what if I'm wrong?"

"For now, I think we should keep him alive. Out in front of the wagon, Tom will have a clear view of him. If we're wrong, well, Tom is very quick with his knife." Richard let out a shallow breath. "I've already learned something important."

"What?"

His hand in the small of her back started her moving. "Let's get going and I'll tell you about it."

Kahlan could see the wagon waiting in the distant darkness. Tom's eyes followed the man as he ran out in front of the big draft horses and stood waiting. Jennsen and Cara were in the back of the wagon. Friedrich sat up on the seat beside Tom.

"How many?" Richard called to Cara as they approached the wagon.

"With the four out in the hills that Tom took care of, and this one, here, twenty-eight."

"That's all of them, then," Richard said with relief.

Kahlan felt his hand on the small of her back slip away. He staggered to a halt. Kahlan paused beside him, not knowing why he'd stopped. Richard sank to one knee. Kahlan dropped down by him, throwing an arm around him for support. He squeezed his eyes shut in pain. With his arm pressed across his abdomen, he doubled over.

Cara leaped over the side of the wagon and raced to their side.

Despite how exhausted Kahlan was, panic jolted her instantly to full alert. "We need to get to the sliph," she said to Cara as well as Richard. "We need to get to Zedd and get some answers—and some help. Zedd can help."

Richard drew labored breaths, unable to speak as he held his breath against a wave of agony. Kahlan felt helpless not knowing what to do to help him.

"Lord Rahl," Cara said, kneeling before him, "you have been taught to control pain. You must do that, now." She seized a fistful of his hair and lifted his head to be able to look into his eyes. "Think," she commanded. "Remember. Put the pain in its place. Do it!"

Richard clutched her forearm as if to thank her for her words. "Can't," he finally managed to say to Kahlan through his obvious suffering. "We can't go in the sliph."

"We must," she insisted. "The sliph is the fastest way."

"And if I step down into the sliph, breathe in that quicksilver creature—and my magic fails?"

Kahlan was frantic. "But we must go in the sliph to get there in a hurry." She feared to say "in time."

"And if anything is wrong, I'll die." He panted, trying to catch his breath against the pain. "Without magic, breathing the sliph is death. The sword is failing me." He swallowed, coughed, gasped for breath. "If my gift is causing the headaches, and that's making magic falter in me, and I enter the sliph, I will be dead after I take the first breath. There's no way to test it."

An icy wave of terror shot through her veins. Getting to Zedd was Richard's only hope. That had been her plan. Without help, the headaches of the gift would kill him.

She feared, though, that she knew why the magic of his sword was failing, and it wasn't the headaches. She feared that it was in fact the same thing that had caused the seal to be broken. The warning beacon testified that she was the cause of that. If it was true, then she was the cause of that and much more.

If she was right, she realized, if it was true, then Richard was right about the sliph—going into the sliph would indeed be death. If she was right, then he wouldn't even be able to call the sliph, much less travel by it.

"Richard Rahl, if you're going to throw mud on my best ideas then you had better have an idea of your own to offer in its place."

He was gasping, now, in the clutch of violent pain. And then Kahlan saw blood when he coughed.

"Richard!"

Tom, looking alarmed, raced up beside them. When he saw the blood running down Richard's chin, he turned ashen.

"Help him to the wagon," Kahlan said, trying to keep her voice steady.

Cara put her shoulder under his arm. Tom circled an arm around Richard and helped Kahlan and Cara lift him to his feet.

"Nicci," Richard said.

"What?" Kahlan asked.

"You wanted to know if I had an idea. Nicci." He gasped in pain and struggled to get his breath. Yet more blood came when he coughed. It was dripping off his chin.

Nicci was a sorceress, not a wizard. Richard needed a wizard. Even if they had to travel overland, they could race there. "But Zedd would be better able—"

"Zedd is too far," he said. "We need to get to Nicci. She can use both sides of the gift."

Kahlan hadn't thought of that. Maybe she really could help.

Halfway to the wagon, Richard collapsed. It was all they could do to hold up his dead weight. With Tom gripping him under the backs of his shoulders and Cara and Kahlan each holding a leg, they ran the rest of the way to the wagon.

Tom, without the need of help from Cara and Kahlan, hoisted Richard into the back of the wagon. Jennsen hurriedly unfurled another bedroll. They laid Richard out as carefully as they could. Kahlan felt as if she were watching herself react, move, talk. She refused to allow herself to give in to panic.

Kahlan and Jennsen tried to lean in, to see how he was, but Cara shoved them back out of the way. She bent over Richard, putting her ear to his mouth, listening. Her fingers felt for a pulse at the side of his throat. Her other hand cupped the back of his neck, no doubt preparing to hold him to give him the breath of life if she had to. Mord-Sith were knowledgeable about such things; they knew how to keep people alive in order to extend their torture. Cara knew how to use that knowledge to help save lives, too.

"He's breathing," Cara said as she straightened. She laid a comforting hand on Kahlan's arm. "He's breathing easier now."

Kahlan nodded her thanks, unwilling to test her voice. She moved in closer to Richard, on the other side, while Cara wiped the blood from his chin and mouth. Kahlan felt helpless. She didn't know what to do.

"We'll ride all night," Tom said over his shoulder as he climbed up into the driver's seat.

Kahlan forced herself to think. They had to get to Nicci.

"No," she said. "It's a long way to Altur'Rang. We're not near any roads; picking our way cross-country in the dark is foolhardy. If we're reckless and push too hard we'll just end up killing the horses—or they could break a leg, which would be just as bad. If we lose the horses, we can't very well carry Richard all the way and expect to make it in time.

"The wisest thing to do is to go just as fast as we possibly can, but we also have to get rest along the way to be ready should we be attacked again. We have to use our heads or we'll never make it."

Jennsen held Richard's hand in both of hers. "He has that headache, and he fought all those men—maybe if he can just get some sleep, he'll be better, then."

Kahlan was buoyed by that thought, even though she didn't think it was that simple. She stood in the wagon bed, looking out at the man waiting for her to command him.

"Are there any more of you? Any more sent to attack us or capture us? Did this Nicholas send anyone else?"

"Not that I'm aware of, Mistress."

Kahlan spoke softly to Tom. "If he even looks like he's going to cause any trouble, don't hesitate. Kill him."

With a nod, Tom readily agreed. Kahlan dropped back down and felt Richard's brow. His skin was cold and wet.

"We'd best go on until we find a place that will be easier to defend. I think Jennsen is right that he needs rest; I don't think bouncing around in the back of this wagon is going to help him. We'll all need to get some rest and then start out at first light."

"We need to find a horse," Cara said. "The wagon is too slow. If we can find a horse, I'll ride like the wind, find Nicci, and start back with her. That way we don't have to wait all the way until we get there in the wagon."

"Good idea." Kahlan looked up at Tom. "Let's get going—find a place to stop for the night."

Tom nodded as he threw off the brake. At his urging, the horses heaved their weight against the harness and the wagon lurched ahead.

Betty, puling softly, lay beside an unconscious Richard and put her head down on his shoulder. Jennsen stroked Betty's head.

Kahlan saw tears running down Jennsen's cheeks. "I'm sorry about Rusty."

Betty's head came up. She let out a pitiful bleat.

Jennsen nodded. "Richard will be all right," she said, her voice choked with tears as she took Kahlan's hand. "I know he will."

CHAPTER 17

Zedd thought he heard something.

His hand, holding a spoonful of stew, paused before his waiting mouth. He remained motionless, listening.

The Keep often had sounded alive to him, as if it were breathing. Once in a while it even sounded as if it were letting out a small sigh. Ever since he was a boy, Zedd had, on occasion, heard loud snaps that he never could trace. He suspected such sounds were most likely the massive stone blocks moving just a tad, popping as they yielded ground against a neighbor. There were stone blocks down in the foundations of the Keep that were the size of small palaces.

Once, when Zedd was no more than ten or twelve, a loud crack had rung through the entire Keep as if the place had been struck with a giant hammer. He ran out of the library, where he'd been studying, to see other people coming out of rooms all up and down the hall, looking about, whispering their worries to one another. Zedd's father had later told him that it was found to be nothing more than one of the huge foundation blocks cracking suddenly, and while it posed no structural problem, the abrupt snap of such a enormous piece of granite had been heard throughout the Keep. Although such occurrences were rare, it was not the last time he heard such a harmless, but frightening, sound in the Keep.

And then there were the animals. Bats flew unrestricted through parts of the Keep. There were towers that soared to dizzying heights, some empty inside but for stone stairs curving up around the inside of the outer wall on their way up to a small room at the top, or an observation deck. In the dusty streamers of sunlight penetrating the dark interiors of those towers there could be seen myriad bugs flitting about. The bats loved the towers.

Rats, too, lived in parts of the Keep. They scurried and squeaked, sometimes causing a fright. Mice were common in places, making noise scratching and gnawing at things. And then there were the cats, offspring of former mousers and pets, but now all wild, that lived off the rats and the mice. The cats also hunted the birds that flew in and out of uncovered openings to feed on bugs, or to build nests up in high recesses.

There were sometimes awful sounds when a bat, a mouse, a bird, or even a cat went somewhere they weren't permitted. The shields were meant to keep people away from dangerous or restricted areas, but they were also placed to prevent unauthorized access to many of the items stored and preserved in the Keep. The shields guarded against life; they made no distinction between human and non-human life.

Otherwise, after all, a pet dog that innocently wandered into a restricted area could theoretically retrieve a dangerous talisman and proudly take it to a child master who could be put in peril by it. Those who placed the shields were aware that it was also possible for unscrupulous people to train animals to go to restricted areas, snatch whatever they might be able to carry, and bring it to them. Not knowing what animal might potentially be trained for such a task, the shields were made to ward off all life. If a bat flew into the wrong shield, it was incinerated.

There were shields in the Keep that even Zedd could not get through because they required both sides of the gift and he had only the Additive.

Some of the shields took the form of a barrier of magic that physically prevented passage in some way, either by restricting movement or by inducing a sensation so unpleasant that one couldn't force oneself beyond. Those shields were meant to prevent ungifted people or children from entering certain areas, not to prevent entrance to the gifted, so it was not necessary for those shields to kill.

But such shields only worked for those who were ungifted.

In other places, entrance was strictly forbidden to anyone but those with not only the appropriate ability, but proper authority. Without both the appropriate ability and authority granted by spells keyed to the particular defenses in that area, such as metal plates that had to be touched by an authorized wizard, the shields killed whatever entered them. The shields killed animals as infallibly, as effectively, as they would kill any intruder.

Such dangerous shields gave warnings of heat, light, or tingling as a warning so as to prevent people from unintentionally going near them—after all, with the size of the place, it was easy enough to become lost. Such warnings worked for the animals, too, but occasionally a cat chased a panicked mouse into a lethal shield, and sometimes the cat, racing after, would run right into it as well.

As Zedd waited, listening, the silence stretched on, unbroken. If he really had heard something, it could have been the Keep moving, or an animal squeaking when it approached a shield, or even a gust of wind coming through one of the hundreds of openings. Whatever it was, it was silent, now. The wooden spoonful of stew finally completed its journey.

"Umm . . ." Zedd declared to no one in particular. "Good!"

To his great disappointment when he'd first tasted it, he had found that the stew wasn't done. Rather than hurry the process with a bit of magic, and possibly incur Adie's wrath for meddling with her cooking, Zedd had sat down on the couch and resigned himself to doing a bit of reading.

There was no end to the reading. Books offered the potential of valuable information that could aid them in ways they couldn't foretell. From time to time, as he read, he checked the progress of the stew, rather patiently, he thought.

Now, as he tasted it, it finally seemed to be done. The chunks of ham were so tender they would fall apart when his tongue pressed them to the roof of his mouth. The whole delightfully bubbling pot had taken on the heady melding of onions and oils, carrots and turnips, a hint of garlic and a dizzying swirl of complementary spices, all crowded with nuggets of ham, some still with crisp fat along one edge.

To his great annoyance, Zedd had long ago noticed that Adie

hadn't made any biscuits. Stew went well with biscuits. There should be biscuits. He decided that a bowl of stew would hold him until she returned and made some. There should be biscuits. It was only right.

He didn't know where Adie had gone. Since he had been down in Aydindril most of the day, he reasoned that she had probably gone off to one of the libraries to search through books for anything that might be of help. She was a great help ferreting potentially relevant books out of the libraries. Being from Nicobarese, Adie sought out books in that language. There were books all over the Keep, so there was no telling where she was.

There were also storerooms filled with racks and racks of bones. Other rooms contained rows of tall cabinets, each with hundreds of drawers. Zedd had seen bones of creatures there that he had never seen in life. Adie was an expert of sorts on bones. She had lived for a good portion of her life in seclusion in the shadow of the boundary. People living in the area had been afraid of her; they called her the bone woman because she collected bones. They had been everywhere in her house. Some of those bones protected her from the beasts come out of the boundary.

Zedd sighed. Books or bones, there was no telling where she was. Besides that, there were any number of other things in the Wizard's Keep that would be of great interest to a sorceress. She might even have simply wanted to go for a walk, or up on a rampart to gaze at the stars and think.

It was much easier to wait for her to come back to her stew than for him to go looking for her. Maybe he should have put one of the bells around her neck.

Zedd hummed a merry tune to himself as he spooned stew into a wooden bowl. No use waiting on an empty stomach, he always said; that only made a person grouchy. It was really better to have a snack and be in good humor than to wait and be miserable. He would only be bad company if he was miserable.

On the eighth spoon of stew into the bowl, he heard a sound.

His hand froze above the bubbling pot.

He thought he'd heard a bell tinkle.

Zedd wasn't given to flights of imagination or to being unreasonably jumpy, but a cold shiver tingled across his flesh as if he'd been touched by the icy fingers of a spirit reaching out from another world. He stood motionless, partly bent toward the pot in the fire, partly turned toward the hall, listening.

It could be a cat. Maybe he hadn't tied the thin cord high enough and as a cat went under the line its tail had swished up and rung the bell. Maybe a cat was being mischievous and as it sat on its haunches, tail swishing back and forth, it had batted a bell. It could be a cat.

Or maybe a bird had landed on the line to roost for the night. A person couldn't get past the shields in order to trip a belled cord. Zedd had placed extra shields. It had to be an animal—a cat, or a bird.

If so, if no one could get past the regular shields and the extras he had placed, then why had he strung bells?

Despite the likely explanations, his hair was trying to stand on end. He didn't like the way the bell had rung; there was something about the character of the sound that told him it wasn't an animal. The sound had been too firm, too abrupt, too quick to stop.

He realized fully, now, that a bell had in fact rung. He wasn't imagining it. He tried to recreate the sound in his mind so that he might be able to put shape to the form that had tripped the cord.

Zedd silently set the bowl down on the side of the granite hearth. He rose up, listening with an ear turned toward the passage from where he had heard the bell. His mind raced through a map of all the bells he'd placed.

He needed to be sure.

He slipped through the door and into the passageway, the back of his shoulder brushing the plastered wall as he moved down to the first intersection on his right, watching not just ahead but behind as well. Nothing moved in the hallway ahead. He paused, leaning ahead to take a quick glance down the hall to the right. When he found it clear, he took the turn.

Zedd moved quickly past closed doors, past a tapestry of vineyards that he had always thought was rather poorly executed, past an empty doorway to a room with a window that looked out over a deep shaft between towers on a high rampart, and past three more intersections until he reached the first stairway. He swept around the corner to the right, up the stairs that curved around to the left as they climbed up and crossed over the hall he'd just been in. In this way he could head back toward a network of halls where he'd placed a web of bells without using those same halls.

Zedd followed a mental map of a complex tangle of passages, halls, rooms, and dead ends that, over a lifetime, he had come to know intimately. Being First Wizard, he had access to every place in the Keep except those places that required Subtractive Magic. There were a few places where he could get confused, but this was not one of them.

He knew that unless someone was following in his footsteps, they would have to either go back or pass a place where he had set traps of elaborate magic as well as simple string. Then, if they didn't see the cord, they would ring another bell. Then he would be sure.

Maybe it was Adie. Maybe she simply hadn't seen the inky cord stretched across a doorway. Maybe she had been annoyed that he'd strung bells and maybe she'd rung one just to vex him.

No, Adie wasn't like that. She might shake her finger at him and deliver a scathing lecture on why she didn't agree with him that stringing bells was an effective thing to do, but she wouldn't pull a trick about something she would recognize as intended to warn of danger. No, Adie might possibly have accidentally rung the bell, but she wouldn't have rung it deliberately.

Another bell rang. Zedd spun to the sound and then froze.

The bell had come from the wrong direction—from where he'd set a bell on the other side of a conservatory. It was too far from the first for anyone to have made it this soon. They would have had to go up a tower stairway, across a bridge to a rampart, along a narrow walkway in the dark, past several intersections to the correct turn that would descend a spiral ramp and make it down through a snarl of passageways in order to break the cord.

Unless there was more than one person.

The bell had chimed with a quick jerk and then clattered as it skittered across stone. It had to be a person tripping over the cord and sending the bell skipping across the stone floor.

Zedd changed his plan. He turned and raced down a narrow passageway to the left, climbing the first stairwell, running up the oak treads three at a time. He took the right fork at the landing, raced to the second circular stairwell of cut stone and climbed as fast as his legs would carry him. His foot slipped on the narrow wedges of spiraling steps and he banged his shin. He paused to wince only for a second. He used the time to consult his mental map of the Keep, and then he was moving again.

At the top, he dashed down a short paneled hall, sliding to a stop on the polished maple floor. He shouldered open a small, round-topped oak door. A starry sky greeted him. He sucked deep draughts of cool night air as he raced along the narrow rampart. He paused twice along the way to peer down through the slots in the crenellated battlements. He didn't see anyone. That was a good sign—he knew where they had to be if they weren't moving by an outer route.

He ran on across the swaying span between towers, robes flying behind, crossing over the entire section of the Keep where both bells had rung far below, going over the top of the area in order to get behind whoever had tripped the cords. While they had tripped bells on opposite sides of the conservatory, they had to have come in through the same wing—he knew that much. He wanted to get behind them, bottle them in before they could get to an unprotected section where they would encounter a bewildering variety of passageways. If they were to make it there and hide in that area, he could have a time of it rooting them out.

His mind raced as fast as his feet as he tried to think, tried to recall all the shields, tried to figure how someone could have gotten past the defenses to get to that specific wing where the bells that had rung were placed. There were shields that should have made it impossible. He had to consider thousands of corridors and passageways in the Keep, trying to come up with all the potential routes. It was like a complex multilevel puzzle, and despite how thorough he'd been, it was possible he'd missed something. He had to have missed something.

There were rooms or even entire sections that were shielded and could not be entered, but often they could be circumvented. Even if a hall was shielded at both ends, so as to prevent anyone from getting to the rooms in that hall, you could still usually get around to the other end of the hall and make your way to whatever lay beyond. That was deliberate; while the rooms might have held dangerous items of magic that had to be kept contained, there needed to be ways to get to them, and get beyond to other rooms that might, from time to time, also have to be restricted. Most of the Keep was like that—a three-dimensional maze with almost endless possible routes.

For the unwary, it could also be a killing field of traps. There were places layered with warning barriers and other devices that would keep any innocent person away. Beyond those protective layers, the shields gave no warning before they killed. Trespassers would not know there were shields embedded beyond, and that they were stepping into a trap. Such shields were designed that way in order to kill invaders who penetrated that deep; the lack of warning was deliberate.

Zedd supposed it was possible for someone to bypass all the shields and work their way into the depths of the place in order to ring those particular bells, but for the life of him, he couldn't trace all the steps necessary. But whoever it was, no matter how lucky they were, they would soon get themselves stuck in the labyrinth and then, if they weren't killed by a shield, he could deal with them.

Zedd gazed out past towers, ramparts, bridges, and open stairs to rooms projecting from soaring walls, out on the city of Aydindril far below, now all dark and dead-looking. How had someone gotten past the stone bridge up to the Keep?

A Sister of the Dark, maybe. Maybe one of them had figured out how to use Subtractive Magic to take his shield down. But even if one had, the shields in the Keep were different. Most of them had been placed by the wizards in ancient times, wizards with both sides of the gift. A Sister of the Dark would not be able to breach such shields—they had been designed to withstand enemy wizards of that time. They were far more powerful than any mere Sister of the Dark.

And where was Adie? She should have been back. He wished now that he had gone and found her. She needed to know that there was someone in the Keep. Unless she already knew. Unless they had her.

Zedd turned and raced down the rampart. At the projecting bastion, he seized the railing to the side to halt his forward rush and spin himself around the corner. He raced down the dark steps as if he were running down a hill.

With his gift, he could sense that there was no one in the vicinity. Since there was no one near, that meant that he had managed to get behind them. He had them trapped.

At the bottom of the steps he threw open the door and flew into the hallway beyond.

He crashed into a man standing there, waiting.

Zedd's momentum knocked the big man from his feet. They fell in a tangle, sliding together along the polished green and yellow marble floor, both grappling for control.

Zedd could not have been more surprised. His gifted sense told him the man was not there. His gifted sense was obviously wrong. The disorientation of encountering a man when he had sensed that the hall was empty was more jarring than the headlong tumble.

Even as he was rolling, Zedd was casting webs to tangle the man in a snare of magic. The man, in turn, lunged to tangle Zedd in meaty arms.

In desperation, despite the close range, Zedd pulled enough heat from the surrounding air to unleash a thunderous blast of lightning and cast it directly into the man. The blinding flash burned a lacing line through the stone block wall beyond him.

Only too late did Zedd realize that the discharge of deadly power had lanced through the man without effect. The hall filled with shards of stone whistling about, ricocheting from walls and ceiling, skipping along the floor.

The man landed on Zedd, driving the wind from him. Desperately yelling for help, the man wrestled Zedd on the slippery floor. Zedd concocted a weak and fumbling defense, to give the man a false sense of confidence, until he was able to suddenly land a knee sharply at the point of his attacker's sternum. The man cried out in surprise as much as in pain as he flipped backward off Zedd, gasping to get his wind back.

Having sucked so much heat from the air had left it as frigid as a winter night. Clouds of their breath filled the cold air as both men panted with the effort of the struggle. The man again cried out for help, hoping to bring comrades to his aid.

Zedd would assume that anyone would fear to attack a wizard by muscle alone. This man, though, had no need to fear magic. Even if he hadn't known that before, certainly the evidence was now all too clear. Yet, despite the man being at least twice the size of his opponent, less than a third his age, and having immunity from the conjuring being thrown at him, Zedd thought that he fought rather . . . squeamishly.

However timid the man was, he was determined. He scrambled to attack again. If he broke Zedd's neck, it wouldn't matter that he did so timidly.

As the man regained his feet and lunged, Zedd drew back his arms, elbows cocked, fingers spread, and cast more of the lightning, but this time he knew better than to waste his effort trying to cut down a man not touched by magic. Instead, Zedd sought to rake the floor with the conjured bolts of power. It slammed into the stone with unrestrained violence, ripping and splintering whole sections, throwing sharp jagged shards streaking through the air.

A fist-sized block of stone hurtling at tremendous speed crashed into the man's shoulder. Above the boom of thunderous power, Zedd heard bones snap. The impact spun the man around and knocked him back against the wall. Since Zedd now knew that this intruder could not directly be harmed by magic, he instead filled the hall with a deafening storm of magic designed not to assail the man directly but to tear the place apart into a cloud of deadly flying fragments.

The man, as he recoiled from striking the wall, again threw himself at Zedd. He was met by a shower of deadly shards whistling through the air toward him. Blood splattered across the wall beyond as the man was ripped to shreds. In a blink, he was killed and dropped heavily to the floor.

From beyond the smoke and dust filling the hall, two more men suddenly flew at Zedd. His gifted sense told him that, like the first man, these men were not there, either.

Zedd threw yet more lightning to rip up the floor and unleash flying stone at the men, but they were already through the flares of power, diving onto him. He crashed to his back, the men atop him. They seized his arms.

Zedd struggled frantically to let loose a blast to bring down the ceiling. He began to whirl the air above the men to tear the hall to pieces, and them with it.

A beefy hand with a filthy white rag clamped down over Zedd's face. He gasped, only to inhale a powerful smell that made his throat want to clench shut, but too late.

With the cloth and the big hand covering his whole face, Zedd couldn't see. The world spun sickeningly.

Soft, silent, blackness pressed in around him as he fought to resist it, until he lost consciousness.

CHAPTER 18

Zedd woke, his head spinning, his stomach heaving with rippling waves of nausea. He didn't think that in his entire life he had ever felt so sick. He hadn't known it was possible to feel so intense an urge to vomit, without actually throwing up. He couldn't lift his head. If he could just die right then, it would be a welcome release from such dizzying agony.

He started to put his hands over the light hurting his eyes, but found his wrists were tied behind his back.

"I think he's waking," a man said in a subservient voice.

Despite his nausea, Zedd instinctively tried to use his gift to sense how many people were around him. For some reason, his gift that ordinarily flowed as easily as thought, as simply as using his eyes to see, his ears to hear, felt thick and slow, as if mired in molasses. He reasoned that it was probably the result of whatever vile substance it was they had soaked the rag in to cause him to pass out when they held it over his face. Still, he managed to sense that there was only one person around him.

Powerful hands seized his robes and yanked him to his feet. Zedd gave himself permission to vomit. Against all expectation, it didn't happen. The dark night swam before his blurred vision. He could make out trees against the sky, stars, and the looming black shape of the Keep.

Suddenly, a tongue of flame ignited in midair. Zedd blinked at the unexpected brightness. The small flame, wavering with a lazy motion, floated above the upturned palm of a woman with wiry gray hair. Zedd saw other people in the shadows; his gifted sense was wrong. Like the man who had attacked him, these, too, had to be people not affected by magic.

The woman standing before him peered at him intently. Her expression twisted with satisfied loathing.

"Well, well, well," she said with patronizing delight. "The great wizard himself awakes."

Zedd said nothing. It seemed to amuse her. Her fearsome scowl and humped nose lit from the side by the flame she held above her palm, floated closer.

"You are ours, now," she hissed.

Zedd, having waited patiently to gather his resolve, abruptly initiated the required mental twist to the gift all the way down to his soul in order to simultaneously call down lightning, focus air to slice this woman in two, and gather every stone and pebble from all around to crush her under an avalanche of rock. He expected the night to light with such power as he unlocked and sent forth.

Nothing happened.

Not waiting to waste the time to analyze what could be the difficulty, he was forced to abandon attempts at satisfying his emotional preferences, and to ignite wizard's fire itself to consume her.

Nothing happened.

Not only did nothing happen, but it felt as if the attempt itself were but a pebble falling endlessly into a vast, dark well. The expectation withered in the face of what he found within himself: a kind of dreadful emptiness.

Zedd felt as if he couldn't light a tongue of flame to match hers if his life depended on it. He was somehow cut off from forming his ability into much of anything useful other than to use it for a bit of dim awareness. Probably a lingering result of the foul-smelling substance they had pressed over his face to make him lose consciousness.

Since Zedd couldn't muster any power, he did the only thing he could: he spat in her face.

With lightning speed, she backhanded him, knocking him from the arms of the men holding him. Unable to use his hands to break his fall, he hit the ground unexpectedly hard. He lay in the dirt for a time, his ears ringing in the aftereffect of the hit he'd taken, waiting for someone to lean over and kill him.

Instead, they hauled him to his feet again. One of the men seized his hair and pulled his head up, forcing him to look into the woman's face. The scowl he saw there looked like it spent a great deal of time on her face.

She spat in his face.

Zedd smiled. "So, here we have a spoiled child playing the game of tit for tat."

Zedd grunted with the sudden shock of a wallop of pain that twisted inside of his abdomen. Had the men not been holding him under his arms he would have doubled over and fallen to the ground. He wasn't quite sure how she had done it—probably with a fist of air delivered with all the power of her gift behind it. She had left the gathered air loosely formed, rather than focusing it to a sharp edge, or it would have torn him in two. As it was, he knew it would leave his middle black and blue.

It was a long and desperate wait before he was able to at last draw a breath.

The men who his gift said weren't there pulled him straight.

"I'm disappointed to discover I'm in the hands of a sorceress who can be no more inventive than that," Zedd mocked.

That brought a smile to her scowl. "Don't you worry, Wizard Zorander, His Excellency very much wants your scrawny hide. He will be playing a game of tit for tat that I believe you will find quite inventive. I have learned that when it comes to inventive cruelty, His Excellency is peerless. I'm sure he will not disappoint you."

"Then what are we standing around for? I can't wait to have a word with His Excellency."

As the men held his head back for her, she ran a fingernail down the side of his face and across his throat, not hard enough to draw blood, but enough to hint at her own restrained cruelty. She leaned in again. One eyebrow lifted in a way that ran a chill up Zedd's spine.

"I imagine you have grand ideas about such a visit, about what you think you will do or say." She reached out and hooked a finger around something at his neck. When she gave it a firm tug, he realized that he was wearing a collar of some sort. By the way it dug into the flesh at the back of his neck, it had to be metal.

"Guess what this is," she said. "Just guess."

Zedd sighed. "You really are a tedious woman. But I imagine you've heard that ofttimes before."

She ignored his gibe, eager to be the messenger of bad news. Her scowling smile widened. "It's a Rada'Han."

Zedd's sense of alarm rose, but he kept any trace of it from his face.

"Really." He paused for an extended, bored yawn. "Well, I'd not expect a woman of your limited intellect to think up something clever."

She slammed a knee into his groin. Zedd doubled over in pain, unable to contain his groan. He hadn't been expecting something so crude.

The men pulled him up straight, not allowing him pause to recover. Being pulled up straight brought a gasp of agony. His teeth were clenched, his eyes were watering, and his knees wanted to buckle, but the men held him upright.

Her smile was getting annoying. "You see, Wizard Zorander? Being clever isn't necessary at all."

Zedd saw her point but didn't say so.

He was already preparing to unlock the cursed collar from his neck. He'd been "captured" before—by the Prelate herself—and had had a Rada'Han put around his neck, like some boy born with the gift who needed training. The Sisters of the Light put such a collar around those boys so that the gift wouldn't harm them before they could learn to control their gift. Richard had been captured and put in such a Rada'Han right after his gift came to life in him.

The collar was also used to control the young wizard wearing it, to give pain, when the Sisters thought it necessary. Zedd understood the Prelate's reasons for wanting Richard's help, since they knew he had been born with both sides of the gift, and, too, they worried about the dark forces that pursued him, he could never forgive her for putting Richard in a collar. A wizard needed to be trained by a wizard, not some misguided gaggle like the Sisters of the Light.

The Prelate, though, had harbored no delusion of actually training Richard to be a wizard. She had collared him in order to smoke out the traitors among her flock: the Sisters of the Dark.

Unlike Richard, though, Zedd knew how to get such a disgusting contrivance off his neck. In fact, he had done it before, when the Prelate had thought to collar him and thus force his cooperation.

Zedd used a thread of power to probe at the lock, not overtly, so as this woman might notice it, but just enough to find the twist in the spell where he would be able to focus his ability to snap the conjured lock.

When the time was right, when he had his feet solidly under him, when his head stopped spinning long enough, he would break the collar's hold. In that same instant, before she knew what had happened, he would release wizard's fire and incinerate this woman.

She hooked a finger under the collar again and gave it another tug.

"The thing is, my dear wizard, I would expect that a man of your renowned talent might know how to get such a device off."

"Really? I'm renowned?" Zedd flashed her a grin. "That's very gratifying."

Her utter contempt produced a smile of pure disdain. With her finger through the collar she pulled him close to her twisted expression. She ignored his words and went on.

"Since His Excellency would be extremely displeased should you get the collar off, I've taken measures to insure that such a thing would not happen. I used Subtractive Magic to weld it on."

Now, that was a problem.

She nodded to the men. Zedd glanced at them to each side and noticed for the first time that their eyes were wet. It shocked him to realize they were weeping.

Weeping or not, they followed her orders, unceremoniously lifting him and heaving him in the back of a wagon as if he were firewood.

Zedd landed beside someone else.

"Glad to see you be alive, old man," a soft voice rasped.

It was Adie. The side of her face was swollen and bleeding. It looked like they'd clubbed her nearly to death. Her wrists were tied behind her back as well. He saw, too, tears on her cheeks.

It broke his heart to see her hurt. "Adie, what did they do to you?"

She smiled. "Not as much as they intend to, I fear."

In the dim light of a lantern, Zedd could see that she, too, wore one of the awful collars.

"Your stew was excellent," he said.

Adie groaned. "Please, old man, do not mention food to me right now."

Zedd cautiously turned his head and saw more men waiting in the darkness off to the side. They had been behind him, so he hadn't noticed them, before. His gift had not told him they were there.

"I think we're in a great deal of trouble," he whispered to no one in particular.

"Really?" Adie rasped. "What be your first clue?"

Zedd knew she was only trying to make him smile, but he could not even manage a small one.

"I be sorry, Zedd."

He nodded, as best he could lying on his side with his wrists bound behind his back. "I thought I was so clever, laying every kind of trap I could think of. Unfortunately, such traps didn't work for those who are not affected by magic."

"You could not know of such a thing," Adie said in a comforting tone.

His mood sank into bitter regret. "I should have taken it into account after we encountered that one down at the Confessors' Palace, in the spring. I should have realized the danger." He stared off into the darkness. "I served our cause no better than a fool."

"But where did all of them come from?" She looked on the verge of losing herself to panic. "I have never encountered a single such person in my entire life, and now there be a whole gang of them standing there."

Zedd hated to see Adie so distraught. Adie only knew there were a number of them by the telltale sounds they made. At least he could see the men with his eyes, if not his gift.

The men stood around, heads hanging, waiting to be commanded. They didn't look pleased by what was happening. They all looked young, in their twenties. Many were crying. It seemed strange to see such big men weeping. Zedd almost regretted killing one of them. Almost.

"You three," the woman growled to more of the men waiting in the shadows as she lifted another lantern from one of them and sent the flame she held into it, "get in there and start the search."

Adie's completely white eyes turned to Zedd, her expression grave. "Sister of the Dark," she whispered.

And now they had the Keep.

CHAPTER 19

"And just how can you be sure that it was a Sister of the Dark you saw?" Verna asked, absently, as she dipped her pen again.

She scrawled her initials at the bottom of the request for a Sister to travel to a town down south to see to a local sorceress's plans for a defense of their area. Even in the field, the paperwork of the office of the Prelate seemed to have chased after and found her. Their palace had been destroyed, the prophet himself was at large and the real Prelate was off alone chasing after him, some of the Sisters of the Light had pledged their souls to the Keeper of the underworld and in so doing had brought the Keeper a step closer to having them all in the dark forever of eternity, a good number of the Sisters—both Sisters of the Light and Sisters of the Dark—were in the cruel hands of the enemy and doing his bidding, the barrier separating the Old and New World was down, the whole world had been turned upside down, the only man—Richard Rahl—who prophecy named as having a chance of defeating the threat of the Imperial Order was off who-knew-where doing who-knew-what, and yet, the paperwork managed to survive it all and persist to vex her.

Some of Verna's assistants handled the paperwork and the requests, but, as much as she disliked dealing with such tedious matters, Verna felt a sense of duty to keep an eye on it all. Besides, as much as paperwork vexed her, it also occupied her mind, preventing her from dwelling on the might-have-been.

"After all," Verna added, "it could just as easily have been a Sister of the Light. Jagang uses both for their ability with magic. You can't really be sure it was a Sister of the Dark. He's been sending

Sisters to accompany his scouts all winter and spring."

The Mord-Sith placed her knuckles on the small desk and leaned in. "I'm telling you, Prelate, it was a Sister of the Dark."

Verna saw no point in arguing, since it mattered little, so she didn't. "If you say so, Rikka."

Verna turned over the paper to the next in the stack, a request for a Sister to come and speak to children on the calling of the Sisters of the Light, with a lecture on why the Creator would be against the ways of the Imperial Order and on their side. Verna smiled to herself, imagining how Zedd would fume at the very idea of a Sister, in the New World, lecturing her views on such a subject.

Rikka withdrew her knuckles from the desk. "I thought you might say as much."

"Well, there you go, then," Verna mumbled as she read the next message from the Sisters of the Light to the south reporting on the passes through the mountains and the methods that had been used to seal them off.

"Wait right here," Rikka growled before flying out of the tent.

"I'm not going anywhere," Verna said with a sigh as she scanned the written account, but the fiery, blond-headed woman was already gone.

Verna heard a commotion outside the tent. Rikka was delivering a scathing lecture to someone. The Mord-Sith was incorrigible. That was probably why, despite everything, Verna liked her.

Since Warren had died, Verna's heart was no longer in much of anything, though. She did as she had to, did her duty, but she couldn't make herself feel anything but despair. The man she loved, the man she had married, the most wonderful man in the world . . . was gone.

Nothing much mattered after that.

Verna tried to do her part, to do as was needed, because so many people depended on her, but, if truth be told, the reason she worked herself nearly to death was to try to keep her mind occupied, to think of something else, anything thing else, except Warren. It didn't really work, but she kept at it. She knew that people counted on her, but she just couldn't make herself truly care.

Warren was gone. Life was empty of what mattered most to her.

That was the end of it, the end of her caring about much of anything.

Verna idly pulled her journey book from her belt. She didn't know what made her do so, except perhaps that it had been some time since she had last looked for a message from the real Prelate. Ann was having her own crisis of caring ever since Kahlan had laid the blame for so much of what had gone wrong, including being the cause of the war itself, right at the Prelate's feet. Verna thought that Kahlan had been wrong about much of it, but she understood all too well why she thought that Ann had been responsible for tangling up their lives; Verna had felt the same way for a time.

Holding the journey book off to the side with one hand, flipping the pages with a thumb, Verna saw a message flash by.

Rikka swept back into the tent. She plunked a heavy sack down on Verna's desk, right on top of the reports.

"Here!" Rikka said, fury powering her voice.

It was then, when Verna looked up, that she saw for the first time the strange way Rikka was dressed. Verna's mouth fell open. Rikka was not wearing the skintight red leather that the Mord-Sith typically wore, except for occasionally when they were relaxing and then they sometimes wore brown leather, instead. Verna had never seen the woman in anything other than those leather outfits.

Now Rikka had on a dress.

Verna could not remember being so astonished.

Not just a dress, but a pink dress that no decent woman of Rikka's age, probably her late twenties or early thirties, would be caught dead in. The neckline plunged down to reveal ample cleavage. The twin mounds of exposed flesh were shoved up and nearly spilling out the top. Verna was amazed that Rikka's nipples had managed to remain covered, what with the way her breasts heaved with her heated breathing.

"You, too?" Rikka snapped.

Verna finally looked up into Rikka's blazing blue eyes. "Me, too, what?"

"You, too, can't get enough of looking at my chest?"

Verna felt her face go scarlet. She gave her red face an excuse by shaking a finger at the woman.

"What are you doing dressed like that in an army camp! Around all these soldiers! You look like a whore!"

Despite how their leather outfits went all the way up to their necks, the tight leather left little to the imagination. Seeing the woman's flesh, though, was altogether different, and quite shocking.

Verna realized, only then, because she had finally looked up at the woman's face, that Rikka's single braid was undone. Her long blond hair was as free as a horse's mane. Verna had never seen one of the Mord-Sith out in public without her hair done up in the single braid that in large part identified their profession of Mord-Sith.

Even seeing the woman's cleavage exposed was not as shocking as seeing her hair undone. It was that, more than anything, Verna realized, that lent a lewd look to the woman. Something about her braid being undone seemed sacrilegious, even though Verna could not condone a profession dedicated to torture.

Verna remembered, then, that she had asked one of the Mord-Sith, Cara, to do her worst to the young man—a boy, really—who had murdered Warren. Verna had sat up the entire night listening to that young man scream his life away. His suffering had been monstrous, and yet it had not been nearly enough to suit her.

At times, Verna wondered if in the next life the Keeper of the underworld would have something wholly unpleasant in store for her for all eternity in recompense for what Verna had done. She didn't really care; it had been worth whatever the price might be.

Besides, she decided, if she was to be punished for condemning that man to just retribution, then the very concept of justice would have to be invalid, rendering living a life of good or evil to have no meaning. In fact, for the justice she had meted out to that vile amoral animal walking the world of life in the form of a man who had murdered Warren, she should be rewarded in the afterlife by being eternally in the warmth of the Creator's light, along with the good spirit of Warren, or else there was no justice.

General Meiffert swept into the tent, fists at his sides, coming to a halt beside Rikka. He raked his blond hair back when he saw Verna sitting behind her little desk, and cooled visibly.

He'd had the carpenters nail together the tiny desk for her out of scrap furniture left in an abandoned farm. It was nothing like the desks at the Palace of the Prophets, of course, but it had been given with more concern and meaning behind it than the grandest gold-leafed desk she had ever seen. General Meiffert had been proud at seeing how useful Verna found it.

With a quick glance, he took in Rikka's dress and her hair. "What's this about?"

"Well," Verna said, "I'm not sure. Something about one of Jagang's Sisters scouting a pass."

Rikka folded her bare arms atop her nearly bare bosom. "Not just a Sister, but a Sister of the Dark."

"Jagang has been sending Sisters scouting the passes all winter," the young general said. "The Prelate has laid traps and shields." His level of concern rose. "Are you telling us that one of them got through?"

"No, I'm telling you that I went hunting for them."

Verna frowned. "What are you talking about? We lost half a dozen Mord-Sith trying that. After you found the heads of two of your sister Mord-Sith mounted on pikes, the Mother Confessor herself ordered you to stop throwing their lives away on such useless missions."

Rikka at last smiled. It was the kind of satisfied smile, especially coming from a Mord-Sith, that tended to give people nightmares.

"Does this look useless?"

Rikka reached into her sack and pulled out a human head. Holding it by the hair, she brandished it in front of Verna's face. She turned, shook it at General Meiffert as well, and then plunked it down on the desk. Gore oozed out over the reports.

"Like I said, a Sister of the Dark."

Verna recognized the face, even as twisted in death as it was. Rikka was right, it was a Sister of the Dark. The question was, how did she know it was a Sister of the Dark, and not one of the Light?

Outside Verna could hear horses clopping past her tent. Some of the soldiers called out greetings to men returning from patrols. In the distance could be heard conversations and men issuing orders. Hammers on steel rang like bells as men worked hot metal into useful shapes for repairs to equipment. Nearby, horses frisked in a corral. As men made their way past Verna's tent, their gear jingled. Fires crackled as wood was added for the cooks or roared as bellows pumped to turn it white-hot for the blacksmiths.

"You touched her with your Agiel?" Verna asked in a quiet voice. "Your Agiel doesn't work effectively on those the dream walker controls."

Rikka's smile turned sly. She spread her arms. "Agiel? Do you see an Agiel?"

Verna knew that no Mord-Sith would ever let her Agiel out of her control. With a glance to the woman's cleavage, she could only imagine where she had it hidden.

"All right," General Meiffert said, his tone no longer indulgent. "I want to know what's going on, and I want to know right now."

"I was down near Dobbin Pass, checking around, and what do I find but an Imperial Order patrol."

The general nodded as he let out a frustrated sigh. "They've been coming in that way from time to time. But how did you manage to come across such an enemy patrol? Why hadn't one of our Sisters already snared them?"

Rikka shrugged. "Well, this patrol was still on the other side of the pass. Back at that deserted farm." She tapped Verna's desk with her toe. "Where you got the wood for this."

Verna twisted her mouth with displeasure. Rikka wasn't supposed to be beyond the pass. The Mord-Sith, though, recognized no orders but those from Lord Rahl himself. Rikka had only followed Kahlan's orders because, during his absence, Kahlan was acting on Richard's behalf. Verna suspected that it was simpler than that, though; she suspected that they had only followed the Mother Confessor's orders because she was wife to Lord Rahl, and if they didn't it would bring Lord Rahl's wrath down on them. As long as such orders weren't viewed by the Mord-Sith as troublesome, they went along. When they decided otherwise, they did as they wished.

"The Sister was by herself," Rikka went on, "having one powerful-looking headache."

"Jagang," Verna said. "Jagang was issuing his order, or punishing her for something, or giving her a lecture in her mind. He does that from time to time. It isn't pleasant."

Rikka stroked the hair on the woman's head sitting on Verna's desk, making a mess of the reports. "The poor thing," she mocked. "While she was off among the pines staring at nothing while she pressed her fingers to her temples, her men were back at the farm-house, having their way with a couple of young women. The two were squealing and crying and carrying on, but the men weren't put off by it any."

Verna lowered her eyes as she let out a heavy breath. Some people had refused to believe the necessity of fleeing before the arrival of the Imperial Order.

Sometimes, when people refused to recognize the existence of evil, they found themselves having to face precisely that which they had never been willing to admit existed.

Rikka's satisfied smile returned. "I went in and took care of the brave soldiers of the Imperial Order. They were so distracted, they paid no attention as I snuck up behind them. The women were so terrorized that they screamed even though I was saving them. The Sister hadn't been paying any attention to the screaming before, and didn't then, either.

"One of the young women was blond and about my size, so an idea struck me. I put on her dress and took out my braid, so I might be mistaken for her. I gave the one girl some of the men's clothes to wear and told them both to run for the hills, in the opposite direc-tion of the Sister, and not to look back. I didn't have to tell them twice. Then I sat down on a stool outside the barn.

"Sure enough, in a while the Sister came back. She saw me sitting there, hanging my head, pretending to be crying. She thought the other woman was still inside, with the men. She said, "It's time those foolish bastards in there were done with you and your friend. His Excellency wants a report, and he wants it now—he's ready to move.""

Verna came up out of her chair. "You heard her say that?"

"Yes."

"Then what?" General Meiffert asked.

"Then the Sister made for the side door into the barn. When she stormed past me, I rose up behind her and cut her throat with one of the men's knives."

General Meiffert leaned toward Rikka. "You cut her throat? You didn't use your Agiel?"

Rikka gave him a look that suggested she thought he hadn't been paying attention. "Like the Prelate said, an Agiel doesn't work very well on those the dream walker controls. So I used a knife. Dream walker or not, cutting her throat worked just fine."

Rikka lifted the head before Verna again. One of the reports stuck to the bottom of it as it swung by the hair. "I sliced the knife through her throat and around her neck. She was thrashing about quite a bit, so I had a good hold on her as she died. All of a sudden, there was an instant when the whole world went black—and I mean black, black as the Keeper's heart. It was as if the underworld had suddenly taken us all."

Verna looked away from the head of a Sister she had known for a very long time and had always believed was devoted to the Creator, to the light of life. She had been devoted, instead, to death.

"The Keeper came to claim one of his own," Verna explained in a quiet voice.

"Well," Rikka said, rather sarcastically, Verna thought, "I didn't think that when a Sister of the Light died such a thing happened. I told you it was a Sister of the Dark."

Verna nodded. "So you did."

General Meiffert gave the Mord-Sith a hurried clap on the back of the shoulder. "Thanks, Rikka. I'd better spread the word. If Jagang is starting to move, it won't be many days before he's here. We need to be sure the passes are ready when his force finally gets here."

"The passes will hold," Verna said. She let out a silent sigh. "At least for a while."

The Order had to come across the mountains if they were to conquer D'Hara. There were few ways across those formidable mountains. Verna and the Sisters had shielded and sealed those passes as well as it was possible to seal them. They had used magic to bring down walls of rock in places, making the narrow roads impassable. In other places, they had used their power to cleave away roads cut into the steep sides of mountains, leaving no way through, except to clamber over rubble. To prevent that, and in other places, the men had worked all winter constructing stone walls across the passes. Atop those walls were fortifications from which they could rain down death on the narrow passes below. Additionally, in every one of those places, the Sisters had set snares of magic so deadly that coming through would be a bloody ordeal that would only get worse, and that was before they encountered the walls lined with defenders.

Jagang had Sisters of the Dark to try to undo the barriers of both magic and stone, but Verna was more powerful, in the Additive anyway, than any of them. Besides that, she had joined her power with other Sisters in order to invest in those barriers magic that she knew would prove formidable.

Still, Jagang would come. Nothing Verna, her Sisters, and the D'Haran army could do would ultimately be able to withstand the numbers Jagang would throw at them. If he had to command his men to march through passes filled a hundred feet deep with their fallen comrades, he would not flinch from doing so. Nor would it matter to him if the corpses were a thousand feet deep.

"I'll be back a little later, Verna," the general said. "We'll need to get the officers and some of the Sisters together and make sure everything is ready."

"Yes, of course," Verna said.

Both General Meiffert and Rikka started to leave.

"Rikka," Verna called. She gestured down at the desk. "Take the dear departed Sister with you, would you please?"

Rikka sighed, which nearly spilled her bosom out of the dress. She made a long-suffering face before snatching up the head and vanishing out of the tent behind the general.

Verna sat down and put her head in her hands. It was going to start all over again. It had been a long and peaceful, if bitterly cold, winter. Jagang had made his winter encampment on the other side of the mountains, far enough away that, with the snow and cold, it was difficult to launch effective raids against his troops. Just as it had the summer before, the summer Warren had died, now that the weather was favorable, the Order would begin to move. It was starting all over again. The killing, the terror, the fighting, running, hunger, exhaustion.

But what choice was there, other than to be killed? In many ways, life had come to seem worse than death.

Verna abruptly remembered, then, about the journey book. She worked it out of the pocket in her belt and pulled the lamp closer, needing the comfort as well as the light. She wondered where Richard and Kahlan were, if they were safe, and she thought, too, about Zedd and Adie all alone guarding the Wizard's Keep. Unlike everyone else, at least Zedd and Adie were safe and at peace where they were— for the time being, anyway. Sooner or later, D'Hara would fall and then Jagang would return to Aydindril.

Verna tossed the small black book on the desk, smoothed her dress beneath her legs, and scooted her chair closer. She ran her fingers over the familiar leather cover on an object of magic that was over three thousand years old. The journey books had been invested with magic by those mysterious wizards who so long ago had built the Palace of the Prophets. A journey book was twinned, and as such, they were priceless; what was written in one appeared at the same time in its twin. In that way, the Sisters could communicate over vast distances and know important information as it happened, rather than weeks or even months later.

Ann, the real Prelate, had the twin to Verna's.

Verna herself, had been sent by Ann on a journey of nearly twenty years to find Richard. Ann had known all along where Richard had been. It was for that reason that Verna could understand Kahlan's rage at how Ann had seemed to twist her and Richard's life. But Verna had come to understand that the Prelate had sent her on what was actually a mission of vital importance, one that had brought change to the world, but also brought hope for the future.

Verna opened the journey book, holding it a little sideways to see the words in the light.

Verna, Ann wrote, *I believe I have discovered where the prophet is hiding*.

Verna sat back in surprise. After the palace had been destroyed,

Nathan, the prophet, had escaped their control and had since been roaming free, a profound danger.

For the last couple of years, the rest of the Sisters of the Light had believed that the Prelate and the prophet were dead. Ann, when she'd left the Palace of the Prophets with Nathan on an important mission, had feigned their death and named Verna Prelate to succeed her. Very few people other than Verna, Zedd, Richard, and Kahlan knew the truth. During that mission, however, Nathan had managed to get his collar off and escape Ann's control. There was no telling what catastrophe that man could cause.

Verna leaned over the journey book again.

I should have Nathan within days, now. I can hardly believe that after all this time, I nearly have my hands on that man. I will let you know soon.

How are you, Verna? How are you feeling? How are the Sisters and how go matters with the army? Write when you can. I will be checking my journey book nightly. I miss you terribly.

Verna sat back again. That was all there was. But it was enough. The very notion of Ann finally capturing Nathan made Verna's head swim with relief.

Even that momentous news, though, failed to do much to lift her mood. Jagang was about to launch his attack on D'Hara and Ann was about to finally have Nathan under control, but Richard was somewhere off to the south, beyond their control. Ann had worked for five hundred years to shape events so that Richard could lead them in the battle for the future of mankind, and now, on the eve of what could very well prove to be that final battle, he was not there with them.

Verna drew the stylus out of the journey book's spine and leaned over to write Ann a report.

My dearest Ann, I'm afraid that things here are about to become very unpleasant.

The siege of the passes into D'Hara is about to begin.

CHAPTER 20

The sprawling corridors of the People's Palace, seat of power in D'Hara, were filled with the whisper of footsteps on stone. Ann pushed herself back a little on the white marble bench where she sat stuffed between three women on one side and an older couple on the other, all gossiping about what people were wearing as they strolled the grand halls, or what other people did while they were here, or what they most wanted to see. Ann supposed that such gossip was harmless enough and probably meant to take people's minds off the worries of the war. Still, it was hard to believe that at such a late hour people would rather be out gossiping than in a warm bed asleep.

Ann kept her head down and pretended to be pawing through her travel bag while at the same time keeping a wary eye on the soldiers passing not too far away as they patrolled. She didn't know if her caution was necessary, but she would rather not find out too late that it was.

"Come from far?" the closest women to her asked.

Ann looked up, realizing that the women had spoken to her. "Well, yes, I guess it has been a bit of a journey."

Ann put her nose back in her bag and rummaged in earnest, hoping to be left alone.

The woman, middle-aged with her curls of brown hair just starting to carry a bit of gray, smiled. "I'm not all that far from home, myself, but I do so like to spend a night at the palace, now and then, just to lift my spirits."

Ann glanced around at the polished marble floors, the glossy red stone columns below arches, decorated with carved vines, that supported the upper balconies. She gazed up at the skylights that allowed the light to flood in the place during the day, and peered off at the grand statues that stood on pedestals around a fountain with life-sized stone horses galloping forever through a shimmering spray of water.

"Yes, I see what you mean," Ann murmured.

The place didn't lift her spirits. In fact, the place made her as nervous as a cat in a doghouse with the door closed. She could feel that her power was frighteningly diminished in this place.

The People's Palace was more than any mere palace. It was a city all joined together and under countless roofs atop a huge plateau. Tens of thousands of people lived in the magnificent structure, and thousands more visited it daily. There were different levels to the palace itself, some where people had shops and sold goods, others where officials worked, some that were living quarters. Many sections were off limits to those who visited.

Sprawled around the base of the plateau were informal markets where people gathered to buy, sell, and trade goods. On the climb all the way up through the interior of the plateau to reach the palace itself, Ann had passed many permanent shops. The palace was a center of trade, drawing people from all over D'Hara.

More than that, though, it was the ancestral home of the House of Rahl. As such, it was grand for arcane reasons beyond the awareness or even understanding of most of the people who called it home or visited it. The People's Palace was a spell—not a place spelled, as had been the Palace of the Prophets where Ann had spent most of her life, but the place itself was the spell.

The entire palace had been built to a careful and precise design: that of a spell drawn on the face of the ground. The outer fortified walls contained the actual spell form and the major congregations of rooms formed significant hubs, while the halls and corridors themselves were the drawn lines—the essence of the spell itself, the power.

Like a spell being drawn in the dirt with the point of a stick, the halls would have had to have been built in the sequence required by the specific magic the spell was intended to invoke. It would have been enormously expensive to build it in that manner, ignoring the typical requirements of construction and accepted methods of the trade of building, but only by doing so would the spell work, and work it did.

The spell was specific. It was a place of safety for any Rahl. It was meant to give a Rahl more power in the place, and to leach power away from anyone else who entered. Ann had never been in a place where she felt such a waning of her Han, the essence of life and the gift within. She doubted that in this place her Han would for long be vital enough to light a candle.

Ann's jaw dropped in astonishment as another element of the spell abruptly occurred to her. She looked out at the halls—part of the lines of the spell—filled with people.

Spells drawn with blood were always more effective and powerful. But when the blood soaked into the ground, decomposed, and dissipated, the power of the spell would often fade as well. But this spell, the drawn lines of the spell itself—the corridors—were filled with the vital living blood of all the people moving through them. Ann was struck dumb with awe at such a brilliant concept.

"So, you're renting a room, then."

Ann had forgotten the woman beside her, still staring at her, still holding the smile on her painted lips. Ann forced herself to close her mouth.

"Well . . ." Ann finally admitted, "I haven't actually made arrangements yet as to where I will sleep."

The woman's smile persisted, but it looked as if it was taking more and more effort all the time. "You can't curl up on a bench, you know. The guards won't allow it. You have to rent a room, or be put out at night."

Ann understood, then, what the woman was driving at. To these people, most dressed in their finest clothes for their visit to the palace, Ann must look like a beggar in their midst. After all the gossip about what people were wearing, this woman must have been disconcerted to find herself beside Ann.

"I have the price of a room," Ann assured her. "I just haven't found where they are yet, that's all. After such a long journey, I meant to go there right away and get myself cleaned up, but I just needed to rest my weary feet for a bit, first. Could you tell me where to find the rooms to rent?"

The smile looked a little easier. "I'm off to my own room and I could take you. It isn't far."

"That would be kind of you," Ann said as she rose now that she saw the guards moving off down the corridor.

The woman stood, bidding her two benchmates a good night.

If Ann was tired, it was only from being caught up in the afternoon devotion to the Lord Rahl. A bell in an open square had tolled, and everyone had moved to gather there and bow down. Ann had noticed then that no one missed the devotion. Guards moved among the crowd watching people gather. She felt like a mouse being watched by hawks so she joined with the other people moving toward the square.

She had spent nearly two hours on her knees, on a hard clay tile floor, bowed down with her forehead touching the ground like everyone else, repeating the devotion in concert with all the other somber voices.

Master Rahl guide us. Master Rahl teach us. Master Rahl protect us. In your light we thrive. In your mercy we are sheltered. In your wisdom we are humbled. We live only to serve. Our lives are yours.

Twice a day, those in the palace were expected to go to the devotion. Ann didn't know how people endured such torture.

Then she remembered the bond between the Lord Rahl and his people that prevented the dream walker from entering their minds, and she knew how they could endure it. She, herself, had briefly been a prisoner of Emperor Jagang. He had murdered a Sister right before her eyes, just to make a point.

In the face of brutality and torture, she guessed that she knew how people endured a mere devotion.

For her, though, such a spoken devotion to the Lord Rahl, to Richard, was hardly necessary. She had been devoted to him for nearly five hundred years before he had even been born.

Prophecy said that Richard was their only chance to avoid catastrophe. Ann peered carefully around the halls. Now she just needed the prophet himself.

"This way," the woman said, tugging at Ann's sleeve.

The woman gestured for Ann to follow her down a hallway to the right. Ann pulled her shawl forward, covering the pack she carried, and hugged her travel bag closer as she followed along the wide corridor. She wondered how many people sitting on benches and low marble walls around fountains were gossiping about her.

The floor had a dizzying pattern of dark brown, rust, and pale tan-colored stone running across the hall in zigzag lines meant to look three-dimensional. Ann had seen such traditional patterns before, down in the Old World, but none on this grand scale. It was a work of art, and it was but the floor. Everything about the palace was exquisite.

Shops were set back under a mezzanine to each side. Some of them looked to sell items travelers might want. There was a variety of small food and drink stands, everything from hot meat pies, to sweets, to ale, to warm milk. Some places sold nightclothes. Others sold hair ribbons. Even at this late hour, some of the shops were still open and doing brisk business. In a place such as this, there would be people who worked at night and would have need of such shops. The places that offered to do up a woman's hair, or paint her face, or promised to do wonders with her fingernails, were all closed until morning. Ann doubted they could pull off wonders with her.

The woman cleared her throat as they strolled down the broad corridor, gazing at the shops to each side. "And where have you traveled from?"

"Oh, far to the south. Very far." Ann took note of the woman's focused attention as she leaned in a bit. "My sister lives here," Ann said, giving the woman something more to chew on. "I'm here to visit my sister. She advises Lord Rahl on important matters."

The woman's eyebrows lifted. "Really! An advisor to Lord Rahl himself. What an honor for your family."

"Yes," Ann drawled. "We're all proud of her."

"What does she advise him on?"

"Advise him on? Oh, well, matters of war."

The woman's mouth fell open. "A woman? Advising Lord Rahl on warfare?"

"Oh yes," Ann insisted. She leaned over and whispered. "She's a sorceress. Sees into the future, you know. Why, she wrote me a letter and told me she saw me coming to the palace for a visit. Isn't that amazing?"

The woman frowned a bit. "Well, that does seem rather remarkable, since here you are and all."

"Yes, and she told me that I'd meet a helpful woman."

The woman's smile returned, it again looked forced. "She sounds to be quite talented."

"Oh, you have no idea," Ann insisted. "She is so specific in her forecasts about the future."

"Really? Had she anything else to say about your visit, then? Anything specific?"

"Oh yes indeed. Why, do you know that she told me I would meet a man when I came here?"

The woman's gaze flicked around the halls. "There are a lot of men here. That hardly seems very specific. Surely, she must have said more than that . . . I mean, if she is so talented, and an advisor to Lord Rahl and all."

Ann put a finger to her lip, frowning in feigned effort at recollection. "Why, yes, she did, now that you mention it. Let's see if I can remember . . ." Ann laid a hand on the woman's arm in a familiar manner. "She tells me about my future all the time. My sister is always telling me so many things about my future in her letters that I sometimes feel as if I'm having trouble catching up with my own life! I sometimes have trouble remembering it all."

"Oh do try," the woman said, eager for the gossip. "This is so fascinating."

Ann returned the finger to her lower lip as she gazed at the ceiling, pretending to be engaged in deep thought, and noticed for the first time that the ceiling was painted like the sky, with clouds and all. The effect was quite clever.

"Well," Ann finally said when she was sure she had the woman's full attention, "my sister said that the man I would meet was old." She returned the hand to the woman's arm. "But very distinguished. Not old and decrepit, but tall—very tall—with a full head of white hair that comes all the way down to his broad shoulders. She said that he would be clean-shaven, and that he would be ruggedly handsome, with penetrating dark azure eyes."

"Dark azure eyes . . . my, my," the woman tittered, "but he does sound handsome."

"And she said that when he looks at a woman with those hawklike eyes of his, their knees want to buckle."

"That is precise," the woman said, her face getting flushed. "Too bad she didn't know this handsome fellow's name."

"Oh, but she did. What kind of advisor to the Lord Rahl would she be if she wasn't talented enough to know such things?"

"She told his name, too? She can really do such tellings of the future?"

"Oh my, yes," Ann assured her.

She strolled along for a time, watching people making their way up and down the hall, stopping at some of the shops that were still open, or sitting on benches, gossiping.

"And?" the woman asked. "What is the name your sister foretold? The name of this tall distinguished gentleman."

Ann frowned up at the ceiling again. "It was N something. Nigel or Norris, or something. No, wait—that wasn't it." Ann snapped her finger and thumb. "The name she said was Nathan."

"Nathan," the woman repeated, looking almost as if she had been ready to pluck the name off Ann's tongue if she didn't spit it out. "Nathan."

"Yes, that's it. Nathan. Do you know anyone here at the palace by that name? Nathan? A tall fellow, older, with long white hair, broad shoulders, azure eyes?"

The woman peered up at the ceiling in thought. This time it was Ann leaning in, waiting for word, watching intently for any reaction.

A hand seized Ann's dress at her shoulder and brought her to an abrupt halt. Ann and the woman turned.

Behind them stood a very tall woman, with a very long blond braid, with very blue eyes, wearing a very dark scowl and an outfit of very red leather.

The woman beside Ann went as pale as vanilla pudding. Her mouth fell open. Ann forced her own mouth to stay shut.

"We've been expecting you," the woman in red leather said.

Behind her, back up the hallway a short distance, spread out to block the hall, stood a dozen perfectly huge men in perfect leather armor carrying perfectly polished swords, knives, and lances.

"Why, I think you must have me mistaken for—"

"I don't make mistakes."

Ann wasn't nearly as tall as the blond woman in red leather. She hardly came up past the yellow crescent and star across her stomach.

"No, I don't suppose you do. What's this about?" Ann asked, losing the timid innocent tone.

"Wizard Rahl wanted us to bring you in."

"Wizard Rahl?"

"Yes. Wizard Nathan Rahl."

Ann heard a gasp from the woman beside her. She thought the woman was going to faint, and so took hold of her arm.

"Are you all right, my dear?"

She stared, wide-eyed, at the woman in red leather glowering down at her. "Yes. I have to go. I'm late. I must go. Can I go?"

"Yes, you had better go," the tall blond said.

The woman dipped a quick bow and muttered "Good night" before scurrying off down the hall, looking over her shoulder only once.

Ann turned back to the scowl. "Well I'm glad you found me. Let's be off to see Nathan. Excuse me . . . Wizard Rahl."

"You won't be having an audience with Wizard Rahl."

"You mean, not tonight, I won't be having an . . . audience with him tonight."

Ann was being as polite as she could be, but she wanted to clobber that troublesome man, or wring his neck, and the sooner the better.

"My name is Nyda," the woman said.

"Pleased to meet—"

"Do you know what I am?" She didn't wait for Ann to answer. "I am Mord-Sith. I give you this one warning as a courtesy. It is the only warning, or courtesy, you will receive, so listen closely. You came here with hostile intent against Wizard Rahl. You are now my prisoner. Use of your magic against a Mord-Sith will result in the capture of that magic by me or one of my sister Mord-Sith and its use as a weapon against you. A very, very unpleasant weapon."

"Well," Ann said, "in this place my magic is not very useful, I'm afraid. Hardly worth a hoot, as a matter of fact. So, you see, I'm quite harmless."

"I don't care how useful you find your magic. If you try to so much as light a candle with it, your power will be mine."

"I see," Ann said.

"Don't believe me?" Nyda leaned down. "I encourage you to try to attack me. I haven't captured a sorceress's magic for quite a while. Might be . . . fun."

"Thank you, but I'm a bit too tired out—from my travels and all—to be attacking anyone just now. Maybe later?"

Nyda smiled. In that smile Ann could see why Mord-Sith were so feared. "Fine. Later, then."

"So, what is it you intend to do with me in the meantime, Nyda? Put me up in one of the palace's fine rooms?"

Nyda ignored the question and gestured with a tilt of her head. Two of the men a short way back up the hall rushed forward. They towered over Ann like two oak trees. Each grasped her under an arm.

"Let's go," Nyda said as she marched off down the hall ahead of them.

The men started out after her, pulling Ann along with them. Her feet seemed to touch the floor only every third or fourth step. People in the hall parted for the Mord-Sith. Passersby pressed themselves up against the walls to the side, a goodly distance away. Some people disappeared into the open shops, from where they peered out windows. Everyone stared at the squat woman in the dark dress being hauled along by the two palace guards in burnished leather and gleaming mail. Behind she could hear the jangle of metal gear as the rest of the men followed along.

They turned into a small hall to the side going back between columns holding a projecting balcony. One of the men rushed forward to unlock the door. Before she knew it, they'd all swept through the little door like wine through a funnel.

The corridor beyond was dark and cramped—nothing like the marble-lined hallways most people saw. Not far down the hall, they turned down a stairway. The oak treads creaked underfoot. Some of the men handed lanterns forward so Nyda could light her way. The sound of all the footsteps echoed back from the darkness below.

At the bottom of the steps, Nyda led them through a maze of dirty stone passageways. The seldom-used halls smelled musty, and in places damp. When they reached another stairwell, they continued down a square shaft with landings at each turn, descending into the dark recesses of the People's Palace. Ann wondered how many people in the past were taken by routes such as this, never to be seen again. Richard's father, Darken Rahl, and his father before him, Panis, were rather fond of torture. Life meant nothing to men such as those.

Richard had changed all that.

But Richard wasn't at the palace, now. Nathan was.

Ann had known Nathan for a very long time—for nearly a thousand years. For most of that time, as Prelate, she had kept him locked in his apartments. Prophets could not be allowed to roam free. Now, though, this one was free. And, worse, he had managed to establish his authority in the palace—the ancestral home of the House of Rahl. He was an ancestor to Richard. He was a Rahl. He was a wizard.

Ann's plan suddenly started to seem very foolish. Just catch the prophet off guard, she'd thought. Catch him off guard and snap a collar back around his neck. Surely, there would be an opening and he would be hers again.

It had seemed to make sense at the time.

At the bottom of the long descent, Nyda swept to the right, following a narrow walk with a stone wall soaring up on the right and an iron railing on the left. Ann gazed off over the railing, but the lantern light showed nothing but inky darkness below. She feared to think how far it might drop—not that she had any ideas of a battle with her captors, but she was beginning to worry that they just might heave her over the edge and be done with her.

Nathan had sent them, though. Nathan, as irascible as he could sometimes be, wouldn't order such a thing. Ann considered then, the centuries she had kept him locked away, considered the extreme measures it had sometimes taken to keep that incorrigible man under control. Ann glanced over the iron rail again, down into the darkness.

"Will Nathan be waiting for us?" she asked, trying to sound cheerful. "I'd really like to talk to him. We have business we must discuss."

Nyda shot a dark look back over her shoulder. "Nathan has nothing to talk to you about."

At an uncomfortably narrow passageway tunneling into the stone on the right, Nyda led them into the darkness. The way the woman rushed lent a frightening aspect to an already frightening journey.

Ann at last saw light up ahead. The narrow passageway emptied into a small area where several halls converged. Ahead and to the right they all funneled down steep stairs that twisted as they descended. As she was prodded down the stairs, Ann gripped the iron rail, fearful of losing her footing, although the big hand holding a fistful of her dress at her right shoulder would probably preclude any chance of falling, to say nothing of running off.

In the passageway at the bottom of the stairs, Nyda, Ann, and the guards came to a halt under the low-beamed ceiling. Wavering light from torches in floor stands gave the area a surreal look. The place stank of burning pitch, smoke, stale sweat and urine. Ann doubted that any fresh air ever penetrated this deep into the People's Palace.

She heard a hacking cough echoing from a dim corridor to the right. She peered into that dark hall and saw doors to either side. In some of the doors fingers gripped iron bars in small openings. Other than the coughing, no sound came from the cells holding hopeless men.

A big man in uniform waited before an iron-bound door to the left. He looked as if he might have been hewn from the same stone as the walls. Under different circumstances, Ann might have thought that he was a pleasant enough looking fellow.

"Nyda," the man said by way of greeting. When his eyes turned back up after a polite bow of his head, he asked in his deep voice, "What have we here?"

"A prisoner for you, Captain Lerner." Nyda seized the empty shoulder of Ann's dress and hauled her forward as if showing off a pheasant after a successful hunt. "A dangerous prisoner."

The captain's appraising gaze glided briefly over Ann before he returned his attention to Nyda. "One of the secure chambers, then."

Nyda nodded her approval. "Wizard Rahl doesn't want her getting out. He said she's no end of trouble."

At least half a dozen curt responses sprang to mind, but Ann held her tongue.

"You had better come with us, then," Captain Lerner said, "and see to her being locked in behind the shields."

Nyda tilted her head. Two of her men dashed forward and pulled torches from stands. The captain finally found the right key from a dozen or so he had on a ring. The lock sprang open with a strident clang that filled the surrounding low corridors. It sounded to Ann like a bell being tolled for the condemned.

With a grunt of effort, the captain tugged the heavy door, urging it to slowly swing open. In the long hallway beyond, Ann saw but a couple of candles bringing meager light to the small openings in doors to each side. Men began hooting and howling, like animals, calling vile curses at who might be entering their world. Arms reached out, clawing the air, hoping to net a touch of a passing person.

The two men with torches swept into the hall right behind Nyda, the firelight illuminating her in her red leather so all those faces pressed up against the openings in their doors could see her. Her Agiel, hanging on a fine chain at her wrist, spun up into her fist. She glared at the openings in the doors to each side. Filthy arms drew back in. Voices fell silent. Ann could hear men scurry to the far recesses of their cells.

Nyda, once certain there would be no misbehavior, started out again. Big hands shoved Ann ahead. Behind, Captain Lerner followed with his keys. Ann pulled the corner of her shawl over her mouth and nose, trying to block the sickening stench.

The captain took a small lamp from a recess, lit it from a candle to the side, and then stepped forward to unlock another door. In the low passageway beyond, the doors were spaced closer together. A hand covered with infected lesions hung limp out of one of the tiny openings to the side.

The hall beyond the next door was lower, and no wider than Ann's shoulders. She tried to slow her racing heart as she followed the rough, twisting passageway. Nyda and the men had to stoop, arms folded in, as they made their way.

"Here," Captain Lerner said as he came to a halt.

He held up his lantern and peered into the small opening in the door. On the second try, he found the right key and unlocked the door. He handed his small lamp to Nyda and then used both hands to pull the lever. He grunted and tugged with all his weight until the door grated partway open. He squeezed around the door and disappeared inside.

Nyda handed in the lamp as she followed the captain in. Her arm, sheathed in red leather, came back out to seize a fistful of Ann's dress and drag her in after.

The captain was opening a second door on the other side of the tiny room. Ann could sense that this was the room containing the shield. The second door grated open. Beyond was a room carved from solid bedrock. The only way out was through the door, and the outer room that contained the shield, and then the second door.

The House of Rahl knew how to build a secure dungeon.

Nyda's hand gripped Ann's elbow, commanding her into the room beyond. Even Ann, as short as she was, had to duck as she stepped over the high sill to get through the doorway. The only furniture inside was a bench carved from the stone of the far wall itself, providing both a seat and a bed off the floor. A tin ewer full of water sat on one end of the bench. At the opposite end was a single, folded, brown blanket. There was a chamber pot in the corner. At least it was empty, if not clean.

Nyda set the lamp on the bench. "Nathan said to leave you this."

Obviously it was a luxury the other guests weren't afforded.

Nyda stepped one leg over the sill, but paused when Ann called her name.

"Please give Nathan a message for me? Please? Tell him that I would like to see him. Tell him that it's important."

Nyda smiled to herself. "He said you would say those words. Nathan is a prophet, I guess he would know what you would say."

"And will you give him that message?"

Nyda's cold blue eyes looked to be weighing Ann's soul. "Nathan said to tell you that he has a whole palace to run, and can't come running down to see you every time you clamor for him."

Those were almost the exact words she had sent down to Nathan's apartments countless times when a Sister had come to her with Nathan's demands to see the Prelate. *Tell Nathan that I have a whole palace to run and I can't go running down there every time he bellows for me. If he has had a prophecy, then write it down and I will look it over when I have the time.*

Until that moment, Ann had never truly realized how cruel her words had been.

Nyda pulled the door shut behind her. Ann was alone in a prison she knew she could not escape.

At least she was near the end of her life, and could not be held as a prisoner for nearly her entire life, as she had held Nathan prisoner for his.

Ann rushed to the little window. "Nyda!"

The Mord-Sith turned back from the second door, from beyond the shield Ann could not cross. "Yes?"

"Tell Nathan . . . tell Nathan that I'm sorry."

Nyda let out a brief laugh. "Oh, I think Nathan knows you're sorry."

Ann thrust her arm through the door, reaching toward the woman. "Nyda, please. Tell him . . . tell Nathan that I love him."

Nyda stared at her a long moment before she pushed the outer door closed.

CHAPTER 21

Kahlan lifted her head. She gently laid a hand on Richard's chest as she turned her ear toward the sound she'd heard off in the darkness. Beneath her hand, Richard's chest rose and fell with his labored breathing, but, even at that, she felt relief—he was still alive. As long as he was alive she could fight to find a solution. She wouldn't give him up. They would get to Nicci. Somehow, they would get to her.

A quick glance to the position of the quarter moon told her that she'd been asleep less than an hour. Clouds, silvery in the moonlight, had silently begun streaming in from the north. In the distant sky she saw, too, the moonlit wings of the black-tipped races that always trailed them.

She hated those birds. The races had been following them ever since Cara had touched the statue of Kahlan that Nicci said was a warning beacon. Those dark wings were never far, like the shadow of death, always following, always waiting.

Kahlan recalled all too well the sand in that hourglass statue trickling out. Her time was running out. She had no actual indication of what would happen when the time that sand had represented finally ran out—but she could imagine well enough.

The place where they had set up camp, before a sharp rise of rock with a stand of bristlecone pine and thorny brush to one side, wasn't as protected or tenable a camp as any of them would have liked, but Cara had confided that she was afraid that if they didn't stop, Richard wouldn't live the night.

That whispered warning had set Kahlan's heart to pounding,

brought cold sweat to her brow, and swept her to the verge of panic.

She had known that the rough wagon ride, slow as it had been while they made their way across open country in the dark, seemed to have made it more difficult for Richard to breathe. Less than two hours after they had started out, after Cara's warning, they'd been forced to stop. After they had stopped, they were all relieved that Richard's breathing became more even, and sounded a little less labored.

They needed to make it to roads so that traveling would be easier on Richard, and so they could make better time. Maybe after he rested the night, they could make swifter progress.

She had to fight constantly to tell herself that they would get him there, that they had a chance, and that the journey's purpose wasn't merely empty hope meant to forestall the truth.

The last time Kahlan had felt this helpless, felt this sense of Richard's life slipping away, she'd at least had one solid chance available to her to save him. She'd had no idea, at the time, that that one chance taken would be the catalyst which would initiate a cascade of events which would begin the disintegration of magic itself.

She was the one who had made the decision to take that chance, and she was the one responsible for all that was now coming to pass. Had she known what she now knew, she would have made the same decision—to save Richard's life—but that made her no less liable for the consequences.

She was the Mother Confessor, and, as such, was responsible for protecting the lives of those with magic, of creatures of magic. And, instead, she might very well be the cause of their end.

Kahlan sprang to her feet, sword in hand, when she heard Cara's whistled birdcall to alert them to her return. It was a birdcall Richard had taught her.

Kahlan slid the shutter on the lantern open all the way to provide more light. She saw Tom, hand resting on the silver-handled knife at his belt, rise from the nearby rock where he'd been sitting as he watched over both the camp and the man Kahlan had touched with her power. The man still lay on the ground at Tom's feet where Kahlan had ordered him to stay.

"What is it?" Jennsen whispered as she appeared at Kahlan's side, hastily rubbing the sleep from her eyes.

"I'm not sure, yet. Cara signaled, so she must have someone with her."

Cara walked in out of the darkness, and, as Kahlan had suspected, she was pushing a man ahead of her. Kahlan frowned, trying to recall where she'd seen him before. She blinked, then, realizing it was the young man they had come across a week or so back—Owen.

"I tried to get to you sooner!" Owen cried out when he saw Kahlan. "I swear, I tried."

Holding him by the shoulder of his light coat, Cara marched the man closer, then yanked him to a halt in front of Kahlan.

"What are you talking about?" Kahlan asked.

When Owen caught sight of Jennsen standing behind Kahlan's shoulder, he paused with his mouth hanging open for an instant before he answered.

"I meant to get to you earlier, I swear," he said to Kahlan, sounding on the verge of tears. "I went to your camp." He clutched his light coat closed at his chest as he began to tremble. "I, I saw . . . I saw all the . . . remains. Dear Creator, how could you be so brutal?"

Kahlan thought Owen looked like he might throw up. He covered his mouth and closed his eyes as he shook.

"If you mean all those men," Kahlan said, "they tried to capture us, to kill us. We didn't collect them from their rocking chairs beside their hearths and bring them out into this wasteland where we slaughtered them. They attacked us; we defended ourselves."

"But, dear Creator, how could you . . ." Owen stood before her, unable to control his shivering. He closed his eyes. "Nothing is real. Nothing is real. Nothing is real." He repeated it over and over, as if it were an incantation meant to protect him from evil.

Cara forcibly dragged Owen back a bit and sat him down on a shelf of rock. Eyes closed meditatively, he mumbled "Nothing is real" to himself continually while Cara took up a position to the left side of Kahlan.

"Tell us what you're doing here," Cara commanded in a low growl. Although she didn't say it, the "or else" was clear enough.

"And be quick about it," Kahlan said. "We have enough trouble and we don't need you added on top of it."

Owen opened his eyes. "I went to your camp to tell you about it, but . . . all those bodies . . ."

"We know about what happened back there. Now, tell us why you're here." Kahlan was at the end of her patience. "I'm not going to ask you again."

"Lord Rahl," Owen wailed, tears bursting forth at last.

"Lord Rahl what?" Kahlan demanded through gritted teeth.

"Lord Rahl has been poisoned," he blurted out as he wept.

Gooseflesh prickled up Kahlan's legs. "How can you possibly know such a thing is true?"

Owen stood, clutching twisted wads of his coat at his chest. "I know," he cried, "because I'm the one who poisoned him."

Could it be? Could it be that it wasn't really the runaway power of the gift killing Richard, but poison? Could it be that they had it all wrong? Could it be that it was all caused by this man poisoning Richard?

Kahlan felt her sword's hilt slip from her fingers as she started for the man.

He stood watching her come, like a fawn watching a mountain lion about to leap.

Kahlan knew there was something strange about this man. Richard, too, had thought there was something unsettling about him, something not quite right.

Somehow, this quaking stranger had poisoned Richard.

Richard barely hung on to life. He was suffering and in pain. This man had been the cause of it all. Kahlan would know why, and she would know the truth of it.

Kahlan closed the distance quickly. She would not risk his escape. She would not risk his lies.

She would have his confession.

Her hand started coming up toward him. Her power was recovered—she could feel it there, in the core of her being, at the ready.

This man had tried to kill Richard. She intended to find out if there was a way to save him. This man could tell her.

She committed herself to taking him.

It was not necessary for Kahlan to invoke her birthright, but merely to withdraw her restraint of it. Her feelings about what this man had done faded away; they no longer mattered in this. Only the truth would serve her now. She was a being of raw commitment.

He had no chance. He was hers.

She saw him standing frozen, watching her come, saw his blue eyes widen, saw the tears running down his cheeks. Kahlan felt the cold coil of power straining for release, demanding to be freed. As her hand rose toward this man who had harmed Richard, she wanted nothing so much as what she would have.

He was hers.

Cara abruptly jumped in between them.

Kahlan's sight of the man was blocked by the Mord-Sith. Kahlan tried to brush Cara aside, but she was ready and firmly held her ground. Cara seized Kahlan by the shoulders and forced her back three paces.

"No. Mother Confessor, no."

Kahlan was still focused on Owen, even if she couldn't see him. "Get out of my way."

"No. Stop."

"Move!" Kahlan tried to shove Cara aside, but the woman had her feet spread and couldn't be budged. "Cara!"

"No. Listen to me."

"Cara, get out of—"

She shook Kahlan so hard that Kahlan thought her neck would snap. "Listen to me!"

Kahlan panted in rage. "What?"

"Wait until you hear what he says. He came here for a reason. When he finishes, you can use your power if you want, or you can let me make him scream until the moon covers its ears, but first we need to hear what he says."

"I'll find out soon enough what he says, and I'll know the truth. When I touch him he will confess every detail."

"And if Lord Rahl dies as a result? Lord Rahl's life is hanging in the balance. We must think of that first."

"I am. Why do you think I'm going to do this?"

Cara pulled Kahlan close to hear her whisper. "And what if using your power on this man kills him for some reason we don't yet even know about? Remember when we didn't know everything in the past? Remember Marlin Pickard announcing he had come to assassinate Richard? It was too easy then, and it's too easy this time.

"What if your touching this man is someone's design?—a trick, with this man sent as bait of some sort? What if they want you to do it for some reason? What if you do what they intend you to do— then what? It won't be a simple mistake that we can work to fix. If Lord Rahl dies we can't bring him back."

Cara's fierce blue eyes were wet. Her powerful fingers dug into Kahlan's shoulders. "What can it hurt to hear him first, before you touch him? You can then touch him, if you still think it's necessary— but hear him first. Mother Confessor, as a sister of the Agiel, I'm asking you, please, for the sake of Lord Rahl's life, wait."

More than anything, it was Cara's reluctance to use force that gave Kahlan pause. If there was anyone who would be more than willing to use physical force to protect Richard, it was Cara.

In the dim light of the lantern, Kahlan studied the emotion in Cara's expression. Despite everything Cara said, Kahlan didn't know if she could afford to take the chance, to hesitate.

"What if it's a stab in the dark?" Jennsen asked from behind.

Kahlan glanced back over her shoulder at Richard's sister, at the worry on her face.

Kahlan had made a mistake before in not acting quickly enough, and it resulted in Richard being captured and taken from her. Then it was his freedom; this time it was his life at stake.

She knew that while hesitation had been a mistake in that instance, that didn't mean that immediate action was always right.

She looked back into Cara's eyes. "All right. We'll hear what he has to say." With a thumb, she brushed a tear from Cara's cheek, a tear of terror for Richard, a tear of terror at the thought of losing him. "Thanks," Kahlan whispered.

Cara nodded and released her. She turned and folded her arms, fixing Owen in her glare.

"You had better not make me sorry for stopping her."

Owen peered about at all the faces watching him—Friedrich, Tom, Jennsen, Cara, Kahlan, and even the man Kahlan had touched, lying on the ground not far away.

"In the first place, how could you possibly have poisoned Richard?" Kahlan asked.

Owen licked his lips, fearful of telling her, even though that was apparently why he had returned. His gaze finally broke toward the ground.

"When I saw the dust rising from the wagon, and I knew that I was near, I dumped out what water I had left, so it would appear I had none. Then, when Lord Rahl found me, I asked for a drink. When he gave me his waterskin so I could have a drink, I put poison in it, just before I handed it back. I was relieved that you had showed up, too. It was my intention to poison both Lord Rahl and you, Mother Confessor, but you had your own water and didn't take a drink when he offered it to you. But I guess it doesn't matter. This will work just as well."

Kahlan couldn't make sense of such a confession. "So you intended to kill us both, but you were only able to poison Richard."

"Kill . . . ?" Owen looked up in shock at the very idea. He shook his head emphatically. "No, no, nothing like that. Mother Confessor, I tried to get to you earlier, but those men went to your camp before I got there. I needed to get the antidote to Lord Rahl."

"I see. You wanted to save him—after you'd poisoned him—but when you got to our camp, we'd gone."

His eyes filled with tears again. "It was so awful. All the bodies— the blood. I've never see such brutal murder." He covered his mouth.

"It would have been murder—our murder," Kahlan said, "had we not defended ourselves."

Owen seemed not to hear her. "And you were gone—you'd left. I didn't know where you'd gone. It was hard to follow your wagon's trail in the dark, but I had to. I had to run, to catch up with you. I was afraid the races would get me, but I knew I had to reach you tonight. I couldn't wait. I was afraid, but I had to come."

The whole story was nonsense to Kahlan.

"So you're like one of those people who starts a fire, calls out an alarm, and then helps put it out—all so you can be a hero."

Startled, Owen shook his head. "No, no, nothing like that. Nothing like that at all—I swear. I hated doing it. I did. I hated it."

"Then why did you poison him?"

Owen twisted his light coat in his fists as tears trickled down his cheeks. "Mother Confessor, we have to give him the antidote, now, or he will die. It's already so very late." He clasped his hands prayerfully and gazed skyward. "Dear Creator, let it not be too late, please." He reached out for Kahlan, as if to urgently beg her as well, to assure her of his sincerity, but at the look on her face, drew back. "There's no more time, Mother Confessor. I tried to get to you earlier—I swear. If you don't let him have the remedy now, it will be the end of him. It will all be for naught—everything, all of it, all for nothing!"

Kahlan didn't know if she dared trust in such an offer. It made no sense to poison a man and then save him.

"Where's the antidote?" she asked.

"Here." Owen hurriedly pulled a small vial from a pocket inside his coat. "Here it is. Please, Mother Confessor." He held the square-sided vessel out toward her. "He must have this now. Please, hurry, or he will die."

"Or this will finish him," Kahlan said.

"If I wanted to finish him, I could have done so when I slipped the poison into his waterskin. I could have used more of it, or I could simply not have come with the antidote. I'm not a killer, I swear—that's why I had to come in the first place."

Owen wasn't making a whole lot of sense. Kahlan wasn't confident in such an offer. It was Richard's life that would be forfeit if she chose wrong.

"I say we give Richard Owen's antidote," Jennsen whispered.

"A stab in the dark?" Kahlan asked.

"You said that there were times when there is no choice but to act immediately, but even then it must be with your best judgment, using all your experience and everything you do know. Earlier, in the wagon, I heard Cara tell you that she didn't know if Richard would live the night. Owen says he has an antidote. I think this is one of those times we must act."

"If it means anything," Tom offered in a confidential tone, "I'd have to agree. I don't see as there really is any choice. But if you have an alternative that might save Lord Rahl, I think now would be the time to add it to the stew."

Kahlan didn't have any alternative, except getting to Nicci, and that was looking more and more like an empty hope.

"Mother Confessor," Friedrich offered in a hushed tone, "I agree as well. I think you should know that if you let him have the remedy, would all be in agreement that it was the best choice to be made."

If the antidote killed Richard, they wouldn't blame her. That was what he was saying.

Jennsen stepped toward Owen, pulling Betty along with her. "If you're lying about this being an antidote, you will have to answer to me, and to Cara, and then to the Mother Confessor—if there's even anything left of you by then. You do understand that, don't you?"

Owen shrank from her, his head turned away, as he nodded vigorously, apparently fearing to look up at her, or at Betty. Kahlan thought that he looked more afraid of Jennsen than of any of the rest of them.

Cara leaned toward Kahlan and whispered. "He has to have an antidote. What purpose would it be to place himself in danger of all we'll do to him if he's lying? Why even come back here, if he only wanted to poison Lord Rahl? He had already poisoned him and gotten away. Mother Confessor, I say that we give Lord Rahl the antidote, and we do it quickly."

"Then why poison him in the first place?" Kahlan whispered back. "If you intend to give a man the antidote, then why poison him?"

Cara let out a frustrated sigh. "I don't know. But right now, if Lord Rahl dies . . ."

Cara's words trailed off at the unthinkable.

Kahlan looked over at Richard lying unconscious. She went weak at the thought of him never waking. How could she live in a world without Richard?

"How much do we give him?" she asked Owen.

Owen rushed forward, past Jennsen. "All of it. Make him drink it all down." He pressed the small, square-sided bottle into Kahlan's hands. "Hurry. Please hurry."

"You've hurt him," Kahlan said with unrestrained menace. "Your poison hurt him. He's been coughing up blood, and he passed out from the pain. If you think I'll ever forget that and be pleased with you for now returning to save his life, you're wrong."

Owen nervously licked his lips. "But I tried to get to you. I was bringing you the antidote so that wouldn't happen. I never intended him such pain. I tried to get to you—but you slaughtered all those men."

"So, it's our fault, then?"

Owen smiled just a bit as he nodded, a small smile of satisfaction that she'd finally seen the light and at last understood that it wasn't his fault at all, but their own.

While Jennsen watched Owen, keeping him back out of the way, Tom watched the man Kahlan had touched, and Friedrich watched Betty, Kahlan and Cara knelt and lifted Richard so they could try to get him to drink the antidote. Cara propped his back against her thigh while Kahlan cradled his head in her arm.

She pulled the stopper with her teeth and spit out the cork. Careful not to spill and waste any of the antidote, she put the bottle to his lips and tipped it up. She watched it wet his lips. She tilted his head back more, so that his mouth would fall open a bit, and tipped the bottle some more. Carefully, she let some of the clear liquid dribble into his mouth.

Kahlan didn't know if what was in the bottle really was an antidote. It was colorless and looked to her just like water. As Richard smacked his lips a little, swallowing what she had poured in his mouth, Kahlan smelled the bottle. The liquid had the slight aroma of cinnamon.

She dribbled more of it into Richard's mouth. He coughed, but then swallowed. Cara used a finger to swipe up a drop that ran down his chin and return it to his mouth.

Kahlan, her heart pounding with worry, poured the rest of the liquid past his lips. Holding the empty bottle between her thumb and first finger, she used the palm of her hand to push Richard's jaw up, forcing his head back, forcing him to swallow.

She sighed with relief when he swallowed several times, taking all the cure. At least she'd been able to get him to swallow it.

Carefully, Kahlan and Cara laid Richard back down. As Cara stood, Owen rushed forward.

"Did you give him all of it? Did he drink it all?"

Cara's Agiel spun into her fist. As Owen, in his exuberance to get to Richard, charged forward, Cara rammed it into his shoulder.

Owen tottered back a step. "I'm sorry." He rubbed his shoulder where Cara had jabbed her Agiel into him. "I only wanted to see how he is. I don't mean any harm. I want him to be well, I swear."

Kahlan stared in astonishment. Cara glanced down at her Agiel, then at Owen.

Her Agiel hadn't worked on him. He wasn't affected by magic.

Even Jennsen was staring at Owen. He was just like her—a pillar of Creation, born pristinely ungifted and unaffected by magic. While Jennsen understood what that meant, it didn't seem that Owen did. He had no idea that Cara had done anything more than poke him good and hard to get him to stand back.

Her Agiel should have dropped him to his knees.

"Richard drank all the antidote. Now it must do its work. In the meantime, I think we had better get some sleep." Kahlan gestured with a tilt of her head. "See to the watches, would you, Cara? I'll stay with Richard."

Cara nodded. She gave Tom a look, which he understood.

"Owen," Tom said, "why don't you come over by me and spend the night over here, with this fellow."

Owen blanched at the look on the face of the big D'Haran, and understood that he wasn't being offered a choice. "Yes, all right." He turned back to Kahlan. "I'll pray that he got the antidote in time. I'll pray for him."

"Pray for yourself," she said.

When everyone had gone, Kahlan lay down beside Richard. Now that she was alone with him, tears of worry finally began to seep out. Richard was shivering with cold, even though it was a warm night. She drew the blanket back up around him and then put her hand on his shoulder as she cuddled close, not knowing if when the new day came he would still be with her.

CHAPTER 22

Richard opened his eyes, only to squint at the light, even though it was far from sunny. By the layered streaks of violet tinting the iron gray sky, it appeared to be just dawn. A heavy overcast hung low overhead. Or it could be sunset—he wasn't really sure. He felt strangely disoriented.

The dull throbbing in his head ached back down through his neck. His chest burned with every breath he drew. His throat was raw. It hurt to swallow.

The heavy pain, though, the pain that had squeezed so hard it had taken his breath and had made the world go black, seemed to have ebbed. The bone-chilling grip of cold had lifted, too.

Richard felt as if he had lost contact with the world for a time— how long a time he didn't know. It seemed like it had been an eternity, as if the world of life was a distant memory from his past. He also felt as if he had come close to never waking again. It brought a flash of sweat to his brow to feel that he had been close to losing his life, to realize that he might never have awakened.

The surroundings were different to those he remembered. Close by, a wall of straw-colored rock with sharp fractured edges rose nearly straight up. To the side he saw a stand of twisted bristlecone pine. Pale, bare wood stood out in naked relief where sections of dark bark had peeled open. The imposing mountains loomed closer than he remembered, and there were more trees on the slopes of the nearby hills.

Jennsen lay curled up in a blanket beside Betty, her back against the rear wheel of the wagon. Tom was asleep not too far away right beside his draft horses. Friedrich sat on a rock standing watch. Richard couldn't make sense of the two men who lay at Friedrich's feet. Richard thought one of them must be the man Kahlan had touched with her power. The other one, though, he wasn't sure of, although Richard thought there was something familiar about him.

Kahlan was sound asleep up against him. His sword lay on his other side, close by his hand. On the other side of Kahlan lay her sword, sheathed, but at the ready.

All the Seekers who had used the Sword of Truth before Richard, the good and the evil, had left within the sword's magic the essence of their skill. By mastering the sword as the true Seeker for whom the makers of the sword intended its power, Richard had learned to tap that ability and make it his own, to draw on all the skill and knowledge of those before him. He had become a master of the blade, in more ways than one, and part of that had come from the blade itself.

Kahlan had been taught to use a sword by her father, King Wyborn Amnell, once king of Galea before Kahlan's mother had taken him for her mate. Richard had completed Kahlan's training, teaching her how to use a sword in ways she had never been shown, ways that used her size and speed to her best advantage, rather than fighting like the enemy and depending on strength.

Despite his pounding head, and the pain when he drew a breath, the warm feel of Kahlan against his side brought him a smile. She looked so beautiful, even with her hair all in a tangle. She made his heart ache with longing. He had always loved her long beautiful hair. He loved to watch her sleep almost as much as he loved to gaze into her arresting green eyes. He loved to make her hair a tangled mess.

He remembered, back when he had first met her, watching her sleep on the floor of Adie's home, watching her slow heartbeat in the vein in her neck. He remembered, as he'd watched, being struck by the life in her. She was just so alive, so passionately filled with life. He couldn't stop smiling as he looked at her.

Gently, he bent and kissed the top of her head. She stirred, nuzzling up tighter to him.

Suddenly, she jerked upright, sitting on a hip as she stared wide-eyed at him.

"Richard!"

She threw herself down beside him, her head on his shoulder, her arm across his chest. She clutched him for dear life. A single gasp of a sob that terrified him with its forlorn misery escaped her throat.

"I'm all right," he soothed as he smoothed her hair.

She pushed herself up again, slower, gazing at him as if she hadn't seen him in an eternity. Her special smile, the one she gave only him, spread incandescent across her face.

"Richard . . ." She seemed only able to stare at him and smile.

Richard, still lying back trying to let his head clear, lifted an arm just enough to point. "Who is that?"

Kahlan looked back over her shoulder. She turned back and took up Richard's hand.

"Remember that fellow a week or so back? Owen? That's him."

"I thought I recognized him."

"Lord Rahl!" Cara dropped to the ground on the side of him opposite Kahlan. "Lord Rahl . . ."

She, too, seemed to have trouble finding words. Instead, she took up his free hand. That, in itself, said a world to him.

Richard took the hand back, kissed his first two fingers and touched the fingers to her cheek.

"Thanks for watching out for everyone."

Jennsen hobbled over, the blanket still tangled around her legs. "Richard! The antidote worked! It worked, dear spirits it worked!"

Richard rose up onto an elbow. "Antidote?" He frowned at the three women around him. "Antidote to what?"

"You were poisoned," Kahlan told him. She aimed a thumb back over her shoulder. "Owen. When he came to us the first time, you gave him a drink. In thanks, he put poison in your waterskin. He intended to poison me with it, too, but only you drank it."

Richard's glare settled on the men at Friedrich's feet, watching them. He nodded his confirmation that it was true, as if he should be commended for it.

"One of those little mistakes," Jennsen said.

Richard puzzled at her. "What?"

"You said that even you made mistakes, and even a little one could cause big trouble. Don't you remember? Cara said you were always making mistakes, especially simple ones, and that's why you need her around." Jennsen flashed him a teasing smile. "I guess she was right."

Richard didn't correct the story, but said, as he stood, "It just goes to show how you can be taken by surprise by something as simple as that fellow over there."

Kahlan was watching Owen. "I have a suspicion he isn't so simple."

Cara put her arm out for Richard to grab hold of in order to steady himself.

"Cara," he said as he had to sit down on a nearby crate from the wagon, "bring him over here, would you?"

"Gladly," she said as she started across their camp. "Don't forget to tell him about Owen," Cara said to Kahlan.

"Tell me what?"

Kahlan leaned close as she watched Cara haul Owen to his feet. "Owen is pristinely ungifted—like Jennsen."

Richard raked his hair back, trying to make sense of it. "Are you saying that he's also my half brother?"

Kahlan shrugged. "We don't know that; we know only that he's pristinely ungifted." A wrinkle of puzzlement tightened on her brow. "By the way, back at the camp where those men attacked us, you were about to tell me something important you figured out when we were questioning the man that I touched, but you never got the chance."

"Yes"—Richard squinted, trying to recall what the man had told them—"it was about the one he said gave the orders sending him to capture us: Nicholas . . . Nicholas something."

"The Slide," Kahlan reminded him. "Nicholas the Slide."

"Right. Nicholas told him where to find us—at the eastern edge of the wasteland, heading north. How could he know?"

Kahlan mulled over the question. "Come to think of it, how could he know? We've seen no one, at least no one we were aware of, who could have reported where we were. Even if someone had seen us, by the time they reported our position and Nicholas sent the men, we would have been far from here. Unless Nicholas is close."

"The races," Richard said. "It has to be that he's the one watching us through the races. We've seen no one else. That's the only way anyone could have known where we were. This Nicholas the Slide had to have seen us, to have seen where we were, through those birds that have been shadowing us. That's how he was able to give our location along with the orders."

Richard rose as the man approached.

"Lord Rahl," Owen said, arms spread in a gesture of relief as he scurried forward, Cara holding a fistful of his coat at his shoulder to keep him reined in. "I'm so relieved you're better. I never meant for the poison to hurt you as it did—and it never would have, had you had the antidote sooner. I tried to get to you sooner—I meant to—I swear I did, but all those men you slaughtered . . . it wasn't my fault." He added a small smile to the pleading expression he gave Kahlan. "The Mother Confessor knows, she understands."

Kahlan folded her arms as she looked up at Richard from under her frown. "It's our fault, you see, that Owen didn't make it to us sooner with the antidote to the poison. Owen got to our last camp, intending to hand over the antidote to cure you, only to find that we had murdered all those men and then up and left. So, it's not his fault—his intentions were good and he tried; we spoiled his effort. Very inconsiderate of us."

Richard stared, not sure if Kahlan was giving him a sarcastic summation of what Owen had told her, or an accurate portrayal of Owen's excuse, or if his head still wasn't clear.

Richard's mood turned as dark as the thick overcast.

"You poisoned me," he said to Owen, wanting to be sure he had the man's story straight, "and then you brought an antidote to where we were camped, but when you got to that camp, you came across the men who had attacked us and you found we had gone."

"Yes." His cheer that Richard had it right abruptly faded. "Such savagery from the unenlightened is to be expected, of course." Owen's blue eyes filled with tears. "But still, it was so . . ." He hugged himself and closed his eyes as he rocked his weight from side to side, from one foot to the other. "Nothing is real. Nothing is real. Nothing is real."

Richard seized the man's shirt at his throat and yanked him closer. "What do you mean, nothing is real?"

Owen paled before Richard's glare. "Nothing is real. We can't know if what we see, if anything, is real or not. How could we?"

"If you see it, then how can you possibly think it isn't real?"

"Because our senses all the time distort the truth of reality and deceive us. Our senses only delude us into the illusion of certainty. We can't see at night—our sight tells us that the night is empty— but an owl can snatch up a mouse that with our eyes we couldn't sense was there. Our reality says the mouse didn't exist—yet we know it must, in spite of what our vision tells us—that another reality exists outside our experience. Our sight, rather than revealing truth, hides the truth from us—worse, it gives us a false idea of reality.

"Our senses deceived us. Dogs can smell a world of things we can't, because our senses are so limited. How can a dog track something we can't smell, if our senses tell us what is real and what isn't? Our understanding of reality, rather than being enhanced by, is instead limited by, our flawed senses.

"Our bias causes us to mistakenly think we know what is unknowable—don't you see? We aren't equipped with adequate senses to know the true nature of reality, what is real and what isn't. We only know a tiny sampling of the world around us. There is a whole world hidden from us, a whole world of mysteries we don't see—but it's there just the same, whether we see it or not, whether we have the wisdom to admit our inadequacies to the task of knowing reality, or not. What we think we know is actually unknowable. Nothing is real."

Richard leaned down. "You saw those bodies because they were real."

"What we see is only an apparent reality, mere appearances, a self-imposed illusion, all based on our flawed perception. Nothing is real."

"You didn't like what you saw, so you choose, instead, to say it isn't real?"

"I can't say what's real. Neither can you. To say otherwise is unenlightened arrogance. A truly enlightened man admits his woeful ineffectiveness when confronting his existence."

Richard pulled Owen closer. "Such whimsy can only bring you to a life of misery and quaking fear, a life wasted and never really lived. You had better start using your mind for its true purpose of knowing the world around you, instead of abandoning it to faith in irrational notions. With me, you will confine yourself to the facts of the world we live in, not fanciful daydreams as concocted by others."

Jennsen tugged on Richard's sleeve, pulling him back to hear her as she whispered. "Richard, what if Owen is right—not necessarily about the bodies, but about the general idea?"

"You mean you think his conclusions are all wrong, and yet, somehow, the convoluted idea behind them must be right?"

"Well, no—but what if what he says really is true? After all, look at you and me. Remember the conversation we had a while back, the one where you were explaining how I was born without eyes to see"—she glanced briefly at Owen and apparently abbreviated what she had intended to say—"certain things. Remember that you said that, for me, such things don't exist? That reality is different for me? That my reality is different from yours?"

"You're getting what I said wrong, Jennsen. When most people get into a patch of poison ivy, they blister and itch. Some rare people don't. That doesn't mean the poison ivy doesn't exist or, more to the point, that its existence depends on whether or not we think it's there."

Jennsen pulled him even closer. "Are you so sure? Richard, you don't know what it's like to be different to everyone else, to not see and feel what they do. You say there's magic, but I can't see it, or feel it. It doesn't touch me. Am I to believe you on faith, when my senses say it doesn't exist? Maybe because of that I can understand a little better what Owen means. Maybe he doesn't have it all wrong. It makes a person wonder what's real and what's not, and if, like he says, it's only your own point of view."

"The information our senses give us must be taken in context. If I close my eyes the sun doesn't stop shining. When I go to sleep I'm consciously unaware of anything; that doesn't mean that the world ceases to exist. You have to use the information from your senses in context with what you've learned to be true about the nature of things. Things don't change because of the way we think about them. What is, is."

"But, like he says, if we don't experience something with our own senses, then how can we know it's real?"

Richard folded his arms. "I can't get pregnant. So would you argue that for me women don't exist?"

Jennsen backed away, looking a little sheepish. "I guess not."

"Now," Richard said, turning back to Owen, "you poisoned me—you admit that much." He tapped his fist against his own chest. "It hurts in here; that's real. You caused it.

"I want to know why, and I want to know why you brought the antidote. I'm not interested in what you think of the camp where the men who attacked us lay dead. Confine yourself to the matter at hand. You brought the antidote for the poison you gave me. That can't be the end of it. What's the rest?"

"Well," Owen stammered, "I didn't want you to die, that's why I saved you."

"Stop telling me your feelings about what you did and tell me instead what you did and why. Why poison me, and why then save me? I want the answer to that, and I want the truth."

Owen glanced around at the grim faces watching him. He took a breath as if to gather his composure.

"I needed your help. I had to convince you to help me. I asked, before, for your help and you refused, even though my people have great need. I begged. I told you how important it was for them to have your help, but you still said no."

"I have my own problems I must deal with," Richard said. "I'm sorry the Order invaded your homeland—I know how terrible that is—but I told you, I'm trying to bring them down and our doing so will only help you and your people in your effort to rid yourselves of them. You aren't the only one who has had their home invaded by those brutes. We have men of the Order murdering our loved ones as well."

"You must help us, first," Owen insisted. "You and those like you, the unenlightened ones, must free my people. We can't do it ourselves—we are not savages. I heard what you all had to say about eating meat. Such talk made me ill. Our people are not like that— we can't be, because we are enlightened. I saw how you murdered all those men back there. I need you to do that to the Order."

"I thought that wasn't real?"

Owen ignored the question. "You must give my people freedom."

"I already told you, I can't!"

"Now, you must." He looked at Cara, Jennsen, Tom, and Friedrich. His gaze settled on Kahlan. "You must see to it that Lord Rahl does this—or he will die. I have poisoned him."

Kahlan seized Owen's shirt. "You brought him the antidote to the poison."

Owen nodded. "That first night, when I told you all of my great need, I had just given him the poison." His gaze returned to Richard. "You had just drunk it, within hours. Had you agreed to give my people the freedom they need, I would have given you the antidote then, and you would be free of the poison. It would have cured you.

"But you refused to come with me, to help those who cannot help themselves, as is your duty to those in need. You sent me away. So, I did not offer you the antidote. In the time since, the poison has worked its way through your body. Had you not been selfish, you would have been cured back then.

"Instead, the poison is now established in you, doing its work. Since it was so long since you drank the poison, the antidote I had with me was no longer enough to cure you, only to make you better for a while."

"And what will cure me?" Richard asked.

"You will have to have more of the antidote to rid you of the rest of the poison."

"And I don't suppose you have any more."

Owen shook his head. "You must give my people freedom. Only then, will you be able to get more of the antidote."

Richard wanted to shake the answers out of the man. Instead, he took a breath, trying to stay calm so that he could understand the truth of what Owen had done and then think of the solution.

"Why only then?" he asked.

"Because," Owen said, "the antidote is in the place taken by the Imperial Order. You must rid us of the invaders if you are to be able to get to the antidote. If you want to live, you must give us our freedom. If you don't, you will die."

CHAPTER 23

Kahlan reached in to seize Owen by the throat. She wanted to strangle him, to choke him, to make him feel the desperate, panicked need of breath that Richard had endured, to make him suffer, to show him what it was like. Cara went for Owen as well, apparently having the same thought as Kahlan. Richard thrust his arm out, holding them both back.

Holding Owen's shirt in his other fist, Richard shook the man. "And how long do I have until I get sick again? How long do I have to live before your poison kills me?"

Owen's confused gaze flitted from one angry face to another. "But if you do as I ask, as is your duty, you will be fine. I promise. You saw that I brought you the antidote. I don't wish to harm you. That is not my intent—I swear."

Kahlan could only think of Richard in crushing pain, unable to breathe. It had been terrifying. She couldn't think of anything else but him going through it again, only this time never to wake.

"How long?" Richard repeated.

"But if you only—"

"How long!"

Owen licked his lips. "Not a month. Close to it, but not a month, I believe."

Kahlan tried to push Richard away. "Let me have him. I'll find out—"

"No." Cara pulled Kahlan back. "Mother Confessor," she whispered, "let Lord Rahl do as he must. You don't know what your touch would do to one such as he."

"It might do nothing," Kahlan insisted, "but it might still work, and then we can find out everything."

Cara restrained her with an arm around her waist that Kahlan could not pry off. "And if only the Subtractive side works and it kills him?"

Kahlan stopped struggling as she frowned at Cara. "And since when have you taken up the study of magic?"

"Since it might harm Lord Rahl." Cara pulled Kahlan back farther away from Richard. "I have a mind, too, you know. I can think things through. Are you using your head? Where is this city? Where is the antidote within the city? What will you do if using your power kills this man and you are the one who condemns Lord Rahl to death when you could have had the information we need had you not touched him?

"If you want, I will break his arms. I will make him bleed. I will make him scream in agony. But I will not kill him; I will keep him alive so that he can give us the information we need to rid Lord Rahl of this death sentence.

"Ask yourself, do you really want to do this because you believe it will gain you the answers we need, or because you want to lash out, to strike out at him? Lord Rahl's life may hang on you being truthful with yourself."

Kahlan panted from the effort of the struggle, but more from her rage. She wanted to lash out, to strike back, just as Cara said—to do whatever she could to save Richard and to punish his attacker.

"I've had it with this game," Kahlan said. "I want to hear the story—the whole story."

"So do I," Richard said. He lifted the man by his shirt and slammed him down atop the crate. "All right, Owen, no more excuses for why you did this or that. Start at the beginning and tell us what happened, and what you and your people did about it."

Owen sat trembling like a leaf. Jennsen urged Richard back.

"You're frightening him," she whispered to Richard. "Give him some room or he will never be able to get it out."

Richard took a purging breath as he acknowledged Jennsen's words with a hand on her shoulder. He walked off a few paces, standing with his hands clasped behind his back as he stared off in the direction of the sunrise, toward the mountains Kahlan had so often seen him studying. It had been on the other side of the range of the smaller, closer mountains, tight in the shadows of those massive peaks thrusting up through the iron-gray clouds, where they had found the warning beacon and first encountered the black-tipped races.

The clouds that capped the sky all the way to the wall of those distant peaks hung heavy and dark. For the first time since Kahlan could remember, it looked like a storm might be upon them. The expectant smell of rain quickened the air.

"Where are you from?" Richard asked in a calm voice.

Owen cleared his throat as he straightened his shirt and light coat, as if rearranging his dignity. He remained seated atop the crate.

"I lived in a place of enlightenment, in a civilization of advanced culture . . . a great empire."

"Where is this noble empire?" Richard asked, still staring off into the distance.

Owen stretched his neck up, looking east. He pointed at the far wall of towering peaks where Richard was looking.

"There. Do you see that notch in the high mountains? I lived past there, in the empire beyond those mountains."

Kahlan remembered asking Richard if he thought they could make it over those mountains. Richard had been doubtful about it.

He looked back over his shoulder. "What's the name of this empire?"

"Bandakar," Owen said in a reverent murmur. He smoothed his blond hair to the side, as if to make himself a respectable representative of his homeland. "I was a citizen of Bandakar, of the Bandakaran Empire."

Richard had turned and was staring at Owen in a most peculiar manner. "Bandakar. Do you know what that name, Bandakar, means?"

Owen nodded. "Yes, *bandakar* is an ancient word from a time long forgotten. It means 'the chosen'—as in, the chosen empire."

Richard seemed to have lost a little of his color. When his eyes met Kahlan's, she could see that he knew very well what the word meant, and Owen had it wrong.

Richard seemed to suddenly remember himself. He rubbed his brow in thought. "Do you—do any of your people—know the language that the ancient word, *bandakar*, is from?"

Owen gestured dismissively. "We don't know of the language; it's long forgotten. Only the meaning of this word has been passed down, because it is so important to our people to hold on to the heritage of its meaning: chosen empire. We are the chosen people."

Richard's demeanor had changed. His anger seemed to have faded away. He stepped closer to Owen and spoke softly.

"The Bandakaran Empire—why isn't it known? Why does no one know of your people?"

Owen looked away, toward the east, seeing his distant homeland through wet eyes. "It is said that the ancient ones, the ones who gave us this name, wanted to protect us—because we are a special people. They took us to a place where no one could go, because of the mountains all around. Such mountains as only the Creator could impose to close off the land beyond, so that we are protected."

"Except that one place"—Richard gestured east—"that notch in the mountain range, that pass."

"Yes," Owen admitted, still staring off toward his homeland. "That was how we entered the land beyond, our land, but others could enter there as well; it was the one place where we were vulnerable. You see, we are an enlightened people who have risen above violence, but the world is still full of savage races. So, those ancient people, who wanted our advanced culture to survive, to thrive without the brutality of the rest of the world . . . they sealed the pass."

"And your people have been isolated for all this time—for thousands of years."

"Yes. We have a perfect land, a place of an advanced culture that is undisturbed by the violence of the people out here."

"How was the pass, the notch in the mountains, how was it sealed?"

Owen looked at Richard, somewhat startled by the question. He thought it over a moment. "Well . . . the pass was sealed. It was a place that no one could enter."

"Because they would die if they entered this boundary."

With an icy wave of understanding, Kahlan suddenly understood what composed the seal to this empire.

"Well, yes," Owen stammered. "But it had to be that way to keep outsiders from invading our empire. We reject violence unconditionally. It's unenlightened behavior. Violence only invites ever more violence, spiraling into a cycle of violence with no end." He fidgeted with the worry of such a trap catching them up in the allure of its wicked spell. "We are an advanced race, above the violence of our ancestors. We have grown beyond. But without the boundary that seals that pass and until the rest of the world rejects violence as we have, our people could be the prey of unenlightened savages."

"And now, that seal is broken."

Owen stared at the ground, swallowing before he spoke. "Yes."

"How long ago did the boundary fail?"

"We aren't sure. It is a dangerous place. No one lives near it, so we can't be positive, but we believe it was close to two years ago."

Kahlan felt the dizzying burden of confirmation of her fears.

When Owen looked up, he was a picture of misery. "Our empire is now naked to unenlightened savages."

"Sometime after the boundary came down, the Imperial Order came in through the pass."

"Yes."

"The land beyond those snowcapped mountains, the Empire of Bandakar, is where the black-tipped races are from, isn't it?" Richard said.

Owen looked up, surprised that Richard knew this. "Yes. Those awful creatures, innocent though they are of malice, prey on the people of my homeland. We must stay indoors at night, when they hunt. Even so, people, especially children, are sometimes surprised and caught by those fearsome creatures—"

"Why don't you kill them?" Cara asked, indignantly. "Fight them off? Shoot them with arrows? Dear spirits, why don't you bash their heads in with a rock if you have to?"

Owen looked shocked by the very suggestion. "I told you, we are above violence. It would be even more wrong to commit violence on such innocent creatures. It is our duty to preserve them, since it is we who entered into their domain. We are the ones who bear the guilt because we entice them into such behavior which is only natural to them. We preserve virtue only by embracing every aspect of the world without the prejudice of our flawed human views."

Richard gave Cara a stealthy gesture to be quiet. "Was everyone in the empire peaceful?" he asked, pulling Owen's attention away from Cara.

"Yes."

"Weren't there occasionally those who . . . I don't know, misbehaved? Children, for example. Where I come from, children can sometimes become rowdy. Children where you come from must sometimes become rowdy, too."

Owen shrugged a bit with one shoulder. "Well, yes, I guess so. There are times when children misbehave and become unruly."

"And what do you do with such children?"

Owen cleared his throat, plainly uncomfortable. "Well, they are . . . put out of their home for a time."

"Put out of their home for a time," Richard repeated. He lifted his arms in a questioning shrug. "The children I know will usually be happy to be put outside. They simply go play."

Owen shook his head emphatically at the serious nature of the matter. "We are different. From the time we are born, we are together with others. We are all very close. We depend on one another. We cherish one another. We spend all our waking hours with others. We cook and wash and work together. We sleep in a sleeping house, together. Ours is an enlightened life of human contact, human closeness. There is no higher value than being together."

"So," Richard asked, feigning a puzzled look, "when one of you—a child—is put out, that is a cause of unhappiness?"

Owen swallowed as a tear ran down his cheek. "There could be nothing worse. To be put out, to be closed off from others, is the worst horror we can endure. To be forced out into the cold cruelty of the world is a nightmare."

Just talking about such a punishment, thinking about it, was making Owen start to tremble.

"And that's when, sometimes, the races get such children," Richard said in a compassionate tone. "When they're alone and vulnerable."

With the back of his hand Owen wiped the tear from his cheek. "When a child must be put out to be punished, we take all possible precautions. We never put them out at night because that is when the races usually hunt. Children are put out for punishment only in the day. But when we are away from others, we are vulnerable to all the terrors and cruelties of the world. To be alone is a nightmare.

"We would do anything to avoid such punishment. Any child who misbehaves and is put out for a while will not likely misbehave again anytime soon. There is no greater joy than to finally be welcomed back in with our friends and family."

"So, for your people, banishment is the greatest punishment."

Owen stared into the distance. "Of course."

"Where I come from, we all got along pretty well, too. We enjoyed each other's company and had great fun when many people would gather. We valued our times together. When we're away for a time, we inquire about all the people we know and haven't seen in a while."

Owen smiled expectantly. "Then you understand."

Richard nodded, returning the smile. "But occasionally there will be someone who won't behave, even when they're an adult. We try everything we can, but, sometimes, someone does something wrong—something they know is wrong. They might lie or steal. Even worse, at times someone will deliberately hurt another person—beat someone when robbing them, or rape a woman, or even murder someone."

Owen wouldn't look up at Richard. He stared at the ground.

As he spoke, Richard paced slowly before the man. "When someone does something like that where you come from, Owen, what do your people do? How do an enlightened people handle such horrible crimes some of your people commit against others?"

"We attack the root cause of such behavior from the beginning," Owen was quick to answer. "We share all we have to make sure that everyone has what they need so that they don't have to steal. People steal because they feel the hurt of others acting superior. We show these people that we are no better than they and so they need not harbor such fears of others. We teach them to be enlightened and reject all such behavior."

Richard shrugged nonchalantly. Kahlan would have thought that he would be ready to strangle the answers out of Owen, but, instead, he was behaving in a calm, understanding manner. She had seen him act this way before. He was the Seeker of Truth, rightfully named by the First Wizard himself. Richard was doing what Seekers did: find the truth. Sometimes he used his sword, sometimes words.

Even though this was the way Richard often disarmed people when he questioned them, in this case it struck Kahlan that such a manner was precisely what Owen would be most accustomed to, most comfortable with. This gentle manner was pulling answers from the man and filling in a lot of information Kahlan had never thought of trying to get.

She had already learned that she was the cause of what had befallen these people.

"We both know, Owen, that, try as we might, such efforts to change people's ways don't always work. Some people won't change. There are times when people do evil things. Even among civilized people, there are some who will not behave in a civil manner despite all your best efforts. What's worse is that, if allowed to continue, these few jeopardize the whole community.

"After all, if you have a rapist among you, you can't allow him to continue to prey on women. If a man committed murder, you couldn't allow such a man to threaten the empire with his ways, now could you? An advanced culture, especially, can't be faulted for wanting to stop such dangers to enlightened people.

"But you've shunned all forms of violence, so you can hardly punish such a man physically—you couldn't put a murderer to death—not if you've truly rejected violence unconditionally. What do you do with such men? How does an enlightened people handle grave problems, such as murder?"

Owen was sweating. It seemed not to have occurred to him to deny the existence of murderers—Richard had already led him past that, had already established the existence of such men. Before Owen could think to object, Richard was already beyond, to the next step.

"Well," Owen said, swallowing, "as you say, we are an enlightened people. If someone does something to harm another, they are given . . . a denunciation."

"A denunciation. You mean, you condemn their actions, but not the man. You give him a second chance."

"Yes, that's right." Owen wiped sweat from his brow as he glanced up at Richard. "We work very hard to reform people who make such mistakes and are given a denunciation. We recognize that their actions are a cry for help, so we counsel them in the ways of enlightenment in order to help them to see that they are hurting all our people when they hurt one, and that since they are one of our beloved people, they are only hurting themselves when they hurt another. We show such people compassion and understanding."

Kahlan caught Cara's arm, and with a stern look convinced her to remain silent.

Richard paced slowly before Owen, nodding as if he thought that sounded reasonable. "I understand. You put a great deal of effort into making them see that they can never do such a thing again."

Owen nodded, relieved that Richard understood.

"But then there are times when one of those who has received a denunciation, and has been counseled to the very best of your ability, goes out and does the same crime again—or one even worse.

"It's clear, then, that he refuses to be reformed and that he's a threat to public order, safety, and confidence. Left to his own devices, such a person, by himself, will bring the very thing you unconditionally reject—violence—to stalk among your people and win others to his ways."

A light mist had begun to fall. Owen sat on the crate, trembling, frightened, alone. Only a short time ago he had been reluctant to answer even the most basic question in a meaningful way; now Richard had him speaking openly.

Friedrich stroked the jaw of one of the horses as he quietly watched. Jennsen sat on a rock, Betty lying at her feet. Tom stood behind Jennsen, a hand resting gently on her shoulder, but keeping an eye on the man Kahlan had touched with her power. That man sat off to the side, listening dispassionately as he waited to be commanded. Cara stood beside Kahlan, ever watchful for trouble, but obviously caught up in the unfolding story of Owen's homeland, even if she was having a hard time holding her tongue.

For her part, Kahlan, while she could sympathize with Cara's difficulty in holding her tongue, was transfixed by the tale of a mysterious empire that Richard casually, effortlessly, drew from this man who had poisoned him. She couldn't imagine where Richard was going with his matter-of-fact questions. What did this empire's forms of punishment have to do with Richard being poisoned? It was clear to her, though, that Richard knew where he was headed, and that the path he was following was wide and sunlit.

Richard paused before Owen. "What do you do in those instances?—when you can't reform someone who has become a danger to everyone. What do an enlightened people do with that kind of person?"

Owen spoke in a soft voice that carried clearly in the misty early-morning hush. "We banish them."

"Banish them. You mean, you send them into the boundary?"

Owen nodded.

"But you said that going into the boundary is death. You couldn't simply send them into the boundary or you would be executing them. You must have a place to send them through. A special place. A place where you can banish them, without killing them, but a place where you know they can never return to harm your people."

Owen nodded again. "Yes. There is such a place. The pass that is blocked by the boundary is steep and treacherous. But there is a path that leads down into the boundary. Those ancient ones who protected us by placing that boundary placed the path as well. The path is said to allow passage out. Because of the way the mountain descends, it is a difficult path, but it can be followed."

"And just because of how difficult it is, it's not possible to climb back up? To enter the Bandakaran Empire?"

Owen chewed his lower lip. "It goes down through a terrible place, a narrow passageway through the boundary, a lifeless land, where it is said that death itself lies to each side. The person banished is given no water or food. He must find his own, on the other side, or perish. We place watchers at the entrance of the path, where they wait to be sure that the one banished has gone through and is not lingering in the boundary only to return. The watchers wait and watch for several weeks to be sure that the one banished has gone beyond in search of water and food, in search of his new life away from his people.

"Once beyond, the forest is a terrible place, a frightening place, with roots that descend over the edge like a land of snakes. The path takes you down under that cascade of roots and running water. Then, even lower, you find yourself in a strange land where the trees are far above, reaching for the distant light, but you see only their roots twisting and stretching down into the darkness toward the ground. It is said that once you see that forest of roots towering all around you, you have made it through the boundary and the pass through the mountains.

"There is said to be no way to enter our land from that other side—to use the pass to return to our empire.

"Once banished, there is no redemption."

Richard moved up close beside Owen and placed a hand on his shoulder.

"What did you do to be banished, Owen?"

Owen sank forward, putting his face in his hands as he finally broke down sobbing.

CHAPTER 24

Richard left his hand on Owen's shoulder as he spoke in a compassionate tone. "Tell me what happened, Owen. Tell me in your own way."

Kahlan was startled to hear, after all Owen had said, that he had become one of the banished. She saw Jennsen's jaw fall open. Cara lifted an eyebrow.

Kahlan could see that Richard's hand on Owen's shoulder was an emotional lifeline for the man. He finally sat up, sniffling back the tears. He wiped his nose on his sleeve.

He looked up at Richard. "Should I tell you the whole story? All of it?"

"Yes. I'd like to hear it all, from the beginning."

Kahlan was struck at how much Richard reminded her, at that moment, of his grandfather, Zedd, and the way Zedd always wanted to hear the whole story.

"Well, I was happy among my people, with them all around me. They held me to their breast when I was young. I was always safe in their welcoming arms. While I knew of other children who became unruly and were put out as punishment, I never did anything to be put out. I hungered to learn to be like my people. They taught me the ways of enlightenment. For a time I served my people as the Wise One.

"Later, my people were pleased with how enlightened I was, how I embraced them all, and so they made me the speaker of our town. I traveled to nearby towns to speak the words of what the people of my town all believed as one. I went to our great cities for the same reason. I was always happiest, though, when I was home with my closest people.

"I fell in love with a woman from my town. Her name is Marilee."

Owen stared off into his memories. Richard didn't rush him, but waited patiently until he began again at his own pace.

"It was spring, a little more than two years ago, when we fell joyfully in love. Marilee and I spent time talking, holding hands, and, when we could, sitting together while among all the others. Among all the others, though, I only had eyes for Marilee. She only had eyes for me.

"When we were with others, it felt like we were alone in the world, Marilee and I, and the world belonged to us alone, that only we had the eyes to see all its hidden beauty. It is wrong to feel this way, to be so alone in our hearts is to be selfish and to think our eyes can see so clearly is sinful pride, but we could not help ourselves. The trees blossomed just for us. The water in the streams burbled their music just for us. The moon rose for us alone." Owen slowly shook his head. "You could not understand how it was . . . how we felt."

"I understand quite well how it was," Richard assured him in a quiet voice.

Owen glanced up at Richard, then his gaze moved to Kahlan. She nodded to him that it was so. His brow twitched with wonder. He looked away then, perhaps, Kahlan thought, in guilt.

"Well," Owen said, going back to his story, "I was the speaker of our town—the one who speaks what all decide that must be decided as being true. I also sometimes helped other people resolve questions of what is right according to the tenets of an advanced culture." Owen flicked his hand in a self-conscious manner. "As I said, I once served my people as the Wise One, so the people trusted me."

Richard just nodded, not interrupting, even though Kahlan knew that he didn't quite understand the meaning of many of the details of what Owen was saying any more than she did. The gist of the story, though, was becoming all too clear.

"I asked Marilee if she would be my wife, if she would marry me and no other. She said that it was the happiest day of her life, to be asked by me, for I said I wanted no other but her. It was the happiest day of my life when she said she would have me as her husband.

"Everyone was very pleased. Everyone loved us both, and kept us sheltered in their arms for a long time to show their joy. As we sat together with everyone, we all talked about the plans for the wedding and how much we would all be pleased that Marilee and I would be husband and wife and bring children among our people."

Owen stared off in his thoughts. It seemed that he might have forgotten that he'd stopped speaking.

"So, was it a grand wedding?" Richard finally prompted.

Owen still stared off. "The men of the Order came. That was when we first realized that the seal, that had protected our people since the beginning times, had failed. There was no longer a barrier protecting us.

"Our empire was now naked to savages."

Kahlan knew that what she had done had caused the boundary to fail, resulting in these people being defenseless. She had had no choice, but that didn't make it any easier to listen.

"They came to our town, where I was speaker. Our town, like others, has walls all around; those who gave us our name, Bandakar, proclaimed that towns should be built such as this. It was wise of them to tell us this. The walls protect us from the beasts of the forests, make us safe, without having to harm any creatures.

"The men of the Order set up a camp outside our walls. There was really no place for them to stay in the town—we have no accommodations to house so many people because we never have great numbers of visitors from other towns. Worse, I was fearful of having such men as they looked sleeping under our roof with us. It was wrong to have such fear; it is my failing, not theirs, I know, but I had the fear.

"Since I was the speaker for my town, I went out to their camp with food and offerings. I was filled with my sinful failing of being afraid of them. They were big, some with long, dark, greasy, tangled hair, some with shaved heads, many with filthy beards of coarse hair—none of them with fair sun-golden hair like our people. It was shocking to see them wearing hides of animals, leather plates, chains and metal, and straps with sharp studs. Hanging on their belts, they all carried vicious-looking implements the likes of which I had never in my life imagined, but which I later learned were weapons.

"I told these strange men that they were welcome to share what we had, that we would honor them. I told them that they were invited to sit with us, to share their words with us."

Everyone waited in silence, not wanting to say a word as tears ran down Owen's face and dripped off his jaw.

"The men of the Order did not sit with us. They did not share their words with us. Though I spoke to them, they acted as if I were not worthy of their recognition, other than to grin at me as if they intended to eat me.

"I sought to allay their fears, since it is the fear of others that causes hostility. I assured the men that we were peaceful and intended them no ill will. I told them that we would do our best to accommodate them among us.

"The man who was their speaker, a commander he called himself, spoke to me then. He told me that his name was Luchan. His shoulders were twice as wide as mine, even though he was no taller than me. This man, Luchan, said that he did not believe me. I was horrified to hear this. He said that he thought my people meant him harm. He accused us of wishing to kill his men. I was shaken that he would think such a thing of us, especially after I had told him of our open welcome to his men. I was shaken to know that I had done something to cause him to feel we were threatening to him and his men. I assured him of our desire to be peaceful with them.

"Luchan smiled at me then, not a smile of happiness, not a smile like I had ever seen before. He said that they were going to burn down our town and kill all the people in it to prevent us from attacking his men as they slept. I begged him to believe our peaceful ways, to sit with us and share his worries and we would do what we needed to do to dispel such doubts and show him our love of him for being our fellow man.

"Luchan said, then, that he would not burn down our town and kill us all upon a condition, as he called it. He said that if I would surrender my woman to him as a token of my sincerity and goodwill he would then believe our words. He said that if, on the other hand, I failed to send her out to him, what happened would be my fault, would be on my head, for not cooperating with them, for not showing my sincerity and goodwill toward them.

"I went back to hear the words of my people. Everyone agreed and said that I must do this—that I must send Marilee out to the men of the Order so that they would not burn down our town and murder everyone. I asked them not to decide so quickly, and offered the idea that we could close the gates in the wall to keep the men from coming in and harming us. My people said that men such as these would find a way to break the wall, and then they would murder everyone for shutting our gates and shaming them with our bigotry toward them. The people all spoke up loudly that I must show the man Luchan goodwill and our peaceful intent, that I must allay his fears of us.

"I never felt so alone among my people. I could not go against the word of everyone, for it is taught that only the voices of people joined together in one voice can be wise enough to know the true way. No one person can know what is right. Only consensus can make a thing right.

"My knees trembled as I stood before Marilee. I heard myself ask if she wished me to do as the men wanted—as our people wanted. I told her that I would run away with her if she would wish it. She wept as she said that she would not hear such sinful talk from me, for it would mean the death of everyone else.

"She said that she must go to the men of the Order to appease them or there would be violence. She told me that she would tell them of our peaceful ways and thus gentle them toward us.

"I was proud of Marilee for upholding the highest values of our people. I wanted to die for being proud of such a thing as would take her from me.

"I kissed Marilee a last time, but I could not stop my tears. I held her in my arms and we wept together.

"Then, I took her out to the man who was their commander, Luchan. He had a thick black beard, a shaved head, and a ring through one ear and one nostril. He said that I had made a wise choice. His sun-darkened arms were nearly as big around as Marilee's waist. His big filthy hand took Marilee by her arm and bore her away with him as he turned back and told me to 'scurry back' to my town, to my people. His men laughed at me as they watched me go back up the road.

"The men of the Order left my town and my people alone. We had peace I had purchased with Marilee.

"I had no peace in my heart.

"For a time, the men of the Order were gone from our town. They returned, then, one afternoon, and called for me to come out. I asked Luchan about Marilee, if she was well, if she was happy. Luchan turned his head and spat, then said he didn't know, that he never asked her. I was worried, and asked if she spoke with him of our peaceful ways, assured him of our innocent intent toward him. He said that when he was with women he wasn't much interested in them for their talking.

"He winked at me. Though I had never seen anyone wink in such a fashion, I knew his meaning.

"I was very frightened for Marilee, but I reminded myself that nothing is real, that I could not really know anything from what I was hearing. I was only hearing what this one man said of things, as he saw them, and I knew that I was only sensing part of the world. I could not know reality from my eyes and ears alone.

"Luchan said then that I should open the town gates lest they think we were acting in a hostile way toward them. Luchan said that if we failed to do as he asked, it would begin a cycle of violence.

"I went back and spoke his words to all the people gathered around me. My people all spoke in one voice, and said that we must open the gates and invite them in to prove that we held no hostility, no prejudice, toward the men.

"The men of the Order came in through those gates we let stand wide for them and seized nearly all the women, from those still the age of girls to grandmothers. I stood with the other men, begging them to leave our women be, to leave us be. I told them that we had agreed to their demands to prove to them that we meant them no harm, but it did no good. They would not listen.

"I told Luchan that I had sent Marilee to him as his condition for peace. I told him that they must honor their agreement. Luchan and his men laughed.

"I cannot say if what I saw then was real. Reality is in the realm of fate, and we, in this place we think we know as the world, cannot know it in full truth. That day, fate swept down on my people; we had no say in it. We know that we must not fight against fate, for it has already been foreordained by the true reality we cannot see.

"I watched as our women were dragged away. I watched, unable to do anything, as they screamed our names, as they reached out for us, as the hands of those big men held our women and bore them away from us. I had never heard such screams as I heard that day."

The overcast seemed as if it would soon brush the tops of the trees. In the thick silence, Kahlan heard a bird in the bristlecone pines singing. Owen was alone, off in his solitary world of terrible memories. Richard stood, arms folded, watching the man, but saying nothing.

"I went to other towns," Owen finally said. "In a couple of places, the Order had been there before me. The men of the Order did much the same to those towns as they had done to my town; they took the women. In some places they also took a few men.

"In other places I went, the Order had not come yet. As the speaker of my town, I told them of what had befallen my town and I urged others to do something. They were angry with me and said it was wrong to resist, that to resist was to give in to violence, to become no better than the savages. They urged me to renounce my outspoken ways and to heed the wisdom of the joined voices of our people that had brought enlightenment and thousands of years of peace. They told me that I was only looking at events through my limited eyes, and not the better judgment of the group.

"I went then to one of our important cities and told them again that the seal on the pass was broken and that the Imperial Order was upon us, and that something must be done. I urged them to listen to me and to consider what we could do to protect our people.

"Because I was so inconsiderately assertive, the assembly of speakers took me to the Wise One so that I might have his counsel. It is a great honor to have the words of the Wise One. The Wise

One told me that I must forgive those who had done these things against my people, if we were to end the violence.

"The Wise One said that the anger and hostility shown by the men of the Order was a mark of their inner pain, a cry for help, and they must be shown compassion and understanding. I should have been humbled by such clear wisdom as could only come from the Wise One, but instead I spoke out of my wish for Marilee and all the other people to be returned from such men, and for the speakers to help me in this.

"The Wise One said that Marilee would find her own happiness without me and that I was guilty of selfishness for wanting to keep her for myself. He said that fate had come for the other people and it was not my place to make demands of fate.

"I asserted to the speakers and the Wise One that the men of the Order had not upheld the agreement made by Luchan for Marilee to be sent to them. The Wise One said that Marilee had acted properly by going in peace to the men so that the cycle of violence would end. He said that it was selfish and sinful for me to put my wants above peace she selflessly worked toward and that my attitude toward them was probably what had provoked the men to anger.

"I asked what I was to do, when I had acted honestly but they had not. The Wise One said that I was wrong to condemn men I did not know, men I had not first forgiven, or tried to embrace, or even to understand. He said that I must encourage them in the ways of peace by throwing myself before them and begging them to forgive me for acting in a way that kindled their inner pain by reminding them of past wrongs done to them.

"I told the Wise One, then, in front of all the other speakers, that I did not want to forgive these men or to embrace these men, but that I wanted to cast them out of our lives.

"I was given a denunciation."

Richard handed Owen a cup of water but said nothing. Owen sipped at the water without seeing it.

"The gathering of speakers commanded me to go back to my town and seek the advice of those among whom I lived, commanding that I ask my people to counsel me back to our ways. I went back intending to redeem myself, only to discover that it had become worse than before.

"Now, the Order had returned to take whatever they wanted from the town—food and goods. We would have given them whatever they wanted, but they never asked, they just took. More of our men had been taken away, too—some of the boys and some of those who were young and strong. Other men, who had in some way offended the dignity of the men of the Order, had been murdered.

"People I knew stood staring with empty eyes at blood where our friends had died. In other such places, people gathered to mound remembrances over the blood. These places had become sacred shrines and people knelt there to pray. The children would not stop crying. No one would counsel me.

"Everyone in my town trembled behind doors, but they cast their eyes down and opened those doors when the men of the Order knocked, lest we offend them.

"I could not stand to be in our town any longer. I ran to the country, even though I was terrified that I would be alone. There, in the hills, I found other men, selfish as I, hiding in fear for their lives. Together, we decided to try to do something, to try to bring an end to the misery. We resolved to restore peace.

"At first, we sent representatives to speak with the men of the Order, to let them know that we meant them no harm, and that we only sought peace with them, and to ask what we could do to satisfy them. The men of the Order hung these men by their ankles from poles at the edge of our town and skinned them alive.

"I knew these men all my life, these men who had counseled me, advised me, broken fasts with me, sheltered me in their arms with joy when I had told them Marilee and I wanted to be wed. The men of the Order left these poor men to hang by their ankles as they screamed in agony in the hot summer sun, where the black-tipped races came and found them.

"I reminded myself that what I saw that day was not real, and that I should not believe such sights, that possibly my eyes were deceiving me as punishment for having improper thoughts, and that my mind could not possibly know if this sight was real or an illusion.

"Not every man that had gone to speak with the men of the Order was killed. A few of our men were sent back to us with word from the Order. They said that if we did not come down out of the hills and return to their rule in our town, to show that we did not intend to attack them, then they would begin skinning a dozen people a day, and hanging them on poles for the races, until either we returned to demonstrate our peaceful intent, or until every last person left in the town was skinned alive.

"Many of our men wept, unable to stand to think that they would be the cause of a cycle of violence, so they went back to the town to show that they intended no harm.

"Not all of us went back. A few of us remained in the hills. Since most returned, and the Order had no count of us, they thought all had complied with their command.

"Those few of us who were left in the hills hid, living off the nuts, fruits, and berries we could find or the food we snuck back and stole. We slowly gathered together supplies to see us through. I told the other men with me that we should find out what the Order was doing with our people they had taken away. Since the men of the Order didn't know us, we could sometimes mingle in with people working the fields or tending to animals and sneak back into our town without the Order knowing who we were—without knowing that we were men from the hills. Over the next months, we followed and watched the men of the Order.

"The children had been sent away, but the men of the Order had taken all the women to a place they built—an encampment they called it—that they fortified against attack."

Owen put his face in his hands again as he spoke through sobs. "They were using our women as breeding stock. They sought to have them bear children—as many children as they could birth—children of their soldiers. Some women were already pregnant. Most of those who weren't already pregnant became pregnant. Over the next year and a half, many children were born. They were nursed for a time, and then they were all sent away as their mothers were gotten pregnant again.

"I don't know where these children were taken—somewhere

beyond our empire. The men who had been taken from the towns were also taken away beyond our empire.

"The men of the Order did not watch their captives well, since our people shunned violence, so a couple of men escaped and ran to the hills, where they found us. They told us that the Order had taken them to see the women, and told them that if they did not do as they were told, if they did not follow all the orders they were given, then all these women before them would die—that they would be skinned alive. These men who escaped did not know where they were to be taken, or what it was they were to do, only that if they did not follow the instructions given them, then they would be the cause of the violence to our women.

"After a year and a half of hiding, of meeting with others, we learned that the Order had spread to other places in our empire, taken other towns and cities. The Wise One and the speakers went into hiding. We discovered that some towns and cities had invited the Order to come in, to be among them, in an attempt to appease them and keep them from doing harm.

"No matter how hard our people tried, their concessions failed to placate the belligerence of the men of the Order. We could not understand why this was true.

"In some of the largest cities, though, it was different. The people there had listened to the speakers of the Order and had come to believe that the cause of the Imperial Order was the same as our cause—to bring an end to abuse and injustice. The Order convinced these people that they abhorred violence, that they had been enlightened as were our people, but they had to turn to violence to defeat those who would oppress us all. They said that they were champions of our people's cause of enlightenment. The people there rejoiced that they were at last in the hands of saviors who would spread our words of enlightenment to the savages who did not yet live by peace."

Richard, a thunderstorm building, could hold his tongue no longer. "And even after all the brutality, these people believed the words of the Imperial Order?"

Owen spread his hands. "The people in those places were swayed by the words of the Order—that they were fighting for the same ideals as we lived by. They told our people in those cities that they had only acted as they did because my town and some of the other places like it had sided with the savages from the north—with the D'Haran Empire.

"I had heard this name before—the D'Haran Empire. During the year and a half that I lived in the hills with the other men, I sometimes traveled out of our land, out into the surrounding places, to see what I could discover that might help us to cast the Imperial Order out of Bandakar. While I was out of my land, I went to some of the cities in the Old World, as I learned it was called. In one place, Altur'Rang, I heard whispers of a great man from the north, from the D'Haran Empire, who brought freedom.

"Other of my men also went out to other places. When we returned, we all told each other what we had seen, what we had heard. All those who came back told of the same thing, told of hearing of one called Lord Rahl, and his wife, the Mother Confessor, who fought the Imperial Order.

"Then, we learned where the Wise One was being kept safe, as were most of our greatest speakers. It was in our greatest city, a place where the Order had not yet come. The Order was busy with other places and so they were in no hurry. My people were going nowhere—they had nowhere to go.

"The men who were with me wanted me to be their speaker, to go to talk with these great speakers, to convince them that we must do something to stop the Imperial Order and cast them out of Bandakar.

"I journeyed to the great city, a place I had never been before, and I was inspired at seeing a place that such a great culture as ours had built. A culture about to be destroyed, if I could not convince these great speakers and the Wise One to think of something to do to stop the Order.

"I spoke before them with great urgency. I told them of all the Order had done. I told them of the men I had in hiding, waiting for word of what they were to do.

"The great speakers said that I cannot know the true nature of the Order from what I and a few men had seen—that the Imperial Order was a vast nation and we saw only a tiny speck of their people.

They said that men cannot do such cruel acts as I described because it would cause them to shrink back in horror before they could complete them. To prove it, they suggested that I try to skin one of them. I admitted that I could not, but I told them that I had seen the men of the Order do this.

"The speakers scorned my insistence that it was real. They said I must always keep in mind that reality is not for us to know. They said that the men of the Imperial Order were probably frightened that we might be a violent people, and simply wanted to test our resolve by tricking us into believing that the things I described were real so that they could see how we reacted—if peace was really our way, or if we would attack them.

"The great speakers said, then, that I could not know if I really saw all the things I said, and that even if I did, I could not judge if they were for the bad, or the good—that I was not the person to judge the reasons of men I did not know, that to do so would be to believe that I was above them, and to put myself above them would be an act of prejudiced hostility.

"I could only think of all the things I had seen, of the men with me who all agreed that we must convince the great speakers to act to preserve our empire. I could only see in my mind the face of Luchan. And then, I thought of Marilee in the hands of this man. I thought of the sacrifice she had made, and how her life was cast away into this horror for nothing.

"I stood up before the great speakers and screamed that they were evil."

Cara snorted a laugh. "Seems you can tell what's real, when you put your mind to it."

Richard shot her a withering glare.

Owen glanced up and blinked. His thoughts had been so distant as he told his story that he hadn't really heard her. He looked up at Richard.

"That was when they banished me," he said.

"But the boundary seal had failed," Richard said. "You had already come and gone through the pass. How could they enforce a banishment with the boundary down?"

Owen waved dismissively. "They do not need the wall of death. Banishment is in a way a sentence of death—the death of the person as a citizen of Bandakar. My name would be known throughout the empire, at least what was left of it, and every person would shun me. I would be turned away from every door. I was one of the banished. No one would want to have any contact with me. I was now an outcast. It does not matter that they could not put me beyond the barrier; they put me beyond my people. That was worse.

"I went back to my men in the hills to collect my things and confess to them that I had been banished. I was going to go out beyond our homeland, as I had been commanded by the will of our people through our great speakers.

"But my men, those in the hills, they would not see me go. They said that the banishment was wrong. These men had seen the things I had seen. They had wives, mothers, daughters, sisters who had been taken away. They all had seen their friends murdered, seen the men skinned alive and left to suffer in agony as they died, seen the races come to circle over them as they hung on those poles. They said that since all our eyes had seen these things, then these things must be true, must be real.

"They all said that we had gone into the hills because we love our land and want to restore the peace we once had. They said that the great speakers were the ones whose eyes did not see and they were condemning our people to murder at the hands of savage men and those of our people who lived to a cruel life under the rule of the Imperial Order, to be used as breeding stock or as slaves.

"I was shocked that these men would not reject me for being banished—that they wanted me to stay with them.

"It was then that we decided that we would be the ones to do something, to come up with the plan we always wanted the speakers to decide. When I asked what would be our plan, everyone said the same thing.

"They all said that we must get Lord Rahl to come and give us freedom. They all spoke with one voice.

"We decided, then, what we would do. Some men said that one such as the Lord Rahl would come to cast out the Order when we asked. Others thought you might not be willing, since you are unenlightened and not of our ways, not of our people. When we considered that possibility, we decided that we must have a way to insure you would have to come, should you refuse us.

"Since I was banished, I said that it was upon me to do this thing. Except to live in the hills with my men, I could have no life among our people unless we cast out the Imperial Order and our ways were restored to us. I told the men that I did not know where I could find the Lord Rahl, but that I would not give up until I did so.

"First, though, one of the men, an older man who had spent his life working with herbs and cures, made me the poison I put into your waterskin. He made me the antidote as well. He told me how the poison worked, and how it could be counteracted, since none of us wished to consider that it would come to murder, even of an unenlightened man."

By the sidelong look Richard gave her, Kahlan knew that he wanted her to hold her tongue, and knew that she was having difficulty doing so. She redoubled her effort.

"I was worried about how I would find you," Owen said to Richard, "but I knew I had to. Before I could go in search of you, though, I had to hide the rest of the antidote, as was our plan.

"While in a city where the Order had won the people to their side, I heard some people at a market say that it was a great honor that the very man who had come to their city was the most important man among all those of the Imperial Order in Bandakar. The thought struck me that this man might know something of the man the Order hated most—Lord Rahl.

"I stayed in the city for several days, watching the place where this man was said to be. I watched the soldiers come and go. I saw that they sometimes took people in with them, and then later the people came back out.

"One day I saw people come back out and they did not appear to be harmed, so I made my way close to them to hear what they might say. I heard them talk that they had seen the great man himself. I could not hear much of what they said of their visit inside, but none said that they were hurt.

"And then I saw the soldiers come out, and I suspected that they might be going to get more people to take them in to see this great man, so I went before them into a central gathering square. I waited, then, near the open isles between the public benches. The soldiers rushed in and gathered up a small crowd of people and I was swept up with the others.

"I was terrified of what would happen to me, but I thought this might be my only chance to go in the building with this important man, my only chance to see what he looked like, to see the place where he was so I could know where to sneak back and listen, as I had learned to do when living in the hills with my men. I had resolved to do this to see if I could learn any information on Lord Rahl. Still, I was trembling with worry when they took us all into the building and down halls and up stairs to the top floor.

"I feared that I was being led to the slaughter and wanted to run, but I thought then of my men back in the hills, depending on me to find the Lord Rahl and get him to come to Bandakar and give us freedom.

"We were taken through a heavy door into a dim room that filled me with fear because it stank of blood. The windows on two walls of the stark room were closed off by shutters. I saw that across the room there was a table with a broad bowl and, nearby, a row of fat, sharpened wooden stakes standing nearly as tall as my chest. They were stained dark with blood and gore.

"Two women and a man with us fainted. Out of anger, the soldiers kicked them in the heads. When the people did not rise, the soldiers dragged them away by their arms. I saw blood trails smear along the floor behind them. I didn't want to have my head caved in by the boot of one of these gruesome men, so I resolved not to faint.

"A man swept into the room, suddenly, like a chill wind. I had not ever been afraid of any man, even Luchan, like I was afraid of this man. He was dressed in layer upon layer of cloth strips that flowed out behind as he moved. His jet-black hair was swept back and smoothed with oils that made it glisten. His nose seemed to stick out even more than it would have, had he not slicked back his hair. His small black eyes were rimmed in red. When those beady eyes fixed on me, I had to remind myself that I had vowed not to faint.

"He peered at each person in turn as he slowly walked past us, as if he were picking out a turnip for dinner. It was then, as his knobby fingers came out from his odd clothes to point in a waving manner at one person and then another until he had pointed out five people, that I saw that his fingernails were all painted as black as his hair.

"His hand waved, dismissing the rest of us. The soldiers moved between the five people this man had pointed out and the rest of us. They started pushing us toward the door, but just then, before we could be ushered out, a commander with a nose that had been flattened to the side, as if from being broken repeatedly, came in and said that the messenger had arrived. The man with the black hair ran his black nails back through his black hair and told the commander to tell the messenger to wait, that by morning he would have the latest information.

"I was then led out and down the stairs along with the rest of the people. We were taken outside and told to go away, that our services wouldn't be needed. The solders laughed when they said this. I left with the others, so as not to make the men angry. The people all whispered about having seen the great man himself. I could think only of what the latest information might be.

"Later, after dark, I sneaked back, and in the rear of the building I discovered, behind a gate through a high wooden fence, a narrow alleyway. In the dark, I entered the alley and hid myself inside a doorway entrance to the back hall of the building. There were passageways beyond, and, in the candlelight, I recognized one passage as the place I had been earlier.

"It was late and there was no one in the halls. I moved deeper into the passageways. Rooms and recesses lined each side of the hall, but with the late hour no one came out. I sneaked up the stairs and crept to the big thick door to the room where I had been taken.

"It was there, in that dark hall before the big door, that I heard the most horrifying cries I have ever heard. People were begging and weeping for their lives, crying for mercy. One woman pleaded endlessly to be put to death to end her suffering.

"I thought I would vomit, or faint, but one thought kept me still and hidden, kept me from running as fast as my legs would carry me. That was the thought that this was the fate of all my people if I did not help them by bringing Lord Rahl.

"I stayed there all night, in a dark recess in a hall across from the big door, listening to those poor people in unimaginable agony. I don't know what the man was doing to them, but I thought I would die of sorrow for their slow suffering. The whole of the night, the moans of agony never ceased.

"I shivered in my hiding place, weeping, and told myself that it wasn't real, that I shouldn't be afraid of what was not real. I imagined the people's pain, but told myself that I was putting my imagination on top of my senses—the very thing I had been taught was wrong. I put my thoughts to Marilee, the times we had been together, and ignored the sounds that were not real. I could not know what was real, what these sounds really were.

"Early in the morning the commander I had seen before returned. I peeked carefully out from my dark hiding place. The man with the black hair came to the door. I knew it was him because when his arm came out of the room to hand the man a scrolled paper, I saw his black fingernails.

"The man with the black hair said to the commander with the flattened, crooked nose, he called him 'Najari,' that he had found them. That's what he said—'them.' Then he said, "They've made it to the east edge of the wasteland and are now heading north.' He told the man to give the messenger the orders right away. Najari said, "Shouldn't be long, then, Nicholas, and you will have them and we'll have the power to name our price.'"

C H A P T E R 25

Richard spun around. "Nicholas? You heard him say that name?"

Owen blinked in surprise. "Yes. I'm sure of it. He said Nicholas."

Kahlan felt a weary hopelessness settle over her, like the cold, wet mist.

Richard gestured urgently. "Go on."

"Well, I wasn't sure that they were talking about you—about the Lord Rahl and the Mother Confessor—when the commander said 'them,' but by the grim excitement in their voices I had the impression that it was so. Their voices reminded me of the first time the Order came, at the way Luchan smiled at me in a way I had never seen before, like he might eat me.

"I thought that this information was my best chance to find you. So I started out at once."

Borne on a light gust, drizzle replaced the morning mist. Kahlan realized that she was shivering with the cold.

Richard pointed at the man sitting on the ground not far away, the man with the notch in his right ear, the man Kahlan had touched. Some of the storm within Richard boiled to the surface.

"There is the man the orders from Nicholas were sent to. He brought with him those men you saw at our last camp. Had we not defended ourselves, had we put our own sincere hatred of violence above the nature of reality, we would be as lost as Marilee."

Owen stared at the man. "What is his name?"

"I don't know and it doesn't matter to me in the least. He fought for the Imperial Order—fought to uphold a view of all life, including his, as unimportant, interchangeable, expendable in the mindless pursuit of an ideal that holds individual lives as worthless in themselves—a tenet that demands sacrifice to others until you are nothing.

"He fights for the dream of everybody to be nobody and nothing.

"The beliefs of the Order hold that you had no right to love Marilee, that everyone is the same and so your duty should be to marry someone who could best use your help. In that way, through selfless sacrifice, you would properly serve your fellow man. Despite how you struggle not to see what's before your eyes, Owen, I think somewhere beneath all your regurgitated teachings, you know that that is the greatest horror brought by the Order—not their brutality, but their ideas. It is their beliefs that sanction brutality, and yours that invite it.

"He didn't value his own life, who he was; why should I care what his name was? I give him what was his greatest ambition: nothingness."

When Richard saw Kahlan shivering in the cold drizzle, he withdrew his hot glare from Owen and retrieved her cloak from her pack in the wagon. With the utmost gentleness and care, he wrapped it around her shoulders. By the look on his face, he seemed to have had all he could take of listening to Owen.

Kahlan seized his hand, holding it to her cheek for a moment. There was some small good in the story they had heard from Owen.

"This means that the gift isn't killing you, Richard," she said in a confidential tone. "It was the poison."

She was relieved that they hadn't run out of time to get him help, as she had so feared on that brief, eternal wagon ride when he'd been unconscious.

"I had the headaches before I ran into Owen. I still have the headaches. The sword's magic as well faltered before I was poisoned."

"But at least this now gives us more time to find the solutions to those problems."

He ran his fingers back through his hair. "I'm afraid we have worse problems, now, and not the time you think."

"Worse problems?"

Richard nodded. "You know the empire Owen comes from? Bandakar? Guess what 'Bandakar' means."

Kahlan glanced at Owen sitting hunched on the crate and all by himself. She shook her head as her gaze returned to Richard's gray eyes, troubled more by the suppressed rage in his voice than anything else.

"I don't know, what?"

"In High D'Haran it's a name. It means 'the banished'. Remember from the book, *The Pillars of Creation*, when I was telling you what it said about how they decided to send all the pristinely ungifted people away to the Old World—to banish them? Remember that I said no one ever knew what became of them?

"We just found out.

"The world is now naked before the people of the Bandakaran Empire."

Kahlan frowned. "How can you know for certain that he is a descendant of those people?"

"Look at him. He's blond and looks more like full-blooded D'Harans than he does the people down here in the Old World. More importantly, though, he's not affected by magic."

"But that could be just him."

Richard leaned in closer. "In a closed place like he comes from, a place shut off from the rest of the world for thousands of years, even one pillar of Creation would have spread that ungifted trait throughout the entire population by now.

"But there wasn't just one; they were all ungifted. For that, they were banished to the Old World, and in the Old World, where they tried to establish a new life, they were again all collected and banished to that place beyond those mountains—a place they were told was for the *bandakar*, the banished."

"How did the people in the Old World find out about them? How did they keep them all together, without a single one surviving to spread their ungifted trait to the general population, and how did they manage to then put them all in that place—banish them?"

"Good questions, all, but right now not the important ones.

"Owen," Richard called as he turned back to the others, "I want you to stay right there, please, while the rest of us decide what will be our single voice about what we must do."

Owen brightened at a method of doing things with which he identified and felt comfortable. He didn't seem to detect, as did Kahlan, the undercurrent of sarcasm in Richard's voice.

"You," Richard said to the man Kahlan had touched, "go sit beside him and see that he waits there with you."

While the man scurried to do as he was told, Richard tilted his head in gesture to the rest of them, calling them away with him. "We need to talk."

Friedrich, Tom, Jennsen, Cara and Kahlan followed Richard away from Owen and the man. Richard leaned back against the chafing rail of the wagon and folded his arms as they all gathered close around him. He took time to appraise each face looking at him.

"We have big problems," Richard began, "and not just from the poison Owen gave me. Owen isn't gifted. He's like you, Jennsen. Magic doesn't touch him." His gaze remained locked on Jennsen's. "The rest of his people are the same as he, as you."

Jennsen's jaw fell open in astonishment. She looked confused, as if unable to reconcile it all in her mind. Friedrich and Tom looked nearly as startled. Cara's brow drew down in a dark frown.

"Richard," Jennsen finally said, "that just can't be. There's too many of them. There's no way that they can all be half brothers and sisters of ours."

"They aren't half brothers and sisters," Richard said. "They're a line of people descended from the House of Rahl—people like you. I don't have time right now to explain all of it to you, but remember how I told you that you would bear children who were like you, and they would pass that pristinely ungifted trait on to all future generations? Well, back a long time ago, there were people like that spreading in D'Hara. The people back then gathered up all these ungifted people and sent them to the Old World. The people down here then sealed them away beyond those mountains, there. The name of their empire, Bandakar, means 'the banished.'"

Jennsen's big blue eyes filled with tears. She was one of those people, people so hated that they had been banished from the rest of the people in their own land and sent into exile.

Kahlan put an arm around her shoulders. "Remember how you

said that you felt alone in the world?" Kahlan smiled warmly. "You don't have to feel alone anymore. There are people like you."

Kahlan didn't think her words seemed to help much, but Jennsen welcomed the comfort of the embrace.

Jennsen abruptly looked back up at Richard. "That can't be true. They had a boundary that kept them locked in that place. If they were like me they wouldn't be affected by a boundary of magic. They could have come out of there any time they wished. Over all this time, at least some of them would have come out into the rest of the world—the magic of the boundary couldn't have held them back."

"I don't think that's true," Richard said. "Remember when you saw the sand flowing sideways in that warning beacon that Sabar brought us? That was magic, and you saw it."

"That's right," Kahlan said. "If she's a pillar of Creation, then how is such a thing possible?"

"That's right," Jennsen agreed. "How could that be, if I'm truly ungifted?" Her eyebrows went up. "Richard—maybe it's not true after all. Maybe I have a bit of the spark of the gift—maybe I'm not really, truly ungifted."

Richard smiled. "Jennsen, you're as pure as a snowflake. You saw that magic for a reason. Nicci wrote us in her letter that the warning beacon was linked to the wizard who created it—linked to him in the underworld. The underworld is the world of the dead. That means that the statue functioned partly through Subtractive Magic— magic having to do with the underworld. You may be immune to magic, but you are not immune to death. Gifted or not, you're still linked to life, and thus death.

"That's why you saw some of the magic of the statue—the part relating to the advancement of death.

"The boundary was a place in this world where death itself existed. To go into that boundary was to enter the world of the dead. No one returns from the dead. If any pristinely ungifted person in Bandakar had gone into the boundary, they would have died. That was how they were sealed in."

"But they could banish people through the boundary," Jennsen pressed. "That would have to mean that the boundary didn't really affect them."

Richard was shaking his head even as she was protesting. "No. They were touched by death, the same as anyone. But there was a way left through the boundary—much like the one that once divided the three lands of the New World. I got through that boundary without being touched by it. There was a pass through it, a special, hidden place to get through the boundary. This one was the same."

Jennsen wrinkled her nose. "That makes no sense, then. If that was true, and it wasn't hidden from them—since they all knew of this passage through the boundary—then why couldn't they all just leave if they wanted to? How could it seal the rest of them in, if they could send banished people through?"

Richard sighed, wiping a hand across his face. It looked to Kahlan as if he wished she hadn't asked that question.

"You know the area we passed a while back?" Richard asked her. "That place where nothing grew?"

Jennsen nodded. "I remember."

"Well, Sabar said he came through another one, a little to the north of here."

"That's right," Kahlan said. "And it ran toward the center of the wasteland, toward the Pillars of Creation—just like the one we saw. They had to be roughly parallel."

Richard was nodding to what she was beginning to suspect. "And they were to either side of the notch into Bandakar. They weren't very far apart. We're in that place right now, between those two boundaries."

Friedrich leaned in. "But Lord Rahl, that would mean that if someone was banished from the Bandakaran Empire, when they emerged from that boundary they would find themselves trapped between the walls of these two boundaries out here, and there wasn't much room between them. A person would have nowhere to go but . . ."

Friedrich covered his mouth as he turned west, looking off into the gloom.

"The Pillars of Creation," Richard finished with quiet finality.

"But, but," Jennsen stammered, "are you saying that someone made it that way? Made these two boundaries deliberately to force anyone who was sent out of the Bandakaran Empire to go into that place—the Pillars of Creation? Why?"

Richard looked into her eyes for a long moment. "To kill them."

Jennsen swallowed. "You mean, whoever banished these people wanted anyone they in turn sent out, anyone they exiled, to die?"

"Yes," Richard said.

Kahlan pulled her cloak tighter around herself. It had been hot for so long she could hardly believe that the weather had so suddenly turned cold.

Richard swiped a lock of wet hair back off his forehead as he went on. "From what Adie told me once, boundaries have to have a pass to create balance on both sides, to equalize the life on both sides. I suspect that those down here in the Old World who banished these people wanted to give them a way to get rid of criminals and so told the people about the existence of the pass. But they didn't want such people to be loosed on the rest of the world. Criminals or not, they were ungifted. They couldn't be allowed to run free."

Kahlan immediately saw the problem with his theory. "But all three boundaries would have had to have a pass," she said. "Even if the other two passes, in the remaining two boundaries, were secret, that still left the possibility that anyone exiled and sent through the notch might find one of them and so not try to escape through the Pillars of Creation where they would die. That left the chance that they might still escape into the Old World."

"If there really were three boundaries, such might be the case," Richard said. "But I don't think there were three. I think there really was only one."

"Now you're not making any sense," Cara complained. "You said there was the one going north and south blocking the pass, and then there were these two parallel ones out here, going east and west, to funnel anyone who came out of the empire through that first boundary, toward the Pillars of Creation where they would die."

Kahlan had to agree. It seemed that there might be a chance for someone to escape through one of the other two.

"I don't think there were three boundaries," Richard repeated. "I think there was only one. That one boundary wasn't straight—it was bent in half." He held two fingers up, side by side. "The bottom of the bend went across the pass." He pointed at the web between the two fingers. "The two legs extended out here, parallel, going off to where they ended at the Pillars."

Jennsen could only ask "Why?"

"It seems to me, by how elaborate the whole design was, that the ones who sealed those people in wanted to give them a way to rid themselves of dangerous people, possibly knowing from what they had learned of their beliefs that they would balk at executing anyone. When these people were banished here to the Old World, they may have already had at least the core of the same beliefs they hold now. Those beliefs leave them completely vulnerable to those who are evil. Protecting their way of life, without executing criminals, meant they had to cast such people out of their community or be destroyed by them.

"The banishment away from D'Hara and the New World, across the barrier into the Old World, must have terrified them. They stuck together as a means of survival, a common bond.

"Those down here in the Old World who put them behind that boundary must have used those people's fear of persecution to convince them that the boundary was meant to protect them, to keep others from harming them. They must have convinced those people that, since they were special, they needed such protection. That, along with their well-established need to stick together, had to have reinforced in them a terrible fear of being put out of their protected place. Banishment had a special terror to those people.

"They must have felt the anguish of being rejected by the rest of the peoples of the world because they were ungifted, but, together as they were, they also felt safe behind the boundary.

"Now that the seal is off, we have big problems."

Jennsen folded her arms. "Now that there's more than one of us—more than one snowflake—you're having worries about a snowstorm?"

Richard fixed her with a reproachful look. "Why do you think the Order came in and took some of their people?"

"Apparently," Jennsen said, "to breed more children like them. To breed precious magic out of the race of man."

Richard ignored the heat in her words. "No, I mean why would they take men?"

"Same reason," Jennsen said. "To mate with regular women and give them ungifted children."

Richard drew in a patient breath and let it out slowly. "What did Owen say? The men were taken to see the women and told that if they didn't follow orders those women would be skinned alive."

Jennsen hesitated. "What orders?"

Richard leaned toward her. "What orders, indeed. Think about it," he said, looking around at the rest of them. "What orders? What would they want ungifted men for? What is it they would want ungifted men to do?"

Kahlan gasped. "The Keep!"

"Exactly." Richard's unsettling gaze met each of them in turn. "Like I said, we have big problems. Zedd is protecting the Keep. With his ability and the magic of that place he can no doubt single-handedly hold off Jagang's entire army.

"But how is that skinny old man going to resist even one young ungifted man who is untouched by magic and comes up and grabs him by the throat?"

Jennsen's hand came away from her mouth. "You're right, Richard. Jagang, too, has that book—*The Pillars of Creation*. He knows how those like me aren't touched by magic. He tried to use me in that very way. That's why he worked so hard to convince me that you were trying to kill me—so that I would think my only chance was to kill you first. He knew I was ungifted and couldn't be stopped by magic."

"And, Jagang is from the Old World," Richard added. "In all likelihood he would have known something about the empire beyond that boundary. For all we know, in the Old World Bandakar might be legendary, while those in the New World, beyond the great barrier for three thousand years, would never have known what happened to those people.

"Now, the Order has been taking men from there and threatening them with the brutal murder of their defenseless women—women who are loved ones—if those men don't follow orders. I think those orders are to assault the Wizard's Keep and capture it for the Imperial Order."

Kahlan's legs shook. If the Keep fell, they would lose the one real advantage, however limited, they had. With the Keep in the hands of the Order, all those ancient and deadly things of magic would be available to Jagang. There was no telling what he might unleash. There were things in the Keep that could kill them all, Jagang included. He had already proven with the plague he'd unleashed that he was willing to kill any number to have his way, that he was willing to use any weapon, even if such weapons decimated his own people as well.

Even if Jagang did nothing with the Keep, just him having control of it denied the D'Haran Empire the possibility of finding something there that could help them. That was, in addition to protecting the Keep, what Zedd was doing while he was there—trying to find something that would help them win the war, or at least find a way to put the Imperial Order back behind a barrier of some kind and confine them to the Old World.

Without the Keep, their cause would likely be hopeless. Resistance would be nothing more than delaying the inevitable. Without the Keep on their side, all resistance to Jagang would eventually be crushed. His troops would pour into every part of the New World. There would be no stopping them.

With trembling fingers Kahlan clutched her cloak closed. She knew what awaited her people, what it was like when the Imperial Order invaded and overpowered places. She had been with the army for nearly a year, fighting against them. They were like a pack of wild dogs. There was no peace with such animals after you. They would be satisfied only when they could tear you apart.

Kahlan had been to cities, like Ebinissia, that had been overrun by Imperial Order soldiers. In a wild binge of savagery that went on for days, they had tortured, raped, and murdered every person trapped in the city, finally leaving it a wasteland of human corpses. None, no matter their age, had been spared.

That was what the people of the New World had to look forward to.

With enemy troops overrunning all of the New World, any trade that was not already disrupted would be brought to a standstill. Nearly all businesses would fail. The livelihood of countless people would be lost. Food would quickly become scarce, and then simply unavailable at any cost. People would have no means of supporting themselves and their families. People would lose everything for which they had worked a lifetime.

Cities, even before the troops arrived, would be in a destructive panic. When the enemy troops arrived, most people would be burned out of their homes, driven from their cities and their land. Jagang would steal all supplies of food for his troops and give conquered land to his favored elite. The true owners of that land would perish, or become slaves working their own farms. Those who escaped before the invading horde would desperately cling to life, living like animals in wild areas.

Most of the population would be in flight, running for their lives. Hundreds of thousands would be out in the elements without shelter. There would be little food, and no ability to prepare for winter. When the weather turned harsh, they would perish in droves.

As civilization crumbled and starvation became the norm, disease would sweep across the land, catching up those on the run. Families would collapse as those they depended on suffered agonizingly slow and painful deaths. Children and the weak would be alone, to be preyed upon as a source of food for the starving.

Kahlan knew what such widespread disease was like. She knew what it was to watch people dying by the thousands. She had seen it happen in Aydindril when the plague was there. She saw scores stricken without warning. She had watched the old, the young— such good people—contract something they could not fight, watched them suffer in misery for days before they died.

Richard had been stricken with that plague. Unlike everyone else, though, he had gotten it knowingly. Taking the plague deliberately had been the price to get back to her. He had traded his life just to be with her again before he died.

That had been a time beyond horror.

Kahlan knew, at first hand, savage desperation. It was then that she had taken the only chance available to her to save his life. It was then that she had loosed the chimes. That act had saved Richard's life. She hadn't known at the time that it would also be a catalyst that would set unforeseen events into motion.

Because of her desperate act, the boundary to this empire had lost its power and failed. Because of her, all magic might eventually fail.

Now, because of that boundary failing, the Wizard's Keep, their last bastion to work a solution against the Order, was in terrible jeopardy.

Kahlan felt as if it was all her fault.

The world was on the brink of destruction. Civilization stood at the threshold of obliteration in the name of the Order's mindless idea of a greater good. The Order demanded sacrifice to that greater good; what they were determined to sacrifice was reason, and, therefore, civilization itself. Madness had cast its shadow across the world and would have them all.

They now stood in the edge of the shadow of a dark age. They were all on the eve of the end times.

Kahlan couldn't say that, though. She couldn't tell them how she felt. She dared not reveal her despair.

"Richard, we simply can't allow the Order to capture the Keep." Kahlan could hardly believe how calm and determined her voice sounded. She wondered if anyone else would believe that she thought they still stood a chance. "We have to stop them."

"I agree," Richard said.

He sounded determined, too. She wondered if he saw in her eyes the true depths of her despair.

"First," he said, "the easy part: Nicci and Victor. We have to tell them that we can't come now. Victor needs to know what we would say to him. He will need to know that we agree with his plans—that he must proceed and that he can't wait for us. We've talked with him; he knows what to do. Now, he must do it, and Priska must know that he has to help.

"Nicci needs to know where we're going. She needs to know that we believe we've discovered the cause of the warning beacon. She has to know where we are."

He left unsaid that she had to come to help him if he couldn't get to her because his gift was killing him.

"She needs to know, too," Richard said, "that we only had a chance to read part of her warning about what Jagang was doing with the Sisters of the Dark in creating weapons out of people."

Everyone's eyes widened. They hadn't read the letter.

"Well," Kahlan said, "with all the other problems we have, at least that's one we won't have to deal with for now."

"We have that much on our side," Richard agreed. He gestured to the man watching, the man waiting for Kahlan to command him. "We'll send him to Victor and Nicci so they will know everything."

"And then what?" Cara asked.

"I want Kahlan to command him that when he's finished with carrying out that part of his orders, he's then to go north and find the Imperial Order army. I want him to pretend to be one of them to get close enough to assassinate Emperor Jagang."

Kahlan knew how implausible such a scheme was. By the way everyone stared in astonishment, they had a good idea, too.

"Jagang has layers of men to protect him from assassination," Jennsen said. "He's always surrounded by special guards. Regular soldiers can't even get close to him."

"Do you really think he has any chance at all to accomplish such a thing?" Kahlan asked.

"No," Richard admitted. "The Order will most likely kill him before he can get to Jagang. But he will be driven by the need to fulfill your orders. He will be single-minded. I expect he will be killed in the effort, but I also suspect he will at least make a good attempt of it. I want Jagang to at least lose some sleep knowing that any of his men might be assassins. I want him to worry that he will never know who might be trying to kill him. I don't want him ever to be able to sleep soundly. I want him to be haunted by nightmares of what might be coming next, of who among his men might be waiting for an opening."

Kahlan nodded her agreement. Richard appraised the grim faces waiting for the rest of what he had to say.

"Now, to the most important part of what must be done. It's vital we get to the Keep and warn Zedd. We can't delay. Jagang is ahead of us in all this—he's been planning and acting and we never realized what he was up to. We don't know how soon those ungifted men might be sent north. We haven't a moment to lose."

"Lord Rahl," Cara reminded him, "you have to get to the antidote before time runs out. You can't go running off to the Keep to . . . Oh, no. Now, you just wait a minute—you're not sending me to the Keep again. I'm not leaving you at a time like this, at a time when you're next to defenseless. I won't hear of it and I won't go."

Richard laid a hand on her shoulder. "Cara, I'm not sending you, but thanks for offering."

Cara folded her arms and shot him a fiery scowl.

"We can't take the wagon up into Bandakar—there's no road—"

"Lord Rahl," Tom interrupted, "without magic you'll need all the steel you have." He sounded only slightly less emphatic than Cara had.

Richard smiled. "I know, Tom, and I agree. It's Friedrich who I think must go." Richard turned to Friedrich. "You can take the wagon. An older man, by himself, will raise less suspicion than would any of the rest of us. They won't see you as a threat. You will be able to make better time with the wagon and without having to worry that the Order might snatch you and put you in the army. Will you do it, Friedrich?"

Friedrich scratched his stubble. A smile came to his weathered face. "I guess I'm at last being called upon to be a boundary warden, of sorts."

Richard smiled with him. "Friedrich, the boundary has failed. As the Lord Rahl, I appoint you to the post of boundary warden and ask that you immediately undertake to warn others of the danger come from out of that boundary."

Friedrich's smile departed as he put a fist to his heart in salute and solemn pledge.

CHAPTER 26

Somewhere back in a distant room, where his body waited, Nicholas heard an insistent noise. He was absorbed in the task at hand, so he ignored the sound. The light was fading, and although light helped to see, darkness would not hinder eyes such as he used.

Again, he heard the noise. Indignant that the sound kept calling him, kept annoying him, kept demanding his attention, he returned to his body.

Someone was banging a fist on the door.

Nicholas rose from the floor, where his body sat cross-legged, taking his body with him. It was always, at first, disorienting to have to be in his body again, to be so limited, so confined. It felt awkward to have to move it about, to use his own muscles, to breathe, to see, to hear with his own senses.

The knock came again. Irate at the interruption, Nicholas went not to the door but to the windows, and threw the shutters closed. He cast a hand out, igniting the torch, and finally stalked to the door. Layered strips of cloth covering his robes flowed out behind, like a heavy mantle of black feathers.

"What is it?" He threw open the heavy door and peered out.

Najari stood just outside, in the hall, his weight on one foot, his thumbs hooked behind his belt. His muscular shoulders nearly touched the walls to each side. Nicholas saw, then, the huddled crowd behind the man. Najari's crooked nose, flattened to the left in some of the numerous brawls his temper got him into, cast an oddly-shaped shadow across his cheek. Anyone unfortunate enough to find themselves in a brawl with Najari usually suffered far worse than a mere broken nose.

Najari waggled a thumb over his shoulder. "You asked for some guests, Nicholas."

Nicholas raked his nails back through his hair, feeling the silken smooth pleasure of oils gliding against his palm. He rolled his shoulders, ruffling away his pique.

Nicholas had been so absorbed in what he had been doing that he had forgotten that he had requested that Najari bring him some bodies.

"Very good, Najari. Bring them in, then. Let's have a look at them."

Nicholas watched as the commander led the gaggle of people into the flickering torchlight. Soldiers in the rear herded the stragglers through the door and into the large room. Heads swiveled around, looking at the strange, stark surroundings, at the wooden walls, the torches in brackets, the plank flooring, the lack of furniture other than a stout table. Noses twitched at the sharp smell of blood.

Nicholas watched carefully as people spotted the sharpened stakes standing in a line along the wall to their right, stakes as thick as Najari's wrists.

Nicholas studied the people, watching for the telltales of fear as they spread out along the wall beside the door. Eyes flitted about, worried, and at the same time eager to take it all in so they could report to their friends what they had seen inside. Nicholas knew that he was an object of great curiosity.

A rare being.

A Slide.

No one knew what his name meant. This day, some would learn.

Nicholas glided past the undulating mob. They were a curious people, these odd, ungifted creatures, curious like mockingbirds, but not nearly so bold. Because they were without any spark whatsoever of the gift, Nicholas had to handle them in special ways in order for them to be of any use to him. It was a bother, but it had its rewards.

Some necks craned in his wake, trying to better see the rare man. He ran his nails through his hair again just to feel the oils slide against his hand. As he leaned close to some of the people he passed, observing individuals in the gathering, one of the women before him closed her eyes, turning her face away. Nicholas lifted a hand toward her, flicking out a finger. He glanced to Najari to be sure he saw which one had been picked.

Najari's gaze flicked from the woman up to Nicholas; he had noted the selection.

A man back against the wall stood stiff, his eyes wide. Nicholas flicked a finger at him. Another man twisted his lips in an odd manner. Nicholas glanced down and saw that the man, in a state of wild fright, had wet himself. Nicholas's finger flitted out again. Three selected. Nicholas walked on.

A thin whine escaped the throat of a woman in the front, right before him. He smiled at her. She peered up, trembling, unable to take her wide-eyed gaze from him, from his red-rimmed black eyes, unable to halt the puling sound escaping her throat. She had never seen one so human . . . yet not. Nicholas tapped her shoulder with a long-nailed finger. He would reward her unspoken revulsion with service to a greater good. His.

Jagang had sought to create something . . . unusual, for himself. A bauble of flesh and blood. A magical trinket crafted from a wizard. A lapdog . . . with teeth.

His Excellency had gotten what he wanted, and more. Oh, so much more.

Nicholas would enjoy seeing how the emperor liked having a puppet without strings, a specially-crafted creation with a mind of its own, and talents to fulfill his wishes.

A man at the rear, against the wall, appeared to be somewhat uninterested, as if impatient for the exhibition to be over so he could go back to his own affairs. While none of these people could be said to think of themselves as important individuals with consequential sway over any meaningful aspects of life in their empire, a few occasionally exhibited tendencies, even if inconsistent, toward self-interest. Nicholas flicked his finger for the fifth time. The man would soon have reason to be highly interested in the proceedings, and he would find that he was no better than anyone else. He would be going nowhere—at least not in body.

Everyone stared in silence as Nicholas chuckled alone at his own joke.

His amusement ended. Nicholas tipped his head toward the door in a single nod. The soldiers jumped into action.

"All right," Najari growled, "move along. Move! Get going. Out, out, out!"

The feet of the crowd shuffled urgently through the door as ordered. Some people cast worried glances back over their shoulders at the five Najari had cut out of the flock. Those five were shoved back when they sought to stay with the rest. A stiff finger to the chest backed them up as effectively as would a club or a sword.

"Don't cause any trouble," Najari warned, "or you will be making trouble for the others."

The five remaining huddled close to one another, rocking nervously side to side like a covey of quail before a bird-dog.

When the soldiers had driven the rest of the people out, Najari closed the door and stood before it, hands clasped behind his back.

Nicholas returned to the windows, opening the shutters on the west wall. The sun was down, leaving a red slash across the sky.

Soon they would be on the wing, on the hunt.

Nicholas would be with them.

Casting an arm back without needing to turn to look, he doused the torch. The flickering light was a distraction during this cusp of time, the transient twilight that was so fragile, so brief. He would need the light, but, at the moment, he wanted only to see the sky, to see the glorious, unbounded sky.

"Are we going to be able to leave soon?" one of the people asked in a timid squeak.

Nicholas turned and peered at them. Najari's eyes revealed which one had spoken. Nicholas followed his commander's gaze. It was one of the men—the one who had been impatient to leave, of course.

"Go?" Nicholas asked as he swept in close to the man. "You wish to go?"

The man stood with his back bent, leaning away from Nicholas. "Well, sir, I was only wondering when we would be going."

Nicholas stooped in even more, peering deeply into the man's eyes. "Wonder in silence," he hissed.

Returning to the windows, Nicholas rested his hands on the sill, his weight on his arms, as he breathed in deeply the gathering night while taking in the sweep of crimson sky.

Soon, he would be there, be free.

Soon, he would soar as no one else but he could.

Impulsively, he sought them.

Eyes bulging with the effort, he cast his senses where none but his could go.

"There!" he screeched, throwing his arm out, pointing a long black nail at what none but he could see. "There! One has taken to wing."

Nicholas spun around, strips of cloth lifting, floating up. Panting through a rush of fluttering excitement, he gazed at the eyes staring at him. They could not know. They could not understand one such as he, understand what he felt, what he needed. He hungered to be on the hunt, to be with them, ever since he had imagined such a use for his ability.

He had reveled in the experience, dedicating himself to it as he learned his new abilities. He had been off with those glorious creatures as often as he could afford the time, ever since he had come here and discovered them.

How ironic it now seemed that he had resisted. How odd that he once had feared what those gruesome women, those Sisters of the Dark, had conspired to do to him . . . what they had done to him.

His duty, they had called it.

Their vile magic had cut like a red-hot blade through him. He had thought his eyes might burst out of his head from the pain that had seared through him. Tied spread-eagled to stakes in the ground in the center of their wicked circle, he had dreaded what they were going to do to him.

He had feared it.

Nicholas smiled.

Hated it, even.

He had been afraid because of the pain, the pain of what they were doing to him, and the even greater pain of not knowing what more they intended to do to him. His duty, they had called it, to a greater good. His ability bore responsibilities, they had insisted.

He watched through glazed eyes as Najari bound the hands of the five people behind each of their backs.

"Thank you, Najari," he said when the man had finished.

Najari approached. "The men will have them by now, Nicholas. I told them to send enough men to insure that they would not escape." Najari grinned at the prospect. "There's no need to worry. They should all be on their way back to us."

Nicholas narrowed his eyes. "We will see. We will see."

He wanted to see it himself. With his own vision—even if his own vision was through another's eyes.

Najari yawned on his way to the door. "See you tomorrow, then, Nicholas."

Nicholas opened his mouth wide, mimicking the yawn, even though he didn't yawn. It felt good to stretch his jaws wide. Sometimes he felt trapped inside himself and he wanted out.

Nicholas closed the door behind Najari and bolted it. It was a perfunctory act, done more to add to the aura of peril than out of necessity. Even with their hands tied behind their backs, these people could, together, probably overpower him—knock him down and kick in his head, if nothing else. But for that, they would have to think, to decide what they ought to do and why, to commit to act. Easier not to think. Easier not to act. Easier to do as you are told.

Easier to die than to live.

Living took effort. Struggle. Pain.

Nicholas hated it.

"Hate to live, live to hate," he said to the silent, ghostly white faces watching him.

Out the window the streaks of clouds had gone dark gray as the touch of the sun passed beyond them and night crept in to embrace them. Soon, he would be among them.

He turned back from the window, taking in the faces watching him. Soon, they would all be out there, among them.

C H A P T E R   27

Nicholas seized one of the nameless men. Powered by muscles crafted of the Sisters' dark art, he hoisted the man into the air. The man cried out in surprise at being lifted so easily. He struggled hesitantly against muscle he would not be able to resist were he even to put daring into it. These people were immune to magic, or Nicholas would have used his power to easily lift them aloft. Absent the necessary spark of the gift, they had to be manhandled.

It made little difference to Nicholas. How they got to the stakes was unimportant. What happened to them once there was all that mattered.

As the man in his arms cried out in terror, Nicholas carried him across the room. The other people withdrew into a far corner. They always went to the far corner, like chickens about to be dinner.

Nicholas, his arms around the man's chest, lifted him high in the air, judging the distance and angle as he raced ahead.

The man's eyes went wide, his mouth did likewise. He gasped with the shock, then grunted as Nicholas, hugging the man tight in his arms, drove him down onto the stake.

The man's breath came in short sharp gasps as the sharpened stake penetrated up through his insides. He went still in Nicholas's powerful arms, fearing to move, fearing to believe what was happening to him, fearing to know it was true . . . trying to deny to himself that it could be true.

Nicholas straightened to his full height before the man. The man's back was as straight and stiff as a board as he sat impaled on the sharpened stake. His eyebrows pushed his sweat-beaded brow up in furrows as he writhed in slow agony, his legs trying to touch the ground that was too far away.

Into that confusion of sensation, Nicholas reached out with his mind, at the same time clawing his hands before the man with the effort as he slid his own being, his own spirit, into the core of this living creature, slid into this man's open mind, into the cavernous cracks between his abrupt and disconnected thoughts, there to feel his agony and fright. There to take control. Once he had slipped his own mind in there with this man, seeped through his conscious-ness, Nicholas drew his essence out and into himself.

With a staggering fusion of destructive and creative power dealt by the Sisters that day, Nicholas had been born into a new being, part him, and yet more. He had become what no man had ever been before—what others wished to make of him, what others wished him to be.

What had been unleashed in him by those Sisters all linked in their ability to harness powers they could never have touched alone and should never have invoked together, they instilled in him. They engendered in him powers few could ever have imagined: the power to slide into another living person's thoughts, and withdraw their spirit.

He drew his closed fists back toward his own abdomen with the effort of drawing with him the spirit of this man on the cusp of life and death, drew onward the marrow of this man's soul. Nicholas felt the slick heat of this other spirit slide into his, the hot rush of sensa-tion at feeling himself filled with another spirit.

Nicholas left the body there, impaled on the first stake, as he rushed to the windows, his head spinning with the first intoxicating wave of excitement at the journey only now just begun, at what was to come, at what power he would control.

He opened his mouth wide again in a yawn that was not a yawn, but a call carrying more than just his silent voice.

His eyes swam with wavering images. He gasped in the first scent of the forests out beyond, where his intent had been cast.

He rushed back and seized a woman. She begged as she wept, begged to be spared as he bore her to her stake.

"But this is nothing," he told her. "Nothing compared to what I have endured. Oh, you cannot imagine what I have endured."

He had been staked naked to the ground, in the center of a circle of those smug women. He had been nothing to them. He had not been a man, a wizard. He had been nothing but the raw material, the flesh and blood innervated by the gift, that they needed for what they wanted, that they used in yet another of their trials, all to be twisted by their tinkering at creation.

He had the ability, so duty required he sacrifice it.

Nicholas had been the first to live through their tests, not because they took care—not because they cared—but because they had learned what didn't work, and so avoided their past errors.

"Scream, my dear. Scream all you want. It will help you no more than it helped me."

"Why?" she screamed. "Why?"

"Oh, but I must, if I am to have your spirit to soar on the wings of my distant friends. You will go on a glorious journey, you and I."

"Please!" she wailed. "Dear Creator, no!"

"Oh, yes, dear Creator," he mocked. "Come and save her—like you came and saved me."

Her wailing did her no good. His hadn't either. She had no idea how immeasurably worse his agony had been than hers would be. Unlike her, he had been condemned to live.

"Hate to live, live to hate," he murmured in a comforting whisper. "You will have the glory and the reward that is death."

He drove her down onto the stake. He reckoned her not far enough onto the stake, and shoved her down another six inches, until he judged it deep enough within her, deep enough to produce the necessary pain and terror, but not deep enough to lance anything inside that would kill her right off. She thrashed, trying desperately, hands helpless behind her back, to somehow remove herself.

He was only dimly aware of her cries, her worthless words. She thought they might somehow make a difference.

Pain was his goal. Their complaints of it only confirmed that he was achieving his goal.

Nicholas stood before the woman, hands clawed, as he slid his own spirit through her sundered thoughts and into the core of her being. With mental strength far superior to his physical strength, he pulled her back. He gasped as he felt her spirit slide into his.

For now, he slipped their spirits out of tortured, dying bodies while those spirits existed in the netherworld between the worldly form they knew was lost to them, but still alive, and the world of the dead already calling them in from beyond. Life could no longer hold them, but death could not yet have them. In that time of spiritual transition, they were his, and he could use those spirits for things only he could imagine.

And he had not yet really even begun to imagine.

Such ability as he possessed was not something that could be taught by another—there was no other but he. He was still learning the extent of his powers, the things he could do with the spirit of another. He had only scratched the surface.

Emperor Jagang had sought to create something akin to himself, a dream walker, a brother, of sorts. One who could enter another's mind. He had gotten far more than he could have ever imagined. Nicholas didn't simply slide into another's thoughts, as Jagang did; he could slide into their very soul, and draw their spirit back into himself.

The Sisters hadn't counted on that aberration of their tinkering with his ability.

Rushing to the window, his mouth pulled open as wide as it would go in a yawn that wasn't a yawn. The room swam behind him. It was only partly there, now. Now, he was beginning to see other places. Glorious places. See them with new vision, with spirits no longer bound to their paltry bodies.

He rushed to the third person, no longer aware even if they were man or woman. Their soul was all that mattered—their spirit.

He drove them onto a stake with urgent effort, slid into them and drew their spirit into his, shuddering with the power of it entering him.

He rushed to the window once more, opening wide his mouth again, twisting his head side to side again with the thrill of it, the slick, silken, sliding ecstasy of it . . . the loss of physical orientation, the exaltation of being above his corporeal existence, the former bounds of his mere worldly form—carried aloft not simply with his own efforts, but by the spirits of others that he had freed from their bodies.

What a glorious thing it was.

It was almost like the joy he imagined death would be.

He seized the fourth weeping person and with delirious expectation ran with them across the room, to the stakes, to the fourth stake, and drove them screaming onto it.

As he lurched back from them, he thrust himself into their wildly racing, confused, swirling thoughts, and took what was there for the taking. He took their spirit into himself.

When he controlled a person's spirit, he controlled their very existence. He became life and death for them. He was their savior, their destroyer.

He was in many ways like those spirits he took, trapped in a worldly form, hating to live, to endure the pain and agony that was life, yet fearing to die even while longing for the promise of its sweet embrace.

With four spirits swirling through him, Nicholas staggered to the fifth person, cowering in the corner.

"Please!" the man wailed, trying to ward what he would not commit to warding. "Please, don't!"

The thought occurred to Nicholas that the stakes were really a hindrance; using them required him to carry people around like woolly sheep to have their souls sheared. Yes, he was still learning what he could do and how to control what he did, but to have to use the stakes was limiting. When he thought about it, it was actually insulting that a wizard of his ability would have to use so crude a device.

What he really wanted to do was to slide into another's spirit and take it without any warning—without needing to bring people to the stakes.

When he was fully able to do that—to simply walk up to another, say "Good day," and slide like the thrust of a dagger into the heart of their spirit, there to draw it into his—then he would be invincible.

When he was able to do that, then no one could challenge him. No one would be able to deny him anything.

As the man shrank down before him, Nicholas, before he fully realized what it was he was doing, driven by an angry need, by hatred, thrust out his hand as he thrust his own mind into this man, into the spaces between thought.

The man stiffened, just as those on the stakes stiffened, when Nicholas had impaled them with his ability.

He drew back his closed fist toward his middle as he drew in this man's spirit. He gasped with the heat of it, with the silky-slick feel of it sliding into him.

They stared at each other, each in shock, each considering what this meant for them.

The man slumped back against the wall, sliding down, in soundless, silent, terrible empty agony.

Nicholas realized that he had just done what he had never done before. He had just taken a soul by his will alone.

He had just freed himself to take what he wanted, when he wanted, where he wanted.

C H A P T E R 28

Nicholas, his vision a blur, staggered to the window.

All five were his, now.

This time, as his mouth opened wide, a cry at last came forth, a cry of the five spirits joining his as he drew them together into one force guided by his will alone. Their worldly agony was a distant concern to them. Five spirits gazed out of the windows along with him, five spirits now waiting to soar out into the night, to where he chose to send them.

Those Sisters had not known what they unleashed that night. They could not have known the power they fused into him, the ability they burned into him.

They had achieved what none had achieved for thousands of years—the altering of a wizard into something more, honing him into a weapon of specific intent. They had imbued him with power beyond that of anyone living. They had given him dominion over the spirits of others.

Most had escaped, but he had killed five of them.

The five were enough. After he had slid into their souls and pulled their spirits back into his that night, he had appropriated their Han, their force of life, their power, for himself.

It was only fitting, as their Han was not natural to them, but was male Han they had stolen from young wizards—a birthright they had sucked from those to whom it belonged in order to give them-selves abilities they had not been born with, could not be born with. Yet more nameless people with ability to be sacrificed to those who needed it, or simply wanted it.

Nicholas had taken it all back from their trembling bodies, pulled it out of them as he had clawed their living insides open. They had been sorry that they had done Jagang's bidding, that they had twisted him into something Creation never intended.

Not only had they made him into a Slide, they had given up their Han to him, and made him that much more powerful for it.

After each of those five women had died, the world had gone darker than dark for an instant when the Keeper had come and taken them to his realm.

The Sisters had destroyed him that day, and they had created him.

He had a lifetime to explore and discover what he could do with his new abilities.

And, to be sure, Jagang would grant him payment for that night. Jagang would pay, but he would pay gladly, for Nicholas would give him something none but Nicholas the Slide could give him.

Nicholas would be rewarded with things enough to repay him for what had been done to him . . . He hadn't decided, yet, what that reward would be, but it would be worthy of him.

He would use his ability to hold sway over lives—important lives. He no longer needed to cart people to the stakes. He knew how to take what he wanted, now.

Now he knew how to slip into their minds at the time of his choosing and take their souls.

He would trade those lives for what he would have in power, wealth, splendor. It would have to be something appropriate . . .

He would be an emperor.

It would have to be more than this petty empire of sheep, though. He would frolic in rule. He would have his every whim fulfilled, once he was given dominion over . . . over something important. He hadn't decided just what, yet. It was an important decision, what he would have as his reward. No need to rush it. It would come to him.

He turned from the window, the five spirits swirling within his, soaring through him.

It was time to use what he had pulled together.

Time to get down to business, if he was to have what he wanted.

He would get closer, this time. He was frustrated from not being closer, from not seeing better. It was dark, now. He would get closer, this time, under cover of the darkness.

Nicholas took the broad bowl from the table and placed it on the floor before the five who still owned the spirits within him. They writhed in otherworldly agony, even the man not on a stake, an agony of both body and soul.

Nicholas sat cross-legged on the floor before the bowl. Hands on his knees, he threw his head back, eyes closed, as he gathered the power within, the power created by those wicked women, those wonderful wicked women.

They had considered him a pathetic wizard of little worth except as flesh and blood and gift to toy with—a sacrifice to a greater need.

When he had time, he would go after the rest of them.

With a more immediate task at hand, Nicholas dismissed the Sisters from his mind.

Tonight, he would not merely watch through other eyes. Tonight, he would again go with the spirits he cast.

Tonight, he would not merely watch through other eyes. Tonight, his spirit would travel to them.

Nicholas opened his mouth as wide as it would go, his head rocking from side to side. The joined spirits within released a part of themselves into the bowl, whirling in a silken, silvery swirl lit with the soft glow of their link to the life behind him, placekeepers for their journey, a stitch in the world holding the knot in the thread of their travels.

His spirit, too, let slip a small portion to remain with his body, to drift in the bowl with the others.

Fragments of the five spirits revolved with the fragment of his, their light of life glowing softly in this safe place as he prepared to journey. He cast his own spirit away, then, leaving behind the husk of a body sitting on the floor behind him as he fled out into the dark sky, borne on the wings of his invested power.

No wizard before had ever been able to do as he did now, to leave his body and have his spirit soar to where his mind would send him. He raced through the night, fast as thought, to find what he hunted.

He felt the rush of air flowing over feathers. As quick as that, he had raced away through the night and was with them, pulling the five spirits along with him.

He summoned the dark forms into a circle with him, and, as they gathered around, cast the five spirits into them. His mouth was still open in a yawn that was not a yawn that back in a room somewhere distant let forth a cry to match the five.

As they circled, he felt the rush of air beneath their wings, felt their feathers working the wind to direct them as effortlessly as his own thought directed not only his spirit but the other five as well.

He sent those five racing through the night, to the place where he had sent the men. They raced over hills, turning to scan the open country, to look out over the barren land. The cloak of darkness felt cool, encasing him in obscure black night, obscure black feathers.

He caught the scent of carrion, sharp, cloying, tantalizing, as the five spiraled down toward the ground. Through their eyes that saw in the darkness Nicholas saw then the scene below, a place littered with the dead. Others of their kind had gathered to feed in a frenzy of ripping and gorging.

No. This was wrong. He didn't see them.

He had to find them.

He willed his charges up from the gory feast, to search. Nicholas felt a pang of urgency. This was his future that had slipped away from him—his treasure slipping through his grasp. He had to find them. Had to.

He spurred his charges onward.

This way, that way, over there. Look, look, look. Find them, find them. Look. Must find them. Look.

This was not supposed to be. There had been enough men. No one could escape that many experienced men. Not when they came by stealth and attacked with surprise. They had been selected for their talents. They knew their business.

Their bodies lay sprawled all about. Beak and claw ripped at them. Screeches of excitement. Hunger.

No. Must find them.

Up, up, up. Find them. He had to find them.

He had suffered the agony of a new birth in those dark woods, those terrible woods, with those terrible women. He would have his reward. He would not be denied. Not now. Not after all that.

Find them. Look, look, look. Find them.

On powerful wings, he soared into the night. With eyes that saw in the dark, he searched. With creatures that could catch the scent of prey at great distance, he tried for a whiff of them.

Through the night they went, hunting. Hunting.

There, there he saw their wagon. He recognized their wagon. Their big horses. He had seen it before—seen them with it before. His minions circled in close on nearly-silent wings, dropping in closer to see what Nicholas sought.

Not there. They weren't there. A trick. It had to be a trick. A diversion. Not there. They had sent the wagon away to trick him, to send him off their trail.

With wings powered by anger, he soared up, up, up to search the countryside. Hunt, hunt. Find them. He flew with his five in an ever wider pattern to search the ground beneath the night. They flew on, searching, searching. His hunger was their hunger. Hunt for them. Hunt.

The wings grew weary as he drove them onward. He had to find them. He would not allow rest. Not allow failure. He hunted in expanding swaths, searching, hunting, hunting.

There, among the trees, he saw movement.

It was only just dark. They wouldn't see their pursuers—not in the dark—but he could see them. He forced the five down, circling, circling, forced them in close. He would not fail this time to see them, to get close enough. Circling, holding him there, circling, watching, circling, watching, seeing them there.

It was her! The Mother Confessor! He saw others. The one with red hair and her small four-legged friend. Others, too. He must be there, too. Had to be there, too. He would be there, too, as the small group moved west.

West. They moved west. They had traveled to the west of where he had seen them last.

Nicholas laughed. They were coming west. The captors sent for them all lay dead, but here they came anyway. They were coming west.

Toward where he waited.

He would have them.

He would have Lord Rahl and the Mother Confessor.

Jagang would have them.

It came to him, then—his reward. What he would have in return for the prizes he would deliver.

D'Hara.

He would have the rule of D'Hara in return for these two paltry people. Jagang would reward him with the rule of D'Hara, if he wanted those two. He would not dare deny Nicholas the Slide what he wanted. Not when he had what Jagang wanted most, more than any other prize. Jagang would pay any price for these two.

Pain. A scream. Shock, terror, confusion raged through him. He felt the wind, the wind that carried him so effortlessly, now ripping at him like fists snatching at feathers as he tumbled in helpless pain.

One of the five falling at blinding speed smacked the ground.

Nicholas screamed. One of the five spirits had been lost with its host. Back somewhere distant, in some far-off room with wooden walls and shutters and bloody stakes, back, back, back in another place he had almost forgotten existed, back, back, back far away, a spirit was ripped from his control.

One of the five back there had died at the same instant the race had crashed to the ground.

Scream of hot pain. Another tumbled out of control. Another spirit escaped his grasp into the waiting arms of death.

Nicholas struggled to see in the confusion, forcing the remaining three to hold his vision in place so he could see. Hunt, hunt, hunt. Where was he? Where was he? Where? He saw the others. Where was Lord Rahl?

A third scream.

Where was he? Nicholas fought to hold his vision despite the hot agony, the bewildering plummet.

Pain ripped through a fourth.

Before he could gather his senses, hold them together, force them with the power of his will to do his bidding, two more spirits were yanked away into the void of the underworld.

Where was he?

Talons at the ready, Nicholas searched.

There! There!

With violent effort, he forced the race over into a dive. There he was! There he was! Up high. Higher than the rest. Somehow up high. Up on a ledge of rock above the rest. He wasn't down there with them. He was up high.

Dive for him. Dive down for him.

There he was, bow drawn.

Ripping pain tore through the last race. The ground rushed up at him. Nicholas cried out. He tried frantically to stop the spinning. He felt the race slam into the rock at frightening speed. But only for an instant.

With a gasp, Nicholas drew a desperate breath. His head spun with the burning torture of the abrupt return, an uncontrolled return not of his doing.

He blinked, his mouth open wide in an attempt to let out a cry, but no sound came. His eyes bulged with the effort, but no cry came. He was back. Whether or not he wanted to be, he was back.

He looked around at the room. He was back, that was the reason no cry came. No screech of a race joined his own. They were dead. All five.

Nicholas turned to the four impaled on stakes behind him. All four were slumped. The fifth man lay slouched in the far corner. All five limp and still. All five dead. Their spirits gone.

The room was as silent as a crypt. The bowl before him glowed only with the fragment of his own spirit. He drew it back in.

He sat in the stillness for a long time, waiting for his head to stop spinning. It had been a shock to be in a creature as it was killed— to have a spirit of a person in him as they died. As five of them died. It had been a surprise.

Lord Rahl was a surprising man. Nicholas hadn't thought, back that first time, that he would be able to get all five. He had thought it was luck. A second time was not luck. Lord Rahl was a surprising man.

Nicholas could cast his spirit out again if he wanted, seek out new eyes, but his head hurt and he didn't feel up to it; besides, it didn't matter. Lord Rahl was coming west. He was coming to the great empire of Bandakar.

Nicholas owned Bandakar.

The people here revered him.

Nicholas smiled. Lord Rahl was coming. He would be surprised at the kind of man he found when he arrived. Lord Rahl probably thought he knew all manner of men.

He did not know Nicholas the Slide.

Nicholas the Slide, who would be emperor of D'Hara when he gave Jagang the prizes he sought most: the dead body of Lord Rahl, and the living body of the Mother Confessor.

Jagang would have them both for himself.

And in return, Nicholas would have their empire.

CHAPTER 29

Ann heard the distant echo of footsteps coming down the long, empty, dark corridor outside the far door to her forgotten vault under the People's Palace, the seat of power in D'Hara. She was no longer sure if it was day or night. She'd lost track of time as she sat in the silent darkness. She saved the lamp for times when they brought food, or the times she wrote to Verna in the journey book. Or the times she felt so alone that she needed the company of a small flame, if nothing else.

In this place, within this spell of a palace for those born Rahl, her power was so diminished that it was all she could do to light that lamp.

She feared to use the little lamp too often and run out of oil; she didn't know if they would give her more. She didn't want to run out and only then find they would give her no more. She didn't want not to have at least the possibility of that small flame, that small gift of light.

In the dark she could do nothing but consider her life and all she had worked so hard to accomplish. For centuries she had led the Sisters of the Light in their effort to see the Creator's light triumph in the world, and see the Keeper of the underworld kept where he belonged, in his own realm, the world of the dead.

For centuries she had waited in dread of the time that prophecy said was now upon them.

For five hundred years she had waited for the birth of the one who had the chance to succeed in leading them in the struggle to see the Creator's gift, magic, survive against those who would cast that light out of the world. For five hundred years she had worked to insure that he would have a chance to do what he must if he was to have a chance to stop the forces that would extinguish magic.

Prophecy said that only Richard had the chance to preserve their cause, to keep the enemy from succeeding in casting a gray pall over mankind, the only one with a chance to prevent the gift from dying out. Prophecy did not say that he would prevail; prophecy said only that Richard was the only one to have a chance to bring them victory. Without Richard, all hope was lost—that much was sure. For this reason, Ann had been devoted to him long before he was born, before he rose up to become their leader.

Kahlan saw all of Ann's efforts as meddling, as tinkering with the lives of others. Kahlan believed that Ann's efforts were in fact the cause of the very thing she feared most. Ann hated that she sometimes thought that maybe Kahlan was right. Maybe it was meant to be that Richard would be born and by his free will alone would choose to do those things that would lead them to victory in their battle to keep the gift among men. Zedd certainly believed that it was only by Richard's mind, by his free will, by his conscious intent, that he could lead them.

Maybe it was true, and Ann, in trying to direct those things that could not be and should not be directed, had brought them all to the brink of ruin.

The footsteps were coming closer. Maybe it was time to eat and they were bringing dinner. She wasn't hungry.

When they brought her food, they put it on the end of a long pole and then threaded that pole through the little opening in the outer door, all the way across the outer shielded room, through the opening in the second, inner door, and finally in to Ann. Nathan would risk no chance for escape by having her guards open her cell door merely to give her food.

They passed in a variety of breads, meats, and vegetables along with waterskins. Although the food was good, she found no satisfaction in it. Even the finest fare could never be satisfying eaten in a dungeon.

At times, as Prelate, she had felt as if she were a prisoner of her post. She had rarely gone to the dining hall where the Sisters of the Light had eaten—especially in the later years. It put everyone on edge having the Prelate among them at dinner. Besides, done too often it took the edge off their anxiety, their discomposure, around authority.

Ann believed that a certain distance, a certain worried respect, was necessary in order to maintain discipline. In a place that had been spelled so that time slowed for those living there, it was important to maintain discipline. Ann appeared to be in her seventies, but with her aging process slowed dramatically while living under the spell that had covered the Palace of the Prophets, she had lived close to a thousand years.

Of course, a lot of good her discipline had done her. Under her watch as Prelate the Sisters of the Dark had infested her flock. There were hundreds of Sisters, and there was no telling just how many of them had taken dark oaths to the Keeper. The lure of his promises was obviously effective. Such promises were an illusion, but try to tell that to one so pledged. Immortality was seductive to women who watched everyone they knew outside the palace grow old and die while they remained young.

Sisters who had children saw those children sent out of the palace to be raised where they could have a normal life, saw those children grow old and die, saw their grandchildren grow old and die. To a woman who saw such things, saw the constant withering and death of those she knew while she herself all the time seemed to remain young, attractive, and desirable, the offer of immortality grew increasingly tempting when her own petals began to wilt.

Growing old was a final stage, the end of a life. Growing old in the Palace of the Prophets was a very long ordeal. Ann had been old for centuries. Being young for a very long time was a wonderful experience, but being old for a very long time was not—at least it was not for some. For Ann, it was life itself that was wonderful, not so much her age, and all she had learned. But not everyone felt that way.

Now that the palace had been destroyed, they would all age at the same rate as everyone else. What had only a short time ago been a future of maybe another hundred years of life for Ann was suddenly perhaps no more than a blink of a decade—certainly not much more.

But she doubted she would live all that long in such a dank hole, away from light and life.

Somehow, it didn't seem as if she and Nathan were close to a thousand years old. She didn't know what it felt like to age at the normal rate outside the spell, but she believed she felt little different to those outside the palace felt as they aged. She believed that the spell that slowed their aging also altered their perception of time; to a degree, anyway.

The footsteps were getting closer. Ann wasn't looking forward to another meal in this place. She was beginning to wish they would let her starve and get it over with. Let her die.

What good had her life been? When she really thought about it, what good had she really accomplished? The Creator knew how she tried to guide Richard in what needed to be done, but in the end it seemed that it was Richard's choice to act as he did, in most cases against what she thought needed to be done, that turned out to be correct. Had she not tried to guide events, bring him to the Palace of the Prophets in the Old World, maybe nothing would have changed and that would have been the way he was to save them all— by not having to act and letting Jagang and the Imperial Order eventually wither and die in the Old World, unable to spread their virulent beliefs beyond. Maybe she'd brought it all to ruin with her efforts alone.

She heard the door at the end of the passageway to her cell scrape open. She decided that she wouldn't eat. She wouldn't eat again until Nathan came to speak with her, as she had requested.

Sometimes, with the food, they sent in wine. Nathan sent it in to vex her, she was sure of that. From his confinement in the Palace of the Prophets, Nathan had sometimes requested wine. Ann always saw the report when such a request was made; she declined every such request.

Wizards were dangerous enough, prophets—who were wizards with the talent of prophecy—were potentially vastly more dangerous, and drunken prophets were the most dangerous of all.

Prophecy given out willy-nilly was an invitation to calamity. Even simple prophecy escaping the confines of the stone walls of the Palace of the Prophets had started wars.

Nathan had sometimes requested the company of women. Ann hated those requests the most, because she sometimes granted them. She felt she had to. Nathan had little of life, confined as he was to his apartments, his only real crime being the nature of his birth, his abilities. The palace could easily afford the price of a woman to sometimes visit him.

He made a mockery of that, often enough—giving out prophecy that sent the woman fleeing before they could speak with her, before they could silence her.

Those without the proper training were not meant to see prophecy. Prophecy was easily misinterpreted by those without an understanding of its intricacies. To divulge prophecy to the uninitiated was like casting fire into dry grass.

Prophecy is not meant for the unenlightened.

At the thought of the prophet being loose, Ann's stomach tightened into a knot. Even so, she had sometimes secretly taken Nathan out herself, to go on important journeys with her—mostly journeys having to do with guiding some aspect of Richard's life, or, more accurately, trying to insure that Richard would be born and have a life. Besides being trouble on two feet, Nathan was also a remarkable prophet who did have a sincere interest in seeing their side triumph. After all, he saw in prophecy the alternative, and when Nathan saw prophecy, he saw it in all its terrible truth.

Nathan always wore a Rada'Han—a collar—that enabled her, or any Sister, to control him, so taking him on those journeys wasn't actually putting the world at risk from the man. He had to do as she said, go where she said. Whenever she had taken him out on a mission with her, he was not really free, since he wore a Rada'Han and she could thus control him.

Now he was without a Rada'Han. He was truly free.

Ann didn't want any supper. She resolved to turn it away when they passed the pole in to her. Let Nathan fret that she might refuse food altogether and die while under his fickle control. Ann folded her arms. Let him have that on his conscience. That would bring the man down to see her.

Ann heard the footsteps come to a halt outside the far door. Muffled voices drifted in to her. Had she ready access to her Han, she would have been able to concentrate her hearing toward those voices and easily hear their words. She sighed. Even that ability was useless to her here, in this place, under the power invoked by the spell form of the layout of the palace. It would hardly make sense to create such elaborate plans to curtail another's magic and allow them to hear secrets whispered inside the walls.

The outer door squealed in protest as it was pulled open. This was new. No one had opened the outer door since the day they shut her in the place.

Ann rushed to the door to her small room, to the faint square of light that was the opening in the iron door. She grabbed hold of the bars and pulled her face up close, trying to see who was out there, what they were doing.

Light blinded her. She staggered back a few steps, rubbing her eyes. She was so used to the dark that the harsh lantern light felt as if it had burned her vision with blazing light.

Ann backed away from the door when she heard a key clattering in the lock. The bolt threw back with a reverberating clang. The door grated open. Cool air, fresher than the stale air she was used to breathing, poured in. Yellow light flooded around the room as the lantern was thrust into the room at the end of an arm encased in red leather.

Mord-Sith.

C H A P T E R 30

Ann squinted in the harsh glare as the Mord-Sith stepped over the sill and ducked in through the doorway into the room. Unaccustomed to the lantern light, Ann at first could only discern the red leather outfit and the blond braid. She didn't like to contemplate why one of the Lord Rahl's elite corps of torturers would be coming down to the dungeon to see her. She knew Richard. She could not imagine that he would allow such a practice to continue. But Richard wasn't here. Nathan seemed to be in charge.

Squinting, Ann at last realized that it was the woman she had seen before: Nyda.

Nyda, appraising Ann with a cool gaze, said nothing as she stepped to the side. Another person was following her in. A long leg wearing brown trousers stepped over the sill, followed by a bent torso folding through the opening. Rising up to full height, Ann saw with sudden surprise who it was.

"Ann!" Nathan held his arms open wide, as if expecting a hug. "How are you? Nyda gave me your message. They are treating you well, I trust?"

Ann stood her ground and scowled at the grinning face. "I'm still alive, no thanks to you, Nathan."

She of course remembered how tall Nathan was, how broad were his shoulders. Now, standing before her, the top of his full head of long gray hair nearly touching the stone chisel marks in the ceiling, he looked even taller than she remembered. His shoulders, filling up so much of the small room, looked even broader. He wore high boots over his trousers and a ruffled white shirt beneath an open vest. An elegant green velvet cape was attached at his right shoulder. At his left hip a sword in an elegant scabbard glimmered in the lamp-light.

His face, his handsome face, so expressive, so unlike any other, made Ann's heart feel buoyant.

Nathan grinned as no one but a Rahl could grin, a grin like joy and hunger and power all balled together. He looked like he needed to sweep a damsel into his powerful arms and kiss her without her permission.

He waved a hand casually around at her accommodations. "But you are safe in here, my dear. No one can harm you while under our care. No one can bother you. You have fine food—even wine now and again. What more could you want?"

Fists at her side, Ann stormed forward at a pace that brought the Mord-Sith's Agiel up into her fist, even though she stayed where she was. Nathan held his ground, held his smile, as he watched her come.

"What more could I want!" Ann screamed. "What more could I want? I want to be let out! That's what more I could want!"

Nathan's small, knowing smile cut her to her core. "Indeed," he said, a single word of quiet indictment.

Standing in the stony silence of the dungeon, she could only stare up at him, unable to bring forth an argument that he would not throw back at her.

Ann turned a glare on the Mord-Sith. "What message did you give him?"

"Nyda said that you wanted to see me," Nathan answered in her place. He spread his arms. "Here I am, as requested. What is it you wanted to see me about, my dear?"

"Don't patronize me, Nathan. You know very well what I wanted to see you about. You know why I'm here, in D'Hara—why I've come to the People's Palace."

Nathan clasped his hands behind his back. His smile had finally lost its usefulness.

"Nyda," he said, turning to the woman, "would you leave us alone for now. There's a good girl."

Nyda appraised Ann with a brief glance. No more was needed;

Ann was no threat to Nathan. He was a wizard—no doubt he had told her that he was the greatest wizard of all time—and was within the ancestral home of the House of Rahl. He had no need to fear this one old sorceress—not anymore, anyway.

Nyda gave Nathan an if-you-need-me-I'll-be-right-outside kind of look before contorting her perfect limbs through the doorway with fluid grace, the way a cat went effortlessly through a hedge.

Nathan stood in the center of the cell, hands still clasped behind his upright back, waiting for Ann to say something.

Ann went to her pack, sitting on the far end of the stone bench that had been her bed, her table, her chair. She flipped back the flap and reached inside, feeling around. Her fingers found the cold metal of the object she sought. Ann drew it out and stood over it, her shadow hiding it.

Finally, she turned. "Nathan, I have something for you."

She lifted out a Rada'Han she had intended to put around his neck. Right then, she didn't quite know how she had thought she could accomplish such a feat. She would have, though, had she put her mind to it; she was Annalina Aldurren, Prelate of the Sisters of the Light. Or, at least, she once had been. She had given that job to Verna before feigning her and Nathan's death.

"You want me to put that collar around my neck?" Nathan asked in a calm voice. "That's what you expect?"

Ann shook her head. "No, Nathan. I want to give this to you. I've been doing a lot of thinking while I've been down here. Thinking about how I'd probably never leave my place of confinement."

"What a coincidence," Nathan said. "I used to spend a great deal of time thinking that very same thought."

"Yes," Ann said, nodding. "I expect you did." She handed him the Rada'Han. "Here. Take this. I never want to see one of these again. While I did what I thought best, I hated every minute of it, Nathan. I hated to do it to you, especially. I've come to think that my life has been a misguided mess. I'm sorry I ever put you behind those shields and kept you a prisoner. If I could live my life over again, I'd not do it the same way.

"I expect no leniency; I showed you none."

"No," Nathan said. "You didn't."

His azure eyes seemed to be looking right into her. He had a way of doing that. Richard had inherited that same penetrating Rahl gaze.

"So, you are sorry you kept me a prisoner all my life. Do you know why it was wrong, Ann? Are you even aware of the irony?"

Almost against her better judgment, she heard herself ask, "What irony?"

"Well," he said as he shrugged, "what is it we're fighting for?"

"Nathan, you know very well what we're fighting for."

"Yes, I do. But do you? Tell me, then, what it is we're struggling to protect, to preserve, to insure remains alive?"

"The Creator's gift of magic, of course. We fight to see that it continues to exist in the world. We struggle for those who are born with it to live, for them to learn to use their ability to its full extent. We fight for each to have and to celebrate their unique ability."

"I think that's kind of ironic, don't you? The very thing you think is worth fighting for is what you feared. The Imperial Order proclaims that it's not in the best interest of mankind for a gifted individual to possess magic, so that unique ability must be stripped away from them. They claim that, since all do not have this ability in identical and equal measure, it's dangerous for some to have it—that man must cast aside the belief that a man's life is his own to live. That those who were born with magic must therefore be expunged from the world in order to make the world a better place for those who don't have such ability.

"And yet, you worked under that very premise, acted on those same wicked beliefs. You locked me away because of my ability. You saw what I am able to do, that others cannot do, as an evil birthright that could not be allowed to be among mankind.

"And yet, you work to preserve that very thing which you fear in me—my unique ability—in others. You work to allow everyone born with magic to have the inalienable right to their own life, to be the best of what they can be with their own ability . . . and yet you locked me away to deny me that very same right."

"Just because I want the Creator's wolves to run free to hunt, as they were intended, doesn't mean that I want to be their dinner."

Nathan leaned toward her. "I am not a wolf. I am a human being. You tried, convicted, and sentenced me to life in your prison for being who I was born, for what you feared I might do, simply because I had the ability. You then soothed your own inner conflict by making that prison plush in an attempt to convince yourself that you were kind—all the while professing to believe that we must fight to allow future people to be who they are.

"You qualified your prison as right because it was lavish, in order to mask from yourself the nature of what you were advocating. Look around, Ann." He swept his arm out at the stone. "This is what you were advocating for those you decided did not have the right to their own life. You decided the same as the Order, based on an ability you did not like. You decided that some, because of their greater potential, must be sacrificed to the good of those less than they. No matter how you decorated your dungeon, this is what it looks like from the inside."

Ann gathered her thoughts, as well as her voice, before she spoke. "I thought I had come to understand something like that while I sat all alone down here, but I realize now that I hadn't, really. All those years I felt bad for locking you away, but I never really examined my rationale for doing so.

"You're right, Nathan. I believed you held the potential for great harm. I should have helped you to understand what was right so you could act rationally, rather than expect the worst from you and lock you away. I'm sorry, Nathan."

He put his hands on his hips. "Do you really mean it, Ann?"

She nodded, unable to look up at him, as her eyes filled with tears. She always expected honesty from everyone else, but she had not been honest with herself. "Yes, Nathan, I really do."

Confession over, she went to her bench and slumped down. "Thank you for coming, Nathan. I'll not trouble you to come down here again. I will take my just punishment without complaint. If you don't mind, I think I'd like to be alone right now to pray and consider the weight on my heart."

"You can do that later. Now get up off your bottom, on your feet, and pick up your things. We have matters to attend to and we have to get going."

Ann looked up with a frown. "What?"

"We have important things to do. Come on, woman. We're wasting time. We need to get going. We're on the same side in this struggle, Ann. We need to act like it and work together toward preserving our causes." He leaned down toward her. "Unless you've decided to retire to sit around the rest of your life. If not, then let's be on our way. We have trouble."

Ann hopped down from the stone bench. "Trouble? What sort of trouble."

"Prophecy trouble."

"Prophecy? There is trouble with a prophecy? What trouble? What prophecy?"

Fists on his hips, Nathan fixed her with a scowl. "I can't tell you about such things. Prophecy is not meant for the unenlightened."

Ann pursed her lips, about to launch into scolding him up one side and down the other, when she caught the smile working at the edges of his mouth. It caught her up in a smile of her own.

"What's happened?" she asked in the tone of voice friends used when they had decided that past wrongs were recognized and matters now set on a correct path.

"Ann, you'll not believe it when I tell you," Nathan complained. "It's that boy, again."

"Richard?"

"What other boy do you know who can get in the kind of trouble only Richard can get into?"

"Well, I no longer think of Richard as a boy."

Nathan sighed. "I suppose not, but it's hard when you're my age to think of one so young as a man."

"He's a man," Ann assured him.

"Yes, I guess he is." Nathan grinned. "And, he's a Rahl."

"What sort of trouble has Richard gotten himself into this time?"

Nathan's good humor evaporated. "He's walked off the edge of prophecy."

Ann screwed up her face. "What are you talking about? What's he done?"

"I'm telling you, Ann, that boy has walked right off the edge of prophecy itself—walked right off into a place in prophecy where prophecy itself doesn't exist."

Ann recognized that Nathan was sincerely troubled, but he was making no sense. In part, that was why some people were afraid of him. He often gave people the impression he was talking gibberish when he was talking about things that no one but he could even understand. Sometimes no one but a prophet could truly understand completely what he grasped. With his eyes, the eyes of a prophet, he could see things that no one else could.

She had spent a lifetime working with prophecy, though, and so she could understand, perhaps better than most, at least some of his mind, some of what he could grasp.

"How can you know of such a prophecy, Nathan, if it doesn't exist? I don't understand. Explain it to me."

"There are libraries here, at the People's Palace, that contain some valuable books of prophecy that I've never had a chance to see before. While I had reason to suspect that such prophecies might exist, I was never certain they actually did, or what they might say. I've been studying them since I've been here and I've come across links to other known prophecy we had down in the vaults at the Palace of the Prophets. These prophecies, here, fill in some important gaps in those we already know about.

"Most importantly, I found an altogether new branch of prophecy I've never seen before that explains why and how I've been blind to some of what's been going on. From studying the forks and inversions off this branch, I've discovered that Richard has taken a series of links that follow down a particular pathway of prophecy that leads to oblivion, to something that, as far as I can tell, doesn't even exist."

One hand on a hip, the other tracing invisible lines in the air, Nathan paced the small room as he talked. "This new link alludes to things I've never seen before, branches that I've always known must be there, but were missing. These branches are exceedingly dangerous prophecies that have been kept here, in secret. I can see why. Even I, had I seen them years ago, might have misinterpreted them. These new branches refer to voids of some sort. Since they are voids, their nature can't be known; such a contradiction can't exist.

"Richard has gone into this area of void, where prophecy can't see him, can't help him, and worse, can't help us. But more than not seeing him with prophecy, it's as if where he is and what he is doing do not exist.

"Richard is dealing in something that is capable of ending everything we know."

Ann knew that Nathan would not exaggerate about something of this nature. While she was in the dark about precisely what he was talking about, the essence of it gave her the cold sweats.

"What can we do about it?"

Nathan threw up his arms. "We have to go in there and get him. We have to bring him back into the world that exists."

"You mean, the world that prophecy says exists."

Nathan's scowl was back. "That's what I said, isn't it? We have to somehow get him back on the thread of prophecy where he shows up."

Ann cleared her throat. "Or?"

Nathan snatched up the lamp, then her pack. "Or, he will cease to be part of viable lines of prophecy, never to be involved with matters of this world again."

"You mean, if we don't get him back from wherever his is, he will die?"

Nathan gave her a curious look. "Have I been talking to the walls? Of course he will die! If that boy isn't in prophecy, if he breaks all the links to prophecy where he plays a role, then he voids all those lines of prophecy where he exists. If he does that, then they become false prophecy and those branches with word of him will never come to pass. None of the other links contain any reference to him— because in the origin of those links, he dies, first."

"And what happens on those links that don't contain him?"

Nathan took up her hand as he pulled her toward the door. "On those links, a shadow falls over everyone. Everyone who lives, anyway. It will be a very long and very dark age."

"Wait," Ann said, pulling him to a halt.

She returned to the stone bench and placed the Rada'Han in the center. "I don't have the power to destroy this. I think maybe it should be locked away."

Nathan nodded his approval. "We will lock the doors and instruct the guards that it is to remain in here, behind the shields, for all time."

Ann held a warning finger up before him. "Don't get the idea that just because you're not wearing a collar I will tolerate misbehavior."

Nathan's grin returned. He didn't come right out and agree. Before he went through the door, he turned back to her.

"By the way, have you been talking to Verna through your journey book?"

"Yes, a little. She's with the army and pretty busy, right now. They're defending the passes into D'Hara. Jagang has begun his siege."

"Well, from what I've been able to gather from military commanders here at the palace, the passes are formidable and will hold for a while, at least." He leaned toward her. "You have to send a message to her, though. Tell her that when an empty wagon rolls into their line, to let it through."

Ann made a face. "What does that mean?"

"Prophecy is not meant for the unenlightened. Just tell her."

"All right," Ann said with breathless difficulty as Nathan pulled her through the tight doorway. "But I'd best not tell her you're the one who said it, or she will likely ignore the advice. She thinks you're daft, you know."

"She just never got a chance to come to know me very well, that's all." He glanced back. "What with me being unjustly locked away, and all."

Ann wanted to say that perhaps Verna knew Nathan all too well, but decided better of it right then. As Nathan started to turn toward the outer door, Ann snatched his sleeve.

"Nathan, what else about this prophecy you found aren't you telling me? This prophecy where Richard disappears into oblivion."

She knew Nathan well enough to know by his agitation that he hadn't told her everything, that he thought he was being gallant by sparing her worry. With a sober expression, he gazed into her eyes for a time before he finally spoke.

"There is a Slide on that fork of prophecy."

Ann frowned as she turned her eyes up in thought. "A Slide. A Slide," she muttered to herself, trying to recall the name. It sounded familiar. "A Slide . . ." She snapped her fingers. "A Slide." Her eyes went wide. "Dear Creator."

"I don't think the Creator had anything to do with this."

Ann impatiently waved in protest. "That can't be. There has to be something wrong with this new prophecy you found. It has to be defective. Slides were created in the great war. There couldn't be a Slide on this link of prophecy—don't you see? The prophecy must be out of phase and long ago expired." Ann chewed her lower lip as her mind raced.

"It isn't out of phase. Don't you think that was my first thought, too? You think me an amateur at this? I worked through the chronology a hundred times. I ran every chart and calculation I ever learned—even some I invented for the task. They all came out with the same root. Every link came out in order. The prophecy is in phase, chronology, and all its aspects are aligned."

"Then it's a false link," Ann insisted. "Slides were conjured creatures. They were sterile. They couldn't reproduce."

"I'm telling you," Nathan growled, "there is a Slide on this fork with Richard and it's a viable prophetic link."

"They couldn't have survived to be here." Ann was sure of what she was saying. Nathan knew more about prophecy than she, there was no doubt of that, but this was one area where she knew exactly what she was talking about—this was her area of expertise. "Slides weren't able to beget children."

He was giving her one of those looks she didn't like. "I'm telling you, a Slide walks the world again."

Ann tsked. "Nathan, soul stealers can't reproduce."

"The prophecy says he wasn't born, but born again a Slide."

Ann's flesh began to tingle. She stared at him a time before finding her voice. "For three thousand years there have been no wizards born with both sides of the gift but Richard. There is no way anyone . . ."

Ann paused. He was watching her, watching her finally realize what had to be. "Dear Creator," she whispered.

"I told you, the Creator had nothing to do with this. The Sisters of the Dark mothered him."

Shaken to her core, Ann could think of nothing to say.

There was no worse news she could have heard.

There was no defense against a Slide.

Every soul was naked to a Slide's attack.

Outside the second door, Nyda waited in the hall, her face as grim as ever, but not as grim as Ann's. The hall was dark but for the dim light coming from the still flames of a few candles. No breath of wind ever made it this deep into the palace. The only color among the dark rock soaking up that small bit of light was the blood red of Nyda's red leather.

Being pulled along by the hand, feeling a jumble of emotions, Ann leaned toward the woman and vented a pent-up fiery scowl. "You told him what I said to tell him, didn't you?"

"Of course," Nyda answered as she fell into step behind the two of them.

Turning halfway around, Ann shook a finger at the Mord-Sith. "I'll make you sorry you told him."

Nyda smiled. "Oh, I don't think so."

Ann rolled her eyes and turned back to Nathan. "By the way, what are you doing wearing a sword? You, of all people—a wizard. Why are you wearing a sword?"

Nathan looked hurt. "Why, Nyda thinks I look dashing with a sword."

Ann fixed her eyes on the dark passageway ahead. "I just bet she does."

CHAPTER 31

Standing at the edge of a narrow rim of rock, Richard looked down on the ragged gray wisps of clouds below. Out in the open, the cool damp air that drifted over him carried the aromas of balsam trees, moss, wet leaves, and saturated soil. He inhaled deeply the fragrant reminders of home. The rock, mostly granite, cracked and weather-worn into pillowed blocks, looked much the same as that in his Hartland woods. The mountains, however, were far larger. The slope rising up behind him was dizzying.

To the west before him, far below, lay a vast stretch of fractured ground and ever-rising rugged hills carpeted in forest. To his left and right, because he knew what he was looking for, he could just make out the strip of ground, devoid of trees, where the boundary had been. Farther off to the west rose up the lesser mountains, mostly barren, that bordered the wasteland. That wasteland, and the place called the Pillars of Creation, was no longer visible. Richard was happy to have left it far behind.

The sky was empty of black-tipped races—for the moment, anyway. The huge birds most likely knew that Richard, Kahlan, Cara, Jennsen, Tom, and Owen were heading west.

Richard had shot the last five races as they had begun gathering in their circling behavior, surprising them by being high up the side of the mountain above the others in his group, closer to where the races flew. After killing the races, Richard had led the rest of his small company into denser woods. He didn't think that the races they'd been seeing up until then had spotted them since. Now that they were traveling through forests of towering trees Richard thought that, if he was careful, they might be able to lose their watchers.

If this man, Nicholas, had seen them through the eyes of those five races, then he knew they had been headed west. But, now that they were hidden, he couldn't assume that they would continue west. If Richard could disappear from where the birds would look for him, and failed to appear where they would expect him, then Nicholas might have second thoughts. He might realize they could have changed direction and gone north, or south. Nicholas might then begin to realize that they had used that period of confusion to run away somewhere else, to flee him.

It was possible that Richard could keep them hidden under the cover of the trees and in so doing keep Nicholas from discovering them. Richard didn't want the man to know where they'd gone, or to have any idea where they were at any given time. It was hardly a certainty that he could deceive Nicholas in this way, but Richard intended to try.

Shielding his eyes with the flat of his hand, Richard scanned the rise of dense forest before them in order to get the lay of the land fixed in his mind before he headed back in under the thick vegetation where the others waited. The trailers of clouds below were but the tattered castoffs of the churning blanket of gloom above them. The mountainside ascended sharply into that wet overcast.

As Richard evaluated the rock, the slope, and the trees, he finally found what he sought. He studied the ascent of the mountain one last time before scanning the sky again to make sure it was clear. Seeing no races—or any other birds, for that matter, he headed in to where the others waited. He knew that just because he didn't see any birds that didn't mean they weren't there watching him. There could be a few dozen races sitting in trees where he would likely never spot them. But, for the moment, he was still where they would expect him, so he wasn't greatly concerned.

He was about to do what they would not expect.

Richard climbed back up the slick bank of moss, leaves, and wet roots. If he fell, he would have only the one chance to grab the small ledge where he'd been standing before tumbling out into the clear air and a drop of several thousand feet. The thought of that drop made him hold tighter to the roots to help him climb, and made him test carefully every score in the rock where he placed his boot before committing his weight to it.

At the top of the bank he ducked under overhanging branches of scrawny mountain maple that grew in the understorey of hardwoods leaning out beside the towering pines in an effort to capture the light. Leaves of the ash and birch rising above the mountain maple collected the drizzle, until their leaves had as much as they could hold and released it to patter down in fat drops that slapped the lower leaves above Richard's head. When a light breeze caught those upper leaves, they released their load to rain down in sudden but brief torrents.

Stooping under low-spreading branches of fir trees, Richard followed his track back through thickets of huckleberry into the more open ground of the hushed woods beneath the canopy of ancient evergreens. Pine needles had been woven by the wind into sprawling mats that cushioned his steps. Spiraling webs hung by spiders to catch the small bugs that zigzagged all about had instead netted the mist and were now dotted with shimmering drops of water, like jeweled necklaces on display.

Back in the sheltering cover of rock and the thick growth of young spruce, Kahlan stood when she saw Richard coming. When she stood, everyone else then saw him, and came to their feet as well. Richard ducked in under the wispy green branches.

"Did you see any races, Lord Rahl?" Owen asked, clearly nervous about the predators.

"No," Richard told him as he picked up his pack and slung it over a shoulder. He slipped his other arm beneath the second strap as he pulled the pack up onto his back. "That doesn't mean they didn't see me, though."

Richard hooked his bow over the back of his left shoulder, along with a waterskin.

"Well," Owen said, wringing his hands, "we can still hope they won't know where we are."

Richard paused to look at the man. "Hope is not a strategy."

As the rest of them all started collecting their things from the brief break, hooking gear on belts and shouldering packs, Richard drew Cara by the arm out of the cover of small trees and pulled her close.

"See that rise through there?" he asked as he held her near him so she could see where he was pointing. "With the strip of open ground that passes in front of the young oak with the broken dead limb hanging down?"

Cara nodded. "Just after where the ground rises and goes over that trickle of water running down the face of the rock, staining it green?"

"That's the spot. I want you to follow up over that area, then cut to the right, taking that cleft up—that one there beyond the split in the rock, there—and see if you can scout a trail up to the next shelf up above these trees here."

Cara nodded. "Where will you be?"

"I'm going to take the rest of us up to the first break in the slope. We'll be there. Come back and tell us if you find a way over the projection."

Cara hoisted up her pack onto her back and then picked up the stout staff Richard had cut for her.

"I didn't know that Mord-Sith could cut trails," Tom said.

"Mord-Sith can't," Cara said. "I, Cara, can. Lord Rahl taught me."

As she vanished into the trees, Richard watched her walk. She moved gracefully, disturbing little as she made her way into the trackless woods. She moved with an economy of effort that would conserve her energy. It had not always been so; she had learned well the lessons he had given her. Richard was pleased to see that the lessons had stuck and his efforts had not been wasted.

Owen came forward, looking agitated. "But, Lord Rahl, we can't go that way." He waggled a hand back over his shoulder. "The trail goes that way. That is the only way up and through the pass. There lies the way down, and with it the way back up, now that the boundary is gone. It's not easy, but it's the only way."

"It's the only way you know of. By how well that trail looks to be traveled, I think it's the only way Nicholas knows of as well. It appears to be the way the Order troops move in and out of Bandakar.

"If we go that way the races will be watching. If, on the other hand, we don't show up, then he won't know where we went. I want to keep it that way from now on. I'm tired of playing mouse to his owl."

Richard let Kahlan lead them up through the woods, following the natural route of the land when the way ahead was reasonably evident. When she was in doubt she would glance back at him for direction. Richard would look where she was to go, or nod in the direction he wanted her to take, or, in a few cases, he needed to give her instruction.

By the lay of the land, Richard was pretty sure that there was an ancient trail up through the mountain pass. That pass, that from afar looked like a notch in the wall of mountains, was in reality no mere notch but a broad area twisting as it rose back up between the mountains. Richard didn't think that the path the Bandakar people used to banish people through the boundary was the only way through that pass. With the boundary in place it may well have been, but the boundary was no longer there.

From what he'd seen so far, Richard suspected that there once had been a route that in ancient times had been the main way in and out. Here and there he was able to discern depressions that he believed were remnants of that ancient, abandoned route.

While it was always possible that the old passage had been abandoned for good reason, such as a landslide that made it impassable, he wanted to know if that once-traveled way was still usable. It would, at the least, since it was in a different part of the mountains than the known path, take them away from where the races were likely to be looking for them.

Jennsen walked up close beside Richard when the way through towering pines was open enough. She tugged Betty along by her rope, keeping her from stopping to sample plants along the way.

"Sooner or later the races will find us, don't you think?" Jennsen asked. "I mean, if we don't show up where they expect to find us, then don't you think they will search until they do find us? You were the one who said that from the sky they could cover great distances and search us out."

"Maybe," Richard said. "But it will be hard to spot us in the woods if we use our heads and stay hidden. In forests they can't search nearly as much area as they could in the same amount of time out in the wasteland. In open ground they could spot us miles away. Here, they will have a hard time of it unless they're really close and we are careless.

"By the time we don't show up where the known trail makes it up into Bandakar, they will have a vast area they suddenly will need to search and they won't have any idea which direction to look. That compounds the problem for them in finding us.

"I don't think that the viewing Nicholas gets through their eyes can be very good, or he wouldn't need to gather the races now and again to circle. If we can stay out of sight long enough, then we'll be among the people up in Bandakar and then Nicholas, through the eyes of the races, will have a hard, if not impossible, time picking us out from others."

Jennsen thought it over as they entered a stand of birch. Betty went the wrong way around a tree and Jennsen had to stop to untangle her rope. They all hunched their shoulders against the wet when a breeze brought down a soaking shower.

"Richard," Jennsen asked in a voice barely above a whisper as she caught back up with him, "what are you going to do when we get there?"

"I'm going to get the antidote so I don't die."

"I know that." Jennsen pulled a sodden ringlet of red hair back from her face. "What I mean is, what are you going to do about Owen's people?"

Each breath he drew brought a slight stitch of pain deep in his lungs. "I'm not sure, yet, just what I can do."

Jennsen walked in silence for a moment. "But you will try to help them, won't you?"

Richard glanced over at his sister. "Jennsen, they're threatening to kill me. They've proven that it isn't an empty threat."

She shrugged uncomfortably. "I know, but they're desperate." She glanced ahead to make sure that Owen wouldn't hear. "They didn't know what else to do to save themselves. They aren't like you. They never fought anyone before."

Richard took a deep breath, the pain pulling tight across his chest when he did so. "You'd never fought anyone before, either. When you thought I was trying to kill you, as our father had, and you believed that I was responsible for your mother's death, what did you do? I don't mean were you correct about me, but what did you do in response to what you believed was happening?"

"I resolved that if I wanted to live I would have to kill you before you killed me."

"Exactly. You didn't poison someone and tell them to do it or they would die. You decided that your life was worth living and that no one else had the right to take it from you.

"When you are willing to meekly sacrifice your ultimate value, your life, the only one you will ever have, to any thug who on a whim decides to take it from you, then you can't be helped. You may be able to be rescued for one day, but the next day another will come and you will again willingly prostrate yourself before him. You have placed the value of the life of your killer above your own.

"When you grant to anyone who demands it the right of life or death over you, you have already become a willing slave in search of any butcher who will have you."

She walked in silence for a time, thinking about what he'd said. Richard noticed that she moved through the woods as he had taught Cara to move. She was nearly as at home in the woods as he was.

"Richard." Jennsen swallowed. "I don't want those people to be hurt any more. They've already suffered enough."

"Tell that to Kahlan if I die from their poison."

When they reached the meeting place, Cara wasn't there yet. They all were ready for a brief rest. The spot, a break in the slope back against granite that rose up steeply to the next projection in the mountain, was protected high overhead by huge pines and closer down by brush. After so long out in the heat of the desert, none of them was yet accustomed to the wet chill. While they spread out to find rocks for seats so they wouldn't have to sit in the wet leaf litter, Betty happily sampled the tasty weeds. Owen sat to the far side, away from Betty.

Kahlan sat close to Richard on a small lump of rock. "How are you doing? You look like you have a headache."

"Nothing to be done about it for now," he said.

Kahlan leaned closer. The warmth of her felt good against his side.

"Richard," she whispered, "remember Nicci's letter?"

"What about it?"

"Well, we assumed that this boundary into Bandakar being down was the reason for the first warning beacon. Maybe we're wrong."

"What makes you think so?"

"No second beacon." She pointed with her chin off to the northwest. "We saw the first way back down there. We're a lot closer to the place where the boundary was and we haven't spotted a second beacon."

"Just as well," he said. "That was where the races were waiting for us."

He remembered well when they found the little statue. The races were perched in trees all around. Richard hadn't known what they were at the time, other than they were large birds he'd never seen before. The instant Cara picked up the statue, the black-tipped races had all suddenly taken to wing. There had been hundreds.

"Yes," Kahlan said, "but without the second beacon, maybe this isn't the problem that we thought caused the first."

"You're assuming that the second beacon will be for me—that I'm the one it will be meant for and so we would have seen it. Nicci said that the second beacon is for the one who has the power to fix the breach in the seal. Maybe that's not me."

Looking at first startled by the idea, Kahlan thought it over. "I'm not sure if I'd be pleased about that or not." She leaned tighter against him and hooked an arm around his thigh. "But no matter who is meant to be the one who can seal the breach again, the one who's supposed to restore the boundary, I don't think they will be able to do so."

Richard ran his fingers back through his wet hair. "Well, if I'm the one this dead wizard once believed could restore the boundary, he's wrong. I don't know how to do such a thing."

"But don't you see, Richard? Even if you did know how, I don't think you could."

Richard looked at her out of the corner of his eye. "Jumping to conclusions and letting your imagination get carried away, again?"

"Richard, face it, the boundary failed because of what I did. That's why the warning beacon was for me—because I caused the seal to fail. You aren't going to try to deny that, are you?"

"No, but we have a lot to learn before we know what's really going on."

"I freed the chimes," she said. "It's not going to do us any good to try to hide from that fact."

Kahlan had used ancient magic to save his life. She had freed the chimes in order to heal him. She'd had no time to spare; he would have died within moments if she had not acted.

Moreover, she'd had no idea that the chimes would unleash destruction upon the world. She hadn't known they had been created three thousand years before from underworld powers as a weapon designed to consume magic. She had been told only that she must use them to save Richard's life.

Richard knew what it felt like to be convinced of the facts behind events and to have no one believe him. He knew she was now feeling that same frustration.

"You're right that we can't hide from it—if it is a fact. But right now we don't know that it is. For one thing, the chimes have been banished back to the underworld."

"And what about what Zedd told us, about how once the destructive cascade of magic begins—which it did—then there is no telling if it can be stopped even if the chimes are banished. There is no experience of such an event upon which to base predictions."

Richard didn't have an answer for her, and was at a disadvantage because he didn't have her education in magic. He was saved from having to speculate when Cara came in through a tight patch of young balsam trees. She pulled her pack off her shoulders and let it slip to the ground as she sat on a rock facing Richard.

"You were right. We can get through there. It looks to me like I can see a way to continue on up from the ledge."

"Good," Richard said as he stood. "Let's get going. The clouds are getting darker. I think we need to find a place to stop for the night."

"I spotted a place under the ledge, Lord Rahl. I think it might be a dry place to stay."

"Good." Richard hoisted her pack. "I'll carry this for you for a while, let you have a break."

Cara nodded her appreciation, falling into line as they moved through the tight trees and immediately had to start to climb up the steeply rising ground. There was enough exposed rock and roots to provide good steps and handholds. Where some of those steps were tall, Richard stretched down to give Kahlan a hand.

Tom helped Jennsen and passed Betty up a few times, even though the goat was better at scrambling up over rock than they were. Richard thought he was doing it more for Jennsen's peace of mind than Betty's. Jennsen finally told Tom that Betty could climb on her own.

Betty proved her right, bleating down at Tom after effortlessly clambering up a particularly trying spot.

"Why don't you help me up, then," Tom said to the goat.

Jennsen smiled along with Richard and Kahlan. Owen just watched as he skirted the other way around the rock. He was afraid of Betty. Cara finally asked for her pack back, having entertained long enough the possibility of being considered frail.

Shortly after the rain started, they found the low slit of an opening under a prominent ledge, just as Cara had said they would. It wasn't a cave, but a spot where a slab from the face of the mountain above had broken off and fallen over. Boulders on the ground held the slab up enough to create a pocket beneath. It wasn't large, but Richard thought they would all fit under it for the night.

The ground was dirty, scattered with collected leaf litter and forest debris of bark, moss, and a lot of bugs. Tom and Richard used branches they'd cut to quickly sweep the place out. They then laid down a clean bed of evergreen boughs to keep them up off the water that did run in.

The rain was starting to come down harder, so they all squatted down and hurried to move in under the rock. It wasn't a comfortable-looking spot, being too low for them to stand in, but it was fairly dry.

Richard dared not let them have a fire, now that they had left the regular trail, lest the smoke be spotted by the races. They had a cold supper of meats, leftover bannock, and dried goods. They were all exhausted from climbing all day, and while they ate engaged in only a bit of small talk. Betty was the only one with enough room to stand. She pushed up against Richard until she got his attention and a rub.

As darkness slowly enveloped the woods, they watched the rain fall outside their cozy shelter, listening to the soft sound, all no doubt wondering what lay ahead in a strange empire that had been sealed away for three thousand years. Troops from the Imperial Order would be there, too.

As Richard sat watching out into the dark rain, listening to the sounds of the occasional animal in the distance, Kahlan cuddled up beside him, laying her head on his lap. Betty went deeper into the shelter and lay down with Jennsen.

Kahlan, under the comfort of his hand resting tenderly on her shoulder, was asleep in moments. As weary as he was from the day's hard journey, Richard wasn't sleepy.

His head hurt and the poison deep within him made each breath catch. He wondered what would strike him down first, the power of his gift that was giving him the headaches, or Owen's poison.

He wondered, too, just how he was going to satisfy the demands of Owen and his men to free their empire so that he could have the antidote. The five of them, he, Kahlan, Cara, Jennsen, and Tom, hardly seemed the army needed to drive the Order out of Bandakar.

If he didn't, and if he couldn't get to the antidote, his life was coming to a close. This very well could be his final journey.

It seemed like he had just gotten back together with Kahlan after being separated from her for half his life. He wanted to be with her. He wanted the two of them to be able to be alone.

If he didn't think of something, all they had in each other, all they had ahead of them, was just about over. And that was without even considering the headaches of the gift.

Or the Imperial Order capturing the Wizard's Keep.

CHAPTER 32

Richard gripped the edge of the rock at the face of the opening to help pull himself up and out from the dark hole in the abrupt rise of granite before them. Once out, he brushed the sharp little granules of rock from his hands as he turned to the others.

"It goes through. It isn't easy, but it goes through."

He saw a dubious look on Tom's face, and a look of consternation on Owen's. Betty, her floppy ears perked ahead in what Richard thought could only be a goat frown, peered down into the narrow chasm and bleated.

"But I don't think we can," Owen complained. "What if . . ."

"We get stuck?" Richard asked.

Owen nodded.

"Well, you have an advantage over Tom and me," Richard said as he picked up his pack from nearby to the side where he'd left it. "You're not quite as big. If I made it through and back, then you can make it, Owen."

Owen waved a hand up the steep ascent to his right. "But what about that way? Couldn't we just go around?"

"I don't like going into dark, narrow places like this, either," Richard said. "But if we go around that way we have to go out on the ledges. You heard what Cara said; it's narrow and dangerous. If it were the only way it would be another matter, but it's not.

"The races could spot us out there. Worse, if they wanted, they could attack us and we could easily fall or be forced over the edge. I don't like going in places like this, but I don't think I'd like to be out there on a windblown ledge no wider than the sole of my boot, with a fall of thousands of feet straight down if I make one slip, and then have one of those races suddenly show up to rip into me with their talons or those sharp beaks of theirs. Would you prefer that?"

Owen licked his lips as he bent at the waist and looked into the narrow passageway. "Well, I guess you're right."

"Richard," Kahlan asked in a whisper as the rest of them started taking off their packs so they could more easily fit through, "if this was a trail, as you suspect, why isn't there a better way through?"

"I think that sometime only in the last few thousand years this huge section of the mountain broke away and slid down, coming to rest at this angle, leaving a narrow passageway beneath it." He pointed up. "See up there? I think this entire portion down here used to be up there. I think it's now sitting right where the trail used to be."

"And there's no other way but this cave or the ledges?"

"I'm not saying that. I believe there's other old routes, but we would have to backtrack for most of a day to take the last fork I saw, and then there isn't any guarantee with that one, either. If you really want, though, we can go back and try."

Kahlan shook her head. "We can't afford to lose any time. We need to get to the antidote."

Richard nodded. He didn't know how he was supposed to rid an entire empire of the Imperial Order so they could get to the antidote, but he had a few ideas. He needed to get the antidote; he saw no reason he had to play by Owen's rules—or the Order's.

Kahlan gave the narrow, dark tunnel another look. "You're sure there aren't any snakes in there?"

"I didn't see any."

Tom handed Richard his sword. "I'll go last," he said. "If you make it through, I can."

Richard nodded as he laid the baldric over his shoulder. He turned the scabbard at his hip in order to clear the rock and then started in. He hugged his pack to his abdomen as he crouched to make it into the small space. The slab of rock above him lay at an angle, so that he couldn't remain upright, but had to twist sideways and back as he went into the darkness. The farther in he went, the darker it became. As the others followed him into the narrow passage, it blocked much of the light, making it even darker.

The rains of recent days had finally ended, but runnels and runoff continued to flow from the mountain. Their wading through ankle-deep water standing in the bottom of the cavern sent echoes through the narrow confines. The waves in the water played gloomy light along the wet walls, providing at least some illumination.

The thought occurred to him that if he was a snake, this would make a good spot to call home. The thought also occurred to him that if Kahlan, right behind him, happened upon a snake in such cramped quarters, she would not be pleased with him in the least for taking her in.

Things that were frightening outside were different when you couldn't maneuver, couldn't run. Panic always seemed to lurk in tight places.

As it became darker, Richard had to feel his way along the cold stone. In places where water seeped down the rock, the walls were slimy. In some spots there was mud, in other places dry rock to walk on. Most of it, though, was wet muck. Spongy leaves had collected in some of the irregular low places.

By the smell, it was obvious that some animal had died and was decomposing somewhere in the sodden grotto. He heard moans and complaints from behind when the rest of them encountered the stench. Betty bleated her unhappiness. Jennsen's echoing whisper told the goat to be quiet.

Even the displeasure of the smell was forgotten as they worked their way under the immense curtain of rock draped over where the trail used to be. This wasn't a true cave, like underground caves Richard had encountered before. It was only a narrow crack under what was, in essence, a big rock. There were no chambers and different routes to worry about; there was only one narrow void under the rock, so lighting their way wasn't critical. He knew, too, that it wasn't all that long. It only felt that way in the dark.

Richard reached the spot where the way ahead abruptly started up at a steep angle. Feeling the walls all around to find places to grab, he started the difficult climb. In places he had to wedge his back against one wall and use his feet against the opposite wall to brace himself while grappling for any ledge or crack in the rock he could find to help pull himself up. He had to balance his pack in his lap as he went, and keep his sword from getting wedged. It was slow going.

Richard finally reached the high table where the rock from above had first come down. The hollow left under the mountain of rock was basically horizontal, rather than vertical, as it had been. Rock rested along the edge of most of the shelf, but there was one place with ample room for them to make it through, over the edge and then in under the slab above them. Once up onto the flat, he leaned over as far as he could, extending a hand down to help Kahlan.

He heard the grunts of effort from below Kahlan as the rest of the small company worked their way up the precipitous passage.

From his place atop the table of rock, Richard could finally see light ahead and light above. He had scouted the route and knew that they were close to being out the other side, but first they had to make it across the shelf of rock where the slab left little room above them. It was uncomfortably confining.

Richard didn't like such places. He knew, though, that there was no other way through. This was the place he worried most about. Tight as it was, it was fortunately close to the end.

"We have to crawl on our bellies from here," he told Kahlan. "Hold my ankle. Have everyone behind do the same."

Kahlan peered ahead toward the light coming from the opening. The glare of that light made it difficult to see to the sides. "Richard, it doesn't look big enough. It's just a crack."

Richard pushed his pack out onto the rock. "There's a way. We'll be out soon."

Kahlan let out a deep breath. "All right. The sooner the better."

"Listen to me," he called back into the darkness. "We're almost out."

"If you make us walk through any more rotting animals, I'll clobber you," Jennsen called up to him. Everyone laughed.

"No more of that," Richard said. "But there is a difficult spot ahead. I've been through it, so I know we can all make it. But you have to listen to me and do as I say. Crawl on your stomach, pushing your pack ahead of you. Hold the ankle of the person in front of you. That way you'll all follow in the right place.

"You'll see the light ahead of you. You can't go toward the light. That isn't the way out. The ceiling drops down too low and the slope of the rock starts pitching down to the left. If you slip down in there it gets even tighter; you'll not be able to get out. We have to go around the low place in the ceiling. We have to go around on the right side, where it's dark, but not as low. Does everyone understand?"

Agreement echoed up from the darkness.

"Richard," Jennsen called in a small voice, "I don't like being in here. I want out."

Her voice carried a thread of panic.

"I don't either," he told her. "But I've been through and out the other side. I made it through and back. You'll be fine. Just follow me and you won't have a problem."

Her voice drifted up to him from the darkness. "I want to go back."

Richard couldn't let her go back. The ledges, where they were exposed to the races, were too dangerous.

"Here," Kahlan told her, "you come ahead of me. Take hold of Richard's ankle and you'll be out before the rest of us."

"I'll see that Betty watches you go through and follows," Tom offered.

That seemed to break the impasse. Jennsen moved up to the ledge and handed her pack up. Richard, lying on his stomach in the low slit of the shelf, took her hand to help her up.

When she saw in the light how low and tight it was, that Richard had to lie on his stomach, she started to tremble. When Richard helped pull her up, and her face came up close to him, he could see her tears in the dim light.

Her wide blue eyes took in the way ahead, how low it was.

"Please, Richard, I'm afraid. I don't want to go in under there."

He nodded. "I know, but it's not far. I won't let you stay in here.

I'll see that you get out." He cupped a hand to the side of her face. "I promise."

"How do I know you'll keep your promise?"

Richard smiled. "Wizards always keep their promises."

"You said you don't know much about being a wizard."

"But I know how to keep promises."

She at last agreed and let him help her the rest of the way up. When he pulled her all the way up onto the shelf of the mountainside, and she actually felt how the roof of rock didn't allow her any room to get up and that she had to lie flat just to fit, and worse, that the roof of rock was only scant inches above her back, she started to shiver with terror.

"I know how you feel," he told her. "I do, Jennsen. I hate this, too, but we have no choice. It's not dangerous if you just follow me through the place where there's room. Just follow me and we'll be out before you know it."

"What if it comes down and crushes us? Or what if it comes down just enough to pin us so we can't move or breathe?"

"It won't," he insisted. "It's been here for ages. It isn't going to come down. It's not."

She nodded but he didn't know if she really heard him. She began to whimper as he turned himself around so he could lead her out.

"Take my ankle," he called back to her. "Here, push your pack up to me and I'll take care of it for you. Then you'll only have to worry about holding on to my ankle and following behind."

"What if it gets too tight and I can't breathe? Richard, what if I can't breathe?"

Richard kept his voice calm and confident. "I'm bigger than you, so if I fit, you will."

She only nodded as she shivered. He extended his hand back and had to tell her again to pass her pack forward before she did as he instructed. Once he had her pack, he tied the straps to his and pushed them both on ahead. She seized his ankle as if it were the only thing keeping her from falling into the arms of the Keeper of the underworld. He didn't complain, though, about how hard she held him; he knew her fear.

Richard pushed the packs out ahead and started inching his way forward. He tried not to think about the rough ceiling of rock only a hand-width above his back. He knew it would become narrower before they got out. The shelf of rock sloped upward to the right slightly, into the dark. The light was to the left, and down.

It looked like the easiest way out was to go straight toward the opening. It wasn't far. They had to go, instead, up into the darkness and around the narrowing of the cleft in order to get around to a place where they could fit through. Forcing himself to go up, into the dark where it felt tighter and more closed in, rather than toward the light of the opening, felt wrong, but he had already scouted the route and he knew that his feelings were wrong about this.

As he moved deeper into the darkness, going around the impassable area in the center of the chamber, he reached the spot where the rock above lowered. Advancing in farther, it came down until it pressed against his back. He knew it wasn't far, not more than a dozen feet but, without being able to take a full breath, the cramped passage was daunting.

Richard pushed the packs ahead as he wriggled and wormed his way along. He had to push with the toes of his boots and, with his fingers finding any purchase available, pull his chest through, force himself to make headway into the dark, away from the light.

Jennsen's fingers had an iron grip on his ankle. That was fine with Richard, because he could then help pull her through with him. He wanted to be able to help pull her through when she reached the spot that would compress her chest.

And then she suddenly let go of his ankle.

CHAPTER 33

Off behind him, Richard could hear Jennsen scrambling away.

"Jennsen? What's going on? What are you doing?"

She was crying out, whining in terror, as she bolted toward the light at the opening.

"Jennsen!" Richard called to her. "Don't go that way! Stay with me!"

Wedged in as he was, he couldn't easily turn to see. He forced himself ahead, crabbing sideways, trying to spot her. Jennsen was clambering toward the light, ignoring him as he called to her.

Kahlan wormed her way up to him. "What's she doing?"

"She's trying to get out. She sees the opening, the light, and won't listen."

Richard shoved the packs and frantically worked his way ahead, moving into the area beyond the tight spot, to where it was open enough that he could at last get a full breath and almost get up on his hands and knees.

Jennsen screamed. Richard could see her clawing frantically at the rock, but she wasn't making any headway. In a frenzy of effort, she tried to push herself forward, but, instead, she'd slipped sideways farther down the slope, wedging herself in tighter.

Each exaggerated, panting breath as she strained and stretched ratcheted her in deeper.

Richard called to her, trying to get her to listen, to do as he said. In her desperation, she wasn't responding to any of his instructions. She saw the opening, wanted out, and would not listen to him.

Fast as he could, Richard scrambled through the darkness and around toward the opening, guiding Kahlan, Owen, Cara, and Tom through the only way he knew they could make it. Kahlan held tight to his ankle and he could hear by the panting of effort that the rest of them were all following in a line behind her.

Jennsen screamed in terror. She struggled madly, but couldn't move. Wedged in as she was, with rock compressing her ribcage top and bottom, it was becoming difficult for her to breathe.

"Jennsen! Take a slow breath! Slow down!" Richard called to her as he scurried around toward the opening. "Breathe slow! Breathe!"

Richard finally reached the opening. He emerged from the dark crevasse, squinting in the sudden light. On his knees, he leaned in and helped pull Kahlan out. Betty scrambled out, somehow having passed the rest of the people. As Owen and then Cara clambered out of the opening, Richard pulled the baldric over his head and handed his sword to Kahlan.

Tom called out that he was going back in to try to reach Jennsen.

As soon as the rest were safely out, Richard dove back into the fissure. Headfirst, on his hands and knees, he scuttled into the dark. He could see that Tom, from his angle of approach, had no chance to get to her.

"Tom, I'll get her."

"I can reach her," the man said even as he was getting himself wedged tight.

"No you can't," Richard said in a stern tone. "Wishing won't make it so. You'll just get yourself stuck. Listen to me. Back out, now, or your weight will help push you downhill and get you stuck so hard that we won't be able to get you out. Back up, now, while you're still able to. Go. Let me get her."

Tom watched Richard moving around behind him, and then, making a face that showed how unhappy he was to be doing it, he started pushing himself back up into the darkness, where there was a few precious inches' more room that would let him make it back out.

Richard worked his way through the tight spot and then moved down the slope so that he wouldn't be facing downhill as he tried to help Jennsen and possibly wedge himself in tighter than he wanted.

If he wasn't careful, he would do the same thing Tom had been about to do. Down in the darkness, Jennsen cried in panic.

Richard, flat on his belly, wiggled and snaked his way deeper, all the while moving to his left, down the pitch in the shelf of rock. "Jennsen, breathe. I'm coming. It's all right."

"Richard! Please don't leave me here! Richard!"

Richard spoke in a calm, quiet voice as he moved around behind her down into the tighter part of the cave. "I'm not going to leave you. You'll be fine. Just wait for me."

"Richard! I can't move!" She grunted with effort. "I can't breathe! The ceiling is coming down! It's moving—I can feel it coming down. It's squeezing me! Please help me! Richard—please don't leave me!"

"You're fine, Jennsen. The ceiling isn't moving. You're just stuck. I'll have you out in a minute."

Even as he worked his way into the low spot, trying to get up close behind her, she was still struggling to move forward, making it worse—there was no way she could go forward and make it out. As she kept struggling, though, she was slowly slipping deeper down the slope and with every frantic breath wedging herself in tighter. He could hear how desperately she was trying to breathe, to draw each shallow breath against the immovable compression of rock.

Finally all the way back around behind her, Richard started pushing himself in the way she'd gone. She had gone into a narrow channel that closed down on the uphill side of her, so there could be no moving her sideways up the slope; he had to get her to back up the way she'd gone in. He had to get her to go away from the light and back into what she feared.

The roof of rock scraped against his back, making it difficult to draw a full breath. He had to take shallow breaths as he moved deeper. The farther he went, he could not even breathe that deeply.

The need for air, for a deep breath, made the pain of the poison feel like knives twisting in his ribs. Arms stretched forward, Richard used his boots to force himself in deeper, trying to ignore his own rising sense of panic. He reasoned with himself that there were others who knew where he was, that he wasn't alone. With the powerful feeling that a mountain of rock was crushing him, reasoning with himself was difficult, especially when the shallow split of rock he was pressed into hardly let him get any air as it was and he was desperately working himself deeper trying to reach Jennsen. He knew that he had to help pull her out of where she was stuck or she would die there.

"Richard," she cried, "it hurts. I can't breathe. I'm stuck. Dear spirits, I can't breathe. Please, Richard, I'm scared."

Richard stretched, trying to reach her ankle. It was too far away. He had to turn his head sideways to advance. Both ears scraped against rock. He wiggled, inching in tighter even though his better judgment was telling him that he was already in trouble.

"Jennsen, please, I need you to help me. I need you to push back. Push back with your hands. Push back toward me."

"No! I have to get out! I'm almost there!"

"No, you're not almost there. You can't make it that way. You have to trust me. Jennsen, you've got to push back so I can reach you."

"No! Please! I want out! I want out!"

"I'll get you out, I promise. Just push back so I can reach you."

With her blocking the light he couldn't tell if she was doing as he instructed or not. He squirmed in another inch, then another. His head was almost stuck. He couldn't imagine how she had gotten in as far as she had.

"Jennsen, push back." His voice was strained. He couldn't get enough of a breath to talk and to breathe, too.

His fingers stretched forward, reaching, stretching, reaching. His lungs burned for air. He just wanted to take a deep breath. He desperately needed a breath. Not being able to draw one was not only painful, but frightening. His heartbeat pounded in his ears.

As high as they were in the mountains, the air was already thin and it was difficult to get enough air the way it was. Limited to taking shallow breaths was making him lightheaded. If he didn't get back to where he could breathe soon, the two of them were going to be forever in this terrible place.

The tips of Richard's fingers caught the edge of the sole of Jennsen's boot. He couldn't get a good grip on her foot, though.

"Push back," he whispered into the dark. It was all he could do to keep his own panic in check. "Jennsen, do as I say. Push back. Do it."

Jennsen's boot moved back into his hand. He snatched it in a tighter grip and immediately worked his way back a few inches. Pulling with all his might, he strained to drag her back with him. Try as he might, she wouldn't budge. She was either stuck tight, or was fighting to go forward.

"Push back," he whispered again. "Use your hands, Jennsen. Push back toward me. Push."

She was sobbing and crying something he couldn't make out. Richard wedged his boots, top and bottom, in the tight cleft and then pulled with all his might. His arm shook with the effort. He managed to draw her back a few inches.

He wiggled himself back an equal distance and pulled again. With agonizing effort, he slowly, painstakingly, started drawing her out of the dead end she had fled into in her panicked attempt to get out.

At times, she tried to squirm back toward the light. Richard, the rock compressing him tight, kept a firm hold of her boot and muscled her back yet more, not allowing her to take back any of the distance he gained.

He couldn't straighten his head. That made it more difficult to use his muscles to move the both of them. With his head lying on the right, he reached back with his left arm and gripped a small lip of rock in the ceiling, using it to help haul them back. With his right arm, stretched forward and holding her by the boot, he drew her back inch by inch.

As he reached back again for another handhold, Richard saw something not far to his left, down the slope, wedged where the rock narrowed. At first he thought it was a rock. As he struggled to draw Jennsen back, he stared at the thing also stuck in the rock. He reached to the side and touched it. It was smooth and didn't feel at all like the granite.

As he began to make good progress backward he stretched to the side and managed to get his fingers around the thing. He pulled it to his side and continued to wiggle back.

With great relief, he was finally back far enough to where he was able to get enough air. He lay still for a time, just catching his breath. Almost as much as air, though, he wanted out.

While he talked to Jennsen, distracting her with instructions she only intermittently followed, he began forcing her back and to the right, where there was more room. Finally, he managed to move up beside her and seize her wrist. Once he had her, he started moving her back up the slope, into the darkness, into the tight place that he knew was the only true way out.

With him up beside her, she was a little more cooperative. All the while, he kept reassuring her. "This is the way, Jennsen. This is the way. I'll not leave you. I'll get you out. This is the way. Just come with me and we'll be out in a few minutes."

When they worked their way up into the dark, tight spot, she began struggling again, trying again to scramble for the light of the opening, but he was blocking her way. He stayed close at her side as he kept them both moving forward. She seemed to find strength in his constant assurances and his firm grip on her wrist. He was not about to let her get away from him again.

When they pushed through to the place where the roof rose up a bit, she started weeping with expectant joy. He knew the feeling. Once the ceiling rose up a foot or two, he hurried as fast as he could to get her to the opening, to the light.

The others were waiting right at the entrance to help pull them out. Richard held the thing he'd retrieved under his left arm as he helped push Jennsen out first. She rushed into Tom's waiting arms, but only until Richard crawled out and got to his feet. Then, crying with relief, Jennsen fled into his arms, clinging to him for dear life.

"I'm so sorry," she said over and over as she cried. "I'm so sorry, Richard. I was so afraid."

"I know," he comforted as he held her.

He'd been in a similar situation before where he thought he might never get himself out of such a terrifying place, so he did understand. In such a stressful circumstance, where you feared you were about to die, it was easy to be overpowered by the blind need to escape—to live.

"I feel so confused."

"I don't like such tight places, either," he said. "I understand."

"But I don't understand. I've never been afraid of places like that. Ever since I was very young I've hid in tight little places. Such places always made me feel safe because no one could find me or get to me. When you spend your life running and hiding from someone like Darken Rahl, you come to appreciate small, dark, concealed places.

"I don't know what came over me. It was the strangest thing. It was like these thoughts that I wouldn't get out, that I couldn't breathe, that I would die, just started coming into my head. Feelings I've never had before just started to seep into me. They just seemed to overwhelm me. I've never done anything like that before."

"Do you still feel these strange feelings?"

"Yes," she said as she wept, "but they're starting to fade, now that I'm out, now that it's over."

Everyone else had moved off a ways to give her the time she needed to set herself straight. They sat not far off waiting on an old log turned silver in the weather.

Richard didn't try to rush her. He just held her and let her know she was safe.

"I'm so sorry, Richard. I feel like such a fool."

"No need. It's over, now."

"You kept your promise," she said through her tears.

Richard smiled, happy that he had.

Owen, his face tense with worry, looked like he couldn't help himself from asking a question. "But, Jennsen," he asked as he stepped forward. "Why didn't you do magic to help yourself?"

"I can't do magic any more than you can."

He rubbed his palms on his hips. "You could if you let yourself. You are one who is able to touch magic."

"Other people might be able to do magic, but I can't. I don't have any ability for it."

"What others think is magic is only themselves tricking their senses and only blinds them to real magic. Our eyes blind us, our senses deceive us—as I explained before. Only those who have never seen magic, only those who have never used, sensed, perceived it, only those who do not have any ability or faculty for it, can actually understand it and therefore only they can be true practitioners of real magic. Magic must be based entirely on faith, if it is to be real. You must believe, and then you truly can see. You are one who can do magic."

Richard and Jennsen stared at him.

"Richard," Kahlan said in an odd voice before he could say anything to Owen. "What's that?"

Richard blinked at her. "What?"

She pointed. "That, there, under your arm. What is it?"

"Oh," he said. "Something I found wedged in the rock near Jennsen, back in where she was stuck. In the dark, I couldn't tell what it was other than that it wasn't rock."

He pulled it out to have a look.

It was a statue.

A statue in his likeness, wearing his war wizard's outfit. The cape was fixed in place as it swirled to the side of the legs, making the base wider than the waist.

The lower portion of the figure was a translucent amber color, and through it could be seen a falling trickle of sand that had nearly filled the bottom half.

The statue was not all amber, though, as Kahlan's had been. Near the middle, obscuring the narrowing where the sand dribbled through, the translucent amber of the bottom began darkening. The higher up the figure, the darker it became.

The top—the shoulders and head—were as black as a night stone.

A night stone was an underworld thing, and Richard remembered all too well what that wicked object had looked like. The top of the statue looked to be made of the same sinister material, all glossy and smooth and so black that it looked as if it might suck the light right out of the day.

Richard's heart sank at seeing himself represented in such a way, as a talisman touched by death.

"She made it," Owen said, shaking an accusatorial finger at Jennsen still sheltered under Richard's right arm. "She made it with magic.

I told you she could. She spun it of evil magic back in that cave when she wasn't thinking. The magic took over and came out of her, then, when she wasn't thinking about how she couldn't do magic."

Owen didn't have any idea what he was talking about. This was not a statue Jennsen made.

This was the second warning beacon, meant to warn the one who could seal the breach.

"Lord Rahl . . ."

Richard looked up. It was Cara's voice.

She was standing off a ways, her back to them, looking up at a small spot of sky off through the trees. Jennsen turned in his arms to see what had put the odd tone in Cara's voice. Holding his sister close, Richard stepped up behind Cara and peered up through the trees where she was looking.

Through a thin area in the canopy of pine, he could see the rim of the mountain pass above them. Silhouetted against iron-gray clouds stealing past was something man-made.

It looked like a huge statue sitting atop the pass.

CHAPTER 34

Icy wind tore at Richard's and Kahlan's clothes as they huddled close together at the edge of a thick stand of spruce trees. Low, ragged clouds raced by as if to escape the colossal, dark, swirling clouds building above them. Fat flakes of snow danced in the cold gusts. Richard's ears burned in the numbing cold.

"What do you think?" Kahlan asked.

Richard shook his head. "I don't know." He glanced behind them, back into the shelter of the trees. "Owen, are you sure you don't know what it is? You don't have any idea at all?"

The roiling clouds made an ominous backdrop for the imposing statue sitting up on the ridge.

"No, Lord Rahl. I've never been here before; none of us ever traveled this route. I don't know what it could be. Unless . . ." His words trailed off into the moan of the wind.

"Unless what?"

Owen shrank back, twisting the button on his coat as he glanced to the Mord-Sith on one side of him and Tom and Jennsen on the other. "There is a foretelling—from the ones who gave us our name and protected us by sealing the pass. It is taught that when they gave our empire its name, they also told us that one day a savior would come to us."

Richard wanted to ask the man just what exactly it was he thought they needed saving from—if they had lived in such an enlightened culture where they were safe from the unenlightened "savages" of the rest of the world. Instead, he asked a simpler question he thought Owen might be able to answer.

"So you think that maybe that's a statue of him, your savior?"

Owen fidgeted, his shoulders finally working into a shrug. "He is not just a savior. The foretelling also says that he will destroy us."

Richard frowned at the man, hoping this was not going to be another of his convoluted beliefs. "This savior of yours is going to destroy you. That makes no sense."

Owen was quick to agree. "I know. No one understands it."

"Maybe it's meant to say that someone will come to save your people," Jennsen suggested, "but he will fail and so only end up destroying them in the attempt."

"Maybe." Owen's face twisted with the displeasure of having to contemplate such an outcome.

"Maybe," Cara suggested in a grim tone, "it means this man will come, and, after seeing your people, decide they aren't worth saving" —she leaned toward Owen— "and decide to destroy them instead."

Owen, as he stared up at Cara, seemed to be considering her words as a real possibility, rather than the sarcasm Richard knew them to be.

"I don't think that is the meaning," Owen finally told her after earnest consideration. He turned back to Richard. "The foretelling, as it has been taught to us, you see, says, first, that a man will come who will destroy us. It then goes on to say that he is the one who will save us. 'Your destroyer will come and he will redeem you,'" Owen quoted. "That is how we have been taught the words, how they were told to my people when we were put here, beyond this pass."

"'Your destroyer will come and he will redeem you,'" Richard repeated. He took a patient breath. "Whatever it originally said has probably been confused and all jumbled up as it's been passed down. It probably no longer resembles the original saying."

Rather than disagree, as Richard expected, Owen nodded. "Some believe, as you say, that over the time since we were protected and given our name, maybe the true words have been lost, or confused. Others believe that it has been passed down intact and must have important meaning. Some believe that the foretelling was meant to say only that a savior will come. Others think it means only that a destroyer will come."

"And what do you believe?" Richard asked.

Owen twiddled the button on his coat until Richard thought it might come off. "I believe that the foretelling is meant to say that a destroyer will come—and I believe that he is this man Nicholas, of the Order—and then that a savior will come and save us. I believe that man is you, Lord Rahl. Nicholas is our destroyer. You are our savior."

Richard knew from the book that prophecy didn't function with these people, with pillars of Creation.

"What your people think is a foretelling," Richard said, "is probably nothing more than an old adage that people have gotten mixed up."

Owen held his ground, if hesitantly. "We are taught that this is a foretelling. We are taught that those who named us told us this foretelling and that they wanted it passed down so all might know of it."

Richard sighed, the wind pulling out a long cloud of his breath. "So you think that up there is a statue of me, put there thousands of years ago by the ones who protected you behind the boundary? How would they know, long before I was born, what I would look like in order to make a statue of me?"

"The true reality knows everything that will be," Owen said by rote. He forced a half smile as he shrugged again. "After all, it made that little statue that you found look like you."

Unhappy to be reminded of that, Richard turned away from the man. The small figure had been made to look like him by magic tied to the boundary and, possibly, to a dead wizard in the underworld.

Richard scanned the sky, the rocky slopes all around, the treeline. He didn't see any sign of life. The statue—they still couldn't quite make out what it was—sat distant upon a treeless, rocky rise. It was yet quite a climb up to that rim of the pass, to that statue.

Richard was not going to like it if it did indeed turn out to be a statue of him beneath the gathering gloom.

He already didn't like it one bit that the second warning beacon was meant for him. It bound him to a responsibility, a duty, he neither wanted nor could accomplish.

He had no idea how to restore the seal on Bandakar. Zedd had once created boundaries that were probably similar to the one that had been down here in the Old World, but even Zedd had used constructed magic he had found in the Keep. Such constructed spells had been created by ancient wizards with vast power and knowledge of such things. Zedd had told him that there were no more such spells.

Richard certainly had no idea how to call forth a spell that could create such a boundary. More to the point, he didn't see how it would do any good even if he knew how. What had really been freed from Bandakar when the boundary failed was the trait of being born without any trace of the gift—that was why they had all been banished here in the first place. The Imperial Order was already breeding women from Bandakar in order to breed the gift out of mankind. There was no telling how far that trait had already spread. Breeding the women, as it sounded like they were doing, now, would gain them more children who were pristinely ungifted, children who would be indoctrinated in the teachings of the Order.

When they started using the men for breeding, the number of such children would vastly increase. A woman could have a child every year. In the same time, a man could sire a great number of children bearing his pristinely ungifted trait.

Despite the Order's creed of self-sacrifice, they had not yet, it would seem, been willing to sacrifice their women to such an under-taking. Raping the women in Bandakar and proclaiming it for the good of mankind was fine with the men of the Order. For the men ruling the Imperial Order to give over their own women to be bred, however, was quite another matter.

Richard had no doubt that they eventually would start using their own women to this purpose, but that would come later. In the mean-time, the Order would probably soon start using all the women captured and held as slaves for this purpose, breeding them to men from Bandakar. The Order's conquest of the New World would provide them with plenty more women for breeding stock.

Whereas in ancient times those in the New World tried to limit the trait from spreading in man, the Imperial Order would do what-ever they could to accelerate it.

"Richard," Kahlan asked in a low voice, so the others farther back in the trees wouldn't hear, "what do you think it means that the second warning beacon, the one for you, is turning black like the night stone? Do you think it means to show you the time you have left to get the antidote?"

Since he had only just found it, he hadn't given it much thought. Even so, he could interpret it only as a dire warning. The night stone was tied to the spirits of the dead—to the underworld.

It could be, as Kahlan suggested, that the darkening was meant to show him how the poison was taking him, and that he was running out of time. For a number of reasons, though, he didn't believe that was the explanation.

"I don't know for sure," he finally told her, "but I don't think it's a warning about the poison. I think that the way the statue is turning black is meant to represent, materially, how the gift is failing in me, how it's slowly beginning to kill me, how the underworld, the world of the dead, is slowly enshrouding me."

Kahlan's hand slipped up on his arm, a gesture of comfort as well as worry. "That was my thought, too. I was hoping you would argue against it. This means that the gift might be more of a problem than the poison—if, after all, this dead wizard used the beacon to warn you about it."

Richard wondered if the statue up on the ridge of the pass would hold any answers. He certainly didn't have any. To make it up there and see, they would have to leave the shelter of the forest and travel out in the open.

Richard turned and signaled the others forward.

"I don't think the races would be expecting us here," he said as they gathered around him. "If we really did manage to lose them they won't know where we went, in which direction, so they won't know to look for us here. I think we can make it up there without the races, and therefore Nicholas, knowing."

"Besides," Tom said, "with those low clouds hugging most of the mountains, they may not be able to search."

"Maybe," Richard said.

It was getting late. In the distant mountains a wolf howled. On another slope across a deep cleft in the mountains, a second wolf answered. There would be more than two.

Betty's ears perked toward the howls as she crowded against Jennsen's legs.

"What if Nicholas uses something else?" Jennsen asked.

Cara gripped the blond braid lying over the front of her shoulder as she scanned the woods to the sides. "Something else?"

Jennsen pulled her cloak tighter around herself as the wind tried to lift it open. "Well, if he can look through a race's eyes, then maybe he can look through the eyes of something else."

"You mean a wolf?" Cara asked. "You think that wolf you heard might be him."

"I don't know," Jennsen admitted.

"For that matter," Richard said, "if he can look through the black eyes of the races, maybe he could just as easily look through the eyes of a mouse."

Tom swiped his windblown blond hair back from his forehead as he cast a wary glance at the sky. "Why do you think he always seems to use the races, then?"

"Probably because they're better able to cover great distances," Richard said. "After all, he'd have a lot of trouble finding us with a mouse.

"More than that, though, I think he likes the imagery of being with such creatures, likes thinking of himself as being part of a powerful predator. He is, after all, hunting us."

"So you think we only have to worry about the races, then?" Jennsen asked.

"I think he would prefer to watch through the races, but that isn't his end, only the means," Richard said. "He's after Kahlan and me. Since getting us is his end, I think he will turn to whatever means he must, if necessary. He very well might look through even the eyes of a mouse if it would help him get us."

"If his end is having you," Cara said, "then Owen is helping his ends by bringing you right to him."

Richard couldn't argue with that. For the moment, though, he had to go along with Owen's wishes. Soon enough, Richard intended to start doing things his own way.

"For now," Richard said, "he's still trying to find us, so I expect that he will stick to the races, since they can cover great distances. But, since I've killed races with arrows, he must realize that we at least suspect someone is watching us through their eyes. As we get closer to him, I see no reason that in the future he might not use something else so we won't know he's watching us."

Kahlan looked to be alarmed by the idea. "You mean, something like a wolf or, or . . . I don't know, maybe an owl?"

"Owl, pigeon, sparrow. If I had to guess, then I'd guess that at least until he finds us he will use a bird."

Kahlan huddled close beside him, using his body to block the wind. They were up high enough in the mountains that they were just beginning to encounter snow. From what Richard had seen of the Old World, it generally appeared too warm for snow. For there to be snow this time of year it could only be in the most imposing of mountains.

Richard gestured to the icy flakes swirling in the air. "Owen, does it get cold in winter in Bandakar? Do you get snow?"

"Winds come down from the north, following down our side of the mountains, I believe. In winter it gets cold. Every couple of years, we get a bit of snow, but it does not last long. Usually in the winter it rains more. I do not understand why it snows here, now, when it is summer."

"Because of the elevation," Richard answered idly as he studied the rising slopes to each side.

Higher yet, the snowpack was thick, and in places, where the wind blew drifts into overhangs, it would be treacherous. Trying to cross such precipitous, snow-covered slopes would be perilous, at best. Fortunately, they were nearing the highest point they would have to climb to make it over the pass, so they wouldn't have to traverse heavy snow. The bitterly cold wind, though, was making them all miserable.

"I want to know what that thing is," Richard finally said, gesturing up at the statue on the rise. He looked around at the others to see if anyone objected. No one did. "And, I want to know why it's there."

"Do you think we should wait for dark?" Cara asked. "Darkness will hide us better."

Richard shook his head. "The races must be able to see pretty well in the dark—after all, that's when they hunt. If given a choice, I'd rather be in the open during the daylight, when I can see them coming."

Richard hooked his bow under his leg and bent it enough to attach the bowstring. He drew an arrow from the leather quiver over his shoulder and nocked it, holding it at rest against the bow with his left hand. He scanned the sky, checking the clouds, and looking for any sign of the races. He wasn't entirely sure about the shadows among the trees, but the sky was clear of races.

"I think we'd better be on our way." Richard's gaze swept across all their faces, first, making sure they were paying attention. "Walk on the rocks if at all possible. I don't want to leave a trail behind in the snow that Nicholas could spot through the eyes of the races."

Nodding their understanding, they all followed after him, in single file, out onto the rocks. Owen, in front of the ever-watchful Mord-Sith, kept a wary eye toward the sky. Jennsen and Betty watched the woods to the sides. In the strong gusts, they all hunched against the wind and the stinging bite of icy crystals hitting their faces. In the thin air it was tiring climbing up the steep incline. Richard's legs burned with the effort. His lungs burned with the poison.

By the look of the sheer walls of rock rising up into broken clouds to either side, Richard didn't see any way, other than the pass, for people to make it over the imposing mountains, at least, not without a journey of tremendous difficulty, hardship, and probably a great loss of life. Even then, he wasn't really certain that it was even possible.

In places, as they trudged up the edge of the steep rise, he could see back through gaps in the rock walls of the mountains, under the dark bottom of clouds, to sunlight beyond the pass.

None of them spoke as they climbed. From time to time they had to pause to catch their breath. They all kept an eye to the churning sky. Richard spotted a few small birds in the distance, but nothing of any size.

As they approached the top, following a zigzagging course so they could more easily make it up without having to scale rock faces or jutting ledges, Richard caught glimpses of the statue sitting on a massive base of granite.

From the high vantage point in the pass, he could now see that the rock on either side of the rise fell away in precipitous drops. The gorge at the bottom of either side dead-ended at vertical climbs of what would have to be thousands of feet. Whatever routes might have branched off lower down, they would have to converge before going up this rise; by the lay of the land, it became clear to him that this was the only way to make it through this entire section of the pass.

He realized that anyone approaching Bandakar by this route would have to climb this ridge in the rise, and they would unavoidably come upon the monument.

As he mounted the final cut between the snow-dusted boulders standing twice his height, Richard was able at last to take in the entire statue guarding the pass.

And guarding the pass it was. This was a sentinel.

The noble figure sitting atop a vast stone base was seated as he watchfully guarded the pass. In one hand the figure casually held a sword at the ready, its point resting on the ground. He appeared to be wearing leather armor, with his cape resting over his lap. The vigilant pose of the sentinel gave it a resolute presence. The clear impression was that this figure was set to ward what was beyond.

The stone was worn by centuries of weather, but that weathering failed to wear away the power of the carving. This figure had been carved, and placed, with great purpose. That it was out in the middle of nowhere, at the summit of a mountain pass no longer traveled and a trail possibly abandoned after this was set here, made it, to Richard, all the more arresting.

He had carved stone, and he knew what had gone into this. It was not what he would call fine work, but it was powerfully executed. Just looking at it gave him goose bumps.

"At least it doesn't look like you," Kahlan said.

At least there was that.

But this thing being there all alone for what very well might have been thousands of years was worrisome.

"What I'd like to know," Richard said to her, "is why this second beacon was down there, down the hill, in that cave, and not up here."

Kahlan shared a telling look with him. "If Jennsen hadn't done what she did, you would never have found it."

Richard walked around the base of the statue, searching—for what he didn't know. Almost as soon as he started looking, he saw, on the front of the base, on the top of one of the decorative moldings, an odd void in the snow. It looked as if something had been sitting there and had then been taken away. It was a track, of sorts, a tell-tale.

Richard thought the barren spot looked familiar. He pulled the warning beacon from his pack and checked the shape of the bottom. His thought confirmed, he placed the figure of himself in the void in the snow collected on the rim of the base. It was a perfect fit.

The little figure had been here, with this statue.

"How do you think it came to be down in the cave?" Cara asked in a suspicious voice.

"Maybe it fell," Jennsen offered. "It's pretty windy up here. Maybe the wind blew it off and it tumbled down the hill."

"And just managed to roll through the woods without being stopped by a tree, and then, neat as can be," Richard said, "roll right into the small opening of the cave, and then just happened to come to be stuck in the rock right near where you, by coincidence, ended up stuck. Stuck, I might add, in a terrifying place you aren't terrified of."

Jennsen blinked in wonder. "When you put it like that . . ."

Standing at the crown of the pass, in front of the statue right where the warning beacon would have rested, and now again rested, Richard could see that the spot held a commanding view of the approach to Bandakar. The mountains blocking off the view to either side were as formidable as anything he'd ever seen. The rise where the sentinel sat overlooked the approach into the pass back between those towering, snowcapped peaks. As high as they were, they were still only at the foothills of those mountains.

The statue was not looking ahead, as might be expected of a guardian, but rather, its unflinching gaze was fixed a little to the right. Richard thought that was a bit odd. He wondered if maybe it was meant to show this sentinel keeping a vigilant eye on everything, on every potential threat.

Standing as he was, directly in front of the statue's base, in front of where the warning beacon sat, Richard looked to the right, in the direction the man in the statue was looking.

He could see the approach of the pass up through the mountains. Farther out, in the distance, he could see vast forests to the west, and beyond that, the low, barren mountains they had crossed.

And, he could see a gap in those mountains.

The eyes of the man in the statue were resolutely fixed upon what Richard now saw.

"Dear spirits," he whispered.

"What is it?" Kahlan asked. "What do you see?"

"The Pillars of Creation."

CHAPTER 35

Kahlan, standing beside Richard, squinted into the distance. From the base of the statue they had a commanding view of the approaches from the west. It seemed as if she could see half a world away. But she couldn't see what he saw.

"I can't see the Pillars of Creation," she said.

Richard leaned close, having her sight down his arm where he pointed. "There. That darker depression in the expanse of flat ground."

Richard's eyes were better at seeing distant things than were hers. It was all rather hazy-looking, being so far away.

"You can recognize where it lies by the landmarks, there" —he pointed off to the right, and then a little to the left— "and there. Those darker mountains in the distance that are a little higher than the rest have a unique shape. They serve as good reference points so you can find things."

"Now that you point them out, I can see the land we traveled from. I recognize those mountains."

It seemed amazing, looking back on where they'd been, how high they were. She could see, spread out into the distance, the vast wasteland beyond the barren mountain range and, even if she couldn't make out the details of the dreadful place, she could see the darker depression in the valley. That depression she knew to be the Pillars of Creation.

"Owen," Richard asked, "how far is this pass from your men— the men who were hiding with you in the hills?"

Owen looked baffled by the question. "But, Lord Rahl, I have never been up in this portion of the pass before. I have never seen this statue. I have never been anywhere close to here before. It would be impossible for me to tell such a thing."

"Not impossible," Richard said. "If you know what your home is like, you should be able to recognize landmarks around it—just as I was able to look out to the west and see the route we traveled to get here. Look around at those mountains back through the pass and see if you recognize anything."

Owen, looking skeptical, walked the rest of the way up behind the statue and peered off to the east. He stood in the wind for a time, staring. He pointed at a mountain in the distance, through the pass.

"I think I know that place." He sounded astonished. "I know the shape of that mountain. It looks a little different from this spot, but I think it's the same place I know." He shielded his eyes from the gusts of wind as he gazed to the east. He pointed again. "And that place! I know that place, too!"

He rushed back to Richard. "You were right, Lord Rahl. I can see places I know." He stared off then he whispered to himself, "I can tell where my home is, even though I've not been here. Just by seeing places I know."

Kahlan had never seen anyone so astounded by something so simple.

"So," Richard finally prompted, "how far do you think your men are from here?"

Owen looked back over his shoulder. "Through that low place, then around that slope coming from the right . . ." He turned back to Richard. "We have been hiding in the land near where the seal on our empire used to be, where no one ever goes because it is near the place where death stalks, near the pass. I would guess maybe a full day's steady walk from here." He suddenly turned hesitant. "But I am wrong to be confident of what my eyes tell me. I may just be seeing what my mind wants me to see. It may not be real."

Richard folded his arms and leaned back against the granite base of the statue as he gazed out toward the Pillars of Creation, ignoring Owen's doubt. Knowing Richard as she did, Kahlan imagined that he must be considering his options.

Standing beside him, she was about to lean back against the stone of the statue's base, but instead paused to first brush the snow off from beside where the warning beacon rested. As she brushed the snow away, she saw that there were words carved in the top of the decorative molding.

"Richard . . . look at this."

He turned to see what she saw, and then started hurriedly brushing away more of the snow. The others crowded around, trying to see what was written in the stone of the statue's base. Cara, on the other side of Richard, ran her hand all the way to the end to clean off the entire ledge.

Kahlan couldn't read it. It was in another language she didn't know, but thought she recognized.

"High D'Haran?" Cara asked.

Richard nodded his confirmation as he studied the words. "This must be a very old dialect," he said, half to himself as he scrutinized it, trying to figure it out. "It's not just an old dialect, but one with which I'm not familiar. Maybe because this is so distant a place."

"What does it say?" Jennsen wanted to know as she peered around Richard, between him and Kahlan. "Can you translate it?"

"It's difficult to work it out," Richard mumbled. He swiped his hair back with one hand as he ran the fingers of his other lightly over the words.

He finally straightened and glanced up at Owen, standing to the side of the base, watching.

Everyone waited while Richard looked down at the words again. "I'm not sure," he finally said. "The phraseology is odd . . ." He looked up at Kahlan. "I can't be sure. I've not seen High D'Haran written this way before. I feel like I should know what it says, but I can't quite get it."

Kahlan didn't know if he really couldn't be sure, or if he didn't want to speak the translation in front of the others.

"Well, maybe if you think it over for a while, it might come to you," she offered, trying to give him a way of putting it off for the time being if he wanted to.

Richard didn't take her offer. Instead, he tapped a finger to the words on the left of the warning beacon. "This part is a little more clear to me. I think it says something like 'Fear any breach of this seal to the empire beyond. . . '"

He wiped a hand across his mouth as he considered the rest of the words. "I'm not so sure about the rest of it," he finally said. "It seems to say, "for beyond is evil: those who cannot see.'"

"Of course," Jennsen muttered in angry comprehension.

Richard raked his fingers back through his hair. "I'm not at all sure I have it right. Something about it still doesn't make sense. I'm not sure I have it right."

"You have it perfectly right," Jennsen said. "Those who cannot see magic. This was placed by the gifted who sealed those people away from the rest of the world because of how they were born." Her fiery eyes filled with tears. "Fear any breach of this seal to the empire beyond, for beyond is evil—those who cannot see magic. That's what it means, those who cannot see magic."

No one argued with her. The only sound was the rush of the wind across the open ground.

Richard spoke softly to her. "I'm not sure that's it, Jenn."

She folded her arms and turned away, glaring out toward the Pillars of Creation.

Kahlan could understand how she felt. Kahlan knew what it was like to be shunned by almost everyone except those who were like you. Confessors were thought of as monsters by many people. Given the chance, Kahlan was sure that much of the rest of humanity would be happy to seal her away for being a Confessor.

But just because she could understand how Jennsen felt, that didn't mean Kahlan thought the young woman was right. Jennsen's anger at those who banished these people was justified, but her anger at Richard and the rest of them for having the same spark of the gift, which made them in that way the same, was not.

Richard turned his attention to Owen. "How many men do you have waiting in the hills for you to return?"

"Not quite a hundred."

Richard sighed in disappointment. "Well, if that's all you have, then that's all you have. We'll have to see to getting more later.

"For now, I want you to go get those men. Bring them here, to me. We'll wait here for you to return. This will be our base from where we work a plan to get the Order out of Bandakar. We'll set up a camp down there, in those trees, where it's well protected."

Owen looked down the incline to where Richard pointed, and then off toward his homeland. His confused frown returned to Richard. "But Lord Rahl, it is you who must give us freedom. Why not just come with me to the men, if you want to see them?"

"Because I think this will be a safer place than where they are now, where the Order probably knows they're hiding."

"But the Order does not know that there are men hiding, or where they are."

"You're deluding yourselves. The men in the Order are brutal, but they aren't stupid."

"If they really know where the men are, then why hasn't the Order come to call them in?"

"They will," Richard said. "When it suits them, they will. Your men aren't a threat, so the men of the Order are in no hurry to expend any effort to capture them. Sooner or later they will though, because they won't want anyone to think they can escape the Order's rule.

"I want your men away from there, to a place they've not been: here. I want the Order to think they're gone, to think they've run away, so they won't go after them."

"Well," Owen said, thinking it over, "I guess that would be all right."

Tom stood watch near the far corner of the statue's base, giving Jennsen room to be alone. She looked angry and he looked like he thought it best just to leave her be. Tom looked as if he felt guilty for having been born with the spark of the gift that allowed him to see magic, that same spark possessed by those who had banished people like Jennsen.

"Tom," Richard said, "I want you to go with Owen."

Jennsen's arms came unfolded as she turned toward Richard. "Why do you want him to go?" She suddenly sounded a lot less angry.

"That's right," Owen said. "Why should he go?"

"Because," Richard said, "I want to make sure that you and your men get back here. I need the antidote, remember? The more men I have back here with me who know where it is, the better. I want them safely away from the Order for now. With blond hair and blue eyes, Tom will fit in with your people. If you run into any soldiers from the Order they will think he's one of you. Tom will make sure you all get back here."

"But it could be dangerous," Jennsen objected.

Richard fixed her in his challenging stare. He didn't say anything. He simply waited to see if she would dare to attempt to justify her objections. Finally, she broke eye contact and looked away.

"I guess it makes sense, though," she finally admitted.

Richard turned his attention back to Tom. "I want you to see if you can bring back some supplies. And I'd like to use your hatchet while you're gone, if that's all right."

Tom nodded and pulled his hatchet from his pack. As Richard stepped closer to take the axe, he started ticking off a list of things he wanted the man to look for—specific tools, yew wood, hide glue, packthread, leather and a list of other things Kahlan couldn't hear.

Tom hooked his thumbs behind his belt. "All right. I doubt I'll find it all right off. Do you want me to search out what I can't find before I return?"

"No. I need it all, but I need those men back here more. Get what's readily available and then get back here with Owen and his men as soon as possible."

"I'll get what I can. When do you want us to leave?"

"Now. We don't have a moment to lose."

"Now?" Owen sounded incredulous. "It will be dark in an hour or two."

"Those couple of hours may be hours I need," Richard said. "Don't waste them."

Kahlan thought that he meant because of the poison, but he could have had the gift in mind. She could see how much pain he was in because of the headache caused by the gift. She ached to hold him, to comfort him, to make him better, but she couldn't make it all just go away; they had to find the solutions. She glanced at the small figure of Richard standing on the base of the statue. Half of that figure was as dark as a night stone, as dark and dead as the deepest part of the underworld itself.

Tom swung his pack up over his shoulder. "Take care of them for me, will you, Cara?" he asked with a wink. She smiled her agreement. "I'll see you all in a few days, then." He waved his farewell, his gaze lingering on Jennsen, before shepherding Owen around the statue and toward the man's homeland.

Cara folded her arms and leveled a look at Jennsen. "You're a fool if you don't go kiss him a good journey."

Jennsen hesitated, her eyes turning toward Richard.

"I've learned not to argue with Cara," Richard said.

Jennsen smiled and ran over the ridge to catch Tom before he was gone. Betty, at the end of a long rope, scampered to follow after.

Richard stuffed the small figure of himself into his pack before picking up his bow from where it leaned against the statue. "We'd better get down into the trees and set up a camp."

Richard, Kahlan, and Cara started down the rise toward the concealing safety of the huge pines. They had been long enough out in the open, as far as Kahlan was concerned. It was only a matter of time before the races came in search of them—before Nicholas came looking for them.

As cold as it was up in the pass, Kahlan knew they didn't dare build a fire; the races could spot the smoke and then find them. They needed instead to build a snug shelter. Kahlan wished they could find a wayward pine to protect and hide them for the night, but she had not seen any of those down in the Old World and wishing wasn't going to grow one.

As she stepped carefully on dry patches of rock, avoiding the snow so as not to leave tracks, she checked the dark clouds. It was always possible that it might warm just a little and that the precipitation could turn to rain. Even if it didn't, it still would be a miserably cold night.

Jennsen, Betty following behind, returned, catching up with them as they zigzagged down through the steep notches of ledge. The wind was getting colder, the snow a little heavier.

When they reached a flatter spot, Jennsen caught Richard's arm.

"Richard, I'm sorry. I don't mean to be angry with you. I know you didn't banish those people. I know it's not your fault." She gathered up the slack on Betty's rope, looping it into coils. "It just makes me angry that those people were treated like that. I'm like them, and so it makes me angry."

"The way they were treated should make you angry," Richard said as he started away, "but not because you share an attribute with them."

Taken aback by his words, even looking a little hurt, Jennsen didn't move. "What do you mean?"

Richard paused and turned back to her. "That's how the Imperial Order thinks. That's how Owen's people think. It's a belief in granting disembodied prestige, or the mantle of guilt, to all those who share some specific trait or attribute.

"The Imperial Order would like you to believe that your virtue, your ultimate value, or even your wickedness, arises entirely from being born a member of a given group, that free will itself is either impotent or nonexistent. They want you to believe that all people are merely interchangeable members of groups that share fixed, preordained characteristics, and they are predestined to live through a collective identity, the group will, unable to rise on individual merit because there can be no such thing as independent, individual merit, only group merit.

"They believe that people can only rise above their station in life when selected to be awarded recognition because their group is due an indulgence, and so a representative, a stand-in for the group, must be selected to be awarded the badge of self-worth. Only the reflected light off this badge, they believe, can bring the radiance of self-worth to others of their group.

"But those granted this badge live with the uneasy knowledge that it's only an illusion of competence. It never brings any sincere self-respect because you can't fool yourself. Ultimately, because it is counterfeit, the sham of esteem granted because of a connection with a group can only be propped up by force.

"This belittling of mankind, the Order's condemnation of everyone and everything human, is their transcendent judgment of man's inadequacy.

"When you direct your anger at me for having a trait borne by someone else, you pronounce me guilty for their crimes. That's what happens when people say I'm a monster because our father was a monster. If you admire someone simply because you believe their group is deserving, then you embrace the same corrupt ethics.

"The Imperial Order says that no individual should have the right to achieve something on his own, to accomplish what someone else cannot, and so magic must be stripped from mankind. They say that accomplishment is corrupt because it is rooted in the evil of self-interest, therefore the fruits of that accomplishment are tainted by its evil. This is why they preach that any gain must be sacrificed to those who have not earned it. They hold that only through such sacrifice can those fruits be purified and made good.

"We believe, on the other hand, that your own individual life is the value and its own end, and what you achieve is yours.

"Only you can achieve self-worth for yourself. Any group offering it to you, or demanding it of you, comes bearing chains of slavery."

Jennsen stared at him for a long moment. A smile finally overcame her. "That's why, then, I always wanted to be accepted for who I was, for myself, and always thought it unfair to be persecuted because of how I was born?"

"That's why," Richard said. "If you want to be proud of yourself because of what you accomplish, then don't allow yourself to be chained to some group, and don't in turn chain other individuals to one. Let your judgment of individuals be earned.

"This means I should not be hated because my father was evil, nor should I be admired because my grandfather is good. I have the right to live my own life, for my own benefit. You are Jennsen Rahl, and your life is what you, alone, make of it."

They made their way the rest of the way down the hill in silence. Jennsen still had a faraway look as she thought about what Richard had said.

When they reached the trees, Kahlan was relieved to get in under the sheltering limbs of the ancient pines and even more so when they entered the secluded protection of the lower, thicker, balsam trees. They made their way through dense thickets, into the quiet solitude of the towering trees, and farther down the slope, to a place where an outcropping of rock offered protection from the elements. It would be easier to construct a shelter in such a place by leaning boughs against it in order to make a relatively warm shelter.

Richard used Tom's hatchet to cut some stout poles from young pines in the understorey which he placed against the rock wall. While he lashed the poles together with wiry lengths of pine roots he pulled up from the mossy ground, Kahlan, Jennsen, and Cara started collecting boughs to make dry bedding and to cover over the shelter.

"Richard," Jennsen asked as she dragged a bundle of balsam close to the shelter, "how do you think you are going to rid Bandakar of the Imperial Order?"

Richard laid a heavy bough up high on the poles and tied it in place with a length of the wiry pine root. "I don't know that I can. My primary concern is to get to the antidote."

Jennsen looked a bit surprised. "But aren't you going to help those people?"

He glanced back over his shoulder at her. "They poisoned me. No matter how you dress it up, they're willing to murder me if I don't do as they wish—if I don't do their dirty work for them. They think we're savages, and they're above us. They don't think our lives are worth as much—because we are not members of their group. My first responsibility is to my own life, to getting that antidote."

"I see what you mean." Jennsen handed him another balsam bough. "But I still think that if we eliminate the Order there, and this Nicholas, we'll be helping ourselves."

Richard smiled. "I can agree with that, and we're going to do what we can. But to truly help them, I need to convince Owen and his men that they must help themselves."

Cara snorted a derisive laugh. "That will be a good trick, teaching the lambs to become the wolves."

Kahlan agreed. She thought that convincing Owen and his men to defend themselves would be more difficult than the five of them ridding Bandakar of the Imperial Order by themselves. She wondered what Richard had in mind.

"Well," Jennsen said, "since we're all in this, all going to face the

Order up in Bandakar, don't you think that I have a right to know everything? To know what you two are always making eyes at each other about and whispering about?"

Richard stared at Jennsen a moment before he looked back at Kahlan.

Kahlan laid her bundle of branches down near the shelter. "I think she's right."

Richard looked unhappy about it, but finally nodded and set down the balsam bough he was holding. "Almost two years ago, Jagang managed to find a way to use magic to start a plague. The plague itself was not magic; it was just the plague. It swept through cities killing people by the tens of thousands. Since the firestorm had been started with a spark of magic, I found a way to stop the plague, using magic."

Kahlan did not believe that such a nightmare could be reduced to such a simple statement and even begin to adequately convey the horror they had gone through. But by the look on Jennsen's face, she at least grasped a little bit of the terror that had gripped the land.

"In order for Richard to return from the place where he had to go to stop the plague," Kahlan said, leaving out terrible portions of the story, "he had to take the infection of plague. Had he not, he would have lived, but lived alone for the rest of his life and died alone without ever seeing me or anyone else again. He took the plague into himself so that he could come back and tell me he loved me."

Jennsen stared, wide-eyed. "Didn't you know he loved you?"

Kahlan smiled a small bitter smile. "Don't you think your mother would come back from the world of the dead to tell you she loves you, even though you know she does?"

"Yes, I suppose she would. But why would you have to become infected just to return? And return from where?"

"It was a place, called the Temple of the Winds, that was partially in the underworld." Richard gestured up the pass. "Something like that boundary was part of the world of the dead but was still here, in this world. You might say that the Temple of the Winds was some-thing like that. It was hidden within the underworld. Because I had to cross a boundary of sorts, through the underworld, the spirits set a price for me to return to the world of life."

"Spirits? You saw spirits there?" Jennsen asked. When Richard nodded, she asked, "Why would they set such a price?"

"The spirit who set the price of my return was Darken Rahl."

Jennsen's jaw dropped.

"When we found Lord Rahl," Cara said, "he was almost dead. The Mother Confessor went on a dangerous journey through the sliph, all alone, to find what would cure him. She succeeded in bringing it back, but Lord Rahl was moments away from death."

"I used the magic I recovered," Kahlan said. "It was something that had the power to reverse the plague that the magic had given him. The magic I invoked to do this was the three chimes."

"Three chimes?" Jennsen asked. "What are they?"

"The chimes are underworld magic. Summoning their assistance keeps a person from crossing over into the world of the dead.

"Unfortunately, or perhaps fortunately, at the time I didn't know anything else about the chimes. It turns out that they were created during the great war to end magic. The chimes are beings of sorts, but without souls. They come from the underworld. They annul magic in this world."

Jennsen looked confused. "But how can they accomplish such a thing?"

"I don't know how they work, exactly. But their presence in this world, since they are part of the world of the dead, begins the destruction of magic."

"Can't you get rid of the chimes? Can't you find a way to send them back?"

"I already did that," Richard said. "But while they were here, in this world, magic began to fail."

"Apparently," Kahlan said, "what I began that day when I called the chimes into the world of life began a cascade of events that continues to progress, even though the chimes have been sent back to the underworld."

"We don't know that," Richard said, more to Kahlan than to Jennsen.

"Richard is right," Kahlan told Jennsen, "we don't know it for sure, but we have good reason to believe it's true. This boundary locking away Bandakar failed. The timing would suggest that it failed not long after I freed the chimes. One of those mistakes I told you about, before. Remember?"

Jennsen, staring at Kahlan, finally nodded. "But you didn't do it to hurt people. You didn't know it would happen. You didn't know how this boundary would fail, how the Order would go in there and abuse those people."

"Doesn't really make any difference, does it? I did it. I caused it. Because of me, magic may be failing. I accomplished what the Order is working so hard to bring about. As a result of what I did, all those people in Bandakar died, and others are now out in the world where they will once again do as they did in ancient times—they will begin breeding the gift out of mankind.

"We stand at the brink of the end times of magic, all because of me, because of what I did."

Jennsen stood frozen. "And so you regret what you caused? That you may have done something that will end magic?"

Kahlan felt Richard's arm around her waist. "I only know a world with magic," she finally said. "I became the Mother Confessor—in part—to help protect people with magic who are unable to protect themselves. I, too, am a creature of magic—it's inextricably bound into me. I know profoundly beautiful things of magic that I love; they are a part of the world of life."

"So you fear you may have caused the end of what you love most."

"Not love most." Kahlan smiled. "I became the Mother Confessor because I believe in laws that protect all people, give all individuals the right to their own life. I would not want an artist's ability to sculpt to be stopped, or a singer's voice to be silenced, or a person's mind to be stilled. Nor do I want people's ability to achieve what they can with magic to be stripped from them.

"Magic itself is not the central issue, not what this is about. I want all the flowers, in all their variety, to have a chance to bloom. You are beautiful, too, Jennsen. I would not chose to lose you, either. Each person has a right to life. The idea that there must be a choice of one over another is counter to what we believe."

Jennsen smiled at Kahlan's hand on her cheek. "Well, I guess that in a world without magic, I could be queen."

On her way by with balsam boughs, Cara said, "Queens, too, must bow to the Mother Confessor. Don't forget it."

CHAPTER 36

Light flooded in as the lid of the box suddenly lifted. The rusty hinges groaned in protest of every inch the lid rose. Zedd squinted at the abrupt, blinding light of day. Beefy arms flipped the hinged lid back. If there had been any slack in the chain around his neck, Zedd would have jumped at the booming bang when the heavy cover flopped back, showering him in dirt and rusty grit.

Between the bright light and the dust swirling through the air, Zedd could hardly see. It didn't help, either, that the short chain around his neck was bolted to the center of the floor of the box, leaving only enough slack for him to be able to lift his head a few inches. With his arms bound in iron behind his back, he could do little more than lie on the floor.

While Zedd was forced to lie there on his side, his neck near the iron bolt, he at least could breathe in the sudden rush of cooler air. The heat in the box had been sweltering. On a couple of occasions, when they had stopped at night, they had given him a cup of water. It had not been nearly enough. He and Adie had been fed precious little, but it was water he needed more than food. Zedd felt like he might die of thirst. He could hardly think of anything but water.

He had lost track of the number of days he had been chained to the floor of the box, but he was somewhat surprised to find himself still alive. The box had been bouncing around in the back of a wagon over the course of a long, rough, but swift journey. He could only assume that he was being taken to Emperor Jagang. He was also sure that he would be sorry if he was still alive at the end of the journey.

There had been times, in the stifling heat of the box, when he had expected that he would soon fade into unconsciousness and die. There were times when he longed to die. He was sure that falling into such a fatal sleep would be far preferable to what was in store for him. He had no choice, though; the control the Sister exerted through the Rada'Han prevented him from strangling himself to death with the chain, and it was pretty hard, he had discovered, to will himself to die.

Zedd, his head still held to the floor of the box by the stub of chain, tried to peer up, but he could see only sky. He heard another lid bang open. He coughed as another cloud of dust drifted over him. When he heard Adie's cough, he didn't know if he was relieved to know that she, too, was still alive, or sorry that she was, knowing what she, like he, would have to endure.

Zedd was, in a way, ready for the torture he knew he would be subjected to. He was a wizard and had passed tests of pain. He feared such torture, but he would endure it until it finally ended his life. In his weakened condition, he expected that it wouldn't take all that long. In a way, such a time under torture was like an old acquaintance come back to haunt him.

But he feared the torture of Adie far more than his own. He hated above all else the torture of others. He hated to think of her coming under such treatment.

The wagon shuddered as the front of the other box dropped open. A cry escaped Adie's throat when a man struck her.

"Move, you stupid old woman, so I can get at the lock!"

Zedd could hear Adie's shoes scraping the wooden crate as, hands bound behind her back, she tried to comply. By the sounds of fists on flesh, the man wasn't happy with her efforts. Zedd closed his eyes, wishing he could close his ears as well.

The front of Zedd's confining box crashed open, letting in more light and dust. A shadow fell across him as a man approached. Because his face was pinned to the floor by the chain, Zedd couldn't see the man. A big hand reached in, fitting a key to the lock. Zedd kept his head stretched as far away as possible to give the man all the room available to let him do his work. Such effort earned Zedd a heavy punch in the side of his head. The blow left his ears ringing.

The lock finally sprang open. The man's big fist seized Zedd by the hair and dragged him, like a sack of grain, out of the box and toward the rear of the wagon. Zedd pressed his lips together, to keep from crying out as his bones bumped over protruding wooden runners in the wagon bed. At the back edge of the wagon he was summarily dumped off the back to slam down onto the ground.

Ears ringing, head spinning, Zedd tried to sit up when he was kicked, knowing it was a command. He spat out dirt. With his hands tied behind his back he was having difficulty complying. After three kicks, a big man grabbed him by the hair and lifted him upright.

Zedd's heart sank to see that they sat among an army of astounding size. The dark mass of humanity blighted the land as far as he could see. So, it would seem, they had arrived.

Out of the corner of his eye, he saw Adie sitting in the dirt beside him, her head hanging. She had a livid bruise on her cheek. She didn't look up when a shadow fell across her.

A woman in a long drab skirt moved in before them, distracting him from his appraisal of the enemy forces. Zedd recognized the brown wool dress. It was the Sister of the Dark who had put the collar around their necks. He didn't know her name; she'd never offered it. In fact, she hadn't spoken to them since they were chained in their boxes. She stood over them, now, like the strict governess of incorrigible children.

The ring through her lower lip, marking her as a slave, in Zedd's mind irrevocably tarnished her air of authority.

The ground was covered with horse manure, most, but not all, old and dried. Out beyond the Sister, horses stood picketed seemingly without any order among the soldiers. Horses that looked like they might belong to the cavalry were well kept. Workhorses were not so healthy. Among the horses and men, wagons and stacks of supplies dotted the late-day landscape.

The place had the foul stink of shallow latrines, horses, manure, and the filthy smell of crowded human habitation failing to meet common sanitary needs. Zedd blinked when acrid woodsmoke from one of the thousands of cook fires drifted across him, burning his eyes.

The air was also thick with mosquitoes, gnats, and flies. The flies were the worst. The mosquito bites would itch later, but the flies stung the instant they bit, and, with his arms bound behind his back, there wasn't much he could do about it other than shake his head to try to keep them out of his eyes and nose.

The two soldiers who had freed Zedd and Adie from their boxes stood patiently to the sides. Beyond the woman's skirts a vast encampment spread out as far as the eye could see. There were men everywhere, men engaged in work, at rest, and at recreation. They were dressed in every variety of clothing, from leather armor, chain mail, and studded belts to hides, dirty tunics, and trousers in the process of rotting into rags. Most of the men were unshaven, and all were as filthy as feral recluses living in mad seclusion. The mass encampment generated a constant din of yells, whistles, men hollering and laughing, the jangle and rattle of metal, the ring of hammers or rhythm of saws and, piercing through it all, the occasional cry of someone in agonizing pain.

Tents by the thousands, tents of all sorts, like leaves after a big wind, lay littering the gently rolling landscape at the foothills of towering mountains to the east. Many a tent was decorated with loot; gingham curtains hung at an entrance, a small chair or table sat before a tent, here and there an item of women's personal clothing flew as a flag of conquest. Wagons and horses and gear were all jammed together among the rabble in no seeming plan. The ground had been churned to a fine dust by the masses in this mock city devoid of skeletal order.

The place was a nightmare of humanity reduced to the savagery of a mob on the loose, the scope of their goals no more than the impulse of the moment. Though their leaders had ends, these men did not.

"His Excellency has requested you both," the Sister said down to them.

Neither Zedd nor Adie said anything. The men hauled them both to their feet. A sharp shove started them moving behind the Sister after she marched away. Zedd noticed, then, that there were more soldiers, close to a dozen, escorting them.

The wagon had delivered them to the end of a road, of sorts, that ran a winding course through the sprawling encampment. The end of the road, where wagons sat in a row, appeared to be the entrance to an inner camp, probably a command area. The regular soldiers outside a ring of heavily armed guards ate, played dice, gambled, bartered loot, joked, talked, and drank as they watched the prisoners being escorted.

The thought occurred to Zedd that if he called out, proclaiming that he was the one who was responsible for the light spell that had killed or wounded so many of their chums, maybe the men would riot, set upon them, and kill them before Jagang had a chance to do his worst.

Zedd opened his mouth to try out his plan, but saw the Sister glance back over her shoulder. He discovered that his voice was muted through her control of the collar around his neck. There would be no speaking unless she allowed it.

Following the Sister, they walked past the standing row of wagons in front of the one that had brought them. There were well over a dozen freight wagons all lined up before the cordoned-off area with the larger tents. None of the wagons were empty, but all were loaded with crates.

With sinking realization, Zedd understood. These were wagons with goods looted from the Wizard's Keep. These were all wagons that had made the journey with them. They were all full of the things those ungifted men, at the Sister's orders, had taken out of the Keep. Zedd feared to think what priceless items of profound danger sat in these crates. There were things in the Keep that became hazardous to anyone should they be removed from the shields that guarded them. There were rare items that, if removed from their protective environment, such as darkness, for even a brief time, would cease to be viable.

Guards in layered hides, mail, leather, and armed with pikes set with long steel points flanked by sharpened winged blades, huge crescent axes, swords, and spiked maces prowled the restricted area. These grim soldiers were bigger and more menacing-looking than the regular men out in the camp—and those were fearsome enough.

While the special guards patrolled, ever watchful, the unconcerned regular soldiers just outside the perimeter carried on with their business.

The guards led the Sister, Zedd, and Adie through an opening in a line of spiked barricades. Beyond were the smaller of the special tents. Most were round and the same size. Zedd thought that these were probably the tents of the staff the emperor would keep close, his attendants and personal slaves. Zedd wondered if the Sisters were all held within the emperor's compound.

Up ahead, the palatial vision of the grand tents of an emperor and his entourage rose up in the late-afternoon light. No doubt some of these comfortable tents set about the center compound, within the ring of tents for servants and attendants, were accommodations for high-ranking officers, officials, and the emperor's most trusted advisors.

Zedd wished he had a light spell and the ability to ignite it. He could probably decapitate the Imperial Order right then and there.

But he knew that such confusion and turmoil would only be a temporary setback for the Imperial Order. They would provide another brute to enforce their message. It would take more than killing Jagang to end the threat of the Order. He wasn't even sure anymore just what it would take to free the world of the oppression and tyranny of the Imperial Order.

Despite the seductively simplistic notions held by most people, the Emperor Jagang was not the driving force of this invasion. The driving force was a vicious ideology. To exist, it could not permit successful lives to be lived in sight of the suffering masses produced as a result of the beliefs and dictates of the Imperial Order. The freedom and resulting success of the people living in the New World put the lie to all the Order preached. It was blasphemy to succeed on your own; since the Order taught that it could not be done, it could only be sinful. Sin had to be eliminated for the greater good. Therefore, the freedom of the New World had to be crushed.

"These the ones?" a guard with short-cropped hair asked. The rings hanging from his nose and ears reminded Zedd of a prized pig decorated for the summer fair. Of course, prized pigs would have been washed and clean and would have smelled better.

"Yes," the Sister said. "Both of them, as instructed."

With deliberate care the man's dark-eyed gaze took in Adie and then Zedd. By his scowl, he apparently thought himself a righteous man who was displeased with what he saw: evil. After noting the collars they both wore, showing that they would be no danger to the emperor, he stepped aside and lifted a thumb, directing them through a second barricade beyond the tents of the attendants, servants, and slaves. The guard's glare followed the sinners on their way to meet their proper fate.

Other men, from inside the inner compound, swept in to surround them. Zedd saw that these men wore more orderly outfits. They were layered in similar leather and mail, wearing heavy leather weapons belts, their chests crisscrossed with studded straps. There was a uniformity to them, a sameness, that showed these were special guards. The weapons hung on those wide belts were better made, and they carried more of them. By the way they moved, Zedd knew that these were not typical men rounded up to be soldiers, but trained men with highly developed talents for warfare.

These were the emperor's elite bodyguards.

Zedd looked longingly at the nearly full water bucket set out for the men standing guard in the heat. It wouldn't do, if you were an emperor, to have your elite guards falling over from lack of water. Knowing what the response was likely to be, Zedd didn't ask for a drink. A sidelong glance showed Adie licking her cracked lips, but she, too, remained silent.

Up a slight rise sat by far the largest and grandest of the tents, among the impressive but lesser quarters of the emperor's retinue. The emperor's tent appeared more a traveling palace, actually, than a tent. It boasted a tri-peaked roof pierced by high poles bearing colorful standards and flags. Brightly embroidered panels adorned the exterior walls. Red and yellow banners flapped lazily in the hot, late-day air. Tassels and streamers all around it made it look like a central gathering tent at a festival.

A guard flanking a doorway met Zedd's gaze before he lifted aside the lambskin covered with shields of gold and hammered medallions of silver, allowing them entrance. One of the other guards stiff-armed Zedd's shoulder, nearly knocking him sprawling. Zedd staggered through the doorway into the dimly lit interior, Adie stumbling in after him.

Inside, the raucous noise of the encampment was muted by layers of rich carpets placed haphazardly. Hundreds of silk and brocade pillows lined the edge of the floor. Colorfully decorated hangings divided up the murky interior space and covered the outer walls. Openings overhead, screened with gauzy material, let in little light but did allow some air to move through the quiet gloom of the grand tent. It was so dim, in fact, that lamps and candles were needed.

In the middle of the room, toward the back, sat an ornate chair draped with rich, red silks. If this was Emperor Jagang's throne, he was not in it.

While guards surrounded Zedd and Adie, keeping them restricted in place, one of the men went off behind the fabric walls from where a glow of light came. The guards standing close around Zedd stank of sweat. Their shoes were caked with manure. For all the sumptuous surroundings doing their best to simulate a reverent aura, a sacred setting, an abiding barnyard stench permeated the place. The horse manure and human sweat of the men who had entered the tent with Zedd and Adie was only making it worse.

The man who had gone behind the walls poked his head back out, signaling the Sister forward. He whispered to her and then she, too, disappeared behind the walls.

Zedd stole a look at Adie. Her completely white eyes stared ahead. He shifted his weight as an excuse to lean toward her and stealthily touched her shoulder with his, a message of comfort where there could be none. She returned a slight push; message received, and appreciated. He longed to embrace her, but knew he probably never would again.

Muffled words could be heard, but the heavy wall hangings muted them so that Zedd couldn't understand any of it. Had he access to his gift, he would have been able to hear it all, but the collar cut him off from his ability. Even so, the nature of the Sister's report, the words, were short and businesslike.

Those slaves working in the tent at brushing carpets, or polishing fine vases, or waxing cabinets, paid no attention to the people the guards had brought in, but the sudden, low tone of menace that came from beyond the wall caused them all to put markedly more attention into their work. While no doubt prisoners were brought before the emperor often enough, Zedd was sure that it would not be wise for those working in the grand tent to pay any notice to the emperor's business.

From beyond walls composed of woven scenes also came the warm smell of food. The variety of scents Zedd was able to detect was astonishing. The stink of the place, though, tended to make the fragrant aromas of meats, olive oil, garlic, onions, and spices some-what repugnant.

The Sister stepped out from behind the wall of colorful hangings. The ring through her lower lip stood out in stark relief against her ashen skin. She gave a slight nod to the men to either side of the prisoners.

Powerful fingers gripping their arms, Zedd and Adie were ushered toward the opening and the glow of light beyond.

CHAPTER 37

Dragged to an abrupt halt, Zedd, at last, stood shackled before the intent glower of the dream walker himself, Emperor Jagang.

Enthroned in an ornately carved high-backed chair behind a grand dining table, Jagang leaned on both elbows, a goose leg spanning his fingers as he chewed. Points of candlelight reflecting off the sides of his shaved head danced as the tendons all the way up through his temples rippled with his chewing. A thin mustache, growing down from the corners of his mouth and at the center under his lower lip, moved rhythmically in time with his jaw, as did the fine chain connected to gold loops in his ear and nose. Greasy goose fat covering his meaty, ringed fingers glistened in the candlelight and ran down his bare arms.

From his place behind his table, Jagang casually studied his latest captives.

Despite the candles set about the table and on stands to either side, the inside of the tent had the murky feel of a dungeon.

To each side of him on the broad table sat plates of food, goblets, bottles, candles, bowls and, here and there, books and scrolls. There being no room for all of the silver platters among the multitude, some of them had to be strategically balanced atop small decorated pillars. There looked to be enough food for a small army.

For all the Order's talk of sacrifice for the betterment of mankind being their noble cause, Zedd knew that such abundance at the emperor's table was meant to send a contradictory message, even when there was no one but the emperor himself to see it.

Slaves stood lined up along the wall behind Jagang, some holding additional platters, some in stiff poses, all awaiting command. Some of those in back were young men—young wizards, from what Zedd had heard—dressed in loose-fitting white trousers and nothing else. This was where wizards in training at the Palace of the Prophets had ended up, along with the captured Sisters who had been their teachers. All were now captives of the dream walker. The most accomplished of men, men with enormous potential, were used as houseboys to perform menial tasks. This, too, was a message sent by the emperor of the Imperial Order to show everyone that the best and the brightest were to be used to clean chamber pots, while brutes ruled them.

The younger women, Sisters of both the Dark and the Light, Zedd assumed, wore outfits that ran from neck to wrist to ankle, but were so transparent that the women might as well have been naked. This, too, was meant to show that Emperor Jagang thought little of these women's talents, and valued them only for his pleasure. The older, less attractive women standing off to the sides wore drab clothes. These were probably Sisters who served the emperor in other menial ways.

Jagang delighted in having under his control, as slaves, some of the most gifted people in the world. It suited the nature of the Order to demean those with ability, rather than to celebrate them.

Jagang watched Zedd taking in the house slaves, but showed no emotion. The dream walker's bull neck made him look almost other than human. The muscles of his chest, as well as his massive shoulders, were displayed by an open, sleeveless lamb's-wool vest. He was as powerful and brawny a man as Zedd had seen, an intimidating presence even at rest.

As Zedd and Adie stood mute, Jagang's teeth tore off another chunk of meat from the goose leg. In the tense silence, he watched them as he chewed, as if deciding what he might do with his newest plunder.

More than anything, it was his inky black eyes, devoid of any pupils, irises, or whites, that threatened to halt the blood in Zedd's veins. The last time he had seen those eyes, Zedd had not been shackled, but that ungifted girl had prevented Zedd from finishing the man. That was going to turn out to be the missed opportunity that Zedd would most regret. His chance to kill Jagang had slipped through his fingers that day, not because of the vast power of all the skilled Sisters and troops arrayed against him, but all because of a single ungifted girl.

Those black eyes, the eyes of a mature dream walker, glistened in the candlelight. Across their dark voids, dim shapes shifted, like clouds on a moonless night.

The directness of the dream walker's gaze was as obvious as was Adie's when she looked at Zedd with her pure white eyes. Under Jagang's direct glare, Zedd had to remind himself to relax his muscles, and remember to breathe.

The thing about those eyes that most terrified him, though, was what he saw in them: a keen, calculating mind. Zedd had fought against Jagang long enough to have come to understand that one underestimated this man at great peril.

"Jagang the Just," the Sister said, holding an introductory hand out to the nightmare before them. "Excellency, this is Zeddicus Zu'l Zorander, First Wizard, and a sorceress by the name of Adie."

"I know who they are," Jagang said in a deep voice as heavy with threat as with distaste.

He leaned back, hanging one arm over the back of the chair and one leg over a carved arm. He gestured with the goose leg.

"Richard Rahl's grandfather, as I hear told."

Zedd said nothing.

Jagang tossed the partially eaten leg onto a platter and picked up a knife. With one hand he sawed a chunk of red meat off a roast and stabbed it. Elbow on the table, he waved the knife as he spoke. Red juice ran down the blade.

"Probably not the way you had hoped to meet me."

He laughed at his own joke, a deep, resonating sound alive with menace.

With his teeth, Jagang drew the chunk of meat off the knife and chewed as he watched them, as if unable to decide on a wealth of delightfully terrible options parading through his thoughts.

He washed the meat down with a gulp from a jeweled silver goblet, his gaze never leaving them. "I can't tell you how pleased I am that you have come to visit me."

His grin was like death itself. "Alive."

He rolled his wrist, circling the knife. "We have a lot to talk about." His laugh died out, but the grin remained. "Well, you do, anyway. I'll be a good host and listen."

Zedd and Adie remained silent as Jagang's black-eyed gaze went from one to the other.

"Not so talkative, just yet? Well, no matter. You will be babbling soon enough."

Zedd didn't waste the effort telling Jagang that torture would gain him nothing. Jagang would not believe any such boast, and even if he did, it would hardly stay his wish to see it done.

Jagang fingered a few grapes from a bowl. "You are a resourceful man, Wizard Zorander." He popped several grapes in his mouth and chewed as he spoke. "All alone there in Aydindril, with an army surrounding you, you managed to gull me into thinking I had trapped Richard Rahl and the Mother Confessor. Quite a trick. I must give you credit where credit is due.

"And the light spell you ignited among my men, that was remarkable." He put another grape in his mouth. "Do you have any idea how many hundreds of thousands of them were caught up in your wizardry?"

Zedd could see the corded muscles in the man's hairy arm draped over the back of the chair stand out as he flexed his fist. He relaxed the hand then and leaned forward, using his thumb to gouge out a long chunk of ham.

He waved the meat as he went on. "It's that kind of magic I need you to do for me, good wizard. I understand, from the stupid bitches I have who call themselves the Sisters of the Light, or the Sisters of the Dark, depending on who they've decided can offer better favors in the afterlife, that you probably didn't conjure that little bit of magic on your own but rather, you used a constructed spell from the Wizard's Keep and simply ignited it among my men with some kind of trick, or trigger—probably some small curiosity that one of them picked up and in the act of having a look, they set it off."

Zedd was somewhat alarmed that Jagang had been able to learn so much. The emperor took a big bite off the end of the piece of ham as he watched them. His indulgent look was beginning to wear thin.

"So, since you can't do such marvelous magic yourself, I've had a few items brought from the Keep so you can tell me how they work, what they do. I'm sure there must be a great number of intriguing items among the inventory. I'd like to have some of those conjured spells so they can blow open a few of the passes into D'Hara for us. It would save me some time and trouble. I'm sure you can understand my eagerness to be into D'Hara and have this petty resistance finally over with."

Zedd heaved a deep breath and finally spoke. "For most of those items, you could torture me to the end of time and I still wouldn't be able to tell you anything because I don't have any knowledge of them. Unlike you, I know my own limits. I simply don't know what such a spell might look like. Even if I did, that doesn't mean I would know how to work it. I was simply lucky with that one I used."

"Maybe, maybe, but you do know about some of the items. You are, after all, as I hear told, First Wizard; it is your Keep. To claim ignorance of the things in it is hardly credible. Despite your claim of luck, you managed to know enough about that constructed light web to ignite it among my men, so you obviously have knowledge about the most powerful of the items."

"You don't know the first thing about magic," Zedd snapped. "You have a head full of grand ideas and you think all you have to do is command they be done. Well, they can't. You're a fool who doesn't know the first thing about real magic or its limits."

An eyebrow lifted over one of Jagang's inky eyes. "Oh, I think I know more than you might think, wizard. You see, I love to read, and I, well, I have the advantage of perusing some of the most remarkably gifted minds you can imagine. I probably know a great deal more about magic than you give me credit for."

"I give you credit for bold self-delusion."

"Self-delusion?" He spread his arms. "Can you create a Slide, Wizard Zorander?"

Zedd froze. Jagang had heard the name, that was all. The man liked to read. He'd read that name somewhere.

"Of course not, and neither can anyone else alive today."

"You can't create such a being, Wizard Zorander. But you have no idea how much I know about magic. You see, I've learned to bring lost talents back to life—arts that have long been believed to be dead and vanished."

"I give you the grandiosity of your dreaming, Jagang, but dreaming is easy. Your dreams can't be made real just because you dream them and decide that you wish them to come alive."

"Sister Tahirah, here, knows the truth of it." Jagang gestured with his knife. "Tell him, darlin. Tell him what I can dream and what I can bring to life."

The woman hesitantly stepped forward several paces. "It is as His Excellency says." She looked away from Zedd's frown to fuss with her wiry gray hair. "With His Excellency's brilliant direction, we were able to bring back some of the old knowledge. With the expert guidance of our emperor, we were able to invest in a wizard named Nicholas an ability not seen in the world for three thousand years. It is one of His Excellency's greatest achievements. I can personally assure you that it is as His Excellency says; a Slide again walks the world. It is no fancy, Wizard Zorander, but the truth.

"The spirits help me," she added under her breath, "I was there to see the Slide born into the world."

"You created a Slide?" Fists still bound behind his back, Zedd took an angry stride toward the Sister. "Are you out of your mind, woman?" She retreated to the back wall. Zedd turned his fury on Jagang. "Slides were a catastrophe! They can't be controlled! You would have to be crazy to create one!"

Jagang smiled. "Jealous, wizard? Jealous that you are unable to accomplish such a thing, can't create such a weapon against me, while I can create one to take Richard Rahl and his wife from you?"

"A Slide has powers you couldn't possibly control."

"A Slide is no danger to a dream walker. My ability is quicker than his. I am his better."

"It doesn't matter how quick you are—it isn't about being quick!

A Slide can't be controlled and he isn't going to do what you want!"

"I seem to be controlling him just fine." Jagang leaned in on an elbow. "You think magic is necessary to control those you would master, but I don't need magic. Not with Nicholas nor with mankind.

"You seem to be obsessed with control, I am not. I managed to find a people those like you didn't want to walk freely among their fellow man, a people cast out by the gifted, a people reviled for not having any spark of your precious gift of magic—a people hated and banished because your kind wasn't able to control them. That was their crime: being outside the control of your magic."

Jagang's fist slammed the table. The slaves all jumped with the platters.

"This is how your kind wants mankind's future to be; your kind wants only those with a spark of the gift to be allowed to walk free. This, so you can use your gift to control them! Like that collar around your neck, your lust is to collar all of mankind with magic.

"I found those outcast ungifted people and have brought them back into the fold of their fellow man. Much to your disapproval and the loathing of your kind, they can't be touched by your vile magic."

Zedd couldn't imagine where Jagang had found such people. "And so now you have a Slide to control them for you."

"Your kind condemned and banished them; we have welcomed them among us. In fact, we wish to model man himself after them. Our cause is theirs by their very nature—purity of mankind without any taint of magic. In this way the world will be one and at last at peace.

"I have the advantage over you, wizard; I have right on my side. I don't need magic to win; you do. I have mankind's best future in mind and have set our irreversible course.

"With the help of these people, I took your Keep. With their help, I have recovered invaluable treasures from within. You couldn't do a thing to stop them, now could you? Man will now set his own course, without the curse of magic darkening his struggle.

"I now have a Slide to help us to that noble end. He is working with those people for the benefit of our cause. In doing so, Nicholas has already proved invaluable.

"What's more, that Slide, which your kind could never control, has vowed to deliver to me the two I want most: your grandson and his wife. I have great things planned for them—well, for her, anyway." His red-faced rage melted into a grin. "For him, not so great things."

Zedd could hardly contain his own rage. Were it not for the collar stifling his gift, he would have reduced the entire place to ash by now.

"Once this Nicholas becomes adept at what he can do, you will find that he will want revenge of his own, and a price you may find far too high."

Jagang spread his arms. "There, you are wrong, wizard. I can afford whatever Nicholas wants for Lord Rahl and the Mother Confessor. There is no such thing as a price too high.

"You may think me greedy and selfish, but you would be wrong. While I enjoy the spoils, I most relish the role I play in bringing heathens to heel. It is the end that truly concerns me, and in the end I will have mankind bow as they should to our just cause and the Creator's ways."

Jagang seemed to have spent his flash of intensity. He leaned back and scooped walnuts from a silver bowl.

"Zedd be wrong," Adie finally spoke up. "You have shown us that you know what you be doing. You will be able to control your Slide just fine. May I suggest you keep him close, to aid you in your efforts."

Jagang smiled at her. "You, too, my dried-up old sorceress, will be telling me all you know about what is in those crates."

"Bah," Adie scoffed. "You be a fool with worthless treasures. I hope you pull a muscle carrying them with you everywhere."

"Adie's right," Zedd put in. "You are an incompetent oaf who is only going to—"

"Oh, come, come, you two. Do you think you will throw me into a fit of rage and I'll slaughter the both of you on the spot?" His wicked grin returned. "Spare you the proper justice of what is to come?"

Zedd and Adie fell silent.

"When I was a boy," Jagang said in a quieter tone as he stared off into the distance, "I was nothing. A street tough in Altur'Rang. A bully. A thief. My life was empty. My future was the next meal.

"One day, I saw a man coming down the street. He looked like he might have some money and I wanted it. It was getting dark. I came up silently behind him, intending to bash in his head, but just then he turned and looked me in the eye.

"His smile stopped me in my tracks. It wasn't a kindly smile, or a weak smile, but the kind of smile a man gives you when he knows he can kill you where you stand if it pleases him.

"He pulled a coin from his pocket and flipped it to me, and then, without a word, turned and went on his way.

"A few weeks later, in the middle of the night, I woke up in an alley, where I slept under old blankets and crates, and I saw a shadowy form out by the street. I knew it was him before he flipped me the coin and moved off into the darkness.

"The next time I saw him, he was sitting on a stone bench at the edge of an old square that some of the less fortunate men of Altur'Rang frequented. Like me, no one would give these men a chance in life. People's greed had sucked the life out of them. I used to go there to look at them, to tell myself I didn't want to grow up to be like them, but I knew I would, a nobody, human refuse waiting to pass into the shadow of oblivion in the afterlife. A soul without worth.

"I sat down on the bench beside the man and asked him why he'd given me money. Instead of giving me some answer that most people would give a boy, he told me about mankind's grand purpose, the meaning of life, and how we are here only as a brief stop on the way to what the Creator has in store for us—if we are strong enough to rise to the challenge.

"I'd never heard such a thing. I told him that I didn't think that such things mattered in my life because I was only a thief. He said that I was only striking back from the injustice of my lot in life. He said that mankind was evil for making me the way I was and only through sacrifice and helping those like me could man hope to be redeemed in the afterlife. He opened my mind to man's sinful ways.

"Before he left, he turned back and asked me if I knew how long eternity was. I said no. He said that our miserable time in this world was but a blink before we entered the next world. That really made me think, for the first time, about our greater purpose.

"Over the next months, Brother Narev took the time to talk to me, to tell me about Creation and eternity. He gave me a vision of a possible better future where before I had none. He taught me about sacrifice and redemption. I thought I was doomed to an eternity of darkness until he showed me the light.

"He took me in, in return for helping him with life's chores.

"For me, Brother Narev was a teacher, a priest, an advisor, a means to salvation" —Jagang's gaze rose to Zedd— "and a grandfather, all rolled into one.

"He gave me the fire of what mankind can and should be. He showed me the true sin of selfish greed and the dark void of where it would lead mankind. Over time, he made me the fist of his vision. He was the soul, I was the bone and muscle.

"Brother Narev allowed me the honor of igniting the revolution. He placed me at the fore of the rise of mankind over the oppression of sinfulness. We are the new hope for the future of man, and Brother Narev himself allowed me to be the one to carry his vision in the cleansing flames of mankind's redemption."

Jagang leaned back in his chair, fixing Zedd with as grim a look as Zedd had ever seen.

"And then this spring, while carrying Brother Narev's noble challenge to mankind, to those who had never had a chance to see the vision of what man can be, of the future without the blight of magic and oppression and greed and groveling to be better than others, I came to Aydindril . . . and what do I find?

"Brother Narev's head on a pike, with a note, "Compliments of Richard Rahl.'

"The man I admired most in the world, the man who brought to us all the hallowed dream of mankind's true purpose in this life as charged by the Creator himself, was dead, his head stuck on a pike by your grandson.

"If ever there was a greater blasphemy, a greater crime against the whole of mankind, I don't know of it."

Sullen shapes shifted across Jagang's black eyes. "Richard Rahl will be dealt justice. He will suffer such a blow, before I send him to the Keeper. I just wanted you to know your fate, old man. Your grandson will know something of that kind of pain, and the additional torment of knowing that I have his bride and will make her pay dearly for her own crimes." A ghost of the grin returned. "After he has paid this price, then I will kill him."

Zedd yawned. "Nice story. You left out all the parts where you slaughter innocent people by the tens of thousands because they don't want to live under your vile rule or Narev's sick, twisted vision.

"On second thought, don't bother with the sorry excuses. Just cut off my head, put it on a pike, and be done with it."

Jagang's smile returned in its full glory. "Not as easily as that, old man. First you have some talking to do."

CHAPTER 38

"Ah, yes," Zedd said. "The torture. I almost forgot."

"Torture?"

With two fingers Jagang signaled a woman to the side. The older Sister standing wringing her hands flinched at seeing his gaze on her and immediately rushed off behind a curtain of wall hangings. Zedd could hear her whispering urgent instructions to people beyond, and then the thump of feet rushing across the carpets and out of the tent.

Jagang went back to his leisurely meal while Zedd and Adie stood before him, starving, dying of thirst. The dream walker finally set his knife across a plate. Seeing this, the slaves sprang into action, clearing away the variety of dishes, most having been tasted, but that hardly made a dent in them. In a matter of moments the entire table was emptied of the food and drink, leaving only the books, scrolls, the candles, and the silver bowl of walnuts.

Sister Tahirah, the Sister who had captured Zedd and Adie at the Keep, stood to the side, her hands clasped before her as she watched them. Despite her obvious fear of Jagang, and her servile fawning over the man, the knowing smirk at Zedd and Adie betrayed the pleasure she was deriving from what was to come.

When half a dozen grisly men entered the room and stood off to the side, Zedd began to understand what it was that pleased Sister Tahirah. They were unkempt, brawny, and as merciless-looking as any men Zedd had ever seen. Their hair was wildly tangled and greasy. Their hands and forearms were spattered with sooty smears, their fingernails ragged and foul. Their filthy clothes were stained dark with dried blood from the labor of their profession.

These men worked at torture.

Zedd looked away from the Sister's steady gaze. She hoped to see fear, panic, or perhaps sobbing.

Then a group of men and women were ushered into the dim room in the emperor's tent. They looked to be farmers or humble working folk, probably picked up by patrols. The men embraced their wives as children huddled around the women's skirts like chicks around hens. The people were herded over to the side of the room, opposite the line of torturers.

Zedd's eyes suddenly turned to Jagang. The dream walker's black eyes were watching him as he chewed a walnut.

"Emperor," said the Sister who had brought the families in, "these are some of the local people, people from the countryside, as you requested." She held an introductory hand out. "Good people, this is our revered emperor, Jagang the Just. He brings the light of the Imperial Order to the world, guided by the Creator's wisdom, that we might all lead better lives and find salvation with the Creator in the afterlife."

Jagang surveyed the cluster of Midlanders as they awkwardly bowed and curtsied.

Zedd felt sick at seeing the timid terror on their faces. They would have had to walk through the encampment of Order soldiers. They would have seen the size of the force that had overrun their homeland.

Jagang lifted his arm toward Zedd. "Perhaps you know this man? This is First Wizard Zorander. He is one who has ruled you with his command of magic. As you can see, he is now shackled before us. We have freed you from the wicked rule of this man and those like him."

The people's eyes darted between Zedd and Jagang, unsure of their role in the emperor's tent, or what they were supposed to do. They finally bobbed their heads, mumbling their thanks for their liberation.

"The gifted, like these two, could have used their ability to help mankind. Instead, they used it for themselves. Where they should have sacrificed for those in need, they were selfish. It is criminal to behave as they have, live as they have, with all they have. It makes me angry to think of all they could do for those in need, those like you poor people, were it not for their selfish ways. People suffer and die without the help they could have had, without the help these people could have given, were they not so self-centered.

"This wizard and his sorceress are here because they have refused to help us free the rest of the people of the New World by telling us the function of the vile things of magic we have captured along with them—things of magic they scheme to use to slaughter untold numbers of people. This selfish wizard and sorceress do this out of spite that they could not have their way."

All the wide eyes turned to Zedd and Adie.

"I could tell you people of the vast number of deaths this man is responsible for, but I fear you would be unable to fathom it. I can tell you that I simply cannot allow this man to be responsible for tens of thousands more deaths."

Jagang smiled at the children then and gestured with both hands, urging them to come to him. The children, a dozen or so, from six or seven to maybe twelve, clung to their parents. Jagang's gaze rose to those parents as he again motioned the children to come to him. The parents understood and reluctantly urged their children to do as the emperor bid of them.

The clump of innocence haltingly approached Jagang's outstretched arms and wide grin. He embraced them woodenly as they shuffled in close around him. He tousled the blond hair of a boy, and then the straight sandy hair of a girl. Several of the younger ones peered pleadingly back at parents before cringing at Jagang's meaty hand on their backs, his jovial pat on their cheek.

Silent terror hung thick in the air.

It was as frightening a sight as Zedd had ever witnessed.

"Well, now," the smiling emperor said, "let me get to the reason I have called upon you people."

His powerful arms gathered the children before him. As a Sister blocked a boy wanting to return to his parents, Jagang put his huge hands on a young girl's waist and set her upon his knee. The girl's wide eyes stared up at the smiling face, the bald head, but mostly at the nightmare void of the dream walker's inky eyes.

Jagang looked from the girl back to the parents. "You see, the wizard and sorceress have refused to offer their help. In order to save a great many lives, I must have their cooperation. They must answer honestly all my questions. They refuse. I'm hoping you good people can convince them to tell us what we need to know in order to save the lives of a great many people, and free a great many more from the oppression of their magic."

Jagang looked toward the row of men standing silently against the opposite wall. With a single tilt of his head, he commanded them forward.

"What are you doing?" a woman asked, even as her husband tried to restrain her. "What do you intend?"

"What I intend," Jagang told the crowd of parents, "is for you good people to convince the wizard and the sorceress to talk. I'm going to put you in a tent alone with them so that you can persuade them to do their duty to mankind—persuade them to cooperate with us."

As the men began seizing the children, they finally burst out in frightened crying. The parents, seeing their red-faced children bawling in terror, cried out themselves and rushed forward to retrieve them. The big men, each holding one or two little arms in a fist, shoved the parents back.

The parents fell to hysterical screaming for the children to be freed.

"I'm sorry, but I can't do that," Jagang said over the wail of the children. He tilted his head again and the men started carting the twisting, screaming children out of the tent. The parents were wailing as well, trying to reach in past big filthy arms to touch what was most precious to them in the world.

The parents were bewildered and horrified, fearing to cross a line that would bring wrath down on their children, yet not wanting them to be carted away. Against their urgent pleading, the children were swiftly whisked away.

As the children were taken out, the sisters immediately blocked the doorway behind them, keeping the parents from following. The tent fell into pandemonium.

With the single word "silence" from Jagang, and his fist on the table, everyone fell silent.

"Now," Jagang said, "these two prisoners are going to be confined to a tent. All of you are going to be in there, alone, with them. There will be no guards, no watchers."

"But what about our children?" a woman in tears begged, caring nothing about Zedd and Adie.

Jagang pulled a squat candle toward him on the table. "This will be the tent with these two, and you good people." He circled a finger around the candle. "All around this tent with you and the criminals, there will be other tents close."

Everyone stared at his ringed finger going round and round the candle. "Your children will be close by, in these tents." Jagang scooped up a handful of walnuts from the silver bowl. He dribbled some onto the table around the candle and put the rest into his mouth.

The room was silent as they all stared at him, watching him chew the walnuts, afraid to ask a question, afraid to hear what he might say next.

Finally a woman could no longer hold her tongue. "Why will they be there, in those tents?"

Jagang's black eyes took them all in before he spoke, making sure none would miss what he had to tell them.

"Those men who took your children to those tents will be torturing them."

The parents' eyes widened. Blood drained from their faces. One woman fainted. Several others bent to her. Sister Tahirah squatted beside the woman and touched a hand to the woman's forehead. The woman's eyes popped open. The Sister told the women to get her to her feet.

When Jagang was satisfied that he had everyone's attention, he circled a finger around the candle again, over the walnuts around it. "The tents will be close by so you can all clearly hear your children being tortured, to be sure that you understand that they will not be spared the worst those men can do."

The parents stood frozen, staring, seemingly unable to believe the reality of what they were hearing.

"Every few hours, I will come to see if you good people have convinced the wizard and the sorceress to tell us what we need to know. If you have not succeeded, then I will go off to other business and when I have the time I will return again to check if these two have decided to talk.

"Just be sure that this wizard and sorceress do not die while you convince them to be reasonable. If they die, then they can't answer our questions. Only when and if they answer questions will the children be released."

Jagang turned his nightmare eyes on Zedd. "My men have a great deal of experience at torturing people. When you hear the screams coming from the tents all around, you will have no doubt as to their skill, or their determination. I think you should know that they can keep their guests alive under torture for days, but they cannot work miracles. People, especially such young, tender souls, cannot survive indefinitely. But, should these children die before you agree to cooperate, there are plenty more families with children who can take their place."

Zedd could not halt the tears that ran down his face to drip off his chin as Sister Tahirah took his arm and pulled him toward the doorway. The crowd of parents fell on him, clawing at his clothes, screaming and crying for him to do as the emperor asked.

Zedd dug in his heels and struggled to a stop before the table. Desperate hands clutched at his robes. As he looked around at their tearstained faces, meeting the eyes of each, they fell silent.

"I hope you people can now understand the nature of what it is we are fighting. I am so sorry, but I cannot dull the pain of this darkest hour of your lives. If I were to do as this man wants, countless more children would be subjected to this tyrant's brutality. I know that you will not be able to weigh this against the precious lives of your children, but I must. Pray the good spirits take them quickly, and take them to a place of eternal peace."

Zedd could not say more to them, to their desperate gazes. He turned his watery eyes to Jagang. "This will not work, Jagang. I know you will do it anyway, but it will not work."

Behind the heavy table, Jagang slowly rose. "Children in this land of yours are plentiful. How many are you prepared to sacrifice before you allow mankind to be free? How long are you willing to persist in your stubborn refusal to allow them to have a future free from suffering, want, and your uninspired morals?"

The heavy gold and silver chains around his neck, the looted medallions and ornaments resting against his muscled chest, and the rings of kings on his fingers all sparkled in the candlelight.

Zedd felt the numb weight of a hopeless future under the yoke of the monstrous ideals of this man and his ilk.

"You cannot win in this, wizard. Like all those who fight on your side to oppress mankind, to allow the common people to be left to cruel fate, you are not even willing to sacrifice for the sake of the lives of children. You are brave with words, but you have a cold soul and a weak heart. You don't have the will to do what must be done to prevail. I do."

Jagang tilted his head and the Sister shoved Zedd toward the door. The screaming, crying, begging crowd of people closed in around Zedd and Adie, clawing and pawing at them in wild desperation.

In the distance, Zedd could hear the horrifying screams of their terrified children.

CHAPTER 39

"They aren't far," Richard said as he stepped back among the trees. He stood silently watching as Kahlan straightened the shoulders of her dress.

The dress showed no ill-effects from its long confinement in their packs. The almost white, satiny smooth fabric glistened in the eerie light of the churning overcast. The flowing lines of the dress, cut square at the neck, bore no lace or frills, nothing to distract from its simple elegance. The sight of Kahlan in that dress still took his breath away.

She looked out through the trees when they heard Cara's whistle. The warning signal Richard had taught Cara was the plaintive, high, clear whistle of a common wood pewee, although Cara didn't know that's what it was. When he'd first told Cara that he wanted to teach her a pewee bird call as a warning signal, she said she wasn't going to learn the call of any bird named a pewee. Richard gave in and told her that he would instead teach her the call of the small, fierce, short-tailed pine hawk, but only if she would be willing to work hard at getting it right, since it was more difficult. Satisfied to have her way, Cara had agreed and readily learned the simple whistle. She was good at it and used it often as a signal. Richard never told her that there was no such thing as a short-tailed pine hawk, or that hawks didn't make whistles like that.

Out through the screen of branches, the dark form of the statue stood guard over an area of the pass that for thousands of years had been deserted. Richard wondered again why the people back then would have put such a statue in a pass no one was likely to ever again visit. He thought about the ancient society that had placed it, and at what they must have thought, sealing people away for the crime of not having a spark of the gift.

Richard brushed pine needles off the back of the sleeve of Kahlan's dress. "Here, hold still, let me look at you."

Kahlan turned back, arms at her sides, as he smoothed the fabric at her upper arms. Her unafraid green eyes, beneath eyebrows that had the graceful arch of a raptor's wings in flight, met his gaze. Her features seemed to have only grown more exquisite since he had first met her. Her look, her pose, the way she gazed at him as if she could see into his soul, struck a chord in him. Clearly evident in her eyes was the intelligence that had from the first so captivated him.

"Why are you looking at me like that?"

Despite everything, he couldn't hold back his smile. "Standing there like that, in that dress, your long hair so beautiful, the green of the trees behind you . . . it just suddenly reminded me of the first time I saw you."

Her special smile, the smile she gave no one but him, spread radiantly through her bewitching eyes. She put her wrists on his shoulders and locked her fingers behind his neck, pulling him into a kiss.

As it always did, her kiss so completely consumed him with his need of her that he momentarily lost track of the world. She melted into his embrace. For that moment there was no Imperial Order, no Bandakar, no D'Haran Empire, no Sword of Truth, no chimes, no gift turning its power against him, no poison, no warning beacons, no black-tipped races, no Jagang, no Nicholas, no Sisters of the Dark. Her kiss made him forget everything but her. In that moment there was nothing but the two of them. Kahlan made his life complete; her kiss reaffirmed that bond.

She pulled back, gazing up into his eyes again. "Seems like you've had nothing but trouble ever since that day you found me."

Richard smiled. "My life is what I've had since that day I found you. When I found you, I found my life."

Holding her face in both hands, he kissed her again.

Betty nudged his leg and bleated.

"You two about ready?" Jennsen called down the hill. "They'll be here, soon. Didn't you hear Cara's whistle?"

"We heard," Kahlan called up to Jennsen. "We'll be right there."

Turning back, she smiled as she looked him up and down. "Well, Lord Rahl, you certainly don't look like the first time I saw you." She straightened the tooled leather baldric lying over the black tunic banded in gold. "But you look exactly the same, too. Your eyes are the same as I saw that day." She cocked her head as she smiled up at him. "I don't see the headache of the gift in your eyes."

"It's been gone for a while, but after that kiss, it would be impossible to have a headache."

"Well, if it comes back," she said with intimate promise, "just tell me and I'll see what I can do to make it go away."

Richard ran his fingers through her hair and gazed one last time into her eyes before slipping his arm around her waist. Together they walked through the cathedral of trees that was their cover off to the side near the crown of the ridge, and out toward the open slope. Between the trunks of the pines, he could see Jennsen running down the hill, leaping from rock to rock, avoiding the patches of snow. She rushed in to meet them just within the small cluster of trees.

"I spotted them," she said, breathlessly. "I could see them down in the gorge on the far side. They'll be up here soon." A grin brightened her face. "I saw Tom leading them."

Jennsen took in the sight of both of them, then—Kahlan in the white dress of the Mother Confessor and Richard in the outfit he had in part found in the Keep that had once been worn by war wizards. By the surprise on Jennsen's face, he thought she might curtsy.

"Wow," she said. "That sure is some dress." She looked Richard up and down again. "You two look like you should rule the world."

"Well," Richard said, "let's hope Owen's people think so."

Cara pushed a spruce bough aside as she ducked in under the limbs of the trees. Dressed again in her skintight, red leather outfit, she looked as intimidating as the first time Richard had seen her in the grand halls of the People's Palace in D'Hara.

"Lord Rahl once confided in me that he intended to rule the world," Cara said, having heard Jennsen's pronouncement.

"Really?" Jennsen asked.

Richard sighed at her awe. "Ruling the world has proven more difficult than I thought it would be."

"If you would listen more to the Mother Confessor and to me," Cara advised, "you would have an easier time of it."

Richard ignored Cara's cockiness. "Would you get everything together? I want to be up there with Kahlan before Tom arrives with Owen and his men."

Cara nodded and started collecting the things they'd been working so hard to make, stacking some and taking a count of others. Richard laid a hand on Jennsen's shoulder.

"Tie Betty up so that she'll stay here for now. All right? We don't need her in the way."

"I'll see to it," Jennsen said as she fussed with ringlets of her red hair. "I'll make sure she won't be able to bother us or wander off."

It was plainly evident how eager she was to see Tom again. "You look beautiful," Richard assured her. Her grin returned to overpower the anxious expression.

Betty's tail was a blur as she peered up at them, eager to go wherever the rest of them were going. "Come on," Jennsen said to her friend, "you're staying here for a while."

Jennsen snatched Betty's rope, holding her back, as Richard, Kahlan close at his side, made his way out past the last of the trees and onto the open ledge. Somber clouds hung low against the face of surrounding mountains. With the towering snowcapped peaks hidden by the low, ominous clouds, Richard thought it was as if they were near the roof of the world.

The wind down at ground level had died away, leaving the trees motionless and, by contrast, making the boiling movement of the cloud masses seem almost alive. The flurries of the day before had ended and then the sun had made a brief appearance to shrink the patches of snow on the pass. He didn't think there was much chance of seeing the sun this day.

The towering stone sentinel waited at the top of the trail, watching forever over the pass and out toward the Pillars of Creation. As they approached it, Richard scanned the surrounding sky but saw only some small birds—flycatchers and white-breasted nuthatches—flitting among the nearby stand of spruce trees. He was relieved that the races had remained absent ever since they had taken this ancient trail up through the pass.

The first night up in the pass, farther back down the slope in the heavier forests, they had worked hard to build a snug shelter, just managing to get it done as darkness had settled into the vast woods. Early the next day, Richard had cleared snow off the statue and all around the ledges of the base.

He had discovered more writing.

He now knew more about this man whose statue had been placed there in the pass. Another small flurry had since dusted snow over the writing, burying again the long dead words.

Kahlan placed a comforting hand on his back. "They will listen, Richard. They will listen to you."

With every breath, pain pulled at him from deep inside. It was getting worse. "They'd better, or I'll have no chance to get the antidote to this poison."

He knew he couldn't do it alone. Even if he had known how to call upon his gift and command its magic, he still would not be able to wave a hand or perform some grand feat of conjuring that would cast the Imperial Order out of the Bandakaran Empire. He knew that such things were beyond the scope of even the most powerful magic. Magic, properly used, properly conceived, was a tool, much like his sword, employed to accomplish a goal.

Magic was not what would save him. Magic was not a panacea. If he was to succeed, he had to use his head to come up with a way to prevail.

He no longer knew if he could even depend on the magic of the Sword of Truth. Nor did he know how long he had before his own gift might kill him. At times, it felt as if his gift and the poison were in a race to see which could do him in first.

Richard led Kahlan the rest of the way up and around to the back of the statue, to a small prominence of rock at the very top of the pass where he wanted to wait for the men. From that spot they could see through the gaps in the mountains and back into Bandakar. Out at the edge of the level area, Richard spotted Tom down below leading the men through the trees and up the switchback trail.

Tom peered up as he ascended the trail and spotted Richard and Kahlan. He saw how they were dressed, where they stood, and gave no familiar wave, realizing that doing so would be inappropriate. Through breaks in the trees, Richard could see men following Tom's gaze up above them.

Richard lifted his sword a few inches, checking that it was clear in its scabbard. Overhead, the dark, towering clouds all around seemed to have gathered, as if they were crowding into the confines of the pass to watch.

Standing tall as he gazed off to the unknown land beyond, to an unknown empire, Richard took Kahlan's hand.

Hand in hand, they silently awaited what would be the beginning of a challenge that would either change forever the nature of the world; or be the end of Richard's chance at life.

C H A P T E R 40

As the men following Tom emerged from the trees below and into the open, Richard was dismayed to see that their numbers were far less than Owen said had been hiding with him in the hills. Rubbing the furrows on his brow with his fingertips, Richard stepped back up to the short plateau where Kahlan waited.

Her own brow drew down with concern. "What's wrong?"

"I doubt they brought fifty men."

Kahlan took up his hand again, her voice coming in gentle assurance. "That's fifty more than we had."

Cara came up behind them, dropping her load off to the side. She took up station behind Richard to his left, on the opposite side to Kahlan. Richard met her grim gaze. He wondered how the woman always managed to look as if she fully expected everything to happen just as she wished it to happen, and that was the end of it.

Tom stepped up over the edge of the rock, the men following. Though he was sweating from the exertion of the climb, a tight smile warmed his face when he saw Jennsen just coming up the other side of the rise. She returned the brief smile and then stood in the shadows beside the base of the statue, back out of the way.

When the unkempt band of men caught sight of Richard in his black pants and boots, black tunic trimmed with a band of gold around the edge, the broad leather belt, the leather-padded silver wristbands with ancient symbols circling them, and the gleaming silver-and-gold-wrought scabbard, they seemed to lose their courage. When they saw Kahlan standing beside him, they cowered back toward the edge, bowing hesitantly, not knowing what they were supposed to do.

"Come on, then," Tom told them, prompting them all to come up onto the expanse of flat rock in front of Richard and Kahlan.

Owen whispered to the men as he moved among them, urging them to come forward as Tom was gesturing. They complied timidly, shuffling in a little closer, but still leaving a wide safety margin between themselves and Richard.

As the men all gazed about, unsure as to what they were supposed to do next, Cara stepped forward and held an arm out toward Richard.

"I present Lord Rahl," she said in a clear tone that rang out over the men gathered at the top of the pass, "the Seeker of Truth and wielder of the Sword of Truth, the bringer of death, the Master of the D'Haran Empire, and husband to the Mother Confessor herself."

If the men had looked timid and unsure before, Cara's introduction made them all the more so. They looked from Richard and Kahlan back to Cara's penetrating blue eyes; then, seeing her waiting, they all went to a knee in a bow before Richard.

When Cara stepped deliberately to the fore, in front of the men, turned, and went to her knees, Tom got the message and did the same. Both bent forward and touched their foreheads to the ground.

In the silent, late-morning air, the men waited, still unsure what it was they were to do.

"Master Rahl guide us," Cara said in a clear voice so the men could all hear her. She waited.

Tom looked back over his shoulder at all the blond-headed men watching. When Tom frowned with displeasure, the men understood that they were expected to follow the lead. They all finally went to both knees and bowed forward, imitating Tom and Cara, until their foreheads touched the cold granite.

"Master Rahl guide us," Cara began again, never lifting her forehead from the ground.

This time, led by Tom, the men all repeated the words after her. "Master Rahl guide us," they said with a decided lack of unity.

"Master Rahl teach us," Cara said when they all had finished the beginning of the oath. They followed her lead again, but still hesitantly and without much coordination.

"Master Rahl protect us," Cara said.

The men repeated the words, their voices coming a little more in unison.

"In your light we thrive."

The men mumbled the words after her.

"In your mercy we are sheltered."

They repeated the line.

"In your wisdom we are humbled."

Again they spoke the words after her.

"We live only to serve."

When they finished repeating the words, she spoke the last line in a clear voice: "Our lives are yours."

Cara rose up on her knees when they finished and glared back at the men, all still bowed forward but peeking up at her. "Those are the words of the devotion to the Lord Rahl. You will now speak it together with me three times, as is proper in the field."

Cara again put her forehead to the ground at Richard's feet.

"Master Rahl guide us. Master Rahl teach us. Master Rahl protect us. In your light we thrive. In your mercy we are sheltered. In your wisdom we are humbled. We live only to serve. Our lives are yours."

Richard and Kahlan stood above the people as they spoke the second and third devotion. This was no empty show put on by Cara for the benefit of the men; this was the devotion as it had been spoken for thousands of years and Cara meant every word of it.

"You may rise now," she told the men.

The men cautiously returned to their feet, hunched in worry, waiting silently. Richard met all their eyes before he began.

"I am Richard Rahl. I am the man you men decided to poison so as to enslave me and thus force me to do your bidding.

"What you have done is a crime. While you may believe that you can justify your action as proper, or think of it as merely a means of persuasion, nothing can give you the right to threaten or take the life of another who has done you no harm nor intended none. That, along with torture, rape, and murder, is the means by which the Imperial Order rules."

"But we meant you no harm," one of the men called out in horror that Richard would accuse them of such a ghastly crime. Other men spoke up in agreement that Richard had it all wrong.

"You think I am a savage," Richard said in a tone of voice that silenced them and put them back a step. "You think yourselves better than me and so that somehow makes it all right to do this to me— and to try to do it to the Mother Confessor—because you want something and, like petulant children, you expect us to give it to you.

"The alternative you give me is death. The task you demand of me is difficult beyond your imagination, making my death from your poison a very real possibility, and likely. That is the reality of it.

"I already came close to dying from your poison. At the last possible instant I was granted a temporary stay of my execution when one of you gave me a provisional antidote. My friends and loved ones believed I would die that night. You were the cause of it. You men consciously decided to poison me, thereby accepting the fact that you might be killing me."

"No," a man insisted, his hands clasped in supplication, "we never intended to harm you."

"If there was not a credible threat to my life, then why would I do as you wish? If you truly mean me no harm and are not committed to killing me if I don't go along with you, then prove it and give me the antidote so that I can have my life back. It's my life, not yours."

This time no one spoke up.

"No? So you see, then, it is as I say. You men are committed to either murder or enslavement. The only choice I have in it is which of those two it will be. I will hear no more of your feelings about what you intended. Your feelings do not absolve you of your very real deeds. Your actions, not your feelings, speak the truth of your intent." Richard clasped his hands behind his back as he paced slowly before the men. "Now, I could do as you people are fond of doing, and tell myself that I can't know if any of it is true. I could do as you would do, declare myself inadequate to the task of knowing what's real and refuse to face reality.

"But I am the Seeker of Truth because I do not try to hide from reality. The choice to live demands that the truth be faced. I intend to do that. I intend to live.

"You men must today decide what you will do, what will be the future of your lives and the lives of the ones you love. You are going to have to deal with reality, the same as I must, if you are to have a chance at life. Today you will have to face a great deal of the truth, if you are to have that which you seek." He gestured to Owen. "I thought you said there were more men than this. Where are the rest?"

Owen took a step forward. "Lord Rahl, to prevent violence, they turned themselves over to the men of the Order."

Richard stared at the man. "Owen, after all you've told me, after all those men have seen from the Order, how could they possibly believe such a thing?"

"But how are we to know that this time it will not stop the violence? We can't know the nature of reality or—"

"I told you before, with me you will confine yourself to what is, and not repeat meaningless phrases you have memorized. If you have real facts I want to hear them. I'm not interested in meaningless nonsense."

Owen pulled his small pack off his back. He fished around inside and came up with a small canvas pouch. Tears welled up in his eyes as he gazed at it. "The men of the Order found out that there were men hiding out in the hills. One of those men hiding with us has three daughters. In order to prevent a cycle of violence, someone in our town told the men of the Order which girls were his daughters.

"Every day the men of the Order tied wire to a finger of each one of these three girls. One man held the girl while another pulled on the wire until her finger tore off. The men of the Order told a man from our town to go to the hills and give the three fingers to our men. Every day he came."

Owen handed the bag to Richard. "These are the fingers from each of his daughters. The man who brought them to our men was in a daze. They said he no longer seemed human. He talked in a dead voice. He repeated what he had been bidden to say. He had decided that since nothing was real, he would see nothing and do as he was told.

"He said that the men of the Order told him that some of the people from our town had given the names of the men in the hills and that they had the children of those other men, as well. They said that unless the men returned and gave themselves up, they would do the same to the other children.

"A little more than half the men hiding in the hills could not stand to think of themselves being the cause of such violence, and so they went back to our town and gave themselves over to the men of the Order."

"Why are you giving me this?" Richard asked.

"Because," Owen said, his voice filled with tears, "I wanted you to know why our men had no choice but to turn themselves in. They could not stand to think of their loved ones suffering such terrible agony because of them."

Richard looked out at the mournful men watching him. He felt his anger boiling up inside, but he kept it in check as he spoke. "I can understand what those men were trying to do by giving themselves up. I can't fault them for it. It won't help, but I couldn't fault them for desperately wanting to spare their loved ones from harm."

Despite his rage, Richard spoke in a soft voice. "I'm sorry that you and your people are suffering such brutality at the hands of the Imperial Order. But understand this: it is real, and the Order is the cause of it. Those men of yours, if they did as the Order commanded or if they failed to, were not the cause of violence. The responsibility for causing violence is entirely the Order's. You did not go out and attack them. They came to you, they attacked you, they enslave and torture and murder you."

Most of the men stood in slumped poses, staring at the ground.

"Do any of the rest of you have children?"

A number of the men nodded or mumbled that they did.

Richard ran his hand back through his hair. "Why haven't the rest of you turned yourselves in, then? Why are you here and not trying to stop the suffering in the same way the others did?"

The men looked at each other, some seeming confused by the

question while others appeared unable to put their reasons into words. Their sorrow, their distress, even their hesitant resolve, was evident on their faces, but they could not come up with words to explain why they would not turn themselves in.

Richard held up the small canvas bag containing the gruesome treasure, not allowing them to avoid the issue. "You all knew about this. Why did you not return as well?"

Finally one man spoke up. "I sneaked to the fields at sunset and talked to a man working the crops, and asked what happened to those men who had returned. He said that many of their children had already been taken away. Others had died. All the men who had come in from the hills had been taken away. None were allowed to return to their homes, to their families. What good would it do for us to go back?"

"What good, indeed," Richard murmured. This was the first sign that they grasped the true nature of the situation.

"You have to stop the Order," Owen said. "You must give us our freedom. Why have you made us make this journey?"

Richard's initial spark of confidence dimmed. While they might have in part grasped the truth of their troubles, they certainly weren't facing the nature of any real solution. They simply wanted to be saved. They still expected someone to do it for them: Richard.

The men all looked relieved that Owen had at last asked the question; they were apparently too timid to ask it themselves. As they waited, some of the men couldn't help stealing glances at Jennsen, standing to the rear. Most of the men also appeared troubled by the statue looming behind Richard. They could only see the back of it and didn't really know what it was meant to be.

"Because," Richard finally told them, "in order for me do as you want, it's important that you all come to understand everything involved. You expect me to simply do this for you. I can't. You are going to have to help me in this or you and all of your loved ones are lost. If we are to succeed, then you men must help the rest of your people come to understand the things I have to tell you.

"You have gone this far, you have suffered this much, you have made this much of a commitment. You realize that if you do the same as your friends have been trying to do, if you apply those same useless solutions, you, too, will be enslaved or murdered. You are running out of options. You all have made a decision to at least try to succeed, to try to rid yourselves of the brutes killing and enslaving your people.

"You men here are their last chance . . . their only chance.

"You must now hear the rest of what I have to tell you and then make up your minds as to what will be your future."

The haggard, ragtag men, all dressed in worn and dirty clothes, all looking like they'd had a very difficult time of living in the hills, either spoke up or nodded that they would hear him out. Some even looked as if they might be relieved by how directly and honestly he spoke to them. A few even looked hungry for what he might say.

CHAPTER 41

"Three years ago from the coming autumn," Richard began, "I lived in a place called Hartland. I was a woods guide. I had a peaceful life in a place I loved among those I loved. I knew very little about the places beyond my home. In some ways I was like you people before the Order came, so I can understand some of what you felt about how things changed.

"Like you, I lived beyond a boundary that protected us from those who would do us harm."

The men broke out in excited whispering, apparently surprised and pleased that they could relate to him in this way, that they had something so basic in common with him.

"What happened, then?" one of the men asked.

Richard couldn't help himself; he couldn't hold back the smile that overwhelmed him.

"One day, in my woods"—he held his hand out to the side—"Kahlan showed up.

"Like you, her people were in desperate trouble. She needed help. Rather than poison me, though, she told me her story and how trouble was coming our way. Much like you, the boundary protecting her people had failed and a tyrant had invaded her homeland. She also came bearing a warning that this man would soon come to my homeland, too, and conquer my people, my friends, my loved ones."

All the faces turned toward Kahlan. The men stared openly, as if seeing her for the first time. It looked to be astonishing to them that this statuesque woman before them could be a savage, as they thought of outsiders, and have the same kind of trouble they'd had. Richard was leaving out vast chunks of the story: he wanted to keep it simple enough to be clear to these men.

"I was named the Seeker of Truth and given this sword to help me in this important struggle." Richard lifted the hilt clear of the scabbard by half the length of the blade, letting the men all see the polished steel. Many grimaced at seeing such a weapon.

"Together, side by side, Kahlan and I struggled to stop the man who sought to enslave or destroy us all. In a strange land, she was my guide, helping me not only to fight against those who would kill us, but helping me to come to understand the wider world I had never before considered. She opened my eyes to what was out there, beyond the boundary that had protected me and my people. She helped me to see the approaching shadow of tyranny and know the true stakes involved—life itself.

"She made me live up to the challenge. Had she not, I would not be alive today, and a great many more people would be dead or enslaved."

Richard had to turn away, then, at the flood of painful memories, at the thought of all those lost in the struggle. At the victories so hard won.

He put his hand to the statue for support as he remembered the gruesome murder of George Cypher, the man who had raised him, the man who, until that struggle, Richard had always believed was his father. The pain of it, so distant and far away, came rushing back again. He remembered the horror of that time, of suddenly realizing that he would never again see the man he dearly loved. He had forgotten until that moment how much he missed him.

Richard gathered his composure and turned back to the men. "In the end, and only with Kahlan's help, I won the struggle against that tyrant I had never known existed until the day she had come into my woods and warned me.

"That man was Darken Rahl, my father, a man I had never known."

The men stared in disbelief. "You never knew?" one asked in an astonished voice.

Richard shook his head. "It's a very long story. Maybe another time I will tell you men all of it. For now, I must tell you the important parts that are relevant to you and those you love back there in your homes."

Richard looked at the ground before him, thinking, as he paced in front of the disorderly knot of men.

"When I killed Darken Rahl, I did it to keep him from killing me and my loved ones. He had tortured and murdered countless people and that alone earned him death, but I had to kill him or he would have killed me. I didn't know at the time that he was my real father or that in killing him, since I was his heir, I would become the new Lord Rahl.

"Had he known who I was, he might not have been trying to kill me, but he didn't know. I had information he wanted; he intended to torture it out of me and then kill me. I killed him first.

"Since that time, I have come to learn a great deal. What I learned connects us—" Richard gestured to the men and then placed a hand on his own chest as he met their gazes— "in ways you must come to understand, as well, if you are to succeed in this new struggle.

"The land where I grew up, Kahlan's land, and the land of D'Hara, all make up the New World. As you have learned, this vast land down here outside where you grew up is called the Old World. After I became Lord Rahl, the barrier protecting us from the Old World failed, much as your own boundary failed. When it did, Emperor Jagang of the Imperial Order, down here in the Old World, used the opportunity to invade the New World, my home, much as he invaded your home. We've been fighting him and his troops for over two years, trying to defeat them or at least to drive them back to the Old World.

"The barrier that failed had protected us from the Order, or men like them, for around three thousand years, longer, even, than you were protected. Before that barrier was placed at the end of a great war, the enemy at the time, from the Old World, had used magic to create people called dream walkers."

The men fell to whispering. They had heard the name, but they didn't really understand it and speculated on what it could mean.

"Dream walkers," Richard explained, when they had quieted, "could enter a person's mind in order to control them. There was no defense. Once a dream walker took over your mind, you became his slave, unable to resist his commands. The people back then were desperate.

"A man named Alric Rahl, my ancestor, came up with a way to protect people's minds from being taken over by the dream walkers. He was not only the Lord Rahl who ruled D'Hara at the time, but also a great wizard. Through his ability he created a bond that, when spoken earnestly or given in a more simple form with heartfelt sincerity, protected people from dream walkers entering their minds. Alric Rahl's link of magic to his people, through this bond, protected them.

"The devotion you men all gave is the formal declaration of that bond. It has been given by the D'Haran people to their Lord Rahl for three thousand years."

Some of the men in front stepped forward, their faces etched with anxiety. "Are we protected, then, from the dream walkers, Lord Rahl, because we gave this oath? Are we protected from the dream walkers entering our minds and taking us?"

Richard shook his head. "You and your people need no protection. You are already protected in another way."

Relief swept through the crowd of men. Some gripped the shoulder of another, or placed a hand in relief on a friend's back. They looked as if they feared that dream walkers were stalking them, and they had just been spared at the last instant.

"But how is it that we can be protected?" Owen asked.

Richard took a deep breath, letting it out slowly. "Well, that's the part that in a way connects us. You see, as I understand it, magic needs balance in order to function."

There were knowing nods all around, as if these pristinely ungifted men all had an intimate understanding of magic.

"When Alric Rahl used magic to create this bond in order to protect his people," Richard went on, "there needed to always be a Lord Rahl to complete the bond, to maintain its power. Not all wizards bear children who also possess this gifted ability, so part of what Alric Rahl did when he created this bond was to make it so that the Lord Rahl would always bear one son who had magic, who had the gift, and could complete this bond with the people of D'Hara. In this way they would always be protected."

Richard held up a finger to make his point as he swept his gaze over the crowd of men. "What they didn't know at the time was that this magic inadvertently created its own balance. While the Lord Rahl always produced a gifted heir—a wizard like him—it was only discovered later that he also occasionally produced offspring who were entirely without any magic."

Richard could see by the blank looks that the men didn't grasp what he was telling them. He imagined that for people living such isolated lives, his story must seem rather confusing, if not far-fetched. He remembered his own confusion about magic before the boundary had come down and he'd met Kahlan. He hadn't been raised around magic and he still didn't understand most of it himself. He'd been born with both sides of the gift, and yet he didn't know how to control it.

"You see," he said, "only some people have magic—are gifted, as it's called. But all people are born with at least a very tiny spark of the gift, even though they can't manipulate magic. Until just recently, everyone thought of these people as ungifted. You see? The gifted, like wizards and sorceresses, can manipulate magic, and the rest of the people can't, so they were believed to be ungifted.

"But it turns out that this isn't accurate, since there is an infinitesimal spark of the gift in everyone born. This tiny spark of the gift is actually what allows people to interact with the magic in the world around them, that is, with things and creatures that have magical properties, and with people who are gifted in a more comprehensive sense—those who do have the ability to manipulate magic."

"Some people in Bandakar have magic too," a man said. "True magic. Only those who have never seen—"

"No," Richard said, cutting him off. He didn't want them losing track of his account. "Owen told me about what you people believe is magic. That's not magic, that's mysticism. That's not what I'm talking about. I'm talking about real magic that produces real results in the real world. Forget what you've been taught about magic, about how faith supposedly creates what you believe in and that is real magic. It's not real. It's just the fanciful illusion of magic in people's imaginations."

"But it is real," someone said in a respectful but firm voice. "More real than what you see and feel."

Richard turned a harsh look on the men. "If it's so real, then why did you have to use a known poison on me that was mixed by a man who had worked his whole life with herbs? Because you know what's real, that's why; when it was vital to your self-interest, to your lives, you resorted to dealing in reality, to what you know really works."

Richard pointed back at Kahlan. "The Mother Confessor has real magic. It's no fanciful curse put on someone and when they die ten years later people believe the curse was the cause. She has real magic that is in elemental ways linked to death, so it affects even you. She can touch someone, with this real magic, and in an instant they will be dead. Not ten years from now—right now, on the spot."

Richard stood resolutely in front of the men, gazing from eye to eye. "If someone doesn't believe that is real magic, then let's have a test. Let them perform their faith-based magic and put a spell on me—to kill me right here and now. After they've done that, then they will come forward and be touched by the Mother Confessor's very real, lethal power. Then everyone else will be able to see the results and judge for themselves." He looked from face to face. "Anyone willing to take up the test? Any magicians among all you ungifted people willing to try it?"

When the men remained silent, no one moving, Richard went on.

"So, it would seem that you men do have some understanding of what's real and what isn't. Keep that in mind. Learn from it.

"Now, I told you how the Lord Rahl always bore a son with magic so he could pass on the rule of D'Hara and his gifted ability in order to make the bond work. But, as I said, the bond that Alric Rahl created may have had an unintended consequence.

"Only later was it discovered that the Lord Rahl, possibly as a means of balance, also sometimes produced offspring that were entirely without any magic—not just ungifted in the way most people are, but unlike any people ever born before: they were pristinely ungifted. These pristinely ungifted people had absolutely no spark of the gift whatsoever.

"Because of that, because they were pristinely ungifted, they were unable to interact with the real magic in the world. They were unable to be touched by magic at all. For them, magic might as well not exist because they were not born with the ability to see it or to interact with it. You might say they were like a bird that could not fly. They looked like a bird, they had feathers, they ate bugs, but they couldn't fly.

"Back then in that time, three thousand years ago, after the bond had been created to protect people from dream walkers in the war, the wizards finally succeeded in placing a barrier between the Old and the New World. Because those in the Old World could no longer come to the New World to wage war, the great war ended. Peace finally came.

"The people of the New World discovered, though, that they had a problem. These pristinely ungifted offspring of the Lord Rahl passed this trait on to their children. Every offspring of a marriage with at least one of these pristinely ungifted partners bears pristinely ungifted children—always, every time. As these offspring married and had children and then grandchildren and then great-grandchildren, as there were more and more of them, that pristinely ungifted trait began spreading throughout the population.

"People, at the time, were frightened because they depended on magic. Magic was part of their world. Magic was what had saved them from the dream walkers. Magic had created the barrier that protected them from the horde from the Old World. Magic had ended the war. Magic healed people, found lost children, produced beautiful creations of art that inspired and brought joy. Magic could help guide people in the course of future events.

"Some towns grew up around a gifted person who could serve people's needs. Many gifted people earned a living performing such services. In some things, magic gave people control over nature and thus made the lives of everyone better. Things accomplished with the aid of magic improved the living conditions of nearly everyone. Magic was a force of individual creation and thus individual accomplishment. Nearly everyone derived some benefit from it.

"This is not to say that magic was or is indispensable, but that it was a useful aid, a tool. Magic was like their right arm. Yet it's the mind of man, not his magic, that is indispensable—much as you could survive without your right arm, but you couldn't survive without your mind. But magic had become intertwined in the lives of everyone, so many believed that it was absolutely indispensable.

"The people came to feel that this new threat—the pristinely ungifted trait spreading through the population—would be the end of everything they knew, everything that they thought was important, that it would be the end of their most vital protection—magic."

Richard gazed out at all the faces, waiting to make sure that the men had grasped the essence of the story, that they understood how desperate the people must have been, and why.

"So, what did the people do about these new pristinely ungifted people among them?" a man in the back asked.

In a quiet tone, Richard said, "Something terrible."

He pulled the book from a leather pouch on his belt and held it up for all the men to see as he again paced before them. The clouds, laden with storms of snow, rolled silently through the frigid valley pass, bound for the peaks above them.

"This book is called *The Pillars of Creation*. That's what the wizards back then called these pristinely ungifted people—pillars of Creation—because they had the power, with this trait that they passed along to their offspring, to alter the very nature of mankind. They were the foundation of an entirely new kind of people—people without any connection to magic.

"I only just a short time ago came across this book. It's meant for the Lord Rahl, and others, so that they will know about these pristinely ungifted people who are unaffected by magic. The book tells the history of how these people came about—through those born to the Lord Rahl—along with the history of what was discovered about them. It also reveals what the people back then, thousands of years ago, did about these pillars of Creation."

Men rubbed their arms in the cold air as Richard slowly paced before them. They all looked caught up in the story.

"So," Owen asked, "what did they do?"

Richard came to a stop and stood watching their eyes before he spoke. "They banished them."

Astonished whispering broke out among the men. They were stunned to hear the final solution. These people understood banishment, they understood it all too well, and they could sympathize with these banished people of so long ago.

"That's terrible," a man at the front said, shaking his head.

Another frowned and held up a hand. "Weren't these pillars of Creation related to some of the other people? Weren't they part of the towns? Didn't the people feel sorrow at banishing these ungifted people?"

Richard nodded. "Yes. They were friends and family. Those banished people were intimately intertwined in the lives of nearly everyone. The book tells how heavy-hearted the people felt at the decision that had been reached about these pristinely ungifted people. It must have been an awful time, a dreadful choice that no one liked, but those in charge at the time decided that in order for them to preserve their way of life, to preserve magic and all it meant to them, to preserve that attribute of man, rather than value the lives of individuals for who they were, they had to banish these pristinely ungifted people.

"What's more, they also decreed that all future offspring of the Lord Rahl, except his gifted heir, should be put to death to insure that no pillar of Creation ever again came among them."

This time there was no whispering. The men looked saddened by the story of these mysterious people and the terrible solution of how to deal with them. Heads hung as the men thought about what it must have been like back in such a grim time.

Finally, a man's head came up. His brow twitched. He finally asked the question Richard expected to be asked, the question he had been waiting for.

"But where were these pillars of Creation banished to? Where were they sent?"

Richard watched the men as other eyes turned up, curious about the historic mystery, waiting for him to go on.

"These people were not affected by magic," Richard reminded them. "And the barrier holding back the Old World was a barrier created of magic."

"They sent them through the barrier!" a man guessed aloud.

Richard nodded. "Many wizards had died and given their power into that barrier so that their people would be protected from those in the Old World who wanted to rule them and to end magic. That was a large part of what the war had been fought over—those in the Old World had wanted to eradicate magic from mankind.

"So, those people in the New World sent these pristinely ungifted people, these people without any magic, through the barrier to the Old World.

"They never knew what became of them, those friends and family and loved ones they had banished, because they had been sent beyond a barrier that none of them could cross. It was thought that they would establish new lives, would make a new beginning. But, because the barrier was there, and it was enemy territory beyond, the people of the New World never knew what became of those banished people.

"Finally, a few years ago, that barrier came down. If these banished people had made a life for themselves in the Old World, they would have had children and spread their pristinely ungifted attribute"— Richard lifted his arms in a shrug— "but there is no trace of them. The people down here are just the same as the people up in the New World—some born gifted but all born with at least that tiny spark of the gift that enables them to interact with magic.

"Those people from ancient times seemed just to have vanished."

"So now we know," Owen reasoned as he stared off in thought, "that all those people sent to the Old World so long ago tragically died out . . . or maybe were killed."

"I had thought as much myself," Richard said. He turned and faced the men, waiting until all eyes were on him before going on.

"But then I found them. I found those long-lost people."

Excited whispering broke out again. The men appeared inspired by the prospect of such people surviving against all odds.

"Where are they, then, Lord Rahl," a man asked, "these people with whom you share ancestry? These people who had to endure such cruel banishment and hardship?"

Richard leveled a cutting gaze at the men. "Come with me, and I will tell you what became of these people."

Richard led them around the statue, to the front, where, for the first time, they could see the full view of the sentinel in stone. The men were awestruck at finally seeing the statue from the front. They talked excitedly among themselves about how real it looked, at how they could clearly see the stalwart features of the man's face.

By the utter shock in their voices and by what the men were saying, Richard got the distinct impression that they'd never seen a statue before, at least no statue as monumental as this one. It appeared that for these men the statue must be something akin to a manifestation of magic, rather than, as Richard knew it to be, a manifestation of man's ability.

Richard placed a hand on the cold stone of the base. "This is an ancient statue of an Old World wizard named Kaja-Rang. It was carved, in part, as a tribute to the man because he was a great and powerful wizard."

Owen lifted a hand to interrupt. "But I thought the people in the Old World wanted to be without magic? Why would they have a great wizard—and why, especially, would they pay a tribute to such a man of magic?"

Richard smiled at Owen catching the contradiction. "People don't always act in a consistent manner. What's more, the more irrational are your beliefs, the more glaring the inconsistencies. You men, for example, try to gloss over incongruities in your behavior by applying your convictions selectively. You claim that nothing is real, or that we cannot know the true nature of reality, and yet you fear what the Order does to you—you believe firmly enough in the reality of what they're doing that you want it to stop.

"If nothing were real, then you would have no reason to want to stop the Imperial Order. In fact, it's counter to your professed beliefs to try to stop them, or even to feel that their presence is real, much less detrimental, since you assert that man is inadequate at the task of knowing reality.

"Yet you grasp the reality of what's happening at the hands of the men of the Order, and know very well that it's abhorrent, so you selectively suspend the precepts of your beliefs in order to send Owen to poison me in an attempt to get me to rid you of your very real problem."

Some of the men looked confused by what Richard said while others looked to be embarrassed. A few looked astonished. None looked willing to challenge him, so they let him go on without interrupting.

"The people in the Old World were the same way—they still are. They claimed they didn't want magic, and yet when faced with that reality, they didn't want to do without it. The Imperial Order is like this. They've come to the New World claiming to be a champion of freeing mankind of magic, proclaiming themselves to be noble for holding such a goal, and yet they use magic in the pursuit of this professed goal. They contend that magic is evil, and yet they embrace it.

"Their leader, Emperor Jagang, uses those with magic to help accomplish his ends, among which, he claims, is the eradication of magic. Jagang is a dream walker descended from those dream walkers of so long ago. His ability as a dream walker is magic, yet he does not disqualify himself from leading his empire. Even though he has magic, which he claims makes people unfit to have any say in the future, he calls himself Jagang the Just.

"Despite what they declare they believe, their goal is to rule people, plain and simple. They seek power but dress it up in noble-seeming robes. Every tyrant thinks he is different. They are all the same. They all rule by brute force."

Owen was frowning, trying to grasp it all. "So, those in the Old World did not live by their word, by what they claimed they believed. They lived in conflict. They preached that man was better without magic, but they continued to want to use magic."

"That's right."

Owen gestured up at the statue. "What of this man, then? Why is he here, if he is against what they preached?"

Dark clouds roiled above the towering statue. The still air hung cold, heavy, and damp. It felt as if a storm were holding back its onslaught, waiting to hear the rest.

"This man is here because he fought to save the people of the Old World from something they feared more than magic itself," Richard said.

He gazed up at the resolute face with its eyes fixed forever on the place called the Pillars of Creation.

"This man," Richard said in a quiet voice, "this wizard, Kaja-Rang, collected all of those pristinely ungifted people, those pillars of Creation, who had been banished down here from the New World, along with any people who while they lived here had joined with them, and he sent them all there."

Richard pointed off into the distance behind the statue.

"He put all those people in that place, protected by the mountains all around, and then he placed a boundary of death before them, across this pass, so that they could never again come out to be among the rest of the people of the world.

"Kaja-Rang gave these people their name: the Bandakar. The name *bandakar* is from a very old language called High D'Haran. It means 'the banished'. This man, Kaja-Rang, is the one who sealed them in and saved his people from the pristinely ungifted, from those without magic.

"You," Richard said to the men before him, "are the descendants of those banished people. You, are the descendants of Alric Rahl, of the people sent into exile in the Old World. You, are all descendants of the House of Rahl. Your ancestors and mine are the same men. You, are the banished people."

The top of the pass before the statue of Kaja-Rang was dead silent. The men stared in shock.

And then pandemonium broke out. Richard made no effort to stop them, to keep them quiet. Rather, he stood close beside Kahlan as he let them take it in. He wanted to give them the time they needed to come to grasp the enormity of what he had told them.

Arms in the air, some men cried out with outrage at what they'd heard, others wailed in horror at the story, some wept in sorrow, many argued, a few protested various points that others answered, while yet others repeated key elements to one another almost as if to hear the words again so they could test them, agreeing finally that it might very well be so.

But through it all, they all slowly began to grasp the enormity of what they'd heard. They all began to hear the ring of truth in the story. Chattering like magpies, all talking at once, they expressed disbelief, outrage, wonder, and even fear, as they came to the heady comprehension of who they really were.

At the whispered urging of some among the group, after having gotten over the initial shock, the men all quieted and at last turned back to Richard, hungry to know more.

"You are this gifted man, the favored heir, the Lord Rahl, and we are the ones banished by your kind," one of the men said, expressing what looked to be a common fear, the unspoken question of what this would mean for them.

"That's right," Richard said. "I am the Lord Rahl, the leader of the D'Haran Empire, and you are the descendants of the pillars of Creation who were banished. I am gifted as have been my ancestors, every Lord Rahl before me. You are ungifted as were your ancestors."

Standing before the statue of Kaja-Rang, the man who had banished them, Richard looked out at all the tense faces.

"That banishment was a grievous wrong. It was immoral. As Lord Rahl, I denounce the banishment and declare it forever ended. You are no longer the Empire of Bandakar, the banished ones, you are now once again, as you once were, D'Harans, if you choose to be."

Every man seemed to hold his breath, waiting to see if he meant it, or would add more, or if he might even recant it.

Richard put his arm around Kahlan's waist as he calmly gazed out at all the hopeful expressions. He smiled. "Welcome home."

And then they were all falling at his feet, kissing his boots, his pants, his hands, and for those who couldn't crowd in close enough, the ground before him. In short order, they were kissing the hem of Kahlan's dress.

They had found a relation, and were in turn welcoming him among them.

CHAPTER 42

As the men crowded around their feet, openly offering their gratitude for ending their sentence of banishment, Richard shared a sidelong glance with Kahlan. Cara looked decidedly displeased by the display but didn't interfere.

Trying to bring a halt to the tearful tribute, Richard gestured for the men to get up. "There is much more to tell you. Listen to me, now."

The smiling, tearful men drew back, hands clasped while gazing at him as if he were a long-lost brother. There were a few older men among the crowd and some of a middle age, but most ranged from young, like Owen, to a little older, like Richard. They were all men who had been through terrible times.

The most difficult part still lay ahead; Richard had to make them face up to what was to come.

Looking over at Jennsen, standing alone off to the side, he gestured for her to come forward.

Jennsen emerged from the shadows of the statue, catching the attention of all eyes as she made her way toward Richard. The men all watched her coming into the light. She looked so beautiful that Richard couldn't help smiling as she stepped across the rocks. Pulling on a red ringlet, she cast a shy glance at the men.

When Richard held an arm out, she sought protection under the shelter of that arm as she gazed nervously out at men who were like her in one important way.

"This is my sister, Jennsen Rahl," Richard said. "She was born pristinely ungifted, just like all of you. Our father tried to kill her, as has been done for thousands of years with ungifted offspring."

"And you?" a man asked, still skeptical. "You will not reject her?"

Richard hugged Jennsen with the one arm. "For what? For what crime should I reject her? Because she was born a woman, instead of a man like me? Because she isn't as tall as me? Because she has red hair, instead of hair like mine? Because her eyes are blue and not gray . . . ? Because she is ungifted?"

The men shifted their weight to the other foot or folded their arms. Some, after all he had already said, averted their eyes, looking embarrassed to have even asked the question.

"She's beautiful, smart, and uses her head. She, too, fights for her right to live, and does so through reasoned means. She is as you men, pristinely ungifted. Because she shares an understanding of the value of life, I embrace her."

Richard heard the bleat and turned. Betty, her rope trailing behind, trotted up the rise. Jennsen rolled her eyes as Betty came close, peering up, her tail wagging in a blur.

Jennsen snatched up the rope, inspecting the end. Richard could see that it had been chewed through.

"Betty," she scolded, shaking the end of the rope at the unrepentant goat, "what did you do?"

Betty bleated her answer, clearly proud of herself.

Jennsen heaved a sigh as she shrugged an apology at Richard.

The men had all taken several steps back, murmuring their dread to one another.

"I'm not a witch," Jennsen told them in a heated tone. "Just because I have red hair that doesn't mean I'm a witch."

The men looked thoroughly unconvinced.

"I've had dealings with a very real witch-woman," Richard told them. "I can assure you, red hair is no mark of a witch. It just isn't true."

"It is true." One of the men insisted. He pointed at Betty. "There is her attendant spirit."

Richard's brow wrinkled. "Attendant spirit?"

"That's right," another told him. "A witch always has a familiar with her. She called her attendant spirit and it came to her."

"Called her?" Jennsen brandished the frayed end of the rope at the men. "I tied her to a tree and she chewed through her rope."

Another man shook his finger at her. "You called her with magic and she came."

Fists at her sides, Jennsen took a step toward the men. They took a collective step back.

"You men all had family and friends—a community of people. I had no friends and could have none because my mother and I had to run from my father my whole life to keep from being caught. He would have tortured and murdered me had he caught me—the same as he would have done with you. I could have no childhood friends, so my mother gave me Betty. Betty was just newborn; we grew up together. Betty chewed through her rope because I'm the only family she's ever known and she simply wanted to be close to me.

"I was banished from everyone for my crime of birth, just like your ancestors. You all know the injustice of such banishment and you know its pain. And now you foolish men would banish me from your acceptance because I have red hair and a goat as a pet? You are spineless cowards and hypocrites!

"First you poison the only person in the world brave enough to end our banishment from the rest of mankind and now you fear me and reject me because of silly superstitions. If I did have magic, I'd burn you all to a cinder for your cruel attitudes!"

Richard put a hand on her shoulder and drew her back. "It will be all right," he whispered to her. "Just let me talk to them."

"You tell us that you're a wizard," an older man in the back called out, "and then you expect us to believe it's so—on faith—because you say it is, while you claim that we should not hold to our beliefs, such as our fear that she could be a witch with her familiar, because it's held only on faith."

"That's right," another said. "You claim your belief is in real magic, while you dismiss our belief. A lot of what you say makes sense, but I don't agree with all of it."

There could be no partial agreement. To reject part of the truth was to reject it all. Richard considered his options, how he could convince people without magic, who could not see magic, that real magic existed. From their perspective, he seemed guilty of the same error he was telling them they were making. How could he demonstrate a rainbow of color to the blind?

"You have a point," Richard said. "Give me a moment and I will show you the reality of the magic I talk about."

He motioned Cara closer. "Get me the warning beacon," he said in a confidential tone.

Cara immediately took off down the hill. He saw that Jennsen's angry blue eyes were filled with tears but she didn't cry. Kahlan pulled her back farther as Richard addressed the men.

"There is more I must tell you—some things you need to understand. I have ended the banishment, but that does not mean that I unconditionally accept each of you back as one of our people."

"But you said that we were welcomed home," Owen said.

"I'm stating the obvious—that you have a right to your own life. Out of goodwill I welcome you all to be part of D'Hara if you wish— part of what D'Hara now stands for. But by welcoming you back, that does not mean that I welcome people unconditionally.

"All men should be free to live their own lives, but make no mistake, there is a vast difference between that freedom and anarchy.

"If we triumph in our struggle, you are welcome to be free people of a D'Haran Empire which holds a belief in specific values. For example, you can think whatever you wish and try to persuade others of the value of your beliefs, but you cannot act on a view that those who fight to gain that freedom are savages or criminals, even though you expect to enjoy the fruits of their struggle. At a minimum, they have earned your respect and gratitude. Their lives are no less than yours and are not expendable for your benefit. That is slavery."

"But you have savage ways and engage in violence for a land we have never even seen," one of the younger men said. He pointed an arm back toward Bandakar. "The only land we have ever known is here and we unconditionally reject your love of violence."

"Land?" Richard spread his arms. "We do not fight for land. We are loyal to an ideal—an ideal of liberty wherever man lives. We do not guard territory, bleed for a piece of dirt. We don't fight because we love violence. We fight for our freedom as individuals to live our own lives, to pursue our own survival, our own happiness.

"Your unconditional rejection of violence makes you smugly think of yourselves as noble, as enlightened, but in reality it is nothing less than abject moral capitulation to evil. Unconditional rejection of self-defense, because you think it's a supposed surrender to violence, leaves you no resort but begging for mercy or offering appeasement.

"Evil grants no mercy, and to attempt to appease it is nothing more than a piecemeal surrender to it. Surrender to evil is slavery at best, death at worst. Thus, your unconditional rejection of violence is really nothing more than embracing death as preferable to life.

"You will achieve what you embrace.

"The right, the absolute necessity, of vengeance against anyone who initiates force against you is fundamental to survival. The morality of a people's self-defense is in its defense of each individual's right to life. It's an intolerance of violence, made real by an unwavering willingness to crush any who would launch violence against you. The unconditional determination to destroy any who would initiate force against you is an exaltation of the value of life. Refusing to surrender your life to any thug or tyrant who lays claim to it, is in fact embracing life itself.

"If you are unwilling to defend your right to your own lives, then you are merely like mice trying to argue with owls. You think their ways are wrong. They think you are dinner.

"The Imperial Order preaches that mankind is corrupt and evil, and therefore life is of little value. Their actions certainly bear this out. They moralize that you can only win salvation and happiness in some other world, and then only by sacrificing your life in this one.

"Generosity is fine, if it's by your free choice, but a belief in the primacy of self-sacrifice as a moral requisite is nothing less than the sanctioning of slavery. Those who tell you that it is your responsibility and duty to sacrifice yourselves are trying to blind you to the chains they are slipping around your neck.

"As D'Harans, you will not be required to sacrifice your life to another, and by the same token you cannot demand that others sacrifice themselves for you. You may believe as you wish, you may even feel that you cannot take up arms and fight directly for our survival, but you must help support our cause and you may not contribute materially or spiritually to the destruction of our values and therefore our lives—that is treason and will be treated as such.

"The Imperial Order has violently invaded innocent lands like yours. They have enslaved, tortured, raped, and murdered in order to seize rule. They have done no less in the New World. They have forfeited their right to be heard. There is no moral dilemma involved, no ethical question open to debate; they must be ground into dust."

A man stepped forward. "But common decency in dealing with our fellow man requires that we must show them mercy for their misguided ways."

"There is no greater value than life—and that's what you partially recognize by your confused notion of granting mercy. Their conscious, deliberate act of murder takes the irreplaceable value of life from another. A murderer, by his own choice to kill, forfeits the right to his own life. Mercy for such evil is nothing short of excusing it and thus allowing evil to prevail—it codifies the taking of innocent life by not making the murderer forfeit their own guilty life.

"Mercy grants value to the life of a killer, while, at the same time, it strips away the value of the life of the innocent victim. It makes the life of a killer more important than the life of an innocent. It is thus a trade of the good for the evil. It is the victory of death over life."

"So," Owen wondered aloud, "because the Order has attacked your land and murdered its people, you intend to try to kill every living person in the Old World?"

"No. The Order is evil and from the Old World. That does not mean that the people of the Old World are evil simply because they happen to have been born on a patch of ground ruled by evil men. Some actively support these rulers and therefore embrace evil, but not everyone does. Many of the people in the Old World are also the victims of the rule of the Imperial Order and suffer greatly under its brutality. Many struggle against this evil rule. As we speak, many risk their lives to rid themselves of these evil men. We fight for the same thing: liberty.

"Where those who seek liberty were born is irrelevant. We believe in the value of the individual's life. That means that where someone lives does not make them evil—it's their beliefs and actions that matter.

"But make no mistake—many people are an active part of the Imperial Order and its murderous ways. Actions must have consequences. The Order must be eradicated."

"Surely you would allow some compromise," one of the older men said.

"If, hoping to appease it, you willingly compromise with unrepentant evil, you only allow such evil to sink its fangs into you; from that day on its venom will course through your veins until it finally kills you."

"But that's too harsh a sentiment," the man said. "It's just being stubborn and obstructing a constructive path. There is always room for compromise."

Richard tapped his thumb against his chest. "You men decided to give me poison. That poison will kill me; that makes it evil. How would you suggest I compromise with poison?"

No one had an answer.

"In trade between willing parties who share moral values and who deal fairly and honestly with one another, compromise over something like price is legitimate. In matters of morality or truth, there can be no compromise.

"Compromising with murderers, which is precisely what you are suggesting, grants them moral equivalence where none can rightfully exist. Moral equivalence says that you are no better than they, therefore, their belief—that they should be able to torture, rape, or murder you—is just as morally valid as your view—that you have the right to live free of their violence. Moral compromise rejects the concept of right and wrong. It says that everyone is equal, all desires are equally valid, all action is equally valid, so everyone should compromise to get along.

"Where could you compromise with those who torture, rape, and murder people? In the number of days a week you will be tortured? In the number of men to be allowed to rape your loved ones? In how many of your family are to be murdered?

"No moral equivalence exists in that situation, nor can it exist, so there can be no compromise, only suicide.

"Even to suggest compromise can exist with such men is to sanction murder."

Most of the men appeared shocked and startled to hear someone speaking to them in such a straightforward manner. They seemed to be losing interest in their supply of empty adages. Some of the men looked to be moved by Richard's words. A few even looked inspired by their clarity; he could see it in their eyes, as if they were seeing things for the first time.

Cara came up behind Richard and handed him the warning beacon. Richard wasn't sure, but it seemed as if the inky black had taken over more of the surface of the small figure than the last time he'd seen it. Inside, the sand continued to trickle down onto the accumulated pile in the bottom.

"Kaja-Rang placed the boundary across this pass to seal your people in. He is the one who named you. He knew your people shunned violence and he feared you might end up being prey to criminals. He is the one who gave you a way to banish them from your land so that you could continue to have the kind of life you wanted. He told your people of the passage through the boundary so that you could rid yourselves of criminals if you rallied the will."

Owen looked troubled. "If this great wizard, Kaja-Rang, didn't want our people among the population of the Old World because we would mix with them and spread our pristinely ungifted trait, as you call it, then what about the criminals we banish? Sending those men out into the world would cause the thing they feared. Making this pass through the boundary and telling our ancestors about it would seem to defeat the whole purpose of the boundary."

Richard smiled. "Very good, Owen. You are beginning to think for yourself."

Owen smiled. Richard gestured up at the statue of Kaja-Rang.

"You see where he's looking? It's a place called the Pillars of Creation. It's a deathly hot place where nothing lives—a land stalked by death. The boundary that Kaja-Rang placed had sides to it. When you sent people out of your land, through the boundary, the walls of death to the sides prevented those banished people from escaping into the world at large. They had only one way they could go: the Pillars of Creation.

"Even with water and supplies, and knowing where you must go to get past it, trying to go through the valley known as the Pillars of Creation is almost certain death. Without water and supplies, without knowing the land, without knowing how to travel it and where you must go to escape such a place, those you banished faced certain death."

The men stared, wide-eyed.

"Then, when we banished a criminal, we were actually executing them," one of the men said.

"That's right."

"This Kaja-Rang tricked us, then," the man added. "Tricked us into what was actually the killing of those men."

"You think that a terrible trick?" Richard asked. "You people were deliberately setting known criminals loose on the world to prey on unsuspecting people. You were knowingly setting free violent men, and condemning unsuspecting people outside your land to be victims of violence. Rather than put murderers to death, you were, as far as you knew—had you given it any thought—knowingly assisting them in going on to kill others. In the blind attempt to avoid violence at all cost, you actually championed it.

"You told yourselves that those other people didn't matter, because they weren't enlightened, like you, that you were better than they because you were above violence, that you unconditionally rejected violence. If you even thought about it, you considered these people beyond the boundary to be savages, their lives unimportant. For all intents and purposes, you were sacrificing their innocent lives for the lives of those men you knew to be evil.

"What Kaja-Rang was doing, besides keeping the pristinely ungifted from being at large in the world, was executing those criminals you banished before they could harm other people. You think yourselves noble in rejecting violence, but your actions would have fostered it. Only Kaja-Rang's actions prevented it."

"Dear Creator. It is far worse than that." Owen sank down, sitting heavily. "Far worse than you even realize."

Other men, too, looked to be stricken with horror. Some had to lower themselves to the ground as Owen had. Others, their faces in their hands, turned away, or walked off a few paces.

"What do you mean?" Richard asked.

Owen looked up, his face ashen. "The story I told you about our land . . . about our town and the other great cities? How in my town we all lived together and were happy with our lives?" Richard nodded. "Not all were."

Kahlan crossed her arms and leaned toward Owen. "What do you mean, not all were?"

Owen lifted his hands in a helpless gesture. "Some wanted more than our simple joyful life. Some people . . . well, they wanted to change things. They said they wanted to make things better. They wanted to improve our life, to build places for themselves, even though this is against our ways."

"Owen is right," an older man said in a grim tone. "In my time I have seen a great many of these people who were unable to endure what some called the chafing principles of our empire."

"And what happened when people wanted to make these changes, or could not endure the principles of your empire?" Richard asked.

Owen looked to each side, to the other dispirited faces. "The great speakers renounced their ideas. The Wise One said they would only bring strife among us. Their hopes for new ways were turned aside and they were denounced." Owen swallowed. "So these people decided they would leave Bandakar. They went out of our land, taking the path through the opening in the boundary, to find a new life for themselves. Not a single one ever returned to us."

Richard wiped a hand across his face. "Then they died looking for their new life, a better life than what you had to offer."

"But you don't understand." Owen rose to his feet. "We are like those people." He swept his arm back at his men. "We have refused to go back and give ourselves over to the men of the Order, even though we know that people are being tortured because we hide. We know it will not stop the Order, so we don't go back.

"We have gone against the wishes of our great speakers, and the Wise One, to try to save our people. We have been denounced for what we choose to do. We have gone out of the pass to seek information, to find a way to rid ourselves of the Imperial Order. Do you see? We are much the same as those others throughout our history.

Like those others, we chose to leave and try to change things rather than to endure the way things were."

"Then perhaps you are beginning to see," Richard said, "that everything you were taught showed you only how to embrace death, not life. Perhaps you see that what you called the teaching of enlightenment was no more than blinders pulled over your eyes."

Richard put his hand on Owen's shoulder. He gazed down at the statue of himself in his other hand and then looked around at the tense faces.

"You men are the ones left after all the rest have failed the tests. You alone got this far. You alone have started to use your minds to try to find a solution for you and your loved ones. You have much more to learn, but you have at least started to make some of the right choices. You must not stop now; you must meet with courage what I will call upon you to do, if you are to truly have a chance to save your loved ones."

For the first time they looked at least a little proud. They had been recognized, not for how well they repeated meaningless sayings, but for the decisions they reached on their own.

Jennsen was frowning in thought. "Richard, why couldn't people get back in through the passage out through the boundary? If they wanted to go off and have a new life but then discovered that they would have to go through the Pillars of Creation, why wouldn't they go back, at least to get supplies, to get what they needed so they could make it through?"

"That's right," Kahlan said. "George Cypher went through the boundary at Kings' Port and then returned. Adie said that the boundary had to have a passage, a vent, like where these people banished criminals, so why couldn't people come back in? There was a pass out, so why did they never return?"

The men nodded, curious to hear why no one ever came back.

"From the first, I've wondered the same thing." Richard rubbed a thumb along the glossy black surface of the statue of himself. "I think that the boundaries in the Midlands had to have an opening through them because they were so big—so long. This boundary, here, is nothing compared to those; I doubt that the same kind of vent would be needed.

"Because it was just one bent section of a boundary and not very long, I suspect that Kaja-Rang was able to put in a pass that allowed criminals to be banished through it, but would not allow passage back in. After all, if a criminal was banished and found he couldn't escape, he would return. Kaja-Rang wouldn't have wanted that to happen."

"How could such a thing work?" Jennsen asked.

Richard rested his left hand on the hilt of his sword. "Certain snakes can swallow prey much larger than themselves. Their teeth are angled back so that as the prey is devoured, it's impossible for it to come back out, to escape. I suppose that the pass through the boundary could have been somehow like that—only able to be traversed in one direction."

"Do you think such a thing is possible?" Jennsen asked.

"There is precedent for such safeguards," Kahlan said.

Richard nodded his agreement. "The great barrier between the New and the Old World had defenses to allow certain people, under specific conditions, one passage through and back, but not two." He pointed the warning beacon up at the statue. "A wizard of Kaja-Rang's ability would surely have known how to craft a pass through the boundary that did not allow any return. After all, he called it up out of the underworld itself and it remained viable for nearly three thousand years."

"So then anyone who went out of this boundary, died," Owen said.

Richard nodded. "I'm afraid so. Kaja-Rang appeared to have made elaborate plans that functioned as he intended for all this time. He even made contingencies should the boundary fail."

"That's something I don't understand," a young man said. "If this wizard was so great, and his magic was so powerful that he could make a wall of death to keep us separated from the world for three thousand years, then how could it possibly fail? In the last two years it simply went away. Why?"

"I believe it was because of me," Kahlan said.

She took a step closer to the men. Richard didn't try to stop her. At this point, it wouldn't do to appear as if he were withholding information from them.

"A couple of years ago, in a desperate act to save Richard's life, I inadvertently called forth underworld power that I believe may be slowly destroying magic in our world. Richard banished this evil magic, but it had been here in the world of life for a time, so the effects may be irreversible."

Worried looks passed among the men. This woman before them had just admitted that because of something she'd done, their protection had failed. Because of her, horrifying violence and brutality had befallen them. Because of her, their way of life had ended.

CHAPTER 43

"You still have not shown us your magic," one of the men finally said.

Richard's hand slipped away from the small of Kahlan's back as he stepped toward the men.

"Kaja-Rang devised a facet to his magic, linked to the boundary he placed here, to help protect it." Richard held up the small figure of himself for all the men to see. "This was sent to warn me that the boundary to your land had failed."

"Why is the top part of it that strange black?" asked a man standing in the front.

"I believe that it's an indication of how I'm running out of time, how I may be dying."

Worried whispering swept through the group of men. Richard held up a hand, urging them to listen to him as he went on.

"This sand inside—can you all see this sand?"

Stretching their necks, they all tried to get a look, but not all were close enough, so Richard walked among them, holding up the statue so that they could all see that it looked like him, and see the sand falling inside.

"This is not really sand," he told them. "It's magic."

Owen's face twisted with skepticism. "But you said we couldn't see magic."

"You are all pristinely ungifted and aren't touched by magic, so you can't see regular magic. The boundary, however, still prevented you from going out into the world, didn't it? Why do you suppose that was so?"

"It was a wall of death," an older man spoke up, seeming to think that it was self-evident.

"But how could it harm people who are not affected by magic? Going into the boundary itself meant death for you the same as for anyone else. Why?

"Because the boundary is a place in this world where the underworld also existed. The underworld is the world of the dead. You may be ungifted, but you are mortal; since you are linked to life so, too, are you linked to death." Richard again held the statue up. "This magic, as well, is tied to the underworld. Since you are all mortal, you have a connection to the underworld, to the Keeper's power, to death. That's why you can see the sand that shows how my time trickles away."

"I don't see anything magical about sand trickling down," a man grumbled. "Just because you say it's magic, or that it's your life trickling away, that doesn't seem to prove anything."

Richard turned the statue sideways. The sand continued to flow, but sideways.

Gasps and astonished whispering broke out among the men as they watched the sand flowing laterally. They crowded in close like curious children to see the statue as Richard held it up, on its side, so they could see magic. Some reached out and tentatively touched the inky black surface as Richard held the figure of himself out for them to inspect. Others leaned close, peering in to see the sand flowing askew in the lower part, where the figure was still transparent.

The men spoke of what a wonder it was, but they weren't sure about his explanation of underworld magic.

"But we all see this," one of the men said. "This doesn't show us that we're really different from you or anyone else, as you say we are. This shows us only that we are all able to see this magic, the same as you. Maybe we aren't this pristinely ungifted people you seem to think we are."

Richard thought about it a moment, thought about what he could do to show them the true aspects of magic. Even though he was gifted, he didn't know a great deal about controlling his own gift, except that it was in part powered by anger linked to need. He couldn't simply demonstrate some bit of magic the way Zedd could and besides, even if he could do something magical, they wouldn't be able to see it.

Out of the corner of his eye, Richard saw Cara standing with her arms folded. An idea came to him.

"The bond between the Lord Rahl and his people is a bond of magic," Richard said. "That same magic powers other things, besides the protection that the bond affords against the dream walker."

Richard gestured for Cara to come forward. "In addition to being my friend, Cara is also a Mord-Sith. For thousands of years Mord-Sith have been fierce protectors of the Lord Rahl." Richard lifted Cara's arm for the men to see the red rod hanging from the fine gold chain at her wrist. "This is an Agiel, the weapon of a Mord-Sith. The Agiel is powered by a Mord-Sith's connection to the Lord Rahl—to me."

"But it has no blade on it," a man said as he looked closely at the Agiel swinging on the end of the gold chain. "It has nothing of any use as a weapon."

"Take a closer look at it," Richard suggested as he held Cara's elbow and guided her forward, among the men. "Look at it closely to satisfy yourself that what this man has observed, that it has no blade, that it is nothing more than this slender rod, is true."

The men leaned in close as Cara walked among them, holding her arm up, letting the men touch and inspect her Agiel as it dangled from its chain. When they had all had a look, inspecting the length of it, looking at the end, hefting it to see that it wasn't heavy and couldn't really be used as a club, Richard told Cara to touch it to the men. The Agiel spun up into her fist. Men flinched back at the grim look on her face as she came at them with the thing that Richard had told them was a weapon.

Cara touched her Agiel to Owen's shoulder.

"She touched me with this red rod before," he assured his men. "It does nothing."

Cara pressed the Agiel to every man close enough for her to reach. A few cringed back, fearful of being harmed, even though it had harmed none of their fellows. Many of the men, though, felt the touch of her Agiel and were satisfied that there was no ill effect.

Richard rolled up his sleeve. "Now, I will show you that this really is a powerful weapon of magic."

He held his arm out to Cara. "Draw blood," he said in a calm voice that did not betray what he really thought of being touched by an Agiel.

Cara stared at him. "Lord Rahl, I don't—"

"Do it," Richard commanded as he held his arm out.

"Here," Tom said, thrusting his bared arm in front of her. "Do it to me, instead."

Cara immediately saw this as a preferable test.

"No!" Jennsen objected, but too late.

Tom cried out as Cara touched the end of her Agiel to his arm. He staggered back a step, a trickle of blood running down his arm. The men stared, unsure what they were seeing.

"It must be a trick of some kind," one suggested.

As Jennsen comforted Tom, Richard held his arm out again.

"Show them," he told Cara. "Show them what a Mord-Sith's Agiel can do with magic alone."

Cara looked into his eyes. "Lord Rahl . . ."

"Do it. Show them, so they understand." He turned to the men. "Gather around closer so you can see that it does its terrible task with no visible means. Watch closely so that you can all see that it's magic alone doing its grisly work."

Richard clenched his fist as he held the inside of his arm up for her to touch. "Do it so that they can clearly see what it will do, otherwise it will be for nothing. Don't make me do this for nothing."

Cara pressed her lips tight with the displeasure of his command. She looked once more at the resolve in his eyes. When she did, he could see in her blue eyes the pain it gave her to hold the Agiel. He clenched his teeth and nodded that he was ready. With an iron visage, she laid the Agiel against the inside of his forearm.

It felt as if lightning had hit him.

The touch of the Agiel was out of all proportion to what it would appear it should feel like. The thunderous jolt of pain shot up his arm. The shock of it slammed into his shoulder. It felt as if the bones in his arm shattered. Teeth gritted, he held his trembling arm out as Cara slowly dragged the Agiel down toward his wrist. Blood-filled blisters rose in its wake. Blood gushed down his arm.

Richard held his breath, kept his abdominal muscles tight, as he went to one knee, not because he intended to, but because he couldn't remain standing under the weight of pain as he held his arm up for Cara as she pressed the Agiel to it. The men gasped as they watched, shocked at the blood, the obvious pain. They whispered their astonishment.

Cara withdrew the weapon. Richard released the rigid tension in his muscles, bending forward as he panted, trying to catch his breath, trying to remain upright. Blood dripped off his fingers.

Kahlan was there beside him with a small scarf Jennsen pulled from a pocket. "Are you out of your mind?" she hissed heatedly as she wrapped his bleeding arm.

"Thanks," he said in response to her care, not wanting to address her question.

He couldn't make his fingers stop trembling. Cara had held little back. He was sure that she hadn't broken any bones, but it felt as if she had. He could feel tears of pain running down his face.

When Kahlan finished, Cara put a hand under his arm and helped him to his feet. "The Mother Confessor is right," she growled under her breath. "You are out of your mind."

Richard didn't argue the need of what he'd had her do, but instead turned to the men. He held his arm out. A wet crimson stain slowly grew along the length of the scarf-bandage.

"There is powerful magic for you. You can't see the magic, but you can see the results. That magic can kill, should Cara wish it." The men cast worried glances her way, viewing her with newfound respect. "But it could not harm you men because you have no ability to interact with such magic. Only those born with the spark of the gift can feel the touch of an Agiel."

The mood had changed. The sight of blood had sobered everyone.

Richard paced slowly before the men. "I've given you the truth in all that I've told you. I've kept nothing important or relevant from you, nor will I. I've told you who I am, who you are, and how we've come to this point. If there is anything you wish to know, I will give you my truthful answer."

When Richard paused, the men looked around at one another, seeing if anyone would ask a question. No one did.

"The time has come," Richard said, "for you men to decide your future and the future of your loved ones. Today is the day upon which that future hinges." Richard gestured toward Owen. "I know that Owen had a woman he loved, Marilee, who was taken away by the Order. I know that each of you has suffered great loss at the hands of the men of the Imperial Order. I don't know all your names, yet, or the names of the loved ones taken from you, but please believe me when I tell you that I know such pain.

"While I understand how you came to the point where you thought you had no options but to poison me, it wasn't right for you to have done so." Many a man looked away from Richard's gaze, casting their own downward. "I'm going to give you a chance to set the proper course for yourselves and your loved ones."

He let them consider this a moment before going on. "You men have passed many tests to make it this far, to have survived this long in such a brutal situation as you have all faced, but now you must make a choice."

Richard rested a hand on the hilt of his sword. "I want to know where you've hidden the antidote to the poison you've given me."

Worried looks spread through the crowd. Men glanced to the side, trying to judge the feelings of their fellows, trying to see what they would do.

Owen, too, tried to gauge the reaction of his friends, but, being just as uncertain as he, they offered no firm indication of what they wanted to do. Finally he licked his lips and timidly asked a question. "If we say that we will tell you where the antidote is, will you agree to first give us your word that you will help us?"

Richard resumed his measured pacing. The men nervously waited for his answer as they watched blood drip off his fingers, leaving a trail of crimson drops on the stone.

"No," Richard said. "I will not allow you to link two separate issues. It was wrong to poison me. This is your chance to reverse that wrong. Linking it to any concession perpetuates the fallacy that it can somehow be justified. Telling me where you've hidden the antidote is the only proper thing for you to do, now, and must be without condition. This is the day you must decide how you will live your future. Until you give me your decision, I will tell you nothing more."

Some of the men looked on the verge of panic, some on the verge of tears. Owen prodded them all back, away from Richard, so that they could discuss it among themselves.

"No," Richard said, his pacing coming to a halt. The men all fell silent and turned back toward him. "I don't want any of you coming to a decision because of what another says. I want each of you to give me your own personal decision."

The men stared. A number spoke up all at once, wanting to know what he meant.

"I want to know, without any preconditions, what each individual chooses to do—to free me of the poison, or to use it as a threat on my life to gain my cooperation. I want to know each man's choice."

"But we must reach a consensus," one man said.

"For what purpose?" Richard asked.

"In order for our decision to be correct," he explained. "No proper decision about the right course of action in any important situation can be made without a consensus."

"You are attempting to give moral authority to mob rule," Richard said.

"But a consensus points to the proper moral judgment," another man insisted, "because it is the will of the people."

"I see," Richard said. "So what you're saying is that if all of you men decide to rape my sister here, then it's a moral act because you have a consensus to rape her and, if I oppose you, I'm immoral for standing alone and failing to have a consensus behind me. That about the way you men see it?"

The men shrank back in confused revulsion. One spoke up.

"Well . . . no, not exactly—"

"Right and wrong are not the product of consensus," Richard said, cutting him off. "You are trying to make a virtue of mob rule. Rational moral choices are based on the value of life, not a consensus. A consensus can't make the sun rise at midnight, nor can it change a wrong into a right, or the other way around. If something is wrong, it matters not if a thousand other men are for it; you must still oppose it. If something is just, no amount of popular outcry should stay you from your course.

"I'll not hear any more of this empty gibberish about a consensus. You are not a flock of geese; you are men. I will know the mind of each of you." He gestured to the ground at their feet. "Everyone, pick up two pebbles."

Richard watched as the bewildered men hesitantly bent and did his bidding.

"Now," Richard said, "you will put either one or both pebbles in a closed fist. Each of you will come up to me, to the man you poisoned, and you will open your fist so that I can see your decision but the others can't.

"One pebble will mean 'no,' you will not tell me where the antidote is located unless I first pledge to try to free your people. Two pebbles in your one fist will mean 'yes,' you agree to tell me, without any precondition, where to find the antidote to the poison you've given me."

"But what will happen if we agree to tell you?" one of the men asked. "Will you still give us our freedom?"

Richard shrugged. "After each of you has given me your answer, you will all find out mine. If you tell me the location of the antidote, I may help you, or, once I'm free of your poison, I may leave you and return to taking care of my own urgent problems. You will only find out after you've given me your answer.

"Now, turn away from your friends and put either one pebble in your fist for no or two pebbles to agree to reveal the location of the antidote. When you've finished, come forward one at a time and open your hand to show me your own individual decision."

The men milled around, casting sidelong glances at one another but, as he'd instructed, they refrained from discussing the matter. Each man finally set about privately slipping pebbles into his fist.

While the men were thus occupied, Cara and Kahlan moved in close around Richard. It looked as if the two of them had been reaching conclusions of their own.

Cara seized his arm. "Are you crazy?" she whispered in an angry tone.

"You've both asked me that today."

"Lord Rahl, need I remind you that you once before called for a vote and it only got you into trouble? You said you would not do such a foolish thing again."

"Cara is right," Kahlan argued in a low voice so the men couldn't hear.

"This time is different."

"It's not different," Cara snapped. "It's trouble."

"It's different," he insisted. "I've told them what's right and why; now they must decide if they will choose to do the right thing or not."

"You're allowing others to decide your future," Kahlan said. "You're placing your fate in their hands."

Richard let out a deep breath as he gazed into Kahlan's green eyes and then the icy blue eyes of the Mord-Sith. "I have to do this. Now, let them come up and show me their decision."

Cara stormed off to stand back by the statue of Kaja-Rang. Kahlan gave his arm a squeeze, offering her silent support, accepting his decision even if she didn't understand his reasons. A brief smile of appreciation was all he could manage before she turned and walked back to stand by Cara, Jennsen, and Tom.

Richard turned away, not wanting to let Kahlan see how much pain he was in. The ache from the poison was slowly creeping back up his chest. Every breath hurt. His arm still trembled with the lingering ache of being touched by an Agiel. The worst, though, was the headache. He wondered if Cara could see it in his eyes. After all, the business of Mord-Sith was pain.

He knew he couldn't wait until after helping these men fight off the Order before getting the antidote to the poison. He had no idea how to rid their empire of the Imperial Order. He couldn't even rid his own empire of the invaders.

Worse, though, he could feel that he was running out of time. His gift was giving him the headaches, and if not attended to, would eventually kill him; but worse, it was weakening him, allowing the poison to work faster. With each passing day he was having more and more difficulty working past the poison.

If he could get these men to agree to do this, to tell him where they'd hidden the antidote, then he might be able to recover it in time.

If not, then his chance to live was as good as over.

C H A P T E R 44

The men milled around the top of the pass, some staring off into their own thoughts, some gazing up at the statue of Kaja-Rang, the man who had banished their people. Some of the men snatched glimpses at their companions. Richard could see that they were aching to ask friends what they would do, but they kept to Richard's orders and didn't speak.

Finally, when Richard stepped up before them, one of the younger men came forward. He had been one of the men eager to hear Richard's words. He'd looked as if he had listened carefully and considered the things Richard had told them. Richard knew that if this man said no, then there was no chance that any of the others would agree.

When the young, blond-headed man opened his fist, two pebbles lay in his palm. Richard let out an inner sigh that at least one of the men had actually chosen to do the right thing.

Another man came forward and opened his fist, showing two pebbles sitting in his palm. Richard nodded in acknowledgment, without showing any reaction, and let him move aside. The rest of the men had lined up. Each stepped forward in turn and silently opened his hand. Each showed him two pebbles, showing that he would recant his death threat, and then moved off so that the next man could show his choice.

Owen was the last in line. He looked up at Richard, pressed his lips tight, and then thrust out his hand. "You have done us no harm," he said as he opened his fist. There in his palm lay two pebbles.

"I don't know what will happen to us, now," Owen said, "but I can see that we must not cause you harm because we are desperate for your help."

Richard nodded. "Thank you." The sincerity in his voice brought smiles to many of the faces watching. "You have all shown two pebbles. I'm encouraged that you've all chosen to do the right thing. We now have common ground upon which to find a future course."

The men looked around at one another in surprise. Then cheerfully gathered in close to their friends, talking excitedly to one another about how they had all made the same decision. They looked gleeful that they were united in that decision. Richard moved back to where Kahlan, Cara, Jennsen, and Tom stood.

"Satisfied?" he asked Kahlan and Cara.

Cara folded her arms. "What would you have done had they all chosen to keep the antidote's location a secret until after you helped them?"

Richard shrugged. "I'd be no better off than I was, but no worse off, either. I'd have had to help them, but at least I would know that I dared not trust any of them."

Kahlan still didn't look pleased. "And what if most of them had said yes, but some stuck to their ways and said no?"

Richard looked into her resolute green eyes. "Then, after the ones who agreed had told me where to find the antidote, I would have had to kill those who said no."

Understanding the seriousness of his explanation, Kahlan nodded. Cara smiled her satisfaction. Jennsen looked shocked.

"If any had said no," he explained to Jennsen, "then they would have been choosing to continue to enslave me, to hold a sentence of death over my head in order to manipulate my life to get what they wanted from me. I would never be able to trust them in what I must ask the rest of them to do. I couldn't trust our lives to such treachery. But, now, that's one less problem we have to worry about."

Richard turned to the waiting men. "Each of you has decided to return my life to me."

The faces watching him turned serious as they waited to hear what he would do now. Richard gazed down at the small figure of himself, at the sand trickling down, at the eerie black surface that had already descended over the top of the statue, like the underworld itself slowly claiming his life. His fingers had left smears of blood across the surface of the figure.

The clouds had lowered in around them, thickening so that the afternoon light seemed more like the gloom of dusk.

Richard lowered the statue and looked back up at the men. "We will do our best to see if we can help you get rid of the Order."

A cheer rose into the thin, cold air. The men hooted their excitement as well as their relief. He hadn't yet seen any of them smile quite this broadly before. Those smiles, more than anything, revealed the depth of their wish to be free of the men of the Order. Richard wondered how they would feel about it when he finally told them their part.

He knew that as long as Nicholas the Slide was able to seek them out through the eyes of the races, he would remain a threat that would haunt them wherever they went and endanger all of their work to get the Old World to rise up and overthrow the Imperial Order. More than that, though, Nicholas would be able to direct killers to find them. The thought of Nicholas seeing Kahlan and knowing where to find her give Richard chills. He had to eliminate Nicholas. It was possible that in doing so, in eliminating their leader, would also help these people drive the Order from their homes.

Richard gestured for the men to gather in closer. "First, before we get to the matter of freeing your people, you need to show me where you've hidden the antidote."

Owen squatted down and selected a stone. With it, he scratched a chalky oval on the face of a flat spot in the rock. "Say that this line is the mountains surrounding Bandakar." He set the stone at the end of the oval closest to Richard. "Then this is the pass into our land, where we are now." He plucked three pebbles from the ground. "This is our town, Witherton, where we lived," he said as he set the first pebble down not far from the rock that represented the pass. "Some of the antidote is there."

"And this is where all of you men were hiding?" Richard asked as he circled a finger over the first pebble. "In the hills surrounding Witherton?"

"Mostly to the south," Owen said, pointing to the area. He placed the second pebble near the middle of the oval. "Here there is another vial of the antidote, in this city, here, called Hawton." He placed the third pebble near the edge of the oval. "Here is the third vial, in this city, Northwick."

"So then," Richard summed up, "I just need to go to one of those three places and recover the antidote. Since your town is the smallest, that would probably be our best chance."

Some of the men shook their heads; others looked away.

Owen, looking troubled, touched each of the three pebbles. "I'm sorry, Lord Rahl, but one of these is not enough. Too much time has passed. Even two will be insufficient by now. The man who made the poison said that if too much time passed, all four would be necessary to insure a remedy.

"He said that if you did not immediately take the first antidote I brought, then it would only halt the poison for a while. He said that then the other three vials would all be needed. He said that in this case, the poison would possibly go through three states. If you are to be free of the poison, you must drink all of the three remaining antidotes. If you don't, you will die."

"Three states? What does that mean?"

"The first state will be pain in your chest. The second state will be dizziness that makes standing difficult." Owen looked away from Richard's gaze. "In the third state the poison makes you blind." He looked up and touched a hand to Richard's arm, as if to dispel his worry. "But taking three vials of the antidote will cure you, make you well."

Richard wiped a weary hand across his brow. The pain in his chest told him that he was in the poison's first state.

"How much time do I have?"

Owen looked down as he straightened his sleeve. "I'm not sure, Lord Rahl. We have already taken a lot of time traveling this far since you had that first vial. I think we have no time to lose."

"How much time?" Richard asked in as calm a voice as he could manage.

Owen swallowed. "To be truthful, Lord Rahl, I'm surprised that you are able to stand the pain from the first state of the poison. From what I was told, the pain would grow as time passed."

Richard simply nodded. He didn't look up at Kahlan.

With soldiers of the Imperial Order occupying Bandakar, getting in to recover the antidote from one place sounded difficult enough, but retrieving it from all three places sounded beyond difficult.

"Well, since time is short, I have a better idea," Richard said. "Make me more of the antidote. Then we won't have to worry about getting what you've hidden and we can then simply worry about how best to take on the men of the Order."

Owen shrugged one shoulder. "We can't."

"Why not?" Richard leaned in. "You made it before—you made the antidote that you hid. Make it again."

Owen shrank back. "We can't."

Richard took a patient breath. "Why not?"

Owen pointed off at the small bag he'd brought, now lying off to the side—the bag containing the fingers of three girls. "The father of those girls was the man who made the poison and made the antidote. He is the only one among us who knew how to make such complex things with herbs. We don't know how—we don't even know many of the ingredients he used.

"There may be others in the cities who could make an antidote, but we don't know who they are, or if they are still alive. With men of the Order in those places we wouldn't even be able to find these people. Even if we could, we don't know what was used to make up the poison, so they would not know how to make an antidote. The only chance you have to live is to recover the three vials of antidote."

Richard's head was hurting so much that he didn't know if he could stand much longer. With only three vials in existence, and all three needed if he was to live, he had to get to them before anything happened to any one of them. Someone could find one and throw it out. They could be moved. They could be broken, the antidote draining away into the ground. With every breath, he felt stitches of pain pull inside his chest. Panic gnawed at the edges of his thoughts.

When Kahlan rested her hand on his shoulder, Richard laid a grateful hand over hers.

"We will help you get the antidote, Lord Rahl," one of the men said.

Another nodded. "That's right. We will help you get it."

The men all spoke up, then, saying that they would all help to get the antidote so that Richard could rid himself of the poison.

"Most of us have been to at least two of these places," Owen said. "Some of us have been to all three. I hid the antidote, but I told the others the places, so we all know where it is. We know where we have to get in to recover it. We will tell you, too."

"Then that's what we'll do." Richard squatted down as he studied the stone map. "Where is Nicholas?"

Owen leaned in and tapped the pebble in the center. "Here, in Hawton, is this man Nicholas."

Richard looked up at Owen. "Don't tell me. You hid the antidote in the building where you saw Nicholas."

Owen shrugged self-consciously. "At the time, it seemed like a good idea. Now, I wish I had thought better of it."

Standing behind Richard, Cara rolled her eyes in disgust. "I'm surprised you didn't hand it to Nicholas and ask him to hold on to it for you."

Appearing eager to change the subject, Owen pointed at the pebble representing Northwick. "In this city is where the Wise One is hiding. Maybe we can get help from the great speakers. Maybe the Wise One will give us his blessing and then people will help us in our effort to rid our land of the Imperial Order."

After all he'd learned about the people who lived beyond the boundary in Bandakar, Richard didn't think he could count on any meaningful help from them; they wanted to be free of marauding brutes, but condemned their only real means to be free. These men had at least proven a degree of resolve. These men would have to work to change other people's attitudes, but Richard had his doubts that they would garner much immediate help.

"In order to accomplish what you men rightfully want—to erad-icate the Order, or at least make them leave your homes—you are going to have to help. Kahlan, Cara, Jennsen, Tom, and I aren't going to be able to do it alone. If it's to work, you men must help us."

"What is it you wish us to do?" Owen asked. "We already said we will take you to these places where the antidote is hidden. What more can we do?"

"You are going to have to help us kill the men of the Order."

Instantly, heated protests erupted. All of the men talked at once, shaking their heads, warding off the notion with their hands. Although Richard couldn't make out all their words, their feelings about what he said were obvious enough. What words he did hear were all objections that they couldn't kill.

Richard rose up. "You know what these men have done," he said in a powerful voice that brought them to silence. "You ran away so you wouldn't also be killed. You know how your people are being treated. You know what's being done to your loved ones in captivity."

"But we can't harm another," Owen whined. "We can't."

"It's not our way," another man added.

"You banished criminals through the boundary," Richard said. "How did you make them go through if they refused?"

"If we had to," one of the older men said, "a number of us would hold him, so that he could harm no one. We would tie his hands and bear him to the boundary. We would tell such a banished man that he must go out of our land. If he still refused, we would carry him to a long steep place in the rock where we would lay him down and push him feet first so that he would slide down the rock and go beyond. Once we did this, they weren't able to return."

Richard wondered at the lengths these people went to not to harm the worst animals among them. He wondered how many had to suffer or die at the hands of such criminals before the people of Bandakar were sufficiently motivated to take what were to them extreme measures.

"We understand much of what you have told us," Owen said, "but we cannot do what you ask. We would be doing wrong. We have been raised not to harm another."

Richard snatched up the bag containing the girls' fingers and shook it at the men. "Every one of your loved ones back there is thinking of nothing but being saved. Can any of you even imagine their terror? I know what it's like to be tortured, to feel helpless and alone, to feel like you will never escape. In such a situation you want nothing more than for it to stop. You would do anything for it to stop."

"That's why we needed you," an older man said. "You must do this. You must rid us of the Order."

"I told you, I can't do it alone." Richard gestured emphatically with an arm wrapped in a bloody bandage. "Surrendering your will to the men of the Order who would do such things as this solves nothing. It simply adds more victims. The men of the Order are evil; you must fight back."

"But if only you would talk to those men like you talked to us, they would see their misguided ways. They would change, then."

"No, they wouldn't. Life doesn't matter to them. They've made their choice to torture, rape, and kill. Our only chance to survive, our only chance to have a future, is to destroy them."

"We can't harm another person," one of the men said.

"It's wrong to harm another," Owen agreed.

"It's always immoral to hurt, much less kill, another person," a middle-aged man said to the mumbled agreement of his fellows. "Those who do wrong are obviously in pain and need our under-standing, not our hate. Hate will only invite hate. Violence will only begin a cycle of violence that never solves anything."

Richard felt as if the ground he had gained with these men was slipping away from him. He was about to run his fingers back through his hair when he saw that they were covered in blood. He dropped his arm and shifted his approach.

"You poisoned me to get me to kill these men. By that act, you've already proven that you accept the reality that it's sometimes neces-sary to kill in order to save innocent lives—that's why you wanted me. You can't hold a belief that it's wrong to harm another and at the same time coerce me to do it for you. That's simply killing by proxy."

"We need our freedom," one of them said. "We thought that

maybe because of your command as a ruler you could convince these men, for fear of you, to leave us be."

"That's why you have to help me. You just said it—for fear of me. You must help me in this so that the threat, the fear, is credible. If they don't believe the threat is real then why would they leave your land?"

One of the others folded his arms. "We thought you might rid us of the Order without violence, without killing, but it is up to you to do such killing if that is your way. We cannot kill. From our very beginning, our ancestors have taught us that killing is wrong. You must do this."

Another, nodding his agreement, said, "It's your duty to help those who cannot bring themselves to do what you can do."

Duty. The polite name put to the chains of servitude.

Richard turned away, closing his eyes as he squeezed his temples between fingers and thumb. He'd thought that he was beginning to get through to these men. He'd thought he would be able to get them to think for themselves—in their own best interest—rather than to function spontaneously according to the rote dictates of their indoctrination.

He could hardly believe that after all he'd told them, these men would still rather have their loved ones endure torture and brutal murder than harm the men committing the crimes. By refusing to face the nature of reality, these men were willingly giving the good over to evil, life over to death.

He realized then that it was even more basic than that. In the most fundamental sense, they were willfully choosing to reject the reality of evil.

Deep inside him, every breath pulled a stitch of pain. He had to get the antidote. He was running out of time.

But that alone would not solve his problems; his gift was killing him just as surely as the poison. He felt so sick from the pounding pain of his headache that he thought he might throw up. Even the magic of his sword was failing him.

Richard feared the poison, but in a more fundamental way, he feared the encroaching death from within, from his gift. The poison, as dangerous as it was, had a clearly-defined cause and cure. With his gift, he felt lost.

Richard looked back into Kahlan's troubled eyes. He could see that she had no solution to offer. She stood in a weary pose, her arm hanging straight with the weight of the warning beacon that seemed to tell him only that he was dying, but offered no answers. Its whole reason for being was to call him to a proclaimed duty to help replace the boundary, as if his life was not his own, but belonged to anyone who laid claim to it by shackling him with a declaration of duty.

That concept—duty—was no less a poison than that which these men had given him . . . a call to sacrifice himself.

Richard took the small statue from Kahlan's hand and stared down at it. The inky black had already enveloped half the length of the figure. His life was being consumed. The sand continued to trickle away. His time was running out.

The stone figure of Kaja-Rang, the long-dead wizard who had summoned him with the warning beacon and charged him with an impossible task, loomed over him as if in silent rebuke.

Behind him, the men huddled close, affirming to one another their beliefs, their ways, their responsibility to their ancient ideals, that the men of the Order were acting as they were because they were misguided and could still be reformed. They spoke of the Wise One and all the great speakers who had committed them to the path of peace and nonviolence. They all reaffirmed the belief that they must follow the path that had been laid down for them from the very beginning by their land's founders, who had given them their customs, their beliefs, their values, their way of living.

Trying to elevate these men to understand what was right and necessary seemed as difficult as trying to lift them by a slender thread. That thread had broken.

Richard felt trapped by the deluded convictions of these people, by their poison, by the headaches, by Nicholas hunting them, and by a long-dead wizard who had reached out from the underworld to try to enslave him to a long-dead duty.

Anger welling up inside him, Richard cocked his arm and heaved the warning beacon at the statue of Kaja-Rang.

The men ducked as the small figure shot by just over their heads to shatter against the stone base of the statue. Amber fragments and inky black shards flew in every direction. The sand from inside splattered in a stain across the front of the granite pedestal.

The cowering men fell silent.

Overhead, wisps trailing from the sullen clouds drifted by, almost close enough to reach up and touch. A few icy flakes of snow floated along in the still air. All around, a frigid fog had moved in to envelope the surrounding mountains, leaving the top of the pass with the stone sentinel feeling isolated and otherworldly, as if this were all there was to existence. Richard stood in the dead quiet center of everyone's attention.

The words written in High D'Haran on the statue's base echoed through Richard's mind.

Fear any breach of this seal to the empire beyond . . . for beyond is evil: those who cannot see.

The High D'Haran words streamed again and again through his mind. The translation of those words just didn't feel right.

"Dear spirits," Richard whispered in sudden realization. "I had it wrong. That's not what it says."

CHAPTER 45

Kahlan felt as if her heart were being crushed by the ordeal these men were putting Richard through. Just when she'd thought he had gotten them to understand the truth of what was needed, it seemed to have slipped away as they reverted to their willful blindness.

Richard, though, seemed almost to have forgotten the men. He stood staring at where the warning beacon had shattered against the statue. Kahlan stepped closer to him and whispered.

"What do you mean, you had it wrong, and that's not what it says? What are you talking about?"

"The translation," he said in what sounded like startled comprehension. He stood motionless, facing the towering statue of Kaja-Rang. "Remember how I told you that it was an odd way to phrase what it said?"

Kahlan glanced to the statue and then back to Richard. "Yes."

"It wasn't odd at all; I just had it wrong. I was trying to make it say what I thought it would say—that those beyond couldn't see magic—instead of just seeing what was before me. What I told you before isn't what it says . . ."

When his voice trailed off, Kahlan reached up and gripped his arm to draw his attention. "What do you mean, that's not what it says?"

Richard gestured toward the statue. "I see what I did wrong with the phrasal sequence, why I was having trouble with it. I told you I wasn't sure of the translation. I was right to have doubts. It doesn't say 'Fear any breach of this seal to the empire beyond, for beyond is evil: those who cannot see.'"

Jennsen leaned in close beside Kahlan. "Are you sure?"

Richard looked back at the statue, his voice distant. "I am now."

Kahlan pulled on his arm, making him look at her. "So what does it say?"

His gray eyes met her gaze briefly before turning to the eyes of the statue of Kaja-Rang staring out at the Pillars of Creation, at his final safeguard protecting the world from these people. Instead of answering her, he started away.

The men parted as Richard strode toward the statue. Kahlan stayed close on his heels, Cara following in her wake. Jennsen gathered up Betty's rope and pulled her along. The men, already backing out of the way for Richard, kept a wary eye on the goat and its mistress as they passed. Tom stayed where he was, keeping a careful but unobtrusive watch over all the men.

At the statue, Richard swiped the dusting of snow off the ledge, revealing again the words carved in High D'Haran. Kahlan watched his eyes moving along the line of words, reading them to himself. He had a kind of excitement in his movements that told her he was racing after an important quarry.

She could also see that his headache was gone for the moment. She couldn't understand the way it ebbed from time to time, but she was relieved to see strength in the way he moved. Hands spread on the stone, leaning on his arms, he looked up from the words. Without the headache, there was a vibrant clarity in his gray eyes.

"Part of this story has been puzzling," he said. "I understand now. It doesn't say 'Fear any breach of this seal to the empire beyond, for beyond is evil: those who cannot see.'"

Jennsen's nose wrinkled. "It doesn't? You mean it wasn't meant to be about these pristinely ungifted people?"

"Oh, it was about them, all right, but not in that respect." Richard tapped a finger to the carved words. "It doesn't say 'for beyond is evil: those who cannot see,' but something profoundly different. It says, "Fear any breach of this seal to the empire beyond, *for beyond are those who cannot see evil.*'"

Kahlan's brow drew down. " . . . 'those who cannot see evil.'"

Richard lifted his bandaged arm up toward the figure towering over them. "That's what Kaja-Rang feared most—not those who couldn't see magic, but those who could not see evil. That's his warning to the world." He aimed a thumb back over his shoulder, indicating the men behind them. "That's what this is all about."

Kahlan was taken aback, and a little perplexed. "Do you think it might be that because these people can't see magic they also can't recognize evil," she asked, "or that because of the way they're different they simply don't have the ability to conceive of evil, in much the same way they can't conceive of objective magic as having nothing to do with mysticism?"

"That might in part be what Kaja-Rang thought," Richard said. "But I don't."

"Are you so sure?" Jennsen asked.

"Yes."

Before Kahlan could make him explain, Richard turned to the men. "Here, in stone, Kaja-Rang left a warning for the world. Kaja-Rang's warning is about those who cannot see evil. Your ancestors were banished from the New World because they were pristinely ungifted. But this man, this powerful wizard, Kaja-Rang, feared them for something else: their ideas. He feared them because they refused to see evil. That's what made your ancestors so dangerous to the people of the Old World."

"How could that be?" a man asked.

"Thrown together and banished to a strange place, the Old World, your ancestors must have clung desperately to one another. They were so afraid of rejection, of banishment, that they avoided rejecting one of their own. It developed into a strong belief that no matter what, they should try not to condemn anyone. For this reason, they rejected the concept of evil for fear they would have to judge someone. Judging someone as evil meant they would have to face the problem of removing them from their midst.

"In their flight from reality, they justified their practices by settling on the fanciful notion that nothing is real and so no one can know the nature of reality. That way, they wouldn't have to admit that someone was evil. Better to deny the existence of evil than have to eliminate the evildoer in their midst. Better to turn a blind eye to the problem, ignore it, and hope it went away.

"If they admitted the reality of evil, then eliminating the evildoer was the only proper action, so, by extension, since they had been banished, they thought that they must have been banished because they were evil. Their solution was to simply discard the entire concept of evil. An entire belief structure developed around this core.

"Kaja-Rang may have thought that because they were pristinely ungifted and couldn't see magic, they also couldn't see evil, but what he feared was the infection of their beliefs spreading to others. Thinking requires effort; these people offered beliefs that needed no thought, but merely the adoption of some noble-sounding phrases. It was, in fact, an arrogant dismissal of the power of man's mind— an illusion of wisdom that spurned the requirement of any authentic effort to understand the world around them or the nuisance of validation. Such simplistic solutions, such as unconditionally rejecting all violence, are especially seductive to the undeveloped minds of the young, many of whom would have eagerly adopted such disordered reasoning as a talisman of enlightenment.

"When they began fanatically espousing these empty tenets to others, it probably set off the alarm for Kaja-Rang.

"With the spread of such ideas, with the kind of rabid hold it has over some people, such as it has over you men, Kaja-Rang and his people saw how, if such beliefs ran free, it would eventually bring anarchy and ruin by sanctioning evil to stalk among his people, just as it leaves you men defenseless against the evil of the Imperial Order now come among you.

"Kaja-Rang saw such beliefs for what they were: embracing death, rather than life. The regression from true enlightenment into the illusion of insight spawned disorder, becoming a threat to all of the Old World, raising the specter of a descent into darkness."

Richard tapped his finger on the top of the ledge. "There is other writing up here, around the base, that suggests as much, and what became the eventual solution.

"Kaja-Rang had those who believed these teachings collected— not only all the pristinely ungifted banished from the New World, but also the rabid believers who had fallen under their delusional philosophy—and he banished the whole lot of them.

"The first banishment, from the New World down to the Old, was unjust. The second banishment, from the Old World to the land beyond here, had been earned."

Jennsen, twiddling the frayed end of Betty's rope, looked dubious. "Do you really think there were others banished along with those who were pristinely ungifted? That would mean there were a great many people. How could Kaja-Rang have made all these people go along? Didn't they resist? How did Kaja-Rang make them all go? Was it a bloody banishment?"

The men were nodding to her questions, apparently wondering the same thing.

"I don't believe that High D'Haran was a common language among the people, not down here, anyway. I suspect that it was a dying language only used among certain learned people, such as wizards." Richard gestured to the land beyond. "Kaja-Rang named these people Bandakar—the banished. I don't think the people knew what it meant. Their empire was not called the pillars of Creation, or some name referring only to the ungifted. The writing here suggests that it was because it was not only the pristinely ungifted who were banished, but all those who believed as they did. They all were Bandakar: the banished.

"They thought of themselves, of their beliefs, as enlightened. Kaja-Rang played on that, flattering them, telling them that this place had been set aside to protect them from a world not ready to accept them. He made them feel that, in many ways, they were being put here because they were better than anyone else. Not given to reasoned thinking, these people were easily beguiled in this fashion and duped into cooperating with their own banishment. According to what's hinted at in the writing here around the statue's base, they went happily into their promised land. Once confined to this place, marriage and subsequent generations spread the pristinely ungifted trait throughout the entire population of Bandakar."

"And Kaja-Rang really believed they were such a terrible threat to the rest of the people of the Old World?" Jennsen asked. Again, men nodded, apparently in satisfaction that she had asked the question. Kahlan suspected Jennsen might have asked the question on behalf of the men.

Richard gestured up at the statue of Kaja-Rang. "Look at him. What's he doing? He's symbolically standing watch over the boundary he placed here. He's guarding this pass, watching over a seal keeping back what lies beyond. In his eternal vigilance his hand holds a sword, ever at the ready, to show the magnitude of the danger.

"The people of the Old World felt such gratitude to this important man that they built this monument to honor what he had done for them in protecting them from beliefs they knew would have imperiled their society. The threat was no trifling matter.

"Kaja-Rang watches over this boundary even in death. From the world of the dead he sent me a warning that the seal had been breached." Richard waited in the tense silence until all the men looked back at him before he quietly concluded, "Kaja-Rang banished your ancestors not only because they couldn't see magic, but, more importantly, because they couldn't see evil."

In restless disquiet, the men glanced about at their companions. "But what you call evil is just a way of expressing an inner pain," one of them said, more as a plea than as an argument.

"That's right," another told Richard. "Saying someone is evil is prejudiced thinking. It's a way of belittling someone already in pain for some reason. Such people must be embraced and taught to shed their fears of their fellow man and then they will not strike out in violent ways."

Richard swept his glare across all the watching faces. He pointed up at the statue.

"Kaja-Rang feared you because you are dangerous to everyone— not because you are ungifted, but because you embrace evil with your teachings. In so doing, in trying to be kind, to be unselfish, in trying to be nonjudgmental, you allow evil to become far more powerful than it otherwise would. You refuse to see evil, and so you welcome it among you. You allow it to exist. You give it power over you. You are a people who have welcomed death and refused to denounce it.

"You are an empire naked to the shadow of evil."

* * *

After a moment of thick silence, one of the older men finally spoke up. "This belief in evil, as you call it, is a very intolerant attitude and is far too simplistic a judgment. It's nothing less than an unfair condemnation of your fellow man. None of us, not even you, can judge another."

Kahlan knew that Richard had a great deal of patience, but very little tolerance. He had been very patient with these men; she could see that he had reached the end of his tolerance. She half expected him to draw his sword.

He walked among the men, his raptor glare causing individuals to move back as he passed. "Your people think of themselves as enlightened, as above violence. You are not enlightened, you are merely slaves awaiting a master, victims awaiting killers. They have finally come for you."

Richard snatched up the small bag and stood before the last man who had spoken. "Open your hand."

The man glanced to those at his sides. Finally, he held his hand out, palm up.

Richard reached into the bag and then placed a small finger, its flesh withered and stained with dried blood, in the man's hand.

The man obviously didn't want the little finger sitting in the palm of his hand, but after he looked up into Richard's withering glower, he said nothing and made no attempt to rid himself of the gory trophy.

Richard walked among the men, ordering random men to open their hand. Kahlan recognized the ones he selected as men who had objected to the things he was trying to do to help them. He placed a finger in each upturned hand until the bag was empty.

"What you hold in your hand is the result of evil," Richard said. "You men all know the truth of it. You all knew evil was loose in your land. You all wanted that to change. You all wanted to be rid of evil. You all wanted to live. You all wanted your loved ones to live.

"You all had hoped to do it without having to face the truth.

"I have tried to explain things to you so that you could under-stand the true nature of the battle we all face."

Richard straightened the baldric over his shoulder.

"I am done explaining.

"You wanted me brought to your land. You have accomplished your goal. Now, you are going to decide if you will follow through with what you know to be right."

Richard again stood before them, his back straight, his chin held high, his scabbard gleaming in the gloomy light, his black tunic trimmed in gold standing out in sharp contrast against the fog-shrouded mountains behind him. He looked like nothing so much as the Lord Rahl. He was as commanding a figure as Kahlan had ever seen.

After Richard and Kahlan's beginning so long ago, when they had struck out from those secluded woods of his, Richard had turned the world upside down. From the beginning, he had always been at the heart of their struggle, and was now the ruler of an empire—even if that endangered empire was largely a mystery to him, as was his gift.

His cause, though, was crystal clear.

Together, Kahlan and Richard were at the center of the storm of a war that had engulfed their world. It had now engulfed these men and their land.

Many people saw Richard as their only salvation. Richard seemed forever trying to prove them wrong. For many others, though, he was the single most hated man alive. For them, Richard sought to give them cause; he told people that their life was their own. The Imperial Order wanted him dead for that more than for any blow he had dealt them.

"This is the way things are going to be," Richard finally said in a voice of quiet authority.

"You will surrender your land and your loyalty to the D'Haran Empire, or you will be the subjects of the Imperial Order. Those are your only two choices. There are no others. Like it or not, you must choose. If you refuse to make a choice, events will decide for you and you will likely end up in the hands of the Imperial Order. Make no mistake, they are evil hands.

"With the Order, if you are not murdered, you will be slaves and treated as such. I think you know very well what that entails. Your lives will have no value to them except as slaves, called upon to help them spread their evil.

"As part of the D'Haran Empire, your lives will be your own. I will expect you to rise up and live them as the individuals you are, not as some speck of dirt in a pit of filth you have dug yourselves into.

"The seal to your hiding place, to the Bandakaran Empire, has failed. I don't know how to repair it, nor would I if I could. There is no more Empire of Bandakar.

"There is no way to allow you to be who you were and to protect you. Maybe the Order can be thrown out of your land, but they cannot be effortlessly kept out, for it is their ideas that have come to destroy you.

"So choose. Slaves or free men. Life as either will not be easy. I think you know what life as slaves will be like. As free men you will have to struggle, work, and think, but you will have the rewards that brings, and those rewards will be yours and no one else's.

"Freedom must be won, but then it has to be guarded lest those like the Order come again to enslave those wishing for someone else to do their thinking.

"I am the Lord Rahl. I intend to go get the antidote to the poison you've given me. If you men choose to be part of this struggle, to rid yourselves and your loved ones of evil, then I will help you.

"If you choose not to stand with us, then you may go back and let the Order do with you what they will, or you can run. If you run, you may survive for a time, as you have been doing, but, because that is not the way you wish to live, you will die as frightened animals, never having lived what life has to offer.

"So choose, but if you choose to stand with me against evil, then you will have to relinquish your self-imposed blindness and open your eyes to look around at life. You will have to see the reality of the world around you. There is good and bad in the world. You will have to use your minds to judge which is which so that you can seek the good and reject the bad.

"If you choose to stand with me, I will do my best to answer any honest question and try to teach you how to triumph against the men of the Order and those like them. But I will not suffer your mindless teachings that are nothing more than a calculated rejection of life.

"Take a look at the bloody fingers you or your friends hold. Look at what was done to children by evil men. You should hate such men who would do this. If you don't, or can't, then you have no business being with those of us who embrace life.

"I want each of you to think about those children, about their terror, their pain, their wish not to be hurt. Think of what it was like for them to be alone and in the hands of evil men. You should rightfully hate the men who would do such things. Hold tight to that righteous hatred, for that is the hatred of evil.

"I intend to recover the antidote so that I can live. In the process, I also intend to kill as many of those evil men as I can. If I go alone, I may succeed in getting the antidote, but alone I will not succeed in liberating your homes from the Imperial Order.

"If you choose to go with me, to help me in this struggle, we may have a chance.

"I don't know what I face there, so I can't honestly tell you that we have a good chance. I can only tell you that if you don't help me, then there is likely to be no chance." Richard held up a finger. "Make no mistake. If you choose to join us and we take up this struggle, some of us will probably die. If we do not, all of us will die, not necessarily in body, but in spirit. Under such rule as the Order has shown you, no one lives, even though their body might for a time endure the misery of life as slaves. Under the Order, every soul withers and dies."

The men were silent as Richard paused to meet their gazes. Most could not look away, while some seemed shamed and so they stared at the ground.

"If you choose to side with me in this struggle," Richard said with deliberate care, "you will be called upon to kill men of the Order, evil men. If you once thought that I enjoyed killing, let me assure you that you are very wrong. I hate it. I do it to defend life. I would never expect you to relish killing. It is a necessity to do it, not to enjoy doing it. I expect you to relish life and do what is necessary to preserve it."

Richard picked up one of the items, lying off to the side, that they had made while waiting for Tom and Owen to bring the men up into the pass. It looked like little more than a stout stick. It was in fact made of oak limbs. It was rounded at the back to fit the hand, narrow at a point in the middle, and pointed at the other end.

"You men don't have weapons. While we waited for you to arrive, we've made some." He waggled his fingers, requesting Tom to come forward. "The men of the Order won't recognize these as weapons, at first, anyway. If questioned, you should tell them that they're used to make holes in the ground to plant crops."

With his left hand, Richard seized Tom's shirt at his shoulder, to hold him, and demonstrated the weapon's use by slowly showing how it would be thrust upward, toward a man's middle just under his ribs, to stab him. Some faces among the men twisted with revulsion.

"This can most easily be driven up into a man's soft part, up under his ribs," Richard told them. "Once you thrust it in, give it a quick sideways twist to break it off at the narrow point. That way, the man won't be able to pull it out. With such a thing lodged in his insides, if he can even stand, he won't want to be running after you or trying to wrestle you. You'll be better able to get away."

One of the men lifted a hand. "But a piece of wood like that will be wet and wouldn't break. Many of the wood fibers will just bend over, leaving the handle end attached."

Richard tossed the weapon to the man. After he caught it, he said, "Look at the middle, where it's cut to a narrow neck. You'll see that it's been held over a fire and dried for that very reason. Notice the pointed end, too. You'll see that it's been cut and split into four sections, with the points bent open, like a flower bud, so that as it's thrust into an enemy it has a good chance to break open, the four sides going in different directions to do more damage. With that one thrust, it will be like stabbing him four times.

"When you snap it off in him, he won't be able to fight you because every move he makes will wrench those long oak splinters through his vulnerable insides. If it doesn't hit something vital and kill him immediately, he's certainly likely to die within the day. While he's dying, he'll be screaming in agony and fear. I want such evil men to know that the pain and death they inflict on others will be coming for them. That fear will cause them to begin to think of running. It will make them lose sleep, wear them down, so that when we do get to them they'll be easier to kill."

Richard picked up another item. "This is a small crossbow." He held it high for the men to see as he pointed out its features. "As you can see, the bowstring is locked back on this nut. A stout bolt is laid in this groove, here. Pulling this lever rotates the nut, releasing the string and firing the bolt. It isn't fancy, and you men aren't experienced at using such weapons, but at close range you don't have to be all that good a shot.

"I've started a number of crossbows and have a whole pile of stocks and parts made. With the items that you men brought back, we can finish making them. They're rather crude and, as I said, they won't be good at much of a distance, but they are small and you can hide them under a cloak. No matter how big and strong the enemy is, the smallest of you can kill him. Not even his chain-mail armor will protect against such a weapon fired at close range. I can promise you that they will be very deadly."

Richard showed the men hardwood clubs they would stud with nails. Such weapons could also be concealed. He showed them a simple cord with a small wooden handle at each end that was used to strangle a man from behind when stealth was paramount.

"As we take these men, we'll be able to get other weapons—knives, axes, maces, swords."

"But, Lord Rahl," Owen said, looking beside himself with worry, "even if we were to agree to join you in this, we are not fighters. These men of the Order are brutes who are experienced at such things. We would stand no chance against them."

The others voiced their worried agreement. Richard shook his head as he held up his hands for them to be quiet.

"Look at those fingers you hold. Ask yourself what chance those little girls had against such men. Ask yourselves what chance your mothers, your sisters, your wives, your daughters have. You are the only hope for these people. You are the only hope for yourselves.

"Most likely, you men would not stand a chance against such men, either. But I have no intention of fighting them as you're thinking. That's a good way to get killed." Richard pointed at one of the younger men. "What is it we want? The reason you came to get me?"

The man looked confused. "To get rid of the men of the Order?"

"Yes," Richard said. "That's right. You want to be rid of murderers. The last thing you want is to fight them."

The man gestured at the weapons Richard had shown them. "But these things . . ."

"These men are murderers. Our task is to execute them. We want to avoid fights. If we fight them, we risk being hurt or killed. I am not saying that we won't have to fight them, but that isn't our goal. There will be times when there may be limited numbers of them and we can be sure that with surprise we can take them out before a fight has a chance to erupt. Keep in mind that these men have been conditioned to none of your people putting up any resistance. We hope to kill them before it occurs to them to draw a weapon.

"But if we don't have to face them, all the better. Our goal is to kill them. To kill every one of them we can. Kill them when they sleep, when they are looking the other way, when they are eating, when they are talking, when they are drinking, when they are out for a stroll.

"They are evil. We must kill them, not fight them."

Owen threw up his hands. "But, Lord Rahl, if we were to start killing them, they would take revenge on all the people they have."

Richard watched the men, waiting until he was sure everyone was paying attention.

"You have just recognized the reality that they are evil. You're right, they will probably start killing captives as a way to convince you to surrender. But they are killing them now. Over time, if left to do as they will, the killing they do will be on a vast scale. The faster we kill them, the sooner it's over and the sooner the murder will stop. Some people will lose their lives because of what we do, but in doing it, we will free all the rest. If we do nothing, then we condemn those innocent people to the mercy of evil and evil grants no mercy. As I've said before, you can't negotiate with evil. You must destroy it."

A man cleared his throat. "Lord Rahl, some of our people have sided with the men of the Order—believed their words. They will not want us to harm the men of the Order."

Richard let out a heavy breath. He looked away for a moment, gazing off into the gloom, before turning his attention once more to the men. "I've had to kill people I knew my whole life because they sided with the Order, much the same as you are saying. They came to believe the men of the Imperial Order and, because I was opposed to the Order, they tried to kill me. It's a terrible thing to have to kill someone like that, someone you know. I believe the alternative is worse."

"The alternative?" the man asked.

"Yes, letting them murder me. That's the alternative: losing your life and losing the cause for which you fight—the lives of your loved ones." Richard's expression had turned grave. "If some of your people have joined with the Order, or work to protect them, then it may be that you could end up facing them. It will be their life, or yours. It could even mean the lives of the rest of us. If they side with evil, then we must not allow them to stop us from eliminating evil.

"This is part of what you must weigh in your decision to join us or not. If you take up this struggle, you must accept that you may have to kill people you know. You must weigh this in the choice you will make."

The men no longer seemed shocked by his words. They looked solemn as they listened.

Kahlan saw small birds flitting past, looking to roost for the night. The sky, the icy fog, was getting darker. She scanned the sky, ever watchful for black-tipped races. With the weather in the pass so dreadful, she doubted they would be around. The fog, at least, was comforting for that reason.

Richard looked exhausted. She knew how hard it was for her to breathe in the high, thin air, so it had to be far worse for him; she feared how, because of the poison, the thin air robbed Richard of his strength. They needed to be down out of the high pass.

"I have told you the truth and all I can for now," Richard told the men. "Your future is now up to each of you."

He quietly asked Cara, Jennsen, and Tom to collect their things. He put a gentle hand on Kahlan's back as he turned to the men and gestured down the hill.

"We're going back down to our camp in those woods. You men decide what you will do. If you are with us, then come down there in the protection of the trees, where the races won't be able to spot us when the weather lifts. We will need to finish making the weapons you will carry.

"If any of you choose not to join us, then you're on your own. I plan not to be here, at this camp, for long. If the Order captures you they will likely torture you and I don't want to be anywhere nearby when you scream your lungs out as you reveal where our camp was."

The forlorn men stood huddled in a group.

"Lord Rahl," Owen asked, "you mean we must choose now?"

"I've told you all I can. How much longer can those being tortured, raped, and murdered wait for you? If you wish to join us and be part of life, then come down to our camp. If you choose not to be on our side, then I wish you luck. But please don't try to follow us or I'll have to kill you. I was once a woods guide; I will know if any of you follow us."

One of the men, the one who had been the first to show Richard two pebbles to say that he would reveal the location of the antidote, stepped forward, away from the rest of the men.

"Lord Rahl, my name is Anson." Tears filled his blue eyes. "I wanted you to know that, to know who I am. I am Anson."

Richard nodded. "All right, Anson."

"Thank you for opening my eyes. I've always had some of the thoughts that you explained. Now I understand why, and I understand the darkness kept over my eyes. I don't want to live like that anymore. I don't want to live by words that don't mean anything and I don't want the men of the Order to control my life.

"My parents were murdered. I saw my father's body hanging from a pole. He never hurt anyone. He did nothing to deserve such a murder. My sister was taken. I know what those men are doing to her. I can't sleep at night thinking about it, thinking about her terror.

"I want to fight back. I want to kill these evil men. They've earned death. I want to grind them into dust, as you have said.

"I choose to join with you and fight to gain my freedom. I want to live free. I want those I love to live free."

Kahlan was stunned to hear one of them say such things, especially without first consulting with the rest of the men. She had watched the eyes of the other men as Anson spoke. They all listened keenly to everything Anson said.

Richard smiled as he placed a hand on the young man's shoulder. "Welcome to D'Hara, Anson. Welcome home. We can use your help." He pointed off at Cara and Tom picking up the weapons they'd brought to show the men. "Why don't you help them take those things back down to our camp."

Anson grinned his agreement. The soft-spoken young man had broad shoulders and a thickly muscled neck. He was genial, but looked determined. If she were in the Imperial Order, Kahlan would not want to see such a powerfully-built man coming after her.

Anson eagerly tried to take the load from Cara's arms. She wouldn't relinquish it, so he picked up the rest of the things and followed Tom down the hill. Jennsen went along, too, pulling Betty behind by her rope, tugging for the first few steps because Betty wanted them to stay with Richard and Kahlan.

The other men watched as Anson started down the hill with Cara, Tom and Jennsen. They then moved off to the side, away from the statue, while they whispered among themselves, deciding what they would do.

Richard glanced at the figure of Kaja-Rang before starting down the hill. Something seemed to catch his eye.

"What's the matter?" Kahlan asked.

Richard pointed. "That writing. On the face of the pedestal, below his feet."

Kahlan knew there had been no writing in that spot before, and she was still too far away to really tell if she could see writing in the flecked granite. She glanced back to see the others making their way down the hill, but instead followed Richard when he started toward the statue. The men were still off to the side, busily engaged in their discussion.

She could see the spot on the face of the pedestal where the warning beacon had shattered. The sand from inside the statue representing Richard was still splattered across the face of the pedestal.

As they got closer, she could hardly believe what she was beginning to see. It looked as if the sand had eroded the stone to reveal lettering. The words had not been there before, that much she was sure of.

Kahlan knew a number of languages, but she didn't know this one. She recognized it, though. It was High D'Haran.

She hugged her arms around herself in the chill wind that had come up. The somber clouds stirred restlessly. She peered around at the imposing mountains, many hidden by a dark shroud of fog. Swirling curtains of snow obscured other slopes in the distance. Through a small, brief opening in the wretched weather, the valley she could see off through the pass offered the promise of green and warmth.

And the Imperial Order.

Kahlan, close beside Richard, wished he would put a warm arm around her. She watched as he stared at the faint letters in the stone. He was being far too quiet for her peace of mind.

"Richard," she whispered, leaning close to him, "what does it say?"

Transfixed, he ran his fingers slowly, lightly over the letters, his lips soundlessly pronouncing the High D'Haran words.

"Wizard's Eighth Rule," Richard whispered in translation. "Talga Vassternich."

CHAPTER 46

Following behind the messenger, Verna stepped aside as a tight pack of horses raced by. Their bellies were caked with mud, their nostrils flared with excitement. The eyes of the cavalry soldiers bent over their withers showed grim determination. With the constant level of activity of recent weeks, she had to maintain a careful vigil whenever she stepped out of a tent lest she be mowed down by one thing or another. If it wasn't horses charging through the camp, it was men at a run.

"Just up ahead," the messenger said over his shoulder.

Verna nodded to his young face as he glanced back. He was a polite young man. His curly blond hair and his mannerly behavior combined to remind her of Warren. She was defenseless against the wave of pain that cut through her with the memory of Warren being gone, at the emptiness of each day.

She couldn't remember this messenger's name. There were so many young men; it was hard to recall all their names. Though she tried her best, she couldn't keep track of them. At least for a while now they hadn't been dying at a terrifying rate. As harsh as the winters were up in D'Hara, such weather had at least been a respite from the battles of the previous summer, from the constant fighting and dying. With summer again upon them, she didn't think that the relative quiet was going to last much longer.

For now the passes held against the Imperial Order. In such narrow and confined places, the enemy's weight of numbers didn't mean so much. If only one man would fit through a narrow hole in a stone wall, it meant little that there were a hundred waiting behind him to go through, or a thousand. Defending against one man, as it were, was not the impossible task that it was trying to fight the onslaught of Jagang's entire force.

When she heard the distant thunder, felt it rolling through the ground, she glanced up at the sky. The sun had not made an appearance in two days. She didn't like the look of the clouds building against the slopes of the mountains. It appeared that they could be in for a nasty storm.

The sound might not have been thunder. It was possible that it was magic the enemy hammered against the shields across the passes. Such battering would do them no good, but it made for uneasy sleeping, so, if for no other reason, they kept at it.

Some of the men and the officers passing in the other direction gave her a nod in greeting, or a smile, or a small wave. Verna didn't see any Sisters of the Light. Many would be at the passes, tending shields, making sure none of the Imperial Order soldiers could get through. Zedd had taught them to consider every possibility, no matter how outlandish, and guard against it. Day and night Verna ran every one of those places through her mind, trying to think if there was anything they had overlooked, anything they had missed, that might allow the enemy forces to flood in upon them.

If that happened, if they broke through, then there was nothing to stop their advance into D'Hara except the defending army, and the defending army was no match for the numbers on the other side of those mountains. She couldn't think of any chink in their armor, but she worried constantly that there might be one.

It seemed that the final battle might be on them at any moment. And where was Richard?

Prophecy said that he was vital in the battle to decide the future course of mankind. With it appearing that they very well could be one battle from the end of it all, of freedom's final spark, the Lord Rahl ran the very real risk of missing the moment of his greatest need. She could hardly believe that for centuries prophecy had foretold of the one who would lead them, and when the time finally arrived, he was off somewhere else. Lot of good prophecy was doing them.

Verna knew Richard's heart. She knew Kahlan's heart. It wasn't right to doubt either of them, but Verna was the one staring into the eyes of Jagang's horde and Richard was nowhere to be found.

From what little information Verna had gleaned from Ann's messages in the journey book, there was trouble afoot. Verna could detect in Ann's writings that she was greatly troubled by something. Whatever the cause, Ann and Nathan were racing south, back down through the Old World. Ann avoided explaining, possibly not wanting to burden them with anything else, so Verna didn't press. She had enough trouble conceiving of why Ann would have joined with the prophet rather than collaring him. Ann said only that a journey book was not a good place to explain such things.

Despite the good work the man sometimes did, Verna considered Nathan dangerous in the extreme. A thunderstorm brought life-giving rain, but if you were the one struck by its lightning, it didn't do you much good. For Ann and Nathan to join forces, as it were, must be indicative of the trouble they were all in.

Verna had to remind herself that not everything was going against them, not everything was hopeless and dismal. Jagang's army had, after all, suffered a stunning blow at the hands of Zedd and Adie, losing staggering numbers of soldiers in an instant and suffering vast numbers of casualties. As a result the Imperial Order had turned away from Aydindril, leaving the Wizard's Keep untouched. Despite the dream walker's covetous hands, the Keep remained out of his reach.

Zedd and Adie had the defense of the Keep well in hand, so it was not all trouble and strife; there were valuable assets on the side of the D'Haran Empire. The Keep might yet prove decisive in helping to stop the Imperial Order. Verna missed that old wizard, his advice, his wisdom, though she would never admit it aloud. In that old man she could see where Richard got many of his best qualities.

Verna halted when she saw Rikka striding across in front of her. Verna snatched the Mord-Sith's arm.

"What is it, Prelate?" Rikka asked.

"Have you heard what this is about?"

Rikka gave her a blank look. "What what's about?"

The messenger stopped on the other side of the intersection of informal roads. Horses trotted past in both directions, one pulling a cart of water barrels. Fully-armed men crossed on the side road. The encampment, one of several, surrounded by a defensive berm, had evolved into a city of sorts, with byways through its midst for men, horses, and wagons.

"Something is going on," Verna said.

"Sorry, I haven't heard anything."

"Are you busy?"

"Nothing urgent."

Verna took a good grip on Rikka's arm and started her walking. "General Meiffert sent for me. Maybe you'd best come along. That way if he wants you, too, we won't have to send someone looking for you."

Rikka shrugged. "Fine by me." The Mord-Sith's expression turned suspicious. "Do you have any idea what's wrong?"

Verna kept an eye on the messenger ahead of her weaving his way among men, tents, wagons, horses, and repair stations, then glanced over at Rikka. "Nothing that I know of." Verna's expression contorted a bit as she tried to put her queasy mood into words. "Did you ever wake up and just feel like there was something wrong, but you couldn't explain why it seems it's going to be a bad day?"

"If it's to be a bad day, I see to it that it's someone else's, and I'm the cause of it."

Verna smiled to herself. "Too bad you're not gifted. You would make a good Sister of the Light."

"I would rather be Mord-Sith and be able to protect Lord Rahl."

The messenger stopped at the side of the camp road. "Back there, Prelate. General Meiffert said to bring you to that tent by the trees."

Verna thanked the young man and made her way across the soft ground, Rikka at her side. The tent was away from the main activity of the camp, in a quieter area where officers often met with scouts just back from patrols. Verna's mind raced, trying to imagine what news scouts could have brought back. There was no alarm, so the passes still held. If there was trouble, there would be a flurry of activity in the camp, but it seemed about the same as any other day.

Guards saw Verna coming and ducked into the tent to announce her arrival. Almost immediately, the general stepped out of the tent and rushed to meet her. His blue eyes reflected iron determination. The man's face, though, was ashen.

"I saw Rikka," Verna explained as General Meiffert dipped his head in a hurried greeting. "I thought I ought to bring her just in case you needed her, too."

The tall, blond-headed D'Haran glanced briefly at Rikka. "Yes, that's fine. Come in, please, both of you."

Verna snatched his sleeve. "What's this about? What's going on? Is something wrong?"

The general's gaze moved to Rikka and back to Verna. "We've had a message from Jagang."

Rikka leaned in, her voice taking on an edge. "How did a messenger from Jagang get through without someone killing him?"

It was standard practice that no one came through for any reason. They didn't want so much as a mouse making it through. There was no telling if it might be some kind of trick.

"It was a small wagon, pulled by a single horse." He tilted his head toward Verna. "The men thought the wagon was empty. Remembering your instructions, they let it through."

Verna was somewhat surprised that Ann's warning to let an empty wagon through had been so correct. "A wagon came of its own accord? An empty wagon drove itself in?"

"Not exactly. The men who saw it thought it was empty. The horse appears to be a workhorse that is used to walking roads, so it plodded along the road as it had been trained." General Meiffert pressed his lips together at the confusion on Verna's face and then turned away from the tent. "Come on, and I'll show you."

He led them to the third tent down the line and held the flap aside. Verna ducked in, followed by Rikka and the general. On a bench inside sat a young novice, Holly, with her arm around a very frightened-looking girl no more than ten years old.

"I asked Holly to stay with her," General Meiffert whispered. "I thought it might make her less nervous than a soldier standing over her."

"Of course," Verna said. "Very wise of you. She's the one who brought the message, then?"

The young general nodded. "She was sitting in the back of the wagon, so the men seeing it coming at first thought it was empty."

Verna now understood why such a messenger got through. Soldiers weren't nearly so likely to kill a child, and the Sisters could test her to insure she was no threat. Verna wondered if Zedd would have something to say about that; threat often came in surprising packages. Verna approached the pair on the bench, smiling as she bent down.

"I'm Verna. Are you all right, young lady?"

The girl nodded.

"Would you like something to eat?"

Trembling slightly as her big brown eyes took in the people looking at her, she nodded again.

"Prelate," Holly said, "Valery already went to get her something."

"I see," Verna said, holding the smile in place. She knelt down and gently patted the girl's hands in her lap to reassure her. "Do you live around here?"

The girl's big brown eyes blinked, trying to judge the danger of the adult before her. She calmed just a little at Verna's smile, and kind touch. "A bit of travel to the north, ma'am."

"And someone sent you to see us?"

The big brown eyes filled with tears, but she didn't cry. "My parents are back there, down over the pass. The soldiers there have them. As guests, they said. Men came and took us to their army. We've had to stay there for the last few weeks. Today they told me to take a letter over the pass to the people here. They said that if I did as I was told, they would let my mother and father and me go home."

Verna again patted the girl's small hands. "I see. Well, that's good of you to help your parents."

"I just want to go home."

"And you shall, child." Verna straightened. "We'll get you some food, dear, so you have a full tummy before you go back to your parents."

The girl stood and curtsied. "Thank you for your kindness. May I go back after I eat, then?"

"Certainly," Verna said. "I'll just go read the letter you brought while you have a nice meal, and then you can return to your parents."

As she sat back up on the bench, squirming her bottom back beside Holly, she couldn't help keeping a wary eye on the Mord-Sith.

Trying not to show any apprehension, Verna smiled her goodbye to the girl before leading the others out of the tent. She couldn't even imagine what Jagang was up to.

"What's in the letter?" Verna asked as they hurried to the command tent.

General Meiffert paused outside the tent, his thumb burnishing a brass button on his coat as he met Verna's gaze. "I'd just as soon you read it for yourself, Prelate. Some of it is plain enough. Some of it, well, some if it I'm hoping you can explain to me."

Stepping into the tent, Verna saw Captain Zimmer waiting off to the side. The square-jawed man no longer had his usual infectious smile. The captain was in charge of the D'Haran special forces, a group of men whose job it was to go out and spend their days and nights sneaking around in hostile territory, killing as many of the enemy as possible. There seemed to be an endless supply. The captain seemed determined to use up the supply.

The men in Captain Zimmer's corps were very good at what they did. They collected strings of ears they took from the enemy they killed. Kahlan used to always ask to see their collection whenever they returned. The captain and his men dearly missed her.

They all glanced up at a flash of lightning. The storm was getting closer. After a moment's pause, the ground shook with the rolling rumble of thunder.

General Meiffert retrieved a small folded paper from the table and handed it to Verna.

"This is what the girl brought."

Looking briefly at the two men's grim expressions, Verna unfolded the paper and read the neat script.

I have Wizard Zorander and a sorceress named Adie. I now hold the Wizard's Keep in Aydindril and all it contains. My Slide will soon present me with Lord Rahl and the Mother Confessor.

Your cause is lost. If you surrender now and open the passes, I will spare your men. If you do not, I will put every one of them to death.

Signed, Jagang the Just.

The arm holding the paper in her trembling fingers lowered. "Dear Creator," Verna whispered. She felt dizzy.

Rikka snatched the paper from her hand and stood facing away as she read it. She cursed under her breath.

"We have to go get him," Rikka said. "We have to get Zedd and Adie away from Jagang."

Captain Zimmer shook his head. "There is no way we could accomplish such a thing."

Rikka's face went red with rage. "He's saved my life before! Yours too! We have to get him out of there!"

In contrast to Rikka's anger, Verna spoke softly. "We all feel the same about him. Zedd has probably saved all of our lives more than once. Unfortunately, Jagang will do all the worse to him for it."

Rikka shook the message before their faces. "So we are just going to let him die there? Let Jagang kill him? We sneak in, or something!"

Captain Zimmer rested the heel of his hand on a long knife at his belt. "Mistress Rikka, if I told you that I had a man hidden somewhere in this camp, in one of the hundreds of thousands of tents, and no one would bother you or ask you any questions, but would allow you to freely go about a search, how long do you think it would take you to find such a hidden man?"

"But they won't be in just any tent," Rikka said. "Look at us, here. This message came. Did it go to just any random tent in the whole camp? No, it went to a place where such things are handled."

"I've been to the Imperial Order encampment too many times to count," Captain Zimmer said as he cast his arm out toward the enemy over the mountains to the west. "You can't even imagine how big their camp is. They have millions of men there.

"Their encampment is a quagmire of cutthroats. It's a place of chaos. That disorder allows us to slip in, kill some of them, and get out fast. You don't want to be there very long. They recognize outsiders, especially blond outsiders.

"Moreover, there are layers of different kinds of men. Most of the soldiers are little more than a mob of thugs that Jagang turns loose from time to time. None of them are allowed beyond a certain point within their own camp. The men guarding the areas with higher security are not nearly so stupid and lazy as the common soldiers.

"The men in those protected areas aren't as numerous as the common soldiers, but they are trained professionals. They are alert, vigilant, and deadly. If you could somehow manage to get through the sea of misfits to reach the island at the core where the torture and command tents are, those professional soldiers would have you on the end of a pike in no time.

"Even they are not all the same. The outer ring of this core, besides having these professionals guarding it, is where the Sisters are. They both live there and use magic to watch for intruders. Beyond them are further rings, starting with the elite guards, and then, finally, the emperor's personal guards. These are men who have been fighting with Jagang for years. They kill anyone, even the elite guard officers, if they become at all suspicious of them. If they even hear word of someone saying disparaging things about the emperor, they hunt them down and have them tortured. After being tortured, if they live through it, they are then put to death.

"I'm not saying that my men and I would be unwilling to risk our lives trying to get Zedd out of there; I'm saying that we would be giving our lives up for nothing."

The mood in the tent could not have been more hopeless.

The general gestured with the paper when Rikka handed it back. "Any idea what a Slide is, Prelate?"

Verna met his blue-eyed gaze. "A soul stealer."

The general frowned. "A what?"

"In the great war—three thousand years ago—the wizards of that time created weapons out of people. Dream walkers, like Jagang, were one such weapon. The best way I can explain it to you is that a Slide is in some ways like a dream walker. A dream walker can enter a person's mind and seize control of them. A Slide, I believe, is something like that, only he seizes your spirit, your soul."

Rikka made a face. "Why?"

Verna lifted her hands in frustration. "I don't really know. To control their victim, perhaps.

"Altering gifted people was an ancient practice. They sometimes changed gifted people with magic to suit a specific purpose. With Subtractive Magic they took away traits they didn't want, and then they used Additive Magic to add to or enhance a trait they did want. What they created were monsters.

"I'm not really well versed in the subject. When I became Prelate I had access to books I had never seen before. That's where I saw the reference to Slides. They were used to slip into another person's being and steal the essence of who they were—their spirit, their soul.

"Altering people in such a way as to create these Slides is a long-dead art. I'm afraid that I don't know a great deal about the subject. I do remember reading that the ones called Slides were exceedingly dangerous."

"Long-dead art," the general muttered. He looked as if he was making a great effort to restrain himself. "The wizards of that time made such weapons as Slides, but how could Jagang? He's no wizard. Could it be that he's lying?"

Verna thought about the question for a moment. "He has gifted people under his direct control. Some are able to use underworld magic. As I said, I don't know a great deal about it, but I suppose it's possible that he was able to do it."

"How?" the general demanded. "How could Jagang do such things? He's not even a wizard."

Verna clasped her hands before herself. "He has Sisters of the Light and the Dark. In theory, I suppose he has what he needs. He is a man who studies history. I know from personal experience that he puts great value in books. He has an extensive and quite valuable collection. Nathan, the prophet, was very concerned about this very thing, and destroyed a number of important volumes before they could fall into Jagang's possession.

"Still, the emperor possesses a great many others—in fact, he has a huge collection. Now that he has captured the Keep, he has access to important libraries. Those books are dangerous, or they wouldn't have been sealed away in the Wizard's Keep in the first place."

"And now Jagang has control of them." General Meiffert ran his fingers back through his hair. He gripped the back of the chair set before the small table and leaned his weight on his arms. "Do you think he really has Zedd and Adie?"

The question was a plea for some thread of hope. Verna swallowed as she carefully considered the question. She answered in an honest voice, not wanting to be the founder of a false faith. Since she'd read the message from Jagang, she had been searching for that same thread of hope. "I don't think he's a man who would find any satisfaction in bragging about something he hadn't actually accomplished. I think he must be telling us the truth and wants to gloat over his accomplishment."

The general released his grip on the chair and turned as he considered Verna's words. Finally, he asked a question worse yet.

"Do you think he's telling the truth that this Slide has Lord Rahl and the Mother Confessor? Do you think this terrible creation, this Slide, will soon deliver the two of them to Jagang?"

Verna wondered if this was the reason for Ann and Nathan's headlong rush down through the Old World. Verna knew that Richard and Kahlan were down there, somewhere. There could be no more urgent reason for Ann and Nathan to race south. Was it possible that this Slide had already captured them, or captured their souls? Verna's heart sank. She wondered if Ann already knew that the Slide had Richard, and that was why she wasn't saying much about her mission.

"I don't know," Verna finally answered.

"I think Jagang just made a mistake," Captain Zimmer said.

Verna lifted an eyebrow. "Such as?"

"He has just betrayed to us how much trouble he's having with the passes. He's just told us how well our defenses are working and how desperate he is. If he doesn't get through this season, his whole army will have to sit out another winter. He wants us to let him through.

"D'Haran winters are hard, especially on men such as his, men not used to the conditions. I saw with my own eyes good indications of how many men he lost last winter. Hundreds of thousands of men died from disease."

"He has plenty of men," General Meiffert said. "He can afford the losses. He has a steady supply of new troops to replace the ones who died from the fevers and sickness last winter."

"So, you think the captain is wrong?" Verna asked.

"No, I agree that Jagang would like very much to get it over with, I just don't think he cares how many of his men die. I think he's eager to rule the world. Patient as he generally is, he sees the end at hand, the goal within his grasp. We're the only thing standing in his way, keeping his prize from falling to him. His men, too, are impatient for the plunder.

"His choice to split the New World first by driving up to Aydindril has left him close to his goal, but in some ways, even more distant from it. If he can't make it through the passes, he may decide to pick up his army and make a long march back south again, to the Kern River valley, to where he can then come over and up into D'Hara. Once his army takes to the open ground down south, there's no way for us to stop them.

"If he can't break through the passes now, it means a long march and a long delay, but he will still have us in the end. He would rather have us now and is willing to offer the lives of our men to close a deal."

Verna stared off. "It's a grave mistake to try to appease evil."

"I agree," General Meiffert said. "Once we opened the passes, he would slaughter every last man."

The mood in the tent was as gloomy as the sky outside.

"I think we should send him back a letter," Rikka said. "I think we should tell him that we don't believe him that he has Zedd and Adie. If he expects us to believe him, he should prove it; he should send us their heads."

Captain Zimmer smiled at the suggestion.

The general tapped a finger on the table as he thought it over. "If it's as you say, Prelate, and Jagang really does have them, then there's nothing we can do about it. He will kill them. After what Zedd did to Jagang's force back in Aydindril, to say nothing of all the havoc he caused the Imperial Order last summer when the Mother Confessor was with us, I know it won't be an easy death, but he will kill them in the end."

"Then you agree that nothing else can be done," Verna said.

General Meiffert wiped a hand across his face. "I hate admitting it, but I'm afraid they're lost. I don't think we should give Jagang the satisfaction of knowing how we truly feel about it."

Verna's head spun at the thought of Zedd and Adie being put to torture, of them being in the hands of Jagang and his Sisters of the Dark. She quailed at the thought of the D'Haran forces losing Zedd. There simply was no one else with his experience and knowledge. There was no one who could replace him.

"We write Jagang a letter, then," Verna said, "and tell Jagang we don't believe he has Zedd and Adie."

"The only thing we can do," Rikka said, "is to deny Jagang what he wants most. What he wants is for us to give up."

General Meiffert pulled out the chair at the table, inviting Verna to sit and write the letter. "If Jagang is angered by such a letter, he just might send us their heads. If he did, that would spare them terrible suffering. That's the only thing we can do for them—the best we could do for them."

Verna took stock of the grim faces and saw only resolve at what had to be done. She sat in the chair the general held for her, wiggled the stopper out of the ink bottle, and then took a piece of paper from a small stack in a box to the side.

She dipped the pen and stared at the paper for a moment, trying to decide how to phrase the letter. She tried to imagine what Kahlan would write. As it came to her, she bent over the table and began writing.

I don't believe you are competent enough to capture Wizard Zorander. If you were, you would send us his head to prove it. Don't bother me anymore with your whining for us to open the passes for you because you are too inept to do it yourself.

Reading over Verna's shoulder, Rikka said, "I like it."

Verna looked up at the others. "How should I sign it?"

"What would make Jagang the most angry—or worried?" Captain Zimmer asked.

Verna tapped the back of the pen against her chin as she thought. Then it came to her. She put pen to paper.

Signed, the Mother Confessor.

CHAPTER 47

Richard scanned the site off in the broad, green valley, watching for any sign of troops. He looked over at Owen.

"That's Witherton?"

Hands pressed against the rich forest floor at the crown of a low ridge, Owen pulled himself closer to the edge. He stretched his neck to see over the rise and finally nodded before pulling back.

Richard had thought it would be bigger. "I don't see any soldiers."

Owen crawled back away from the edge. In the shadowed cover among ferns and low scrub, he stood and brushed the moist crumbles of leaves from his shirt and trousers. "The men of the Order mostly stay inside the town. They have no interest in helping to do the work. They eat our food and gamble with the things they have taken from our people. When they do these things they are interested in little else." His face heated to red. "At night, they used to collect some of our women." Since the reason was obvious enough, Owen didn't put words to it. "In the daytime they sometimes come out to check on our people who work in the fields, or watch to see that they come back in at night."

If the soldiers had once camped outside the city walls, they no longer did. Apparently, they preferred the more comfortable accommodations within the town. They had learned that these people would offer no resistance; they could be cowed and controlled by words alone. The men of the Imperial Order were safe sleeping among them.

The wall around Witherton blocked much of Richard's view of the place. Other than through the open gates, there wasn't much to see. The wall was constructed of upright posts not a great deal taller than the height of a man. The posts, a variety of sizes no bigger around than a hand's width, were bound tightly together, top and bottom, with rope. The wavy wall snaked around the town and leaned in or out in places. There was no bulwark, or even a trench before the wall. Other than keeping out grazing deer or maybe a roaming bear, the walls certainly didn't look strong enough to withstand an attack from the Imperial Order soldiers.

The soldiers had no doubt made a point of using the gate into the town for reasons other than the strength of the wall. Opening the gates for soldiers of the Imperial Order had been a symbolic sign of submission.

Broad swaths of the valley were clear of trees, leaving fields of grain to grow alongside row crops in communal gardens. Tree limbs knitted into fencing kept in cows. There, the wild grasses were chewed low. Chickens roamed freely near coops. A few sheep grazed on the coarse grass.

The smells of rich soil, wildflowers, and grasses carried on a light breeze into the woods where Richard watched. It was a great relief to have finally descended from the pass. It had been getting difficult to breathe in the thin air up on the high slopes. It was considerably warmer, too, down out of the lofty mountain pass, although he still felt cold.

Richard checked the sweep of open valley one last time and then he and Owen made their way back into the dense tangle of woods toward where the others waited. The trees were mostly hardwoods, maple and oak, along with patches of birch, but there were also stands of towering evergreens. Birds chirped from the dense foliage. A squirrel up on the limb of a pine chattered at them as they passed. The deep shade below the thick forest crown was interrupted only occasionally by mottled sunlight.

Some of the men, swatting at bugs, stood in a rush when Richard led Owen into the secluded forest opening. Richard was glad to stand in the warmth of sunlight slanting in at a low angle.

It appeared that the open area in the dense woods had been created when a huge old maple had been hit by lightning. The maple split and fell in two directions, taking other trees down with it. Kahlan hopped down off her seat on the trunk of the fallen monarch. Betty, her tail wagging in a blur, greeted Richard eagerly looking for attention, or a treat. Richard scratched behind her ears, the goat's favorite form of attention.

More of the men came into the open from behind upturned roots that had become silvered by years of exposure to the elements. A crop of spruce, none more than chest high, had sprung up in the sunny spot created when the old maple had died such a sudden and violent death. Dotted between Kahlan, Cara, Jennsen and Tom were the rest of the men—his army.

Back up in the pass, Anson saying that he wanted to help rid his people of the Imperial Order soldiers seemed to have galvanized the rest of the men, and the balance had finally tipped. Once it had, a lifetime of darkness and doubt gave way to a hunger to live in the light of truth. The men all declared, in a breathtaking moment of determination, that they wanted to join with Richard to be part of the D'Haran Empire and fight the soldiers of the Imperial Order to gain their freedom.

They had all decided that the men of the Order were evil and deserved death, even if they themselves had to do the killing.

When Tom glanced down to see Betty going back to browsing on weeds, Richard noticed that the man's brow was beaded with sweat. Cara fanned herself with a handful of big leaves from a mountain maple. Richard was about to ask them how they could be sweating when it was such a cool day, when he realized that it was the poison making him cold. With icy dread, he recalled how the last time he had gotten cold, the poison had nearly killed him that awful night.

Anson and another man, John, took off their packs. They were the ones planning to slip in among the field-workers returning to town at nightfall. Once they sneaked into town, the two men planned to recover the antidote.

"I think I'd better go with you," Richard said to Anson. "John, why don't you wait here with the others."

John looked surprised. "If you wish, Lord Rahl, but there is no need for you to go."

It wasn't supposed to be a foray that would result in any violence, only the recovery of the antidote. The attack on the Imperial Order soldiers was to be after the antidote had been safely recovered and they had assessed the situation, the number of men, and the layout.

"John is right," Cara said. "They can do it."

Richard was having difficulty breathing. He had to make an effort not to cough. "I know. I just think I had better have a look myself."

Cara and Kahlan cast a sidelong glance at each other.

"But if you go in there with Anson," Jennsen said, "you can't take your sword."

"I'm not going to start a war. I just want to get a good look around the place."

Kahlan stepped closer. "The two of them can scout the town and give you a report. You can rest—they will only be gone a few hours."

"I know, but I don't think I want to wait that long."

By the way she appraised his eyes, he thought she must be able to see how much pain he was in. She didn't argue the point further but instead nodded her agreement.

Richard pulled the baldric and sword-belt off over his head. He slipped it all over Kahlan's head, laying the baldric across her shoulder.

"Here. I pronounce you Seeker of Truth."

She accepted the sword and the honor by planting her fists on her hips. "Now don't you go starting anything while you're in there. That's not the plan. You and Anson will be alone. You wait until we're all together."

"I know. I just need to get the antidote and then we'll be back in no time."

Besides getting the antidote, Richard wanted to see how the enemy forces were placed, and the layout of the town. Having the men draw a map in the dirt was one thing, seeing it for himself was another; these men didn't know how to evaluate threat points.

One of the men took off his light coat, something a number of the men wore, and held it out to Richard. "Here, Lord Rahl, wear this. It will make you look more like one of us."

With a nod of thanks, Richard drew the coat on. He had changed out of his war wizard's outfit into traveling clothes, so he didn't think he would look out of place with the way the men from the town of Witherton looked. The man was nearly Richard's size, so the coat fit well enough. It also hid his belt knife.

Jennsen shook her head. "I don't know, Richard. You just don't look like one of them. You still look like Lord Rahl."

"What are you talking about?" Richard held out his arms, looking down at himself. "What's wrong with the way I look?"

"Don't stand up so straight," she said.

"Hunch your shoulders and hang your head a little," Kahlan offered.

Richard took their advice seriously; he hadn't thought about it, but the men did tend to hunch a lot. He didn't want to stand out. He had to blend in if he didn't want to raise the suspicions of the soldiers. He bent over a little.

"How's that?"

Jennsen screwed up her mouth. "Not much different."

"But I'm bending down."

"Lord Rahl," Cara said in a soft voice as she gave him a meaningful look, "you remember how it was to walk behind Denna, when she held the chain to the collar around your neck. Make yourself like that."

Richard blinked at her. The mental image of his time as a captive of a Mord-Sith hit him like a slap. He pressed his lips tight, not saying anything, and conceded with a single nod. The memory of that forsaken time was depressing enough that he would have no trouble using it to fall into the role.

"We had better be on our way," Anson said. "Now that the sun is falling behind the mountains, darkness comes quickly." He hesitated, then spoke again. "Lord Rahl, the men of the Order will not know you—I mean they probably will not realize you aren't from our town. But our people do not carry weapons; if they see that knife, they will know you are not from our town, and they will send up an alarm."

Richard lifted open the coat, looking at the knife. "You're right." He loosened his belt and removed the sheath holding the knife. He handed it to Cara for safe-keeping.

Richard cupped a hand quickly to the side of Kahlan's face as a way of saying his good-bye. She seized the hand in both of hers and pressed a quick kiss to the backs of his fingers. Her hands looked so small and delicate holding his. He sometimes kidded her that he didn't see how she could possibly get anything done with such small hands. Her answer was that her hands were a normal size and perfectly adequate, and his were simply outsized.

The men all noticed Kahlan's gesture of affection. Richard was not embarrassed that they did. He wanted them to know that other people were the same as they in important, human ways. This was what they were fighting for—the chance to be human, to love and cherish loved ones, to live their lives as they wished.

The light faded quickly as Richard and Anson made their way through the woods running beside fields of wild grasses. Richard wanted to work around to where the forest came in closer to the men out weeding in the gardens and tending to animals. With the nearby mountains to the west being so high, the sun vanished behind them earlier than what would normally be sunset, leaving the sky a swath of deep bluish green and the valley in an odd golden gloom.

By the time he and Anson had reached the place where they would leave the woods, it was still a little too light, so they waited a short while until Richard felt the murky light in the fields was dim enough to hide them. The town was some distance away and since Richard couldn't make out any men outside the gates, he reasoned that if soldiers were watching, then they couldn't see him, either.

As they moved quickly through the field of wild grass, staying low and out of sight, Anson pointed. "There, those men going back to town, we should follow them."

Richard spoke quietly back over his shoulder. "All right, but don't forget, we don't want to catch up with them or they might recognize you and make a fuss. Let them stay a good distance ahead of us."

When they reached the town walls, Richard saw that the gates were no more than two sections of the picket walls. A couple of posts no bigger than Richard's wrist had been tied sideways to stiffen two sections of wall and make them into gates. The ropes that tied the posts together served as the hinges. The sections were simply lifted and swung around to open or close them. It was far from a secure fortification.

In the murky twilight, the two guards milling around just inside the gates watching workers return couldn't really see much of Richard and Anson. To the guards, they would appear to be two more workers. The Order understood the value of workers; they needed slaves to do the work so that the soldiers might eat.

Richard hunched his shoulders and hung his head as he walked. He remembered those terrible times as a captive when, wearing a collar, he walked behind Denna, devoid of all hope of ever again being free. Thinking of that inhuman time, he shuffled through the open gates. The guards didn't pay him any attention.

Just as they were nearly past the guards, the closest one reached out and snatched Anson's sleeve, spinning him back around.

"I want some eggs," the young soldier said. "Give me some of the eggs you collected."

Anson stood wide-eyed, not knowing what to do. It seemed ludicrous that these two young men were allowed to serve their cause by being bullies. Richard stepped up beside Anson and spoke quickly, remembering to bow his head so that he wouldn't loom over the man.

"We have no eggs, sir. We were weeding the bean fields. I'm sorry. We will bring you eggs tomorrow, if it pleases you."

Richard glanced up just as the guard backhanded him, knocking him flat on his back. He instantly took a firm grip on his anger. Wiping blood from his mouth, he decided to stay where he was.

"He's right," Anson said, drawing the guard's attention. "We were weeding beans. If you wish it, we will bring you some eggs tomorrow—as many as you want."

The guard grunted a curse at them and swaggered off, taking his companion with him. They headed for a nearby long, low structure with a torch lashed to a pole outside a low door. In the flickering light of that torch, Richard couldn't make out what the place was, but it appeared to be a building dug partway into the ground so that the eaves were at eye level. After the two soldiers were a safe distance away, Anson offered Richard a hand to help him up. Richard didn't think he'd been hit that hard, but his head was spinning.

As they started out, faces in doorways and around dark corners peered out to watch them. When Richard looked their way, the people ducked back in.

"They know you are not from here," Anson whispered.

Richard didn't trust that one of those people wouldn't call the guards. "Let's hurry up and get what we came for."

Anson nodded and hurriedly led Richard down a narrow street with what looked like little more than huts huddled together on each side. The single torch burning outside the long building where the soldiers had gone provided little light down the street. The town, at least what Richard could see of it in the dark, was a pretty shabby-looking place. In fact, he wouldn't call it a town so much as a village. Many of the structures appeared to be housing for livestock, not people. Only rarely were there any lights coming from any of the squat buildings and the light he did see looked as if came from candles, not lamps.

At the end of the street, Richard followed Anson through a small side door into a larger building. The cows inside mooed at the intrusion. Sheep rustled in their pens. A few goats in other pens bleated. Richard and Anson paused to let the animals settle down before making their way through the barn to a ladder at the side. Richard followed Anson as he climbed quickly to a small hayloft.

At the end of the loft, Anson reached up over a low rafter to where it tied into the wall behind a cross-brace. "Here it is," he grimaced, stretching his arm up into the hiding place.

He came out with a small, square-sided bottle and handed it to Richard. "This is the antidote. Hurry and drink it, and then let's get out of here."

The large door banged open. Even though it was dark outside, the torch down the street provided just enough light to silhouette the broad shape of a man standing in the doorway. By his demeanor, he had to be a soldier.

Richard pulled the stopper from the bottle. The antidote had the slight aroma of cinnamon. He quickly downed it, hardly noticing its sweet, spicy taste. He never took his eyes off the man in the doorway.

"Who's in here?" the man bellowed.

"Sir," Richard called down, "I'm just getting some hay for the livestock."

"In the dark? What are you up to? Get down here right now."

Richard put a hand against Anson's chest and pushed him back into the darkness. "Yes, sir. I'm coming," Richard called to the soldier as he hurried down the ladder.

At the bottom of the ladder, he turned and saw the man coming toward him. Richard reached for his knife under the coat he was wearing, only then remembering that he didn't have his knife. The soldier was still silhouetted against the open barn door. Richard was in the darkness and the man probably wouldn't be able to see him. He silently moved away from the ladder.

As the soldier passed near him, Richard stepped in behind him and reached to his side, seizing the knife sheathed behind the axe hanging on his belt. Richard gingerly drew the knife just as the man stopped and looked up the ladder to the hayloft.

As he was looking up, Richard snatched a fistful of hair with one hand and reached around with the other, slicing deep through the soldier's throat before he realized what was happening. Richard held the man tight as he struggled, a wet gurgling the only sound coming from him. He reached back, frantically grabbing at Richard for a moment before his movements lost their energy and he went limp.

"Anson," Richard whispered up the ladder as he let the man slip to the ground, "come on. Let's go."

Anson hurried down the ladder, coming to a halt as he reached the bottom and turned around to see the dark shape of the dead man sprawled on the ground.

"What happened?"

Richard looked up from his work at undoing the weapons belt around the dead weight of the soldier. "I killed him."

"Oh."

Richard handed the knife, in its sheath, to Anson. "Here you go. Now you have a real weapon—a long knife."

Richard rolled the dead soldier over to pull the belt the rest of the way out from under the man. As he tugged it free, he heard a noise and turned just in time to see another soldier running in toward them.

Anson slammed the long knife hilt-deep into the man's chest. The man staggered back. Richard shot to his feet, bringing the weapons belt with him. The soldier gasped for breath as he clutched at the knife handle. He dropped heavily to his knees. One hand clawed at the air above him as he swayed. Pulling a final gasp, he toppled to his side.

Anson stood staring at the man lying in a heap, the knife jutting from his chest. The he bent down and pulled his new knife free.

"Are you all right?" Richard whispered when Anson stood.

Anson nodded. "I recognize this man. We called him the Weasel. He deserved to die."

Richard gently clapped Anson on the back of the shoulder. "You did well. Now, let's get out of here."

As they made their way back up the street, Richard asked Anson to wait while he checked down alleyways and between low buildings, searching for soldiers. As a guide, Richard often scouted at night. In the darkness he was in his element.

The town was a lot smaller than he had expected. It was also much less organized than he thought it would be, with no apparent order to where the simple structures had been built. The streets through the haphazard town, if they could be called streets, were in most cases little more than footpaths between clusters of small, single-roomed buildings. He saw a few handcarts, but nothing more elaborate. There was only one road through the town, leading back to the barn where they had recovered the antidote and run into the two soldiers, that was wide enough to accommodate a wagon. His search didn't turn up any patrolling soldiers.

"Do you know if all the men of the Order stay together?" Richard asked when he returned to Anson, waiting in the shadows.

"At night they go inside. They sleep in our place, near where we came in."

"You mean that low building where the first two soldiers went?"

"That's right. That's where most people used to gather at night, but now the men of the Order use it for themselves."

Richard frowned at the man. "You mean you all slept together?"

Anson sounded mildly surprised by the question. "Yes. We were together whenever possible. Many people had a house where they could work, eat, and keep belongings, but they rarely slept in them. We usually all slept in the sleeping houses where we gathered to talk about the day. Everyone wanted to be together. Sometimes people would sleep in another place, but mostly we slept there together so we could all feel safe—much as we all slept together at night as we made our way down out of the pass with the statue."

"And everyone just . . . lay down together?"

Anson averted his eyes. "Couples often slept apart from others by being with one another under a single blanket, but they were still together with our people. In the dark, though, no one could see them . . . together under a blanket."

Richard had trouble imagining such a way of life. "The whole town fit in that sleeping building? There was enough room?"

"No, there were too many of us to all sleep in one sleeping house. There are two." Anson pointed. "There is another on the far side of the one you saw."

"Let's go have a look, then."

They moved quickly back toward the town gates, such as they were, and toward the sleeping houses. The dark street was empty. Richard didn't see anyone on the paths between buildings. What people were left in the town had apparently gone to sleep or were afraid to come out in the darkness.

A door in one of the small homes opened a crack, as if someone inside were peering out. The door opened wider and a thin figure dashed out toward them.

"Anson!" came the whispered voice.

It was a boy, in his early teens. He fell to his knees and clutched Anson's arm, kissing his hand in joy to see him.

"Anson, I am so happy that you are home! We've missed you so much. We feared for you—feared that you were murdered."

Anson grabbed the boy by his shirt and hauled him to his feet.

"Bernie, I'm well and I'm happy to see you well, but you must go back in now. The men will see you. If they catch you outside . . ."

"Oh, please, Anson, come sleep at our house. We're so alone and afraid."

"Who?"

"Just me and my grandfather, now. Please come in and be with us."

"I can't right now. Maybe another time."

The boy peered up at Richard, then, and when he saw that he didn't recognize him, shrank back.

"This is a friend of mine, Bernie—from another town." Anson squatted down beside the boy. "Please, Bernie, I will return, but you must go back inside and stay there tonight. Don't come out. We fear there might be trouble. Stay inside. Tell your grandfather my words, will you now?"

Bernie finally agreed and ran back into the dark doorway. Richard was eager to get out of the town before anyone else came out to pay their respects. If he and Anson weren't careful, they would end up attracting the attention of the soldiers.

They moved quickly the rest of the way up the street, using buildings for cover. Pressing up against the side of one at the head of the street, Richard peered around the corner at the squat daub-and-wattle sleeping house where the guards had gone. The door was open, letting soft light spill out across the ground.

"In there?" Richard whispered. "You all slept in there?"

"Yes. That is one of the sleeping houses, and beyond it the other one."

Richard thought about it for a moment. "What did you sleep on?"

"Hay. We put blankets over it, usually. We changed the hay often to keep it fresh, but these men do not bother. They sleep like animals in dusty old hay."

Richard looked out through the open gates at the fields. He looked back at the sleeping house.

"And now the soldiers all sleep in there?"

"Yes. They took the place from us. They said it was to be their barracks. Now our people—the ones still alive—must sleep wherever they can."

Richard made Anson stay put while he slipped through the shadows, out of the light of the torch, to survey the area beyond the first building. The second long structure also had soldiers inside laughing and talking. There were more men than were needed to guard such a small place, but Witherton was the gateway into Bandakar—and the gateway out.

"Come on," Richard said as he came up beside Anson, "let's get back to the others. I have an idea."

As they made their way to the gate, Richard looked up, as he often did, to check the starry sky for any sign of black-tipped races. He saw instead that the pole to each side of the gate held a body hanging by the ankles. When Anson saw them, he paused, held frozen by the horror of the sight.

Richard laid a hand on the man's shoulder and leaned close. "Are you all right?"

Anson shook his head. "No. But I will be better when the men who come to us and do such things are dead."

CHAPTER 48

Richard didn't know if the antidote was supposed to make him feel better, but if it was it hadn't yet done its work. As they crept through the pitch-black fields, his chest hurt with every breath he took. He paused and closed his eyes briefly against the pain of the headache caused by his gift. He wanted nothing more than to lie down, but there was no time for that. Everyone started out once more when he did, quietly making their way through the fields outside of Witherton.

It felt good, at least, to have his sword back, even if he dreaded the thought of having to draw it for fear of finding its magic was no longer there for him. Once they recovered the other two bottles of the antidote and he was rid of the poison, then maybe they could make it back to Nicci so that she could help him deal with his gift.

He tried not to worry if a sorceress could help a wizard once his gift had gone out of control, as his had. Nicci had vast experience. As soon as he reached her, she would help him. Even if she couldn't help him, he felt confident that she would at least know what he had to do in order to get the help he needed. After all, she had once been a Sister of the Light; the purpose of the Sisters of the Light had been to help those with the gift to learn to control it.

"I think I see the outer wall," Kahlan said in a quiet voice.

"Yes, that's the place." Richard pointed. "There's the gate. See it?"

"I think so," she whispered back.

It was a dark night, with no moon. While the others were having difficulty seeing much of anything as they made their way through the dark, Richard was glad for the conditions. The starlight was enough for him to see by, but he didn't think it was enough to give the soldiers any help in seeing them.

As they crept closer, the sleeping house came into view through the open gate. The torch still burned outside the door to the building where the soldiers slept. Richard signaled everyone to gather around. They all crouched low. He grabbed the shoulder of Anson's shirt and pulled him up closer yet, then did the same with Owen.

Both now carried battle-axes. Anson also carried the knife he'd earned. The rest of the men carried the weapons they had helped finish making.

When Richard and Anson had returned to the forest clearing, Anson had told the waiting men everything that had happened. When he said that he had killed the man called the Weasel, Richard held his breath, not sure exactly how the men would react to hearing that one of their own had actually killed a man. There was a brief moment of astonished silence, and then spontaneous joy at the accomplishment.

Every man wanted to shake Anson's hand to congratulate him, to tell him how proud they were. At that moment, any lingering doubts Richard harbored had vanished. He had allowed the men to celebrate briefly while he waited for the night to darken, and then they had started making their way through the fields.

This was the night when Witherton would gain its freedom.

Richard looked around at all the dark shapes. "All right now, remember all the things we've told you. You must stay quiet and hold the gates steady while Anson and Owen cut the ropes where they hinge. Be careful not to let the gates fall once the ropes are cut."

In the dim starlight Richard could just make out the men nodding to his instructions. Richard carefully checked the sky, looking for any sign of black-tipped races. He didn't see any. It had been a long time since they'd seen any races.

It seemed that the trick of taking to the forests just before they changed their expected route and being careful to stay out of sight from the sky had worked. It was possible that they had succeeded in slipping out from under Nicholas the Slide's surveillance. If they really had escaped his observation, then he wouldn't know where to begin looking for them.

Richard briefly squeezed Kahlan's hand and then started for the opening in the town wall. Cara crouched close at his other side. Tom was bringing up the rear, along with Jennsen, making sure there were no surprises from behind.

They had left Betty not only tied up, but confined to a makeshift pen to be sure she didn't follow after them and give them away at the wrong moment. The goat had been unusually distraught to be left behind, but with lives at stake they couldn't risk Jennsen's goat causing trouble. She would be happy enough after they returned.

When they reached the fields close to the town gates, Richard motioned for everyone to get down and stay where they were. Along with Tom, Richard moved up to the gates, taking cover in the shadow of the wall. There was a soldier just inside the gate, pacing slowly in his lonely night-time sentry duty. He wasn't being very careful, or he would not be doing such duty in the light of the torch.

As the soldier turned to walk away from them, Tom slipped up behind the man and swiftly silenced him. As Tom dragged the dead man through the gates to hide him in the darkness outside the wall, Richard moved in through the gates, staying in the shadows away from the torch burning outside the sleeping house. The door to the sleeping house stood open, but no light or sound came from inside. This late, the men were bound to be asleep.

He moved past the first long building to the second, and there came upon another guard. Quickly, silently, Richard seized the man and cut his throat, holding him tight as he struggled. When he finally went limp, Richard laid him in the darkness at the head of the second sleeping house, around the corner from the torchlight.

In the distance, the men had already swarmed over the gates, holding them up while Anson and Owen worked quickly at cutting the ropes that acted as hinges. In moments, both sections of gate were freed. Richard could hear the soft grunts of effort as the heavy gates were manhandled around by the two gangs of men.

Jennsen handed Richard his bow, the string already strung. Then she handed him one of the special arrows, holding the rest at the ready for him. Kahlan slipped up to the torch on the pole outside the first building and lit several small torches, handing each of them off to the men. She kept one for herself.

Richard nocked the arrow and then glanced around at the faces seeming to float before him in the wavering torchlight. In answer to the unspoken question, they all nodded that they were ready. He checked the men balancing the two gates and saw their nod. The bow in one hand, with his fist holding the arrow in place, Richard gave hand signals to the men, starting them moving.

What had been a slow, careful approach from the woods into the town suddenly transformed into a headlong rush.

Richard held the head of the arrow nocked in his bow in the flame of the torch Kahlan held out for him. As soon as it caught, he ran to the open door of the sleeping house, leaned into the darkness, and fired the arrow toward the back.

As the blazing arrow flew the length of the building, it illuminated row upon row of men sleeping on the bed of straw. The arrow landed at the far end, spilling flame across the straw. A few heads lifted at the confusing sight. Jennsen handed Richard another. He immediately drew string to cheek and the arrow shot toward the middle of the interior.

As Richard pulled back from the doorway, two men with torches dripping flaming drops of pitch heaved them just inside. They hissed as they flew through the air, landing amid the sleeping men, bouncing and tumbling through the straw, igniting a wall of flame.

In a matter of only a few heartbeats since the attack started, the first sleeping house was afire from one end to the other. The largest blaze, by design, was the fire spread by the pitch-laden torches, at the end of the building nearest the door. Confused cries came from inside, muted by the thick walls. The still-sleepy soldiers scrambled to their feet.

Richard checked that the men with the heavy gates were coming, then he ran around the sleeping house to the second building. Jennsen, following close behind, handed him an arrow, the flames around its head wrapped in oil-soaked cloth making a whooshing sound as he ran.

One of his men pulled the torch from the stand outside the building where the guard Richard killed had been patrolling. Richard leaned in the doorway only to see a big man charging at him out of the dark interior. Richard pressed his back against the doorjamb and kicked the man squarely in the chest, driving him back.

Richard drew the bowstring back and shot the flaming arrow off into the interior. As it lit the interior in its track through the building, he could see that some of the men had been awakened and were getting up. Turning to take the second flaming arrow from Jennsen, he saw smoke pouring up from the first building. As soon as he drew string to cheek and loosed the second arrow, he leaned away and men heaved the torches in.

One torch fell back out of the doorway. It had bounced off the chest of a man rushing for the doorway to see what was happening. The pitch from the torch caught his greasy beard afire. He let out a bloodcurdling scream. Richard kicked him back inside. In an instant, men by the dozens were racing for the door, not only to escape the burning building, but to meet the attack. Richard saw the flash of weapons being drawn.

He sprang back from the doorway as the men carrying the heavy section of gate rushed in. They turned the gate sideways and rammed it in under the eaves, but before they could bring the bottom down to wedge it against the ground, the weight of bellowing men inside crashed into the section of gate and drove it back. The men carrying it fell back, the weight knocking them from their feet, the gate landing atop them.

Suddenly, men were pouring from the doorway. Richard's men were ready and fell on them, driving the wooden weapons into their soft underbellies and snapping the handles off as man after man spilled out of the doorway. Standing to the side of the door, others used their maces to bash in the skulls of soldiers who emerged. When one soldier came out with his sword raised, the man to the side clubbed his arm as another rushed in and drove a wooden stake in up under his ribs. The more men who fell at the doorway, the more those trying to get out were slowed and could be dispatched.

The soldiers were so stunned to see these people fighting that in some cases they fought back only ineffectually. As a soldier leaped over the bodies in the doorway and lifted a sword, a man jumped on his back and seized his arm while another stabbed him. Another, crying orders, charged Jennsen, only to have the bolt of a crossbow fired into his face. A few soldiers escaped the burning building and managed to slip past Richard's men only to meet Cara's Agiel. Their screams, worse than the cries of men on fire, briefly brought the gaze of every man, from both sides of the battle.

Fallen knives and swords were scooped up by the men of the town and turned on the men from the Imperial Order. Richard fired an arrow into the center of the chest of a man emerging from the smoke that rolled out of the doorway. As he was falling, a second arrow felled the man behind him. As more men rushed out, they fell over those piled around the doorway and were hacked to death with commandeered axes or stabbed with confiscated swords. Since they could emerge only one at a time, the soldiers couldn't mount a coordinated attack, but these waiting could.

As Richard's men fought back those struggling to get out of the doorway to the burning building, other men rushed to help lift the gate so those under it could get up and get control of it. Once the gate was lifted, the men swung it around and with a cry of joint effort, ran with it toward the building. They drove the top up under the eaves first, but when they brought the bottom edge down, the bodies piled in the doorway prevented them from getting the bottom down so they could wedge it in place.

Richard called out orders. Some of his men rushed in and seized an arm or a leg of a dead man and dragged the body aside so the others could finally bring the bottom of the gate down against the building to close off the opening.

One man from inside squeezed through just before they had the gate in place. The weight of the door pinned him against the building. Owen leaned in and with a sword he'd picked up decisively stabbed the man through the throat.

As men inside pounded at the gate covering the doorway and threw their weight against it, men on the outside piled around to push it down and hold it in place. Other men fell to their knees and drove stakes into the ground to lock the gate section in place, trapping the soldiers inside.

Behind them, streamers of flame leaked out from under the eaves of the first building and leaped up into the night sky. The roof of the building ignited all at once, explosively engulfing the entire sleeping house in sparks and flames. Screams of men being burned alive ripped the night.

The waves of heat coming off the massive fire as the first building was consumed by the flames began to carry the heavy aroma of cooking meat. It reminded Richard that, for the killing he did, his gift demanded the balance of not eating meat. After all the killing of this night, since his gift was already spinning out of control, he would have to be even more careful to avoid eating any meat.

His head was already hurting so much that he was having trouble focusing his vision; he couldn't afford to do anything that would further unbalance his gift. If he wasn't careful, the poison wouldn't get the chance to be the first thing to kill him.

Heavy black smoke billowed out from around the edges of the gate covering the doorway of the second sleeping house. Screams and pleas came from inside. The men of the town moved back, watching, as smoke began rolling up from under its eaves. The battle seemed to have ended as quickly as it had started.

No one spoke as they stood in the harsh glare from the roaring fires. Flames ate through the second building. With a loud whoosh it was engulfed in fire.

The heat drove everyone back from the two sleeping houses. As they moved away from the burning buildings, they encountered the rest of the people of the town, all gathered in the shadows, watching in stunned silence.

One of the older men took a step forward. "Speaker Owen, what is this? You have committed violence?"

Owen stepped away from the men he was with to stand before the people of his town. He held an arm back, pointing toward Richard.

"This is Lord Rahl, of the D'Haran Empire. I went in search of him to help us be free. We have much to tell you, but for now you must know that tonight, for the first time in many seasons, our town is free.

"Yes, we have helped Lord Rahl to kill the evil men who have terrorized us. We have avenged the deaths of our loved ones. We will no longer be victims. We will be free!"

Standing silently, the people seemed only able to stare at him. Many looked confused. Some looked quietly jubilant, but most just looked stunned.

The boy, Bernie, ran up to Anson, peering up in astonishment. "Anson, you and our other people have freed us? Truly?"

"Yes." Anson laid a hand on Bernie's shoulder. "Our town is now free."

"Thank you." The boy broke into a grin as he turned back to the town's people. "We are free of the murderers!"

A sudden, spontaneous cheer rose into the night, drowning out the sound of the crackling flames. The people rushed in around men they had not seen for months, touching them, hugging them, asking them questions.

Richard took Kahlan's hand as he stepped back out of the way, joining Cara, Jennsen, and Tom. These people who were so against violence, who had lived their whole lives avoiding the truth of what their beliefs caused, were now basking in the tearful joy of what it really meant to be freed from terror and violence.

People slowly left their men to come and look at Richard and those standing with him. He and Kahlan smiled at their obvious joy. They gathered in close before him, smiling, staring, as if Richard and those with him were some strange creatures from afar.

Bernie had attached himself to Anson's arm. Others had the rest of the men firmly embraced. One by one, though, the men started pulling away so that they could stand behind Richard and Kahlan.

"We are so happy that you are home, now," people were telling the men. "We have you back, at last."

"Now we are all together again," Bernie said.

"We can't stay," Anson told him.

Everyone in the crowd fell silent.

Bernie, like many of the others, looked heartbroken. "What?"

Buzzing, worried whispers spread through the crowd. Everyone was shaken by the news that the men were not home to stay.

Owen lifted a hand so they would listen. When they went silent, he explained. "The people of Bandakar are still under the cruel power of the men from the Order. Just as you have become free tonight, so must the rest of the people of Bandakar be free.

"Lord Rahl and his wife, the Mother Confessor, as well as his friend and protector Cara, his sister Jennsen, and Tom, another friend and protector, have all agreed to help us. They cannot do it alone. We must be part of it, for this is our land, and more importantly, our people, our loved ones."

"Owen, you must not engage in violence," an older man said. In view of their sudden freedom, it was not an emphathic statement. It seemed to be an objection more out of obligation than anything else. "You have begun a cycle of violence. Such a thing is wrong."

"We will speak with you before we go, so that you may come to understand, as we have, why we must do this to be truly free of violence and brutality. Lord Rahl has shown us that a cycle of violence is not the result of fighting back for your own life, but is the result of a shrinking back from doing what is necessary to crush those who would kill you. If you do as you must in duty to yourself and your loved ones, then you will eradicate the enemy so completely that they can no longer do you any harm. Then there is no cycle of violence, but an end to violence. Then, and only then, will true peace and freedom take root."

"Such actions can never accomplish anything but to start violence," another old man objected.

"Look around," Anson said. "The violence has not begun tonight, but ended. Violence has been crushed, as it should be, by crushing evil men who bring it upon us."

People nodded to one another, the heady relief of being suddenly freed from the grip of the terror brought by the soldiers of the Imperial Order plainly overcoming their objections. Joy had taken over from fear. The reality of having their lives returned had opened their eyes.

"But you must understand, as we have come to understand," Owen said, "that nothing can ever again be the way it once was. Those ways are in the past."

Richard noticed that the men weren't slouching anymore. They stood with their heads held high.

"We have chosen to live," Owen told his people. "In so doing, we have found true freedom."

"I think we all have," said the old man in the crowd.

CHAPTER 49

Zedd frowned with the effort of concentrating on what it was Sister Tahirah had placed on the table before him. He looked up at her, at the way her scowl pinched in around her humped nose.

"Well?" she demanded.

Zedd looked down, squinting at the thing before him. It looked like a leather-covered ball painted with faded blue-and-pink zigzagged lines all around it.

What was it about it that seemed so familiar, yet so distant?

He blinked, trying to focus his eyes better. His neck ached something fierce. A father, hearing his young son in the next tent screaming in appalling agony, had grabbed Zedd by the hair and yanked him away from other parents who, pulling and pawing at him, made desperate demands of their own. Because of the torn muscles in his neck, it was painful to hold up his head. Compared to the torture he'd heard, though, it was nothing.

The dim interior of the tent, lit by several lamps hanging from poles, felt as if it were detached from the ground and swirling around him. The foul place stank. The heat and humidity only made the smell, and the spinning, worse. Zedd felt as if he might pass out.

It had been so long since he'd slept that he couldn't even remember the last time he had actually lain down. The only sleep he got was when he fell asleep in the chair while Sister Tahirah was seeing to another object being unloaded from the wagons, or when she went to bed and the next Sister hadn't yet arrived to take the next stint in their laborious cataloguing of the items brought from the Keep. The catnaps he got were rarely longer than a few precious minutes at a time. The guards had orders not to allow him or Adie to lie down.

At least the screams of the children had ended. At least, as long as he cooperated, those cries of pain had stopped. At least, as long as he went along, the parents had hope.

A violent crack of pain suddenly hammered the side of his head, knocking him back. The chair toppled over, spilling him to the ground. With his arms bound behind his back, he couldn't do anything to break the fall and he hit hard. Zedd's ears rang, not only from the fall, but from the aftermath of the blow of the Sister's power delivered through the collar around his neck.

He hated that wicked instrument of control. The Sisters were not shy about exercising that control. Because the collar locked him away from the use of his own gift, he could not use his ability to defend himself. Instead, they used his power against him.

It took little or no provocation to send one of the Sisters into a fit of violence. Many of these women had once been kindly people devoting their lives to helping others. Jagang had enslaved them to a different cause. Now, they did his bidding. Though they might have once been gentle, they were now, he knew, trying to keep one step ahead of the discipline Jagang meted out to them. That discipline could be excruciating beyond endurance. The Sisters were expected to get results; Jagang would not be interested in the excuse that Zedd was being difficult.

Zedd saw that Adie, too, had been knocked to the ground. Any punishment he received, she, too, endured. He felt more agony for her than for himself.

Soldiers standing to the side moved in to right the chair and lift Zedd into it. With his arms bound behind his back, he couldn't get up by himself. They sat him down hard enough to drive a grunt from his lungs.

"Well?" Sister Tahirah demanded. "What is it?"

Zedd once again leaned in, staring down at the round object sitting by itself in the center of the table. The faint blue-and-pink zigzagging lines stirred deep feelings. He thought he should know this thing.

"It's . . . it's . . ."

"It's what?" Sister Tahirah slammed the book against the edge of the table, causing the round object to bounce up and roll a few inches before it came to a stop closer to Zedd. She tucked the book under one arm as she leaned with the other on the table. She bent down toward him.

"What is it? What does it do?"

"I . . . I can't remember."

"Would you like me to bring in some children?" the Sister said in the soft, sweet tone of a very bitter threat, "and show you their little faces before they are taken to the tent next to us to be tortured?"

"I'm so tired," he said. "I'm trying to remember, but I'm so tired."

"Maybe while the children are screaming you would like to explain to their parents that you are tired and just can't quite seem to remember."

Children. Parents.

Zedd suddenly remembered what the object was. Painful memories welled up. He felt a tear run down his cheek.

"Dear spirits," he whispered. "Where did you find this?"

"What is it?"

"Where did you find it?" Zedd repeated.

Huffing impatiently, the Sister straightened. She opened the book and made a noisy show of turning heatedly through the pages. Finally, she stopped and tapped a finger in the open book.

"It says here that it was found hidden in an open recess in the back of a black six-drawer chest in a corridor. There was a tapestry of three prancing white horses hanging above the chest." She lowered the book. "Now, what is it?"

Zedd swallowed. "A ball."

The sister glared. "I know it's a ball, you old fool. What is it for? What does it do? What is its purpose?"

Staring at the ball no bigger than his fist, Zedd remembered. "It's a ball for children to play with. Its purpose is to bring them pleasure."

He remembered this ball, brightly colored back then, frequently bouncing down the halls of the Wizard's Keep, his daughter giggling and chasing after it. He had given it to her for doing well in her studies. Sometimes she would roll it down the halls, urging it along with a switch, just as if she were walking a pet. Her favorite thing to do was to bounce it on the floor so that it would come up against a wall, after which it would bounce to another wall at an intersection of stone hallways. In that way she made it bounce around a corner. She would watch which hall it went down, left or right, then chase after it.

One day she came to him in tears. He asked her to tell him her troubles. She crawled up in his lap and told him that her ball had gone somewhere and got itself lost. She wanted him to get it unlost. Zedd told her that if she looked, she would likely find it. She spent days despondently wandering the halls of the Keep, searching for it. She couldn't find it.

Finally, starting out one morning at sunrise, Zedd made the long walk down to the city of Aydindril, to the market on Stentor Street. That was where he had first come across a stand where they sold such toys and found the ball with the zigzagged lines. There, he bought her another one—not just like it, but instead one with pink and green stars. He deliberately chose a ball unlike the one she'd lost because he didn't want her to think that wishes could be miraculously fulfilled, but he did want her to know that there were solutions that could solve problems.

He remembered his daughter hugging his legs, thanking him for the new ball, telling him that he was the best father in all the world and that she would be ever so much more careful with the new ball and never lose it. He had smiled as he watched her put a little hand to her heart and recite a little-girl-oath she had invented on the spot.

She treasured the ball with the pink and green stars. Since it was small, it was one of the few things she had been able to take with her, after she was grown, when she and Zedd ran away to Westland, after Darken Rahl had raped her.

When Richard had been young, he had played with that ball. Zedd remembered the smile on his daughter's face as she watched her own child play with that precious ball. Zedd could see in her beautiful eyes the memories of her own childhood as she watched Richard play. She had kept that ball her whole life, kept it until she died.

This ball before him was the very same one his daughter had lost. It must have bounced up behind the chest and fallen into a recess in the back, where it had been for all those long years.

Zedd leaned forward, resting his forehead on the dusty ball surrounded with faded blue-and-pink zigzagged lines, the ball which her little fingers had once held, and wept.

Sister Tahirah seized a fistful of his hair and pulled him upright. "I don't believe you're telling me the truth. It's an object of magic. I want to know what it is and what it does." Holding his head back, she glared into his eyes. "You know that I will not hesitate to do what is necessary to make you cooperate. His Excellency accepts no excuses for failure."

Zedd stared up at her, blinking away his tears. "It's a ball, a toy. That's all it is."

With a sneer, she released him. "The great and powerful Wizard Zorander." She shook her head. "To think that we once feared you. You are a pathetic old man, your courage crushed by nothing more than the cry of a child." She sighed. "I must say, your reputation far exceeds the reality of your mettle."

The Sister scooped up the ball, turning it in her fingers as she inspected it. She huffed with disgust and tossed it aside, as if it were worthless. Zedd watched the ball bounce and roll across the ground, coming to rest at the side of the tent, against the bench where Adie sat. He looked up into her completely white eyes to see her watching him. Zedd turned away, waiting while the Sister made notes in her book.

"All right," she finally said. "Let's go have a look at what they've unloaded in the next tent."

The soldiers lifted him from the chair before he had a chance to try to do it himself. His shoulders ached from his wrists being bound behind his back and from being lifted by his arms. Adie, too, was lifted to her feet. The book snapped closed. Sister Tahirah's wiry gray hair whipped around as she turned and led them out of the tent.

Because the Sisters knew how dangerous items of magic from the Wizard's Keep could be, especially if the wrong combination of magic were to accidentally be allowed to combine or touch, they were cautious enough to bring the items one at a time out of each individual, protected, shielded crate in the wagons. Zedd knew that there were things in the Keep that, by themselves, were not dangerous, but became so in the presence of other things that, by themselves, were also not dangerous. Sometimes it was only the combination of specific items that created a desired outcome.

The Sisters had vast experience in the most esoteric things of magic and so they at least understood the principles involved. They treated the cargo with the care due such potentially hazardous goods. Once each object was uncrated, they placed it, by itself, in a tent to await examination. They took Zedd and Adie from tent to tent so that Zedd could identify each treasure, tell them what it was, explain how it worked.

They had been at it for days—how many, Zedd couldn't remember. Despite his best efforts, the endless days and nights had all begun to melt together in his mind.

Zedd did all he could to stall, but there was only so much he could do. These women knew magic. They would not easily be fooled by any invented explanation. They had made very clear the consequences of any such deception.

And Zedd didn't know how much they knew. At times they feigned ignorance of something which they actually understood quite well, just to see if he was telling the truth.

Fortunately, as of yet they had uncovered nothing that was extravagantly dangerous. Most of the items from the crates were simple-looking objects, but were actually for a narrowly focused purpose—a pole that could remotely judge the depth of water in a well, an iron decoration shaped like a fan of leaves that prevented words from carrying beyond an open door where it was placed, a large looking glass that revealed when a person entered another room. While possibly useful to Emperor Jagang, such items were not all that valuable or dangerous; they were not going to help him to conquer and rule the world.

What dangerous things the Sisters had uncrated and shown him were not really anything that a Sister couldn't easily produce with a spell of her own. The most dangerous item had been a constructed spell held within an ornate vase that, under specific conditions, such as when a vase was filled with water, created a temperature inversion that produced a blast of flame. Zedd was not betraying his cause or putting innocent lives at risk by revealing how the spell worked; any Sister worth her salt could reproduce the same effect. The purpose of the spell was protective; had it touched other stolen items, which, because they were stolen, was a reversal of intended ownership that such a spell recognized, it would have ignited and destroyed those items, keeping them from covetous hands.

None of the things so far discovered would offer Jagang any real benefit. There were things in the Keep, though, that could cause him harm. There were spells there, such as the constructed spell in the vase, that recognized the nature of the person invoking its magic. Opened by the right person, such as Zedd, those things would do nothing but, opened by a thief, they would create calamity.

The Keep had thousands of rooms. The looting of it had netted the Imperial Order a caravan of cargo wagons, but even that much hardly scratched the surface of the contents of the Keep.

So far, Zedd had not seen any plums.

He didn't know if he would live to see any. The ride in the box after his capture had been brutal. He was still not recovered from the injuries inflicted after meeting Jagang. Guards let the parents do what they would to convince Zedd and Adie to give in, but they wouldn't allow the parents to get so carried away that they killed such prize prisoners. The parents had known that they weren't to kill them, but in the heat of such raw passion, Zedd knew that such orders were easy to forget. Zedd yearned for them to kill him and end it. The emperor, though, needed them alive, so the guards stood careful watch.

After the first few horrifying hours of listening to children being subjected to crippling torture, of being among their parents who understandably demanded, quite forcefully, that he cooperate and tell the emperor what he wanted to know, Zedd had given in—not for the sake of the parents so much as to stop those brutal men from what they were doing to the children.

He had figured that he had nothing to lose, really, by giving in. It stopped the torture of the children for the time being. The Keep was vast; the amount of things they brought were only a tiny portion of them. Zedd reasoned that the caravan of wagons probably didn't hold anything of any real value to Jagang. It would take quite a while to catalogue everything—it could be weeks more before they reached the last item. There was no purpose in allowing children to endure torture when there might not be anything useful for Zedd to betray to Jagang.

Once, when they were alone while the Sister had gone to check on the preparations in the next tent, Adie had asked what he would do if they presented him with something that would materially help Jagang win. Zedd hadn't had a chance to answer; the soldiers had come in then and taken the two of them to the Sister in the next tent.

He was hoping to drag out the process for as long as possible. He hadn't counted on how they would keep at it day and night.

It sometimes took quite a while for the Sisters to get out the next treasure and have it ready. They were understandably cautious and took no chances. Those strange men without any trace of the gift who helped them might not be harmed if any errant item of magic were to accidentally be set in motion, but everyone else certainly was vulnerable. Careful as they were, there were enough people working at the preparations that Zedd and Adie were not allowed to sleep for long before they were taken off to unravel the next puzzle for them.

As he and Adie were dragged through the dark camp to the next tent, Zedd's legs would hardly hold him. Seeing his daughter's long-lost ball had sapped much of his remaining strength. He had never felt so old, so feeble. He feared that his will to go on was flagging.

He didn't know how much longer he could keep his sanity.

He wasn't at all sure that he actually still possessed it. The world seemed to have turned into a crazy place. At times the whole thing seemed dreamlike. What he knew and what he didn't know some-times seemed to have all twisted together into a knot of confusion.

As he was marched through the dark camp, through the humid

heat, he began to imagine that he saw things—mostly people—from his past. He began to doubt that he really had seen that ball. He wondered if, like some of the other things he was seeing, he had imagined it as well. Could it maybe have been a simple ball, and he only thought that it was the one his daughter had lost? Had he imagined the zigzagged colors around it? He was beginning to question himself over every little thing.

Looking up at all the people in the crowded encampment, he thought he saw his long-dead wife, Erilyn, in the faces of the women held nearby under guard. They were mothers, their worst nightmares ready to come to life if Zedd didn't cooperate. His gaze passed over children clutching their mother's skirts, or their father's legs. They looked at him, his wavy white hair in disarray, probably thinking he was some crazy man. Maybe he was.

Torches lit the sprawling camp with a kind of flickering light that made everything seem imaginary. The campfires, spread as far as he could see, looked like a star field lying across the ground, as if the world had turned upside down.

"Wait," the Sister said to the guards.

Zedd was jerked to a halt as the Sister ducked inside the tent. Adie cried out as the man holding her wrenched her arm in the act of stopping her.

Zedd swayed on his feet, wondering if he might pass out. The whole night-time camp wavered in his vision.

As he looked at one of the girls held captive across the way, he stared, astonished, thinking he recognized her. Zedd looked up at the emperor's elite guard in the distance holding the child. Zedd blinked his blurred vision. The guard, in leather-and-mail armor, with a belt full of weapons, looked like a man Zedd used to know. Zedd turned away at the memory, only to see a Sister, making her way among the tents not far away, who also looked like someone else he knew. He looked around at soldiers going about their business. Elite soldiers guarding the emperor's compound looked like men he thought he remembered.

Zedd truly was terrified, then. He was sure that he was losing his mind. He couldn't possibly be seeing the people he thought he saw.

His mind was all he had. He didn't want to be some babbling old man sitting by the side of a road begging.

He knew that people sometimes became irrational—lost their mind—when they got old or were pressed past their endurance. He had known people who had snapped, who had gone insane, and saw things that weren't really there. That's what he was doing. He was having visions of people from his past who weren't really there. That was a sure sign of insanity—seeing your past come to life, thinking you were back with long-lost loved ones.

His mind was the most important thing he had.

Now, he was losing that, too.

He was losing his sanity.

CHAPTER 50

Nicholas heard an annoying noise back in another place.

A disturbance of some sort, back where his body waited.

He ignored it, watching the streets, watching the buildings go by. The sun had just set. People, wary people, moved past. Color. Sound. Activity.

It was a dingy place, with buildings crowded close. Watch, watch. Alleyways were dark and narrow. Strangers stared. The street smelled. None of the buildings was more than two stories, he was sure of it. Most were not even that.

Again, he heard the noise back where his body waited. It was forceful, calling his attention.

He ignored the thump, thump, thump back somewhere else as he watched, trying to see where they were going. What's this? Watch, watch, watch. He thought he knew, but he wasn't positive. Look, look. He wanted to be sure. He wanted to watch.

He so enjoyed watching.

More noise. Obnoxious, demanding, thumping noise.

Nicholas felt his body around him as he slammed back to where it waited, sitting cross-legged on the wooden floor. He opened his eyes, blinking, trying to see in the dim room. Slivers of dusk leaking in around the edges of the closed shutters lent only somber light to the room.

He stood, wavering on his feet for a moment, not used to the strange feeling of being back in his own body. He started walking across the room, looking down, watching as he lifted each foot out ahead, shifted his weight with every step. He had been gone so much lately, day and night, that he was not used to having to do such things on his own. He had been so often in another place, another body, that he had difficulty adjusting to his own.

Someone was banging on the door, yelling for him to open it. Nicholas was furious at the uninvited caller, at such a rude intrusion.

With a wobbly gait, he made his way to the door. It felt so confining being back in his own body. It moved in such an odd manner. He rolled his shoulders, resisting the urge to bend forward. He pulled and stretched his neck one way, then the other.

It was bothersome to have to move himself about, to use his own muscles, to feel himself breathe, to see, hear, smell, feel with his own senses.

The door was barred by a heavy bolt to prevent unwelcome callers from entering while he was off elsewhere. It wouldn't do to have someone messing with his body while he wasn't there using it himself. Wouldn't do at all.

Someone pounding on the other side of the door bellowed his name and demanded to be let in. Nicholas lifted the heavy bolt and heaved it over. He threw open the thick door.

A young soldier stood just outside in the hall. A common, grubby soldier. A nobody.

Nicolas stared in stunned fury at the lowly man who would just walk up the stairs to the room everyone knew was off-limits and pound on the forbidden door. Where was Najari's flat, crooked nose when he needed it? Why wasn't someone guarding the door?

A broken bone jutted from the back of the bloody fist the man had been hammering against the door.

Nicholas craned his neck, peering past the soldier out into the dimly-lit hall, and saw the bodies of guards sprawled in pools of blood.

Nicholas ran his fingernails back through his hair, shivering with delight at the silken-smooth feel of oils gliding against his palm. He rolled his shoulders with the pleasure of the sensation.

Then, he fixed his gaze on the wide-eyed, common soldier whom he was about to kill. The man was dressed like many of the Imperial

Order soldiers, at least the better-outfitted soldiers, with leather chest-armor, a sleeve of protective mail on his right arm, and a number of leather straps and belts holding a variety of weapons—a short sword, a mace with a spiked metal head; knives. Despite how deadly all his gear appeared, the expression on his face was one of startled terror.

Nicholas puzzled for a moment at what such a meaningless man could possibly have to say that would be worth his life. "What is it, you insipid fool?"

The man lifted an arm, then the hand, then a single finger in a manner that reminded Nicholas of nothing so much as a puppet having its strings pulled. The finger tipped to one side, then the other, then back again, the way someone might waggle a finger in admonishment.

"Ah, ah, ah." The finger twitched side to side again. "Be polite. Be awfully polite."

The soldier, his eyes wide, seemed surprised by his own haughty words. The voice sounded too deep—too mature—to belong to this young man.

The voice, in fact, sounded dangerous in the extreme.

"What is this?" Nicholas frowned at the soldier. "What's this about?"

The man started into the room, his legs moving in a most peculiar, stilted manner. In some ways it reminded Nicholas of how it must look when he used his own legs after not being in his body for a long spell. He stepped aside as the man walked woodenly into the center of the dim room and turned. Blood dripped from the hand that had been pounding against the door, but the man, his eyes still wide with fear, seemed not to notice what had to be painful injuries.

His voice, though, came out anything but afraid. "Where are they, Nicholas?"

Nicholas approached the man and cocked his head. "They?"

"You promised them to me, Nicholas. I don't like it when people don't keep their word. Where are they?"

Nicholas drew his brow down even farther, leaned in even more. "Who?"

"Richard Rahl and the Mother Confessor!" the soldier bellowed in unrestrained rage.

Nicholas backed away a few paces. He understood, now. He had heard the stories, heard that the man could do such things. Now he was seeing it for himself.

This was Emperor Jagang, the dream walker himself.

"Remarkable," Nicholas drawled. He approached the soldier who was not a soldier and tapped a finger against the side of the man's head. "That you in there, Your Excellency?" He tapped the man's temple again. "That's you, isn't it, Excellency?"

"Where are they, Nicholas?" It was as dangerous-sounding a question as Nicholas had ever heard.

"I told you that you would have them, and you shall."

"I think you're lying to me, Nicholas," the voice growled. "I don't think you have them, as you promised you would."

Nicholas flipped a hand dismissively as he strolled off a few paces. "Oh foo. I have them by a string."

"I think otherwise. I have reason to believe that they aren't down here at all. I have reason to believe that the Mother Confessor herself is far to the north . . . with her army."

Nicholas frowned as he approached the man, leaning in close, peering into the eyes. "Do you completely lose your senses when you go cavorting into another man's mind like that?"

"Are you saying it isn't so?"

Nicholas was losing patience. "I was just watching them when you barged in here to pester me. They were both there—Lord Rahl and the Mother Confessor."

"Are you sure?" came the deep, gravelly voice out of the young soldier's mouth.

Nicholas planted his fists on his hips. "Are you questioning me? How dare you! I am Nicholas the Slide. I will not be questioned by anyone!"

The soldier took an aggressive step forward.

Nicholas held his ground and lifted a finger in warning. "If you want them, then you had better be awfully careful."

The soldier watched with wide eyes, but Nicholas could see more in those eyes: menace.

"Talk, then, before I lose my patience."

Nicholas screwed his mouth up in annoyance. "Whoever told you that they were to the north, that the Mother Confessor is with their army, either doesn't know what they're talking about or is lying to you. I've kept a careful eye on them."

"But have you seen them lately?"

The room was growing dark. Nicholas cast a hand toward the table, sending a small spark of his gift into three candles there, setting their wicks to flame.

"I told you, I was just watching them. They are in a city not far from here. Soon, they will be coming here, to me, and then I will have them. You don't have long to wait."

"What makes you think they're coming to you?"

"I know everything they do." Nicholas held his arms aloft, his black robes slipping up to his elbows, gesturing expansively as he walked around the man, speaking of what he alone knew. "I watch them. I have seen them lying together at night, the Mother Confessor tenderly holding her husband in her arms, holding his head to her shoulder, comforting his terrible pain. It's quite touching, actually."

"His pain?"

"Yes, his pain. They are in Northwick right now, a city not far to the north of here. When they are finished there, if they live through their visit, then they will be coming here, to me."

Jagang in the soldier looked around, taking in the freshly-dead bodies lying against the wall. His attention returned to Nicholas.

"I asked, what makes you think so?"

Nicholas looked over his shoulder and lifted an eyebrow at the emperor. "Well, you see, these fool people here—the pillars of Creation who so fascinate you—have poisoned the poor Lord Rahl. They did it to try to insure his help in getting rid of us."

"Poisoned him? Are you sure?"

Nicholas smiled at the note of interest he detected in the emperor's voice. "Oh, yes, quite sure. The poor man is in a great deal of pain. He needs an antidote."

"Then he will do what he must to get such an antidote. Richard Rahl is a surprisingly resourceful man."

Nicholas leaned his backside against the table and folded his arms. "He may be resourceful, but he's now in a great deal of trouble. You see, he needs two more doses of the antidote. The second is in Northwick. That's why he went there."

"You would be surprised at what that man can accomplish." It would have been impossible to miss the bristling anger in the emperor's voice. "You would be a fool to underestimate him, Nicholas."

"Oh, but I never underestimate anyone, Excellency." Nicholas smiled meaningfully at the emperor watching him through another man's eyes. "You see, I'm reasonably sure that Richard Rahl will retrieve the antidote in Northwick. In fact, I am counting on it. We shall see. I was watching him as you came in, watching what would happen. You spoiled it. But even if he obtains the antidote in Northwick, he will still need to get the last dose. The antidote in Northwick alone will not spare his life."

"Where's this other dose of his antidote?"

Nicholas reached into a pocket and showed the emperor the square-sided bottle, along with a satisfied smile. "I have it."

The man with an emperor inside him smiled. "He may come to take it from you, Nicholas. But, more likely, he will have someone else make him more of the antidote so that he won't even have to bother coming here."

"Oh, I don't think so. You see, Excellency, I am quite thorough in my work. This poison that Lord Rahl took is complex, but not nearly as complex as the antidote. I know, because I had the only man who can make it tortured until he told me what it was, told me all about it, told me its secrets. It contains a whole list of things I couldn't even begin to recall.

"I had the man killed, of course. Then I had the man who tortured the confession out of him, tortured the antidote's list of ingredients out of him, killed as well. It wouldn't do to have the resourceful Richard Rahl find either man and somehow discover from them what was in the cure.

"So, you see, Excellency, there is no one left to make Lord Rahl any more of the antidote." He held the bottle by the neck and wagged it before the man. "This is the last dose. Lord Rahl's last chance at life."

Through the eyes of a young soldier, Jagang watched the bottle Nicholas dangled before him. Any trace of humor had vanished.

"Then Richard Rahl will come here and get it."

Nicholas pulled the cork. He took a whiff. The liquid inside carried the slight aroma of cinnamon.

"You think so, Excellency?"

Making a great show of it, Nicholas poured the liquid out onto the floor.

As Emperor Jagang watched, Nicholas shook the bottle, making sure that the very last drop fell out.

"So, you see, Excellency, I have everything well in hand. Richard Rahl will not be a problem. He will shortly die from the poison—if my men don't manage to get him before then. Either way, Richard Rahl is a dead man—just as you requested."

Nicholas bowed, as if at the conclusion of a grand performance before an appreciative audience.

The man smiled again, a smile of strained forbearance.

"And what of the Mother Confessor?" the emperor asked.

Nicholas noted the clear undertone of restrained wrath. He was displeased not to be roundly admired for his great accomplishment. After all, this Emperor Jagang had not managed to capture the prize he so keenly sought. Nicholas smiled indulgently.

"Well, the way I see it, Excellency, now that I've told you Lord Rahl is soon to join the ranks of the Keeper's flock in the underworld, I have no assurance that you will keep your part of the bargain. I would like a commitment, on your part, before I give you the Mother Confessor."

"What makes you think you can capture her?"

"Oh, I have that well in hand. Her own nature will deliver her into my hands."

"Her own nature?"

"You let me worry about that, Excellency. All you need know is that I will deliver the Mother Confessor to you, alive, as promised. You might say that Lord Rahl was free—a gift on my part—but you will have to pay the price if you are to have the prize you covet: the Mother Confessor."

"And what would be your price?"

Nicholas strolled around the man in the center of the room. He gestured with the empty antidote bottle at the surroundings. "Not my idea of the proper way to live, if one has to live."

"So, you would have riches as a reward for doing your duty to the Creator, to the Imperial Order, and to your emperor."

The way Nicholas saw it, he had done more than his duty that night in the woods with the Sisters. Instead of saying so, he shrugged. "Well, I will let you have the rest of the world you have fought so hard to gain. I only want D'Hara. An empire of worth for my own."

"You wish to rule the land of D'Hara?"

Nicholas performed an exaggerated bow. "Under you, of course, Excellency." He straightened. "I will rule as do you, through fear and terror, all in the name of sacrificing for the betterment of mankind."

The dream walker watched through the eyes of the frightened soldier. The glint in those eyes was looking dangerous again.

"You play a risky game, Slide, making such demands. Your life must mean little to you."

Nicholas showed the emperor a smile that said he was tiring of trifling. "Hate to live, live to hate."

Finally, the emperor's smile returned to the man's lips.

"D'Hara is your wish? It is done. Lord Rahl dead, and the Mother Confessor delivered to me, alive, and you will then have D'Hara to do with as you wish . . . as long as you pay homage to the rule of the Imperial Order."

Nicholas indulged Jagang with a more polite smile as he bowed his head. "But of course."

"Then, when Richard Rahl is dead and I have the Mother Confessor, you shall be named Emperor Nicholas of the land of D'Hara."

"You are a wise emperor."

This was the man who had prescribed Nicholas's fate. This was the man who had sent those Sisters to practice their vile craft, to sunder him with the terrible agony of destroying who he had been, to mother him in an agonizing second Creation. They had decreed that he sacrifice himself to their cause. Nicholas had had no say in it. Now, at least, for the small task of dealing with the petty enemies of the Order, he would have his reward. He would have riches and power that he could never have dared imagine before he had been reborn. They had destroyed him, but they had created him again more powerful than he had ever been.

Now, he was but one step away from being Emperor Nicholas.

It had been a bitter road.

Driven by angry need, by hatred, Nicholas thrust out his hand as he thrust his own mind, like a hot dagger, into the mind of this man before him, into the spaces between his thoughts, into the marrow of his soul.

He hungered to feel the slick heat of this other spirit slide into his own, the hot rush of taking him while Jagang was still within the man's mind.

But there was nothing there.

In that spark of time, Jagang had already slipped away.

The man crashed to the floor, dead.

Nicholas—Emperor Nicholas—smiled at the game only just begun. He was beginning to wonder if he had set the price too low.

CHAPTER 51

As they made their way up the street, Kahlan glanced at the small windows in the surrounding buildings. In the gathering darkness, she doubted that the faces she saw peering out of the windows could tell much about the people they saw out in the street, but she pulled the hood of her cloak forward anyway.

From the stories the men had told, it was not safe to be a woman in Bandakar, so Kahlan, Jennsen and Cara wore hoods to cover their identities to draw as little attention as possible. Kahlan knew that people in fear for their own lives sometimes tried to shift attention away from themselves by offering another to the wolves. Worse, she also knew that there were bitter people devoted to the morbid ideal of the perpetual cannibalism of appeasement that they defined as peace.

Richard slowed and checked the alley as they passed. One hand gripped the front of his simple black cloak so that, if need be, he could lift it open and draw his sword.

Their men were spread out so as not to appear to be a mob moving through Northwick. Any gathering of crowds of men, except in markets, would no doubt be reported and swiftly draw the attention of the Imperial Order soldiers. They had timed their entry into the city to be just as night fell so as to better obscure them, yet not so late that their presence on the streets would be suspicious.

"There," Owen said as they reached the corner, tilting his head to the right. "Down that way."

Richard looked back over his shoulder to make sure that everyone was still with him, then turned down the narrow street. The buildings in the city were mostly single-story, but they were entering a district where a number had a second story, usually hanging several feet out over the street. Kahlan saw nothing taller than the squat two-story buildings.

The area they had turned into reeked with the stench of sewage in a shallow ditch to the side. The dusty streets of Northwick kept making her cough. She imagined that when it rained the place turned into a quagmire that stank even worse. She saw that Richard was making a great effort not to cough. It wasn't always possible. At least when he did, he wasn't coughing up blood.

As they kept to the shadows in under the overhangs and eaves, Kahlan moved up closer to him. Jennsen followed right behind. Anson, out ahead, scouted their route, looking for all the world as if he was by himself.

Richard scanned the sky again. It was empty. They hadn't seen any black-tipped races since before they started up the pass into Bandakar. Kahlan and Cara were glad not to see the huge black birds. Richard, though, seemed as troubled by not seeing them as he once had when he did.

Cara hung back a bit, along with a half-dozen men. Tom and some others were moving up a parallel street. Yet other men, who knew where they were headed, made their way through the city by a different route. Even though there were less than fifty in their force, such numbers together could bring attention and trouble.

For now, they didn't need trouble. They needed the antidote.

"Where is the city's center?" Kahlan asked Owen when she got close enough to be able to speak in a low voice.

Owen swept his arm around, indicating the street they were on. "This is the place. These shops are where the major commerce is, where people come. In the open squares the people sometimes set up markets."

Kahlan saw a leather shop, a bakery, a place that sold cloth, but nothing more elaborate. "This is the center of your great city? These post-and-beam buildings with living quarters over the shops? This is your major business center?"

"Yes," Owen said, sounding half-puzzled and half proud.

Kahlan let out a sigh, but didn't comment. Richard did.

"This is the result of your advanced culture?" He gestured around at the shabby daub-and-wattle buildings. "In close to three thousand years this is what your great culture has accomplished? This is what you have managed to build?"

Owen smiled. "Yes. It is magnificent, is it not?"

Instead of answering the question, Richard said, "I thought you were in Altur'Rang."

"I was."

"Well, even that dingy place was far more advanced than this city of Northwick."

"It was? I am sorry, Lord Rahl, but I did not see much of Altur'Rang. I was afraid to go far into such a place, and I did not stay for long." Owen looked back at Kahlan. "Do you mean to say that the city where you are from is more magnificent than this one?"

Kahlan blinked at the man. How could she possibly explain Aydindril, the Wizard's Keep, the Confessors' Palace, the palaces on Kings Row, the People's Palace, the marble-and-granite work, the soaring columns, the noble works of art, or any of a hundred other places and sights to a man who thought straw-and-dung buildings were an example of advanced culture? In the end, she decided that this was not the time to try.

"Owen, I hope that when we are all free of the oppression of the Imperial Order, Richard and I can show you and your people some other places in the world outside Bandakar—show you some other centers of major commerce and art—some of what mankind else-where has accomplished."

Owen smiled. "I would like that, Mother Confessor. I would like it very much." He stopped abruptly. "Oh, here is the place. It is down here."

A head-high wooden gate weathered to a brownish gray barred the alleyway beyond from sight. Richard checked both ways up the street, looking to see if anyone was watching. The street was empty of everyone but their men. As he kept an eye on the street, he pushed the gate open enough to allow Owen to slip through.

Owen poked his head back out. "Come, it is clear."

Richard gave a hand signal to the men up at the corner. He put his arm around Kahlan's waist, holding her close as he squeezed with her through the gate into the alley.

The walls of the buildings on either side that came to the edge of the narrow, dusty alleyway had no windows. Some of the tightly-packed structures that weren't set so far back had room for small backyards. As they moved cautiously up the alley, more of their men poured in through the gate at the far end. Chickens penned in one of the yards flapped their wings in fright at the people moving close by.

Jennsen pulled Betty along by her rope, keeping the goat close so she couldn't cause any trouble. Betty remained quiet, seeming nervous in the strange surroundings of a city. She wasn't even wagging her tail as she peered up at Richard, Kahlan, and Jennsen for reassurance as they moved deeper into the heart of the jumble of buildings.

Tom appeared at the other end of the alleyway, bringing another group of men. Richard signaled for them to spread out and wait at that end of the alleyway.

Cara came up from behind, the hood of her cloak pulled up like Kahlan and Jennsen's. "I don't like it."

"Good," Richard whispered in answer.

"Good?" Cara asked. "You think it's good that I don't like this place?"

"Yes," Richard said. "If you were ever happy and unconcerned, then I'd be worried."

Cara twisted her mouth with a reply she decided to keep to herself.

"Here," Owen said, grabbing Richard's arm to stop him.

Richard looked where Owen had pointed and then stared down at him. "This is a palace?"

Owen nodded. "One of them. We have several palaces. I told you, we are an advanced culture."

Richard gave Kahlan a sidelong glance, but said nothing.

From what Kahlan could see in the dim light, the backyard was dry dirt with clumps of grass growing here and there. A wooden stairway at the back of the building led up to a small balcony with a door onto the second floor. As they passed through a short gate into the yard, Kahlan saw that under the stairs there was a stairwell going down.

Owen looked around, then leaned close. "They are downstairs. This is where they are hiding the Wise One."

Richard scanned the alley and the surrounding buildings. He rubbed his fingertips across his brow.

"And the antidote is in there?"

Owen nodded. "Do you wish to wait while I go get it?"

Richard shook his head. "We'll go with you."

Kahlan held his arm, wishing she could do more to comfort his pain. The best thing, though, was to get the antidote. The sooner they rid him of the poison, the sooner he could deal with solving the problem of the headaches caused by the gift.

Some of their men waited nearby. She saw in their eyes their fear of being back in a city where the Imperial Order soldiers had control. She didn't know what she and Richard could do to help them free their people of those troops, but she intended to come up with something. Were it not for her desperate act, no matter how unwitting, these people would not be suffering and dying at the hands of the Order.

The last gray glow of twilight made Richard's eyes look as if they were made of steel. He pulled Jennsen close.

"Why don't you and Tom stay out here, with Betty, and stand watch. Stay under the concealment of the stairs and balcony. If you see any soldiers, come let us know."

Jennsen nodded. "I'll let Betty graze on the grass. It would look more natural if any patrols pass by."

"Just keep out of sight," he said. "If soldiers see a young woman like you they won't hesitate to snatch you."

"I'll keep her out of sight," Tom said as he came up into the yard. He aimed a thumb over his shoulder. "I have the men spread out so they won't be so noticeable."

Kahlan and Cara followed Richard and Owen toward the back of the building. At the stairwell down, Owen paused when Richard instead went to the door into the building.

"This way, Lord Rahl."

"I know. Wait while I check the hallway inside, make sure it's clear."

"It is just empty rooms where people sometimes meet."

"I want to check it anyway. Cara, wait here with Kahlan."

Kahlan followed Richard to the door under the balcony. "I'm going with you."

Cara was right on Kahlan's heels. "If you want to check the hall," she told Richard, "then you may come with us."

After a quick glance at Kahlan's eyes, he didn't argue with her. Looking at Cara, he said, "Sometimes . . ."

Cara flashed him a defiant smile. "You wouldn't know what to do without me."

Kahlan saw that as he turned to the door, he couldn't help but smile. Her heart lifted at seeing Richard's smile, and then she felt a sudden pang of sorrow for Cara, knowing how she must miss General Meiffert with their army far to the north in D'Hara. It wasn't often that a Mord-Sith could come to care about someone the way Kahlan knew Cara cared about Benjamin. Cara wouldn't come out and admit it, though, and had put first her wish to protect Richard and Kahlan. When she and Cara had been back with the army, Kahlan had promoted the then captain to general after a battle in which they had lost a number of officers. Captain Meiffert had risen to the occasion. Since then, he had held their army together. While she had complete faith in him, she also feared for his well-being, as Cara certainly must. Kahlan wondered if they would ever again see the young general.

Richard opened the door a crack and peered into the dark hallway beyond. It was empty. Cara, Agiel in hand, pushed through and entered ahead of them, wanting to be sure that it was safe. Kahlan followed Richard in. There were two doors to each side. At the far end of the hall stood a door with a small window.

"What's out there?" Kahlan whispered as Richard looked through the window.

"The street. I see some of our men."

On the way back, Richard checked rooms on one side while Cara checked the rooms on the other. They were all empty, just as Owen had said.

"This might be a good place to hide our men," Cara said.

Richard nodded. "That's what I was thinking. We could make strikes from here, from their midst, rather than risk being spotted coming in from the countryside to attack."

Before they reached the back door, Richard suddenly stumbled, banging a shoulder against the wall before going to one knee. Kahlan and Cara grabbed for him, keeping him from falling on his face.

"What's wrong?" Cara whispered.

He paused a moment, apparently waiting for the bout of pain to lift. His fingers squeezing Kahlan's arm hurt so much that her eyes were watering, but she made herself remain silent.

"I just . . . just got dizzy for a minute." He panted, trying to recover his breath. "The dark hall, I guess."

His fingers released their viselike grip on Kahlan's arm.

"The second state," Kahlan said. "That's what Owen called it. He said that the second state of the poison was dizziness."

Richard looked up at her in the dark. "I'm all right. Let's go get the antidote."

Owen, waiting in the shadows in the stairwell, started down when they reached him. At the bottom of the stairs he pushed the door open and looked in.

"They are still here," he said with relief. "The speakers are still here—I recognize some of their voices. The Wise One must still be here with them. They have not moved to another hiding place as I feared they might."

Owen was hoping the great speakers would agree to help rid their people of the Imperial Order. Since they had refused in the past, Kahlan didn't think they would agree this time, but then, Owen and his men had not at first agreed to fight. Owen believed that with the commitment of the men they had and with what had happened in his town, the assembly of speakers would see that there was a chance of being free again and would be more open to hearing what had to be done. Many of the men shared Owen's confidence that help was at hand.

More important than talking to the speakers, as far as Kahlan was concerned, was that this was where the second bottle of antidote was hidden. That came above all else. They had to secure the antidote. Whenever she thought about the possibility of Richard dying, it made her knees tremble.

Just inside the small vestibule, Owen rapped gently on a door.

Soft candlelight came from inside when the door pulled in a crack. A man peered out for a moment, then his eyes went wide.

"Owen?"

Kahlan didn't think the man intended to open the door. Before he had a chance to think it over, Richard pushed the door open and moved into the room. The man hastily backed out of Richard's way.

Richard pulled Cara close. "Guard the door. None of these people comes out unless I say so."

Cara nodded and took up a position outside the door.

"What is the meaning of this?" the man inside demanded of Owen as he gaped in fear at Richard and Kahlan.

"Great speaker, it is vital that we speak with all of you."

The place was aglow with candles. A dozen and more men sitting around on rugs sipping tea or leaning against pillows lining the walls abruptly fell silent.

The stone walls were the outer foundation of the building. Stone piers marched in two lines down the center of the large room, supporting fat beams far above Richard's head. There was no decoration. It looked like little more than a basement made more comfortable with rugs and pillows where the men congregated at one end of the extensive room. Simple wooden tables against the walls at one end held candles.

Some of the men rose to their feet.

"Owen," one of them said in grave reprimand, "you have been banished. What are you doing here?"

"Honored speaker, we are well past petty issues of banishment." Owen held out an introductory hand. "These are friends of mine, from outside our land."

Kahlan grabbed Owen's shirt at the shoulder and pulled his ear close as she said through gritted teeth, "Antidote."

Owen nodded apologetically. The men, all older, watched indignantly as Owen went to the corner at the far right. At about chest height, he grasped a stone and twisted it from side to side. Richard reached in and helped Owen wiggle the stone loose. When he finally pulled the heavy block out far enough to turn it to the side, Owen reached in behind and came out with the bottle. He wasted no time in handing it to Richard.

When Richard pulled the cork, Kahlan detected the slight aroma of cinnamon. Richard downed the contents.

"You must leave," one of the men growled. "You are not welcome here."

Owen didn't back down. "We must see the Wise One."

"What!"

"The men of the Order have invaded our land. They are torturing and murdering our people. Others, they have taken away."

"Nothing can be done about this," the red-faced speaker said. "We do as we must so that our people can go on with their lives. We do as we must to avoid violence."

"We have ended violence," Owen told the man. "At least, in our town. We killed all the men of the Order who held us in the grip of fear, who raped and tortured and murdered our people. Our people there are now free of these men of the Order. We must fight back and free the rest of our people. It is your duty as speakers to do right by our people and not accommodate their enslavement."

The great speakers were apoplectic.

"We will hear none of this!"

"We will speak of it with the Wise One and see what he has to say."

"No! The Wise One will not see you! Never! You are all denied! You must all leave!"

CHAPTER 52

One of the men came forward and angrily seized a fistful of Richard's shirt, trying to push him out. "You are the cause of this! You are an outsider! A savage! One of the unenlightened! You have brought profane ideas among our people!" He did his best to shake Richard. "You have seduced our people to violence!"

Richard snatched the speaker's wrist and wrenched his arm around, taking him to his knees. The man cried out in pain. Without letting up, Richard leaned down toward him. "We have risked our lives helping your people. Your people are not enlightened, but people the same as anyone else. You are going to listen to us. This night, the future of you and your people will be shaped."

Richard released the man with a shove, then went to the door and stuck his head out. "Cara, go ask Tom to help you get all the rest of the men to come down here. I think they had all better be part of this."

As Cara ran to spread the word that Richard wanted all the men to gather into the basement of the "palace," he ordered the speakers back against the wall.

"You have no right to do this," one protested.

"You are the representatives of the people of Bandakar. You are their leaders," Richard told them. "The time has come for you to lead."

Behind him, men started filing into the candlelit room. It wasn't long before they were all quietly assembled. The basement was large enough that Owen's men took up only part of the available space. Kahlan saw other, unfamiliar people straggle in as well. Knowing the nature of these people, and since Cara was letting them in, Kahlan didn't think that they presented a threat.

Richard gestured toward the quiet gathering watching the speakers. "These men from the town of Witherton have faced the truth of what is happening to their people. They will no longer tolerate such brutality. They will no longer be victims. They wish to be free."

One of the speakers, a man with a narrow, pointed chin, huffed dismissively. "Freedom can never work. It only gives people license to be self-centered. A thoughtful person, dedicated to the welfare of an enlightened mankind, must reject the immoral concept of 'freedom' for what it is—selfish."

"That's right," another agreed, "such simplistic beliefs can only provoke a cycle of violence. This silly notion of 'freedom' leads to viewing things as black or white. Such uninspired morals are obsolete. Individuals have no right to judge others—especially in such authoritarian terms. What is needed is compromise among all sides if there is to be peace."

"Compromise?" Richard asked. "A cycle of violence can only exist if you grant all people, including those who are evil, moral equivalence—if you say that everyone, including those who decide to harm others, has an equal right to exist. That is what you do when you refuse to crush evil—you give moral standing and power to those who murder.

"Devotion to compromise in such arenas is a sick idea that says you must cut off a finger, and then a leg, and then an arm to feed the monster living among you. Evil feeds on the good. If you kill the monster, the violence ends.

"You have two choices before you. Choose to live in cringing fear, on your knees, apologizing endlessly for wishing to be allowed to live as you struggle to appease an ever-expanding evil, or eliminate those who would harm you and free yourselves to live your own lives—which means you must remain vigilant, ever ready to protect yourself."

One of the speakers, his eyes going wide, lifted an arm to point at Richard. "I know you, now. You are the one who was named in prophecy. You are the one that prophecy says will destroy us!"

Whispers carried the accusation back through the crowd.

Richard gazed back at his gathered men, then directed a withering glare at the speakers. "I am Richard Rahl. You're right, I am the one named in the prophecy given to your people so long ago. 'Your destroyer will come and he will redeem you.'

"You're right, this prophecy is about me. But if I had not come along, it would eventually have been another who would have fulfilled those words, whether in another year, or another thousand years, because this prophecy is really about man's honorable commitment to life.

"Your people were banished because they refused to see the truth of the world around them. They chose to close their minds to reality. I have ended that blindness." Richard pointed back at the men with him. "When the truth was put before these men, they chose at last to open their eyes and see it. Now, the rest of your people must meet the same challenge and make a choice as to how they will live their future.

"'Your destroyer will come and he will redeem you,' are words about the potential for a better future. They mean that your way of life—of impeding people from being their best, of restricting them from being all that they can be, of your blind destructive ways that crush the spirit of each individual and over time have caused so many of the best of your people to abandon you and go into the unknown beyond the boundary—are ended.

"The men of the Order may have invaded your land, but, spiritually, they change nothing for you. Their violence is merely more apparent than your slow suffocation of human potential. They offer the same unseeing lives you already live, simply with a more manifest form of brutality.

"I have brought the light of truth to some of your people, and in so doing I have destroyed their dark existence. The rest of your people must now decide whether they will continue to cower in darkness or come into the light I have brought among you.

"In bringing that light to your people, I have redeemed them.

"I have shown them that they can soar on their own wings, aspire to reach for what they want for themselves. I have helped them take back their own lives.

"Yes, I have destroyed the pretext which creates the chains of their repression, but in so doing I have freed the nobility of their spirits.

"That is the meaning of the prophecy. It is up to each of you to rise to the occasion and seek to triumph, or to hide in your self-imposed darkness without trying. There is no guarantee that if you try you will succeed. But without trying, you will assure failure and lives of dread for yourselves and your children. The only difference will be that if you choose to live the same way you do now, if you continue to appease evil, you will now know that it's at the price of your souls."

Richard turned away from the speakers. Before he closed his eyes to rub them with his fingertips, Kahlan saw the terrible agony in those eyes. She wanted nothing more than to get to the last antidote and then to do what they must to rid him of the pain caused by his gift. She knew she was slowly losing him. It seemed to her as if Richard were somewhere all alone, dangling from the edge of a cliff, holding on by his fingertips, and his fingers were slowly slipping.

Owen stepped forward. "Honored speakers, the time has come to hear from the Wise One. If you do not think this crisis for our people warrants it, then nothing does. This is our future, our lives, at stake.

"Bring out the Wise One. We will hear his words, and see if he truly is wise and worthy of our loyalty."

After noting the murmurs of agreement throughout the room, the speakers put their heads together, whispering among themselves to find a consensus as to what to do. Finally, about half of them went off into a back room.

One of the remaining speakers smiled and bowed his bald head. "We will see what the Wise One has to say." Kahlan had seen such contemptuous smiles often enough. Lifting his pointed chin, he serenely clasped his hands before him. "Before all these people, we will put your blasphemous words to the Wise One and hear his wisdom so that this matter may be put to rest."

Men emerged from the back room carrying posts draped with red cloth, notched boards, and planks. Before the door into a back room, they began assembling a simple platform with posts at each corner and the heavy red drapes designed to enclosed it. When the structure was finally completed, they placed a large pillow on the platform and then drew the drapes together. Other men carried over two tables holding a number of candles, and placed one on each side of the draped ceremonial seat of wisdom. In short order, the speakers had created a simple but reverent setting.

Kahlan knew a number of peoples in the Midlands who had magic and functioned in the capacity she imagined that this Wise One did. They also usually had attendants, such as these speakers. She also knew better than to underestimate such simple shamans and their link to the spirit world. There were those who had very real connections and very real power over their people.

What she couldn't imagine was how a people without any magic whatsoever could have such an agent of the spirits. If it was true that they did, and such a person went against them, then all their work would have been for nothing.

The speakers lined up to either side and then drew the curtains in the front just enough to see into the dim interior.

There, sitting cross-legged on the pillow, was what appeared to be a boy in white robes, his hands resting prayerfully in his lap. He didn't look very old, maybe eight or ten at most. A black scarf was tied around his head to cover his eyes.

"He's just a boy," Richard said.

At the interruption, one of the speakers shot Richard a murderous glare. "Only a child is innocent enough of the contamination of life to be free to touch true wisdom. As we grow older we layer our experiences over our once-perfect insight, but we remember those once unadulterated connections and so we realize how only in a child can wisdom itself be so pure."

Heads throughout the room bobbed knowingly.

Richard cast a sidelong glance at Kahlan.

One of the speakers knelt before the platform and bowed his bald head. "Wise One, we must ask your knowing guidance. Some of our men wish to begin a war."

"War solves nothing," the Wise One said in a pious voice.

"Perhaps you would like to hear his reasons."

"There are no valid reasons for fighting. War is never a solution. War is an admission of failure."

The people in the room shrank back, looking ill-at-ease to have brought such crude inquiries before the Wise One, inquiries he had no trouble untangling with simple wisdom that laid bare obvious immorality.

"Very wise. You have shown us wisdom in its true, simple perfection. All men would do well to heed such truth." The man bowed his head again. "We have tried to tell—"

"Why are you wearing a blindfold?" Richard asked, cutting off the speaker kneeling before the platform.

"I hear anger in your voice," the Wise One said. "Nothing can be accomplished until you shed your hate. If you search with your heart, you can find the good in everyone."

Richard put a hand on Owen's back, urging him ahead. He reached back into the crowd of men and grabbed a pinch of Anson's shirt, pulling him forward as well. The three men moved up to the Wise One's platform. Only Richard stood tall. With his foot, he forced the kneeling speaker aside.

"I asked why you're wearing a blindfold," Richard said.

"Knowledge must be denied so as to make room for faith. It is only through faith that real truth can be reached," the Wise One said. "You must believe before you can see."

"If you believe without seeing the truth of what is," Richard said, "then you're simply being willfully blind, not wise. You must see, first, in order to learn and understand."

The men around Kahlan looked uncomfortable that Richard was speaking in this way to their Wise One.

"Stop the hate, or you reap only hate."

"We were talking about knowledge. I haven't asked you about hate."

The Wise One put his hands together prayerfully before himself, bowing his head slightly. "Wisdom is all around us, but our eyes blind us, our hearing deafens us, our minds think and so make us ignorant.

Our senses only trick us; the world can tell us nothing of the nature of reality. To be at one with the greater essence of the true meaning of life, you must first stare blindly inward to discover truth."

Richard folded his arms over his chest. "I have eyes, so I can't see. I have ears, so I can't hear. I have a mind, so I can't know anything."

"The first step to wisdom is to accept that we are inadequate to know the nature of reality, and so nothing we think we know can be real."

"We must eat to live. How is one to track a deer in the woods so you can eat? Blindfold yourself? Stuff wax in your ears? Do it while you're asleep so your mind won't contribute any thinking to the task at hand?"

"We do not eat meat. It is wrong to harm animals just so that we might eat. We have no more right to live than an animal."

"So you eat only plants, eggs, cheese—things like that."

"Of course."

"How do you make cheese?"

In the awkward silence, someone in the back of the room coughed.

"I am the Wise One. I have not been called upon to do this work. Others make cheese for us to eat."

"I see, you don't know how to make cheese for your dinner because no one has ever taught you. That's perfect. Here you are, then, blindfolded and with a clear mind not all clogged up with troublesome knowledge on the subject. So, how do you make cheese? Is it coming to you? Is the method of making cheese being sent to you through your blindfolded divine introspection?"

"Reality cannot be tested—"

"Tell me how, if you were to wear a blindfold so you couldn't see, put wax in your ears so you couldn't hear, and put on heavy mittens so you couldn't feel anything, how you would even do something as simple as picking a radish to eat. Tell you what, you can leave the wax out of your ears, and not bother with the mittens. Just leave that blindfold on and show me how you can pick a radish so you have something to eat. I'll even help you find the door, first, then you're on your own. Come on, then. Off you go."

The Wise One licked his lips. "Well, I . . ."

"If you deny yourself sight, hearing, touch . . . how will you plant food to sustain your life, or how can you even hunt for berries and nuts? If nothing is real, then how long until you starve to death while you wait for some inner voice of 'truth' to feed you?"

One of the speakers rushed forward, trying to push Richard back. Richard shoved the man so hard that it sat him on the ground. The speakers cowered back a few paces. Richard put one boot up on the platform, laid his arm across his knee, and leaned close to the Wise One.

"Answer my questions, 'Wise One.' Tell me what staring blindly inwardly has so far revealed to you about making cheese. Come on, let's hear it."

"But . . . it's not a fair question."

"Oh? A question regarding the pursuit of a value is not fair? Life requires all living things to successfully pursue values if they are to continue to live. A bird dies if it can't succeed at catching a worm. It's basic. People are no different."

"Stop the hate."

"You already have on a blindfold. Why don't you plug your ears and hum a tune to yourself so you won't be thinking about anything" —Richard leaned in and lowered his voice dangerously— "and in your state of infinite wisdom, Wise One, just try to guess what I'm about to do to you."

The boy squealed in fright and scooted back.

Kahlan pushed her way between Richard and Anson and sat back on the platform. She put an arm around the terrified boy and pulled him close to comfort him. He pressed himself into her sheltering protection.

"Richard, you're scaring the poor boy. Look at him. He's shaking like a leaf."

Richard pulled the blindfold off the boy's head. In confused dismay, he peered fearfully up at Richard.

"Why did you go to her?" Richard asked in a gentle tone.

"Because, you were about to hurt me."

"You mean, then, that you were hoping she would protect you?"

"Of course—you're bigger than me."

Richard smiled. "Do you see what you're saying? You were frightened and you hoped to be protected from danger. That wasn't wrong of you, was it? To want to be safe? To fear aggression? To seek help from someone you thought might be big enough to stop the threat?"

The boy looked confused. "No, I guess not."

"And what if I held a knife to you? Wouldn't you want to have someone prevent me from cutting you? Wouldn't you want to live?"

The boy nodded. "Yes."

"That's the value we're talking about, here."

He frowned. "What do you mean?"

"Life," Richard said. "You want to live. That is noble. You don't want someone else to take your life. That is just. All creatures want to live. A rabbit will run if threatened; that's why he has strong legs. He doesn't need the strong legs or big ears to find and eat tender shoots. He has the big ears to listen for threats, and the strong legs to escape.

"A buck will snort in warning if threatened. A snake may shake a rattle to ward off threats. A wolf growls a warning. But if the danger keeps coming and they can't escape, a buck may trample it, the snake may strike, and the wolf may attack. None of them will go looking for a fight, but they will protect themselves.

"Man is the only creature who willingly submits to the fangs of a predator. Only man, through continual indoctrination such as you've been given, will reject the values that sustain life. Yet you instinctively did the right thing in going to my wife."

"I did?"

"Yes. Your ways couldn't protect you, so you acted on the chance that she might. If I really were someone intent on harming you, she would have fought to stop me."

The Wise One looked up into Kahlan's smile. "You would?"

"Yes, I would. I, too, believe in the nobility of life."

He stared in wonder.

Kahlan slowly shook her head. "But your instinctive act of seeking protection would have done you no good had you instead sought the protection of people who live by the misguided teachings you repeat. Those teachings condemn self-preservation as a form of hate. Your people are being slaughtered with the aid of their own beliefs."

He looked stricken. "But, I don't want that."

Kahlan smiled. "Neither do we. That's why we came, and why Richard had to show you that you can know the truth of reality and doing so will help you survive."

"Thank you," he said to Richard.

Richard smiled and gently smoothed down the boy's blond hair. "Sorry I had to frighten you to show you that what you were saying didn't really make any sense. I needed to show you that the words you've been taught can't serve you well—you can't live by them because they are devoid of reality and reason. You look to me like a boy who cares about living. I was like that when I was your age, and I still am. Life is wonderful; take delight in it, look around with the eyes you have, and see it in all its glory."

"No one has ever talked to me about life in this way. I don't get to see much. I have to stay inside all the time."

"Tell you what, maybe, before I go, I can take you for a walk in the woods and show you some of the wonders of the world around you—the trees and plants, birds, maybe we'll even see a fox—and we'll talk some more about the wonders and joy of life. Would you like that?"

The boy's face lit up with a grin. "Really? You would do that for me?"

Richard smiled one of those smiles that so melted Kahlan's heart. He playfully pinched the boy's nose. "Sure."

Owen came forward and ran his fingers affectionately through the boy's hair. "I was once like you—a Wise One—until I got a little older than you."

The boy frowned up at him. "Really?"

Owen nodded. "I used to think that I had been chosen because I was special and somehow only I was able to commune with some glorious otherworldly dominion. I believed that I was gushing great wisdom. Looking back, I am ashamed to see how foolish it all was. I was made to listen to lessons. I was never allowed to be a boy. The great speakers praised me for repeating back the things I had heard, and when I spoke then with great scorn to people, they told me how wise I was."

"Me, too," the boy said.

Richard turned back to the men. "This is what your people have been reduced to as a source of wisdom—listening to children repeating meaningless expressions. You have minds in order to think and understand the world around you. This self-imposed blindness is a dark treason to yourselves."

The men in front, that Kahlan could see from where she sat holding the boy, all hung their heads in shame.

"Lord Rahl is right," Anson said, turning back to the men. "Until today, I never actually questioned it or thought about how foolish it really is."

One of the speakers shook his fist. "It is not foolish!"

Another, the one with the pointed chin, leaned in and snatched Anson's knife from the sheath at his belt.

Kahlan could hardly believe what she had just seen. It felt as if she were watching a nightmare suddenly unfold, a nightmare she wasn't able to stop or even slow. It seemed she knew what was going to happen before she saw it.

With an enraged cry, the speaker suddenly struck out, stabbing Anson before he could react. Kahlan heard the blade hit bone. Driven by blind rage, the speaker swiftly drew back the fist holding the now-bloody knife to stab Anson again. Anson's face twisted in shock as he began to fall.

Points of candlelight reflecting off the polished length of razor-sharp steel blurred into streaks as Richard's sword flashed past Kahlan. Even as the sword swept around, the unique ring of the steel as it was drawn accompanied its terrifying arc toward the threat. Driven by Richard's formidable strength, the tip of the sword whistled through the air. As the speaker's arm reached the apex of its swing, as it once more began a deadly journey down, Richard's blade slammed into the side of the speaker's neck and without seeming to slow in the least ripped through flesh and bone, cleaving off the man's head and one shoulder along with the arm holding high the knife. The lightning slash threw long strings of blood against the stone wall of the foundation of the palace of the Bandakar Empire.

As the speaker's head and the one shoulder with the arm attached tumbled through the air in an odd, wobbling spiral, his body collapsed in a heap. The head smacked the floor with a sickening thud and bounced across the carpets, leaving a trail of blood as it tumbled.

Richard swept the crimson blade around, directing it toward the potential threat of the other speakers. Kahlan pressed the boy's face to her shoulder, covering his eyes.

Some of the men fell in around Anson. Kahlan didn't know how badly he was hurt—or if he was even still alive.

Not far away, the gory head and arm of the dead speaker lay before a table set with candles. The fist still held the knife in a death grip. The sudden carnage lying there before them all, the blood spreading across the floor, was horrifying. Everyone stared in stunned silence.

"The first blood drawn by you great speakers," Richard said in a quiet voice to the cluster of cringing speakers, "is not against those who come to murder your people, but against a man who committed no violence against you—one of your own who simply stood up and told you that he wanted to be free of the oppression of terror, free to think for himself."

Kahlan stood and saw then that there were far more people in the room than there had been before. Most were not their men. When Cara made her way through the silent throng to her side, Kahlan took her by the arm and leaned close.

"Who are all those people?"

"The people from the city. Runners brought them the news that the town of Witherton had been freed. They heard about our men being here to see the Wise One and wanted to witness what would happen. The stairs and halls upstairs are full of them. The words that have been spoken down here have spread up through the whole crowd."

Cara was obviously concerned about being close enough to protect Richard and Kahlan. Kahlan knew that many of the people had been swayed by what Richard had been saying but now she didn't know what they would do.

The speakers seemed to have lost their conviction. They didn't want to be associated with the one among them who had done such a thing. One of them finally left his fellow speakers and made the lone walk over to the boy standing beside the curtain-draped platform, and under Kahlan's protective arm.

"I am sorry," he said in a sincere voice to the boy. He turned to the people watching. "I am sorry. I don't want to be a speaker any longer. The prophecy has been fulfilled; our redemption is at hand. I think we would do best to listen to what these men have to say. I think I would like to live without the fear that the men of the Order are going to murder us all."

There were no cheers, no wild ovation but, rather, silent agreement as all the people Kahlan could see nodded with what looked like expectant hope that their secret wish to be free of the brutality of the Imperial Order was not a sinful, secret thought after all, but was really the right thing.

Richard knelt beside Owen as other men worked at tying a strip of cloth around Anson's upper arm. He was sitting up. His whole arm was soaked in blood, but it looked as if the bandage was slowing the bleeding. Kahlan sighed in relief at seeing that Anson was alive and not seriously hurt.

"It looks as if it will need to be stitched," Richard said.

Some of the men agreed. An older man pushed his way through the crowd and stepped forward.

"I do such things. I also have herbs with which to make a poultice."

"Thank you," Anson said as his friends helped him stand. He looked light-headed and the men had to steady him. Once sure of his feet, he turned to Richard. "Thank you, Lord Rahl, for answering the call in the words of the devotion I spoke: 'Master Rahl protect us.' I never thought I would be the first to bleed for what we have set out to do, or that the blood would be drawn by one of our own people."

Richard gently clapped Anson on the back of his good shoulder, showing his appreciation for his words.

Owen looked around at the crowd. "I think we have all decided to be free again." When the crowd nodded their agreement, Owen turned to Richard. "How will we get rid of the soldiers in Northwick?"

Richard wiped his sword clean on the cloth of the dead speaker's trouser leg. His gaze turned upon the crowd. "Any idea how many soldiers there are here in Northwick?"

There was no anger in his voice. Kahlan had seen, since the moment he had drawn his sword, that the Sword of Truth's attendant magic had been absent from his eyes. There was no spark of the sword's rage in the Seeker's eyes, no magic dangerously dancing there, no fury in his demeanor. He had simply done what was necessary to stop the threat. While it was a relief that he had swiftly succeeded, it was gravely worrisome that the Sword's magic had not come out along with the sword itself.

What had always been there to help him before had apparently finally failed him. This absence of his sword's magic left Kahlan feeling icy apprehension.

People in the crowd looked around at others and then spoke up about hundreds of men of the Order they had seen. Another man said there were several thousand.

An older woman lifted her hand. "Not that many, but approaching it."

Owen turned to Richard. "That's a lot of men for us to take on."

Having never been in a real battle, he didn't know the half of it. Richard didn't seem to hear Owen. He slid his sword back into the scabbard hidden under his black cloak.

"How do you know?" he asked the woman.

"I am one of the people who helps prepare their meals."

"You mean you people cook for the soldiers?"

"Yes," the old woman said. "They do not wish to do it for themselves."

"When do you next have to cook?"

"We have large kettles we are just starting to get ready for tomorrow's meal. It takes us all night to prepare the stew so that we can cook it tomorrow for their evening meal. Besides that, we also have to work all night making biscuits, eggs, and porridge for their morning meal."

Kahlan imagined that the soldiers were probably pleased to have such a ready supply of pliant slaves. Richard paced in a short track between her and Owen. He pinched his lower lip as he considered the problem. With such a small force of their own, nearly two thousand armed men was a lot to take on, especially considering how inexperienced the men were. Kahlan recognized that Richard was scheming something.

He took the arm of the older man tightening the bandage around Anson's wound. "You said you had herbs. Do you know about such things?"

The man shrugged. "Not a great deal, just enough to make simple remedies."

Kahlan's mood sank. She had thought that maybe this man might know something about making more of the antidote.

"Do you have access to lily of the valley, oleander, yew, monkshood, hemlock?"

The man blinked in surprise. "Common enough, I guess, especially just to the north in the wooded areas."

Richard turned to his men standing at the fore of the crowd. "We must eliminate the men of the Order. The less fighting we have to do, the better.

"While it's still dark, we need to slip out of the city and go collect the things we need." He lifted a hand to the woman who had spoken about cooking for the soldiers. "You show us where you're going to do all the cooking of tomorrow's evening meal. We'll bring you some extra ingredients.

"With what we put in the stew, the soldiers will be getting violently sick within hours. We will put different things in different kettles, so the symptoms will be different, to help create confusion and panic. If we can get enough of the poisons into the stew, most of them will die within hours, suffering everything from weakness and paralysis to convulsions.

"Late in the night, we'll go in and finish any who aren't yet dead, or who may not have eaten. If we prepare carefully, Northwick will be free of the Imperial Order without our having to fight. It will be swiftly ended without any of us being hurt."

The room was silent for a moment, then Kahlan saw smiles breaking out among the people. A ray of light had come into their lives.

With the heady thought of imminent freedom, some began to weep as they suddenly felt the need to come forward and tell brief accounts of those they loved who had been raped, tortured, taken away, or murdered.

Now that these people had been given a chance to live, none wanted to turn back. They saw salvation, and were willing to do what had to be done to gain it.

"This will destroy our way of life," someone said, not in bitterness, but in wonder.

"Redemption is at hand," one of the other people in the crowd added.

CHAPTER 53

Standing in dusty streamers of late-day sunlight, Zedd wavered on his feet as he waited not far from the tent where Sister Tahirah had just taken a small crate. While she was inside carefully unpacking and preparing the item of magic for inspection, the guards stood not far off, talking among themselves about their chances of having ale that night. They were hardly worried about a skinny old man with a Rada'Han around his neck and his arms shackled behind his back causing them any trouble or running off.

Zedd used the opportunity to lean against the cargo wagon's rear wheel. He wanted only to be allowed to lie down and go to sleep. Without being obvious, he looked over his shoulder at Adie. She gave him a brief, brave smile.

The wagon he leaned against was full of items looted from the Keep that had yet to be identified. For all Zedd knew, he could be leaning against a wagon full of simple magic meant to entertain and teach children, or something so powerful that it would hand Jagang victory in one blinding instant.

Some of the items brought from the Keep were unknown to Zedd. They had been locked behind shields that he had never been able to breach. Even in his childhood the old wizards at the Keep had not been able to get at what was behind many of the shields.

But the men who had assaulted and taken the Wizard's Keep were untouched by magic and apparently had no trouble getting through shields that had been in place for thousands of years. Everything Zedd knew had been turned upside down. In some ways, it seemed as if this was not only the end of the Wizard's Keep as it had been intended and envisioned, but the end of a way of life as well, and the death of an era.

The items brought from the Keep that Zedd had so far identified were of no great value to Jagang in winning the war. There were a few things, now back in protective crates, that were a mystery to Zedd; for all he knew, they could be profoundly dangerous. He wished that they could all be destroyed before one of the Sisters of the Dark discovered how to use them to create havoc.

Zedd looked up when he saw one of the elite soldiers in leather and mail pause not far away, his attention keenly focused on something. His right ear had a big V-shaped notch taken out of the upper portion, the way some farmers marked their swine. Although he wore the same kind of outfit as the rest of the elite soldiers, his boots weren't the same. Zedd saw, when the man looked around, that his left eye didn't open as wide as his right, but then he moved off into the bands of patrolling soldiers.

As Zedd watched the constantly churning press of soldiers, Sisters, and others moving past, he kept having the disconcerting visions of people from his past, and others he knew. It was disheartening to be having such will-o'-the-wisps—illusions spawned by a mind that from lack of sleep, and perhaps the constant tension, was failing him. The faces of some of the elite guards looked hauntingly familiar. He guessed he had been seeing the men for days and they were beginning to look familiar.

In the distance he saw a Sister walking past who looked like someone he knew. He had probably met her recently, was all. He'd met a number of Sisters recently, and it had never been congenial. Zedd admonished himself that he had to keep a grasp on his wits.

One of the little girls not far away, being held prisoner by a big guard standing over her, was watching Zedd and when he glanced up at her, she smiled. He thought it the oddest thing that a frightened child—amid such chaos of soldiers, prisoners, and military activity—could possibly do. He supposed that such a child could not possibly understand that she was there to be tortured, if necessary, to make sure Zedd told all he knew. He looked away from her long blond hair cascading down around her shoulders, her beautiful, oddly-familiar face. This was madness—in more ways than one.

The hump-nosed Sister emerged from the tent. "Bring them in," she snapped.

The four guards jumped into action, two seizing Adie, the other two taking Zedd. The men were big enough that Zedd's weight was trivial to them. The way they held him up by his arms prevented half his steps from touching the ground. They horsed him into the tent, advanced him around the table, spun him around, and dropped him into the chair with such force that it drove the wind from his lungs in a grunt.

Zedd closed his eyes as he grimaced in pain. He wished they would just kill him so that he wouldn't ever have to open his eyes again. But when they killed him, they would send his head to Richard. Zedd hated to think of the anguish that would cause Richard.

"Well?" Sister Tahirah asked.

Zedd opened his eyes and peered at the object set before him in the center of the table.

His breath caught.

He blinked at what he saw, too astonished to let out the breath. It was magic constructed called a sunset spell.

Zedd swallowed. Surely, none of the Sisters had opened it. No, they wouldn't have opened it. He wouldn't be sitting there if they had.

Before him on the table sat a small box, the size of half his palm. The box was shaped like the upper half of a stylized sun—a half disc with six pointed rays coming out from it, meant to represent the sun setting at the horizon. The box was lacquered a bright yellow. The rays were also yellow, but with lines of orange, green, and blue along their edges.

"Well?" Sister Tahirah repeated.

"Ahh . . ."

She was looking in her book, not at the small yellow box. "What is it?"

"I'm . . . not sure I remember," he said, stalling.

The Sister wasn't in a patient mood. "Do you want me to—"

"Oh, yes," he said, trying to sound nonchalant, "I recall, now. It's a box with a spell that produces a little tune."

That much was true. The Sister was still reading in her book. Zedd glanced back over his shoulder at Adie sitting on the bench. He could see in her eyes that she knew by his demeanor that something was up. He hoped the Sister couldn't detect the same thing.

"It's a music-box, then," Sister Tahirah murmured, more interested in her catalog of magic.

"Yes, that's right. A box that contains a spell for music. When you remove the lid, it produces a melody." Sweat trickled down from his neck, down between his shoulder blades. Zedd swallowed and tried not to let his trembling carry in his voice. "Take the lid off—you'll see."

She peered suspiciously over the top of the book. "You take the lid off."

"Well . . . I can't. My hands are shackled behind my back."

"Use your teeth."

"My teeth?"

The Sister used the back end of her pen to push the yellow half-sun box closer to him. "Yes, your teeth."

He had been counting on her suspicion, but he dared not overplay it. He worked his tongue in his mouth, desperately trying to work up some saliva. Blood would be better, but he knew that if he bit the inside of his lip the Sister would get suspicious. Blood was too common a catalyst.

Before the Sister got leery, Zedd leaned forward and tried to stretch his lips around the box. He worked to get his bottom teeth at the bottom of the sun and his top teeth hooked over a pointed ray. The box was a hair too big. With a hand on the back of his head, Sister Tahirah pushed him down on it. That was all he needed and he captured the lid with his teeth.

He lifted the lid, but the whole box came up off the table. He shook his head and, at last, the top came free. He set the lid aside.

If not opened by a party to the theft of items preserved at the Keep, a sunset spell had to be activated by a wizard whom the spell would recognize. Quickly, before she saw what he was doing, he let some saliva drop into the box in order to activate the spell.

Zedd felt giddy as the music started. It worked. It was still viable. He glanced through the narrow slit of the tent flap. The sun would be down soon.

He wanted to jump up and dance to the merry tune. He wanted to let out a whoop. Even though he didn't have long to live, he still felt exhilarated. The ordeal was almost over. In a short time, all the things of magic that were stolen would be destroyed, and he would be dead. They would never get anything out of him. He would not betray their cause.

He felt bad that the captured families who were being used to help gain his cooperation would also die, but at least they would no longer have to suffer. He felt a sudden pang of sadness that Adie, too, would die. He hated the thought of that nearly as much as the thought of her suffering.

The sister reached in and replaced the lid. "Very cute."

The music stopped. It didn't matter, though. The spell had been activated. The music was simply confirmation—and a warning to get out of range. No chance of that.

It didn't matter.

Sister Tahirah scooped the yellow box off the table. "I'm going to put this back." She leaned down toward Zedd. "While I'm gone, I'm going to have the guards bring in the next child and let you have a good look at her, let you think about what those men in the next tent are going to do to her—without hesitation—if you stall and waste our time like that again."

"But I—"

His words were cut off as she used the Rada'Han around his neck to send a shock of searing pain from the base of his skull down to his hips. His back arched as he cried out, nearly losing consciousness. He slumped back in his chair, his head hanging back, unable to lift it for the moment.

"Come with me," Sister Tahirah said to the guards. "I'll need some help. The guard who brings in the next child can watch them for a few minutes."

Panting from the lingering pain, tears filling his eyes, Zedd stared at the ceiling of the tent. He saw light as the flap was opened. Shadows moved across the canvas as the Sister and the four men left and she sent in the guard with the child. Zedd stared up at the ceiling, not wanting to look at the face of another child.

Finally, recovered from the bout of pain, he sat up.

One of the big elite guards, dressed in leather and mail, and with a broad belt holding an assortment of weapons, stood to the side with a blond-headed girl held before him. It was the girl who had smiled. Zedd closed his eyes a moment in the agony of what they would do to this poor child who reminded him so much of someone he knew.

When he opened his eyes, she smiled again. Then she winked.

Zedd blinked. She lifted up her flower print dress just enough so that Zedd could see two knives strapped to each of her thighs. He blinked again at what he was seeing. He looked up into her smiling face.

"Rachel . . . ?" he whispered.

Her smile widened into a beaming grin.

Zedd looked up at the face of the big man standing guard behind her.

"Dear spirits . . ." Zedd whispered.

It was the boundary warden.

"I hear you've gotten yourself into a bit of trouble," Chase said.

For an instant, Zedd thought that for sure he must be seeing things. Then he realized why Rachel looked so familiar, yet different; she was more than two and a half years older than the last time he'd seen her. Her blond hair, once chopped short, was now long. She had to be nearly a foot taller.

Chase hooked his thumbs behind the broad leather belt. "Adie, as levelheaded as you are, I imagine it had to be Zedd who got you into this fix."

Zedd looked over his shoulder. Adie wore a beautiful, tearful smile. He couldn't remember the last time he had seen her smile.

"He be nothing but trouble," she told the boundary warden.

It had been two and a half years since he'd seen Chase. The boundary warden was an old friend. He was the one who had taken them to meet Adie back then so she could show Richard the way through the boundary before Darken Rahl had brought it down. Chase was older than Richard, but one of his dearest and most trusted friends.

"An older boundary warden, Friedrich, came looking for me," Chase explained. "He said that 'Lord Rahl' had sent him to the Keep to warn you about some trouble. He said that Richard had told him about me, and since you were gone and the Keep had been captured, he came to Westland looking for me. Boundary wardens can always count on one another.

"Rachel and I decided to come pull your scrawny hide out of the fire."

Zedd glanced at the sunlight coming through the tent's narrow opening. "You have to get out of here. Before the sun sets—or you'll be killed. Hurry, get out of here while you can."

Chase lifted an eyebrow. "I've come all this way and I don't intend to leave without you."

"But you don't understand—"

A knife poked through the side of the tent and ran a slit down through the canvas. One of the elite guards pushed his way in through the slit. Zedd stared in astonishment. The man looked familiar, but he didn't look right.

"No!" Zedd called to Chase as the big man went for the axe hanging at his hip.

"Stay where you are," the man coming in through the slit in the side of the tent said to Chase. "There's a man right outside who will put a sword through you if you move."

Zedd's jaw dropped. "Captain Zimmer?"

"Of course. I've come to get you out of here."

"But, but, you have black hair."

The captain flashed one of his infectious smiles. "Soot. Not a good idea to have blond hair in the middle of Jagang's camp. I've come to rescue you."

Zedd was incredulous. "But you all have to get out of here. Hurry, before the sun sets. Get out!"

"Do you have any more men?" Chase asked the captain.

"A handful. Who are you?"

"An old friend," Zedd told him. "Now look here—"

At that, cries and shouts came from outside. Captain Zimmer rushed to the tent's opening. A man poked his head in.

"It's not us," he said in answer to the captain's unspoken question.

In the distance, Zedd could hear the shouts of "Assassin!"

Captain Zimmer rushed behind Zedd and worked a key in the manacles. They broke open. Zedd's arms were suddenly free. The captain hurried to undo Adie's as she stood and turned her back to him.

"Sounds like our chance," Rachel said. "Let's use the commotion to get you out of here."

"The brains of the group," Chase said with a grin.

The first thing Zedd did when his arms were free was to fall to his knees and hug the girl. He couldn't bring forth words, but they weren't needed. To feel her spindly arms around his neck was better than any words.

"I've missed you, Zedd," she whispered in his ear.

Outside the tent, mayhem had broken out. Orders were being shouted, men were running, and in the distance the clash of steel rang out.

The Sister burst back into the tent. She saw Zedd free and immediately released a bolt of power through his collar. The shock sent him sprawling.

Just then, a second young blond Sister in a drab brown wool dress charged in behind Sister Tahirah. Sister Tahirah spun around. The second Sister smacked her so hard it nearly knocked the woman from her feet. Without pause, Sister Tahirah unleashed a bolt of her power that lit the inside of the tent with a blinding flash. Instead of it blasting the second Sister back through the tent's doorway, as Zedd had expected, Sister Tahirah cried out and crumpled to the ground.

"Got you!" the second Sister growled as she planted a boot on Sister Tahirah's neck, keeping her on the ground.

Zedd blinked in astonishment. "Rikka?"

Rikka was already turning, her Agiel in her fist. She held it toward Chase.

"Rikka?" Captain Zimmer asked from the other side of the tent, sounding startled, not just to see who it was, but perhaps to see the Mord-Sith with her blond hair undone from its single braid and flying free.

"Zimmer?" she frowned at his black hair. "What are you doing here?"

"What am I doing here? What are you doing here?" He gestured to her dress. "What are you wearing?"

Rikka grinned that wicked grin she had. "The dress of a Sister."

"Sister?" Zedd asked. "What Sister?"

Rikka shrugged. "One who didn't want to give up her dress. She lost her head over the whole affair." With her finger and thumb Rikka pulled her lower lip out. "See? I borrowed her ring, too. I spread the split and hung it here, so I'd look like a real Sister."

Rikka pulled Sister Tahirah up by her hair and shoved her toward Adie. "Get that thing off her neck."

"I will do no such—"

Rikka drove her Agiel up under the Sister's chin. Blood gushed out over her lower lip. The Sister started choking on it as she gasped in agony.

"I said, get that thing off Adie's neck. And don't you ever question me again."

Sister Tahirah scrambled to Adie to do as the Mord-Sith had commanded.

Chase planted his fists on his hips as he glared down at Zedd, still on the ground. "So what are we going to do now—draw straws to see who gets to rescue you?"

"Bags! Isn't anyone listening? You people have to get out of here!"

Rachel shook a finger at Zedd. "Now Zedd, you know you're not supposed to say bad words in front of children."

Sputtering in frustration, Zedd gaped up at Chase.

"I know," the boundary warden said with a sigh. "She's been a trial for me, too."

"The sun's about to set!" Zedd roared.

"It would be better if we could delay until it did," Captain Zimmer said. "It would be easier to get out of camp in the dark."

A humming noise filled the tent, making the very air vibrate, then there was a sudden metallic pop. Adie cried out with relief as the collar fell away.

"Isn't anyone listening?" Zedd scrambled to his feet and shook his fists. "I've ignited a sunset spell!"

"A what?" Chase asked.

"A sunset spell. It's a protective device from the Keep. It's a shield of sorts. When it recognizes that other shields are being violated and protected items are being taken, it insinuates itself among the stolen goods. When a thief opens it to see what it is, it activates the spell. At the first sunset the spell ignites and destroys everything that has been plundered."

Sister Tahirah shook her fist at him. "You fool!"

Rikka seized his arm. "Then let's get going."

Chase grabbed Zedd's other arm and pulled him back. "Now hold on."

Zedd yanked both arms free and pointed out through the slit in the side of the tent at the setting sun. "We've got mere moments until this place is a fireball."

"How big a fireball?" Captain Zimmer asked.

Zedd threw up his hands. "It will kill thousands. It won't destroy the camp by any means, but this whole area is going to be leveled."

Everyone started talking, but Chase cut them all off with an angry command for silence. "Now listen to me. If we look as if we're escaping, we'll be caught. Captain, you and your men come with me. We'll pretend like Zedd and Adie are our prisoners. Rachel, too—that's how I got in here; I found out they were holding children." He flipped a hand toward Rikka and Sister Tahirah. "They will look like Sisters in charge of prisoners, along with us playing the guards."

"Do you want that thing off your neck, first?" Rikka asked Zedd.

"No time for that now. Let's go."

Adie grabbed Zedd's arm. "No."

"What!"

"Listen to me, old man. There be those families and children in these tents around us. They will die. You go. Get to the Keep. I will get the innocent people out of here."

Zedd didn't like the idea, but arguing with Adie was a fool's task, and besides, there was no time.

"We split up, then," Captain Zimmer said. "My men and I will play the part of guards and get the men, women, and children out of here, back to our lines, along with Adie."

Rikka nodded. "Tell Verna that I'm going to go with Zedd to help take back the Keep. He will need a Mord-Sith to keep him out of trouble."

Everyone looked around to see if there would be any arguments. No one said anything. It suddenly seemed settled.

"Done," Zedd said.

He threw his arms around Adie and kissed her cheek. "Be careful. Tell Verna I'm going to take the Keep back. Help her defend the passes."

Adie nodded. "Be careful. Listen to Chase—he be a good man to come all this way for you."

Zedd smiled and then gasped as Chase grabbed his robe and yanked him out of the tent. "The sun is setting—let's get out of here. Remember, you're our prisoner."

"I know the part," Zedd grumbled as he was dragged out of the tent like a sack of grain. He smiled as Adie, already rushing away, looked over her shoulder one last time. She smiled back, and then was gone.

"Wait!" Zedd called. He quickly reached into one of the wagons and retrieved something he didn't want to be destroyed. He slipped it into a pocket. "All right, let's go."

Outside the tent, the camp was in pandemonium. Elite guards, in a state of high alert and with weapons drawn, raced past on their way toward the command tents. Other men ran to the ring of barricades. Trumpets blared alarms and coded messages that directed men to tasks. Zedd feared his small group might be set upon and held for questioning.

Instead of waiting for that to happen, Chase reached out and snatched a soldier running past. "What's the matter with you? Get me some protection for these prisoners until I can get them to a safe place! The emperor will have our heads if we allow them to be recaptured!"

The soldier quickly collected a dozen men and fell in around Rikka, Sister Tahirah, Chase, Rachel, and Zedd. Rachel was doing a convincing job of bawling in fear. For effect, Chase would occasionally give her a shake and yell at her to shut up.

Zedd glanced back over his shoulder, seeing the sun touch the horizon. He growled at Rikka, out ahead, for her to pick up her pace.

At the barricades, scowling guards looked them over carefully as they approached and then opened their ranks. They were preventing anyone from getting in, and were momentarily confused by such a company of their own men with prisoners making their way out. One man decided to step out to stop and question them.

Chase straight-armed him. "Idiot! Out of our way! Emperor's orders!"

The man frowned as he stared at the procession sweeping past. While he considered what to do, they were past and gone, swallowed up in the larger camp.

In moments, they were out of the heart of the camp. In short order, regular soldiers, seeing Rikka at the lead, moved to block their path. A beautiful woman out among the regular soldiers was asking for trouble, and with the confusion the men saw in the command area, they believed they had an opportunity while those in authority were busy. Rikka and Chase kept their small group moving at a quick pace. The grinning soldiers closed ranks, blocking the way. One of the men, missing his two front teeth, took a step out in front of his men. With one thumb hooked behind his belt, he held up the other hand.

"Hold on there. I think the ladies would like to stay for a visit."

Without pause, Rachel reached under the hem of her dress and pulled a knife. She didn't slow or even look back as she flipped the knife up over her shoulder. In one fluid motion, without missing a step, Chase caught the knife by the tip and heaved it at the toothless man. With a *thunk*, the knife slammed hilt-deep into the man's forehead.

As he was still toppling back, Rachel flipped a second knife up over her shoulder. Chase caught it and sent it on its way. As the second man twisted toward the ground, dead, the rest of the men backed away to let the small group, marching onward, in among them. Deadly fights within the Imperial Order camp were not a rarity.

Elite guards or not, the soldiers were confident in their numbers and, with a beautiful woman in their midst, sure of what they wanted. Men all around closed in.

Zedd snatched a quick glance back. "Now! Hit the ground!"

Rikka, Chase, Rachel, and Zedd dove to the dirt.

For an instant, everyone above them froze, staring in surprise. The soldiers who were accompanying them, weapons already drawn for the fight they expected, also stopped and stood in confusion.

Sister Tahirah saw her opportunity and cried out. "Help! These people are—"

The world ignited with brilliant white light.

An instant later a thunderous blast rocked the ground. A wall of debris followed, driven before a roar of noise.

Men were blown into the air. Some were cut down by flying wreckage. The elite guards who had escorted them tumbled through the air over Zedd.

Sister Tahirah had turned toward the flash. A wagon wheel shot toward them at incredible speed, hitting her chest-high, cutting her in two. The bloodied wheel sailed onward without even being slowed. The Sister's shredded remains were flung across the ground along with the bodies of countless men.

As the blast from behind still rumbled, the screams of terribly wounded men rose into the lingering rays of sunset.

Zedd dearly hoped that Adie had not wasted any time in escaping.

Chase seized Zedd's robes at one shoulder and hauled him to his feet as he swept Rachel up in his other arm. Rikka grabbed Zedd's robes at the other shoulder and pulled him ahead. Together, Zedd's two rescuers rushed with him into the carnage.

Rachel hid her face in Chase's shoulder.

Zedd was about to ask Chase why in the world he would teach a young girl such things with knives, when he recalled that he himself had been the one who had once commanded Chase to teach her everything the boundary warden knew.

Rachel was a special person. Zedd had wanted her to be prepared for whatever life might have in store.

"You should have let me make the Sister take off that collar when we had the chance," Rikka said as they ran.

"If we had taken the time," Zedd answered, "we would have been back there and caught up in that fireball."

"I suppose," she said.

They slowed a bit to catch their breath. Men ran in every direction. In the confusion and disorder, no one noticed that the four of them were making good their escape. As they hastily made their way through the vast Imperial Order encampment, Zedd put an arm around Rikka's shoulders and pulled her closer.

"Thank you for coming to save my life."

She flashed him a cunning smile. "I wouldn't leave you to those pigs—not after all you've done for us. Besides, Lord Rahl has Cara protecting him; I'm sure he would want a Mord-Sith protecting his grandfather as well."

Zedd had been right. The world was turned upside down.

"We have horses and supplies hidden," Chase said. "On our way out of this place, we'd better take a horse for Rikka."

Rachel looked back over Chase's shoulder, her arms around his neck. She gave Zedd a serious frown as she whispered, "Chase is unhappy because he had to leave all his weapons behind and be so lightly armed."

Zedd glanced to the battle-axe at one hip, the sword at his other, and two knives at the small of his back. "Yes, I can see how being so defenseless would make a man grumpy."

"I don't like this place," Rachel whispered in Chase's ear.

He patted her back as she laid her head on his shoulder. "We'll be back in the woods in no time, little one."

Amid the screams and death, it was as tender a sight as Zedd could imagine.

CHAPTER 54

Verna paused when the sentry rushed up in the dark. She moved her hands up on the reins, closer to the bit, to keep her horse from spooking.

"Prelate—I think it might be an attack of some sort," the soldier said in breathless worry.

She frowned at the man. "What might be an attack? What is it?"

"There's something coming up the road." He pointed back toward Dobbin Pass. "A wagon, I think."

The enemy was always sending things at them—men sneaking through the darkness, horses encased in spells designed to blow a breach in their shields running wildly toward them, innocent enough wagons with archers hiding inside, powerful spell-driven winds laced with magic conjuring of every sort.

"Since it's dark, the commander thinks it's suspicious and we shouldn't take any chances."

"Sounds wise," Verna said.

She had to get back to their camp. She had made the rounds herself to get a good look at their defenses, to see the men at the outposts, before their nightly meeting back at camp to go over the day's reports.

"The commander wants to destroy the wagon before it gets too close. I've checked, Prelate—there are no other Sisters at hand. If you don't want to see to this, we can have the men up above drop a rockslide on the wagon and crush it."

Verna had to get back to meet with the officers. "You had better tell your commander to take care of it in whatever manner he sees fit."

The soldier saluted with snap of a fist to his heart.

Verna pulled her horse around and put a foot into the stirrup. Why would the Imperial Order think they could get a wagon through, especially at night? Certainly, they weren't foolish enough to think it wouldn't be seen in the dark. She paused and looked at the soldier hurrying away.

"Wait."

He stopped and turned.

"I changed my mind. I'll go with you."

It was foolish to use the rocks they had ready overhead; they might need them if a full-scale attack suddenly charged up this pass. It was silly to waste such a defense.

She followed the man up the trail to the lookout point where his company waited. The men were all watching out through the trees. The road ahead and below them looked silver in the light of the rising moon.

Verna inhaled the fragrance of balsam firs as she watched the wagon making its way up the silvery road, being pulled by a single, plodding horse. Tense archers waited at the ready. They had a shielded lantern standing by to light fire arrows in order to set the wagon ablaze.

Verna didn't see anyone in the wagon. An empty wagon seemed pretty suspicious. She recalled the strange message from Ann, warning her to let an empty wagon through.

But they had already done that. Verna recalled that the girl with the message from Jagang had come in by this route and method. Verna's heart pounded in worry at the thought of what new message Jagang might be sending, now.

Perhaps it was Zedd and Adie's heads.

"Hold," she called to the archers. "Let it through, but stand at the ready in case it's a trick."

Verna made her way down the narrow path between the trees. She stood behind a screen of spruce, watching. When the wagon was close enough, she opened a small gap in the weave of the vast shield she and the Sisters had spun across the pass. The pattern of magic was barbed with every nasty sort of magic they could conjure.

This pass was small enough that the shields alone could hold it, and if the enemy did come, it was too small for any numbers to come all at once. Even without the formidable shield, the pass was relatively easy to hold.

When the wagon passed through the shield, Verna closed the hole. When it rolled close enough, one of the men ran out of the trees and took control of the horse. As the wagon drew to a halt, dozens of archers behind him and on the other side, behind Verna, drew their weapons. Verna had spun a web of magic and she was prepared to unleash it at the slightest provocation.

The tarp in the bed of the wagon eased back. A little girl sat up. It was the child who had brought the message the last time. Her face lit up at seeing Verna, someone she recognized.

Verna's heart skipped a beat at the thought of what the message might be, this time.

"I brought some friends," the girl said.

People lying in the back of the wagon pulled the tarp aside and started sitting up. They looked like parents with their frightened children.

Verna blinked in shock when she saw some of the people help Adie up. The sorceress looked to be exhausted. Her black-and-gray hair was no longer parted neatly in the middle, but was in as much disarray as Zedd's usually was.

Verna rushed over, leaning in to help the woman. "Adie! Oh, Adie, am I ever glad to see you!"

The old sorceress smiled. "I be awfully happy to see you, too, Verna."

Verna's gaze swept over the people in the wagon, her heart still pounding with apprehension. "Where's Zedd?"

"He escaped as well."

Verna closed her eyes with a silent prayer of gratitude. Her eyes popped open. "If he escaped, then where is he?"

"He be on his way back to the Keep, in Aydindril," Adie said in her raspy voice. "The enemy has captured it."

"We heard."

"That old man intends to have his Keep back."

"Knowing Zedd, I feel sorry for anyone who gets in his way."

"Rikka be with him."

"Rikka! What was she doing over there? I ordered her not to do that!" Verna realized how that must have sounded. "We thought it would be pointless, that she wouldn't have a chance and we would just lose her for nothing."

"Rikka be Mord-Sith. She has a mind of her own."

Verna shook her head. "Well, even though she wasn't supposed to do that, now that I see you again and know Zedd has escaped as well, I'm glad that that obstinate woman didn't listen to me."

"Captain Zimmer be on his way back as well."

"Captain Zimmer!"

"Yes, he and some of his men decided to come to rescue us as well. They be coming back the way they travel, unseen in the night." Adie gestured to the surrounding trees. "They be up around us, protecting the wagon on our way in. The captain feared that some of the enemy might stop the wagon and capture us all over again. He wanted to make sure we be safe."

The captain and his men had special signals that allowed them to move through the pass without being attacked by their own men, or the Sisters, by mistake. The nature of the way Captain Zimmer and his men worked was that they were, for the most part, outside regular command. Kahlan had set it up that way so they could act on their own initiative. While it could at times be aggravating, those men accomplished more than anyone ever expected.

"Zedd wanted me to help these people escape." Adie gave Verna a meaningful look. "There be others we could not help."

Verna glanced over at the people huddling together at the back of the wagon. "I can only imagine what Jagang has been doing with people like that."

"No," Adie said. "I doubt you can."

Verna changed to an even more horrifying subject. "Has Jagang been able to find anything from the Keep, so far, that he will use against us?"

"Thankfully, no. Zedd set a spell that destroyed the things stolen from the Keep. There be a big explosion in the middle of their camp."

"Like the one back in Aydindril that killed so many of them?"

"No, but it still caused much destruction and killed some important people—even some of Jagang's Sisters, I believe."

Verna never thought she would see the day that she would be pleased to hear that Sisters of the Light had died. Those women were controlled by the dream walker, and even when they had been offered freedom, they had been too afraid to believe those trying to rescue them. They had chosen to remain Jagang's slaves.

With a sudden thought, Verna grabbed a fistful of Adie's robes. "Could the spell Zedd ignited possibly have taken out Jagang?"

With her completely white eyes, Adie looked back up Dobbin Pass toward the Imperial Order camp. "I wish I had better news, Prelate, but Captain Zimmer, on the way out, told me that just as we were about to be rescued, an assassin managed to get deep into the inner camp."

"An assassin? Who was it? Where was he from?"

"None of us knows. He appeared much like others from the Old World. The intruder be driven by a single-minded determination to get to Jagang and kill him. He somehow made it into the inner defenses, killed some people, and took the uniform of the elite guards so he might get to Jagang. The guards somehow recognized he not be one of their own. They hacked the man to pieces before he could get close to the emperor.

"Jagang left the area until his men could check over their defenses and make sure there be no more assassins about. Many of the Sisters went with him, helping with his safeguards. That be when Zedd set off the sunset spell. We did not know Jagang had left the area, but it would have made no difference. Zedd had to use the spell when it be put before him. The spell be triggered by the sun setting."

Verna nodded. For a moment, she had been hoping . . .

"Still, you and Zedd escaped, and that's what matters for now. Thank the Creator."

"A surprising number of people showed up all at once to rescue us." Adie lifted an eyebrow. "I do not recall seeing the Creator among them."

The warm breeze ruffled Verna's curly hair. "I suppose not, but you know what I mean."

The crickets in the woods kept up their steady chirping. Life seemed to be a little sweeter, their situation a little less hopeless.

She let out a sigh. "I hope the Creator will at least help Zedd and Rikka take back the Keep."

"Zedd will not need the Creator's help," Adie said. "Another man showed up to help get us out. Chase be an old friend of Zedd, me, and Richard. Chase will have those holding the Keep praying for the protection of the Creator."

"Then we can look forward to the day the Keep is back in our hands and Jagang is denied help in breaking through the passes into D'Hara."

Verna waved her arm, signaling, and the four couples standing at the back of the wagon shuffled forward with their children.

"Welcome to D'Hara," Verna told them. "You will be safe, here."

"Thank you for helping get us out," one of the men said with a bow of his head to Adie. "I feel ashamed, now, of the terrible things I had been thinking of you."

Adie smiled to herself as she tightened her thin fingers on his shoulder. "True. But I could not blame you."

The girl who had brought the message the last time tugged on Verna's dress. "This is my mother and father. I told them how nice you were to me, before."

Verna squatted down and hugged the girl. "Welcome back, child. Welcome back."

C H A P T E R   5 5

Whenever a breath of wind sighed among the branches above, silvery streamers of moonlight cascading down through the forest canopy glided about in the darkness like ghosts on the prowl. Kahlan peered around, barely able to make out the somber shapes of the looming trees as she tried to see if there was anything that did not belong. She heard no chirps of bugs, no small animals scurrying among the leaf litter, no mockingbirds singing throughout the night as there had been. Carefully picking her way over the mossy ground, she did her best to see in the gloom so as not to step in holes and cracks in the rocky places or pools of standing water in the low areas.

Ahead of her, Richard slipped though the open forest like a shadow. At times he seemed to disappear, causing her to fear that he might no longer be with them. He had ordered everyone following behind him not to talk and to walk as quietly as possible, but none of them could move through the woods as silently as he did.

For some reason, Richard was as tense as his bowstring. He felt that something was wrong, but he didn't know what. While it might seem a beautiful moonlit night in the woods, the way Richard was acting, on top of the haunting silence, had draped a pall of foreboding over everyone.

Kahlan was at least pleased that the skies had cleared. The rains of recent days had made travel not just difficult, but miserable. While it hadn't really been cold, the wet made it feel so. Taking shelter had not been an option. Until they had the final dose of the antidote, they had no choice but to press on.

The antidote from Northwick had improved Richard's condition a little, in addition to stopping the advance of the symptoms of his poisoning, but now the temporary improvement was dissipating. Kahlan was so worried for him that she had no appetite.

They now had well over double the number of men with them, and many more than that were making their way toward the city of Hawton by different routes. Those other groups of men planned to eliminate the lesser detachments of Imperial Order soldiers stationed in villages along the way. Richard, Kahlan, and their smaller group were pushing toward Hawton as rapidly as possible, deliberately avoiding contact with the enemy so as to get there before Nicholas and his soldiers knew they were on their way. Stealth would afford them the best chance of recovering the final dose of the antidote.

Once they had the antidote, then they could gather with the rest of the men for an attack. Kahlan knew that if they could first eliminate Nicholas it would make it much easier, and less risky, to defeat the remaining Imperial Order troops. If she could somehow find a way to get close to Nicholas she could touch him with her power. She knew better than to suggest such an idea to Richard; he would never go along with it.

To a certain extent, Kahlan felt responsible for what these people had suffered under the Imperial Order. After all, if not for her freeing the chimes, the boundary protecting Bandakar would still be in place. Yet, if these people could rid themselves of the Imperial Order, the changes that had come about also meant the true freedom they had never really enjoyed and, with it, the opportunity for better lives.

The change in the people in Northwick had been heartening to witness. That night, the men Richard and Kahlan had brought had stayed up most of the night talking to the people there, explaining the things Richard and Kahlan had explained to them. The morning after the annihilation of the soldiers who had taken over their city and held them in the grip of fear, the people had celebrated by singing and dancing in the streets. Those people had learned not only just how precious freedom really was, but also that their old ways provided no real tools for improving the quality of their lives.

After Richard had dissolved the ancient illusions of the Wise One's wisdom and the meaningless tenets the speakers substituted for knowledge, and after the killing of the enemy soldiers, the men of Northwick had not been shy about volunteering to help rid their land of the Imperial Order. Freed from the enforced blindness of a repressive mindset, many now hungered aloud for a future of their own making.

Kahlan unexpectedly came up against Richard's outstretched arm. She put a hand to her chest, over her galloping heart, then immediately turned and passed the signal to stop back to those behind. There was still no sound in the dark woods—not so much as the buzz of a mosquito.

Richard slipped his pack off his back, set it on a low rock, and started quietly searching through it.

Kahlan leaned close to whisper, "What are you doing?"

"Fire. We need light. Pass the word back for some of the men to get out torches."

While Richard pulled out a steel and flint, Kahlan whispered instructions to Cara, who in turn passed them back. In short order, several men tiptoed forward with torches.

The men gathered in close, squatting down beside a low jumble of rock next to Richard. He picked a stick up off the ground and dipped it in a small container from his pack. He then wiped the stick across the top of a high point on the rock.

"I'm putting some pine resin on this rock," he told the men. "Hold your torches over it so that when I strike a spark and the resin flames up, it will light the torches."

Pine resin, painstakingly collected from rotting trees, was valuable for starting fires in the rain. A spark would ignite it even when wet. It burned hot enough to often be able to catch damp wood on fire.

Richard had always seemed at home in the dark. Kahlan had never seen him need to have light like this. She stared intently out into the night, wondering what it was he thought might be out there that they couldn't see.

"Cara," Richard whispered, "pass the word back. I want everyone to get out a weapon. Now."

Without hesitation, Cara turned to pass on the orders. After a seemingly endless span of silence, broken only by the soft whisper of steel sliding past leather, word came back and she leaned down toward Richard. "Done."

Richard looked up at Kahlan and Jennsen. "Both of you, as well."

Kahlan drew her sword, Jennsen her silver-handled dagger with the ornate letter "R" that stood for the House of Rahl.

Richard struck the spark. The pine pitch flamed up with an angry hiss; the torches caught; light ignited in the heart of the dark forest.

In the sudden, harsh glare, everyone turned and looked about to see what might be hiding in the darkness around them.

Men gasped.

In the trees all around them, perched on branches everywhere, sat black-tipped races. Hundreds of them. Beady black eyes watched the people.

In that moment of sudden bright light, everything but the flickering flame was silent and still.

With a burst of wild cries, the races launched their attack.

From all around, all at once, the races descended on them. The night air suddenly filled with a riot of glossy black feathers, the sweep of huge wings, hooked beaks, and reaching talons. After such a long silence, the sound of piercing cries and beating wings was deafening.

Everywhere, the people met the attack with fierce determination. Some of the men were knocked to the ground, or stumbled and fell. Others cried out as they tried to protect themselves with one arm while driving off the attack with the other. Men hacked at the races atop their friends and turned to ward off other screeching beasts that flew in toward them.

Kahlan saw the red-striped breast of a race abruptly appear right before her face. She swung her sword, lopping off a wing, spun around, bringing the sword up to hit another bird coming in from the other side. She stabbed a race on the ground at her feet as it reached in with its beak, like a vulture, to try to rip flesh from her leg.

Richard's sword was a blur of silver slashing through the winged attackers. A cloud of black feathers surrounded him. The birds were attacking everyone, but the assault appeared to be centered around Richard. It almost seemed as if the races were trying to drive the people back from Richard so that more of the birds could get at him.

Jennsen frantically stabbed at birds going for him. Kahlan swung at others, knocking them to the ground, wounded or dead. With measured efficiency, Cara snatched them out of the air and swiftly wrung their necks.

Everywhere men stabbed, cut, and hacked at the onslaught of fierce raptors. Some men used their torches as weapons. The night was filled with the screams of the birds, with the flapping of wings, with the thud of weapons striking home. Birds tumbled and fell as they were hit. More dove in to take their place. The trees all around poured the monstrous birds down on them. Wounded and dying birds struggling on the ground made the forest floor a writhing sea of black feathers.

The ferocity of the attack was frightening.

And then, it was suddenly over.

A few of the birds on the ground, wings spread, still tried to get up, their feathers making a silken rasp as they rubbed against the feathers of dead birds beneath them. Here and there men stabbed or chopped at a bird still alive on the ground at their feet. It wasn't long before all the creatures finally went still. No more races came from the sky.

Dead races mounded up against Richard like snow drifted in a storm.

Men panted as they held torches aloft. They peered into the darkness beyond the light, looking for any sign of more trouble from above. But for the hissing of the torches, the night was silent. The branches of the trees all around appeared to be empty.

Kahlan could see scratches and cuts on Richard's arms and hands. She waded through the sea of dead birds to get to his pack sitting on a nearby rock. The forest floor around him was nearly knee-deep with dead races. She had to flip a dead bird off Richard's pack. Pushing her hand down into his pack, she blindly searched until her fingers found a folded waxed paper that contained a salve.

Cara rushed in close to Richard when she saw him unsteady on his feet. She grasped his arm, lending him support.

"What in the world was that all about?" Jennsen asked, panting, still catching her breath as she pulled strands of red ringlets off her sweaty face.

"I guess they finally decided to try to get us," Owen said.

Jennsen patted Betty's head when the goat stepped unhurt through the corpses of races to get in closer to her friends. "One thing for sure is that they finally found us again."

"There was an important difference this time," Richard said. "They weren't following us. They were here, waiting for us."

Everyone stared at him.

"What do you mean?" Kahlan paused at daubing salve on his cuts. "They've followed us before. They must have seen us."

Betty moved in closer, leaning against Kahlan's leg to stand and watch her and Richard talking. Kahlan wasn't in the mood to be scratching the goat's ears, so pushed her out of the way.

Richard laid a hand on Cara's shoulder to steady himself. Kahlan noticed how he swayed on his feet. At times he was having difficulty standing.

"No. They haven't been following us. The skies have been empty." Richard gestured to the dead birds all around him. "These races weren't following us. They were waiting for us. They knew we were coming here. They lay in wait."

That was a chilling thought—if it were true.

Kahlan straightened, holding the waxed paper in one hand, a finger of her other hand, loaded with salve, waited. "How could they possibly know where we were going?"

"That's what I'd like to know," Richard said.

Nicholas glided back into his body, his mouth still opened wide in a yawn that was not a yawn. He stretched his neck to one side and then the other. He smiled with his delight in the game. It had been dazzling. It had been delicious. His widening grin bared his teeth.

Nicholas staggered to his feet, wavering unsteadily for a moment.

It reminded him of the way Richard Rahl swayed on his feet, dizzy with the effects of a poison that was inexorably doing its deadly work.

Poor Richard Rahl needed the last dose of the antidote.

Nicholas opened his mouth again in a yawn that was not a yawn, twisting his head, eager to be away, eager to learn more. He would return soon enough. He would watch them. Watch them as they worried, as they struggled in vain to understand what was happening, watch them as they approached. They would reach him in mere hours.

The fun was truly about to begin.

Nicholas wound his way across the room, stepping between the bodies sprawled everywhere. They had all died suddenly when the races were killed. Here and there the dead were stacked in piles atop one another, just as the races in those dark woods had been heaped around Richard Rahl.

Such violent deaths. Those spirits had been horrified as they were slaughtered, but there was nothing they could do to stop it.

Nicholas had controlled their souls, their fate. Now they were beyond his control; they now belonged to the Keeper of the dead.

Nicholas ran his fingernails back through his hair, shivering with delight as he felt the slick oils glide through his fingers and against his palm.

He had to drag three bodies aside before he could get at the door. He threw the heavy latch over and opened the thick door.

"Najari!"

The man stood not far away, leaning against the wall, waiting. His muscular form straightened.

"What is it?"

Nicholas opened his arm back in graceful indication, his fingers tipped with black nails stretching wide. "There is a mess in here that needs to be cleaned up. Get some men and have these bodies taken away."

Najari stepped to the door and stretched his neck to peer into the room.

"The whole crowd we brought in?"

"Yes," Nicholas snapped. "I needed them all, and some more I had the soldiers fetch for me. I'm done with them all, now. Get rid of them."

When the races had attacked, each had been driven by the soul of one of these ungifted people, and each of those souls had been driven by Nicholas. It had been a stupendous achievement—the simultaneous command of so many with such precision and coordination. When the races had been killed, though, so too died the bodies back in the room with Nicholas.

He supposed that one day he really should learn how to call back such spirits when their host died. It would save him from having to get new ones each time. But, people were plentiful. Besides if he were to find a way to call them back, then he would have to mind the people once their spirits returned, after they had learned his use of them.

Still, it was annoying when Richard Rahl killed those Nicholas used to help him watch.

"How much longer?" Najari asked.

Nicholas smiled, knowing what the man was curious about. "Soon. Very soon. You must get these people out of here before they arrive. Then, keep our men out of the way. Let them do as they will."

Najari flashed a cunning smile. "As you wish, Nicholas."

Nicholas lifted an eyebrow. "Emperor Nicholas."

Najari chuckled as he started away to get his men. "Emperor Nicholas."

"You know, Najari, I've been thinking."

Najari turned back. "About what?"

"About Jagang. We've worked so hard. What reason is there for me to bow to him? A legion of my silent army could swoop in upon him and that would be that. I wouldn't even need an army. He could mount his horse one day, and I could be there in the beast, waiting to throw him and trample him to death."

Najari rubbed his stubble. "True enough."

"Of what use is Jagang, really? I could just as easily rule the Imperial Order. In fact, I would be better suited to it."

Najari cocked his head. "Then what of the plans we've already laid?"

Nicholas shrugged. "Why change them? But why should I give the Mother Confessor to Jagang? And why let him have the world? Perhaps I will keep her for my own amusement . . . and have the world as well."

CHAPTER 56

Richard pressed his back up against the clapboard wall. He had to pause a moment, waiting for the world to stop spinning. He was so cold he felt numb. As dark as it was, he was having difficulty seeing.

But it was more than the darkness.

He knew that his sight was beginning to fail him.

At night it was worse. He had always been able to see better at night than most other people. Now, he was no better able to see at night than Kahlan. That wasn't a big difference, but he knew it was meaningful.

The third state of the poison had begun.

Fortunately, they were close to having the final dose.

"This is the alleyway, here," Owen whispered.

Richard looked up and down the street. He didn't see anything moving. The city of Hawton was asleep. He wished he could be, too. He was so exhausted and dizzy he could hardly put one foot in front of the other. He had to take shallow breaths to keep from coughing. Coughing brought on the worst pain. At least he wasn't coughing up blood.

Coughing now, though, could be fatal, so he swallowed, trying to stifle the urge. If they made any noise, it might alert the soldiers.

When Owen moved into the alleyway, Richard, Kahlan, Cara, Jennsen, Tom, Anson, and a handful of their men followed in single file. There had been no lights burning in the windows facing the streets. As the small group moved through the alley close to the walls, Richard saw no windows. A few of the walls did have doors.

At a narrow space between buildings, Owen turned in, following the brick path hardly wider than Richard's shoulders.

Richard seized Owen by the arm. "Is this the only way in?"

"No. See there? The walkway goes through to the street in front, and there is another door inside that comes up on the other side of the building."

Satisfied that they had alternate escape routes, Richard gave Owen a nod. They took the dark stairwell down to a room at the bottom under the building. Tom struck flint to steel a number of times until he managed to light a candle.

Once the candle was lit, Richard gazed around at the small, empty, windowless room. "What is this place?"

"The basement of a palace," Owen said.

Richard frowned at the man. "What are we doing here?"

Owen hesitated and glanced at Kahlan.

Kahlan saw the look. She pushed Richard down until he sat and leaned back against the wall. A footsore Betty squeezed between them and lay down beside Richard, pleased to have a rest. Jennsen squatted close, on the other side of Betty. Cara closed him in from the other side.

Kahlan knelt in front of him and then sat back on her heels. "Richard, I asked Owen to bring us here—to a place where we would be safe. We can't all go into that building to get the antidote."

"I suppose not. That's a good idea. Owen and I will go, the rest of you can stay here where no one will spot you."

He started to get up, but Kahlan pushed him back down. "Richard, you have to wait here. You can't go. You're dizzy. You need to save your strength."

Richard gazed into her green eyes, eyes that always captivated him, always made everything else but her seem unimportant. He wished they could be alone somewhere peaceful, like the home he had built for her back in the mountains where he had taken her to recover after she had been hurt . . . when she had lost their unborn child after being beaten nearly to death by those brutes.

She was the most precious thing alive. She was everything. He wanted so much for her to be safe.

"I'm strong enough," he said. "I'll be fine."

"If you start coughing in that place where the soldiers are, then you'll be caught and never get out—much less recover the antidote. You and Owen would both be caught. There is no telling how many soldiers are in there. What will happen to us if you're caught? What would happen if . . ." Her voice trailed off. She hooked a stray strand of hair behind an ear. "Look, Richard, Owen went in there before; he can go in there again."

Richard saw desperation in her eyes. She was terrified of losing him. He hated that he was making her afraid.

"That's right, Lord Rahl," Owen assured him. "I will get the antidote and bring it to you."

"While we're waiting, you can get some rest," Kahlan said. "Some sleep would do you more good than anything else until they bring back the antidote."

Richard couldn't debate how tired he was. He still didn't like the idea of not going himself.

"Tom could go with him," Cara suggested.

Richard looked up into Cara's blue eyes. He looked up into Kahlan's eyes. He knew he had already lost this argument.

"How far is this place?" Richard asked Owen.

"A goodly distance. Here, we are just at the fringe of the city. I wanted to take us to a place where we would be less likely to encounter soldiers. The antidote is at most an hour distant. I thought it best if we were not too far into the city if we had to get back out, but we are close enough so that you will not have long to wait for the antidote."

Richard nodded. "All right. We'll wait here for you and Tom."

Kahlan paced in the small, damp basement as the others sat against the wall, waiting in silence. She couldn't stand the tension. It felt too much like a deathwatch.

They were so close that it made it seem impossibly far. They had waited so long that the small amount of time left seemed an eternity that would never end. Kahlan told herself to calm down. Shortly,

Richard would have the antidote. He would be better, then. He would be cured of the poison, then.

But what if it didn't work? What if he had already waited so long that he was beyond any cure? No, the man who had made the poison and the antidote had told Owen that this last dose would cure Richard of the poison for good. Because of the beliefs of these people, they would be certain that the poison was reversible. They would never have used it if they believed it would risk a life.

But what if what they believed was wrong?

Kahlan rubbed her shoulders as she paced, and admonished herself for inventing problems to worry about. They had enough real problems without letting her imagination get carried away. They would get the antidote and then they would address the problem with Richard's gift. After that, they had to turn their attention to larger issues of Jagang and his army.

When Kahlan glanced over and saw that Richard had fallen sound asleep, she decided to go outside and watch for Owen and Tom. Cara, leaning against the wall beside Richard, guarding him while he slept, nodded when Kahlan whispered to her, telling her where she was going. Jennsen, seeing that Kahlan was heading for the door, quietly followed her out. Betty had fallen asleep beside Richard, so Jennsen left her there.

The moonlit night had cooled. Kahlan thought she should be sleepy, but she was wide awake. She followed the brick path out between the buildings toward the alley.

"Owen will be back soon," Jennsen said. "Try not to worry. It will be over, soon."

Kahlan glanced over in the dark. "Even after he has the antidote, we still have his gift to worry about. Zedd is too far. We're going to have to get to Nicci right away. She is the only one close enough that might know what to do to help him."

"Do you think the trouble with his gift is getting worse?"

Kahlan was haunted by the pain she so often saw in his eyes. But there was more to it. "When he used the sword the last two times I could see that even the sword's magic had failed him. He's in more trouble with his gift than he will admit."

Jennsen chewed her lower lip as she watched Kahlan pace. "Tonight he will have the antidote," she finally said in soft assurance. "Soon, we can be on our way to Nicci."

Kahlan turned when she thought she heard a noise in the distance. It had sounded like the crunch of a footstep. Two dark figures appeared off at the end of the alleyway. By the way one of them towered over the other, Kahlan was pretty sure that it was Tom and Owen. She wanted to run to meet them, but she knew how deadly tricks could be, so she drew Jennsen back with her around the corner of the building, into the darkest part of the shadows. This was no time to get careless.

When the two men reached the narrow walkway and started to turn in, Kahlan stepped out in front of them, prepared to unleash her power if necessary.

"Mother Confessor—it's me, Tom, and Owen," Tom whispered.

Jennsen let out a breath. "Are we ever glad to see you back."

Owen looked both ways down the alley. When he turned to check, Kahlan saw moonlight reflect off tears running down his face.

"Mother Confessor, we have trouble," Tom said.

Owen spread his hands. "Mother Confessor, I, I . . ."

Kahlan grabbed his shirt in both fists. "What's wrong? The antidote was there, wasn't it? You have it, don't you?"

"No." Owen choked back his tears and pulled out a folded piece of paper. "Instead of the bottle of antidote, I found this in its hiding place."

Kahlan snatched it out of his hands. With trembling fingers, she unfolded the paper. She turned as she held it close so she could read it by the light of the moon.

I have the antidote. I also hold by a thread the lives of the people of Bandakar. I can end all their lives as easily as I can end the life of Richard Rahl.

I will give over the antidote and the lives of all the people in this empire in exchange for the Mother Confessor.

Bring the Mother Confessor to the bridge over the river one mile to the east of where you are. In one hour, if I do not have the

Mother Confessor, I will pour the antidote in the river and then I will see to it that all the people of this city die.
  Signed, Emperor Nicholas

Kahlan, her heart racing out of control, started east.

Tom grabbed her arm and held her back. "Mother Confessor, I know what it says."

Kahlan's hands wouldn't stop shaking. "Then you know why I have no choice."

Jennsen put herself in front of Kahlan to stop her from starting out once again. "What does the letter say?"

"Nicholas wants me in exchange for the antidote."

Jennsen put her hands against Kahlan's shoulders to stop her. "What?"

"That's what the letter says. Nicholas wants me in exchange for the lives of everyone else in this empire and the antidote to save Richard's life."

"The lives of everyone else . . . but how could he carry out such a threat?"

"Nicholas is a wizard. There are any number of deadly things available to such a man. If nothing else, he could use wizard's fire and incinerate the entire city."

"But his magic won't harm the people here—they're pristinely ungifted, the same as me."

"If he uses wizard's fire to set a building ablaze, like we did to those soldiers sleeping back in Owen's town, it won't matter to the people inside how the fire started. Once the buildings catch fire, then it's just regular fire—fire that will kill anyone. If not that, Nicholas has soldiers here. He could immediately start executing people. He could have thousands beheaded in hardly any time at all. I can't even imagine what else he could do, but he put this letter where the antidote was hidden, so I know he's not bluffing."

Kahlan stepped around Jennsen and started out again. She couldn't make herself stop trembling. She tried to slow her racing heart, but that didn't work, either. Richard had to have the antidote. That was what mattered. She focused her attention ahead as she marched swiftly up the dark street.

Tom paced along beside her, opposite Jennsen. "Mother Confessor, wait. We have to think this out."

"I already have."

"We can take a force of men to the meeting place—take the antidote by force."

Kahlan kept going. "From a wizard? I don't think so. Besides, if Nicholas were to see such a force coming he would probably pour the antidote in the river. Then what? We have to do as he demands. We have to get our hands on the antidote, get it safely away from him."

"What makes you think that after Nicholas has you he won't then pour it in the river?" Tom asked.

"We'll have to make the exchange in a way that best insures we get the antidote. We aren't going to rely on his goodwill and honesty. Owen and Jennsen are pristinely ungifted. They won't be harmed by his magic. They can help make sure we get the antidote in the exchange."

Jennsen pulled her hair away from her face as she leaned close. "Kahlan, you can't do this. You can't. Please, Richard will go crazy—we all will. Please, for his sake, don't do this."

"At least he will be alive to go crazy."

Tears streamed down Jennsen's face. "But this is suicide!"

Kahlan watched the buildings, the streets, making sure there were no troops to hem them in. "Let's hope Nicholas thinks so, too."

"Mother Confessor," Owen pleaded, "you can't do this. This is what Lord Rahl has shown us is wrong. You can't bargain with a man like Nicholas. You can't try to appease evil."

"I have no intention of appeasing Nicholas."

Jennsen wiped tears from her cheek. "What do you mean?"

Kahlan stiffened her resolve. "What is our best chance of getting rid of the Imperial Order in this city—and all of Bandakar? Eliminating Nicholas. How better to get close to him than to make him think he has won?"

Jennsen blinked in surprise. "You mean you intend to touch him with your power. That's what you're thinking, isn't it? You think you will have a chance to touch him with your Confessor power."

"If I get him in my sight, he's dead."

"Richard would never agree to this," Jennsen said.

"I'm not asking him. This is my decision."

Tom stepped in front of her, blocking the way. "Mother Confessor, I'm sworn to protect the Lord Rahl, and I understand risking your life to protect him—but this is different. You may be acting to try to save his life, but at what cost? We would lose too much. You can't do this."

Owen moved around in front of her, too. "I agree. Lord Rahl will be more than crazy if you exchange yourself for the antidote."

Jennsen nodded her agreement. "He will kill us all. He will take off our heads for allowing you to do this."

Kahlan smiled at their tense expressions. She put a hand to the side of Jennsen's face. "Remember back just after we'd met you, and I told you that there were times when there was no choice but to act?"

Jennsen nodded, her tears returning.

"This is one of those times. Richard is getting sicker by the day. He's dying. If he doesn't get the antidote, he has no chance and will soon be dead. That's the truth of the way things are.

"How can we let this chance slip away from us? There are no more opportunities after this. Our chances to save him will forever be lost. It will be the end. I don't want to live without him. I don't want the rest of our people to live without him.

"If I do this, then Richard will live. If Richard lives, then there will still be a chance for me, too. I can touch Nicholas with my power, or Richard and the rest of you can think of something to do to save me.

"But if Richard dies, then our chances end."

"But, Mother Confessor," Jennsen sobbed, "if you do this, then we'll lose you . . ."

Kahlan looked to each face, her anger rising. "If any of you have a better idea, then put words to it. Otherwise, you are risking me losing the only chance left."

No one had anything to say. Kahlan was the only one with a realistic plan of action. The rest of them had only wishes. Wishing would not save Richard.

Kahlan started out once again, hurrying her pace to get there in time.

CHAPTER 57

Kahlan paused in the quiet darkness not far from the bridge. She could just make out what appeared to be a burly man standing on the other side. He was all alone. She couldn't see his face, or tell what he looked like. She scanned the far bank of the river, along with the trees and buildings she could make out in the moonlight, looking for soldiers, or anyone else.

Jennsen clutched her arm. "Kahlan . . . please." Her voice was choked with tears.

Kahlan felt oddly calm. There were no options for her to weigh, so she suffered no gnawing indecision; there was only one choice. Richard lived, or he died. It was as simple as that. The choice was clear.

Her mind was made up and with that came clarity and determination. She could now focus on what she was to do.

The river through the city was larger than Kahlan had expected. The steep banks to each side, in this area, anyway, were a few dozen feet high and lined with stone blocks. The bridge itself, wide enough for wagons to pass one another, had two arches to make the span and side rails with simple stone caps. The waters below were dark and swift. It was not a river she would want to have to try to swim.

Kahlan approached as far as the foot of the bridge and stopped. The man on the other side watched her.

"Do you have the antidote?" she called over to him.

He lifted what looked like a little bottle high above his head. He lowered the arm and pointed to the bridge. He wanted her to come across.

"Mother Confessor," Owen pleaded, "won't you reconsider?"

She gazed into his wet eyes. "Reconsider what? If I will have Richard live rather than let him succumb to the poison? If I will try to kill Nicholas in order to make it possible to defeat the Imperial Order and for your people to have a better chance to free themselves? How would I ever live with myself if Richard died without the antidote and I knew there was something I could have done that would have saved him and also have given me a chance to get close enough to Nicholas to eliminate him? I couldn't live with myself if I failed to do this.

"We are fighting this war to stop people like this, people who bring death upon us, people who want us dead because they cannot stand that we live our lives as we wish, that we are successful and happy. These people hate life; they worship death. They demand that we do the same and join them in their misery.

"As Mother Confessor, I decreed vengeance without mercy against the Imperial Order. Changing from our course is suicide. I will not reconsider."

"What would you have us tell Lord Rahl?" Tom asked.

She smiled. "That I love him, but he knows that."

Kahlan unbuckled her sword belt and handed it to Jennsen. "Owen, come with me."

Kahlan started out, but Jennsen threw her arms around her and hugged her fiercely. "Don't worry," she whispered. "We'll get the antidote to Richard, and then we'll come back for you."

Kahlan hugged Jennsen briefly, whispered her thanks, and then started onto the bridge. Owen walked at her side, saying nothing.

The man on the far side watched, but stayed where he was.

In the center of the bridge, Kahlan stopped. "Bring the bottle," she called across.

"Come over here and you can have it."

"If you want me, you will come to the center of the bridge and give the bottle to this man to take back, as Nicholas offered."

The man stood for a time, as if considering. He looked like a soldier. He didn't match the description of Nicholas that Owen had given her. Finally, he started onto the arch of the bridge. Owen whispered that it looked like the commander he had seen with Nicholas. Kahlan waited, watching the man walk through the moon-light. He wore a knife at one side and a sword at his other hip.

When he had almost reached her, he came to a halt and waited.

Kahlan held her hand out. "The note said we were to trade. Me for what Nicholas has."

The man, his crooked nose flattened to the side, smiled. "So we were."

"I am the Mother Confessor. Either give me the bottle or you die here, now."

He pulled the square-sided bottle from his pocket and placed it in her hand. Kahlan saw that it was full of clear liquid. She pulled the cork and smelled it. It had the slight aroma of cinnamon, as had the other bottles of the antidote.

"He goes back with this," Kahlan said to the grim-looking man as she handed Owen the bottle.

"And you come with me," the man said as he grabbed her wrist. "Or we all die on this bridge. He may go, as agreed, but if you try to run you will die."

Kahlan glanced to Owen. "Go," she growled.

Owen looked over at the man with black hair, then back to her. He looked as if he had a lot to say, but he nodded and then ran back over the bridge to where Tom and Jennsen stood waiting, watching.

When Owen reached the other two, the man said, "Let's go, unless you'd like to die here."

Kahlan yanked her arm back. When he turned and started out, she followed behind him as they crossed the rest of the way over the bridge. She scanned the shadows among the trees on the far side of the river, the thousand hiding places among the buildings beyond, the streets in the distance. She didn't see anyone, but that didn't really make her feel any better.

Nicholas was there, somewhere, hiding in the darkness, waiting to have her.

Suddenly, the night lit up from behind. Kahlan spun and saw the bridge enveloped in a boiling ball of flame. The fire turned black as it billowed up. Stones sailed into the air above the inferno. As the luminous cloud rose, she could see the bridge beneath the roaring fireball crumpling. The arches caved in on themselves and the entire structure began the long drop into the river.

With icy dread, Kahlan wondered if there were any more bridges across the river. How would she get back to Richard if she succeeded? How was help going to get to her if she didn't?

On the far side, Kahlan could see Tom, Jennsen, and Owen running back up the road toward where Richard slept. They were not about to waste time watching a bridge being destroyed. At the thought of Richard, Kahlan almost let out a sob.

The man unexpectedly shoved her. "Move."

She glared at him, at his self-satisfied smile, at the smug confidence she saw in his eyes.

As she walked ahead of this man and he occasionally shoved her, Kahlan's temper was on a low boil. She had the urge to use her power and take out the despicable brute, but she had to concentrate on the task at hand: Nicholas.

Walking up the street leading away from the river, she was just able to make out soldiers hanging back in the shadows on the dark side streets, blocking every escape route. It didn't matter. At the moment, she wasn't interested in escape, but in her objective. The man behind her, as arrogantly as he was behaving, was also wary and treated her with cautious contempt.

The farther she walked into the city on the far side of the river, the closer the clusters of small buildings were packed together. Side streets of narrow twisting warrens ran off among the ramshackle structures. What trees there were grew crowded in close to the street. Their branches hung out over her like arms raised to snatch her in their claws. Kahlan tried not to think about how deep she was getting into enemy territory, and how many men were surrounding her.

The last time she had been surrounded and trapped by such savage men she had been beaten and had come perilously close to dying. Her unborn child had died. Her child. Richard's child.

She had also lost a kind of innocence that day, a simplistic sense of her invincibility. In its place had come the understanding of how frail life was, how frail her own life was, and how easily it could be lost. She knew how much it had hurt Richard to fear he might lose her. She remembered the terrible agony in his eyes every time he had looked at her. It was completely different to the pain she saw in his eyes from his gift. It had been a helpless suffering for her. She hated the thought of that pain returning to haunt him.

From the shadows to the right side, a man stepped out from behind a building. He wore black robes, covered in layers of what looked like strips of cloth, almost as if he were covered in black feathers. They lifted in the breeze created by his stride, lending him an unsettling, floating fluidity as he moved.

His hair was slicked back with oils that glistened in the moonlight. Close-set, small black eyes rimmed with red peered out at her from an altogether unwholesome face. He held his wrists to his chest, as if he were holding back claws tipped with black fingernails.

Kahlan needed no introduction to know that this was Nicholas the Slide. She had taken confessions from men who appeared to be no more than polite young men, working fathers, or kindly grandfathers but in truth were men who had carried out acts of ruthless cruelty. To look at them behind their bench where they made shoes, or behind a counter where they sold bread, or in a field tending their animals it would be difficult to believe them capable of their vile crimes. But looking at Nicholas, Kahlan saw such utter corruption that it tainted everything about the man, right down to the indecent squint of his eyes.

"The prize of prizes," Nicholas hissed. He reached out, making a fist. "And I have her."

Kahlan hardly heard him. She was already lost to the commitment of wielding her power. This was the man who held the lives of innocent people hostage. This was the man who brought suffering and death in his shadow. This was the man who would kill her and Richard, if given the chance.

She snatched his outstretched wrist capped with his fist.

He appeared no more than a statue before her.

The night, sprinkled with a vault of stars, seemed cold and distant. Beneath her grip of him, Kahlan could feel Nicholas tense, as if to draw back his arm. But it was too late.

He had no chance. He was hers.

Time was hers.

The men all around, who had begun rushing in, were far too distant to matter. They could never reach her in time to save Nicholas. Not even the man who had brought her from the bridge, who now stood not more than a few paces away, was close enough to matter.

Time was hers.

Nicholas was hers.

She gave no thought to what those men would do to her. Right now, it didn't matter. Right now, nothing but her ability to do what needed doing mattered. This man had to be eliminated.

This was the enemy.

This was the man who had invaded a land to torture, rape, and murder innocent people in the name of the Imperial Order. This was a man who had been mutated by magic into a monster designed to destroy them. This man was a tool of conquest, a being of evil.

This was the man who held Richard's life in the balance.

The power within raged to be released.

All her emotions evaporated before the heat of that power. She no longer felt fear, hate, anger, horror. The emotions behind her reasons were now gone. In the all-consuming race of time suspended before the violent rush of her power, she felt only a resolute determination. Her power had become an instrument of pure reason.

All her barriers fell before it.

In an infinitesimal spark of time as she watched the beady eyes staring at her, her power became all.

As she had done countless times before, Kahlan released her restraint on it, and released herself into the flux of violence focused to a singular purpose.

Where she should have felt the exquisite release of merciless force, she felt instead a terrifying emptiness. Where there should have been the fierce twisting of her power through this man's mind, there was . . . nothing.

Kahlan's eyes went wide as she gasped.

As she felt hot pain knife through her.

As she felt the thrust of something foreign and terrible beyond anything she could have imagined.

Hot agony lanced through her consciousness all the way into her very soul.

It felt as if her insides were being ripped apart.

She tried to scream but couldn't.

The night went blacker still.

Kahlan heard laughter echoing through her soul.

CHAPTER 58

Richard's eyes popped open. He felt suddenly, completely, horrifyingly wide awake.

The hair at the back of his neck lifted. It felt as if all his hair wanted to stand on end. His heart raced nearly out of control.

He shot to his feet. Cara, right beside him, caught his arm, surprised to see him suddenly stand up. Looking as if she feared he might fall, she frowned in concern. "Lord Rahl, what's the matter? Are you all right?"

The room was silent. Startled faces all around stared up at him.

"Get out!" he yelled. "Get your things! Everyone out! Now!"

Richard snatched up his pack. He didn't see Kahlan, but saw her pack and grabbed it as well. He wondered if he might still be dreaming. But he never remembered his dreams. He wondered if the feeling might be some lingering dread from a dream. No. It was real.

At first made confused and indecisive by Richard's sudden commands, when the men saw him urgently picking up his gear, everyone scooped up their things and scrambled to their feet. Men everywhere were snatching anything they saw lying about, no matter whose it was.

"Move!" Richard yelled as he pushed hesitant men toward the door. "Go. Move, move, move."

It felt as if something brushed against him, a sliding caress of his flesh, something warm and wicked. Goose bumps tingled up his arms.

"Hurry!"

Men scrambled wildly up the dark stairs ahead of him. Betty, caught up in the mood of panicked escape, shot between his legs and ran up the steps. Cara was close behind him.

The hair at the nape of his neck prickled as if lightning was about to strike. Richard scanned the dark, empty room.

"Where's Kahlan and Jennsen?"

"They went outside before," Cara said.

"Good. Let's go!"

Just as Richard reached the top of the stairs, a fiery blast from back in the room knocked him sprawling. Cara fell on his legs. The stairwell lit up in a flash of yellow and orange light as the entire basement filled with flames. Gouts of fire rolled up the stairwell.

Richard seized Cara's arm and dove with her through the open doorway. As they burst out into the night, the building behind them erupted in a thunderous roar of flames. Parts of the building broke apart, lifting in the billowing blaze. Richard and Cara ducked as flaming boards fell all around them, bouncing and flipping across the ground lit by the glow.

Finally away from the burning building, Richard made a quick appraisal of the alley, looking to see if there were any soldiers about to set upon them. Not seeing anyone he didn't recognize, he started the men moving down the alley to put some distance between them and the burning building.

"We have to get away from here," Richard told Anson. "Nicholas knew we were here. The fire will draw attention and troops. We haven't much time."

Looking around, he still didn't see Kahlan anywhere. His concern rising, he spotted Jennsen, Tom, and Owen running up the alley toward him. By the looks on their faces, he immediately knew that something was wrong.

Richard seized Jennsen's arm as she ran up close. "Where's Kahlan?"

Jennsen gulped air. "Richard—she, she—"

Jennsen burst into tears. Owen waved a square-sided bottle, and a piece of paper, as he, too, wept uncontrollably.

Richard looked at Tom, expecting an answer, and fast. "What's going on?"

"Nicholas found the antidote. He offered it in trade . . . for the Mother Confessor. We tried to stop her, Lord Rahl—I swear we did. She wouldn't listen to any of us. She insisted that she was going to get the antidote and then stop Nicholas. After you have the antidote, if she fails to stop Nicholas and return, she wants you to come for her."

The leaping flames lit the grim faces around him.

"Once her mind is made up," Tom added, "there's no talking her out if it. She has a way of making you do as she says."

Richard knew the truth of that. Amid the roar and crackle of the fire, the building groaned and popped. The roof began to fall in, sending showers of sparks skyward.

Owen urgently handed the square-sided bottle to Richard. "Lord Rahl, she did it to get the antidote. She wanted you to have it so you could be well. She said that comes first—before it is too late."

Richard pulled the cork on the bottle. It had the slight aroma of cinnamon. He took the first swallow, expecting a thick, sweet, spicy taste. It didn't taste that way at all.

He looked at Jennsen and Owen's faces. "This is water."

Jennsen's eyes went wide. "What?"

"Water. Water with a little cinnamon in it." Richard poured it on the ground. "It's not the antidote. She traded herself to Nicholas for nothing."

Jennsen, Owen, and Tom stood in mute shock.

Richard felt a kind of detached calm. It was over. It was the end of everything. He now had a limited amount of time to do what had to be done . . . and then everything was at an end for him.

"Let me see this note," he said to Owen.

Owen handed it over. Richard had no trouble reading by the light coming from the fire. As Cara, Tom, Jennsen, and Owen watched, he read it over three times.

Finally, his arm lowered. Cara snatched the note away and read it for herself.

Richard gazed up the alleyway at the burning building, trying to figure it out. "How did Nicholas know that someone was coming for the antidote? He said we had an hour. How did he know we were here, this close, and coming for it, in order to write in the note that he gave us an hour?"

"Maybe he didn't," Cara said. "Maybe he wrote the note days ago. Maybe he just wrote that to make us rush without thinking."

"Maybe." Richard gestured behind him. "But how did he know we were here?"

"Magic?" Jennsen offered.

Richard didn't like the idea that Nicholas apparently knew so much and was always one step ahead of them.

"How did you know that Nicholas was about to set this place ablaze?" Cara asked him.

"I woke suddenly," Richard said. "My headache was gone and I just knew we had to get out at once."

"So your gift worked?"

"I guess so. It does that—it works sometimes to warn me."

He wished he could somehow make it more dependable. At least, this time, it had been, or they would all be dead.

Tom peered out into the night. "So, you think Nicholas is close? That he knew where we were and set the place afire?"

"No. I think he wants us to believe he's close. He's a wizard. He could have sent wizard's fire from a great distance. I'm no expert on magic; he might have used some other means to set the fire from a distance."

Richard turned to Owen. "Take me to this building where you hid the antidote, where Nicholas was when you first saw him."

Without hesitation, Owen started out. The rest of the small group followed after him.

"Do you think she will be there?" Jennsen asked.

"There's only one way to find out."

By the time they reached the river they were out of breath. Richard was furious to find the bridge gone, with stone blocks from it scattered on the banks far below. The rest of it had apparently vanished beneath the dark water. Owen and some of the other men said that there was another bridge farther to the north, so they took off in that direction, following the road that twisted along beside the river.

Before they reached the bridge, a knot of soldiers rushed out from a side street, weapons raised, yelling battle-cries.

The night rang with the distinctive sound of Richard's sword being drawn. While the blade was free, its magic was not. With the heart-pounding threat, it didn't matter. Richard had anger to spare and met the enemy with a cry of his own.

The first man lunged. Richard's strike was so violent it cleaved the burly man down through the leather armor over his shoulder to his opposite hip. As Richard spun without pause to a soldier coming at him from behind, he brought the sword around with such speed that the man was beheaded before he had cocked his sword arm. Richard drew his elbow back, smashing the face of a man rushing in to stab him from behind. A quick thrust took down another man before Richard could turn to finish the man behind who had dropped to his knees, his hands covering his bleeding face. A moonlit flash of Richard's sword brought measured death.

Tom slashed through the men at the same time as Cara's Agiel took others down. Cries of surprised pain shattered the quiet of the night. All the while, Richard swept through the enemy like a wind-borne shadow.

In mere moments, the night was again silent. Richard, Tom, and Cara had eliminated the enemy squad before any of their men could react to the threat that had come out of the darkness. Scarcely had they caught their breath when Richard was already charging onward to the bridge.

When they reached it, two slouching Imperial Order soldiers stood guard, pikes standing upright. The guards seemed to be surprised that people would be running toward them at night. Probably because the people of Bandakar had never before dared to cause them any trouble, the two guards stood watching Richard come until he pulled his sword from behind and took them down with a rapid thrust to the first man and a powerful sweeping slice that cut the second in two along with the pike standing at his side.

The small company raced unopposed across the bridge and into the darkness among the crowded buildings. Owen directed Richard at every turn as they rushed onward toward the place where Owen had hidden the antidote and where he had recovered, instead of the antidote, the note demanding Kahlan in exchange for Richard's life, in exchange for the lives of an empire naked to the dark talents of Nicholas the Slide.

In the somber heart of the city made up of small, squat, mostly single-story buildings, Owen pulled Richard to a stop. "Lord Rahl, down here, at the corner, we turn to the right. A short distance beyond is a square where people often gather. At the far end of the square will be a building taller than those around it. That is the place. Down a small street to the side of it, there will be an alleyway that runs behind the building. That is the way I got in, before."

Richard nodded. "Let's go."

Without waiting to see if the tired men were with him, he started out, keeping in close to the buildings, to the shadows cast by the moon. Richard moved around the building at the corner. Hung over a small front window was a carved sign displaying loaves of bread. It was still too early for the baker to be at work.

Richard looked up and froze. There before him was the square with trees and benches. The building across the open square was in ruin. Only smoldering timbers remained. A small crowd had gathered around, watching what had hours ago obviously been a large fire.

"Dear spirits," Jennsen whispered in horror. She covered her mouth, fearing to speak aloud the worry on everyone's mind.

"She wouldn't be in there," Richard said in answer to the unspoken fear. "Nicholas wouldn't take her back here just to kill her."

"Then why do this?" Anson asked. "Why burn the place down?"

Richard watched the wisps of smoke slowly curling up into the cool night air, at his hopes disappearing. "To send me a message that he has her and I'll not find her."

"Lord Rahl," Cara said under her breath, "I think we had better get out of here."

From the darkness around the building that had burned down, Richard could just start to make out the sight of soldiers by the hundreds, no doubt waiting to catch them.

"I feared as much," Owen said. "That's why I brought us in by such a circuitous route. See that road over there, where all the soldiers are? That's the road coming from the bridge we crossed."

"How do they always know where we are, or where we will be?" Jennsen whispered in frustration. "And when?"

Cara grabbed Richard's shirt and started pulling him back. "There are too many. We don't know how many more are around us. We need to get out of here."

Richard was loath to admit it, but she was right.

"We have men waiting for us," Tom reminded him. "And a lot more coming."

Richard's mind raced. Where was she?

Finally he nodded. The instant he did, Cara took him by his arm and they dashed off into the darkness.

CHAPTER 59

Under the sweep of stars, Richard willed himself to stand up straight and tall before all the men gathered beneath the spreading branches of the oak trees at the forest's edge. A few candles burned among the gathering so they could all see. By the time they charged into the city of Northwick to make their attack, it would just be light.

Richard wanted nothing more than to get into the city and find Kahlan, but he had to use everything he had at hand to help, or he might waste the chance. He had to do this, first.

Most of these men had never really fought before. Owen and Anson's men from the town of Witherton had been there at the first attack on the sleeping houses and had taken part in the skirmishes there. The rest of the men were from Northwick, where Richard had gone to see the Wise One. They had been in on the clashes with the soldiers who weren't poisoned. There had not been a great many enemy soldiers to fight, but the men had done what had to be done. If anything, those minor but bloody encounters had only served to make the men more determined because it had shown them that they could win freedom themselves, that they were in control of their own destiny.

This, though, was different. This was going to be a battle on a scale they had not experienced. Worse, it was in a city that had, for the most part, willingly joined with the Order's cause. The populace was not likely to offer much help.

Had he more time, Richard might have come up with a better plan that would have chipped away at the enemy's numbers first, but there was no time. It had to be now.

TERRY GOODKIND

Richard stood before the men, hoping to give them something to help them carry the day. He had trouble thinking of anything but finding Kahlan. In order to have the best chance to save her, he put her from his mind and focused on the task at hand.

"I had hoped we wouldn't have to do it this way," he said. "I had hoped we could do it in some manner like we've done before, with the fire, or the poisoning, so that none of you would be hurt. We don't have that option. Nicholas knows we're here. If we run, his men will come after us. Some of us might escape . . . for a while."

"We have finished running," Anson said.

"That's right," Owen agreed. "We have learned that running and hiding brings only greater suffering."

Richard nodded. "I agree. But you must understand that some of us are probably going to die, today. Maybe most of us. Maybe all of us. If any of you choose not to fight, then we must know now. Once we go in, we'll all be depending on each other."

He clasped his hands behind his back as he paced slowly before them. It was hard to make out their faces in the dim light. Richard knew, too, that his time was running out. His sight would only get worse. His dizziness would only get worse.

He knew he was never going to get better.

If he was to have a chance to get Kahlan away from the men of the Order, it had to be at once, with these men or without them.

When none said that they wanted to quit, Richard went on. "We need to get to their commanders for two reasons: to find out where the Mother Confessor is being held, and to eliminate them so that they can't direct their soldiers against us.

"You all have weapons now and, in the limited time we've had, we've done our best to teach you how to use them. There's one other thing you must know. You will be afraid. So will I.

"To overcome this fear, you must use your anger."

"Anger?" one of the men asked. "How can we bring forth anger when we're afraid?"

"These men have raped your wives, your sisters, your mothers, daughters, aunts, cousins and neighbors," Richard said as he paced. "Think about that, when you look into the enemy's eyes as they come at you. They have taken most of the women away. You all know why. They have tortured children to make you give up. Think about the terror of your children as they screamed in fear and pain, dying bloody and alone after being mutilated by these men." The heat of Richard's anger seeped into his words. "Think about that when you see their confident grins as they come at you. These men have tortured people you loved, people who never did anything against them. Think about that as these men come at you with their bloodstained hands.

"These men have sent many of your people away to be used as slaves. Many more of your people have been murdered by these men. Think about that, when they come to murder you, too.

"This is not about a difference of opinion, or a disagreement. There can be no debate or uncertainty about this among moral men. This is about rape, torture, murder." Richard turned and faced the men. "Think about that, when you face these beasts." He tapped a fist to his chest as he ground his teeth. "And when you face these men, men who have done all these things to you and your loved ones, face them with hate in your hearts. Fight them with hate in your hearts. Kill them with hate in your hearts. They deserve no better."

The woods were silent as the men considered his chilling words. Richard knew that he had rage enough, and hate enough, to be eager to get at the men of the Imperial Order.

He didn't know where Kahlan was, but he intended to find out and to have her back. She had done as she had to in order to get the antidote to save his life. He understood what she had done, and couldn't fault her for it—that was the kind of woman she was. She loved him just as fiercely as he loved her. She had done what she had to do.

But he was not going to let her down. She was depending on him to come for her.

The terrible irony was that it had all been for nothing. The antidote she had made such a sacrifice to obtain was no antidote at all.

Richard looked out at all their faces, so intent on what he had to tell them on the eve of such a momentous battle, and remembered, then, the words on the statue at the entrance to this land, the words of the Wizard's Eighth Rule: Talga Vassternich.

"There is one last thing to tell you," he said. "The most important thing of all."

Richard faced them as the leader of the D'Haran Empire, an empire struggling to survive, to be free, and told them those two words in their language.

"Deserve Victory."

It was just turning light as they charged into the city. Only one of them had remained behind: Jennsen. Richard had forbidden her from joining the fight. Besides being young and not nearly as strong as the men they would come up against, she would only create a tempting target. Rape was a sacred weapon of the wicked, and one this enemy used religiously. The men of the Imperial Order would rally for such a prize. Cara was different; she was a trained warrior and more lethal than any of them except Richard.

Jennsen hadn't been pleased to be left behind, but she had understood Richard's reasons and hadn't wanted to give him anything else to worry about. She and Betty had remained behind in the woods.

A man they had sent out to scout because he knew the area well emerged from a side alley. As they reached him they all moved up against the wall, trying to remain out of sight as best they could.

"I found them," the scout said, trying to catch his breath. He pointed to the right of their route into the city.

"How many?" Richard asked.

"I think it must be their main force within the city, Lord Rahl. It's where they sleep. They seem to still be there, as you expected, and not yet up. The place they've taken over contains buildings for city offices and administration. But I bring troubling news, as well. They are being protected by the people of the city."

Richard ran his fingers back through his hair. He had to concentrate to keep from coughing. He gripped the window frame of the building beside him to help himself stand.

"What do you mean, they are being protected?"

"There are crowds of people from the city surrounding the place occupied by the soldiers. The people are there to protect the soldiers—from us. They are there to stop us attacking."

Richard let out an angry breath. "All right." He turned back to the worried, expectant faces of all the men. "Now, listen to me. We are joined in a battle against evil. If anyone sides with evil, if they protect evil men, then they are serving to perpetuate evil."

One of the men looked unsure. "Are you saying that if they try to stop us, we might have to use force against them?"

"What is it these people seek to accomplish? What is their goal? They want to prevent us from eliminating the Imperial Order. Because they hate life, they despise freedom more than slavery."

With grim determination, Richard met the men's gazes. "I'm saying that anyone who protects the enemy and seeks to keep them in power, for whatever reason, has sided with them. It's no more complicated than that. If they try to protect the enemy or hamper us from doing as we must . . . kill them."

"But they aren't armed," a man said.

Richard's anger flared. "They are armed—armed with evil ideas that seek to enslave the world. If they succeed, you die.

"Saving the lives of innocent people and your loved ones—and having far less loss of life in the end—is best served by crushing the enemy as decisively and quickly as possible. Then there will be peace. If these people try to prevent that, then they are, in effect, siding with those who torture and murder—they help them to live another day to murder again. Such people must not be treated any differently than what they in truth are: servants of evil.

"If they try to stop you, kill them."

There was a moment of silence, then Anson put a fist his heart. "With hate in my heart . . . Vengeance without mercy."

Looks of iron determination spread back through the men. They all put fists to their hearts in salute and took up the pledge. "Vengeance without mercy!"

Richard clapped Anson on the side of the shoulder. "Let's go."

They raced out from the long shadows of the buildings and poured around the corner. The people off at the end of the street all turned when they spotted Richard's force coming. More people—men and women from the city—surged into the street in front of the compound of buildings the soldiers had taken up as barracks and a command post. The people looked like a scraggly lot.

"No war! No war! No war!" the people shouted as Richard led the men up the street at a dead run.

"Out of the way!" Richard yelled as he closed the distance. This was no time for subtlety or discussions; the success of their attack depended in large part on speed. "Get out of the way! This is your only warning! Get out of the way or die!"

"Stop the hate! Stop the hate!" the people chanted as they locked arms.

They had no idea how much hate was raging through Richard. He drew the Sword of Truth. The wrath of its magic didn't come out with it, but he had enough of his own. He slowed to a trot.

"Move!" Richard called as he bore down on the people.

A plump, curly-haired woman took a step out from the others. Her round face was red with anger as she screamed, "Stop the hate! No war! Stop the hate! No war!"

"Move or die!" Richard yelled as he picked up speed.

The red-faced woman shook her fleshy fist at Richard and his men, leading an angry chant. "Murderers! Murderers! Murderers!"

On his way past her, gritting his teeth as he screamed with the fury of the attack begun, Richard took a powerful swing, lopping off the woman's head and upraised arm. Strings of blood and gore splashed across the faces behind her even as some still chanted their empty words. The head and loose arm tumbled through the crowd. A man made the mistake of reaching for Richard's weapon, and took the full weight of a charging thrust.

Men behind Richard hit the line of evil's guardians with unrestrained violence. People armed only with their hatred for moral clarity fell bloodied, terribly injured, and dead. The line of people collapsed before the merciless charge. Some of the people, screaming their contempt, used their fists to attack Richard's men. They were met with swift and deadly steel.

At the realization that their defense of the Imperial Order's brutality would actually result in consequences to themselves, the crowd began scattering in fright, screaming curses back at Richard and his men.

Richard's army did not pause as they tore through the ring of protectors, now on the run, but continued on to the maze of buildings among grassy open spaces dotted with trees. The soldiers who were outside began to realize that this time they would have to protect themselves, that the people of the city could no longer do it for them. These were men used to slaughtering defenseless, docile victims. For more than a year of occupation they had not had to fight.

Richard was the first on them, taking down men on his way into their midst. Cara charged in at his right, Tom at his left, the deadly point of a spear driving into soldiers only now pulling free their weapons. These were men used to overwhelming their cowering opponents with sheer numbers, not with fighting resolute opposition. They did so now, and for their lives.

Richard moved through them as if they were statues. They thrust a blade at where he had been, while he cut where they were going and met them there with razor-sharp steel. He came up behind others as they looked both ways, losing track of him, only to have him reach around and draw his sword across their throats. Others he beheaded before they realized he was about to strike.

He wasted no effort with exaggerated movements and wild slashes. He cut with deadly proficiency. He didn't try to best men to show them he was better; he simply killed them. He didn't give them any chance to fight back; he cut them down before they could.

Now that he was committed to the fight, he was committed to the dance with death, which meant one thing: cut. It was his duty, his purpose, his hunger to cut the enemy down quickly, resolutely, and utterly.

They were not prepared for this level of violence unleashed.

As his men fell on the soldiers, a great cry rose up. As men fell, their screams filled the morning.

Seeing a man who looked like an officer, Richard wheeled around him and laid his blade across the man's throat.

"Where is Nicholas and the Mother Confessor?"

The man answered by trying to grab Richard's arm. He wasn't nearly quick enough. Richard pulled his sword across the man's throat, nearly severing his head, as he spun to a man coming at him from behind. The man skidded to a stop in an effort to avoid Richard's blade, only to be stabbed through the heart.

The battle raged on, moving back between the buildings as they took down those men who met the attack. Yet more men, layered in leather, mail, hides, and weapons-belts came out of the barracks at hearing the clash. They were fierce-looking men who appeared better suited to murder than any men Richard had ever seen.

As they came onward, Richard seized anyone who looked like an officer. None of them was able to give him any answers. None of them knew the whereabouts of either Nicholas or Kahlan.

Richard had to fight off the dizziness as well as the soldiers. By focusing on the dance with death and the precepts the sword had taught him in the past, he was able to surmount the effects of the poison. He knew that such efforts couldn't long replace the required strength of endurance, but for the moment he was able to do as he had to.

It was somewhat surprising to see how well his men were doing. They helped each other as they moved deeper into the enemy lines. By fighting in that way, using one another's strengths, they were often able to survive together where one alone would not have.

Some of his men had not survived; Richard saw several lying dead. But the surprised enemy was being slaughtered. The Imperial Order soldiers were not charged with righteous, resolute determination. Richard's men were. The Order soldiers were little more than a gang of thugs allowed to run loose. They now faced men calling them to account. The men of the Order fought a disorderly attempt to spare their own individual lives, without thought for a coordinated defense, while Richard's men fought to a singular purpose of exterminating the enemy's entire force.

Richard heard Cara calling urgently for him from the narrow space between two buildings. At first, he thought she was in trouble, but when he rounded the corner he saw then that she had a husky man on his knees. She held his head up by a fistful of his greasy black hair. One ear displayed a row of silver rings. Cara had her Agiel at his throat. Blood ran down his chin.

"Tell him!" she yelled at the man when Richard ran up.

"I don't know where they are!"

In a fit of fury, Cara slammed the tip of her Agiel to the base of the man's skull. He flinched, his arms shaking with the shattering shock of pain that brought a gasp rather than a scream. His eyes rolled back in his head. Holding him by his tangled hair, Cara bent him back over her knee to hold him upright.

"Tell him," she growled.

"They left," he mumbled. "Nicholas left last night. They carried a woman away with them, but I don't know who she was."

Richard went to a knee and grabbed the man's shirt. "What did she look like?"

The man's eyes were still rolling. "Long hair."

"Where did they go?"

"Don't know. Gone. In a hurry."

"What did Nicholas tell you before he left?"

The man's eyes slowly came into focus. "Nicholas knew you were going to attack at dawn. He told me the route you would take into the city."

Richard could hardly believe what he was hearing. "How could he possibly know that?"

The man hesitated. The sight of Cara's Agiel made him talk. "I don't know. Before he left, Nicolas told me how many men you had, told me when you would attack, and by which route. He told me to get people from the city to shield us from your attack. We gathered our most fanatical supporters and told them that you were coming to murder us, that you wanted to make war."

"When did Nicholas leave? Where did he take this woman?"

Blood dripped from the man's chin. "I don't know. They just left in a hurry last night. That's all I know."

"If you knew we were coming, why didn't you make a better defense?"

"Oh, but we did. Nicholas told me to take care of the city. I assured him that such a small force as yours could not possibly defeat us."

Something was terribly wrong. "Why not?"

For the first time, the man smiled. "Because you don't know how many men we really have. Once I knew where your attack was coming, I was able to call in all my forces." The man's smile widened. "Do you hear that horn in the distance? Here they come." A belly-laugh rolled up. "You are about to die."

Richard gritted his teeth. "You first."

With a mighty thrust, he ran his sword through the officer's heart. The man's eyes widened in shock. Richard gave the blade a twist as he withdrew it to be sure the job was done.

"We'd better get the men out of here," Richard said as he took Cara's arm and ran for the corner of the buildings.

"Looks like we're too late," she said when they came out from behind cover and saw the legions of men pouring in all around them.

How did Nicholas know when and where they were going to attack? There had been no one around—no races, not so much as a mouse had been there when they had made their plans as they moved through the countryside. How could he have known?

"Dear spirits," Cara said. "I didn't think they had this many men in Bandakar."

The roar of the soldiers was deafening as they charged in. Richard was already spent. Each deep breath he pulled was agonizingly painful. He knew that there was no choice.

He had to find a way to get to Kahlan. He had to hold out at least that long.

Richard whistled in a signal to gather his men. As Anson and Owen ran up, Richard looked around and saw most of the others.

"We have to try to break out of here. There's too many of them. Stay together. We're going to try to punch through. If we make it, scatter and try to make it back to the forest."

With Cara at one side, Tom at the other, Richard charged at the head of his men toward the enemy lines. Thousands of the Imperial Order soldiers poured out from the city around them and into the open. It was a frightening sight. There were so many that it almost seemed as if the ground itself were moving.

Before Richard reached the soldiers, the morning suddenly lit with blinding blasts of fire. Thunderous eruptions of flame tore through the enemy lines, killing men by the hundreds. Sod, trees, and men were hurled into the air. Men—their clothes, hair, and flesh burning—tumbled across the ground.

Richard heard a howl coming from behind. It sounded somehow familiar. He turned just in time to see a roiling ball of liquid yellow flame wailing through the air toward them. It expanded as it came, tumbling with seething, deadly intensity.

Wizard's fire.

The incandescent, white-hot inferno roared by just overhead. Once past Richard and his men, it descended, crashing down among the enemy soldiers, spilling a flood of liquid death out among them. Wizard's fire stuck to what it touched, burning with ferocious intensity. A single droplet of it would burn down through a man's leg to the bone. It was horrifyingly deadly. It was said to be so excruciatingly painful that those who lived longed only for death.

The question was, who was it coming from?

To the other side, men of the Order fell as something scythed through their ranks. It almost looked as if a single blade cut them down by the hundreds, ripping them apart with bloody ferocity. But who was doing it?

There was no time to stand around and wonder. Richard and his men had to turn to meet the soldiers who made it through the devastating conjuring. Now that their numbers had been so thinned, the Imperial Order soldiers were unable to mount an effective attack. Their charge fell apart on the blades of Richard's men.

As they fought, more deadly fire came in to catch those trying to run, or those who massed to attack. In other places, Order soldiers fell without Richard or his men touching them. They gasped in great agony, clutching their chests, and fell dead.

Before long, the morning fell silent but for the groans of the wounded. Richard's men rallied around him, unsure of what had happened, worried that whatever had befallen these men might suddenly turn and befall them as well. Richard realized that they didn't see the attack of wizard's fire and magic in the same way as he did; to them it must seem a miracle of salvation.

Richard spotted two people beside one of the buildings off to the side of the grounds. One was taller than the other. He squinted, trying to make them out, but he just couldn't see who they were. With a hand on Tom's shoulder for support, they headed toward the two figures.

"Richard, my boy," Nathan said when Richard made it over to him. "So good to find you well."

Ann, a squat woman in a plain gray dress, smiled that knowing smile of hers, so filled with joy, satisfaction, and at the same time a kind of knowing tolerance.

"I doubt you two could imagine how glad I am to see you," Richard said, still catching his breath, trying not to breathe too deeply. "But what are you doing here? How in the world did you find me?"

Nathan leaned in with a sly smile. "Prophecy, my boy."

Nathan wore high boots and a ruffled white shirt with a vest and an elegant green velvet cape attached at his right shoulder. The prophet cut quite a figure.

Richard saw then that Nathan was wearing an exquisite sword in a polished scabbard. It seemed to Richard rather odd for a wizard who could command wizard's fire to carry a sword. It seemed even more odd to see the man abruptly draw the weapon.

Ann suddenly gasped as someone sprang from behind the building and grabbed her. It was one of the people from the city who had gathered to protect the army—a tall, slender, pinch-faced woman with a formidable scowl and a long knife.

"You are murderers!" she cried, her straight hair whipping side to side. "You are filled with hate!"

The ground around Ann and the woman erupted, chunks of dirt and grass flying up into the air. Ann, a sorceress, was apparently trying to fight off her attacker. The woman was unaffected. Against a pristinely ungifted person, magic wasn't working.

Nathan, not far to the side of Ann, stepped in and without ado ran the tall woman through with his sword. The woman staggered back, his sword through her chest, her face a picture of surprise. She dropped, sliding off the red blade.

Ann, free of her attacker, glanced at the dead woman. She fixed Nathan with a scowl. "Dashing indeed."

Nathan smiled at her private joke. "I told you, they aren't touched by magic."

"Nathan," Richard said, "I still don't understand—"

"Come here, my dear," Nathan said, signaling off behind him.

Jennsen ran out from behind the building. She threw her arms around Richard.

"I'm so glad you're all right," she said. "I hope you aren't angry with me. Nathan showed up in the woods not long after you and the men left. I remembered seeing him before—at the People's Palace in D'Hara. I knew he was a Rahl, so I told him the trouble we were in. He and Ann wanted to help. We came as fast as we could."

Jennsen looked expectantly up at Richard. He answered her worry with a hug.

"You did the right thing," he told her. "You used your head for something the Order didn't anticipate."

Now that the heat of battle had ended, Richard was dizzier than ever. He had to lean on Tom for support.

Nathan put a shoulder under Richard's other arm. "I hear you're having trouble with your gift. Maybe I can help."

"I don't have time. Nicholas the Slide has Kahlan. I have to find her or—"

"Don't play a fool when you aren't," Nathan said. "It won't take long to bring your gift into harmony. You need the help of another wizard to get it under control—like the last time I helped you—or you won't be of any use to anyone. Come on, let's get you inside one of these places where it's quiet, then I can take care of that much of your troubles."

Richard wanted nothing more than to find Kahlan, but he didn't know where to look. He felt like falling into the man's arms and surrendering his destiny to him, to his experience, to his vast knowledge. Richard knew Nathan was right. He felt like crying with relief that help was finally at hand. Who better to help him get his gift back under control than a wizard?

Richard had never even dared to hope to have this opportunity;

he had planned on trying to get to Nicci because she was the only one he could think of who might know what to do. This was infinitely better than a sorceress helping him.

A wizard was the only one really meant to help with this kind of trouble with another wizard's gift.

"Just make it quick," he told Nathan.

Nathan smiled that Rahl smile of his. "Come on, then. We'll have your gift back to right in no time at all."

"Thank you, Nathan," Richard mumbled as he let the big man help him through a nearby doorway.

CHAPTER 60

Richard sat cross-legged on the wood floor facing Nathan. The barren room had no furniture. Nathan said none was needed, that the floor was fine with him. Ann, not far away, sat on the floor as well. Richard was a little surprised that Nathan was allowing her to observe, but didn't question it. There was the possibility that he might want to have her help for some part of it.

Everyone else waited outside. Cara wasn't happy about allowing Richard out of her sight, but Richard calmed her concern by telling her that he would feel more comfortable and able to concentrate on correcting the problem with his gift if he knew she was outside keeping an eye on everything for him.

The two windows had been shuttered, allowing in only dim light and keeping out most of the noise. With his hands on his knees, the prophet pushed his back straighter and, drawing a deep breath, seemed to pull an aura of authority around himself. Nathan was the one who had first taught Richard about his gift, telling him how war wizards, like Richard, weren't like other wizards. Instead of tapping the core of power within themselves, they directed their intent through their feelings.

It had been a difficult concept to grasp. Nathan had told Richard that his power worked through anger.

"Lose yourself in my eyes," Nathan said in a quiet voice.

Richard knew he had to try to put his worry about Kahlan aside.

Trying to keep his breathing steady so as not to cough, he stared into Nathan's hooded, deep, dark, azure eyes. Nathan's gaze drew him in. Richard felt as if he were falling up into clear blue sky. His breath came in ragged pulls, and not of his own doing. He felt Nathan's commanding words more than heard them.

"Call forth the anger, Richard. Call forth the rage. Call forth the hate and fury."

Richard's head was swimming. He concentrated on calling his anger. He thought about Nicholas having Kahlan and he had no trouble summoning rage.

He could feel another force within his own, as if he were drowning and someone was trying to hold his head above water.

He drifted, alone, in a dark and still place. Time seemed to mean nothing.

Time.

He had to get to Kahlan in time. He was her only chance.

Richard opened his eyes. "Nathan, I'm sorry, but . . ."

Nathan was drenched in sweat. Ann was sitting beside him, holding Richard's left hand, Nathan his right. Richard wondered what had happened.

Richard looked from one face to the other. "What's wrong?"

They both looked grim. "We tried," Nathan whispered. "I'm sorry, but we tried."

Richard frowned. They had only just begun.

"What do you mean? Why are you giving up so soon?"

Nathan cast a sidelong glance at Ann. "We've been at it for two hours, Richard."

"Two hours?"

"I'm afraid there is nothing I can do, my boy." By the sound of Nathan's voice, he meant it.

Richard ran his fingers back through his hair. "What are you talking about? You're the one who told me the last time I had this problem that joining with a wizard would set it straight. You said it was a simple matter for a wizard to fix such a disharmony with the gift."

"That's the way it should be. But your gift is somehow tangled up into a knot that's strangling you."

"But you're a prophet, a wizard. Ann, you're a sorceress. Together you both probably know more about magic than anyone who has lived in thousands of years."

"Richard, there has not been another born like you in the last three thousand years. We don't know that much about how your particular gift works." Ann paused to push stray strands of gray hair back into the bun at the back of her head. "We tried, Richard. I swear to you, we both tried our best. Your gift is beyond Nathan's help, even with my ability enhancing his power. We tried everything we know, and even a few things we thought up. None of it had any effect. We cannot help you."

"So, what must I do?"

Nathan's azure eyes turned away. "Your gift is killing you, Richard. I don't know the cause, but I'm afraid that it has spiraled into a phase that is out of control and fatal."

Ann's eyes were wet. "Richard . . . I'm so sorry."

Richard looked from one distraught face to the other.

"I guess it doesn't really matter," Richard said.

Nathan frowned. "What do you mean it doesn't matter?"

Richard rose up, groping for the wall to keep his balance. "I've been poisoned. The antidote is gone . . . There is no cure. I'm afraid that I'm running out of time. I guess the joke is on my gift—something else is going to get me first."

Ann stood and gripped his upper arms. "Richard, we can't help you right now, but you can at least rest while we try to figure out—"

"No." Richard waved off her concern. "No. I can't waste what little time I have left. I have to get to Kahlan."

Ann cleared her throat. "Richard, at the Palace of the Prophets, Nathan and I waited for your birth for a very long time. We worked to clear those obstacles which prophecy showed us lay in your path. The prophecies name you as central to the course of the future of the world. In fact, they say you are the only one with a chance; we need you to lead us in this battle.

"We don't know what is wrong with your gift, but we can work on it. You must be here so that if we come up with a solution, we can set your power right."

"I'll not live for you to cure me. Don't you see? The poison is killing me. It has three states. I'm already entering the third state: blindness. I'm going to die. I must use what time I have left to find

Kahlan. You aren't going to have me to lead you but, if I can get her away from Nicholas, you will have her to lead the struggle in my place."

"You know where she is, then?" Nathan asked.

Richard realized that in the state of focused, concentrated thought, as he was adrift in that quiet place while Nathan was trying to help him, it had come to him where Nicholas most likely had taken Kahlan. He had to get there while Nicholas was still there with her.

"Yes, I believe I do."

Richard pulled open the door. Cara, sitting right outside, shot to her feet. Her expectant expression quickly withered when he shook his head, signaling that it hadn't worked.

"We have to get going. Right away. I think I know where Nicholas took Kahlan. We have to hurry."

"You know?" Jennsen asked, holding Betty close by her rope.

"Yes. We need to leave at once."

"Where is she, then?"

Richard gestured. "Owen, remember how you told us about a fortified encampment the Imperial Order built when they first came to Bandakar and they were worried about their safety?"

"Back near my town," Owen said.

Richard nodded. "That's right. I think Nicholas took Kahlan there. It's a secure place they built to hold some of the women captive. There would be plenty of soldiers to protect him and it's the kind of place built specifically to be defensible, so it would be much more difficult to approach than his place, here, in the city."

"Then how will we approach it?" Jennsen asked.

"We'll have to figure that out once we get there and see the place."

Nathan joined Richard at the door. "Ann and I will go with you. We might be able to help rescue Kahlan from the Slide. While we travel the two of us can work on a solution for untangling your gift."

Richard gripped Nathan's shoulder. "There are no horses in this land. If you can run and keep up with us, you're welcome, but I can't afford to slow for you. I don't have much time, and neither does Kahlan. Nicholas will not likely hold her there long. After he pauses for rest and supplies and then leaves this land, it will be even more difficult to find him. We have no time to lose. We're going to have to travel as swiftly as possible."

Nathan's eyes turned down in disappointment.

Ann drew Richard into a brief hug. "We're far too old to keep up the speed afoot that you and these young people can. When you get her away from the Slide, come back and we'll do our best to help you. We'll work on the problem while you're getting her out of his clutches. Come back then, and we'll have a solution."

Richard knew that he would never live that long, but there was no point in saying it. "All right. What can you tell me about a Slide?"

Nathan drew his thumb along his jaw as he considered the question. "Slides are soul stealers. There is no defense against them. Even I would be powerless to stop them."

Richard didn't suppose that needed any explanation. "Cara, Jennsen, Tom, you can come with me."

"What about us?" Owen asked.

Anson stood close by, looking eager to be included, and nodded at Owen's suggestion. There were others as well, who had stood vigil outside the place where Nathan had tried to help Richard. They were all men who had fought hard. If he was to get Kahlan back, he would likely need some men, at least.

"Your help would be welcome. I think most of the men should stay here with Nathan and Ann. The people here in Hawton need to have you men explain everything to them—help them to understand all that you've learned. They will need to make some changes to adjust to interacting with the world out there now open to them."

As Richard started away, Nathan grabbed hold of his sleeve. "Richard, as far as I know, you have no defense against a soul stealer, but there is one thing I recall from an old tome in the vaults in the Palace of the Prophets."

"I'm listening."

"They somehow travel outside their bodies . . . send their own spirits out."

Richard rubbed his fingertips across his brow as he thought about Nathan's words. "That has to be how he was watching me, tracking me. I believe he watched me through the eyes of huge birds that live here, called black-tipped races. If what you're saying is right, then maybe he leaves his body in order to do this." Richard looked up at Nathan. "How does this help me?"

Nathan leaned closer, cocking his head to peer at him with one azure eye. "That is when they are vulnerable—when they are out of their bodies."

Richard lifted his sword a few inches in the scabbard to be sure it was clear. "Any idea how to catch him outside his body?" He let the sword drop back.

Nathan straightened. "Afraid not."

Richard nodded his thanks anyway and stepped down out of the doorway. "Owen, how far is this fortified encampment?"

"Back close to where the path used to go out through the boundary."

That was why Richard hadn't seen it; they had come in the ancient route used by Kaja-Rang. Ordinarily, it would be a journey of well over a week. They didn't have nearly that long.

He took in all the faces watching him. "Nicholas has quite a head start on us and he will be in a hurry to escape with his prize. If we travel swiftly and don't stop long to rest, there's a good chance we can still catch up with him by the time he reaches their encampment. We need to be on our way at once."

"We're only waiting for you, Lord Rahl," Cara said.

So was Kahlan.

CHAPTER 61

Each day of hard travel, Richard's condition worsened, but his fear for Kahlan drove him relentlessly onward. Most of the time, hour after hour, through sunlight, darkness, and occasional rain, they ran at a steady lope. Richard used a staff he'd cut himself to help keep his balance. When he thought he would be unable to go on, he deliberately picked up the pace to remind himself that he could not give up. They stopped at night only long enough to get a few hours sleep.

The men had trouble keeping up with him. Cara and Jennsen didn't; they were both used to strenuous exertion in the course of difficult journeys. All of them, though, were so exhausted from the unrelenting pace that they talked only when necessary. Richard drove himself doggedly, trying not to think about his own hopeless condition. It didn't matter. He reminded himself that with every step they ran, if it was fast enough, they were gaining on Nicholas and were just that much closer to Kahlan.

In moments of despair, Richard told himself that Kahlan had to be alive, that Nicholas could have killed her long ago if that was his intention. He wouldn't have run if she were dead. Kahlan would be much more valuable to him alive.

In a way, he felt an odd kind of relief. He could push as hard as he needed. He didn't have to worry about his health. There was no antidote to the poison. Given the time, it would kill him. There was no solution to the problem of his gift being out of control; that, too, would kill him. There was nothing Richard could do about either. He was going to die.

The wooded hills were easy enough traveling. They were open, with broad green meadows sprinkled with wildflowers and a patchwork of grassland. Wildlife was abundant. Were he not dying, in pain, and sick with worry about Kahlan, Richard might have enjoyed the beauty of the land. Now, it was just an obstacle.

The sun in his eyes was slipping down behind the towering mountains. Soon, darkness would be upon them. A little earlier, Richard had used his bow to take a buck when the opportunity presented itself. Tom had made quick work of butchering it. The rest of them needed to eat, or they would not be able to keep up the pace. Richard supposed that they would have to stop for a while to cook the meat and get some sleep.

Owen came up beside Richard as they trotted through a sea of grass rolling beneath the breeze. Owen pointed ahead. "There, Lord Rahl. That stream coming out of the hills is getting close to the Order's encampment. Just a little farther, over that line of hills and toward the mountains." He pointed to the right. "Off that way, not far, is my town of Witherton."

Richard changed his course a little to the left, heading for the woods that started at the foot of a gentle rise. They made the trees just as the orange disc of the sun slipped behind the snowcapped mountains.

"All right," Richard said, coming to a breathless halt as they entered a small clearing. "Let's set up camp here. Jennsen, Tom, why don't you two and the men stay here—get some meat cooking while I go with Owen and Cara to scout this fortification and see if I can figure out how we're going to get in."

When Richard started out, using his staff to help balance, Betty started following him. Jennsen snatched Betty's rope.

"Oh no you don't," Jennsen said. "You're staying here. Richard doesn't need you tagging along to attract attention at the worst possible time."

"What should we make for you to eat, Lord Rahl?" Tom asked.

Richard couldn't stand the thought of eating meat. After all the bloody fighting, he needed to balance his gift more than ever. His gift was killing him, but if he did the wrong thing it might hasten the end and then he might not last long enough to get Kahlan away from Nicholas.

"Whatever we have that isn't meat. You have time before we come back, so you could cook some bannocks, some rice, maybe some beans."

Tom agreed to take care of it and Richard followed after Owen. Cara, looking more unhappy than he could ever remember seeing her, put a hand on his shoulder.

"How are you holding up, Lord Rahl?"

He dared not tell her how much pain he was in from the gift, or that he had started to cough up blood. "I'm all right for now."

By the time they dragged back into their camp, almost two hours later, the meat on the spit had been cooked and some of the men had already eaten. They were just curling up in blankets to get some sleep.

Richard was beyond being tired. He was certain that they had been close to Kahlan. It had been agonizing to have to return, to leave the place where Nicholas held her, but he had to use his head. Wild, irrational action would bring only failure. It would not get Kahlan out of there.

Richard was being driven by needs beyond food or sleep, but as he watched Owen sit heavily near the fire, he knew that Owen and Cara were exhausted and he imagined that they had to be hungry. Rather than sit, Cara waited at his side. She would not allow him to get far from her watchful protection. Nor would she voice any concern for herself or her needs.

He could never have imagined, back in the beginning, ever feeling this close to a Mord-Sith.

Jennsen stood and rushed to meet him. "Richard—here, let me help you. Come and sit."

Richard flopped down on the grass near the fire. Betty came over and begged a place beside him. He let her lie down.

"Well?" Tom asked. "What do you think of the place?"

"I don't know. It has well-made timber walls with trenches dug before them. There are snares and traps all around the place. It has a gate—a real gate." Richard sighed as he rubbed his eyes. His sight was getting blurry. It was getting more difficult all the time to see things. "I haven't quite figured it out, yet."

It was hard to think with the smell of the cooking meat, which was making him sick. Richard took a piece of bannock and the bowl of rice and beans Jennsen handed him.

He couldn't eat watching them eat the meat.

Richard stood. "I'm going to go for a walk." He didn't want to make them feel bad about their dinner, or feel guilty for eating meat in front of him. "I need some time alone to think it out." He gestured for Cara to sit back down and stay where she was. "Get some dinner," he told her. "I need you to stay strong."

Richard walked off through the trees, listening to the chirp of crickets, watching the stars through the canopy of leaves. It was a relief to be alone, not to have people asking him anything. It was tiring to have people always depending on him.

Richard found a quiet place where an old oak had fallen. He sat and leaned back against the trunk. He wished he never had to get up. If not for Kahlan, he wouldn't.

Betty showed up. She stood before him, looking at him intently as if to ask what they were going to do next. When Richard said nothing, Betty lay down in front of him. It occurred to him that maybe Betty just wanted to offer him some comfort.

Richard felt a tear run down his cheek. Everything was falling to pieces. He couldn't hold those pieces together any longer. He could hardly breathe past the lump in his throat.

He lay down and put an arm over Betty.

"What am I going to do?" he sniffled. He wiped the back of his hand across his nose.

"Kahlan, what am I going to do?" he whispered in forlorn misery. "I need you so much. What am I going to do?"

He was at the end of all hope.

He had thought, when he'd seen Nathan unexpectedly arrive, that help was at hand. The bright ember of that last hope had been extinguished. Not even a powerful wizard could help him.

Powerful wizard.

Kaja-Rang.

Richard froze.

The words sent to him by Kaja-Rang, those two words emblazoned across the granite base of that statue, echoed through his mind.

Those two words were meant for Richard.

Talga Vassternich.

Deserve Victory.

"Dear spirits . . ." Richard whispered.

He understood.

C H A P T E R   62

Nicholas watched as Lord Rahl made his way back into the camp among his men after his despairing whispered last prayer. So sad. So very sad that the man was going to die. He would soon be with his dear spirits . . . in the Keeper's realm of the underworld.

Nicholas relished the game. The poor Lord Rahl was so lost and confused. Nicholas wished the game could continue for a good long time, but Lord Rahl had little time left. So sad.

But it would be much more fun after Lord Rahl died, after that last detail was finally finished. Jagang thought this pathetic man was resourceful. *Don't underestimate him*, Jagang had warned. Perhaps Jagang was no match for the great Richard Rahl, but Nicholas the Slide was.

His spirit swelled with delight at the expectant thought of Lord Rahl's death. That was going to be something to watch. It would be a grand finale of the play of life. Nicholas intended to see it all, to see every sad moment of the last act. He imagined that Lord Rahl's friends would gather to weep and wail as they stood by, helpless, watching him slip into the welcoming embrace of death, eternity's shepherd, come to help him begin the magnificent, never-ending spiritual journey away from the bitter interlude that had been life.

The final curtain was about to draw closed. Nicholas so loved sad endings. He could hardly wait to watch it played out.

Hate to live, live to hate.

Nicholas wondered, too, as did Lord Rahl, which would get Richard first, the poison or his gift. It seemed to tug first toward one, and then toward the other. For a time the headaches inflicted by his gift nearly put him down, then the poison would tighten its pain and make him gasp in agony. It was a fascinating question, one that, as in any good play, would not be answered until the very end. The tension was delicious.

Nicholas was rooting for the gift to win the fatal contest. Poison was all well and good, but what a vastly more intriguing twist of fate it would be to see a wizard of Lord Rahl's ability and potential, a wizard unlike any to be born since an era long-buried in the dunghill of mankind's history, succumb to his birthright—to his own vast but vain power . . . another victim of men reaching too high in life. That would be a fascinating and fitting end.

Not long to wait.

Not long at all.

Nicholas watched, not wanting to miss a single delectable detail. With the spirit of Richard Rahl's lovely bride beside him, as it were, Nicholas felt almost a part of the family as he attended the approach of such a great man's tragic end.

Nicholas felt it only fair that the Mother Confessor should get to see it all played out, see the sad end to her beloved. As she watched along with Nicholas, she was suffering seeing the agony of it as Richard Rahl walked back into his camp.

Nicholas savored her distress. He had not yet begun to make her suffer. He would soon have a very long time with her to explore her capacity for suffering.

The people there in the woods around the campfire looked up, curious as their master returned among them. They all waited, with Nicholas, watching, with Nicholas, as their Lord Rahl stood over them. His figure wavered in the fire, as it did in Nicholas's vision. It was almost as if he were already but a spirit, about to drift away into the glorious oblivion of the dead.

"I've figured it out," Lord Rahl told them. "I know how to attack the fortification."

Nicholas's ears pricked up. What was this?

"At first light we go in," Lord Rahl said. "Just as the sun breaks over the mountains. Right then, on the east side, we'll come in over the wall. The guards won't be able to see well because the sun will be in their eyes when they look in that direction. Men don't look where it's troublesome to look."

"I like it," one of the other men said.

"So we will sneak in, then, rather than try to attack," another said.

"Oh no, there will be an attack," Lord Rahl said. "A big attack. An attack that will set their heads spinning."

What was this? What was this? Nicholas watched, watched, watched. This was most curious. First Lord Rahl is going to sneak over the wall, and then he would have his men attack? How was he going to set their heads to spinning? Nicholas was fascinated.

He moved in a little closer, fearing to miss a precious word.

"The attack will involve all the rest of you men," Lord Rahl said. "You will all come in toward the gate at first light. While you're attacking through the gate and drawing their attention, I will be slipping over the wall. While you will be there to distract them, in part, you will play an even more vital role that they will never expect."

The game was afoot. Nicholas was in rapture as he listened, as he watched. He so liked the game—especially when he knew all the rules, and could bend them to his wishes. It was going to be a glorious day, tomorrow.

"But Lord Rahl," the big man, Tom, asked, "how are we going to be able to attack through the gate if it's as formidable as you say?"

Nicholas hadn't thought of that. How curious. A key part of Lord Rahl's plan seemed to be faulty.

"That's the real trick," Lord Rahl said. "I've already figured it out and you'll be amazed to hear how you're going to do it."

He had already figured it out? How curious. Nicholas wanted to hear what possible solution could solve such a major hitch in Lord Rahl's plan.

Lord Rahl stretched and yawned. "Look," he said, "I'm exhausted. I can't stand up any more. I need to get some rest before I lay it all out for you. It's complicated, so I'd better wait until just before we leave.

"Wake me up two hours before dawn, and I'll explain the whole thing, then."

"Two hours before dawn," Tom repeated in confirmation of the orders.

Nicholas was furious. He wanted to hear it now. He wanted to know the wonderful, fabulous, complicated plan.

Lord Rahl gestured to his delicious companion, the one named Cara, and then to several of the young men. "Why don't you come with me and get some sleep while the rest finish their meal."

As they started away, Lord Rahl turned back. "Jennsen, I want you to keep Betty here, with you. Make sure she stays here. I need some sleep; I don't need the smell of goat to wake me up."

"Am I going with you in the morning, Richard?" the one called Jennsen asked.

"Yes. You play an important part in the plan." Lord Rahl yawned again. "I'll explain after I've slept. Don't forget, Tom. Two hours before dawn."

Tom nodded. "I will wake you myself, Lord Rahl."

Nicholas would be there as well, to watch, to hear the final piece of Lord Rahl's plan. Nicholas could hardly stand to wait that long. He would be there early. He would hear every word of it.

And then Nicholas would have a surprise waiting for Richard Rahl when he and his men came for a visit.

Maybe neither the poison nor his gift would take Lord Rahl.

Maybe Nicholas would do it himself.

Her spirit a helpless prisoner of the Slide, Kahlan could do nothing but watch along with him. She was unable to answer Richard's forlorn pleas, unable to cry in sorrow for him, unable to do anything. She ached to be able to hold him in her arms again, to comfort his pain, his heartache.

He was near the end. She knew that.

It broke her heart to see his precious life slipping away.

To see his tears.

To hear him cry her name in longing.

To hear him say how much he needed her.

She felt so cold and alone. She loathed the feeling of being adrift.

She desperately wanted to be back in her body. It waited somewhere back in a lonely room in the fortified encampment. Nicholas's body waited there, too. If only she could get back there.

Most of all, she wished there were some way she could warn Richard that Nicholas knew his plan.

C H A P T E R 63

Nicholas lay in wait in the camp, sniffing, listening, watching, eager for the game to continue. He had come early, fearing to miss anything. He was sure it had to be two hours before dawn—time for the last act of the play. It was time for the man, Tom, to wake Lord Rahl. It was time. Watch, watch, watch. Where was he? Somewhere, somewhere. Look, look, look.

Men off through the trees stood guard over the camp. Where was Tom? There he was. Nicholas saw that Tom was one of the men standing vigil as others slept. Didn't want to be late. Lord Rahl's orders. He wasn't sleeping, he was awake, so he should know it was time.

What was the man waiting for? His master had given him a command. Why wasn't he doing as he had been told?

The woman, Jennsen, woke and rubbed her eyes. She looked up and took appraisal of the stars and moon. It was time—she knew it was. She threw off her blanket.

Nicholas followed behind as she rushed past the low glow of the smoldering embers, rushed through the stand of young trees, rushed to the big man leaning against a stump.

"Tom, isn't it time to wake Richard?"

Somewhere back in a distant room in the fortification, where his body waited, Nicholas heard an insistent noise. He was absorbed in the task at hand, in the game, so he ignored the sound.

Probably Najari. The man was eager to have a chance to get at the Mother Confessor, a chance to enjoy her more feminine charms. Nicholas had told Najari that he would have his chance, but he had to wait until Nicholas returned. Nicholas didn't want the man tampering with her body while they were gone. Najari sometimes didn't know his own strength. The Mother Confessor was valuable property and Nicholas didn't want that property damaged.

Najari had proven to be a loyal man and deserved a small reward, but not until later. He would not disobey Nicholas's orders. He would be sorry if he did.

Maybe it was just—

Wait, wait. What was this? Watch, watch, watch. The man stood and put a hand reassuringly on the young woman's shoulder. How very touching.

"Yes, I guess it is about time. Let's go wake Lord Rahl."

Again the noise. Stealthy, sharp yet soft.

Most odd. But it would have to wait.

Through the woods. Hurry. Watch, watch, watch. Hurry. Couldn't they move faster? Didn't they grasp the importance of the occasion? Hurry, hurry, hurry.

"Betty," the Jennsen woman growled, "stop bumping my legs."

Again there was a skulking sound back somewhere with his body.

And then, another, more urgent sound.

This time, the sound ran a sharp shiver through Nicholas's very soul.

It was as deadly a sound as he had ever heard.

As the Sword of Truth cleared its scabbard, the distinctive ring of steel filled the dimly-lit room.

With the sword came ancient magic, unhindered, unrestrained, unleashed.

The sword's power instantly inundated Richard with its boundless fury, a fury that answered only to him. The force of that power flooded into every fiber of his being. It had been so long since he had truly felt it, truly felt the full magnitude of it, that for an instant Richard paused in the exaltation of the profound experience of simply holding such a singular weapon.

His own righteous wrath had already slipped its bonds. Joined now with the pure rage of the Sword of Truth, both spiraled through him like twin storms rampaging unchecked.

Richard gloried that they could, and at being the ultimate master of both.

The Seeker of Truth willed both storms ever onward even as the sword began its fearful journey, the merciless lightning of those thunderheads about to strike.

The tip of the blade whistled through the night air, still two hours before dawn.

Hesitant and uncertain, Nicholas watched as the man, Tom, and the Jennsen woman moved through the woods to awake their dying Lord Rahl.

Somewhere back in a distant room in the fortification, where his body waited, Nicholas heard a scream.

It was not a scream of fear, but a riotous cry of unbridled rage. It sent a shiver through his soul.

With sudden alarm, knowing that it could not be ignored, Nicholas slammed back into his body where it sat on the floor, waiting for him.

Unsteady from the abrupt return, Nicholas blinked as he opened his eyes.

Lord Rahl himself stood before him, feet spread, both hands gripping his sword. It was a picture of sheer muscular force focused by terrifying resolve.

Nicholas's eyes went wide at seeing the gleaming blade arcing through the still air.

Lord Rahl was in the midst of a scream of startling power and rage. Every bit of his might was committed to the swing of his sword.

Nicholas had a sudden and completely unexpected realization: he didn't want to die. He very much wanted to live. As much as he hated life, he realized, now, that he wanted to hold on to it.

He had to act.

He summoned his power, rallied his will.

He had to stop this avenging soul before him.

He reached out with his power to seize this other's spirit.

He felt the horrifying shock of a staggering blow against the side of his neck.

Richard was still screaming as his sword, with every ounce of power and speed he could put behind it, swept around, just clearing the top of Nicholas's left shoulder.

Richard saw every detail as the blade tore through flesh and bone, turning muscle, tendon, arteries, and windpipe inside out, following with precision the path to which the Seeker had justly committed it. Richard had dedicated everything to the swift journey of his sword. Now, he watched as that journey reached its destination, as the blade cleared the neck of Nicholas the Slide, as the man's head, its mouth still opened in the beginning of shock not fully comprehended, his beady eyes still trying to grasp the totality of what they were seeing, lifted into the air, beginning to turn ever so slowly as the sword below it passed along its deadly arc, as curved ropes of the man's blood began tracing a long wet line across the wall behind him.

Richard's scream ended as the sword's swing reached its limit. The world came crashing back around him.

The head hit the floor with a loud, bone-cracking *thunk*.

It was ended.

Richard recalled the rage. He had to get it under control immediately. He had something yet more important to accomplish.

In one fluid motion, Richard slid the bloody blade home into its scabbard as he turned to the second body leaning up against the wall to the right.

The sight of her almost overcame him. To see her there, alive, breathing, seemingly unhurt, brought a wild rush of joy. His worst fears, fears he would not even allow into his conscious mind, evaporated in an instant.

But then he realized that she was not all right. She could not have slept through such an attack.

Richard fell to his knees and took her up in his arms. She felt so light, so limp. Her face was ashen and beaded with sweat. Her eyelids were half closed, her eyes rolled back in her head.

Richard sank back within himself, seeking strength to bring back the one he loved more than life itself. He opened his soul to her. All he wanted, all he needed, as he held her to him, was for her to live, to be whole.

Instinctively, in a way he did not fully understand, he let his power well up from a place deep inside his mind. He released himself into the torrent as it rushed onward. He let his love of her, his need of her, flood through their connection as he hugged her to his breast.

"Come home to where you belong," he whispered to her.

He let the core of his power course through her, intending it to be like a beacon to light her way. If felt as if he were searching through the dark, using the light of ability from deep within to help him. Even though he couldn't define the precise mechanism, he could consciously focus his purpose, his need, and what he wanted to accomplish.

"Come home to me, Kahlan. I'm here."

Kahlan gasped. Even though she hung limp, he felt the intensity of the life in his arms. She gasped again, as if she had nearly drowned and needed air.

At last, she stirred in his arms, her limbs moving, groping. She opened her eyes, blinking, and looked up. Astonished, she sank back into his arms.

"Richard . . . I heard you. I was so alone. Dear spirits, I was so alone. I didn't know what to do . . . I heard Nicholas scream. I was lost and alone. I didn't know how to get back. And then I felt you."

She embraced him tightly, as if she never wanted to let go.

"You led me back through the darkness."

Richard smiled down at her. "I'm a guide, remember?"

She puzzled at him. "How could you do that?" Her beautiful green eyes opened expectantly. "Richard, your gift . . ."

"I figured out the problem with my gift. Kaja-Rang had given me the solution. I'd had the solution long before that, but I never realized it. My gift is fine, now, and the sword's power works again. I was being so blind that I will be ashamed to tell it all to you."

Richard's breath caught, and he coughed, then, unable to hold it back any longer. Nor could he hold back grimacing at the pain.

Kahlan gripped his arms. "The antidote—what happened to the antidote! I sent it back with Owen. Didn't you get it?"

Richard shook his head as he coughed again, the pain feeling as if it ripped him deep inside. He finally regained his breath. "Well, now, that is a problem. It wasn't the antidote. It was just water with a bit of cinnamon in it."

Kahlan's face went ashen. "But . . ." She looked over at Nicholas's body, at his head lying upended at the end of a bloody trail across the floor.

"Richard, if Nicholas is dead, how are we going to get the anti-dote?"

"There isn't any antidote. Nicholas wanted me dead. He would have destroyed the antidote long ago. He gave you a fake to be able to capture you."

Her face had gone from joy to horror.

"But, without the antidote . . ."

CHAPTER 64

"There's no time to worry about the poison just now," Richard told her as he helped her to her feet.

No time? She watched his step falter as he made his way across the room. He groped for the window ledge.

At the small window opening in the outer wall of the fortification he signaled with the high, clear whistle of the common wood pewee—the whistle Cara thought was that of the mythical short-tailed pine hawk.

"I used a ladder pole," he explained. "Cara is on her way."

Kahlan tried to make her way over to him, but her body felt alarmingly unfamiliar to her. She staggered a couple of steps, her legs moving woodenly. She had the urge to get down on her hands and feet to walk. She felt like a stranger inside her own skin. It seemed foreign to have to breathe on her own, to have to look through her own eyes, to have to listen through her own ears. It was a strange, haunting sensation to feel her clothes against her skin.

Richard held out his hand to help steady her. Kahlan thought that as wobbly as she was, she might still be more steady on her feet than Richard.

"We're going to have to fight our way out," he said, "but we'll have some help. I'll get you the first sword I can."

Richard blew out the flame of the single candle before a tin reflector on a small shelf.

"Richard, I'm not yet used to being . . . back inside myself. I don't think I'm ready go out there. I can hardly walk."

"We don't have a lot of choice. We have to get out. Learn as you go. I'll help you."

"You can hardly walk yourself."

Cara, at the top of a pole ladder Richard had cut, leaned forward and wriggled in through the small window.

Halfway in, Cara gaped in delighted wonder. "Mother Confessor—Lord Rahl did it."

"You don't need to sound so surprised," Richard griped as he helped the Mord-Sith the rest of the way in.

Cara only briefly took note of the dead man sprawled across the floor before Kahlan threw her arms around the woman.

"You can't imagine how glad I am to see you," Cara said.

"Well, you can't imagine how glad I am to see you through my own eyes."

"If only the trade you made had worked," Cara added in a whisper.

"We'll find another way," Kahlan assured her.

Richard slowly drew the door open a crack and peeked out. He shut the door and turned back. "It's clear. Doors to the left and around the balcony are the rooms with the women in them. Stairs to the right are the closest that lead down. Some of the rooms at the bottom are for officers, others are barracks for soldiers."

Cara nodded. "I'm ready."

Kahlan looked from one to the other. "Ready for what?"

Richard took her by the elbow. "I need you to help me see."

"Help you see? Is it progressing that fast?"

"Just listen. We're going to move along the balcony to the left and open the doors. Do your best to keep the women calm. We're going to break them out of here."

Kahlan was a bit confused by everything—it was completely different from the plans she had been hearing along with Nicholas. She knew she would just have to follow Richard and Cara's lead.

Outside on the simple wooden balcony there were no lamps or torches. The moon was down behind the black sprawl of the mountains. Kahlan's sight when Nicholas had controlled her had been like looking through a greasy pane of wavy glass. The sparkling vault of stars overhead had never looked so beautiful. In that starlight, Kahlan could see simple buildings lined up around the outer wall of the fortification.

Richard and Cara moved along the balcony, opening doors. At each one, Cara quickly ducked inside. Some of the women came out in their nightshirts, some Kahlan could hear inside rushing to get dressed. In some of the rooms, babies cried.

While Cara was in one of the rooms, Richard opened another door. He leaned close to Kahlan and whispered, "Go in and tell the women inside that we've come to help them escape. Tell them that their men have come to get them out. But they must be as quiet as possible, or we'll be caught."

Kahlan rushed in, as best she could on unsteady legs, and shook the young woman in the bed to the right. She sat up, terrified, but silent. Kahlan reached around and shook the woman in the other bed.

"We've come to help you escape. You mustn't make any noise. Your men are going to help. You have a chance to be free."

"Free?" the first woman asked.

"Yes. It's up to you, but I strongly advise you to take the chance, and to hurry."

The women flew out of their beds and grabbed for clothes.

Richard, Kahlan, and Cara moved farther down the balcony, asking the women who had already come out to help to rouse the others. In a matter of a few minutes, hundreds of women were huddled together out on the balcony. There was no problem keeping them quiet; they were all too familiar with the consequences of causing trouble. They didn't want to do anything to get themselves caught trying to escape. Before long, they had made it all the way around the fortification balcony.

Many of the women had very young babies—ones too young to be taken away. The babies were mostly sound asleep in their mothers' arms, but some of them started to cry. The mothers desperately tried to rock and cuddle them into silence. Kahlan hoped that it was a common enough sound that it wouldn't draw the attention of the soldiers.

"Wait here," Richard whispered to Kahlan. "Keep everyone up here until we get the gate open."

With Cara right behind him, Richard slipped carefully down the steps and started across the open yard. When one of the babies suddenly began bawling, soldiers came out of a building to see what was going on. They spotted Richard and Kahlan. The soldiers yelled, sounding an alarm.

Kahlan heard the distinctive ring of steel as Richard drew his sword. Men rushed out of some of the doors, heading Richard and Cara off. Being used to dealing with these people, the men rushing toward Richard apparently weren't greatly concerned about violence. They were wrong, and fell as soon as they got close enough for Richard to strike. Some, Richard took down as he ran, others Cara caught as they tried to come in from the side.

The screams of some of the men as they fell woke the whole encampment. Men rushed out of barracks below, pulling on their trousers and shirts, dragging weapons belts behind.

In the faint starlight, Kahlan spotted Richard by the dropgate. He took a mighty swing. Sparks showered across the wall as the sword shattered one of the heavy chains holding up the gate. Richard ran to the other side, to cut the other chain. Two men caught up to him there. In one swift movement, Richard cut them both down.

As Cara dropped other men who were rushing in at Richard, he swung the sword again. White-hot fragments of steel filled the air along with the ringing sound of metal shattering. The gate groaned and slowly started to fall outward. Richard heaved his weight against it and it picked up speed. With a resounding crash, it came down, raising clouds of dust.

A great cry rose up as men outside, wielding swords, axes, and battle-maces, charged in across the broken bridge and into the fortification. The soldiers rushed to meet the invasion and there was a great clash of weapons and men.

Kahlan saw, then, that soldiers were racing up the stairway on the opposite side of the balcony.

"Come on!" Kahlan yelled to the women. "We have to get out now!"

Holding the rail to keep her balance, Kahlan raced down the steps, all the women pouring down behind her, a number carrying screaming babies. Richard ran to meet her at the bottom. He snatched up a short sword with a leather-wound grip and tossed it to her. Kahlan caught it by the handle just in time to turn and slash a soldier running up from beneath the balcony.

Owen made his way through the fighting and over to the women. "Come on!" he called to them. "Get to the gate! Run!"

The women, galvanized by his command, started running across the compound. As they reached the fighting, some of the women, instead of running out the gate, instead took the opportunity to leap on the backs of soldiers fighting Owen and his men. The woman bit the men on the backs, beat at their heads, tore at their eyes. The soldiers were not restrained in dealing with the women, and several were brutally killed. It didn't stop others from joining the fight.

If they would only run for the gate, they could escape, but instead, they were attacking the soldiers with their bare hands. They had been held in bondage to these men for a very long time. Kahlan could only imagine what they had gone through and couldn't say she blamed them. She was still having difficulty moving, making her body do what she wanted it to do, or she would have joined them.

Kahlan turned at a sound only to see a man charging in at her. She recognized his flattened nose. Najari—Nicholas's right-hand man. He was one of the men who had carried her to the fortification. He wore a wicked grin as he came for her.

She could have used her power on him, but she feared to trust it right then. Instead, she brought the short sword out from behind her back and slammed it through Najari's gut. He stood stiffly right in front of her, his eyes wide. She could smell the stink of his breath. Kahlan wrenched the handle of the sword to the side. Mouth open wide, he panted, fearing to draw a deep breath, fearing to move and cause any more damage. Kahlan gritted her teeth and swept the sword's handle around in an arc, ripping his insides apart.

She stared into his startled eyes as he slid off her sword. He grunted in pain as he dropped to his knees, holding his wound together as best he could. He never got what Kahlan knew he intended, what Nicholas had promised him. He fell forward onto his face, spilling his insides across the ground at her feet.

Kahlan turned to the attack. Richard was engaged in slashing his way through men trying to surround him as he fought to keep the gate clear. Others, Richard's men, came at the enemy from behind, cutting into them the way Richard had taught them.

Kahlan saw Owen not far away. He was standing in the open, among the fallen and the fighting, staring across the raging battle at a man just outside one of the doors under the balcony.

The man had a thick black beard, a shaved head, and a ring through one ear and one nostril. His arms were as big as tree limbs. His shoulders were twice as wide as Owen's.

"Luchan," Owen said to himself.

Owen started across the open area of the fortification, past men engaged in pitched battle, past those crying out and those falling to blades, past swords and axes sweeping though the air, as if he didn't even see them. His eyes were locked on the man watching him come.

The face of a young woman appeared in the dark doorway behind Luchan. He turned and growled at her to go back inside, that he was going to take care of the little man from her village.

When Luchan turned back around, Owen was standing before him.

Luchan laughed and put his fists on his hips. "Why don't you scurry back into your hole?"

Owen said nothing, gave no warning, made no demands. He simply lit into Luchan with a vengeance—just as Richard had counseled him to do—slamming a knife into the big man's chest over and over before Luchan had a chance to react. He had underestimated Owen. It had cost him his life.

The woman rushed out of the doorway and came to a halt over the body of her former master. She stared down at him, at his one arm splayed out to the side, at the other lying across his bloody chest, at the unseeing eyes. She looked up at Owen.

Kahlan assumed that this was Marilee, and feared that she was going to reject Owen for harming another, that she would castigate him for what he had done.

Instead, she rushed to Owen and threw her arms around him.

The woman went to her knees beside the body and took the bloody knife from Owen's hand. She turned to the fallen Luchan and stabbed him half a dozen times with such force that it drove the knife in up to the hilt with every thrust. Watching her tearful fury, Kahlan didn't have to wonder how she had been treated by the man.

Her anger spent, she stood again and tearfully hugged Owen.

Kahlan needed to get to Richard. She was relieved that her ability to move as she intended was returning. She started making her way around the edge of the battle, staying close to the walls, past men who saw her and thought she would be an easy mark. They didn't know that from a young age she had been taught to use a sword by her father, King Wyborn, and that Richard had later honed her skill to deadly proficiency, teaching her how to use her lighter weight to give her lethal speed. It was the last mistake the men made.

Off across the open area, a mob of soldiers, now fully awake and fully prepared to engage in battle, swarmed out of the barracks. They all charged for Richard. Kahlan knew right away that there were too many of them. Richard's men couldn't stop the flood of soldiers as they streamed across the encampment. All of them crashed in toward Richard.

Kahlan heard a deafening crack like lightning as the walls of the fortification lit with a flash. She had to turn away and shield her eyes. Night turned to day, and, at the same time, a darkness darker than any night was loosed.

A blazing white-hot bolt of Additive Magic twisted and coiled around and through a crackling black void of Subtractive Magic, creating a violent rope of twin lightning joined to a terrible purpose.

It seemed as if the noonday sun crashed down among them. The air itself was drawn into the fierce heat and light. Try as she might, Kahlan couldn't draw a breath against the force of it.

Richard's fury gathered it all into a single point. In an explosive instant, the thunderous ignition of light unleashed a devastating blast of staggering destruction radiating outward across the entire encampment, annihilating the Imperial Order soldiers.

The night fell dark and silent.

Men and women stood stunned among the sea of blood and

viscera, gazing around at the unrecognizable remains of the enemy soldiers.

The battle was over. The people of Bandakar had carried the day. At last, the women fell to wailing and crying, ecstatic to be free. They knew many of the men who had come to free them, and clung to them in gratitude, overwhelmed with joy to be reunited. They hugged friends, relatives, and strangers alike. The men, too, wept with relief and happiness.

Kahlan rushed through the maze of rejoicing people crowded into the open area of the fortification. Men cheered her, thrilled that she, too, had been liberated. Many of the men wanted to talk to her, but she kept running to get to Richard.

He stood to the side, leaning against the wall, Cara helping to hold him up. He still gripped his blood-slicked sword in his fist, the blade's tip resting on the ground.

Owen, too, made his way over to Richard.

"Mother Confessor! I'm so relieved and thankful to have you back!" He looked over at a smiling Richard. "Lord Rahl, I would like you to meet Marilee."

This woman who only a short time ago had savagely stabbed the corpse of her captor, now seemed too shy to speak. She dipped her head in greeting.

Richard straightened and smiled that smile Kahlan so loved to see, a smile filled with the sheer pleasure of life. "I'm very happy to meet you, Marilee. Owen has told us all about you, and about how much you mean to him. Through all that happened, you were always first in his mind and heart. His love for you moved him to act to change this entire empire for the better."

She seemed to be overwhelmed by it all, and by his words.

"Lord Rahl came to us and did something more important than saving us all," Owen told Marilee. "Lord Rahl gave me the courage to come and fight for you, to fight to save you—for all of us to fight for our own lives and the lives of those we love."

Beaming, Marilee leaned in and kissed Richard on the cheek. "Thank you, Lord Rahl. I never knew my Owen could do such things."

"Believe me," Cara said, "we had our doubts about him, too." She clapped Owen on the back of the shoulder. "But he did well."

"I, too, have come to understand the value of what he has done," Marilee said to Richard, "of the things you seem to have taught our people."

Richard smiled at the two of them, but then he could no longer hold back the coughing that so hurt him. The mood of joyous liberation suddenly changed. People rushed in around them, helping to hold him up. Kahlan saw blood running down his chin.

"Richard!" she cried. "No . . ."

They eased him to the ground. He clutched at Kahlan's sleeve, wanting to have her close. Kahlan saw tears running down Cara's cheek.

It seemed that he had spent all the strength he had left. He was slipping into the fatal grasp of the poison, and there was nothing they could do for him.

"Owen," Richard said, panting to catch his breath when the spell of coughing stopped. "How far to your town?" His voice was getting hoarse.

"Not far—only hours, if we hurry."

"The man who made the poison and the antidote . . . he lived there?"

"Yes. His place is still there."

"Take me there."

Owen looked puzzled, but he nodded eagerly. "Of course."

"Hurry," Richard added, trying to get up. He couldn't.

Tom appeared in the crowd. Jennsen was there, too.

"Get some poles!" Tom commanded. "And some canvas, or blankets. We'll make a litter. Four men at a time can carry him. We can run and get him there quickly."

Men rushed to the buildings, searching for what they would need to make a litter.

CHAPTER 65

Kahlan hurriedly pulled the tin off the shelf and opened the lid. The tin contained a yellowish powder. It was the right color. She leaned down and showed it to Richard as he lay in the litter. He reached in and took a pinch.

He smelled it. He put his tongue to it and then nodded.

"Just a little," he whispered, lifting it out to her. Kahlan held out her palm while he dribbled some of the crushed powder in her hand. He threw the rest on the floor, too weak to bother returning it to the tin. Kahlan added the small portion on her palm to one of the pots of boiling water.

Cloth bags of herbs steeped in other pots of hot water. Alkaloids from dried mushrooms were soaking in oil. Richard had other people grating stalks of plants.

"Lobella," Richard said. His eyes were closed.

Owen bent down. "Lobella?"

Richard nodded. "It will be a dried herb."

Owen turned to the shelves and started looking. There were hundreds of little square cubby-holes in the wall of the place where the man who had made Richard's poison, and the antidote, used to work. It was a simple single-roomed building with little light. It was not nearly as well-equipped as the herbalist places Kahlan had seen before, but the man had an extensive collection. More than that, he had once made the antidote, presumably from what was there.

"Here!" Owen said, holding a bag down for Richard to see. "It says *lobella* on the tag."

"Grind a little pile half the size of your thumbnail, sift out the fibers and discard them, then add what's left to the bowl with the darker oil."

Richard knew about herbs, but he didn't know anywhere near enough about herbs to concoct the cure for the poison he had been given.

His gift seemed to be guiding him.

Richard was in a near-trance, almost unconscious, Kahlan wasn't exactly sure which. He was having difficulty breathing. She didn't know what else to do to help him. If they didn't do something, he was going to die, and soon. As long as he lay quietly on the litter he was resting more comfortably, but that was not going to make him recover.

It had been a short run to Witherton, but it had taken too long as far as Kahlan was concerned.

"Yarrow," Richard said.

Kahlan leaned down. "What preparation?"

"Oil," Richard said.

Kahlan fumbled through the shelves of small bottles. She found one labeled *yarrow oil*. She squatted down and held it before Richard.

"How much?"

She lifted one of his hands and put the bottle in it, closing his fingers around it so he could tell its size. "How much?"

"Is it full?"

Kahlan hurriedly wiggled out the whittled wooden stopper. "Yes."

"Half," Richard said. "In with any of the other oils."

"I found the feverfew," Jennsen said as she hopped down from the stool.

"Make a tincture," Richard told her.

Kahlan replaced the stopper in the bottle and squatted down beside Richard. "What next?"

"Make an infusion of mullein."

"Mullein, mullein," Kahlan mumbled as she turned to the task.

As Richard gave them instructions, half a dozen people worked at boiling, blending, crushing, grating, filtering, and steeping. They added some of the preparations together as they were completed, and kept others separate as they worked on them. As they worked, the number of various tasks were combined and reduced at specified points.

Richard gestured for Owen. Owen brushed his hands clean on his trouser legs as he bent down to await instruction.

"Cold," Richard said, his eyes closed. "We need something cold. We need a way to cool it."

Owen thought a moment. "There's a stream not far."

Richard pointed to various stations where people labored. "Pour those bowls of preparations and powders into the boiling water in the kettle, there. Then take it to the stream. Hold the kettle down in the water to cool it." Richard held up a finger in caution. "Don't put it in too deep and let the water from the stream run in over the top, or it will be ruined."

Owen shook his head. "I won't."

He stood impatiently as Kahlan poured the contents of shallow bowls into the boiling pot of water. She didn't know if any of this made sense, but she knew that Richard had the gift, and he certainly had figured out and eliminated the problem he had been having with it. If his gift could guide him in making the antidote, it might save his life.

Kahlan didn't know anything else that would.

She handed the kettle to Owen. He ran out the door to put it in the stream to cool it. Cara followed him out to make sure that nothing happened to what might be the only thing that could save Richard's life.

Jennsen sat on the floor on the other side of Richard, holding his hand. With the back of her wrist, Kahlan pushed her hair off her face. She sat beside Richard and took his free hand to wait for Owen and Cara to return.

Betty stood in the doorway, her ears pricked forward, her tail intermittently going into a hopeful blur of wagging whenever Jennsen or Kahlan looked her way.

It seemed like hours until Owen came running back with the kettle, although Kahlan knew it really hadn't been all that long.

"Filter it through a cloth," Richard said, "but don't squeeze the cloth at the end, just let the liquid run through until you have a half a cup of it. Once you've done that, then add the oils to the liquid you collected in the cup."

Everyone stood watching Kahlan work, snatching up what she needed, tossing it away when she was finished with it. When she had enough liquid from the kettle collected in the cup, she poured in the oils.

"Stir it with a stick of cinnamon," Richard said.

Owen climbed up on the stool. "I remember seeing cinnamon."

He handed a stick down to Kahlan. She stirred the golden liquid, but it didn't seem to be working.

"The oil and water don't want to mix," she told Richard.

His head was rolled to the side away from her. "Keep mixing. A moment will come when they suddenly come together."

Dubious, Kahlan kept stirring. She could see that the oils were sticking together in globs and not mixing with the water she had filtered through the cloth. The more it cooled, the less and less it looked as if it was going to work.

Kahlan felt a tear of desperation run down her cheek and drip off her jaw.

The contents of the cup stiffened. She kept stirring, not wanting to tell Richard that it wasn't working. She swallowed past the growing lump in her throat.

The contents in the cup began to melt. Kahlan gasped. She blinked. Everything in the cup suddenly went together into a smooth, syrupy liquid.

"Richard!" She wiped the tear from her cheek. "It worked. It mixed together. Now what?"

He held his hand out. "It's ready. Give it to me."

Jennsen and Cara helped him to sit up. Kahlan held the precious cup in both hands and carefully put it to his mouth. She tipped it up to help him drink. It took a while to get it down. He had to stop from time to time as he sipped, trying not to cough.

It was a lot more than had been in any of the little square-sided bottles, but Kahlan figured that maybe he needed more, since he was so late in taking it.

When he was finished, she reached up and set the cup on the counter. She licked a drop of the liquid off her finger. The concoction had the slight aroma of cinnamon and a sweet, spicy taste. She hoped that was right.

Richard worked at recovering his breath after the effort of drinking. They gently laid him back down. His hands were trembling. He looked miserable.

"Just let me rest, now," he murmured.

Betty, still standing in the doorway, watching intently, bleated her wish to come in.

"He will be all right," Jennsen said to her friend. "You just stay out there and let him rest."

Betty puled softly and then lay down in the doorway to wait along with the rest of them. It was going to be a long night. Kahlan didn't think she was going to be able to sleep until she knew if Richard would be all right.

Zedd pointed. "There's another one, there, that needs to be cleaned up," he said to Chase.

Chase wore a chain-mail shirt over a tan leather tunic. His heavy black trousers held a black belt set with a large silver buckle emblazoned with the emblem of the boundary wardens. Beneath his black cloak, strapped everywhere—legs, waist, upper arms, over the backs of his shoulders—was a small arsenal of weapons, everything from small, thin spikes held in the fist and used to puncture the skull, to a crescent-shaped battle-axe used to divide a skull cleanly with one blow. Chase was deadly with any of them.

It had been a while now since they had needed the skills of a boundary warden. Chase seemed to be a man without a mission.

The big man walked across the rampart and bent to pull a knife from beneath the body. He grunted in recognition. "There it is." He held the walnut-handled knife up to the light as he inspected it. "I was worried I'd lost it."

He slipped the knife into an empty sheath without having to look. With one hand, he grabbed the waistband of the trousers and picked up the stiff body. He stepped into an opening in the crenellated wall and heaved the body out into the air.

Zedd looked over the edge. It was a drop of several thousand feet before the rock of the mountain flared enough for anything falling to make contact. It was several thousand more feet down a granite cliff before the forest began.

The golden sun was getting low in the mountains. The clouds had taken on streaks of gold and orange. From this distance, the city below was as beautiful as ever, except Zedd knew that it was an empty place without the people to bring it life.

"Chase, Zedd," Rachel called from the doorway, "the stew is ready."

Zedd threw his skinny arms into the air. "Bags! It's about time! A man could starve waiting for stew to cook."

Rachel planted the fist with the wooden spoon on her hip and shook a finger of her other hand at him. "If you keep saying bad words, you'll not get any dinner."

Chase let out a sigh as he glanced over at Zedd. "And you think you have troubles. You wouldn't think that a girl who doesn't come up to my belt buckle could be such a trial."

Zedd followed Chase to the doorway through the thick stone wall. "Is she always this much trouble?"

Chase mussed Rachel's hair on the way past. "Always," he confided.

"Is the stew good?" Zedd asked. "Worth watching my language for?"

"My new mother taught me how to make it," Rachel said in a tempting singsong. "Rikka had some before she went out. She said it was good."

Zedd smoothed back his unruly white hair. "Well, Emma can cook better than any woman I ever met."

"Then be good," Rachel said, "and I'll give you biscuits to go with the stew."

"Biscuits!"

"Sure. Stew wouldn't be stew without biscuits."

Zedd blinked at the child. "Why, that's what I always thought, too."

"You'd better let me see if she made it right, first," Chase said as they passed through the tapestry-lined halls of the Keep. "I'd hate you to go making any firm commitments before we even know if the stew is edible."

"Friedrich helped me with the heavy parts," Rachel said. "He says it's good."

"We'll see," Chase said.

Rachel turned and shook her wooden spoon at him. "You have to wash your hands, first, though. I saw you throwing that dead man over the wall. You have to wash your hands before you come to the table and eat."

Chase gave Zedd a look of strained forbearance. "Somewhere, there's a boy enjoying himself right now, probably carrying around a dead frog, oblivious to the sorry fact that he's someday going to be married to little-miss-wash-your-hands-before-you-eat."

Zedd smiled. When Chase had taken Rachel in to be his daughter, it was just about the best thing Zedd could ever have wished for. Rachel thought so, too, and it looked as if she still did. She was fiercely devoted to the man.

As they sat at the table, before the cheery fire in the hearth, Zedd enjoying his third bowl of stew, he couldn't recall the Keep ever being such a wonderful place. It was because there was a child, along with friends, once again in the halls of the Keep.

Friedrich, the man who had come on Richard's orders to warn Zedd of the impending attack on the Keep, had realized he had not been in time. The man had used his head and sought out Chase, the old friend he had heard Richard talk about.

While Chase had gone to rescue Zedd and Adie, Friedrich had returned to the Keep to spy on the people who had taken it. By watching carefully and staying out of sight of a Sister, Friedrich had been able to provide Chase and Zedd with invaluable information about the number of people occupying the Keep, and their routines. He then helped take the place back.

Zedd liked the man. He was not only frightfully handy with a knife, but entertaining at conversation. Friedrich, since he had been married to a sorceress, was able to converse with Zedd without being intimidated as some were of wizards. Having lived in D'Hara all his life, Friedrich was also able to fill in pieces of information.

Rachel held up a carving of a hawk. "Look what Friedrich made for me, Zedd. Isn't it the most beautiful thing you ever did see?"

Zedd smiled. "It certainly is."

"It's nothing," Friedrich scoffed. "If I had some gold leaf, then I could gild it for you. That used to be what I did for a living." He leaned back and smiled to himself. "Until Lord Rahl made me a boundary warden."

"You know," Zedd drawled offhandedly to both men, "the Keep is even more vulnerable, now, to those who might come and don't have magic, than to those who do. I'm just fine protecting against those who are affected by magic, but not the other kind."

Chase nodded. "Seems so."

"Well, the thing is," he went on, "I was thinking that since there's no boundary any longer, and what with all the trouble about, perhaps you two would like to take on the responsibility of helping to protect the Wizard's Keep. I'm not nearly so fit for the task as would someone trained in such things." Zedd leaned in, his brow lowering. "It's vitally important."

Elbows on the table, Chase chewed a bite of biscuit as he watched Zedd. Finally, he stirred his spoon around in his bowl.

"Well, it could be a disaster if Jagang were to use those ungifted men to get his hands on the place again." He thought about it. "Emma will understand."

Zedd shrugged. "Bring her here."

Chase frowned. "Bring her here?"

Zedd gestured around. "The Keep is certainly big enough."

"But what would we do with our children?" Chase leaned back. "You don't want all my children here in the Keep, Zedd—they'd be running and up and down, playing in the halls. It would drive you batty. Besides," Chase added, peering with one scowling eye at Rachel, "each one's uglier than the next."

Rachel hid her giggle behind a biscuit.

Zedd remembered the sounds of children's laughter in the Keep, the sounds of joy and love.

"Well, it would be a burden," he agreed, "but this is, after all, about the protection of the Keep. What sacrifice wouldn't it be worth making to protect the Keep?"

Rachel looked from Chase to Zedd. "My new sister, Lee, could bring Cat back to you, Zedd."

"That's right!" Zedd said, throwing his hands up. "I haven't seen Cat for ages! Is Lee treating Cat well?"

Rachel nodded earnestly. "Oh, yes. We all take good care of Cat."

"What do you think, Rachel?" Chase finally asked. "Would you want to live here in this dusty old place with Zedd?"

Rachel ran over and hugged Chase's leg. "Oh, yes, can we, please? It would be ever so grand."

Chase sighed. "Then I guess it's settled. But you'll have to behave and not bother Zedd by being too loud."

"I promise," Rachel said. She frowned up at Zedd. "Will Mother have to crawl into the Keep through that little tunnel, like we did?"

Zedd chuckled. "No, no, we'll let her come in the proper way, like the lady she is." He turned to Friedrich. "How about it, boundary warden? Would you be willing to continue doing Lord Rahl's bidding and stay to help guard the Keep?"

Friedrich slowly spun the bird carving by the tip of one wing, thinking.

"You know," Zedd added, "while you're waiting for some fear-some attack, there are any number of old gilded things here at the Keep that are in terrible need of repair. Perhaps you would consider taking on the job of being the Keep's official gilder? We have plenty of gold leaf. And, someday, when the people return to Aydindril, you would have a steady supply of customers."

Friedrich stared down at the table. "I don't know. This one adventure was all well and good, but since my wife, Althea, died, I don't seem to be interested in much."

Zedd nodded. "I know how it is. I used to have a wife. I think it would do you good to get paid to do something that was needed."

Friedrich smiled. "All right, then. I will take your job, wizard."

"Good," Chase said. "I'll have someone to help me when I need to lock troublesome children in the dungeon."

Rachel giggled as he set her on the ground.

Chase pushed his chair back and stood. "Well, Friedrich, if we're going to be Keep wardens, then I think we ought to make some rounds and satisfy ourselves about the security of a few things. As big as this place is, Rikka could use the help."

"Just mind the shields," Zedd reminded them as they headed for the door.

After the two men had gone off, Rachel got Zedd another biscuit to go with the rest of his stew. Her little brow bunched together earnestly. "When we live here, we'll try to be real quiet for you, Zedd."

"Well, you know, Rachel, the Keep is a big place. I doubt you would bother me much if you and your brothers and sisters wanted to play a little bit."

"Really?"

Zedd pulled the leather-covered ball painted with faded blue-and-pink zigzagged lines all around it out of his pocket and set it on the table.

Rachel's eyes lit up in astonishment.

"I found this old ball," he said, gesturing with his biscuit. "I think a ball has a much better time if it has someone to play with it. Do you think you and your brothers and sisters might like to play with this when you live here? You can bounce it down the halls to your heart's content."

Her mouth fell open. "Really, Zedd?"

Zedd grinned at the look on her face. "Really."

"Maybe I can bounce it in the dark hall that makes the funny noises. Then it wouldn't bother you any more than now."

"This old place is full of funny noises—and a bouncing ball isn't liable to cause too much trouble."

She climbed up in his lap and put her little arms around his neck, hugging him tightly.

"It's a lot better hugging you now that you found those things to get that awful collar off your neck."

Zedd rubbed her back as she hugged him. "Yes it is, little one, yes it is."

She leaned back and looked at him. "I wish Richard and Kahlan could be here to play with the ball, too. I miss them something fierce."

Zedd smiled. "Me, too, little one. Me too."

She frowned at him. "Don't get tears, Zedd. I won't make a lot of noise to bother you."

Zedd shook a bony finger at her. "I'm afraid you have a lot to learn about playing with a ball."

"I do?"

"Of course. Laughing goes with playing with a ball like biscuits go with stew."

She frowned at him, not sure if he was telling the truth.

He set her on the floor. "Tell you what. Why don't you come with me and I'll show you."

"Really, Zedd?"

Zedd stood up and mussed her hair. "Really." He scooped the ball off the table. "Let's see if you can show this ball how to have a good time."

C H A P T E R 66

Richard rested his back against a rock in the shade of a stand of white oaks as he gazed off at the line of silver maples shimmering in the breeze. The air smelled fresh after the rain of the day before. The clouds had moved on and left a clear, bright blue sky behind. His head finally felt clear, as well.

It had taken three days, but he was finally recovered from the effects of the poison. His gift had not only helped bring Kahlan back from the brink, but himself as well.

The people of the town of Witherton were just beginning to try to put their lives back together. With all the people they'd lost, it was going to be difficult for them. There were gaping holes where there used to be friends or members of families. Still, now that they were free there was the beginning of a vibrant sense of their future being better.

But just because they were free, that did not mean they would stay that way.

Richard gazed up the broad valley beyond the town. People were out working with their crops and tending to the animals. They were going back to their lives. He was impatient to be on his way, back to his own life. This place had kept them from important business, from people who had been waiting for them.

He guessed that this place had been important business as well. It was hard telling what this all had begun, or what the future would hold.

For sure, the world would never be the same.

Richard saw Kahlan coming out through the gate, Cara beside

her. Betty frolicked along at their side, eager to see where they were going. Jennsen must have let the goat go for a romp. Betty had grown up and spent her entire life on the move. She'd never stayed in one place for long. Maybe that was why she always wanted to follow Richard and Kahlan. She recognized family and wanted to be with them.

"So, what's she going to do?" Richard asked Kahlan as she came close and set her pack down beside Richard's.

"I don't know." With the flat of her hand to her brow, Kahlan shielded her eyes from the sunlight. "I think she wants to tell you first."

Cara set her pack beside Kahlan's. "I think she's torn and doesn't know what to do."

"How do you feel?" Kahlan asked as she reached down and with her fingertips rubbed the back of his shoulder. Her gentle touch was a calming connection.

Richard smiled up at her. "I keep telling you, I'm fine."

He tore off a strip of dried venison and chewed as he watched Jennsen, Tom, Owen, Marilee, Anson, and a small group of the men finally emerge through the gates and make their way across the waving field of waist-high green grass.

"I'm hungry," Kahlan said. "Can I have some?"

"Sure." Richard pulled strips of the meat from his pack, stood, and handed a piece to both Kahlan and Cara.

"Lord Rahl," Anson said, waving, as the group joined Richard, Kahlan, and Cara in the shade of the oaks, "we wanted to come out to say good-bye and see you off. Maybe we will walk with you toward the pass?"

Richard swallowed. "We'd like that."

Owen frowned. "Lord Rahl, why are you eating meat? You just healed your gift. Won't you harm your balance?"

Richard smiled. "No. You see, incorrectly trying to apply a false notion of balance was what caused the problem I was having with my gift."

Owen looked puzzled. "What do you mean? You said that you must not eat meat as the balance to the killing you sometimes must do. After the battle at the fortification, don't you need to balance your gift all the more?"

Richard took a deep breath and let it out slowly as he gazed out over the mountains.

"You see, the thing is," Richard said, "I owe you all an apology. You all listened to me, but I didn't listen to myself.

"Kaja-Rang tried to help me with the words revealed on the statue, the words I told you—Deserve Victory. They were, first of all, meant for me."

"I don't understand," Anson said.

"I told you that your life is your own to live and that you have every right to defend it.

"Yet, I was telling myself that I had to balance the killing I did to defend my life and the lives of my loved ones by not eating meat— in essence, saying my self-defense, my killing of those who attack me and other innocent people, was morally wrong, and so for the killing I'd done I needed to make amends to the magic that helped me by offering it the appeasement of balance."

"But your sword's magic didn't work, either," Jennsen said.

"No, it didn't, and that should have been the thing that made me realize what the problem was, because both my gift and the sword's magic are different entities, yet they reacted logically to the same unreasoned action on my part. The sword's magic began to fail because I myself, by not eating meat, was saying that I did not completely believe that I was justified in using force to stop others who initiate violence.

"The sword's magic functions through the belief-structure of the sword's owner; it only works against what the Seeker himself perceives as the enemy. The sword's magic will not work against a friend. That was the key I should have understood.

"When I thought that the use of the sword had to be balanced, I was, in effect, expressing a belief that my actions were in some way unjustified. Therefore, because I held that remnant of faith in a false concept that had been inculcated in me throughout my life, just as all the people of Bandakar were taught—that killing was always wrong—the sword's magic began to fail me.

"The Sword of Truth's magic, as my gift, could only again be viable when I comprehended—completely—that the magic needs no balance for the killing I've done because the killing I've done is not only moral, but the only moral course of action I could have taken.

"By not eating meat, I was acknowledging that some part of my mind believed the same thing that the people here in Bandakar believed when we first met Owen and his men—that killing is always wrong.

"By thinking that I must not eat meat as a balance, I was denying the moral necessity of self-preservation, denying the essential of protecting the value of life. The very act of seeking 'balance' for what I'm right in doing is a conflict which is what was causing the headaches and also caused the Sword of Truth's power to fail me. I was doing it to myself."

Richard had violated the Wizard's First Rule by believing a lie—that it was always wrong to kill—because he feared it was true. He had also violated the Second Rule, among others, but most grievous of all, he had violated the Sixth Rule. In so doing, he had ignored reason in favor of blind faith. The failure of his gift and the sword's power was a direct result of not applying reasoned thought.

Fortunately, with the Eighth Rule—*deserve victory*—he had come to reexamine his actions and finally realized the flaw in his thinking. Only then was he able to correct the situation.

In the end, he had fulfilled the Eighth Rule.

Richard shifted his weight to the other foot as he gazed at the faces watching him. "I had to come to understand that my actions are moral and need no balance, but are in themselves balanced by my reasoned actions, that killing is sometimes not only justified, but the only right and moral thing to do.

"I had to come to understand the very thing I was asking all of you to understand. I had to understand that I must deserve victory."

Owen looked over at those with him and then scratched his head. "Well, considering everything, I guess we can understand how you could make such a misjudgment."

Jennsen, her red hair standing out against the green of the trees and fields, squinted at him in the sunlight. "Well," she said with a sigh, "I'm glad to be pristinely ungifted. Being a wizard sounds awfully hard."

The men all nodded while voicing their agreement.

Richard smiled at Jennsen. "A lot of things in life are hard to figure out. Like what you've been considering. What have you decided?"

Jennsen clasped her hands and glanced over at Owen, Anson, and all the rest of the people with them.

"Well, this is no longer a banished empire. It's no longer an empire naked to the aggression of tyrants. It's part of the D'Haran Empire, now. These people want the same as us.

"I think I'd like to stay with them for a while and help them come to be part of the wider world, just as I've been starting to do. It's kind of exciting. I'd like to take your suggestion, Richard, and help them in that."

Richard smiled at his sister. He ran his hand down her beautiful red hair.

"On a condition," she added.

Richard let his hand drop back. "Condition?"

"Sure. I'm a Rahl, so . . . I was kind of thinking that I ought to have some proper protection. I could be a target, you know. People want to kill me. Jagang would love to—"

Richard laughed as he drew her into a hug with one arm to silence her.

"Tom, being as you are a protector to the House of Rahl, I'm assigning you to protect my sister, Jennsen Rahl. It's an important job and it means a great deal to me."

Tom lifted an eyebrow. "Are you sure, Lord Rahl?"

Jennsen swatted him with the back of her hand. "Of course he's sure. He wouldn't say it unless he was sure."

"You heard the lady," Richard said. "I'm sure."

The big blond D'Haran smiled with a boyish grin. "All right, then. I swear I will protect her, Lord Rahl."

Jennsen gestured vaguely back at the men and the town behind her. "Since I've been with them, they have come to see that I'm not a witch, and Betty is not a spirit guide—although for a time there I was afraid they might be right about Betty."

Richard peered down at the goat. Betty cocked her head. "I guess none of us except Betty knew the truth of what Nicholas was up to." At the sound of her name, Betty's ears pricked forward and her tail went into a fit of expectant wagging.

Jennsen patted Betty's round middle. "Now that these people understand that I'm not a witch, but I do share some of their traits, I suggested I might play an important role." She drew the knife at her belt and held it up, showing Richard the ornate letter R engraved on the silver handle. "I suggested that I be the official representative of the House of Rahl—if you approve."

Richard grinned. "I think that's an excellent idea."

"I think that would be wonderful, Jennsen." Kahlan pointed to the east with her chin. "But don't wait too long before you get back to Hawton to see Ann and Nathan. They will be a valuable help in insuring that the people here are no longer the prey of the Imperial Order. They will help you."

Jennsen twisted her fingers together. "But aren't they going to want to be going with the both of you? Helping you?"

"Ann thinks she should direct Richard's life," Kahlan said. "I don't think some of her directions have been the best thing." She slipped her arm through Richard's. "He is the Lord Rahl, now. He needs to do things his way, not theirs."

"They both feel responsible for us," Richard explained. "Nathan Rahl is a prophet. Prophecy, because of the way it functions, actually does require balance. The balance to prophecy is free will. I am the balance. I know those two don't like it, but I think I need to be free of them—for now, at least.

"But there is more to it. I think it's more important that they help the people here, first. We already know the uses to which Jagang will put the pristinely ungifted. I think it's vital that these people here, who are willing to value and protect the freedom they've won, are given some guidance in how to do that.

"Ann and Nathan will be able to set up defenses that will help protect the people here. They will also be valuable in teaching you the history that is important for you to know."

After Richard picked up his pack and slipped his arms through the straps, Owen gripped Richard's hand. "Thank you, Lord Rahl, for showing me that my life is worth living."

Marilee stepped forward and hugged him. "Thank you for teaching Owen to be worthy of me."

Richard laughed. Owen laughed. Cara gave Marilee an approving clap on the back. And then all the men laughed.

Betty pushed in and with a flurry of tail-wagging got the point across that she didn't want to be left out.

Richard knelt down and scratched Betty's ears. "And you, my friend, from now on I don't want you letting any Slides using you to spy on people."

Betty pushed her head against his chest as he scratched her ears and bleated as if to say she was sorry.

CHAPTER 67

Alone at last beneath the vast blue sky, the soaring walls of snow-capped mountains, and in among the trees, Richard felt good about being on their way. He would miss Jennsen, but it was only for a time. It would do her good to be on her own, yet among people also discovering how to live their own lives as they learned more about the wider world. He knew he would not trade away all he had learned since he'd left his sheltered life in Hartland. If not for that, he wouldn't be with Kahlan.

It felt good to walk and stretch his legs. He hitched his bow up higher on his shoulder as they made their way through the dappled sunlight of the hushed forest floor. After being so close to death as well as to losing his ability to see, he found everything more vibrant. The mosses looked more lush, the leaves more shimmery, the towering pines more awe-inspiring.

Kahlan's eyes seemed more green, her hair softer, her smile warmer.

As much as he at one time had hated the fact that he had been born gifted, he was now relieved to have his gift back. It was part of him, part of who he was, part of what made him the individual he was.

Kahlan had once asked him if he wished she had been born without her Confessor's power. He had told her that he would never wish that because he loved her for who she was. There was no way to separate out the parts of a person. That was to deny their individuality. He was no different. His gift was part of who he was. His abilities touched everything he did.

His problem with his gift was of his own making. The magic of the Sword of Truth had helped him understand that by failing him. In so doing, it had revealed his own failure to recognize the truth.

To have it back at his hip, and to know that it was once again in harmony with him and ready to defend him and those he loved was a comforting feeling—not because he wished to fight, but because he wished to live.

The day was warm and they made good time climbing the rocky trail up into the pass. By the time they reached the crown of the notch through the formidable mountains, it was colder, but without a biting wind it was not unpleasant.

At the top of the pass they stopped to gaze up at the statue of Kaja-Rang, sitting where it had been for thousands of years, all alone, keeping vigil over an empire of those who once could not see evil.

In some ways, the statue's presence was a monument to failure. Where Kaja-Rang and his people had failed to get these people to see the truth, Richard had succeeded—but not without Kaja-Rang's help.

Richard put his hands on the cold granite, on the words—Talga Vassternich—that had helped save his life.

"Thank you," he whispered up at the face of the man staring off toward the Pillars of Creation, where Richard had discovered his sister.

Cara placed her hands over the words, and Richard was surprised to see her look up at the statue and say, "Thank you for helping to save Lord Rahl."

After they started descending the pass, first crossing the open ledges and then making it down into the dense woods, Richard heard the call of a pewee, the signal he had taught Cara that had served them so well.

"You know," Cara said as she led them down the rocky ground beside a small stream, "Anson knows a lot about birds."

Richard stepped carefully among the tangle of cedar roots. "Really."

"Yes. While you were recovering we spent time talking." She put a hand against the fibrous bark of the reddish trunk of a cedar to keep her balance. She pulled her long blond braid forward over her shoulder as she started out again, running her hand down the length of the braid.

"He complimented me on my bird whistle," Cara said.

Richard glanced at Kahlan. She shrugged to let him know that she didn't have any idea of what Cara was getting at.

"I told you that you learned it well," Richard said.

"I told him that you taught it to me, that it was the call of the short-tailed pine hawk. Anson said that there wasn't any such bird as a short-tailed pine hawk. He said the call I used as a signal—the call you taught me—was a common wood pewee. Me, a Mord-Sith, using the call of a bird named a pewee. Imagine that."

They walked in silence for a moment.

"Am I in trouble?" Richard finally asked.

"Oh yes," Cara answered.

Richard couldn't help smiling, but he made sure the Mord-Sith didn't see it, nor did Cara see Kahlan look back over her shoulder with the special smile she gave no other but him.

Kahlan lifted an arm, pointing. "Look."

Through the gaps in the crowns of the cedars, against the bright blue sky, they saw a black-tipped race circling high above them, riding the mountain air currents. The races were no longer hunting them. This one was simply looking for its dinner.

"What's that old saying?" Cara asked. "Something about a bird of prey circling over you at the beginning of a journey being a warning sign."

"Yes, that's right," Richard said. "But I'm not going to let that old tale bother me; we'll let you come with us anyway."

Kahlan laughed and received a scolding scowl. Kahlan laughed all the more when Richard started laughing, too. Cara couldn't hold out, and, as she turned back to the trail, Richard saw the smile spread across her face.

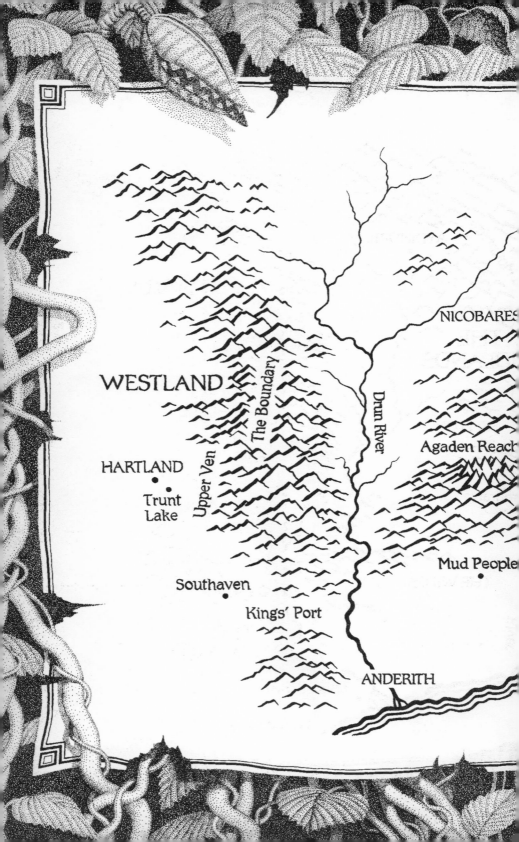

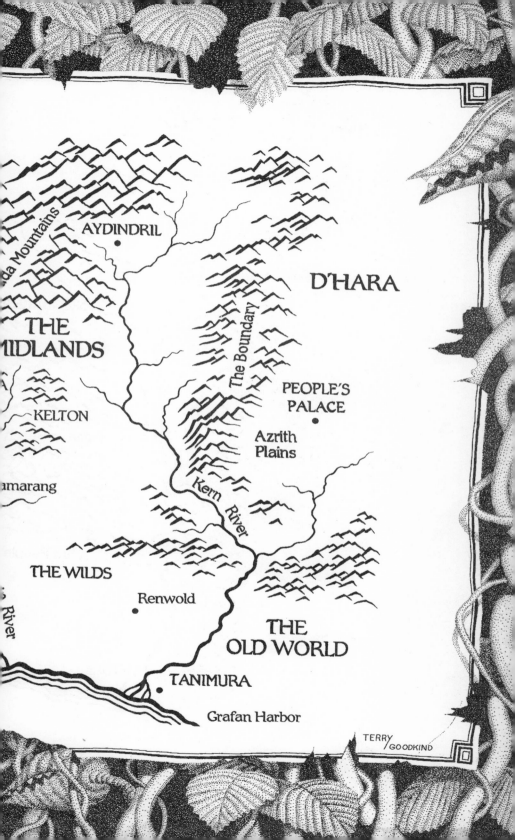